WOOD LEIGHTON

Wood Leighton

or,

A Year in the Country

Mary Howitt

NONSUCH

First published 1836
Copyright © in this edition Nonsuch Publishing, 2007

Nonsuch Publishing
Cirencester Road, Chalford, Stroud, Gloucestershire, GL6 8PE

Nonsuch Publishing (Ireland)
73 Lower Leeson Street, Dublin 2, Ireland

www.nonsuch-publishing.com

Nonsuch Publishing is an imprint of NPI Media Group

For comments or suggestions, please email the editor of this series at:
classics@tempus-publishing.com

British Library Cataloguing in Publication Data.
A catalogue record for this book is available from the British Library.

ISBN 978 1 84588 210 5

Typesetting and origination by Nonsuch Publishing Limited
Printed in Great Britain by Oaklands Book Services Limited

CONTENTS

INTRODUCTION TO THE MODERN EDITION

"Will you walk into my parlour?" said the Spider to the Fly,
"'Tis the prettiest little parlour that ever you did spy;
The way into my parlour is up a winding stair,
And I've a many curious things to shew when you are there."
"Oh no, no," said the little Fly, "to ask me is in vain,
For who goes up your winding stair can ne'er come down
again."

'THE SPIDER AND THE FLY', a classic of children's poetry, is one of those terribly simple works that has managed to work its way into the collective consciousness; it has long reverberated around nursery walls and Sunday school classrooms and been the proud subject of countless children's breathless recitals. It is true it is unlikely to be found next to the works of Heaney or Neruda in any anthology of works that shape the soul, but it clearly has something about it which has made it such a timeless and enduring favourite.

However, while there may be a great many people who have heard it, and who can offer up at least the first line with gusto, there are precious few who would have any knowledge of the author. Like so many works of literature, art and music, it may as well have come into existence fully formed as far as the great majority of people are concerned. But, for the sake of posterity, it should be made clear that this poem certainly had an author, and that her name was Mary Howitt.

Mary Howitt (*née* Botham) was born in 1799, in Coleford, on the western edge of Gloucestershire, at the point where the Royal Forest meets the Wye Valley. This is an area of very great natural beauty, conducive, it might be argued, to the development of her artistic nature. In 1821 she married William Howitt, of Derbyshire, who was some seven years her senior. He had been apprenticed in his youth to a builder, but this did not constitute any form of barrier to William and his new wife setting themselves up as chemists, and this they did in the Hanley area. As a couple, it seems, they were both willing and able to turn their hand to whatever task took their fancy, and their next move, some two years later, was most definitely away from the scientific arena.

The Howitts moved north to Nottingham, and it was here that their remarkable literary output was to take shape. Between the two of them they produced over 180 works across a wide variety of subjects, ranging from poetry, history and fiction to translation work and economic critique. To get a flavour of their versatility, one of William's earlier works was *A History of Priestcraft* (1833), while he was later to produce works on the nature of rural life in Germany and a history of Australia. For Mary's part, one of her major contributions to literary life in England was her translation of the writings of Hans Christian Anderson, through which this standard-bearer of children's literature was first introduced to an English-language readership. Her poetry was also hugely successful in her day, although she was more commercially successful in America, where she was one of the country's most popular foreign poets over the course of the 1830s and '40s. Their literary efforts won them the friendship of some of the giants in the field, including that of such household names as Dickens, Gaskell, Tennyson and Barret Browning.

Allied to these literary efforts and achievements was a voluminous output of fiction writing, for which Mary was largely responsible. Hugely popular in their day, one such work was the story of *Wood Leighton, or A Year in the Country* (1836). A fascinating piece of writing, *Wood Leighton* recounts the tales told in a country village. This flexible literary device allows for a wide range of tone and theme within each story, including an account of an ancient curse and a vow of revenge, together with an intricately woven account of adultery and the sad consequences that result. A blend of the supernatural and the melodramatic, what is created is a charming tapestry of life at the beginning of the Victorian age.

Like so many other writers who have thrown their lot in with fickle posterity, from the Rev'd Edward Bradley to Thomas Chandler Haliburton, Howitt's work has largely faded from view today; as was the case with Bradley and Haliburton, her writings were greatly loved during her own day, and for this alone they would be worth revisiting; but if one was to be drawn to them by a sense of duty, one is more than likely to realise why it was that these writings were so happily received in a different time.

PREFACE

IN PUBLISHING A WORK LIKE the present, wherein an actual locality is given, a few observations are necessary. I have chosen as the scene of the following stories and characters the town and neighbourhood in which my own youth was spent, not only because it afforded ample material for one who desired to make a book characteristic of English country life, but also from the great delight I had in recollecting scenes associated with the pleasures of my earlier years, and from the uncommon beauty of those scenes, as fair specimens of an English Arcadia; and so far my work has indeed been a labour of love.

And now, in especial consideration of the inhabitants of the town intended by Wood Leighton, I must acknowledge that although I have laid the scene of Denborough Park in their neighbourhood, they will look in vain for its site there. The events of that story occurred in a southern county; but in order to preserve the unity of my work I took the liberty of locating it here. The nabob was one of my own ancestors, Major Francis Wood—one of the eight sons of

William Wood, the ill-used Irish patentee, who was ruined by the selfish cunning of Dean Swift—and the brother of Charles Wood, my maternal grandfather, who first introduced platina into Europe.

Major Wood was one of those singular beings who seem born for adventures; and the family traditions preserve many strange passages of his life, untold here, from the day when a lord's daughter fell in love with him, and was slighted by him, to that on which he died, as related in this story, leaving dismay and perplexity behind him.

The story has always appeared to me a strange and melancholy one, more particularly so in the case of this unfortunate legatee, where we see a mind so acted upon by circumstances as to become the very opposite of what appeared to be its original character, and whence followed, almost in fulfilment as it seemed of his enemy's curse, this ruin and misery of his family.

From the foregoing statement I hope it will be clearly understood that though I have a pleasure and pride in acknowledging that the description of Wood Leighton and the country about it is in its main features the description of a real town and neighbourhood, which will be easily recognised by the inhabitants, those inhabitants are not to look for any living portraiture of themselves among the characters, which was totally beside my intentions.

In this new edition which is about to make a portion of the Parlour Library, it is my hope that the re-arrangement which I have made in the contents of the volume, as well as the general correction of the whole, will make Wood Leighton more worthy of the public favour than it was ten years ago, even with the charm of entire novelty about it.

M.H.
The Elms, Clapton,
Dec. 18, 1846

Taking Possession

B Y THE DEMISE OF A distant relative, Mr. John Crumpton, we had the good fortune to find a considerable inheritance fallen to our lot. It lay in a distant county, and in the small town of Wood Leighton.

With the greatest good-will in the world we went to view our new possession, and every step as we advanced within ten miles of the place showed us that it lay in a very land of Goshen. We were exactly in the humour to see every thing and place under the most agreeable aspect; and though we travelled in the gloom of a winter's day towards the end of January—perhaps the most cheerless time of the whole year—we found nothing but cause for admiration. We entered the little town just before the close of the day, when there was just light enough to show us that it was a very antiquated place—what the tourist would call a peer town, with irregular, ill built, and ill-paved streets, lighted with neither gas nor lamps. But these things we did not observe: we only saw many a picturesque old house turning its gabled end or projecting its huge porch into the street; and that a very natural and child-like curiosity brought both men and women to their doors and windows to get a peep at us as our chaise drew up at our new—home it could not be called then, though the cheerful fire that lighted up the most comfortable of old-fashioned parlours, and the curtsying and gracious smiles and welcomes of the old housekeeper, who lighted the candles and spoke her congratulations at the same time, made us feel, even then, that we were received to the comforts and welcome of home.

We found our house, though not large, sufficient for even a considerable family. It stood a little back from the line of the street, within a paved court, separated from the street with iron palisades. The court was filled with laurels and evergreens, and on one side grew a line of remarkably fine Lombardy poplars. The shrubs almost concealed the house, excepting one end, which projected to the street, and was overrun with a prodigal growth of ivy. The kitchens and the hall occupied this side of the house; on the other lay the principal rooms—two old-fashioned, spacious parlours—the common and the best parlour, as our attendant called them, dining and drawing-room being too modern for the style of their late possessor.

It was not till the next day that we saw the whole beauty and value of the place. Then we found our parlours opening into a noble garden—the upper end full of tall, ancient evergreens, junipers, arbor-vitæ, and yews, overtopped by Scotch firs, with a thick undergrowth of bays, laurels, and laurustinus, and with thickets of privet, lilac, and guelder-rose. A broad lawn lay in front, surrounded by a gravel-walk, and here and there corners and openings among the evergreens filled with flower-borders. The remainder and larger portion of the garden lay below this, sloping to the south, and was gained by stone steps from a low parapeted wall which divided the upper garden from the lower. This was the kitchen-garden, well stocked with everything a family could require. At the bottom of all ran a filbert-hedge; and here again a narrow slip of flower-border cut in a broad stripe of grass, sloping down to a beautiful, clear, and swift stream. Beyond this lay a broad meadow, and then green, ascending hilly fields stretching upwards for a mile or more, beautifully adorned with hedge-row timber and clumps of fine wood, with a farm-house seen in the distance; and to the right, where a small valley opened into the flat of meadow-land that bounded our garden, a tributary stream was seen running down among alder-trees, shining like silver in the sun. Nothing could be more tranquilly beautiful than this landscape. It was complete in its kind: there was no sublimity—no expansion of prospect; but as a piece of English Arcadia it was so perfect that the mind desired nothing different, and felt that any addition must destroy its harmony of character.

I can imagine no more delightful circumstances than those in which we were placed. The death of our respected relative had not been untimely, nor had the family connexion been so near as that his loss should sadden our spirits. We knew that, as a shock of corn fully ripe, he had died in his place, after having enjoyed it even beyond the usual term of human life. And here we were, with feelings something like those of our first parents in paradise: all was our own, we were there to enjoy it, and every step made us acquainted with some new object, some new delight.

We traversed the house from cellar to garret, examining every dark room and secret nook, expecting in every one to find some strange mystery or hidden treasure. Curious angular closets there were papered over like the walls, so that the key-hole or the ring by which the door was opened only showed their existence. There were deep, strange-looking nooks that ran far into darkness, by the side of some projecting chimney; and there was a large nondescript piece of furniture, like one clumsy old cabinet set upon another, opening with folding doors, and containing an innumerable quantity of drawers, some of which opened with a secret spring; yet, though the locks of all had been secured and the keys conveyed to us before our arrival, and we now dived down into all their mysterious depths, like divers into the unsunned caves of the ocean, we found nothing but old china, not remarkably fine—old table linen, fine, but much the worse for wear—a considerable quantity of plate—but every article so small, so light and thin with long use, that it could not reckon for much. Other things too we found—a marvellous quantity of dried herbs; the old double-cabinet was full of them, for our relative had been a renowned collector of medical plants, and was famous over the whole country for his snuff made of coltsfoot leaves, the virtues of which, according to his belief, were as numerous as those of any modern panacea whatever; and moreover lumber of every conceivable kind—old chairs dismembered of arm or leg, legs and arms of others without bodies—old bedsteads and balustrades which mouldered to the touch—boards—sticks—boxes without lids, and lids without boxes—matting, carpeting, old bed-hangings and rugs dusty and full of moths; in short, all the accumulated rubbish and lumber which had been stored up in the fourscore years and ten of the life of a man who, we are told, had a remarkable gift for hoarding up almost everything, and was withal the most methodical man in the world. Concealed hoards of money were perhaps out of the question: certain it is, whatever hopes we might have of finding any were disappointed. One thing however we did find—what every old house possesses—a chest of manuscripts;—yes, truly, *manuscripts.* The chest was not curiously carved,—was not opened by a complicated spring-lock, nor yet secured by a huge chain and padlock: it was only a common oak chest with a common lock, and yet it was filled with manuscripts. I was at some trouble, even in the heyday of our exploratory rambles, to delve down and see what treasure of poem or history I might find, and thereby I made my companion very impatient, and was threatened, if I did not desist, with being left by myself in the most dismal and haunted-looking room in the house. I *did* desist, but not before I had delved down among those ancient writings, and found—nothing but dusty and yellow letters tied up in yearly bundles, ditto of yearly expenses, and sundry estimates and bills concerning alterations made in the house long enough before I was born. What further the chest contained I did not discover that day: —But more of this in proper time and season.

The furniture of the house was ample, but of the most old-fashioned and simple description: the frame of a modern looking-glass, which seemed strangely out of place, was the only article made of mahogany, everything else being of oak. The character of every piece of furniture was angular; the backs and arms of the chairs formed the most perfect right angles with the seats, the table legs stood straight without curve or inclination, and all so thin that it seemed wonderful how they could have supported their burdens so lang. Everything seemed to belong to a tall, thin-legged generation: the bed-posts tapered upwards without scroll or curve, supporting testers round which hung the shallowest and most scanty of valances: every chamber was furnished with a round or oval pier-glass set in an ancient gilt frame, about a finger's breadth, equally adorned with the bed-posts; and over each rose rectangularly and close against the wall three or four peacock's feathers. I never saw furniture on which so little ornament had been expended; and yet all the rooms were so thoroughly carpeted, so amply furnished with chests, chairs, and wardrobes, and all so neat and clean, and such a uniformity existed through the whole house—all was so perfectly in keeping, that the effect was anything but mean—it was pleasant and in harmony. In what appeared the most neglected room of the house we found the only picture in it—the portrait of our deceased relative, taken in his younger days, in a sky-blue coat, powdered and with a pig-tail, and in a very handsome pair of ruffles: his hat was under his arm, and his hand rested on his cane;—he seemed to be an amiable, yet a somewhat dry and precise person, as if in his instance Nature had succeeded in what is commonly considered an impossible achievement, that of setting an old head upon young shoulders. We awarded it a place of honour, and having it brought downstairs, we hung it over the chimney-piece of our dining-room. Of books we found but few; the works of Bunyan, De Foe, and Richardson—a few divines—Millar's Gardener's Calendar, and several works on vegetable medicine. There were many, and some very curious, editions of the Bible—many commentaries on it, and several Concordances, together with the five volumes of Calmet. Biblical literature was certainly the good old man's favourite study.

"He might be said to die reading the Bible," observed the housekeeper; and pointing to one which lay on a stand in the chimney corner, "That," she said, "was the book he read; it had good print."

I opened the volume, and between the leaves of the Gospel of St. John lay a pair of silver spectacles.

"Ah," cried the housekeeper, "these are the glasses for which I have had such hunts!—Poor dear master! he was using them the day before he died, and could not tell where he had left them."

I have never seen my worthy relative, but this little circumstance seemed to have the charm of a life-long intercourse; the old man was no longer as a stranger to me; a sentiment like filial reverence bound my heart to his memory; I again placed the spectacles where his own hands had laid them, and glancing at the chapter found it that blessed one where Christ promises the Comforter to his disciples.

The examination of the house abundantly satisfied us; such an abode of family comfort, unostentatious as it was, we had hardly ever seen—room beyond room adapted for every chance and necessity of life; and scarcely had we gone half over it before we said, "What should hinder our taking up our abode here for the present, and till these law questions are settled?" For, gentle reader, whereas thou hast heard that earthly happiness is never without alloy, and that at the heart of the rose lieth the canker, be it known unto thee that certain perplexing law technicalities were the alloy to this our earthly happiness—the determining certain boundaries was the canker at the heart of this our rose.

Upon making this house our home therefore for whatever time might be needful we decided; and accordingly, in little more than one month from that time, being the last day of February, we arrived with such of our household gods as were needful to our different way of life and more modern notions, and established ourselves as inhabitants of Wood Leighton.

One month of a mild winter, verging now on an open spring, had made great improvement in the garden and general aspect of our new abode. The flower-borders were bright with hepaticas, snowdrops, and crocuses, which grew in handfuls, white and yellow and purple; buds were already appearing on the lilacs; and the stems of the laburnum were green and fresh, as if impatient to burst forth with their new vegetable life. The violets under the nut-trees were full of bud, and even some more hardy than the rest had opened into flower; and the nut-trees themselves were gemmed with their minute crimson tufts, and tasselled with their wavering catkins.

Once established at Wood Leighton, in a district so eminently beautiful, the features of which were so peculiarly English, the year passed away as it were in a succession of rural festivals; and among its people we found so much original and singular character, and were enabled to gather up so many pleasant and curious histories, that we were soon induced to put together this Chronicle of Wood Leighton—assuring our readers that, however strange and out of the common chances of probability many of the incidents and characters may appear, all are strictly true, and only serve to show how great a diversity of form and aspect the human character may assume when suffered to run wild, as it did in this out-of-the-world town and neighbourhood

MR. CRUMPTON AND HIS WAY OF LIVING

IT WAS A GREAT SCANDAL in Wood Leighton that there was no sale of Mr. Crumpton's effects. He was an old bachelor, with the decided aversion to the sex, but so well served by his old housekeeper, Mrs. Woodings, that he did not require other female attendants; consequently no gossip of the house went abroad, for she kept as close within doors as her master. The place might have been hermetically sealed for any access there was to it. There was no chance of calling on Mr. Crumpton to inquire the character of a servant, for *his one* was never likely to leave him; and if a lady, as much prompted by curiosity as charity, contrived to get the entrée of his house under the plea of a subscription for a poor family, she was merely admitted into his common parlour: she saw just enough to excite, nothing to satisfy her curiosity. The very circumstance of the place appearing inaccessible created the desire to storm it; and no sooner did the news go abroad that the old gentleman was dead than everybody rejoiced to think that now the whole house would be thrown open to them; there must be a sale!—and already the good gossips had gone in imagination from one mysterious locked-up apartment to another, feasting their senses on hidden treasure and furniture more curiously antique than was contained in any other house in the parish. One had heard rumours of wondrously fine china—another of plate, and another of hoards of bed and table-linen; in short, the discovery of all the thousand-year-old treasures of a buried city would not have afforded them the delight they expected at the sale of Mr. Crumpton's effects.

Great therefore was the consternation when it was told that the people to whom the house had descended, though young, and to appearance not at all of the old school, were going to inhabit it *as it was*, and would have no sale at all. It was an incredible thing; everybody said—"Oh no, there must be a sale. It was impossible that a family used to modern furniture could endure anything so old-fashioned as that—there must be a sale." But when they not only saw us but our children established there they came to another conclusion. The old gentleman, they said, had *tied us off* selling anything. To be sure he was always singular; and that the old furniture must remain as it was, was a condition of the inheritance; and old Mrs. Woodings also was a fixture in the place. "Well," said they, "they have a pretty bargain of it. I would not have the place on such conditions. Only think of all that moth and worm-eaten furniture and those old-fashioned papers on the walls. Why, it must be fifty years since that paper was put up—and what papers they had fifty years ago!" Old fashioned as the people of Wood Leighton were, they fancied the fashion of Mr. Crumpton's house half a century behind them; and all concluded by saying it was a bad day's work for Mr. Smallwood, the upholsterer, who had new-furnished his shop in the expectation of new-furnishing our house. There never was so fertile and yet so unsatisfactory a subject of wonder and speculation since Wood Leighton was a town. And when, beyond all this, it was noised abroad that "the new people" brought servants with them, instead of supplying their domestic establishment from the decent young people of the place, the measure of dissatisfaction was full. We must have been unpopular, for nobody now had any chance of hearing all about us and our children—about the china, the plate, the linen, and the paper on the walls—much less of being enabled to judge for themselves.

As I have said before, I had never seen our worthy relative. I was therefore desirous to obtain all possible information respecting him; and fortunately Mrs. Woodings, the person most capable of satisfying my curiosity, was never weary of talking of him; but in the first place I must endeavour to make my readers acquainted with this queen of ancient housekeepers. She was short and broad, and yet singularly spare in person, her breadth being made up by multiplicity of garments. She appeared at first silent rather than talkative; but once set a-going there was no end to her loquacity. Her habit was silence, but by nature she was communicative. Her dear old master was the never-failing topic. Respect for him and care for his property by long habit had become the ruling sentiment and spring of her actions. She had lived with him forty years, and for the last twenty had been his sole attendant. It would have been impossible but that she must have acquired some peculiarities—and Heaven knows she had many. She would sit with her hands placed together on her knees for an hour at a time perfectly still, with her eyes fixed on the fire, purring to herself like a cat; and from these reveries it often was with difficulty she could be roused. She had the greatest possible aversion to domestic animals and children; and but that it was the less evil of the two to endure them or leave the old place, I do not believe she would have permitted them to set foot within the territories. She was the most orthodox believer in ghosts and spectres of all kinds; she had stories of haunted madhouses, of white ladies that appeared by the sides of lonesome waters, of headless women who sat spinning beside stiles, and of black dogs that haunted bridges. She knew the very farm-kitchen where the household work had been performed by an indefatigable brownie or hobthrush, who however had been driven away by the proffered reward of a hempen shirt. She knew the wagoner whose team of five strong horses was unable to move the wagon which a malicious fairy had tied by the wheel with a rush; and beyond all the rest, she herself had seen ghosts.

"You do not believe me," said she. "Well, well; I'll tell you however one case. I had in my youth a friend—a handsome young woman—by name Hannah Jackson. She was twenty years of age, and the daughter of a small farmer; the most pious and good young woman I ever knew, though she was so unfortunate. As she was everywhere said to be the prettiest girl thereabout, she had to be sure a great many lovers. There was nobody thought of but Hannah Jackson, either at fair or market, at wake or christening, and she was always chosen for the May Queen; and yet, though she was so much admired by the men, the women all said she deserved it, for she was so modest and good as well as beautiful. If she had one she had twenty sweethearts, and might have chosen from among all the best young men of the whole country round. But, poor thing, she chose one that was unworthy of her; and for all her friends could say she would listen to nobody but him. His name was Charles Woolley, a handsome, strong-built young man, the best wrestler and prize-fighter in the county; but he was a wild, unfeeling, bad man—a bad son and bad brother, given to evil company, and the doer of evil deeds.

"Poor Hannah! it was a sad day's work for her when she first gave him her love; and as long as I live I never shall forget what a broken-hearted wretch he made her.

"Well, two months after, in the beginning of winter, I was forced to leave her to take a service in a distant town; and 'Nanny,' says she as we parted, 'I shall die before spring, but you shall see me again before I leave this world.' And not six weeks after that, as I lay in my bed about two o'clock in the morning, I saw a pleasant light in my chamber—not like a candle, but as if daylight could be gathered up into about the size of a woman; and presently the curtains of my bed were softly opened, and I saw poor Hannah Jackson, pale and thin, but, oh, so beautiful and peaceful, gazing down upon me; and I heard her say in the sweetest low voice, 'I am come to say good-bye! All is well with me now; but I shall not see you again.' And with a smile she seemed to go softly away, and the room was dark again. I was not frightened; for at the moment, forgetting how impossible it was for her to have entered the house, I thought it really was herself, come to bid me good-bye before she went to an uncle's at a distance, as had been talked of. But when I came to think I knew it could be no other than her spirit, and I lay musing on it till daybreak. That day was Saturday; and my father, who was a miller and came to the town with flour, called to tell me that poor Hannah had died at two o'clock that very morning."

Such was the story that she told to convince me of the reality of ghosts; and however much inclined I might be to disbelieve such tales in general, I liked this narrative, and my silence passed with the good old woman for conviction.

Among her other qualities Mrs. Woodings was very religious in her way; but she never attended any place of worship except the quakers' meeting, and when I told her I thought a good sermon and a cheerful worship would be more edifying and agreeable, "Nay, nay," she said, "I like the silence."— "Perhaps," said I, "you are a quaker?"—"No, no," she replied; "neither she nor her master: he was a good Church-of-England man, and she might have sat in his pew—he often wanted her to do so; but, for her part, she liked the silence of a quakers' meeting better than any preaching either at church or chapel;" and she continued a regular attender of the silent meetings.

Poor Mrs. Woodings! what a happiness it was to her that things remained in their old state—a sale would have been the death of her! She, however, was not the only living fixture of the place; another made his appearance the second week of our residence there in the person of the old gardener—one who had been used to come, as he himself thought proper, for a day's work or a week's work at a time. He was as perfect in his way as Mrs. Woodings in hers—a little old man, with, like all old gardeners, a stoop in his back—dressed in a blue coat of the most ancient cut, furnished with buttons the size of half-crowns, a red waistcoat with long flaps, black breeches, and blue worsted stockings, and with large silver buckles in his shoes, he had a remarkable way of turning out his toes, so that his feet appeared as if placed horizontally to the front of his leg: his track in the snow might have been known from a thousand. A better model of an old man I never saw; with his large nose and chin, and his hat-brim turning up behind as if to complete the picturesqueness of his costume. There had been some speculation, I have no doubt, as to whether he would be permitted to hold his post of gardener under the new regime;—but when we appeared not only pleased with him, but I pronounced him an ornament to the place, there was nothing further needed to gain the heart of Mrs. Woodings.— "O" exclaimed she, in the fulness of her satisfaction, "that my poor dear master had but known you! for, 'Nanny,' said he, 'when I am gone, you and everything else will go—William and you may look out for other places!'—and, bless you, ma'am, I should have died if I must have left this house!"

"Well, but," said I, seeing her in such good humour, "how did Mr. Crumpton enjoy his time? I cannot conceive what he found to do. You have told me that he never visited, and but rarely saw company at home."

"No," said Mrs. Woodings, "he never did visit of late years, and only three times a-year—on the coronation-day, King George the Third's—on his own birthday, which was the 15th of September— and on Christmas-day, did he see company at home—Mr. Pope, Mr. Somers, and one or two other old gentlemen: he never was fond of much company. And yet I've heard say, when he was young, he used to visit about a good deal that was when Miss Patty was alive—"

"And who was Miss Patty?" interrupted I.

"Bless me!" exclaimed Mrs. Woodings—"and you never heard of Miss Patty! It was before my time long enough; but I've heard say she was the handsomest young lady in these parts—a cousin of my master's, and a sort of ward of his, as I've been told, though he was not so much older than she was either. She was brought up by Madam Crumpton in this very house; and he was to have married her, and very fond he was of her from the time she was a little child. The blue room was Miss Patty's room, and there my poor master's picture hung. I've heard say that that room was never disturbed for many years after her death, but was kept just as she left it, and some roses and flowers that she had placed over the picture were there till they all mouldered sway."

"But what was the cause of Miss Patty's death?" inquired I, shocked to find that we had removed the picture from a sacred place.

"Miss Patty had been dead," continued Mrs. Woodings, "twenty years before my time; but I heard all about her from an old woman who was servant in the family at the time.— She was very handsome, as I told you, and the best creature in the world. What needlework she used to do! All that fine worked furniture in the best chamber was her doing—chair-cushions, window-curtains, and all; and in the four corners of the counterpane you may see, in one, the king's arms—in the other, the Crumpton arms; I warrant ye, she made sure, poor thing! that she should be Mrs. Crumpton,—in another, her dog, and in the other her cat, as natural as could be,— and under them her name, Martha Unwin, aged nineteen—for she was not a Crumpton, but a cousin on the mother's side. She was mighty clever with her needle, poor thing! Well, as I told you, she was very handsome, and having a good fortune, had many lovers, though everybody knew that she was to be married to her cousin.

"Old Madam Crumpton, not my master's mother, but his aunt, a very rich lady, took Miss Patty with her to Bath, and there a young gentleman fell in love with her. It was in vain that they told him she was engaged, he persisted that as long as she was unmarried there was hope for him, and he used to follow her about everywhere. He seldom spoke to her, but only looked tenderly at her, and used to walk backwards and forwards before the house that he might get a sight of her as she came to the window, or as her shadow passed the blind. I never heard of such love as his was; he was very handsome, and used to cast the saddest looks at her, and heave the deepest sighs when he saw her, as must have melted any woman's heart, however hard it might be, or if she had not been promised to a man like my master. Everybody in Bath pitied the young gentleman, and many said in the end he would succeed. I believe Madam Crumpton thought so too, for she sent off in great haste, bidding my master come to them; for she was too ill to leave Bath, and would not part with Miss Patty. Well, my master joined them; and he and the young lady went a deal about together, and everywhere they met the gentleman who seemed now ten times more melancholy than ever and was always sighing and looking as if his heart would break. He never interrupted them in their walks, nor sought to make the acquaintance of my master; but loved at a distance as one may say, following Miss Patty with the most unhappy looks and sighs.

"At last, about a fortnight after my master joined them, and when they had been together at some grand ball, the poor young gentleman blew his brains out under Miss Patty's window. Of course it made a great talk, and then everybody blamed her, as if she had been the cause of his death; and, to be sure, in some sort she might be said to be; but then she had never given him encouragement— not even at the very first.— Well, his friends came, and his mother; and a great piece of work there was, for they found in his will that he had left her a great deal of money; and his mother, who was a very proud woman, grieved less for his death, than that he had been such a fool, as she said, when dozens of ladies were dying for him in his own parts: so she set aside the will, saying he was out of his mind; and Miss Patty, who never had the least desire in the world for either him or his money, gave up all claim, or else it must have come to trial, and everybody said she would have got it, for he was as much in his senses as either you or I—and, bless you, there were plenty of people to swear it.

"But it was a terrible shock to Miss Patty; and though she and madam left Bath directly, and came here, intending that she and my master should be married directly, she somehow never looked up again; but fell into a moping kind of way, and died before that time twelvemonth."

"Poor Miss Patty!" I exclaimed.

"Ay, indeed, poor thing!" continued Mrs. Woodings: "and it was a sad break-down to Mr. Crumpton—he never was the same man again; and even when I came, which was twenty years afterwards,

I've known him to go and sit in Miss Patty's room for hours and hours. He always locked the door upon himself; and the servants who lived here then—for then he had three, a housemaid and footman, besides housekeeper—said it was to indulge his grief for her loss, and that he always seemed much more calm and cheerful after he came out. He never kept much company since I knew the house. There was, to be sure, a Mr. Parnel, a quaker, who used to come from somewhere in the north, that would stay three or four weeks a time with him: he was a sober, good kind of man, a deal older than my master, but a cheerful, comfortable person, who was always writing. There used to be a deal of his writing and a sort of life of himself, which, many years afterwards, when old Thomas the footman was dead; and soon after Nancy, the last housemaid—she was a sad, wild huzzy, and I found I could do a deal better by myself:—well it was the first winter that I was alone, I think, that master, seeing the nights were long and wearisome, and I all alone in the kitchen, called me into the parlour, and 'Nanny,' says he, for he always called me Nanny, 'you remember my friend Mr. Parnel, the quaker?'—'Sure I do,' said I. 'Well, then,' says he, 'bring your knitting and sit down, and I will read you his life—for I know you love the quakers—for he often used to laugh at me about that, as you do, ma'am;—and very pretty reading that journal of Mr. Parnel's was! it was just for the world like the good man talking, and he had been in his grave ten years! I have not seen those writings now for a long time," said Mrs. Woodings, after a pause.

"But I must have a look for them," said I.

"They are somewhere in the chest up-stairs," observed Mrs. Woodings, "for master was always careful of his writings:—'There is no knowing,' said he, 'the value of a bit of paper—a whole estate has sometimes been lost for the want of it.' I'll warrant it, those papers will be found up-stairs."

"And after Miss Patty's death," I inquired, "did Mr. Crumpton ever again think of marrying?"

"Bless you, no!" replied the old woman, almost indignant at the surmise: "he think of marrying, not he! not but that many a one would have been glad to have had him, but he was the sort of person to love only once; and it was many years before he overgot the loss of poor Miss Patty; and then he was getting past middle life, and had fixed his own ways so much he never would have done to marry. Why you never in all your life saw anything so exact as he was! He used to say that the happiest part of his life was after I kept his house; and, that was saying a good deal, and he to have lost a lady like Miss Patty!"

"It must have been very dull for both of you," I remarked.

"Not it!" replied she, as if amazed at the idea. "Day after day went on, and year after year, and it never was dull. Up in the morning at seven, winter and summer; breakfast at eight; dinner at one; tea at five; supper at eight, and all in bed soon after nine;—I warrant ye it never was dull. Then master was very good to the poor: there were seven old pensioners of sixpence a week each, and they all came of a Monday morning; and two pounds in halfpence he gave yearly to the poor on begging Monday. A pretty sight it was to see him neat and clean, as he always was, standing at the hall-door with his basket of money beside him, giving to the poor creatures that came—old folks and women, with three or four children—all two-pence or three-pence apiece, and to hear them bless him and bless him, the whole court full at a time; I am sure I have cried to see it. Then he gave ten pounds away in coals, and ten pounds in bread and beef. And with the company we had three times a year, and the cleaning there was both before and afterwards, besides regular week's work, I assure you the time never passed wearily with me: there was always something to be done: and as for master he would take up a book at any time and read."

"But," persisted I, "your winter evenings must have been long?"

"As to winter evenings," said she, "they were no longer than summer evenings, for aught that I know; but then, as I told you about Mr. Parnel's journal, I did use to take my knitting and sit by the parlour fire while he read."

"And what did he read?" I asked.

"Why, sometimes one thing, and sometimes another. We had the newspaper once a week, Pilgrim's Progress now and then, and one winter we had the Book of Martyrs."

"Terrible reading that!" I said, half amused at the idea of those two solitary old people reading such a book on winter nights.

"Terrible reading, as you say," she replied; "la me! I shall never forget it as long as I live! He read and read night after night, and my blood seemed to curdle within me; I wished not to hear, and yet I dared not to sit alone in my kitchen. Well, I sat knitting and knitting, and trying not to listen, and yet every word came as plain as it could be,—and master was just in the middle of a horrible story about a poor man being sawn in two, when he suddenly stopped short—oh, how it startled me, that stopping of his!—and 'Nanny,' says he, 'do you enjoy this book?'—'No, master,' said I, 'and I have not enjoyed it for a good bit.'—'Nor have I,' says he; 'I only read it, Nanny, because I thought you liked it—but we won't read any more.'—'And I wish,' said I, 'we had not read so much.' And master shut to the book, and carried it home next morning, for he had borrowed it of Mr. Pope."

Wood Leighton and
its Neighbourhood

O F Wood Leighton itself I shall say nothing more, than that it consists of three or four considerable streets, of low, old-fashioned houses; some of antiquated wood-framing, the intervals filled up with regular and uniform brickwork; others, of building of various materials, positions, and dates; and others, of lath and plaster, neatly whitewashed, or greenish with age, and marked and dotted in manifold figures of men, women, and four-footed creatures, or with quaint arabesque patterns, according to the taste of some artist whose head, as an old sibyl of Wood Leighton expressed it, does not ache now. Here and there the regularity of the street is broken by a garden with its old hedge, well barricaded at the bottom with dead sticks and tub-staves, to exclude all the variety of small depredators; here and there, by a wall of old brickwork, entered by a door, and over which hang the dark, thick branches of venerable yews, beyond which may be seen the tall, solid chimneys, or gabled front of some ancient and more important house, the abode of one of the magnates of the place; and beside it, perhaps, stands a crazy wooden barn, or an isolated cottage, at the door of which sits an old man looking with an air of apathy on all that passes; or some little shop, in whose lofty and small bow-window may be seen divers of the multifarious wares in which, as is set forth over the door, Dorothy Smith is a licensed dealer;—or by an old public-house, "The Cross Keys," or "Travellers' Rest," furnished with its wooden horse-block, on the steps of which may be seen two or three idle townsmen smoking their long pipes, and listening to the knot they always assemble round them, who, with folded arms, talk over the affairs of the town or of the nation, and are thence called such-a-one's parliament.

At the pump, which is found in every street, and is in one or two instances an extremely picturesque little edifice of old stone or yet more ancient looking wood, may be found a similar group of female gossips; some old and grotesque, both in figure and costume, standing with arms a-kimbo beside their brown nondescript vessels; and others, young, strong, and graceful, standing firmly yet lightly, balancing with one hand the pitcher on their heads, and with the other perhaps holding by the hand a rosy, impatient child; frequently forming groups of great interest and beauty.

These streets all meet in a shapeless sort of market-place, where may be found the smarter shops, and here and the more modern red brick edifice, square and formal, with a door in the centre, four sash windows, with outside shutters painted yellow oak colour, making a most unpleasant contrast to their ancient and respectable neighbours, the houses of lath and plaster. The ornament and grace of the market-place is its ancient cross and well, both united; the cross worn away and crumbling with time, but yet upon which may still be discovered traces of the rich carved work that once adorned it; its steps, too, worn to the very base with the feet of many generations; but its bountiful well, pure and clear, and fresh as ever pouring out in the dryest summers its free sparkling waters, like a never-stinted blessing. I love these old holy wells and crosses; though they may belong to an age of ignorance and superstition, it was a truly Christian act to place them by the wayside, and in the market-place, for the use and blessing of all.

In one of the less frequented streets stands a range of old buildings of one story, with small windows of little diamond panes, and each window divided by a heavy stone mullion; doors of unpainted oak, ornamented and strengthened with large lozenge pattern of iron nails; and over the central door an inscribed tablet, purporting that "these almshouses were erected and endowed by Elizabeth May and Jane Doubleday, spinsters, for old dames of godly character" and ever and anon one of these two old dames may be seen dismissing some little grandchild, or opening the door for the old cat that sat outside mewing for admittance. At the bottom of the street stands the church, by peeping through the chancel-window of which, a view may be had of the effigies of those charitable spinsters, extended on their common tomb, which moreover immortalizes the person of a favourite dog, and modestly sets forth on its surrounding panels of white marble the genealogies and bountiful nature of the worthy pair.

The church itself is of considerable size, and, though of the simplest Gothic, has a handsome appearance, principally owing to the beauty of a finely-proportioned and lofty spire. The churchyard is one of the pleasantest I ever saw; not locked up from the public, but forming a link to the market-place and the little street I have mentioned, by a broad gravel walk which runs through it; and yet it is as green, quiet, and untrampled as the fairest lawn. It lies upon a pleasant slope to the south, commanding an extensive prospect over that fine pastoral country which on all sides surrounds Wood Leighton, but is on this more particularly rich and smiling, and where, at a distance of half a mile, a bright and classical English river winds through its green meadows like a line of silver.

The monuments and mural tablets in the church are very numerous; its chancel being the burial-place of many old families in the neighbourhood; in some instances, of families now extinct, and, in others, dwindled and decayed, even, as in one case, to the sole survivor being now an inhabitant of an almshouse.

There is an extremely beautiful effigy of alabaster, singularly perfect from having been walled in, and only discovered of late years, of an abbess who, as the tradition says, travelled on foot, perhaps in penance, attended by a lay sister. Night came on as they were approaching Wood Leighton, and they lost their way, for many hours wandering about in a wood below the town—a marshy, desolate wood in those days—and had given themselves up for lost, when they heard the cheering sound of a curfew-bell; their spirits revived, and the sound directed them which way to advance. They reached Wood Leighton, and the abbess, a delicate, feeble woman, took to her bed and died on the third day, leaving a sum of money to be paid yearly to the ringer of the curfew-bell; and to this day the bell is tolled an unusual length of time.

The effigy is wonderfully beautiful; and if the abbess in figure was but half as graceful as she is here represented, she must have indeed been a splendid woman, and the habit of her order admirably ordered to set off the symmetry of her figure. Nothing can be more graceful than the contour of her bust. This circumstance is authenticated by the town records—singular but most interesting documents, preserved from the year 1252, when Wood Leighton was made a borough town. These incidents are thus recorded.

1417, November. The abbess came. Paid for doctor and attendants, seven shillings and fourpence.

The abbess gave the rent of the Spicer's Fie which she had purchased, for the nightly ringing of the curfew-bell, by the space of one quarter of an hour, after the hour of eight at night.

Paid to him that fetched the notary, threepence.

Paid to the three women that laid out the body, sixpence.

Paid for making the vault, and the costs of burial, five pounds ten shillings and threepence.

Paid to the man who rode with the sister Maud to Derby, one shilling.

1410. Paid to the mason and his men who put up the monument and stone figure, seventeen shillings and fivepence. Such records as these are invaluable. The entries made during the wars of the Commonwealth furnish a better history, and give a more vivid picture of the times and their incidents, than many a volume of what is called legitimate history. I will make my extracts from this period.

1642. Paid to them that swept Mr. Ward's hall for King Charles, one shilling.

Paid to the ringers when the king was here, five shillings.

Put in the purse for the king, fifty pounds, nineteen shillings.

Paid for rings for the said purse, two shillings.

Paid for maten, powder, and coals, at some of the town-ends in February, fifteen shillings, one penny.

John Sharratt, for leading clods four days to the bulwarks, sixteen shillings.

To carpenters and labourers at the bulwarks, five pounds fifteen shillings and twopence.

Bestowed on the countrymen when they came to guard the town, two shillings and threepence.

For watching Lord Stanhope and his son at the Crown, eleven shillings.

To a prisoner that came from Hopton Battle, fourpence.

Paid for match, powder, candles, bullets, and coals, for the town-ends, two pounds, ten shillings, and ninepence.

Bestowed on the men that came into trench, fourpence.

Paid for drink to the men of five villages when they came to help the town against Worthley, four shillings.

Paid to the men who fetched in provisions, one shilling and fourpence.

Paid to the three men who watched the ordnance at the Crown door, one shilling and sixpence.

Paid Richd. Cartridge for watching in the church, eightpence.

Ale for the captain and his men, who brought a warrant from Lord Loughborough for fifty pounds, three shillings.

For ale, tobacco, wood, coals, and pay for the guards and sentinels, two pounds, ten shillings, and fourpence.

1644. Paid for a rope to hang the man that killed John Scott, and for rope to pinion the prisoner, one shilling

For 7 cwt. 2 qrs. 7 lbs of cheese to Tutbury, seven pounds, fifteen shillings, and tenpence.

Levies upon the town, six hundred and eight pounds.

1645. Paid to Prince Rupert's cook for his fee, five shillings.

Hay, oats, beer, tobacco, wood, and coals, for the guard, three nights, when the Parliament came against Tutbury castle, one pound, nineteen shillings, and eightpence.

For guides to go a-scouting, three nights, nine shillings.

For a sheet, making a grave, ringing, beer, and burying the soldier slain in the streets, four shillings.

For a warrant to make Hanson give up his corn, eightpence.

For bringing in two soldiers who were maimed at the High Wood, two shillings and sixpence.

Paid for the doctor, seven shillings.

To Widow Allen and her seven children, four shillings.

1610. To two horses and a man to carry bread and cheese to Tutbury in the night, they being in great want, three shillings and fourpence.

Paid to two towns when the people had the plague there, eight pounds.

For quartering General Fairfax's soldiers, twenty pounds.

For quartering Colonel Cromwell's soldiers, twenty pounds.

For quartering Colonel Oakley's men, thirteen pounds, two shillings.

1647. To forty-five travellers, or Egyptians, with a pass from Parliament to travel by the space of six months together to get relief, four shillings.

1648. To two men watching on the steeple when the town was fearful of an insurrection, one shilling and fourpence.

1651. For a warrant to fetch in and search for papists' and delinquents' arms, fourpence.

For proclaiming the Lord Protector, one shilling.

Paid the ringers, five shillings.

Paid for a warrant for the witch, fourpence.

To those who oversaw the ducking, one shilling.

1660. Paid to the ringers when King Charles the Second was proclaimed, eight shillings.

For painting the king's arms, nineteen shillings and twopence.

Ringing on the coronation-day, eight shillings.

Repairing the stocks and the cuck-stool, eight shillings

A warrant for Quakers, one shilling.

For wine and ale at the Crown, two pounds, two shillings, and sixpence.

For coal for the bonfires, eight shillings.

For ale at the High Street bonfire, four shillings.

For ale at the Church-yard bonfire, four shillings.

For ale at the Cross bonfire, four shillings.

Given to two drummers at the same time, two shillings.

Paid for one new flag of fine silk, two pounds.

Here is a perfect history. The good people of Wood Leighton are loyal; Mr. Ward's hall must be swept for the king's reception, and a purse with new rings is given him, containing what we must suppose a handsome bonus. The town is defended for him, and the bells ring while he is there. One can feel the troubles that succeed; the barricading of the town-ends—the digging the trench—the coming in of the countrymen to help—the killing and maiming of the townspeople—the distress of the widow and the seven small children—the raising levies—the sending relief here and there—colonels and captains coming and going with their companies—warrants issued for supplies—laden wagons going out with corn and oats, hay and cheese; all this one can see: what a turmoil was kept up in the little town, and what a consternation through all the district! Still the town is loyal, and Prince Rupert's cook has his fee. Prince Rupert must have been a gourmand to have travelled with his cook at the head of his army in such times as these! Presently one can feel the change that has come over them. The king's party is falling—the Leaguers are helped—Cromwell and Fairfax enter the town with their soldiers, and are quartered there; tradition says the church was converted into barracks; in fact, one may feel a disrespect for the sacred edifice by one little entry—two men watching on the steeple—it is no longer the church—"when the town was fearful of an insurrection;" all had not, therefore, gone over to the ruling powers. But one thing we may be sure of,—he that made this entry was a puritan; papacy and churches were out of fashion, and warrants are issued for searching for papists' and delinquents' arms, and five Wood Leighton men are drafted for the Parliament militia. Who cannot see, too, the little town's wonder as the five-and-forty travelling Egyptians come in with their pass? The place is all astir,—we can see it plainly—we can hear the talk it occasioned at every fireside. The strange men from foreign parts are forgotten; a new event occurs. The Lord Protector is proclaimed, and the bells ring as they did when the king was here. Two years go on, and Cromwell dies; King Charles the Second comes to his own again; the little town is loyal once more, and our chronicle ends merrily. The bells ring, the royal arms are painted and put up in the again-honoured church. Puritanism is out of vogue; the stocks are repaired, and a warrant is issued against the quakers; —but what matter? Coronation-day comes, eight shillings are paid to the ringers, whereas for his father and the Lord Protector they had but five. Loud rang the bells, and Wood Leighton was a joyful town. 'Jovial doings were there at the Crown—this inn must have been out of repute in Cromwell's days. Who cannot see the very landlord himself? The Corporation and the gentlemen had a dinner there, and two guineas were paid for wine: three bonfires were blazing in the town, and there were two extra drummers beside the Wood Leighton band. Who does not see how mad the little town was?—who does not hear the ringing of the bells—the sound of squibs and crackers—the firing of guns—the parading of the band, with the new flag of fine silk displayed abroad, and the tattooing of the two extraordinary drummers? Who does not see all this, and all the people too, the tradesmen and their wives, dressed in their best, walking about, and smiling merrily on this day of great rejoicing?

Leaving the town, I must now beg my readers to accompany me on an April morning, by a footpath, through the little meadow that bounds our garden, to the hilly fields opposite, and so upwards through crofts and by a variety of the most rustic cottages, embowered in orchards, now white over with blossom, to the range of high ground which bounds our home landscape. Arrived here, we find the country stretching onwards for about three miles of pleasantly wooded farm-land to the forest-crowned slopes of Needwood, dark and richly undulating; a belt of magnificent wood of many miles extent, terminated on the left by the ruin-crowned hill of Tutbury, and on the right stretching on towards the cathedral city of Lichfield.

The situation of Wood Leighton, as seen from this height, unites everything of which I can form an idea in the most beautiful pastoral landscapes. About a mile below us, at the foot of those rural enclosures we passed in our ascent, and of which now only here and there a green slip can be seen through their abundant trees, against whose fresh vernal foliage rises the white smoke of their hidden cottages, Wood Leighton is seen, with its clustered buildings and lofty spire, just where a fine valley opens into one still finer, and, indeed into one of the most luxuriant and celebrated vales of England, and down which the river I have mentioned before flows from the wild regions of the Peak of Derbyshire. It is just, too, where this noble and prolific valley changes its course, and leaves a flat of the most abounding meadows in the immediate neighbourhood of the town. Thus, to the right, we command a view along this extensive vale in all its beauty, beyond the wood-embosomed mansions of two noble lords, as far down as the lofty ruins of Tutbury Castle; and before us, beyond the town, over another region of wood, from the midst of which are dimly seen villages and old grey halls, to the blue and shadowy softness of wild bills, at twenty miles' distance, which form the north of the county, and run on into the still wilder hills of the Peak. To the right of Wood Leighton, and overlooking the valley, though at another angle, on the bold brow of a hill, stands a noble mansion, and its dependant village church and delightful

parsonage, half shrouded in surrounding—woods seeming proudly
to survey the animated scene—this plenteous valley—its thousands
of cattle—its river winding through its green expanse, and all
around it a vast extent of undulating country in the highest state
of cultivation.

The situation of Wood Leighton seems to fit it for the capital of
a pastoral district, which, in fact, it may be considered. The spirit
and revolution of manners produced by great manufactories have
scarcely come within twenty miles of it; and the inhabitants of
either town or neighbourhood living fifty years ago might rise and
behold their old haunts little altered, except by the silent attacks of
time, the progress of agriculture, the facilities afforded by excellent
roads, and the general improvement in all modern vehicles. In this
way, however, they certainly would be surprised to see strangers
pass through their out-of-the-world town; some even in splendid
carriages with gay liveries; others, spruce commercial travellers in
gigs, with cloaks and many-caped coats hanging behind, enough to
shelter half a dozen people from the most tremendous storm: but
beyond all would they be astonished to find a stage coach, which,
going from London to the North, diverges a few miles from its
direct course, to take Wood Leighton in its way.* Very different
would these things seem to the scenes of their times, when the
neighbouring gentry deemed a journey to London as serious an
affair as a voyage to the East Indies is reckoned now; and when it
was customary to make their wills before setting out, and to take
a guide and trusty guard to the next market-town to keep them
out of bogs and the danger of robbers. Perhaps, too, they might be
a little surprised at the style in which their children issued from
their old farm-houses, in many a little woody and sequestered
valley, punctually as they themselves were wont on market-days to
their favourite old town and inn, but still in a different guise; some
dressed like country squires, in their short bottle-green coats and
striped waistcoats, booted and spurred, and scouring away on blood-
horses; some even in gigs and jaunty tax-carts; others with seats of
board swung across a tilted cart, a whole family jogging along

together, and a few of the older trotting sedately on their long-tailed, heavy-heeled cart-horses. The shades of the grandmothers, nevertheless, would run a risk of being still more shocked. What, for instance, would a good dame who came to market in her worky-day dress of linsey-woolsey and a blue apron, say to find her lotions of buttermilk, elder-flowers, and May-dew exploded for a green silk parasol, which I saw the first market-day in April, carried by a dainty young damsel who came to the market with eggs?

With the exception, however, of such occasional innovations as this, the two last generations would find all things much as they left them; the country as quiet and pleasant as ever, and inhabited by a race as simple, as hospitable, and as honestly old-fashioned as themselves.

I write of the neighbourhood of Wood Leighton as we found it after the whole summer's experience; and, first making my reader acquainted with its general aspect, we will visit together more particularly its individual scenes and characters. We traversed the country in all directions, and sometimes were ready to believe we were among things of a century ago. There were so many of the scenes and images and persons about us in which the poets of an earlier period so abundantly deal—such antiquated figures and dresses—such homely but hearty greetings in cottage and in grange—such sights and sounds of old English rusticity, and such an air of sylvan solitude and beauty wherever we went, as delighted me doubly, because I thought they had ceased to exist.

At one time we found ourselves seated by the ruins of an old castle, finding interest in every mass of stone, every crumbling turret, and even in the very weeds through which we waded to every forsaken corner. Then we were rambling through the adjoining park, still left in all its olden rudeness; its oaks aged, gnarled, and grey, thinly scattered over hill and dale; the fern springing from its dry and scorched turf; the hare crouched among it, with its large round eye watching us anxiously; the rabbit seen by its little white tuft of tail, scudding to its burrow; the fallow deer trotting lightly at a distance; the old red stag shaking his antlered head in the shade to dismiss those black vampires, the flies; and the heron, slowly wafting herself above the solitary scene.—all seemed full of the spirit of poetry, and conjured up dreams and stories of feudal days. Again, we were exploring the ruined abbey, admiring the sagacity or the good taste of monastic zeal, which delighted always to build its nest, not only in the midst of rural solitude, but also of rural plenty and pastime. On other days we progressed to the old but inhabited hall, surveying its lofty turrets and solemn aspect with a feeling almost of reverence as we advanced slowly between rows of ancient trees up the grassy avenue, and were admitted through its huge and sounding door by a spruce valet or an ancient serving-woman; tracing till we are weary, its tapestried rooms, and galleries hung with sombre portraits of beauties and warriors innumerable, down to the present lord and his favourite horse, or the smiling golden-haired little daughter leading her greyhound with a blue ribbon, now a woman grown and a mother in some distant hall.

But, whatever was the object of our attention, our walk to it was always through scenes of the most pastoral or sylvan character, the remains of the forest, now depopulated of its fairies and its outlaws, but delightful for its recollections and its traditionary tales—for its wild glades, its thickets of black impenetrable holly, and some far-famed oak, shooting from a trunk of many yards' circumference a wide extended shade of mighty branches, and curling up its knotted and sinewy roots into seats, as if for half a hundred woodland revellers; or over untracked and sunny heaths, wrapped in mud solitude, unbroken but by the crow of the pheasant cry of the peewit, aroused by some old woman or a band of little children gathering cranberries. Most commonly, however, our rambles lay through quiet villages, where the Maypole swings aloft its garlands, and on all hands you see groups of children, covered with dust and happiness, delving in the dry banks, making mills and playing at selling sugar,

> Mimicking, with self-important airs,
> Of elder life the business and the cares,—

and where, in short, the dress of old and young, and the peeping from door and window as we went by, showed that strangers there were strangers indeed. Everywhere we met with farm-houses, with their gardens weeded and dug once a year, exhibiting in many cases a curious mixture of flowers and weeds; roses blushing through tall tussocks of grass; wall-flowers, snapdragons, and white lilies springing promiscuously with nettles and dandelions from walls, flower-beds, and foot-paths: horticulture it was evident had not made much progress here. Perhaps, too, a large cat might be seen sleeping amongst them, darting wildly away at the first glimpse of a visiter; or a hen scratling and scratching the dust over her on a dry border. Dark, ample kitchens were there, well stored with ham and bacon flitch in the wide chimney; rows of pewter plates and round dishes of an immense size ranged on the dresser-shelves, in the very position in which they were placed a century ago; and two or three stout country girls, stripped to the stays and green petticoat, with arms and faces glowing with prodigality of health, ever moving about the door employed in their cheerful farmhouse occupations.

Occasionally, however, we found gardens the very reverse of the one I have described; trim and neat, and glowing with the most abundant growth of every antiquated flower that shall be found either in poetry or calendar, all looking the very pictures of their quaint old-fashioned names: polyanthuses, oxlips, daffodils, and gillifowers; sweet-williams and pinks; heart'sease, larkspur, lemon-thyme, and vervain; sweetbriar, and the rose of May; the star of Bethlehem, honesty, and Aaron's rod; and a honeysuckle twined round a little open arbour, within which the quiet farmer and his wife sat enjoying their garden on a Sunday afternoon. To a garden of this sort invariably belonged an ancient orchard of those old-fashioned little red apples and large brown pears which more modem cultivators hold in sovereign contempt.

* Since this was written a greater marvel has entered Wood Leighton in the shape of steam-carriages—a railroad being in preparation which runs along its quiet meadows, nearly cutting through the little town, and startling its inhabitants with a spirit of bustle and enterprise unknown to them before.

M. H.

The Vicar and his Family

At the end of a little wooded lane, as smooth and finely kept as a garden path, and about ten minutes' walk from the church, among tall old elms thickly populated by a colony of rooks, stands the vicarage, an antiquated mansion-like building, of dark purple-coloured bricks, mingled in diamond patterns with those of the common kind. The style of the house is so noble, that the first impression is of its being unusually large; the second, of the perfectly good taste in which it is built, and its appropriateness to its situation. It stands upon the same slope with the churchyard, and commands the same view, excepting rather more confined, and with a more western aspect, and including the church and beautiful churchyard.

The ground-floor is occupied by the kitchens and servants' apartments, and the entrance is gained by a double flight of steps guarded by a heavy stone balustrade. The entrance-hall is in the most exquisite taste, and represents the nave of a church, with side aisles formed by clustered pillars, in which are the doors opening to the different rooms: these pillars, three on each side, support galleries leading in the same way to the chambers. The ceiling is richly finished in stucco-work, representing angels and cherubs flying towards the centre; which is so managed, though a perfectly flat surface, as to represent the hollow of a dome, in which a shadowy company seems to be assembled, with a very grand effect, it is one of the most beautiful and unique ceilings I ever saw. My first inquiry was, who could possibly have been the designer and executor of so singular a work; an original and poetic mind, whoever it might be: but I could gain no satisfactory information. There appeared to be no tradition belonging to it; nor had it excited any attention but had been in a state of great neglect, till the present incumbent came to the living, about five-and-twenty years ago. He brought it into notice, and, like myself, questioned of every one what was its history. No one knew; "the well-fed wits" of Wood Leighton were puzzled; and even Mr. Pope, the antiquarian of the district, could throw no light on it; nor, which was a worse dilemma in his eyes, could he, in any of his ancient tomes, meet with any account of a ceiling that bore a resemblance to it: it was therefore, he wisely concluded, the work of no man of reputation, and was not worth further trouble. The vicar's family thought differently.

The hall is lighted by two lofty windows, one on each side the door, of the old-fashioned casement kind, and glazed with small panes of glass. Opposite the entrance is the broad dark oak staircase, lighted by a similar window, excepting that it contains a good deal of stained glass. The staircase is within a recess which falls back from the square of the hall; and on each side is a large panel on the wall, painted in oil, very dark and old, and yet producing a good effect: the one represents the angels announcing to the shepherds the birth of the Saviour; the other, Christ delivering the keys to Peter. The rest of the house, however, is much plainer than this hall, and only corresponds with it in the solidity of the work and the excellent finish of every part. But before we enter the rooms, let me prepare my reader for those he shall find there.

A finer specimen of an English gentleman never lived than the Rev. Hugh Somers. He was a good deal past middle life; but was one of those temperate, cheerful-spirited men on whom time makes no havoc: the very indications of age in him appeared but like graceful characteristics of person. That he had ever been handsomer than he then was, I could not imagine. His manner you immediately felt was that of one who had mixed much with the best society; it was so perfectly calm and natural, so free from that flutter and anxiety which never can be got rid of by one unaccustomed to society, or who endeavours to appear what he is not. Yet his manners were not those of the finished gentleman merely; his politeness was more the sincerity of a good heart than the etiquette of modern fashion. There was, too, an earnestness and good faith in everything he said and did that assured you, beyond profession, of the high moral tone of his character, and the perfect integrity of his spirit. To all this he added a keen insight into character, a ready wit, and high relish of humour. In his youth he had been chaplain in a noble family, had lived much in London, and afterwards, accompanying his patron abroad, had seen every variety of character and society in the principal cities of Europe. His knowledge, therefore, was not only derived from books, but was the fruit of his own experience, gained under circumstances the most fortunate in the world.

Such a man as this, we sometimes thought, was thrown away on the antiquated people of Wood Leighton; but yet, when we came to consider that his pleasant manners and knowledge of the world made him an acceptable guest at the tables of the best families in the county, and that he occasionally diversified his rural life by joining in those circles, we found that he was not buried, and that, besides, he had those particular tastes which must make a country life pleasant to a person of educated mind. He was fond of all kinds of antiquities, heraldry, tracing of genealogies; and in his library were to be found, placed side by side with the best editions of the classics, and the best English and foreign divines, all sorts of works on antiquity and topography. He was a complete chronicle of the histories of all the old houses and old families in the neighbourhood: you could mention no one but he could tell you all its connexions; trace the descent of the family, its marriages and intermarriages, with many a particular event worthy of narration, but which yet had never found its way into any written narration. He had explored every castle, abbey, mound, embankment, and barrow to be found within fifty miles; and had at his tongue's end all that had ever been conjectured about them, much more known. He was equally fond of natural history with Gilbert White of Selborne; and much resembled him in his delight of rambling in the woods, and watching the habits and goings-on of birds, beasts, and insects. Nothing in the world did the dear old man enjoy more than an excursion to visit some curious object or some pleasant place; some delicious quarter of the old forest; some secluded water; some nondescript race of people, who had settled themselves in some out-of-the-way-region; and I believe he liked us all the better because we furnished him with an excuse for ordering out his low four-wheeled chaise, and his broad, sleek, jolly roan horse, that he might again visit them in our company.

If, however, Mr. Somers found in his parish none who could fully estimate his more sterling qualities and acquirements, this was not the case in his own home: there he lived with the most congenial spirits, and among the most loving and admiring hearts. His family at the time we came to Wood Leighton consisted only of his wife, his daughter, and a youth of seventeen, to whom he was guardian: two sons there were, but they were considerably older than their sister, had married wealthily, and were settled in distant parts of England.

His wife was tall and slender, and remarkably agile. Walking behind her, you would suppose, from the buoyancy of her step and the excellence of her figure, that she was not above thirty years of age; but in reality her countenance was that of a person much older than her husband, and probably your first idea might be that she was much his inferior in intellect. At your first view, you thought her homely; at the second, domestic; at the third, matronly; and as your knowledge of her character grew upon you, you became struck, astonished, and delighted at the wealth of poetic feeling—at the strong sense and extensive general knowledge that she possessed; so that you did not wonder when you heard her husband, as you often afterwards did, say how much he had been indebted in his most difficult moments to her judgment and animated by her energy. These higher qualities of Mrs. Somers were, however, little known beyond her own family; it was the strong benevolence of her nature, the affectionate sympathy she felt for all around her, that made her loved and admired in Wood Leighton. Such were the vicar and his lady.

Their daughter was a happy union of the characteristics and higher qualities of both her parents. In person she was rather above the middle size, delicately fair, and of a lofty style of beauty; the expression of her countenance was that of a superior intellect. The contour of her head was of the purest antique, gracefully set on her fine neck and shoulders—a forehead wonderfully fair and noble—intelligent eyes of that deep, dark colour which defies description; the beholder thought not, however, of the colour—he only felt their sentiment, whether of mirth or tenderness, flashing forth indignation, or spiritualized, as it were, into the very essence of light; hence it was that they have been described of all colours— certain it was that they were among the very finest eyes in the world. Her nose was not either Grecian or Roman, but finely and freely chiselled, and in harmony with the rest of her face; her mouth might have had too strong a character of decision about it, had it not continually relaxed into the most arch and merry—nay, almost mischievous expression; her smile was irresistible, and her laugh the most cordial bursting forth of an uncontrollable joy—the very laugh of a Euphrosyne. Beautiful Elizabeth Somers! she was a creature all glowing with kindness and radiant with happiness, as if her business on earth were create a paradise of the heart wherever she came. At one moment, when you listened to her relation of something tender and touching, her countenance had that calm, angelic aspect that seemed to mark especially her character, and her voice that tone of deep pathos that thrilled and melted you down into the most sorrowful but delightful sympathy. Then, again, you heard a light laugh come from some distant part of the garden, all reckless gaiety;

or you heard her chattering to her mother in that saucy, waggish, familiar merriment, that would have seemed downright irreverence if it were not for that thorough good-nature and purity of heart that marked her whole being. Then, again, you saw her bright face turned back to you, all radiant with smiles, and full of arch meanings, as she sat by her father's side in his little carriage, as he drove on before you along some wooded lane. Beautiful Elizabeth Somers! The charming frankness of her manners—her independence and right-mindedness—the indignation of her spirit against meanness or oppression—the sunny joyousness of her nature—the deep piety and exquisite tenderness of her soul, combine to form a character as delightful to be known as rare to be met with!

Charles Harwood, the ward of Mr. Somers, was the orphan child of a young physician, who had died just as a splendid career of first-rate practice was opening to him in London; his wife had died in giving birth to this their first child. Dr. Harwood had not been sufficiently long in practice to have accumulated any fortune, and the agony of death was embittered tenfold by the desolate prospects of his child, who would be left among relations upon whose judgment and principle he had no dependence, whatever confidence he might have in their well-meaning affection. In this moment of anxious distress he begged the presence of Mr. Somers, to whom he was well known; and while he left his boy under the care of his nearest relatives, delivered him into the hands of Mr. Somers, solemnly conjuring him to exercise the authority of a father on his behalf. All this was cheerfully promised; and the good man remained with him, comforting, cheering, and strengthening his spirit in its last struggle.

Dr. Harwood's relatives, however, with that touchy pride so common to little minds, offended at the preference which seemed shown to another, declined taking charge of the child at all; and Mr. Somers, indignant at their selfish and cold-hearted natures, summoned his wife from Wood Leighton. Her counsel was the most generous and decided—that he should take the entire charge of the friendless orphan on himself; and accordingly the little

Charles, a rosy and happy child of but two years old, was brought home with them to Wood Leighton.

He grew a fine, high-spirited boy, of a frank, bold, and most generous nature—indeed, what a noble nature must have become under such tuition; and, four years the junior of Elizabeth, in every respect he filled the place of the youngest child of the family, never being otherwise thought of than as son and brother; and Mr. Somers, with the noblest consideration for his ward, conducted his education himself, that his little patrimony might accumulate as much as possible; and, though study was not his choice, the boy nobly repaid his instructor. Still, however, there was in him an independence and originality of mind that produced a peculiar character; and, though bred among books, and designed from the first by his guardian for the church, he soon showed propensities and inclinations of another kind. He was of a most stirring, enterprising turn;—the most arduous undertakings—anything in which courage and endurance, whether of mind or body, were required, were the pursuits after which he panted.

While yet a little boy, if any strange accident occurred in the town, Charles was the first to bring tidings of it—was sure to have been in the very way of it; it seemed as if he went out to meet with adventures; and sure it was, wherever he went, adventures fell out and strange incidents happened as if for his behoof:—

Where crowds assembled he was sure to run—
Hear what was said, and muse on what was done.

He knew everybody in the town, and continually astonished his guardian by the intimate knowledge he had of persons and things of the most out-of-the-way, and often equivocal, kind; nor was there a house in the whole town that he was not privileged to enter how and when he liked. The most prominent bent of his mind, however, was a passion for the sea. This, instinct it might be called, where there was no one object, no one person to give birth to it in the child, showed itself very soon after he came under the Somers' roof,

and was seen by them with the greatest pain, and discouraged as
much a possible, from their being aware of this singular fact, that
such a propensity had existed in his family for generations, and
had been most fatal to it. There was scarcely a colony or sea on
the whole globe in which some branch of his family had not been
lost, and in most instances in early life. The propensity, however, was
too strong to be crushed: the child, who could have but the most
vague notions of the sea, sat shaping his little blocks of wood into
boats; and as he grew older, and could consult books, his vessels
were made with the most astonishing skill and accuracy; they were
to be found in every corner of the house—in many a house too
in Wood Leighton—and his own chamber resembled a dock-yard.
It was in vain that all means were used to divert this tendency—it
grew only stronger, becoming every year a more determined part
of his character; and at fourteen, as might be expected, Robinson
Crusoe and the Arabian Tales were the only books he had any
thorough relish for.

He had also a wonderful turn for mechanics—furnished a little
workshop for himself, set up a lathe, and turned cups and balls
for all his little friends—snuff-boxes for all the old men of his
acquaintance; made reels and bodkin-cases, and mended spinning-
wheels for the old women—no wonder he was popular in Wood
Leighton—and presented curious tobacco-stoppers, wafer-seals,
and all sorts of knickknacks in wood and ivory, to everybody, who
would do him the favour to accept them. There was nothing that
seemed beyond his skill, from a gate in the field to a jewel-box: he
made a writing-desk for Elizabeth, and mended her clogs; made a
kitchen-table and a tea-caddy for Mrs. Somers, and presented his
guardian, as an ornament for his study, with the most elaborate piece
of his ship-building. Sorely puzzled was Mr. Somers what to do
in this case—he would rather the boy had made wooden skewers
than the finest ship that ever was built; but he knew it was in the
gratitude of his heart that the poor fellow offered him what he
considered his best piece of work: he accepted it, therefore, cordially,
and placed it on the mantelpiece of his study, little knowing how

dear and invaluable it would one day become. Poor Charles! he was a thorough sailor; in spirit wild, thoughtless, and overflowing with generosity—beloved by every one, and at every one's service. He drove Elizabeth about the country, and everywhere astonished her by introducing her to his acquaintances, from Sir Harry Highflyer down to the Scotch drover on the road; brought home rooks' and lapwings' eggs and hornets' nests for Mr. Somers; and, like a faithful page, was ever ready at Mrs. Somer command, winning at the same time the love of everybody by his original humour, his thorough good-nature, and the irrepressible flow and elasticity of his spirits.

Such was Charles Harwood when we came to Wood Leighton— a handsome, well-grown youth of seventeen, with an open, good-tempered countenance, large blue eyes, and a brown manly complexion;—his whole air was that of a youth designed for the sea. This was the only disputed point between him and his friends. Mr. Somers said, "Charles must go to Cambridge;" Charles said, "I must go to sea!"

Such, gracious reader, was the family at the vicarage.

The rooms opening out of the hall were four: those on the right, a dining-room and small boudoir, called by Elizabeth her bower; on the left, a library and drawing-room. The window of the lesser room on the right opened upon a flagged terrace which ran along the higher part of the garden its whole length, screened at the back by a wilderness of shrubbery, beyond and above which rose the tall elms filled with the voices of their dusky tenants; the garden, which lay below this, was upon the slope I have spoken of, commanding, as indeed the terrace did, that fine Arcadian view, together with the church and part of Wood Leighton, through trees and shrubbery, which could not be seen from the terrace. The garden had been laid out when the house was built—about the time of Queen Anne, and had a corresponding air of stateliness. It had been the good fortune of this place never to have been *improved*; the cypresses grew where they had first been planted—so did a fair cedar-tree, the glory of the garden, spreading forth its horizontal branches magnificently; the pleached walks might have stood from the days of Shakespeare, so might the old grey sun-dial in the middle of the square of fine turf, that was springy and soft to the foot as a turkey carpet. Before the windows of the drawing-room—which, I should have said, opened to the library by folding doors, making a noble apartment—played a small fountain, which fell into a curiously-carved basin representing large scallop shells laid one within the other, from the centre of which, where all the narrow ends of the shells met, sprang the small silvery jet of water, firm and clear as a column of quicksilver, to about the height of a man, and then fell again in a thousand individual streams, that bore a fanciful resemblance to the boughs of a weeping willow carved in frostwork. Nothing more beautiful than this fountain can be imagined; and when the auxiliaries of a fine peacock sunning his stateliness near it, or Elizabeth's doves drinking and sporting themselves in its water, were added, it seemed most like a beautiful piece of eastern luxury—the realization of a picture in the Arabian Tales.

The first bond between Elizabeth Somers and ourselves was the admiration we had of the country about Wood Leighton. "I can get nobody to join with me," said Elizabeth, "in extolling these Arcadian scenes of ours. Mr. Pope merely says, 'Yes, yes, fine coursing country; fine growth of timber; it always had that—prefix to names of places shows it: Wood seat, Wood-ford, Up-wood, Low-wood, and so on;' Mr. Reynolds, to be sure, who is visiting at Captain Kenrock's, does condescend to think it resembles Italy; the Captain and good Mrs. Nelly, dear blind souls, can see nothing at all to admire in it: and my friend, Miss Traintree, the prettiest girl hereabout, thinks the closest street in London preferable to the best view that ever was!"

In us, therefore, Elizabeth found the very quality she missed in others. We not only admired the country, but were willing and able explorers of all the hidden nooks within ten miles; and we never met without planning some fresh excursion; some ride to forest or chase, or some walk to a favourite village: there was always some old hall or castle to be seen, stories and traditions of which she gleaned up with indefatigable zeal, and related with a pathos or humour which I only wish I could transfer to my pages.

BEGGARS AND WAYFARERS

ONE DAY AT THE VICARAGE we were talking of beggars we were remarking that even in so retired a place as Wood Leighton, where old usage seemed of such universal acceptance, the race of picturesque, nay, *respectable* beggars, if one may be allowed a phrase which in these days of vagrant-laws appears somewhat incongruous, seemed extinct. There were no longer, even here, any remains of that privileged race of mendicants, common in the beginning even of the present century, who, having a fixed residence in some town or village, under a roofless hovel, or tumble-down shed perhaps, which nobody else thought worth owning, wandered up and down the country in all seasons, welcomed and authorised visitors, carrying news from one retired district to another, and claiming, year after year, the same cast-off article of wearing apparel from the same family, which was never refused, and by which means they always retained the same uniform characteristic appearance. They had an ancient family-look about them; and, when death at length put an end to their wandering, they were missed from their accustomed haunts in many ways, and were long talked of and remembered with regret. Such objects as these are excellent adjuncts to a landscape, beautiful in their picturesqueness as an ancient and shattered oak or an ivy-clothed ruin.

We had known Tam Hogg, the pilgrim wire-worker, who wheeled in an immense barrow, at a snail's pace, his portable forge, his manufactured goods, and his raw material, from town to town throughout the length and breadth of merry England. We had stood beside him as children, marvelling much at the wise old man, grave and sarcastic, who read much, talked little, kept a tame hedgehog in his barrow, never slept in a house, and who, chained to his moveable workshop, then closed, stood reading his Bible during the whole Sabbath; and lastly who made verses and curious witty acrostics and anagrams on people's names, and epitaphs on the dead, one of which in his own handwriting, we still possess.

We had known Betty Bolsover, the travelling pedlaress, who came once a year to the home of our childhood, a welcome guest, in her long blue cloak and man's hat; a big, bony woman of near six feet high. She carried a flat basket divided into compartments containing thread tied in hanks, white and whitey-brown, combs and buttons, bodkins and bodkin-cases, turned both in bone and wood; she sold "ferreting" for shoe-strings and smart-coloured worsted garters; pins and Whitechapel needles, warranted with gold eyes and not to cut the thread; Whitechapel sharps, which as she averred would sew of themselves: then, too, she had bobbin flat and round, and tapes fine and coarse, all good linen-thread tapes. But of all Betty's wares none equalled, in my childish fancy, the beauty of those tin tea-caddies, some vermillion, on which golden shells laid among bronze seaweed were figured; some yellow round about which went a march of peacocks shining in red and purple and green, and some black, on which were set forth united hearts, united hands, Cupids with torches and Cupids without, a very valentine of a tea-caddy, bordered round with intertwined wedding-rings, and on the front this legend in golden letters—

When two in Hymen's bonds agree,
To live a life of amity,
Let me be chose their tea to keep,
My lock is good, my price is cheap.

Besides these, had she not boxes of horn, and boxes of tin; boxes japanned, and adorned with cross pipes on the top for tobacco, and others of an approved fashion for snuff? and had she not shoeing-horns, and wooden-spoons, and cabbage-nets, and skewers, and bottle-brushes, and bone-spoons; and spoons tied up half a dozen together in brown paper, with a patter spoon on the outside, which she never displayed without rubbing on the inside of her cloak to make it look like silver? Had she not little tin cans at the low price of twopence—things are sold now-a-days for a penny—painted and unpainted, and adorned with red and green and black flowers, or lettered, "A present for my dear boy," or "For a good girl," or "A present for Sarah," or simply with the name "Hannah," "James?" Had she not all these, and many things beside; knives, and scissors, and nut-crackers—round wooden nut-crackers that worked with a screw, and which, in my childish imagination, bore some relationship to the wine-presses of which we read in Scripture? and had she not apple-scoops made out of a mutton shank-bone, fearful things which always looked yellow and charnelhouse-like? What a treasury of a thousand things was that basket! How in the world she could stow them all away into it, was more than I could comprehend: she was a walking store, according to the American word.

But big Betty was welcomed for something beside the multifarious contents of her basket. Hard-featured, weather beaten woman as she was, what could equal the kindliness of her eye, the bland, winning tones of her voice! Then, too, there was something mysterious about her: she wore a broad silver hoop-ring as a charm against the ague; carried double, triple, and even quadruple nuts in her pocket; and tested the goodness of all the silver money she took by scoring it on a large cabalistical-looking black stone. She had silver pen flies, and always many of those heavy, ungainly coin, copper twopenny-pieces about her; and her money she carried in a skin purse. Oh, she was an awful woman, though she spoke sweetly and looked kindly! Then what could be more thrillingly delicious than the narrative she was always ready to tell, of an adventure which befell her once upon a time. How she had been belated one November night, and took shelter from the storm which came on, in a deserted, way-side house, thinking to take up her quarters there, since none better were at hand; and how, a little past midnight, her first sleep was broken by thieves coming in; and how, unconscious of her presence, they had talked over their intended next night's attack on the squire's house; how they had talked of fearful things, and she scarce dared to breathe, lest they should find her and murder her; how they had at last all gone to sleep in the place, and she, at day break, on tiptoe, had stolen out unperceived, and made the best of her way to the squire's; how the squire had set his house in order to receive the robbers; how they had come at midnight and cut away a casement to effect their entrance and then stealing on, with a dark lantern, along dismal, dark passages to the butler's pantry, had secured the plate which was laid out for them, and then proceeded to the housekeeper's room, where the squire and seven servants, and Betty Bolsover herself, armed with weapons, offensive and defensive, stood ready to receive them; and the how the thieves, finding themselves fairly taken, fell upon their knees and prayed for mercy; but were conveyed the next morning to the county gaol: how she had appeared on the trial as evidence; had been complimented by the lord judge; and had heard sentence pronounced on the thieves—transportation for life to Botany Bay; and, lastly, how the squire had settled forty shillings by the year on her for life.

What a tale of breathless interest and wonder was this to be told to a child! Never shall I forget Betty Bolsover! I love all wandering pedlars, with their flat baskets, for her sake!

"We have had itinerants of our own," said an old gentleman in the company—"we have had itinerants of our own; some perhaps, that you may remember, Mr. Somers? There was Tony Collett, the wandering corkcutter: a fine figure of a man was he, tall and straight, setting down his feet as if he had been web-footed, without a joint below the knee, who spoke in nasal tones, and used a Somersetshire dialect; still he was a well grown figure of a man; his costume, too, of an ample, antique cut, such as William Penn, or any of the old quaker worthies, might have put on, beaver and all.

"Then there was old Henry Hiller, or Healer, as he chose to call himself, as being indicative of his profession. A noted man was Henry in my days, though you, perhaps, may not remember him, Mrs. Somers?"

Mrs. Somers confessed that she did not.

"Henry was a son of Galen," continued the other—"a peripatetic philosopher, who read no works inferior to Aristotle, Pedacius Dioscorides, Paulus Ægineta, Serapion the younger, Albucasis or Averrhoës the Arabian. He was what is vulgarly called a quack doctor, but to my knowledge performed more cures with his vervain ointment, and clary or clear-eye, his elecampane and assarabecca, than half a college of M.D.s. A great nostrum with him for the stanching of blood was pounded nettles and a pretty instance of its virtue I saw in the case of old Simeon Davis, who cut his tongue and was bleeding to death: Henry came by and saw him; when what does the old fellow but cut up some nettles, pound them between two stones, clap on a poultice, and the blood stanched presently!"

"But," said I, "none of these people belong to the class we set out by speaking of—the genuine beggars, who carried nothing to sell, professed no art or calling, but gave the passing news of the country or a hearty benediction, in return for the alms they received."

"Of this class was Peter Clare," said Elizabeth Somers, "a well-known mendicant."

"A well-known scoundrel, an impudent impostor," interrupted the old gentleman —"a pretending vagabond, who claimed kindred with all the best families in the county as a plea for asking their charity!"

"He was a wonderfully fine old man," persisted Elizabeth, "nor would his face and head have belied his claim, however high he might have aspired to kinship."

"Miss Somers, he was a knavish fellow! There was not a genealogy in the county but he had it by heart, and pretended to be allied to all families alike. Why, he pretended to be descended from my own progenitors; as if I were likely to relieve him any sooner for making me seven-and-twentieth cousin to a beggar!"

"Oh," said Elizabeth, laughing, "I will give up Peter Clare if he tried to palm off his genealogical knowledge on you; I thought my friend Peter had been less shallow; I will give him up to your tender mercies."

"And in that case," returned the old gentleman, "I would have him put in the stocks to learn better manners."

"There was Doctor Green," said Charles Harwood, "that mad beggar, who, till within the last few years, used to make his periodical incursion on the town—a little, thin, electrical sort of being, that sent off everybody at a tangent; he cleared the streets like a troop of cavalry; people used to look at him from their windows or behind doors; I remember, very well, my own terror at his small, fiery, red eyes. And even now there's poor Tommy Garland, a sylvan, salvage creature—a Caliban—who appears in the town every now and then, drawing a troop of women and children about him—the very reverse of Doctor Green.

"We have an Alsatia too in the town—the seventh heaven of beggars; a lane eschewed by the townspeople, but which I perambulate occasionally for my own divertisement. In it you shall see, at one time, all the ills that flesh is heir to; as many maimed and miserable as peopled the mountain of misery itself; then, again, you shall see the lame walking, the blind seeing, and hear the dumb singing aloud. I have a most vivid notion of what would be the effect of a visit from one of those healing saints in the days of miracles, from witnessing this renovation of human bodies.

"It is inhabited by a sort of circulating population—all the rag-gatherers, the match-makers, the mop and besom makers, the chair and umbrella menders, the fashioners of iron skewers, the wandering tinkers, musicians, and ballad-singers of the next five counties. There you may see some rare specimens of the animal creation: grotesque and squalid old crones, banditti-like men, boys the very images of Flibbertigibbet or of rib-nosed monkeys—brown, shaggy imps, the personification of mischief and grimace: dogs, too, of every possible kind and degree of ugliness, felonious-looking quadrupeds that seem made to be hanged; others one-eyed, snarling, and with turned-up noses; lank and gaunt, like skeleton dogs, who sit on their haunches shivering even in summer; and some overgrown and apoplectic, waddling, with short fat tails and shorter legs: and their asses, too, sometimes stabled in the lower rooms of uninhabited houses, sometimes tied to the door-post, at others to a stake on the opposite side of the lane, for the houses are but on one side; strange, nondescript animals, many of them with cropped ears and tails to personate horses.

"This lane constitutes a kingdom of its own, governed by its own laws and officers. Royalty here, however, is not hereditary, but elective. Nobody in Wood Leighton will forget the coronation and procession of the last, or rather their present majesties."

"That is of very ancient usage," observed the visiter: "old Sylvanus Scrymshaw has told me of a charter and certain immunities that formerly belonged to that lane, but I find nothing of the sort mentioned either in Plott or Cambden. This town, it is true, was erected into a borough in the reign of Henry III which charter was lost in the time of Henry VII: it might be that this quarter of the town enjoyed privilege under that charter."

"Perhaps," said Mr. Somers, raising himself in his large leather-covered reading-chair, "one of the last of the old fashioned and more respectable class of mendicants was Daniel Neale, the Irish beggar, who died near a hundred years old, and who lived, when at home, with his mother, a very ancient woman, in the Finder's Lane. Why he and his mother had fixed their residence there—for they were Irish, and Roman Catholics—nobody knew; and there was no reason why they should know; for why an old Irish beggar

should not have a spice of mystery about him, and possess a secret
of his own, as well as anybody else, I can see no reason. Old Daniel
was exactly of my way of thinking; and so, if had a secret, or a
particular reason for fixing his abode, he kept them to himself. One
thing was evident enough—he was very fond of the old woman.
Whilst she lived, he maintained her by the fruits of his rambles; and,
at her death, he performed the wake for her with great ceremony;
and many a time, in the darkest and most tempestuous nights, to
the amazement of the neighbours, would be heard howling and
lamenting at her grave.

"After her death his visits to the hovel where they had lived
were less frequent, and his stay shorter. He was often encountered
at an amazing distance from home; and often did he surprise those
who knew him, by finding him quietly seated by the roadside, in
the wildest places and in the wildest weather, as if insensible to
the influence of the elements. There would he sit in a great snow,
not such as we have had of late years, but one of your good old-
fashioned snows; one which, in a single night, would block up your
doors and windows, bury cottages, stop mails, and, driven by the
wind, would curl over the tops of high banks and fences in the
most fantastic spires and volumes: there, in a snow hollowed by the
drift, with the contents of his wallet spread before him,—all that
heterogeneous collection of bones, bread, cold meats, and a plentiful
supply of sundries, brought together from the four winds of heaven,
and from many a table whose owners never dreamt of clubbing
viands for the same feast! There would he sit, with his dog at his
foot, watching every motion of his fortunate master with an eye that
devoured every mouthful that old Daniel did, and yet most exactly
'like Patience smiling on a monument.'

"There would the old Irish beggar sat, as happy as a lord, with
a face as ruddy and as cheerful as if basking by a kitchen fire; for
what were frosts and snows, and winds and rains (which, however,
he liked least of all), to him? He had made acquaintance with them;
they had been fellow-travellers for half an age, and had come to
an agreement to be sociable. He was a hardy and picturesque old

object—perfectly Bewickean. His figure was short and considerably bent forward—yet he walked with long strides and a firm step, using his long staff rather as a companion than as a support in his journey, his hat, whatever might be its fashion when given him, always took a peculiar twist of its own; his bushy white locks—his coat buckled round with a broad leathern strap, and capacious wallet, were things which, although common attributes of beggars, distinguished him from all others.

"He was a stout, but not a sturdy beggar; a successful, but not a whining and importunate one. He had an air of service—for at some former time he had been soldier; and of respectability, which neither his calling nor his garb could extinguish. He belonged to no gang; he affected no miseries; he was a solitary, and yet a contented-looking being; and rich and poor gave him with alacrity, because they never saw, if refused, that his 'God bless you all the same!' had the usual meaning of a malediction.

"I became first acquainted with Daniel Neale, the very week after I took possession of this living, in rather a singular way. I was summoned by him to the sudden death-bed of a miserly gentleman in this neighbourhood—one Sir Harbottle Grimstone."

"What an extraordinary story his was!" said Elizabeth.

"It was so," returned the vicar. "I will relate it—our friends are curious in these old histories."

The story was related in brief outline; and afterwards, from various sources, I gathered together much detail, which has enabled me to present it to my readers in a tolerably perfect form.

Denborough Park

Part I

The Heirs Expectant

I

"A VERY EXTRAORDINARY DREAM WAS THAT of mine!" said Mrs Ashenhurst, of Harbury, to her daughter, who sat at her little work-table, preparing her green taffety gown for an evening party.

Mrs. Ashenhurst sat in her usual large chair; the Book of Common Prayer, and the last year's Court Calendar—the only books she ever read—lying before her; her finger instinctively was between the gilt-edged pages of the book of honour, but it remained unopened, and she repeated that hers had been an extraordinary dream.

"But you know, mamma," returned her daughter, "we were talking of my uncle only last night."

"And did I not dream of him the night before?" was the lady's interrogatory reply.

"You did, mamma."

"It is seven-and-twenty years, my love, since your uncle left England. I did not think at that time to have been so completely forgotten."

"Perhaps he is not living," suggested the young lady.

"A man of his consequence could not die even in India without its being known at home. His property must be immense by this time," mused Mrs. Ashenhurst: "fourteen years ago I read in the Bath Journal that he was reckoned about the most fortunate man in India. In person your uncle was very much like our relation Lord Montjoy,—you remember him, love,— tall, and handsomely made; to be sure, he was one of the finest men I ever saw!"

"He must be very much altered now," remarked Miss Ashenhurst: "if he were to return, you would hardly know him."

"My love," said her mother, "do look how you are sowing that tucker in!—give the lace its full depth: that is not lace to put out of sight!"

The young lady drew out her thread, and did as her mother desired her.

"I protest," said Mrs. Ashenhurst, "that it was very unhandsome of Mrs. Parkinson to invite us only yesterday for her party this evening, when I know everybody else was asked a week ago. We should not have been invited at all if she could have made up her number without us; I am only wanted for a fourth at a pool. I do not think I shall go after all; you can say, my love, that I was but indifferent. Mrs. Parkinson will understand what it means. If we had five hundred a-year we should be as much thought of as Mrs. Willoughby and her daughters. No, no, I shall not go, Jane."

"If your dream comes true," replied Jane, "you will be even more thought of than Mrs. Willoughby."

"I should not wish you to wear any ornaments to-night, my love," continued the mother; "those Miss Parkinsons are so overdone with rings, and necklaces, and ear-rings; it is far more ladylike to wear no ornament than to overdo it as they do."

A few moments' pause ensued, in which Jane was thinking of her gown, and Mrs. Ashenhurst of her dream; at length she inquired—

"Did you see that travelling carriage, my dear?"

"Yes," said Jane; "I was walking in the garden as it passed. It was a very handsome carriage; the gentleman was travelling post, and had four servants."

"The gentleman! then there was but one gentleman in it? Lord! how foolish I am!" exclaimed Mrs. Ashenhurst.

"I could not help thinking," said Jane, smiling at her old childishness, "what plenty of room there would have been for you and me, mamma; and of what a charming tour we would make somewhere or other if we were rich enough to command such a carriage."

"Do you know, my love," said Mrs. Ashenhurst, recalled to her own circumstances by her daughter's vision of greatness, "that Betty wants her wages raised. It will not suit me to keep her at advanced wages."

"She is an excellent servant, and always looks so clean and respectable," replied Jane: "I shall be very sorry to part with her."

"But, my love, Betty is unreasonable—such an easy, comfortable place as she has; and I have already advanced her wages half-a-guinea! and every half-guinea, you know, my love, is of importance to us."

At that very moment, as if to verify the saying, "Talk of a person and they'll appear," Betty came hastily into the room, exclaiming—

"Oh, ma'am! here's a poor soldier who has been knocked down by a gentleman's coach and run over for certain! Thomas Thackaray had brought him in," added she with simper, "and I am afeard he's badly hurt."

Mrs. Ashenhurst rose hastily, so did her daughter, and followed Betty into the kitchen. There they found our friend Daniel Neale, wearing his old regimentals—for this was his very first pilgrimage as a beggar,—and though not above forty years of age, looking much older, not only from the wear and tear of hard service, but from his natural conformation both of countenance and figure. The pain he was enduring was indicated rather by the compressed lips and contracted brow than by any verbal expression; and, altogether, his appearance was that of a man of iron nerves, though of somewhat slight person, who would desire to excite admiration by patient endurance rather than compassion by lamentation and complaint. By his side stood the aforesaid Thomas Thackaray; and Betty twisted the corner of her apron between her fingers while she looked on from a distance. When Daniel saw the ladies, he attempted to rise; but Mrs. Ashenhurst insisted on his remaining seated, and inquired concerning the accident.

"It was partly my own fault," said the beggar: "I saw the Colonel in the carriage—General that now is,—and I wanted to make myself known,—more fool me, for any good he could have done me, if he had hurled me a lack of rupees from the coach window!—but I got someway knocked down by the horses, and I think my ribs are broken!"

"Poor man!" said Miss Ashenhurst, and her mother inquired if the gentleman was aware of the accident.

"Oh yes, my lady;" he returned, "and bade me follow him to Wood Leighton, near where he has bought a grand place; but sorrow take me if I do!—I never knew good come of his gifts!"

"And you have served abroad?" said Mrs. Ashenhurst, not regarding the discontents of the beggar.

"Yes, madam—many a long year too, and hard service into the bargain,—and yet I've got no pension for all that—Ugh!" groaned the beggar, between the pain of his bruises and the sense of his ill-rewarded service: "I served under this Colonel—General Dubois, as he is now."

"Dubois!" exclaimed Mrs. Ashenhurst: "Good Heavens! do you say General Dubois passed through the town this morning?"

"In a carriage and four?" asked Jane.

"Yes, my lady," said Daniel, seeing, with that intuitive acuteness so characteristic of the inborn mendicant, that his auditors took a strange interest in his narrative—"the General himself—and mighty well he looks!"

"And where may General Dubois be travelling?" inquired Mrs. Ashenhurst.

"To Wood Leighton, ma'am, or near it: he has a grand seat there."

"My good friend," said the joyful and astonished Mrs. Ashenhurst, "this General Dubois is my own brother—I am the only near relative he has living—I am very much your debtor for this incident. Betty, bring out the cold meat."

Daniel looked well nigh as pleased as Mrs. Ashenhurst herself, but declared he could not eat.

Thomas Thackaray was then despatched for Mr. Bolus, the surgeon—Betty was ordered to throw a blanket over the large kitchen chair, and even the fair hands of the lady herself disdained not to arrange the cushions which were to receive the mendicant. This done, the ladies returned to their sitting-room, impatient to give further outlet to their joyful surprise.

"And that really was my uncle!" cried Jane.

"Good Heavens!" exclaimed the mother, throwing herself into her chair; "and the General was in the town all night!—how could he forget that I lived here?"

"But are you sure it is my uncle?" hinted Jane: "may there not be two Generals Dubois?"

"Oh, no—certainly not; I am sure it is my brother—why should I have been dreaming of him else? I have not been able to get him out of my head these two days. I assure you, love, when Mr. Watkins was announced yesterday, I was in such a flutter I could hardly receive him, for I took it in my head that it was my brother; and when Betty demurred about Mr. Parkinson's name, I was going to say, Dubois, so strongly was I possessed with the idea of him. But, however, I will go and ask a few questions further." Accordingly she went out.

Jane remained in a delightful flutter of imagination and hope. She tried to recall the face she had seen in the carriage, it was that of an elderly person who reclined back, the very picture of luxurious ease—it could be no other than this long-lost uncle, and already she felt as if certain of accomplishing the visioned tour in such a carriage. We need not go through all her ecstatic anticipations, nor detail the dream of delight in which she was lost, when her mother returned to interrupt, but not to dissolve the charm.

"There is no doubt in the world," said the sanguine Mrs. Ashenhurst, "not the shadow of a doubt;—this man went out with General Dubois, who, he says, was a cadet under the auspices of Lord Montjoy—that was the old Lord Montjoy—and his person he exactly describes, even to that peculiar sauvity of manner for which he was remarkable when a boy. There is no doubt, my love—no doubt in the world as to his identity; you will be the heiress of General Dubois—and amazingly rich he must be!"

"I wonder he never wrote to us on his arrival in England," remarked Jane.

"My dear, he may suppose us dead—I must write immediately to him. This poor man's accident was an especial interference of providence in our behalf."

"Poor man!", said Jane; "what must we do for him?!"

"My love, I will see that a comfortable home is provided for him, and settle a little annuity on him into the bargain: he can open a park-gate or so; General Dubois' establishment will furnish us ample means of providing for him."

Mr. Bolus the surgeon arriving, put an end to this Alnaschar vision, and Mrs. Ashenhurst consigned her protegé into his hands. He was pronounced much bruised, and to have one or two ribs broken, as he had supposed: accordingly he was given into the careful hands of Thomas Thackaray, to whose cottage he was to be removed, and where Mr. Bolus had especial charge to attend him. Mrs. Ashenhurst promised to raise the wages of Betty, and then sat down, a happy and self-important woman, to write to this new-found brother. In about an hour her letter was completed and she read as follows to her daughter:—

"*Harbury, May* 21, 17—

"MY DEAR GENERAL,—For two days and nights you have never been out of my mind, so strong are the natural ties of consanguinity. I find you passed through the town this morning, and my daughter got a sight of you. I, too, saw your carriage, but though my mind was strongly influenced by a presentiment of your presence, how little could I believe that it contained so neat and dear a relative! Thank God! you are well,—I need not tell you how much I am rejoiced in your happy return, seven-and-twenty years, my dear brother, have dissolved many precious ties; but for my part, those few that remain are more sacred—more beloved than ever.

"We have known several afflictions since I wrote last, and considerable diminution of income; but, I am thankful to say, have been able to make a genteel and handsome appearance notwithstanding. By the death of good Mrs. Charterhouse I lost thirty pounds a-year, but I have managed to keep two maids ever since then: for, with a daughter now growing up, as mine is, you will acknowledge that it is of vital importance not to sink in the eyes of the world. My daughter is called Jane, as I mentioned many years since: but perhaps the letter was lost, with many others which I wrote, as I received no answers. God knows what a grief this has been to me!—but, blessed be his name, my fears were unfounded—you have returned to Old England once more—and long may you live to make up for the years you spent out of your native land!

"But, as I was going to tell you, my daughter bears your favourite name of Jane. She is just now turned eighteen; is, I flatter myself, passably handsome, and is very much admired, not only for her good looks but for her accomplishments. She sends her dutiful love to you, and is quite set up to have had the first sight of you.

"Our cousin-german Marsden did not behave well to me; but, poor man! his affairs were found to be sadly embarrassed after his death.

"I have learned the place of your abode, and in fact of your happy return, through an old soldier who met you this morning, and speaks in the handsomest manner of you.

"Let me have the pleasure of hearing from you soon; and believe me, my dear brother,

> "Your very affectionate.
> "KATHERINE ASHENHURST."

The letter was pronounced unexceptionable; it was therefore folded, directed, and sealed,—sealed with the properly quartered escutcheon-seal of the Dubois; a seal Mrs. Ashenhurst scrupulously noted, the Ashenhurst family having no distinct cognizance, and the lady holding an unarmorial seal in as much contempt as she had now come to consider a family which could not reckon up seven descents at least. How and why she married Captain Ashenhurst was a matter only solvable by remembering that young ladies of seventeen, when in love, do things which sober women of seven-and-forty would think of very questionable propriety.

The letter was, as we have said, sealed, and being then delivered into the trusty hands of the wages-advanced Betty, with especial orders for her to be careful and hear it drop into the letter-box, Mrs. Ashenhurst altered her mind with regard to the Parkinsons and the evening visit, saying to her daughter—

"Fetch down my violet-coloured tabby—it wants a little repair at the cuffs; and you shall wear your pink mode—it is a remarkably pretty dress, and there is no reason why we should not look as well as our neighbours."

II

Mrs. Ashenhurst was anxious to know whether anybody at Mr. Parkinson's had seen the General's equipage; accordingly she inquired, whilst engaged at whist with Mr. Parkinson, Miss Fame and old Mrs. Burgoyne, if any of them had seen such a carriage, adding, "You might see it change horses at the Queen's Head, Miss Farnel."

"To be sure I did," replied the spinster; "a handsome coach, maroon and black with four horses, and four servants, in a livery of white and scarlet—very splendid equipage!"

"Was it my Lord Montjoy?" asked Mr. Parkinson, meaning to be sarcastic on Mrs. Ashenhurst's well-known love of nobility and the often-told story of his lordship's visit.

"No, sir," returned the triumphant lady; "a nearer relation than his lordship—my own brother—General Dubois."

"Zounds!" shouted the ill-natured Mr. Parkinson, "I would not give a button for such grand relations if they would not call on me!"

"My brother did not know of my living in Harbury," said Mrs. Ashenhurst, who was too charitable with all the world to be offended even with Mr. Parkinson.

"General Dubois?" asked Mrs. Burgoyne, looking up over her spectacles; "what! he that signalised himself so greatly in the taking of Matapan and Furnapore?"

"The same," replied Mrs. Ashenhurst.

"An immensely rich man," continued the good old lady, taking off her spectacles. "I have a nephew in Madras, a cousin of Brian's, who sends me the *Madras Herald*, and there I saw an account of the taking of Furnapore and it was said that because of the great spoil, the General might be called the Nabob of Furnapore. Then, afterwards, I saw a sketch of his military life, and I assure you it spoke with the greatest honour of him: I would not venture to say how rich he was supposed to be."

"Egad!" chuckled Mr. Parkinson, "I should like to be your heir, Mrs. Ashenhurst. Pretty picking there will be for Miss Jane! I tell you what, Mrs. Burgoyne, your nephew there should strike while the iron is hot—first come first served, you know," said he, winking towards the part of the room where Jane was listening with a faint blush to the half-whispered words of Brian Livingstone, the nephew of Mrs. Burgoyne: "'gad! she'll be worth having if she's to come in for the old fellow's rupees!" Then, turning half round on his chair, he shouted to his wife,—"Eh, Mrs. P. have you heard of Mrs. Ashenhurst's luck? Her brother's come home from the Indies as rich as a Jew—the great English Nabob of Burnapoor or some devil of a poor; rich would be nearer the mark!" added he, laughing at his own attempted wit.

Mrs. Parkinson and everybody gathered round the whist table, and Mrs. Ashenhurst told all she had to tell.

"Ah, then, after all," said Mr. Parkinson, when she had done, "you did not see him! I thought he had slept at your house; I'll lay you ten to one he'll turn out no brother after all! Not seen him indeed! I thought he had been at your house—why my Lord Montjoy was better than this!"

Whether the people who listened to this oration wished it might prove Mrs. Ashenhurst's brother, or whether, like Mr. Parkinson, they wished their townswoman to be disappointed, has not come down to us: certain it is, poor Mrs. Ashenhurst had not the satisfaction she had expected in making known her anticipated good fortune; and more earnestly than ever did she hope it would prove to be her brother, were it only to mortify Mr. Parkinson. Jane, too, had never been so critically commented upon before. Some pronounced her proud, some conceited, some thought her a trifle too tall, and others declared she stooped. Nobody but good Mrs. Burgoyne and her nephew said what really was the truth,—that she was a very lovely, extremely well-made and well-dressed young lady: and, what was better, remarkable for good sense and good feeling; "and assuredly," concluded the aunt, "such a one as must delight her nabob uncle, and be an ornament to his splendid mansion in—shire, if it turned out, as she hoped it would, that this stranger was the true General Dubois."

This last wish, the necessity of our true history compels us to confess, was more than Brian Livingstone expected to see accomplished; nor, since the truth must be told, was it what he so ardently desired. Brian was deeply in love, and withal felt himself in a dilemma—his passion was undeclared, and how could he now make it known without some compromise of appearances? Mrs. Ashenhurst, he felt sure, would suspect his motives, and, high-spirited woman as she was, would reject him instantly. In the generosity of his love, therefore, he vowed with himself to offer hand and heart when the certainty of disappointment reached them—for he truly believed disappointment would come—flattering himself that he had so much influence with the daughter as to compensate for the loss of a visionary greatness.

So reasoned Brian through half the wakeful night, and towards morning fell asleep on the comfortable pillow of good intentions. In the morning, however, he altered his plan, and at all risks determined to make known his passion that very day. When Mrs. Burgoyne's breakfast was over, Brian took his customary walk into the fields, partly to tranquillize his mind, and partly to indulge an unrestrained meditation upon his hopes before he risked the future fortune of his life upon the decision of a yes or no. While Brian was thus feeding his passion in the gladness and beauty of that May morning, Jane and her mother were sitting as we first found them at the commencement of our history.

"Well, my love, I think we may expect a letter in about ten days," observed Mrs. Ashenhurst. "And by the way, my dear, your pink mode looks extremely well; and I would have you give that chintz to Mary, and take your green taffety into common wear. It is, not, my love, as if we had no expectations.—But, bless me there's a knock!—I wish you had your other gown on: go, my love, this minute, and change your dress."

Jane vanished at her mother's bidding; and Mrs. Ashenhurst assumed the calm, composed air natural to her; took up the Red Book for the year 17—, and sat with its open pages before her, as if she were deep in the study of them, when Betty announced Mr. Parkinson.

Mr. Parkinson was all smiles and courtesy, and without any demur or difficulty introduced his business. He did not know, he said, till that very morning, that Miss Jane had played the dickens with his son Tom's heart. Tom, he declared, was a good fellow—a steady good fellow, and had carried off three gold medals from—college; and that, for his part, he had no manner of objection to his marrying Miss Ashenhurst, nor could he see that there was any. Tom had a good fortune—two hundred a year now in his own hands, left him by his godmother, besides his profession, which might fairly be reckoned as five or six hundred more, say nothing of what he would have at his father's death.

Nothing could exceed the astonishment and indignation of Mrs. Ashenhurst, and her three first words convinced her visiter of the hopelessness of his mission. Still Mr. Parkinson was not to be utterly quelled by even Mrs. Ashenhurst's scorn. "Tom," he said, "was fittest to plead his own cause—pleading was what he was used to, while he himself was a plain-spoken man; and Jane at that moment entering, all unconscious of what was going forward, in the full grace of the green taffety and lace tucker, which never before had been assumed as an everyday dress, the discomfitted man bluntly appealed to her "whether she did not think his son Tom would make her a good husband?"

Had Jane been convicted of treason she could not have looked more thunderstruck than by this address; but she was spared an answer by her mother rising and assuring Mr. Parkinson with severe dignity that she insisted upon the subject being dismissed, as any connexion with Mr. Thomas Parkinson was out of the question for her daughter. Chagrined and mortified as the unfortunate man was, he wished both Jane and her mother a very good morning, intending to show them that they were below his anger; but he went out wishing with an oath that they might be ten times over deceived and disappointed in this General Dubois; and to make their mortification the greater, he vowed to inform everybody of their extravagant expectations and abominable pride.

After Mrs. Ashenhurst had somewhat exhausted the subject of Mr. Parkinson and his impertinence, she dismissed Jane to request from Mrs. Burgoyne a sight of those Madras papers she had spoken of the evening before; and, by that law of contraries which so perplexes human affairs, scarcely had Jane been gone five minutes one way, when Mrs. Burgoyne, leaning on the arm of her nephew, arrived by the other. The good lady had brought the papers in quest of which her friend had sent; and Mrs. Ashenhurst for the first five minutes gratified her self-love and her family pride by glancing over the papers, and seeing column after column of the same subject, in which the words, "the gallant general," "this spirited commander," "this excellent officer," together with others as significant— "immense spoil," "jewels to the amount of fifty thousand sterling, besides, elephants, arms, and the enemy's state carriage and tents, to the value of many thousands more"—met her eye sufficiently often even to satisfy her ambition. For the moment she asked nothing more, and felt infinitely grateful to her friends; what could she do less than make them her confidants in the affair of Mr. Parkinson? Accordingly it was related "in the strictest confidence," every word falling on the ear of Brian Livingstone like molten lead. "And I can assure you," said Mrs. Ashenhurst, "if an earl were to make proposals for my daughter under existing circumstances, I should suspect his motives, and would dismiss him accordingly."

"Here, then," thought Brian, "is an end of my hopes. These are the natural interpretations and constructions which would be put upon my addresses." It was well for him that neither lady demanded his voice in the question. He heard every word as distinctly as if it had been thundered into his brain; but for his life he could not have spoken a word. He walked to the window, almost unconscious that he had left his seat, and began deliberately to pull to pieces Jane's superb hydrangea; from which he was only roused by the voice of Jane, who at that moment entered, having returned from her fruitless errand, and who laughing merrily begged him to remember that he had given her that plant, and that she would not have it destroyed for the world. These few words would have made Brian happy beyond expression, but for what he had heard before; and as if his evil fortune was leagued against him at every moment when, spite of all these disadvantages, he might have improved the occasion with Jane, she was gone, and Mrs. Burgoyne was informing her of the object of her mission.

"My nephew," said she, "would not rest till he had found the papers; and I am sure nobody rejoices more in your prospects than we do." Brian joined them, but he said nothing.

Mrs. Ashenhurst then went through the history of her dreams and prepossessions; and lastly of the adventure of Daniel Neale; and everything was told that bore in the remotest degree on this interesting subject; wishes were exchanged and probabilities weighed; still the conversation lay between the elder people; for

Brian's silence, as if it had been contagious, had communicated itself to Jane.

Day after day went on, and by this time the news of Mrs. Ashenhurst and her expectations was in everybody's mouth, variously related and commented upon; and the mistress of the post-office kept a strict look-out after all letters directed for Mrs. Ashenhurst; but six days passed on, and no letter had yet arrived in the least degree worthy of suspicion.

All this time Brian Livingstone had absented himself from the house, waiting in torturing anxiety the result of their expectations. He walked, he read, or seemed to read; he sat at his writing for hours together; and good Mrs. Burgoyne wondered what hard problem, or what difficult book in Latin or Greek it was that puzzled him so, praying him a dozen times in the day to have mercy on his poor brains. And let it not be supposed that Jane Ashenhurst took no heed of his absence or melancholy; yet she did not fall into Mrs. Burgoyne's error of the Greek and Latin—she shrewdly guessed that herself had more to do with it than either languages or mathematics, and she wished he had half the boldness of Mr. Parkinson.

Ten days' absence had made Brian Livingstone a stranger, and then he called to take leave. His only and beloved sister was dangerously ill, and he was summoned instantly to her home. He parted from his friends with the warmest and most affectionate wishes for their good fortune: yet perhaps it is questionable if he meant what Mrs. Ashenhurst understood by them; something too his eyes said beyond this, which Jane's heart readily interpreted, and which indescribably relieved the pain of parting. Brian was gone, but she was unusually cheerful; it was a great delight to practise over the new song winch he had given her, words of his own composing, to a favourite air which they had many a time played together; fortunately it was also a favourite with Mrs. Ashenhurst, and Jane sang it three times that one evening.

Daniel Neale also left Harbury that night. He was a restless being, and, like the thistle-down, always kept moving onwards; and weak as he still was, and extraordinary as was the care taken of him, he soon became

tired of the monotony of an invalid's life, and announced his intention
of proceeding on his journey. Mr. Bolus demurred, Mrs. Ashenhurst
declared she never would consent; but Daniel was not to be overruled,
and accordingly a place was taken for him in a stage-wagon which went
within a few miles of Wood Leighton, Daniel assuring his patroness
that he would not fail of being the very first person to welcome her
thither. The beggar's pockets were filled with money, and he made his
adieus, a happy and grateful man, with ten thousand blessings on his
lips.

III

A few mornings after the departure of Brian Livingstone, a letter
arrived with the Wood Leighton post-mark. What might be its
contents? Mrs. Ashenhurst scarcely breathed while she broke the
seal and glanced over it. Jane stood with her hands clasped, and her
eyes riveted on her mother's countenance to read the tenor of the
letter in its expression. Mrs. Ashenhurst gathered up its meaning in
a moment, uttered a scream of joy, and then burst into a passion
of tears. Jane was alarmed, and strove to compose her mother's
agitation; but she put her daughter aside, exclaiming—"Read it!
read it!"

Jane took up the letter, which had dropped to the ground, and
read the following short but satisfactory epistle:—

"*At Denborough Park, June 6, 17—*

"DEAR SISTER,—Your letter gave me infinite pleasure. I rejoice
to hear that you and your daughter are alive and well, and in a
condition to come to me.

"Never mind old troubles and losses; I have enough for us
all. I have a place here which people tell me is vastly beautiful;
I shall be glad of your opinion of it. The sooner you can come
the better; your taste used to be good, and it may be serviceable
to me.

"I am glad to hear that my niece is handsome—beauty is always a good thing for a woman; and if she he as handsome as you were at her age, she will do.

"If I do not hear from you to the contrary, I shall send a carriage for you this day week.

I shall give a banquet here in the course of the autumn. I am yours, &c.

"FRANCIS DUBOIS.

"P.S.—I send you a bill, which you can convert into wearing apparel. I should wish you both to appear in what is handsome."

"Oh, what a generous, kind-hearted, dear uncle this is!" exclaimed Jane; "and here is a bill for two hundred pounds."

By this time Mrs. Ashenhurst was a little composed, and could look her good fortune in the face. "How lucky we are, my love," she exclaimed, "how wonderfully lucky! In a week—let me see—this was written on the sixth, and this is now the ninth; that—will be on Wednesday."

"A carriage?" said Jane, again looking at the letter; "then he must keep more than one. Oh, I cannot believe all this good fortune is really meant for us. And do you not remember when you said you could not afford to lose seven shillings at whist with that tiresome Mrs. Parkinson, and now we have two hundred pounds to spend at once."

"Give me the paper and the ink, my love," said Mrs. Ashenhurst: "I must write to dear Mrs. Burgoyne."

"I wish Mr. Livingstone were here to know our good fortune; " and then while her mother commenced her note, she sang, in her blithe voice that was like the carol of a wood-lark

"And give to me my biggonets,
My bishop-satin gown,
For I maun tell the baillie's wife
That Colin's come to town."

While Mrs. Ashenhurst was pouring out her full-hearted joy upon the most approved of note-paper, and in the most lady-like of Italian caligraphy, Jane went about the room in all the exuberance of youthful spirits. She watered her flowers, she fondled with her bird, and every now and then she glanced at the progress of the note, impatient for its ending, that she might once more be at liberty to talk; then she opened her instrument, and ran over its keys to the last air she had sung with Brian Livingstone, interrupting even the charmed thoughts of that dear friend with the wonder whether her uncle was fond of music. By this time she had the pleasure of seeing the note folded; she lighted the taper therefore to expedite its dismissal, never thinking, poor girl, that she thus hastened the worst possible tidings to Brian. The note was dismissed and delivered to Mrs. Burgoyne the moment she was concluding a letter to her nephew. "How fortunate," said the good old lady, "that my letter was not gone;" and she added this important information as a postscript.

Mrs. Ashenhurst, having unburdened herself of the greatest weight of her good fortune—the bearing it unknown to her neighbours—invited her daughter to consider with her how the money was to be laid out.

"For you see, my dear," said she, "that the General loves show, as he has good right to do, and will feel it a slight unless we appear very handsomely, and suitably to his magnificence."

"But," said Jane, after they had exhausted the subject of silks, satins, lace, gold and silver tissues, and India chintzes, "may we not give a few shillings to those poor old women in the almshouses? I long to make somebody as happy as I am myself."

"You are right, love; and before we go, we must invite our friends for one evening—tea and supper. Let me see: there are the Willoughbys and Mrs. Burgoyne—poor Mr. Livingstone, it is a pity he is not here—Miss Farnel—and all our friends in short. A pretty vexation there will be for the Parkinsons; but I am very glad I have a good reason for not inviting them."

The notes of invitation were despatched; and then the two ladies went into the town, dressed in their ordinary garb; "For," said the elder, "it is much more correct to be under-dressed than over-dressed."

It was a day of triumph indeed; everywhere they were met by congratulations; even Mr. Parkinson, who popped upon them as they turned a corner, veiled his chagrin to make professions of "the happiness the news gave him," and "his pleasure in their good fortune;" adding, "he hoped his son Tom might call to felicitate them on the news."

Mrs. Ashenhurst assumed her most dignified air, and assured him their time would be so entirely occupied that she feared they could not have that pleasure.

"A hollow-hearted sycophant!" said she, when he parted from them; "but for the desire to get your fortune to himself, nothing would have delighted him equal to our being disappointed."

The most beautiful gown-pieces which the best shops in Harbury contained, were purchased that morning; the shopkeeper even protested he had parted with the dresses ordered especially for the lady of Sir John Docket—nay, which had been made expressly for her—and thereby he should lose her custom: but, for all that, he did it with the greatest pleasure in the world—he would rather oblige Miss Ashenhurst than Lady Docket—these dresses would look so exquisite on Miss Ashenhurst's figure, &c. &c.

Miss Shapit, the most approved dressmaker in Harbury, and her two assistants, sat up two nights sewing their fingers to the bone to make up the purchases—"Sweet pretty dresses! beauteous dresses!" as she averred. "But then, to be sure, both Mrs. and Miss Ashenhurst had such delightful taste in dress; and these being made up by her own fingers, how could they help looking handsome!"

So said she, as she exhibited them to her best customers, who had been informed, if they would just drop in on the Tuesday morning, they might see them in her little sitting-room just before they were sent home.

"And, bless my life," said one lady, as tall as a giraffe, with ostrich feathers in her hat, "and who would have thought of all this good luck happening to Mrs. Ashenhurst?"

"She did not carry her head so high for nothing," returned another—a little round woman in a short black silk cloak.

"It is a mighty fortunate thing for her servants!" observed a third, who was folded in a large shawl, put on cloak-fashion, and held so tightly over the shoulder that there was not a fold from head to foot;—"a mighty fortunate thing it is for those poor servants of hers!—there was a close hand held in the house, if all's true that's said out of the kitchen."

"Good gracious!" interrupted one young lady, "will this go round Miss Ashenhurst's waist?"

"Oh, what a train!" exclaimed a second, holding out the gown of purple Genoa velvet which was meant for the state robe of Mrs. Ashenhurst; "and lined, as I live, with white satin!"

"Bless me!" ejaculated the lady of the black mantle; "lined with white satin!"

"Do you know the price of this blue mode, Miss Shapit?" asked the one of the hat and feathers.

"Eight shillings a yard, ma'am."

"It's well for them that they can afford it," returned the querist.

"I hope it may all end well!" observed the lady of the large shawl.

"Oh, my goodness!" screamed one of the juniors; "there's a drop of tallow on this pearl-coloured tabbinet!"

"Nay, sure!" cried the alarmed Miss Shapit.

"I'm sure I wish it may all turn out well!" again repeated the lady, and left the room.

We also will leave the party in deep consultation, as to the best means of extracting a drop of tallow from a pearl-coloured tabbinet.

The leave-taking party at Mrs. Ashenhurst's went off extremely well. She and her daughter were too happy not to be pleased with all the world; yet Mrs. Ashenhurst herself had too much tact and worldly wisdom to obtrude her delight on her guests: she looked so placidly happy, so unostentatiously fortunate, that even the ill-natured Mr.

Parkinson, had he seen her, could have said no more than he did say when he heard of it—that "she knew what she was about."

It was now Tuesday morning. The dresses and the millinery had all come home, and had been approved by their owners, without the grease-spot in the pearl-coloured tabbinet being detected. It is true Miss Shapit contrived to keep it under the folds all the time;—and they ware moreover packed up ready to travel. Betty, too, who was now advanced into lady's woman, and wore her Sunday gown on work-a-days, was full of smiles, talk, and curtsies; and only now and then overshadowed by the prospect of parting with Thomas Thackaray. Mrs. Asheuhurst had set the house in order, and the said Thomas Thackaray, and his mother—who, since the Ashenhursts' good fortune, had been introduced as general domestic assistant—were to be left in charge of the house during the absence of its mistress.

Scarcely was noon past, when a carriage and four—and no longer post-horses, but noble well-fed creatures, than which none finer had ever been seen in Harbury—drove into the town. A happy—a proud woman was Mrs. Ashenhurst. Jane was wild with ecstasy: and she was the next morning to be driven off in that superb vehicle! "Oh, that Brian Livingstone had but been here!" thought she, half in the joy of her good fortune, and half from a habit she had lately got of keeping Brian Livingstone for ever in her thoughts.

The news of a coach and four being come for Mrs. Ashenhurst, and having driven to the Queen's Head, soon circulated through Harbury; and a crowd collected in the inn-yard to get a sight of it, to admire the horses, and to talk with the postillions.

Mrs. Burgoyne came up in the evening for a last leave-taking, and several others of their acquaintance also, now full of professions and congratulations; whereas, only one month ago, Mrs. Ashenhurst was but in their eyes a widow, with a small income and a vast deal of family pride—a person to be noticed for the sake of her breeding and knowledge of the world, but from whom nothing was to be looked for in return. Now, however, the tables were turned; and these time-serving friends professed themselves as having always esteemed and loved her, and that they—every one of them—should be inconsolable for her loss.

Mrs. Burgoyne brought no intelligence of her nephew: he had never written, and she could not tell what to think of it. She was, however, invited to correspond by letter with her old friends, "that we may know," said Mrs. Ashenhurst, "the news of Harbury—"

"And how you go on, dear Mrs. Burgoyne," added Jane; and how poor Miss Livingstone is, and how she likes Harbury, when she comes to see you this autumn."

Mrs. Burgoyne made her adieus the very latest of all the guests: and the mother and daughter were left with less sorrow for the parting than with joyful anticipations for the morrow.

IV

The morrow rose as brightly beautiful as any day could rise for the accomplishment of earthly felicity.

By half-past nine the carriage with its four noble horses stood at the door of Mrs. Ashenhurst's, awaiting her pleasure; the lower order of townspeople gathered in an eager crowd, full of admiration of the four black horses, not one hair different the one from the other—the richly plated harness—the handsomely emblazoned panels of the carriage, as bright and unsullied as a mirror—and of the mute, immovable postillions, who, booted and spurred, in tight smart jackets and caps, and with whip in hand, awaited the word to be off. It was indeed a sight of unimaginable grandeur; and this was to whirl away to a new home, which report represented as an El-Dorado palace, their umquhile Mrs. Ashenhurst and her fair daughter, who, but a few short weeks ago, had walked among them not too great to be approached by the meanest! Had the fiery chariot and the fiery horses of the prophet stood before them, they could not have excited more wonderous admiration.

"Well, there's no saying what may happen to any of us!" was the winding-up of some of the street wisdom; and then the spectators were called upon to witness—first, the strapping on of divers

mails, and the affixing of travelling trunks; then the entrée of Mrs.
Ashenhurst and her lovely daughter into the superb vehicle, with
the most sedulous attention of the demure but handsome serving-
men, as if the business of their lives was to care for these ladies; then
the mounting of these two livened attendants each to his place;
and lastly, the consigning of Betty herself from the vigorous adieus
of Thomas Thackaray, to the gallant assiduities of the taller of the
serving-men.

Thomas Thackaray withdrew a few paces—Betty looked down
from her elevation on her squire—the postillions put spurs to their
horses—and the magnificent equipage swept out of the gate with a
swirl on to the turnpike road, leaving behind it a blank, and drawing
after it a hundred admiring eyes.

A happy pair were the mother and daughter, and very comely
withal. Mrs. Ashenhurst had studied that their dress should not
disgrace their mission—such as should reach the happy medium
between plainness and magnificence. Her daughter wore a new
chintz sack and petticoat, with an apple-blossom-coloured silk
cloak, and a white chip hat, trimmed with pale green gauze: she
herself was habited in what had been her best visiting suit for the
last two years—her violet-coloured tabby—and over her shoulders
a black mode cloak, trimmed, like her daughter's, with rich black
lace, and a hat to match. Jane was in raptures with the luxurious ease
of the carriage, and the stateliness of its appointments; she leaned
back into the corner, and felt as if all human prosperity and bliss
were centered in those few square feet of travelling space. She took
off her hat, and sat, with her rich curling locks, bright and fair as
pale gold, confined only by a ribbon, falling on her shoulders, a very
Hebe in appearance. Her mother looked at her with delight, and
believed their reception would be propitious, were it only for the
sake of her daughter's beauty.

The road was all new to Jane; and with a heart attuned to
happiness as hers was, any landscape would have appeared pleasant;
but this, with its cheerful villages—its abounding meadows filled
with flocks and herds—its woods, yet in the varied and clear

green of early summer—its mansions—its waters, seen by glimpses as they passed the head of some valley, or looked down into its sylvan quiet from higher ground—its occasional ruins, shrouded in trees, or standing bleak and bare upon a hill-top, a mark to the country round—and all this seen under the bright but not burning sky of early June—could not fail to realise dreams of Arcadia and Fairyland;—dreams which her warm imagination had fashioned rather as pastime than as anything to be realised upon the earth.

Little was said either by mother or daughter for the first stage of the journey. A great—inconceivable happiness, in which mingled the tender memory of Brian Livingstone, enveloped Jane's existence. When should they meet again? what would that meeting tend to? would he follow her to her new abode?—surely he would! And oh, the happiness of introducing two such men as her uncle and Brian Livingstone to each other—Brian so handsome, so gentlemanly, so accomplished a scholar; her uncle so kind, so fatherly, so munificent! When did youth ever look through the sunshine of hope and love, and find anything but joy? Happy Jane! her heart danced in the transcendently glorious vision it created; and never thinking that shadow might darken its beauty, in the satiety, as it were, of heart-pleasure, she turned to external things. All again was bright—all was delicious—everything was flattering to her self-love; and, as if awakening from a dream, she exclaimed—"How glorious this morning is! how beautiful this landscape!"

At D— they stayed a couple of hours to refresh the horses before they proceeded the remaining stage. And here Jane could not but remark the amazing difference with which people were received, travelling in an ordinary way—in a post-chaise, perhaps, as she had been used to—or with an equipage and attendants, such as they had now. The bustle which their arrival occasioned throughout the place—the overstrained civilities of the landlord, and of the fine-spoken, curtsying landlady, who seemed as if they would absolutely carry them into their house in their arms—the running to and fro of the servants—the alertness of men and maids—the general solicitude to make them comfortable—the fear lest all, when all was done, was not to their liking—amused her even to laughter.

"What would these people say," she observed to her mother, "if they knew that even within a month it was a debated matter whether we could afford to raise Betty's wages?"

After they had refreshed themselves, they walked into the town, attended by their footman. Mrs. Ashenhurst was not a woman to be inconvenienced by, or to feel her state a burden; on the contrary, all this was extremely grateful to her feelings—she seemed only now in her proper sphere. Jane bore her elevation with much less equanimity, and continually provoked her mother by her inaptitude.

"Who would think," said she, "that I have made a pudding within the last ten days, and see me followed by this smart footman!"

Denborough Park lay five miles on the other side of Wood Leighton. Half-a-mile before they reached town, they crossed the river by its old stone bridge; and here they were greeted by the "God bless you, my lady! and a happy welcome to you, Miss Jane !" of their old acquaintance Daniel Neale, who was standing within one of the angular piers of the bridge.

Mrs. Ashenhurst threw him a gold coin; Jane smiled and nodded to him: and the beggar sent a hundred thousand welcomes and blessings after them.

As they approached Denborough Park, the sun was setting, and the rich crimson light of a summer evening lay over the landscape. The travellers were both silent, both occupied by similar but new sensations; that mysterious awe which will gather about the human spirit when a new and untried existence, even though it promises happiness, lies before them. Neither of them would have confessed to a sentiment of doubt or depression, but each felt that vague, undefinable impression, that will at times creep over in spite of ourselves, whispering of the uncertainty of all earthly things, even at the very moment that delivers them to our grasp. The feeling was one Jane could not endure; she turned to her mother with a burst of admiration for a clump of trees which were kindled into golden light by the setting sun, and her mother was glad to be rid of her own reverie. Neither said a word to the other of the shadow that had passed over her mind, but simultaneously gave themselves up to the beauty of the old park scenery.

And it *was* scenery that deserved unmixed attention: green slopes lying in light contrasted with shadowy hollows; clumps of trees, or some majestic oak of five centuries' growth, which held up aloft, above its green leafiness, a splintered and whitened crown of decaying branches, or yet more grotesquely seemed bowed with the weight of its years, decaying in trunk and branch even while it yet garlanded a few outspreading arms with fresh verdure: here and there, too, lay herds of deer, the image of sylvan repose, or rushed past them, startled from their rest, with a twinkling of horns, and a rush like the passing of a gale. Occasionally, too, they caught glimpses of still lake-like waters lying low and in shadow, bordered round with reeds, or by the green smooth turf which was reflected as in a mirror. Herons were soaring away to their night trees; there was now and then heard the deep, soothing coo of the wood-pigeon; and, advancing down a slope towards the house, under broad, spreading beech-trees they perceived a troop of peacocks, arching their gorgeous necks and extending their long trains on the turf. It was made up of images of grandeur—noble antiquity and present prosperity and ease: no wonder that our sanguine travellers soon forgot that doubt and disappointment have any part in human affairs.

Presently the house came into sight: but this, and their reception there, are too important to fill the end of a chapter.

V

Denborough Hall, or Park, as it was more generally called, was a magnificent pile of buildings standing in the centre of the park, which sloped down to it on three sides from its extreme boundaries of many miles in extent: the hall occupying, as it were, the hollow of an immense irregular basin with one broken side; this fourth or broken side, opening to the south-west a far-seen stretch of country, infinitely diversified and beautiful; on each hand the wooded slopes of the park gradually sinking into the plain beyond. One of these lake-like waters we have mentioned lay in the mid foreground; trees, standing singly or in groups, all disposed with the most exquisite taste, diversified the landscape, which terminated in twenty miles of distance, embracing hamlet spires and towers, woods, waters, and a distant outline of hills, seen clearly against the yet warm sunset sky.

The principal front commanded this view. The house itself stood nobly among its lawns, gardens, and groves, like a pleasure-palace in the gardens of Armida. Its architecture was in unison with its situation, belonging to no one distinct style, but uniting all that was grand and beautiful in each; each separate front presenting styles and ornaments incongruous perhaps in detail, but forming a general effect at once imposing and characteristic.

The approach to it lay through shrubberies of full-grown flowering trees and evergreens, with here and there an oasis of lawn and garden. They passed glades of velvet turf which seemed made for fairy revellers; they saw fountains in green and shadowy places shining out like the fair Una in her shady wood; and everywhere the odour of flowers and trees, and the loud song of a thousand birds, which the smooth gliding on of the carriage over a gravel road as level as a marble pavement could not deaden, greeted them as they went along.

A sweep of the road round a promontory of tree-like flowering shrubs brought them at once to the front of the house; and the carriage drew up to a lofty, pillared and temple-like portico, at which already stood two servants to receive them. Thence they were conducted to a handsome chamber, in a room adjoining to which refreshments of all kinds awaited them, while servants, full of quiet assiduity, attended on them.

In reply to the inquiry of Mrs. Ashenhurst after the General, they were informed that it was not his wish that they should be interrupted either in refreshing themselves or performing their toilet by seeing him, but that he awaited their pleasure as soon after as was agreeable to themselves.

Jane's imagination had pictured rooms as lofty and as large as these; but their details of furniture, accommodation for ease and luxury, the abundance and splendour of the repast, and the profound reverence of the attendants, went beyond what she had visioned of these things,—they excited her almost to emotion. Mrs. Ashenhurst took all that came quietly; she loved state as dearly as the nabob himself, and nothing presented itself to her in the guise of sumptuousness or ceremonial to which she could not accommodate herself. She was charmed with everything she saw, but made uncomfortable by nothing; the very obsequiousness of the silken attendants was received with as much indifference as if she had been used to it all the days of her life. Betty's wonder and agitation were extreme; the poor young woman looked frightened to death, and was, to use her own expression, "all in such a fluster, she could not stick a pin."

Mrs Ashenhurst, who felt so well the proprieties of her position, neither put on a state-robe, nor anything that might appear beyond the ordinary dress of a gentlewoman. She was simply habited in rich green silk, with a point-lace cap, handkerchief, and ruffles. Of her daughter's appearance she was more studious. Her beautiful hair was left to its own way, and fell with a child-like simplicity in heavy curls on her smooth, fair shoulders; her dress was the pink mode we have heard of before, the effect of which her mother knew to be perfect; on her neck she wore pearls, and pearl bracelets on her round fair arms, which her mother was well aware might be displayed with advantage. Thus habited, Betty informed the servant who remained in waiting, that the ladies were ready to be announced.

They were conducted through a long gallery covered with Indian mat, and filled with a variety of Indian spoil—the spoil of war and of the chase, to the saloon; the very room on which the nabob had lavished his utmost care, and to which nothing of luxurious gorgeousness could have been added—it was redolent of silk and gold. They trod on carpets that yielded to the foot like down; the odour as of a celestial land opened upon them from the plants

and flowers of an unimagined splendour, which filled vases of rich
oriental china; and here and there, in golden cages, or perched on
the branches of the shrubs, gaily-coloured Indian birds were seen;
some already nestled to sleep in their gorgeous featheriness, others
seeming to court admiration by the display of crest and wing. These
things, and much beside, were rather perceived than observed; for
midway in the room, which was of great size, they were received by
the lord of the mansion himself, a man tall and stately and deeply
bronzed by Indian suns, but overflowing with courtesy, and with
that, low bland voice of which Mrs. Ashenhurst had spoken many
and many a time. He received them at first with a profound bow;
and then, taking his sister's hand in both his, he saluted her on
the cheek, and bade her welcome. Jane passed through the same
ceremonial, and then both ladies were conducted, one in each hand,
to the couch from which he had just risen. Jane sank into its elastic
softness with an involuntarily sense of the delight of anything so
luxurious.

Seven-and-twenty years of ordinary life could not pass over
any human countenance and leave it scathless: but sorrows and
anxieties in the case of Mrs. Ashenhurst; foreign travel, some years
of hard service, and more of the laying together of treasure, in that
of her brother, had produced their necessary effects, nothing abated.
The brother and sister met even more changed than they had
anticipated; and for the first ten minutes a listener might have been
amused to observe the evident care both parties took not to speak
an unpalatable truth.

"My dear General." said the wary Mrs. Ashenhurst, "I rejoice
to see your good looks; your complexion is altered, but certainly
improved; you look younger than lord Montjoy at the same age."

The courtly man smiled graciously at the flattering assurance, and
declared to the lady that time had used her tenderly, and that "he
missed no charm from the fair face of his sister."

It was tacitly understood between them that each should conceal
whatever truth on this subject might be unflattering. While
these things were being said, and inquiries as to their journey

made and replied to, Jane more narrowly observed her uncle. In appearance he might be sixty years of age; perhaps five years older. His countenance bore traces of care and toil, with those strong lines that indicate resolute if not obstinate character; a deep-set penetrating eye, whose expression did not always seem in accordance with the smooth smile and the remarkably bland voice: still Jane saw nothing to dislike; on the contrary, she saw a man bent to please and to make them pleased with themselves; a luxurious and extremely polite person, whom she was very happy to consider as her uncle, nay, if such should be his pleasure, as her adopted father. What lay below the surface it would have required a much more practised and acute judge of human nature than Jane Ashenhurst to have detected.

His dress, she observed, was in perfect keeping with everything about him, rich and showy; the costume of a private gentleman, in which ornament, however, and the use of precious metals, were as lavishly used as could be, even beyond, what seemed to her, good taste. He was powdered, and wore a brilliantly bright mulberry-coloured velvet coat lined with primrose serge, with gold buttons the size of half-crowns; his cravat was of the most transparently delicate point lace, and fell over his waistcoat of gold and silver embroidered silk, fastened likewise with bullion; he wore black satin breeches with gold knee-buckles, and the buckles of his shoes were of the same metal; his stockings, of black silk, were carefully drawn over his shapely leg, which he evidently displayed at great self-satisffaction; his hands, which were thin and yellow, and displayed age even more than his face, were enveloped in ruffles of the same material as his cravat, and his fingers were loaded with jewelled rings. Never had such an elaborately dressed man met the eyes of his young kinswoman before, and she could not help thinking that the ornaments of his person alone far exceeded her mother's yearly income, which had been husbanded with extraordinary care: she no longer wondered at the bill for the two hundred pounds. Scarcely had she arrived at this last conclusion, when her uncle addressed her.

"He hoped his niece had half the pleasure in visiting him, that he had in welcoming her under his roof."

Jane expressed her unqualified delight.

"We must see," said he, "what we can do to make your time pass pleasantly. Of my neighbours, as yet, I know but little. A young lady, however, will attract where an old bachelor has little chance of pleasing."

Jane protested against any attraction being superior to that of her uncle.

"We will not contest the point, my dear young lady; and nothing will give me greater pleasure than yielding the palm to you."

And so passed compliments between them, all seeming mutually pleased. At length Mrs. Ashenhurst remarked, unable longer to suppress an uneasy sentiment which obtruded itself, that she had expected to find him furnishing his house, whilst on the contrary he appeared to have been established there some time. "How long might it be?"

"Eighteen mouths," was the answer.

"Eighteen months!" reiterated his sister, quite thrown off her guard; "how long then had he been in England?"

"Three years," replied the General in his usual tone of courtesy, as if he were unconscious or totally regardless of the pain this avowal occasioned.

"My dear General!" exclaimed the lady: "and, but for the merest chance in the world, you might have been three years longer, and I should never have known of it!"

The impassive General felt neither reproof nor offence. A silence of a few moments succeeded, in which Mrs. Ashenhurst, however mortified she might feel by the truth thus obtruded on her knowledge, resolved to keep careful hold on the General, now she had the opportunity; and Jane's gratitude and affection for her uncle struggled with the unpleasant belief that he would never have sought them out—that he had no affection for them. But these thoughts were in some measure dissipated by the courtesies of the General; he renewed the conversation with the utmost ease

and cheerfulness; told of the new instrument he had ordered for
his niece, of the fashionable music he had procured for her, of his
own love of music, of the wonderfully fine voice of his sister was
remarkable for, declaring he did not but doubt her daughter's was
equally fine; spoke of the jewels he had already selected for them,
and then called upon his niece to admire his flowers and his birds.
Jane could not resist such devotion; she went the round of the
apartment at his side, listening to the names, the qualities, and the
histories of his various Indian treasures. An elegant supper, in which
their host pledged them in wine of Shiraz, closed this eventful day:
they then retired to the apartments they had before occupied, and
led by the enraptured Betty through a suite of rooms which she
informed them had been fitted for their especial use; and indeed,
unless the nabob had had some other female inmates in view, this
must have been the case, for they were evidently designed for ladies'
use.

A doubt, spite of herself, remained in the mind of Mrs. Ashenhurst
as to the sincerity of her brother; but, for the word, she would not
have confessed as much to any living creature, not even to her
daughter. It was an unpleasant thing to have doubts darkening
prospects as bright as these: still she had sufficient reliance on her
own management to believe herself secure in her present position.
Jane, like her mother, was jealous of confessing the unpleasant effect
of the General's avowal; but she determined, if possible, to forget
what she had heard, or to disbelieve his having been three years in
England.

VI

Mrs Ashenhhurst and her daughter, spite of the aforementioned
annoyance, woke to a golden life. The splendours and riches of
their habitation were exhaustless. All that is read of in books, or
fancied in day-dreams, seemed gathered together in this palace of
splendour. There was silence profound and deep, a dreamy absence
of sound to propitiate repose, and there were instruments of music

to awaken sweet sounds upon. There was in some apartments a twilight at noon, a soft slumberous atmosphere of odour as if for the indulgence of a voluptuous idleness; others were light and airy, filled with birds and flowers, with windows wreathed with trellised plants, thrown open and commanding a landscape which combined grandeur and cheerfulness. Books there were for the studious, if the studious ever came there, and such light and pleasant literature as the age then furnished to suit a lady's reading: pictures there were on the walls, and beautiful rare statues filled each appropriate niche, or steed on marble pedestals looking down on the spectator with their calm, unimpassioned countenances, or casting over the stateliness of those rooms the shadow of some old but immortal agony or woe. Without, lay gardens and groves, all trim and finely kept as if by fairy hands, for no gardener or labourer was ever seen in them, their work being early morning; beyond these lay the park, with its slopes, its shadowy glens, its waters, its old wood and its sylvan creatures. Besides these, carriages, horses, servants, were ever at their command, to convey or attend them when and where they chose.

Mrs. Ashenhurst and her daughter might truly be said to enjoy a golden life. As for the nabob, those who saw him might have believed that they it was for whom he had especially made this earthly paradise, so great seemed not only his contentment in their presence, but his unwearying devotion to them.

So passed on week after week; and so easily does the human mind accustom itself to circumstances, however strange and out of its common track they may at first appear, that not only Mrs. Ashenhurst, but Jane herself, began to feel as perfectly at home, as much accustomed to the grandeur of Denborough Park, as if it had been their residence for years rather than weeks.

But clouds will rise to obscure the brightness of a summer's day and even this golden life had its annoyances; and the first that presented itself, after the memory of the first evening was got over, was owing to a letter from Mrs. Burgoyne. Till then, Jane would have said it was impossible that a letter from her could afford other than unmingled pleasure, seeing it did not announce the death of Miss Livingstone; but so it was. After all good Mrs. Burgoyne's regrets for the loss of her friends and her wishes for their happiness had been gone through; after she had told all the news of Harbury, how one Miss Parkinson had got a lover worth seven hundred a year, and another had lost hers worth a thousand; the good old lady went on to say, "and this in perfect confidence, for she had very likely no business to mention it, but that now his sister was recovering, poor Brian had time to think of himself, and that she believed he was very unhappy that he had allowed dear Miss Ashenhurst to leave Harbury without declaring his love for her, but that it was what Mrs. Ashenhurst had said about Tom Parkinson which had presented his doing so; and now she was afraid he would not come forward, because their prospects were so changed for," added she, "what has Brian in prospect beyond the rectory that has been promised him, and that, though in itself no to be despised, is nothing to entitle him to ask for the hand of General Dubois' heiress." To all this was added a postscript, that she believed she was wrong to have said all this, "for that, now Augusta was better, she believed Brian would pay his respects to his old friends at Denborough Park soon after he was ordained, which would be in a week or two."

The feelings of the mother and daughter were very different on reading this letter. A few weeks ago they would have thought precisely the same—that Brian Livingstone of all men was the most welcome of suitors; Jane's feelings were unchanged, but her mother talked of her altered circumstances, wondered at Mrs. Burgoyne not knowing better than to persuade her nephew to such a step, for she had no doubt it was her doing; that, to be sure, Mr. Livingstone was a gentleman, but what pretension could he have to think of her daughter? who certainly might match with the heir of a dukedom?—besides all this, it was not her place to dispose of her daughter; she considered General Dubois in the place of a father, nor did she think it likely he would give his consent to anything of the kind.

Had Jane heard her mother plotting against church and state, she could not have been more amazed than when, one after another, these reasons were advanced against Brian Livingstone; all selfish, cold-hearted reasons, worthy as she thought of Mr. Parkinson himself. Poor Mrs. Burgoyne, too, that had written such a genuine, confidential letter, so full of old feelings and old friendliness, which but to read was like hearing the dear old lady talk, was she too to be censured? Jane sighed deeply as she said what she felt truly—"that if their greatness here must alienate them thus from their old friends, must change their old feelings and old opinions, she would rather have remained in their small house at Harbury with only two servants, and no better acquaintance than poor Mrs. Burgoyne!"

Day after day went on, and Jane lived in the happy belief that Brian would visit them, and then she was sure all would be well: in the mean time, Mrs. Ashenhurst had replied to the letter according to her new philosophy.

As may well be imagined the new inmates at Denborough Park created no little sensation among the neighbouring gentry; their first appearance in public was by the General's side in his grand pew at church. No sooner was the service over than everybody was engaged on the same topic. "Who were they? What could their being at Denborough Park mean? Had anybody heard of such arrivals being looked for? Was the General married?" that was perhaps the question most anxiously asked. The truth soon got abroad: and then Miss Ashenhurst was declared to be a sweet, pretty creature, so beautifully dressed, and her mother was so much the gentlewoman! Would Miss Ashenhurst be the General's heir? was a very important question.

There was, it must be acknowledged, bitter disappointment in many a lady's soul to find that the General had any female relatives, and particularly such as these; they feared now, he never would marry, and it was a thousand pities—just the man as he was to make a woman happy, and with such a fortune and such a beautiful place! The General had been their neighbour for eighteen months, had visited everybody, had been intimate with everybody, yet no one had ever heard him speak of these his near female relations! Never had the wisdom of the ladies of that division of the county been so much at fault before. It was not extraordinary that Jane Ashenhurst nor her mother, notwithstanding their good looks and handsome dresses, found but little favour in the eyes of the ladies. The gentlemen saw things very differently. They called Jane Ashenhurst a divine creature, and declared she would make Denborough Park all it should be. What an amazing fortune she would be! And they were credibly informed that she and her mother were the sole relatives the nabob had; she would have the best fortune in five counties! Well might they call her the finest girl that ever was seen; with such a complexion! just what a lady's complexion should be. Then her figure! Jane Ashenhurst was voted perfect, and her mother the very next approach to it!

Among the most ardent admirers of the young lady and her fortune was Sir Harbottle Grimstone, and thence rose another of Jane's annoyances; but of this renowned knight we must be allowed to speak a few words.

When General Dubois became a resident at Denborough Park, he heard, wherever he went, and from every one who came near him, of Sir Harbottle Gristmstone, nobody but Sir Harbottle Grimstone! "Did he know Sir Harbottle Grimstone?" "No!" "Oh! but he must know him; he was the man!" "Had not Sir Harbottle Grimstone called?" "No." "When he had the pleasure of knowing Sir Harbottle Grimstone, he would see what the county of S— could boast of!" Was there a man who rode well? It was Sir Harbottle Grimstone. Who gave good dinners? Again it was Sir Harbottle Grimstone. Who sang the best song, he who the ladies vowed the most delectable partner in the dance, was no other than Sir Harbottle Grimstone! Whose equipage was the most splendid, whose hounds and horses the best bred, whose house the best furnished? Again and again he heard of Sir Harbottle Grimstone!

A man who had been used to an omnipotent rule, and who demanded it everywhere he might be, as General Dubois did, was only to be piqued into curiosity, not excited by encomiums such as these of his extraordinary neighbour, who, unlike the rest of the gentry within a dozen miles of the nabob's new residence, seemed slow of making his acquaintance.

At last he met his paragon of a country gentleman at the dinner-table of a mutual friend; he met him, and instantly disliked him.

Sir Harbottle was the antipodes to General Dubois: in age he might be thirty; and having but lately come into possession of his hereditary estate, was full of arrogance and assumption of unaccustomed possession. He was a thoughtless, swaggering, talking man, in the full intoxication of animal spirits and property, who had no conception of living but to enjoy himself, or of enjoyment but in feasting, drinking, and galloping over hedges and five-barred gates. He was what his squiral associates called a good fellow, the ladies a great rake, and the gentlemen a sower of wild oats, born for the destruction of woods and the growth of mortgages, unless marriage tamed him—and Sir Harbottle, they were free to confess, had only to choose and take. This was in fact not saying too much, for, spite of his coarse manners, vulgar tastes, and rather questionable character, by dint of a handsomely manly person, a dashing off-hand address, and that unaccountable inconsistency which makes women too often admire that which all the world blames, Sir Harbottle was their magnus Apollo. Such was the estimation he held in public opinion when the nabob came to reside at Denborough Park: thenceforward things began to change. The amazing wealth which the new-comer was reputed to possess, and the unaccustomed splendour in which he burst forth among them, made instant diversion in his favour; besides this, while everyone supposed the primary object with a man of his caste and character would be to choose associates of the highest class, the very fact of his adapting himself to all his new acquaintance involved the highest possible compliment to each one's self-love. Sumptuous and dignified as he was, he could become a pleasant smiling, chatting, social being, and wherever he went made himself very affably at ease. All this in fact was but a part of his schenme to acquire power and influence; and though in the eyes of some of his neighbours, plain country squires and justices of the peace, he was thought over-polished and effeminate, even to them he was perfectly polite, unostentatious of his superior knowledge and riches, and would seem even to be a willing listener to the details of hunts, the business of quarter-sessions and the pedigree of horses. He was on good terms with all; he had forbearance for them all, except for this much-vaunted Sir Harbottle Grimstone.

Sir Harbottle returned the General's aversion; he was over-shadowed by his greatness; and ever since his introduction among them, his influence with the ladies had begun to increase. At first he was asked, "Have you seen—General Dubois?" "No." "The finest, the most perfectly well-bred man in the world! you must see General Dubois!" "Oh! Sir Harbottle! have you seen the General's new carrriage; his superb black horses? Have you heard of the saloon at Denborough Park? Why, they say the General's only inferior to those of the crown!" "Oh! Sir Harbottle!" exclaimed another fair lady, "you must pay your respects to the General, and bring me a report of him; I am dying to see him!" Such were the exclamations and remarks which beset the falling greatness of Sir Harbottle. "And what the devil care I for this yellow nabob." and "Plague take the old fellow!" were ejaculations he repeated twenty times to himself. They met with some curiosity on both sides, and some latent ill-will; they parted with mutual dislike. "A vulgar low-lived fellow, with less brains than his horse, and less breeding than his dogs!" was the nabob's summing-up of his character. "A purse proud, effeminate, sneaking old coxcomb, that leads those thick-headed squires by the nose with his lies about tiger-hunting and Heaven knows what, and yet without pluck enough to ride at an English fox-hunt!" were the words of Sir Harbottle, as he spurred his horse homeward in great ill-humour. They met again and Sir Harbottle ventured a rough joke upon him; the General returned a caustic retort, which turned the laugh on him, and stung him to the quick. Every subsequent meeting showed him the vast superiority of this new-comer in all matters of intellect and general information, things which he and the ladies had never dreamed before. Presently too, "which was the unkindest cut of all," "the old bachelor beau," as he called him in contempt, was reigning triumphant in the ladies' admiration, the fascinations of Sir Harbottle were in the wane; his jokes were no longer applauded, while the gallant speeches of the General made every woman happy, and his bon-mots were declared to be the only good things that ever were heard.

Such was the state of things when Mrs. Ashenhurst and her daughter became inmates of Denborongh Park; and powerful indeed must have been the impression which Jane made, when even the stout heart, or pride, of Sir Harbottle Grimstone gave way before it. "The yellow old nabob," "the conceited old coxcomb," were suddenly changed in his imagination into "a rich old fellow," "a rather witty old boy; what need he care for him? Denborough Park was quite another place now!" "He would go and make sure of the young lady, that he would, by Jove!" So reasoned and so vowed Sir Harbottle many a day as he sat over his bottle, and many a night as he went to his bed; and accordingly he got up one Monday morning resolute for the achievement—the facing the General, and, more than that, the seeking his acquaintance in his own house; but Sir Harbottle was a bold man, and whatever lover had dared to do he would dare. Accordingly, one burning morning towards the end of July, he presented himself in his riding garb, booted and spurred, in a green coat and buckskins, mounted on his best blood mare, at Denborough Park.

Mrs. Ashenhurst and her daughter were sitting in the shaded coolness of the saloon, when they were startled by the blustering loudness of a strong voice, and a heavy step advancing up the stairs, together with the sound of a riding-whip which, as a sort of accompaniment, was struck upon the balustrades.

"No, hang me, General, if it was want of respect that kept me from Denborough Park. I never am happier than in your company, egad I never am!"

The low voice of the General made an inaudible reply.

"By Jove I thought you'd make this place as complete as you could, General; and now you've brought two such women as can't be matched in the county: ay, ay, you know how to draw about you the treasures of the universe! Upon my soul, cunningest of philosophers; old Epicurus was a fool to you, I'll be hanged if he was not!"

This elegant asseveration brought them sufficiently near to make the General's reply audible.

"I am extremely happy to receive commendation from so distinguished a judge in matters of taste."

"Well, you're a fine fellow, General," was the answer, "and you must let me see the ladies."

"Certainly; the ladies would be in despair not to receive a visit from you; but I must pray you not to be perfectly irrestible, I cannot go picking and choosing as you can, Sir Harbottle!" and with that he bowed him into the saloon.

"I have the honour," said he, "to introduce Sir Harbottle Grimstone; you will oblige me by receiving him with particular attention!"

Both Sir Harbottle and the ladies were for the moment perplexed; but the effrontery of the one, and the ready politeness of the others, came to their help. The nabob threw himself on his couch, enjoying to the utmost this awkward ceremonial, without vouchsafing one word to help forward the conversation. Mrs. Ashenhurst and her daughter recollected all the ridiculous things that had been said of Sir Harbottle, the contempt with which the General had always spoken of him; yet so uncertain did they feel as to the meaning of this introduction, that they could do no other than exert themselves to entertain their guest, supposing all would be explained when he was gone. Sir Harbottle cursed the General by all his gods and yet so charming did Jane look, so desirable the possession of that immense wealth which was but shadowed forth by the sumptuousness of all about him, that he felt every moment deeper and deeper in love, and was almost ready to offer the hand and heart even then, but thought it might be too precipitate.

When every available topic had been talked threadbare, and even Mrs. Ashenhurst was in despair what to say next, the baronet rose to depart, and with him rose the nabob, overwhelming him with sinister politeness meant to be even more annoying than direct sarcasm. But Sir Harbottle was not to be provoked; he returned smile for smile, bow for bow, and even his enemy was not sure whether he had not gone off victor.

Mrs. Ashenhurst, with all her manœuvring, could not fathom, the General's intentions respecting Sir Harbottle Grimstone further than that it was his pleasure he should be well received, and that she and her daughter should be always be at home to him.

"Well, it is his way," said the facile Mrs. Ashenhurst, "we must humour him."

Jane protested in no qualified terms against being compelled to anything so disagreeable.

"Remember my love," was her mother's reply, "as I have said before, and as I have always found 'things never are entirely smooth in this world, we cannot have things all our own way; and I am sure, with all the blessings we enjoy, we must be content to take up with some disagreeables!'"

VII

As Mrs. Ashenhurst had said to her daughter, nothing is altogether smooth in this world; and so they continually found. Bright and untroubled as their lot seemed at a distance, it was but as the distant sunny views of mountains, where even the desolation gives beauty; a nearer approach, a more intimate knowledge, shows the barrenness, the unsightliness—caves of savage creatures—difficulty and painfulness for the wayfarer. All this was an exact type of their fortunes. The external polish, and extreme courtesy of the general's manners veiled cold selfishness, capricious humours, and the most inordinate passion for power,—all which a very short time served to make known to his relatives. Old feelings and old habits they were called upon to sacrifice; they had much to bear and much to forbear; they were no longer free agents; nothing could be done, said or scarcely felt, without considering in the first place how far it might be agreeable to the General. True, he was willing by every indulgence of outward ease and splendour; but Jane soon found that these were but poor compensation for independence of action, thought, and feeling. Mrs. Ashenhurst, whose natural independence of character was much less than her daughter and whose love of state, of wealth, and the influence and indulgence it commands, much greater, felt the conditions less painfully. Whatever was expedient she converted into a duty; it was expedient to maintain her present position, therefore it was her duty to accede to the General's terms; and whatever she could not thus reason away was made endurable by her commonplace wisdom of things never being altogether smooth in this world, or that she had invariably found the rough and the smooth go together.

Besides all this, three months made them aware of other peculiarities in the nabob than those of temper. He was, in spite of his seeming, an unhappy, unsatisfied man. Occasionally he was deeply agitated by unexplained causes, and at times moody and silent of receiving pleasure even of all the multiplied sources of it which he had gathered about him; and many hours were passed within his own chamber, with barred doors, whence the servants reported sounds of human agony to have issued as if he inflicted bodily penance, or underwent mental scrutiny for some untold sin; and, as confirmation strong, he was said to wear a hair-shirt under his delicately fine linen. All these things, the common topic of the servants' hall, were reported to the ladies by Bett, who regarded him as a most awful personage. An immense iron chest too was reported to be kept under his bed, in which it was supposed his treasure was contained,—treasure for which it was surmised he endured that mental or bodily anguish; and, strange to say, this chest, which was reported to be immovable to other hands, was heard to be drawn forth by the nabob with the utmost ease. Stories too were told of glimpses that had been made of jewels so mysteriously splendid that the famous carbuncle must have been dim in comparison.

All this Mrs. Ashenhurst affected to hear with the utmost indifference, as the idle fancy of idle domestics; and Betty, though artfully encouraged to tell all she knew, was chidden for ignorant credulity, her lady the while resolving with herself to watch the nabob narrowly, and to get a peep into his mysterious chamber, which had become fascinating to her imagination as the forbidden closet of Blue-beard was to his wives.

Days and weeks passed on, and Sir Harbottle went and came from Denborough Park as if it had been his home; and the country rang with the strange news that Sir Harbottle was to marry Miss Ashenhurst, after all the bad feeling there had been between him and General Dubois. Even Mrs. Ashenhurst herself began to fear that her daughter was by the General for the bride of Sir Harbottle, and much was the casuisty she employed to persuade her natural love of refinement, and her affection for her daughter, that it certainly was as far as rank and fortune went, not a bad connexion;—that, after all, Sir Harbottle was a good-natured man and would most likely make an excellent husband. But she could not altogether succeed; on the contrary, she even at times questioned if there was not a duty she owed to her daughter more imperative, more sacred, than that which she owed even the General. Poor Mrs. Ashenhurst, she was completely thrown upon both horns of the dilemma! As for Jane herself, she felt that there was a want of self-respect and delicacy in receiving those attentions from Sir Harbottle which she could not pretend to misunderstand. Still she was summoned to his presence by her uncle, and told by him that she must receive him well. Her soul rebelled against it, and she continually showed Sir Harbottle how unpleasant his attentions were; yet she dared not disobey her uncle by offending him, reserving to herself the privilege of refusing him, come what would, whenever his addresses became definite.

Many were the thoughts Jane sent after Mrs. Burgoyne and Brian Livingstone. Why did not the dear old lady write?—why did not Brian visit them as he intended to do? Her intercourse with rude, free-spoken, and jovial Sir Harbottle only made the memory of Brian Livingstone more delightful to her, were it but from the force of contrast.

"Everybody would think and feel the same as I do, even without my particular reasons for liking him," were Jane's reflections as she sat before her glass one morning while Betty was arranging her hair; and as if in confirmation of the thought, Betty, who had been attempting to bring in the subject for the last ten minutes, was now forced to drag it in head and shoulders, to use her own phrase.

"Oh! Miss Jane, if I might but speak my mind!"

"To be sure—what have you to say?" was Jane's encouraging answer.

"Why, it is not for such as me to interfere, if you like him better, Miss Jane; but dear me! I think Sir Harbottle Grimstone is not to be named in the same month with Mr. Livingstone!"

"He is not!" said Jane.

"Laus-a-me, to be sure not! And as for being called my lady, if I may be bold to say it, it's nothin to being Mrs. Livingstone; and only see what a nice, handsome gentleman he is!"

"I cannot understand what all this means," said Jane.

"I hope you are not angry, Miss Jane," said Betty, determined nevertheless to speak her mind; "but ay dear! doesn't everybody believe you are to be married to Sir Harbottle?— more's the pity!— and poor Mr. Livingstone just a-coming, as one may say."

Jane scarcely breathed, and the waitingwoman went on.

"I know it is not my place to talk to you in this way; but, oh! Miss Jane, there's a deal in a word, and a word is soon spoken; and if so be you had promised to Sir Harbottle before the other came, it might be the death of him, so ill as he has been; and you might live to repent it all the blessed days of your life!" And Betty, touched by her own earnestness, wiped the tears from her eyes.

"Ill!" said Jane; "has Mr. Livingstone been ill?"

"Ay dear, yes; ma'am; but Thomas Thackaray says he's better again."

"Thomas Thackaray?"

"Yes, ma'am; Mr. Livingstone has taken him as his servant, now that he has got the rectory; and he came last night to see me," said Betty, hesitatingly; "seven-and-thirty-miles it's a good way; and he came in his new livery, not as grand as what they wear here, but very handsome. And I should not wonder if Mr. Livingstone comes here before he is many months older; he has been very ill, Thomas says; and Mrs. Burgoyne and Miss Augusta are gone to live in Bath."

Nothing could have shown Jane so forcibly as this information, how far removed, how entirely alienated they were from their old friends. "All this had happened: Brian has been ill—he was now rector of Collington-Magna; and her friends were living at Bath. Mrs. Burgoyne had not written! Ah! that showed how entirely changed all things were now!" So thought Jane, in astonishment and sorrow of heart; while poor Betty thought, "it was the strangest thing in the world that Miss Ashenhurst should care no more about Mr. Livingstone than nothing, and only see how easy she seemed to take it!—Well, for her part she might just as well take up with Mr. John, instead of Thomas Thackaray; as if such a thing was possible! as Miss Jane likes Sir Harbottle better than Mr. Livingstone!"

At ths very time Sir Harbottle rose from his bed "with" as the old song says, "his heart full of love."

"By jingo! I'll know what's what," said he, "this day, or my name is not Grimstone!"

Sir Harbottle dressed himself three times that morning;—first in his riding-suit, which was his favourite, and in which he flattered himself he looked most irresitible,—at all events, he looked most unlike the nabob.

"I've a good leg," said he, as he stretched it out to his admiring gaze, after he had finished his toilet, "a well-made leg—and I'm not altogether an ugly fellow, either!"

Thus well satisfied, he ordered his horse to be saddled with the new saddle, and his groom to be ready to attend him precisely at twelve, not a minute later.

Scarcely was breakfast over when he altered his mind—he would go in his phaeton; the order for the horses was countermanded. The nabob had ridiculed him in his hunter's suit, and for this one day he would be on his good behaviour,

Again he performed his toilet, and habited himself somewhat in the fashion of the nabob himself, in a damson-coloured coat lined with rose-coloured silk, and embroidered waistcoat, satin breeches, and white silk stockings. Sir Harbottle was the pink of fashion; he contemplated himself in his mirror, and saluted himself with an oath—"he looked a devilishly deal better in his other dress! women like something manly, and not such finikin finery as this!" said he, as he again unrobed, and assumed his proper habilments.

Again the order in the stables was changed.

"Lord bless my soul!" exclaimed the groom; "when will master know his own mind!"

The horses were at the door to the minute, and Sir Harbottle, in his new boots, mounted into his new saddle, and, attended by his servant, rode up to Denborough Park.

General Dubois was sipping his chocolate; Mrs. Ashenhurst was sitting at a work-table, seeming to work rather than doing so; and Jane was accommpanying herself on her guitar, to that very song of Brian Livingstone's which he had given her when they parted.

The three were thus ocoupied when Sir Harbottle Grimstone was announced. A shade of vexation passed over every countenance, but the General rose and received him with courtesy. Mrs. Ashenhurst did the same; Jane set down the instrument, and stood looking at a parrot, wtithout seeming to see Sir Harbottle.

"Come, Miss Ashenhurst," said her uncle, "you must give Sir Harbottle that song,—Sir Harbottle is an excellent judge of music!"

Jane felt, as if it were profanation to sing it before him, but in obedience she took up her guitar, and blushing over her brow and bosom, she sang—

Heart, what mean these hopse and fears?
Eyes of mine, why flow these tears?
Grief with my few-number'd years
Hath no right to grow!

Pr'y thee, dear heart, tell me why
Thou art sad, although thou try
Joy to win? In times gone by
It was not so!

It is love, sweet love, doth keep
In thy heart's heart sure and deep!
Not for grief is't thou dost weep,
But for joy's excess!

Hast thou love within thy breast,
Hold him fast, let go the rest,
Houses, lands,—supremely blest
If love thee bless!

"My niecee has tolerable execution," said her uncle when she had finished.

"Divine, by Jove!" shouted Sir Sir Harbottle. "Nay, Miss Ashenhurst, you have not done," said he, coming to her side, and looking unutterable things in her eyes, while he sang in his rude voice the words of the song,

Hast thou love within thy breast,
Hold him fast, let him go the rest,
Houses, lands—

Jane looked towards her uncle, to see what he wished her to do.

"Certainly, oblige Sir Harbottle! Can't you make a pretty love-scene out of it, and reply,

—supremely blest,
Thee love shall bless!"

There was the keenest derision in the tone in which the General
said these words; and, utterly confounded and mortified, Jane laid
down the guitar. Sir Harbottle was wild with exultation.

"Egad! my dear General," said he, "you are an emperor. By Jove!
you've hit the right nail on the head! Here am I come this blessed
day to tell Miss Ashenhurst in plain downright English how I adore
her! My dear Miss Jane, will you permit me?" said he, snatching her
hand, and pressing it to his lips.

"Sir Harbottle Grimstone!" exclaimed three voices at once, in
tones that made even the ecstatic Sir Harbottle feel strange.

"Sir Harbottle Grimstone, will you please to explain yourself?"
said the General, rising in such cool wrath as at once silenced
and terrified the ladies, and made the baronet stand on the
defensive.

"What the deuce is all this?" asked Sir Harbottle.

"What the deuce is this, indeed! Why, that you are not to take
liberties with my niece!"

"Bless my life! General Dubois, have I not had your encouragement
to pay attention to Miss Ashenhurst? Miss Ashenhurst, I hope to
God you are my friend! Mrs. Ashenhurst, will not you say one word
for me? Upon my soul, I love Miss Ashenhurst—I adore her; and
here I am come for no other earthly purpose than to offer her my
hand. You will not be so cruel, Miss Ashenhurst!"

"Sir Harbottle Grimstone, there are three descriptions of
persons my niece shall never marry: a widower, a fox-hunter, and
a parson!"

"You are not to decide between Miss Ashenhurst and me,"
said Sir Harbottle, with an earnestness which might pass either
for anger or emotion. "Speak Miss Ashenhurst! Egad, I would
not affront you! I have a good fortune, Miss Jane; what I am you
see!"

"Oh! Sir Harbottle," said Jane, "say no more; I cannot accept your offer!" and overcome almost to fainting by the words of her uncle, she leaned on her mother's arm.

"Sir Harbottle," said the General, triumphantly, "you have lived to see the day when a woman *has* refused you! My God! Did you think it was only to ask and have? I thought it was strange if I could not find a woman who would refuse you!"

Mrs. Ashenhurst saw at once what had been her brother's designs. Sir Harbottle glanced furious anger on his enemy, but he continued to plead with Jane. "Miss Ashenhurst, why should you be overruled by others? I have a good fortune, Mrs. Ashenhurst; my estate is four thousand a year!"

"You have heard what the General has said," obseeved the politic Mrs. Ashenhurst, "it is our pleasure, as well as our duty, to abide by his will!"

"Oho! that's it!—is it? Heaven and earth! is General Dubois to come between you and me, Miss Jane? On my soul, I love you! General Dubois has known it long, and what the devil would he forbid it now for!"

"My neice shall marry neither fox-hunter nor parson!" again exclaimed the General, looking on with as much triumph as anger.

"Let me leave the room!" said Jane Ashenhurst.

"By your permission," said her mother, putting her hand to the door, against which Sir Harbottle had placed his burly person.

"Ladies," returned he, "I never imagined that my devotions had been other than agreeable to you!"

"They were always extremely disagreeable, sir," replied Mrs. Ashenhurst; "and whatever is needful to be said farther on the subject, my brother will say it."

"My dear Miss Ashenhurst," persisted he, addressing Jane, "you cannot be so cruel!"

"I am extremely sorry for what has happened, Sir Harbottle," she replied, with great agitation; "but your attentions never did and never can give me pleasure!"

"Mighty pretty, upon my word!" exclaimed the angry Sir

Harbottle, leaving the ladies at liberty to make their exit,—"mighty pretty! And why the devil was I made a fool of? General Dubois, you have behaved villainously!"

"Sir!" exclaimed the General.

"You have behaved in a rascally manner—in a shabby way, sir!"

"Will you please to leave the house?" said General Dubois.

Sir Harbottle seized his hat and riding-whip, and overturning two stands of flowering plants, and setting the parrot and other birds all in an uproar of fright, went out of the apartment, swearing that the old nabob should live to repent it.

General Dubois' rage rose to its height at the confusion and havoc Sir Harbottle had made; servants were summoned to set things right again, while he wished he had the offender at Furnapore, where, he swore, he had shot many a much better man for a less cause!

Unjustifiable as both mother and daughter felt the General's conduct to have been throughout this affair, it was still a relief to know that Jane was not destined for the wife of Sir Harbottle. Nevertheless, Jane freely censured her uncle: she had been made a tool to pique Sir Harbottle, or to revenge an old affront; there had been no regard for her feelings—it was an unprincipled, selfish piece of cunning; and with great warmth Jane declared that both she and Sir Harbottle had been very ill used.

"Bless me, my dear, how you talk!" replied Mrs. Ashenhurst; "to name yourself and Sir Harbottle in the same breath! Why, sure, love, you had no partiality for him!"

"If I had," said Jane, "I do not see that any regard would have been had to my feelings. But in truth I had not; I detested Sir Harbottle. Yet my uncle saw me daily distressed by his vulgar attentions, which I cannot pretend to have misunderstood, and repeated over and over again that it was his pleasure I should receive him well. This was unfeeling towards me, especially when, after all, Sir Harbottle was to be repulsed."

"My dear," remonstrated her mother, "how can you talk in this way?"

"Then as to Sir Harbottle," continued Jane, " how could he expect such a rebuff? Disguise it as you will, mamma, it has been an unfeeling, not to say a treacherous conduct!"

"Dear love," again said Mrs. Ashenhurst, "I would not for the world that your uncle heard you say so! Your uncle, you must remember, stands in the place of a father to you, and you must bear with his peculiarities. For my part; I think it my duty to study his wishes and his pleasure as much as I can: we cannot, my love, have everything to our own way in this world."

"I think we were much happier at Harbury than we are likely to be here," sighed Jane.

"Oh, love, if you are thinking of Mr. Livingstone, and what your uncle said, I must take his part there. All people, you ought to remember, have their prejudices; and there is nothing uncommon in gentlemen who have lived so long abroad thinking but lightly of the clergy."

"As to him," said Jane, blushing deeply, "he is nothing to me; but I really think, after my uncle had neglected us so long—nor ever, it is my opinion, would have inquired after us—it is hardly right that he should interfere with connexions that might have been formed before he took any thought about us. I do not mean that his determination against my marrying a clergyman can ever signify to me; still, you know, it might have signified, and I do not suppose either your feelings or mine would have been consulted."

"Well, love," returned her mother, "after all I do not think Mr. Livingstone exactly the husband you might look for now. I mean no imputation on him—he is an excellent young man: besides, I dare say his attentions meant nothing. Mrs. Burgoyne loves to talk dearly, and I have no doubt she would be glad that her nephew did so well!"

Jane looked at her mother in amazement. "Nay," said she, "Brian Livingstone is not a man to feign feelings; nor would poor Mrs. Burgoyne say anything she did not believe."

Mrs. Ashenhurst felt reproved; but she added, with apparent

gaiety, "Well, love, when Brian Livingstone comes to pay his address to you, perhaps your uncle may make an exception in his favour. Your uncle is a good, kind creature, and I must not have you think hardly of him: for you may depend upon it, out of a thousand men of his wealth and standing, you would find nine hundred and ninety-nine far more unreasonable than he."

However much Mrs. Ashenburst endeavoured to persuade herself of the General's perfection, she could not help feeling that her daughter spoke with some show of reason; and though she by no means was disposed to quarrel with her present position, even if General Dubois required greater sacrifices than those of feeling and opinion, still she thought it as well to show, or to make the trial at least of independent feelings, as well as to discover, if possible, how far they might reckon upon Denborough Park as their permanent home.

Accordingly, as the General appeared in remarkably condescending humour, a few days afterwards, she took the opportunity of remarking, "that she must now begin to think of her return to Harbury."

"My dear madam," said 'he, "I hope your residence here is made perfectly agreeable—my servants give you no cause of complaint?"

"Nothing in the world could be more entirely to my satisfaction," replied she.

"Then I cannot part with you."

"But, my dear sir," continued Mrs. Ashenhurst, satisfied as to the subject most at heart, "my house at Harbury awaits my return and even now I hear the persons I left in charge of it wish to be at liberty."

"What need for your having a house at Harbury at all? I am not disposed to part with you. I have not yet got my niece married."

"By-the-bye," observed the lady, though it was not quite true, "I cannot understand your behaviour to Sir Harbottle Grimstone."

"What!" exclaimed he, raising himself from his couch, "are you among the worshippers of this fox-hunter, who is hardly better than a barbarian!"

"Good Heavens! my dear General, how could you think of such a thing?—the man always was my aversion!"

"Sir Harbottle Grimstone," returned the nabob, "is a boasting fool; he has bragged in my presence that the woman did not live who could refuse him! He is a vulgar coxcomb—a man whom I hate, and I have humbled him!—Mrs. Ashenhurst, whatever I do, I do with a design—Sir Harbottle is humbled!"

"But, my dear sir, you should consider the feelings of your niece."

"God bless my soul! has the simpleton fallen in love with that brute?"

"No, sir, no! You entirely mistake me; my daughter had the utmost aversion to him. But you must pardon me, my dear General, it is like playing with edge tools—suppose she *had* loved him?"

"Well, then, my good lady, she must have taken the consequence. But as to young ladies' affections, I think them pretty much like their dresses—put on and off at pleasure. However I mean to get her well married, if it's only to annoy this Sir Harbottle! But I would have you understand one thing—she marries neither fox-hunter, widower, nor parson. I have my reasons for what I do, and from you and my niece I look for aquiescence. Had the fox-hunter, instead of Sir Harbottle Grimstone, been his Majesty himself—if the parson in the person of the Archbishop of Canterbury, or the widower as a prince of the blood, Jane Ashenhurst should have none of them!"

"My dear sir, you are infinitely good and generous," said Mrs. Ashenhurst; "but with respect to my residence at Harbury?"

"Ah, let it be disposed of. Your home for the future is with me. I owe you something, my dear lady, for apparent neglect; but upon my word, I had no idea that I had such agreeable relatives."

Mrs. Ashenhurst was flattered and satisfied.

"Whatever you want, ask me freely for it," continued the General; "and to make you less immediately dependant upon me, I will secure to you and to my niece each a thousand pound a year for your own private expenses, to be paid quarterly, begginning with a payment this day: you shall want for nothing!"

Mrs. Ashenhurst certainly at that moment felt that she did want for nothing; she was the most fortunate, the most grateful of women, and in this happy state of feeling left the General to his siesta.

Mrs. Ashenhurst looked round her in proud yet calm complacency: whatever her eyes met of grand or rare would one day be her daughter's. Where would there be an heiress like Jane Ashenhurst? No, no, she must never marry poor Brian Livingstone! The General was entitled to his want and it was their duty to acquiesce with his will and wishes, whatever they might be.

VIII

"To be sure, Jane can never marry Brian Livingstbne, and it is my duty to counteract any such attachment. The idea of her marrying a country parson is quite ridiculous!"

Such was the substance of Mrs. Ashenhurst's thoughts as she entered their own apartments, and found a letter lying on the table; a letter from no other than Brian Livingstone, addressed to her daughter, and bearing the Wood Leighton postmark. "How lucky it is," she exclaimed, "that Jane is absent!" for that her daughter should receive the letter would be, in her opinion, a most unadvised thing. Mrs. Ashenhurst knew it would be much easier to crush the attachment in its present state than after the lovers had exchanged sentiments, even knowing, as they would, existing impediments. "But it shall not come to that," was her fixed determination, as she eyed critically the well-known and scholar-like handwriting of Brian Livingstone, and remarked internally that his seal was handsome and well cut. Mrs. Ashenhurst could conjecture perfectly well how the whole affair stood: her letter to Mrs. Burgoyne—the only one she had written to her from Denborough Park—had had the desired effect; it had offended her; but that was of little consequence. No doubt it had also given much pain to her nephew; it was possible that Jane too might be thought accessory; neither was that of importance. Certain it was, the intended visit and declaration of love had both been withheld, and in all probability there would have been an end of the affair, but for the inopportune death of the old rector of Collington-Magna, which had thus placed Brian in a sufficiently independent state to renew his suit.

"But it shall never be!" exclaimed the cogitating lady—"my daughter shall match with an equal in fortune, or a superior in rank!" And with these words, hastily glancing over the epistle, which overflowed with the eloquence of love, she consigned it to the flames—a far different destination to what the writer had hoped for it!

Having thus taken the affair into her own hands, it behoved her to finish it. A ready plan suggested itself; and, as if fortune played the game for her, who should be announced at that moment but Lady Cornbury. Of this right honourable personage we must be permitted a few words.

Lady Cornbury had taken the place formerly occupied by Mrs. Burgoyne; she was Mrs. Asheuhurst's most favoured and most admired friend—in fact, she was the most elevated in rank of all her acquaintance.

Lord and Lady Cornbury lived at Wilton Hall, ten miles from Denborough Park. They had exchanged visits with General Dubois, but not until Mrs. Ashenhurst had become his inmate, did the acquaintance advance beyond etiquette. Mrs. Ashenhurst and her daughter pleased even them; and her ladyship, dignified, cold, and generally inactive as she was, made extraordinary exertions and unheard-of efforts to do them honour. It was enough for Mrs. Ashenhurst, lover of rank as she was, that her friend was the wife of a peer, and was in herself the representative of a noble line. Nothing more was needed. Mrs. Burgoyne, the only tried friend of many years was dethroned, and the coroneted lady took her place.

A thousand pities it was that Lady Cornbury had no son; a thousand more that the heir of Wilton and the title had quarrelled with them a dozen years ago. Poor Mrs. Ashenhurst had no patience with him; though her ladyship, too indolent to be a good hater, seemed herself already to have forgotten the cause of offence, and spoke of him with kindness, though she persisted that they never should be friends again. Still, Mrs. Ashenhurst consoled herself that Jane's hononrable and noble husband elect would come through the hands of the Cornburys.

Her ladyship was between fifty and sixty years of age; short and plump, fair and smooth, blue-eyed and flaxen-haired, and quiet to a miracle. She had never spoken fifty, nor half fifty consecutive words at one time in the whole course of her life; nor had ever walked a hundred yards, where it was possible by any human contrivance to introduce either carriage or chair; she never read because it tired her eyes; nor did any kind of work, because she had never been used to it. That a being so nearly approaching a nonentity could ever have been in a passion, was a moral impossibility; an equally impossible thing was it, that she could ever have laughed—laughed in the real sense of the word—a side-shaking laughter. Yet there was at all times, and on all occasions, an ever-enduring smile or semblance of a smile on her yet red and perfectly-formed lips, which made the world call her the sweetest-tempered woman in the universe. Care and trouble and anxiety were things that had never come near the smooth current of her existence. As to their darker shades, sorrow and disappointment and anguish, mental or bodily, such things were so far out of her ladyship's comprehension, that nobody could have thought of her sympathising with them. Her nature could only be emblemed by a polished steel mirror, bright, and reflecting back images of splendour or happiness, itself cold and impassive the while.

Lord Cornbury was her counterpart. Public life, its perplexities, its annoyances, and its activities were not for him; he took his seat in the House, but was scarcely seen there again. The greater part of his time he spent at his favourite residence of Wilton: he planted, he farmed, he bred cattle and audited his steward's accounts; besides this, he ate, he drank, he slept.

Mrs. Ashenhurst, with her quiet gentlewomanliness, yet profound veneration for rank, was a prodigious favourite with them, and especially, as after the first advances all activity of friendship,—no, certainly that is not the term—of intimacy, as performed by her: she made four calls for her ladyship's one—went twice a-week invariably—took them all the passing county news; she talked, and they listened.

That Lord and Lady Cornbury were the most insufferably dull people in the world, was an opinion Jane entertained in spite of her mother. Still Wilton was a grand old place, less ostentatious than Denborongh Park; there was a repose and dignity in its old carving and gilding, its old furniture, its old pictures, and its old sober domestics, in their demure murrey-coloured livery, which she preferred to the new magnificence and costly decoration and officious ministration of her own home. Besides this, she was more perfectly at liberty there; was there free to act and think for herself; Lady Cornbury nor asking her to talk, sing, read, or play.—She loved, as she told Mrs. Ashenhurst, to look at Jane: she sat so well, and walked so well, and was really such a lovely creature. It was quite a comfort to have her there. Lord Cornbury said the same.

Could anything have been more fortunate than that her ladyship should come this very morning to request Jane's company for a week or ten days? "For," said she, "they tell me the park is looking so well—but for my part I never notice such things." Mrs. Ashenhurst declared herself delighted with the proposal, and Jane entering at that moment, was informed of the pleasure that was offered her. "I know you love to be with her ladyship, my dear, and the change will do you good."

Jane assented with sincere willingness; for she thought of the rambles she would have in Wilton-Park, unattended even by servants if such were her pleasure;—how she could indulge there her own speculations and fancies, and even perhaps forget that there was such a person in the world as Sir Harbottle Grimstone; and, moreover, she should be ten miles nearer to Collington-Magna.

In a few hours she took her seat by the side of the placid Lady Cornbury; and as she was driven away from Denborough Park, through the fine gloom of an autumnal day, the annoying and soul-sickening memory of the baronet, and of her uncle's prohibitions, gradually gave way before the fair and rose-coloured visions of hope. Little did the poor girl think she was conveying herself away from the very being whom of all others she desired to see;—from the very being who cast a glory over those heart-creations, like the sun over the clouds of his setting.

That was a weary day for Brian Livingstone: the morrow, however, brought the answer to his letter.

"Mrs. Ashenhurst begged the honour of an hour's conversation with the Rev. Brian Livingstone."

It was with an anxious and foreboding heart that he entered the noble demesne. The grandeur of Jane's new home, her unquestionably altered fortunes, fell upon his senses like a crushing weight. It requires no ordinary philosophy to resist the influence of these things; but the man were unworthy of a woman's love who, with an internal consciousness of his own worth—his honourable, upright intentions, would not pass through even a more trying ordeal than this spirit-crushing one. Brian was a man to dare all things, to endure all things; still he had received too ominous a summons not to be alive to all discouraging impressions.

Mrs. Ashenhurst received him with a show of civility, and inquired after Mrs. Burgoyne and his sister, he told of their removal to Bath. She affected no surprise, for her manner was intended to prove that circumstances had placed every one connected with him out of the range of the Denborough Park sympathies. Brian felt the intended sentiment: and assuming a coldness equal to her own, said he was there by her own request, but that he hoped to have the pleasure of seeing Miss Ashenhurst."

"My daughter, sir, left home yesterday, to spend a few days with our friend Lady Cornbury," was her reply.

"Am I to understand that she left home in consequence of a letter I had the honour of addressing to her?" asked he.

"You are at liberty, sir, to form your own conjectures. My daughter knows her duty. I shall not pretend ignorance of the purport of your letter, Mr. Livingstone; and after what I said to Mrs. Burgoyne, I consider it a breach of propriety in you to address my daughter."

"You have seen the letter?" asked Livingstone.

"My daughter did not show me your letter," was Mrs. Ashenhurst's reply; "but it is enough for you to know that such a connexion is undesirable."

Brian felt at this moment perhaps more indignant than a minister of Christ should have felt; yet he condescended to remonstrate, informing Mrs. Ashenhurst that he was in possession of the rectory of Collington-Magna: therefore, perhaps, less presumptuous in declaring an attachment of which he had hoped she was aware before she and Miss Ashenhurst left Harbury.

"Neither my daughter nor myself," replied she, "are entirely at liberty to indulge our own predilections, even supposing they existed. General Dubois stands in the place of a parent to Miss Ashenhurst, and as such has a right to be consulted."

"Let me see General Dubois," said Livingstone, eagerly.

"You mistake me, sir; my brother has certain peculiarities of opinion—prejudices I shall not call them—he is too liberal and noble-minded for prejudices; but he has declared that his niece shall not marry a clergyman. I cannot entirely hold with him, because it might prevent my daughter connecting herself very properly, both as to rank and fortune: still I do not see that we have any right to oppose his opinions—it is our duty to submit."

"A man who would adopt so unreasonable, not to say unchristian, a prejudice," replied he, warmly, "certainly would be very likely to exact implicit obedience."

"I beg, sir, I may hear no insinuations against General Dubois," returned Mrs. Ashenhurst, with equal warmth; "our greatest happiness is to fall in with his wishes."

"Was this declaration with respect to a clergyman made in consequence of my addresses to Miss Ashenhurst?" asked Brian.

"I cannot see, Mr. Livingstone, what right you have to make these inquiries."

"I have a right, and you are in duty bound to answer them, inasmuch as you are bound not to trample on the happiness of a fellow-being."

"It was not made with immediate reference to you," replied Mrs. Ashenhurst, impressed by the solemnity of his manner; "but as an unfolding of his views towards my daughter, when he rejected the suit of Sir Harbottle Grimstone."

"Ha!" said Brian; "Sir Harbottle is then rejected, thank God."

"There is no occasion to say much more on this subject, Mr. Livingstone. This you clearly understand. General Dubois will never consent to his niece marrying a clergyman, were it the Archbishop of Canterbury. This he has declared repeatedly. He is not a man to retract; and, I confess to you, Mr. Livingstone, he is not a man to displease with impunity. We owe this consideration to ourselves; and I must beseech of you, as a minister of the gospel, as a preacher of peace, and a maintaner of the unity of families, that you will never renew this subject. If you value my daughter's happiness, you will not do it."

"God knows," said Brian, "how dear, how sacred the happiness of Miss Ashenhurst must ever be to me! Still, I cannot calmly resign her on these grounds alone. Let me hear from her own lips that there is no hope for me, and I may perhaps then learn to submit without murmuring!"

"My dear sir!" said Mrs. Ashenhurst, who began to be alarmed at the turn things were taking, "I have no wish to impose restrictions, or to place impediments in your way; but I will state the case, and then leave it to your honour. Jane could not marry a clergyman, were he the Bishop of London."

"But," said Brian, "I would willingly believe she might accept the rector of Collington-Magna, while she might reject a more dignified clergyman."

"I do not dispute it," was her answer; "but supposing you yourself were the Archbishop of York, she could not marry you without forfeiting the favour of her uncle; and this she will not do—I know she will not, Mr. Livingstone: Jane is a high-principled girl, and will sacrifice her inclination to her duty, and even you must admire her for such conduct."

"You assure me, then, that I have still an interest in Miss Ashenhurst's heart!"

"I have no right to make confessions for my daughter, Mr. Livingstone; but, I assure you, her peace of mind would not be improved by such an interview, however much yours might; nor should I think it generous in you to persist in the wish."

"I would not for the world give Miss Ashenhurst pain, and yet—"

"And yet," said Mrs. Ashenhurst, interrupting him, "you would desire an interview which must of necessity occasion more uncertainty—more distress of mind than her present determination has cost her. Disguise it as you will, Mr. Livingstone, such a wish on your part is selfish, and, I will candidly tell you, must be fruitless: you would only distress and agitate her to no earthly purpose!"

Brian passed his hand across his brow, and for two seconds made no answer: at length he said,— "It is strange, it is not like her usual consideration, to make no reply to my letter. Three months are not sufficiently long to have deadened a heart naturally noble and generous as Miss Ashenhurst's was, or I could almost have suspected such a cause."

"For that matter, Mr. Livingstone, my daughter knew that all which it was necessary to say, I should say for her. We are not in the situation we were at Harbury; we are not now entirely free agents, as I hinted before. As to my daughter," added she, seeing him about to speak, "you may be sure I can have nothing but her happiness at heart; and when I state how much her equanimity must fruitlessly suffer from such an interview as you desire, I do it in the hope you will spare her the suffering. I leave it to your own good sense, Mr. Livingstone. I believe my daughter is dear to you; nor is there any one who wishes you better than I do, and could this interview serve any good purpose I would not oppose it. Having stated thus much, I leave it to your better judgment."

Mrs. Ashenhurst had strung all these professions together in her most candid manner and most kindly voice to prevent Brian replying, and at the same time to impose upon him a thorough belief in her good faith. He now sat silent and uncertain, his mind agitated by the most painful feelings—disappointment, love, and in some degree self-reproach.

"I have been miserably unfortunate," at length he said, "in delaying what ought to have been avowed before you left Harbury, and which would have been avowed save from sentiments of delicacy. I dreaded the sarcasm and scorn which you heaped on that fool Parkinson! Heaven knows, I ought to have had more self-respect! Certain visions too of romantic generosity made me willing to defer it: I was less sanguine in your expectations from General Dubois than I ought to have been. God knows, I have been punished!" said he, with a voice of the deepest heart-anguish. "I should have been the happiest of men to have offered Miss Ashenhurst a handsome independency had she been disappointed in her expectations!"

"It is useless, Mr. Livingstone, to imagine cases; we have only to do with actualities."

"Very true," said Brian; "but you must allow the man who hast lost his all to indulge some regrets!"

"Again reverting to this interview, Mr. Livingstone, you surely cannot persist in desiring it?" urged Mrs. Ashenhurst.

"I have no reason to doubt your assurances," he replied; "and if I am certainly to believe Miss Ashenhurst by her own wish left this place to avoid seeing me, I have no right to desire it: your assurance of this will be enough."

"It was without any compulsion—by her own will that she embraced the offer of our friends at Wilton to accompany them."

Brian heard it as the criminal hears his sentence from the mouth of the judge. A shade passed over his brow, his lips quivered, and his hands were momentarily clenched. Mrs. Ashenhurst respected the suffering she had inflicted, and was silent. In a few moments he rose, and, without speaking, offered her his hand.

"You are such as I believed you," said she, taking his hand with the utmost kindness; "you are a noble-minded, excellent man. I have no doubt, Mr. Livingstone, but your best days are to come."

"You are more flattering than my own heart," was his reply, in a suppressed tone of bitterness and agony, and, disengaging his hand, he hastily left the room.

This was too important an event to be concealed in the lady's own breast; nor did many hours elapse before the General was possessed of its detail. Of course the value of the sacrifice was heightened: he was called "an old and most highly-valued friend, the nephew of a friend equally dear; but he had been rejected entirely from a desire to conform to the General's wishes;" Mrs. Ashenhurst, declaring that she never was so happy as when evincing her gratitude to her brother. At the same time, she besought him to conceal from Jane this rejection of a suitor to whom she had reason to believe her attached; as she wished by all means to spare her feelings; and she esteemed herself most fortunate, she averred, that the gentleman had come at a time of her absence.

There was something sinister in the General's eye as he professed himself her debtor, declaring that such a proof of attachment should not be forgotten, at the same time wishing she had introduced this gentleman to his acquaintance before she had taken this step, as in all cases he had much rather be consulted.

Upon the whole, there was something in his manner which was unsatisfactory; and poor Mrs. Ashenhurst, with all her plotting, fell thus much short in self-approbation.

IX

Surely the heart is no sorcerer, or the days Jane passed at Wilton, gorgeous and calm as autumn days could be, had not slid on like an uninterrupted festival. At Wilton no events seemed ever to occur; it was a charmed land of untroubled rest; and from morning till night, from night till morning, Jane had full leisure to indulge her own visions and fancies. They were happy days, perhaps happier than most she had passed since she had left Harbury therefore is it that I believe the heart to be no sorcerer.

Never had Jane been in a fitter mood than now to enjoy a sojourn in an old stately mansion like Wilton. She ranged over the house at will, through ancient chambers and galleries, and in imagination peopled them with their long-perished possessors. She made herself familiar with all the old family portraits and their histories; some bright fair histories, that the heart fed upon and took courage from; others-dark and terrible, full of that fearful tragic interest which saddens and thrills the listener, and haunts him for days like a destiny. She turned over the old richly bound and coroneted volumes of the library; books which, by their appearance, had not been opened since the days of the Lady Jacquett as of fearful memory, and the Lord Ernests of olden and darker days. She feasted on Milton and Shakespeare, those treasures of poetry, and heart-philosophy which is the substance of poetry—on the very pages she had so lately turned over with the friend who first opened her soul to the knowledge; she heard, as it were, his deep, thrilling voice read passage after passage—their full meaning unfolded before her—her soul seemed exalted and ennobled by their sublime imaginings, or the depths of her heart laid open before their subtle and truth-searching spirits. Never did Jane know till then how that beloved friend made a part of her soul's existence, how love and poetry had grown together, and how they created those holy and ennobling sentiments which it was her greatest happiness to indulge. All her reading, however, was not poetry in its accepted sense, though certainly poetry in its spirit: here she found Froissart, that grand old chronicler, who united the matter-of-fact observer so wonderfully with the poet, and who has left a Chronicle more valuable for its picture of manners, costume and feelings and for its brave old chivalric spirit, than ever for its circumstantial history. Here she found the old romances, Amadis de Gaul, Morte d'Arthur, Charlemagne, and the quaint but fascinating stories of Chaucer; and here again these old divines, Jeremy Taylor, South, and Barrow, who, in the earnest eloquence of their high right-mindedness, wrote less to produce effect than to touch the heart with eternal truths, and have left works which will be read and read again when more ambitious writers are lost in oblivion, and sects and parties are forgotten.

What a refreshment, what a strengthening of the soul sprang from these studies! The annoying memory of Sir Harbottle Grimstone seemed gone; and even when the heart-wringing consciousness returned that a vow had been registered against Brian Livingstone by her proud uncle and accorded to by her worldly-minded mother, if Jane wept, it was not as one who is utterly forlorn.

At the end of three weeks Jane returned home. Again things fell into their usual course; the leaves had kindled in the gorgeous colouring of autumn, and had then faded and fallen before the winds and frosts of the early winter. Mrs. Ashenhurst and her daughter had now been six months at Denborough Park. According to the feelings of the former, she might have lived there all her days, so completely did she fall into and adopt all the requirings of her situation. That she owed this great and perfect happiness to the accidental laming of a poor soldier, she was in a fair way of forgetting.

Daniel Neale had refused all offers of assistance, as far as fixing him at a park gate or in a shrubbery-cottage went. He took up his residence at Wood Leighton; whence radiating as from a centre in all directions on his vagrant expeditions, he never presented himself at Denborough Park; and as the General invariably spoke of him with contempt and dislike, Mrs. Ashenhurst did not trouble herself farther than by throwing a piece of money occasionally when he came in her way. Jane not satisfied with the indifference of her elders, would have evinced her gratitude in some substantial manner, but the bitterness with which he often spoke of her uncle, and the hints he dropped, "that if she chose he could tell her something," displeased her, and in this respect she so far imitated her mother as to hold no farther intercourse with him than by relieving him liberally whenever they met.

All this time Mrs. Ashenhurst had not let pass without narrowly watching her brother; endeavouring to fathom the hidden guilt, if such there were, that occasionally gloomed his spirit; or how those mysterious penances were performed of which such fearful rumours were abroad. But the General defied all her skill; she knew no more at the end of six months the she had known at the end of two, although the same alternations of spirit and temper remained, and the same portion of each day was spent in the privacy of his own chamber. Into that chamber she never got access, it was only entered by the General, who himself kept the key, and by his valet once a day, and that only while his master remained in a dressing-room or an adjoining apartment. The chamber was as mysterious and as impenetrable as ever. Mrs. Ashenhurst had once, in a propitious moment, as she thought, spoken of his jewels; but he had only glanced upon her his sinister eye, laughed, and assured her that she and her daughter already possessed the most valuable of them: and once she had ventured to speak of the iron chest, but that once sufficed; she would not again have perilled her abode at Denborough Park had she believed the chest and its contents would have been given up to her for her pains. Mrs. Ashenhurst was ever after contented to remain in ignorance, looking back to the time when she had dared so greatly with astonishment at her fool-hardiness. What, however, was the precise mode in which her curiosity was rewarded, she never divulged; we have told as much as ever descended to posterity.

Week after week went on, and the hope that was long deferred made the heart weary; "It is strange, it is passing strange," thought Jane; and in proportion as Brian seemed voluntarily to have resigned her, did the consciousness of her uncle's prohibition lose its weight. She felt that it was unkind thus to give her up to her barren exaltation. What to her was this splendour of the present, or the promise of the future, deserted as she felt herself to be by the only being for whom it could be valued, or with whom it could be enjoyed? He could know nothing of her uncle's prejudices; why, then, was she less worthy of his love than formerly? How happy, how perfectly happy seemed the days of their abiding at Harbury! The unpretending drawing-room—the two quiet maid-servants —even the discarded India chintz gown, the first thing given up as unworthy of their new fortunes—all seemed in her eyes to belong to a preferable order of things. To those days belonged the friendly gossip of the kind-hearted Mrs. Burgoyne; the frequent call from

Brian Livingstone,—the walks taken with him through wood and meadow, and by water-side—dewy early morning-walks, fresh and full of the spirit of gladness, embleming so aptly hopeful and rejoicing youth,—or sunset strolls, when everything about them seemed visible poetry. There were the books they read together, the songs she sang for him, and learned to like for his sake; and over all was the perfect fellowship of mind and heart—the love understood though never formally acknowledged. And all this had been resigned for what?—for a splendour which already palled—for new friends to whom she could not give her heart—for some yet-to-be-found alliance, in which rank and fortune were alone made the requisites. And still more, Jane sorrowfully felt, though she was jealous of acknowledging it to herself, that the feelings and opinions of her mother had all undergone a change—she had sold herself for the possession of worldly greatness.

It was fortunate for Jane Ashenhurst that with deep sensibilities she possessed great strength of character; and when the melancholy fear that Brian Livingstone had voluntarily abandoned her, as time went on became conviction, she saw her duty before her,—to struggle with her own heart, and, with a woman's high principle and purity of sentiment, to eradicate these precious hopes, "which, it may be," argued the poor girl, somewhat against a lingering belief in his good faith, "he may have relinquished with all man's coldness and offended self-love." Jane was thankful that her duty was so plain and clear before her as to admit of no doubt, nor even to need asking counsel on; and the very idea showed her how forlorn she was—for of whom could she ask counsel and not be answered by worldly arguments or unreasonable prejudices?

Time still went on; and week after week passed as uneventfully even at Denborough Park as at Wilton Hall, in spite of a round of Christmas visits, suppers and balls, all stately and dull. But now the grand event approached—the long-talked-of banquet, which was to be celebrated on the 12th of March, the General's birthday, and was to astonish all the world by its magnificence and splendour.

Not a word had been heard of Brian Livingstone; he might have been dead, for any tidings of him that seemed to reach Denborough Park. But again on this long-lost topic. Jane was destined to be enlightened by her faithful abigail; who however, it must be understood, was about leaving Jane's service.

"Ay, dear me, ma'am! and such a preparation as there is! One would think the house was large enough without all this altering and building," said Betty, meaning to make this banquet of which everybody talked an introduction to another subject.

"General Dubois means to surprise everybody; it will be a most magnificent entertainment," was Jane's reply.

"And if I could get your leave," said Betty, "I don't think I should be here to see it."

"How is that?"

"Why, ma'am, if it would make no difference to you, and I could go at the end of next week instead of the week after, I should be much obliged; and as you are to have the niece of Mrs. Ashenhurst's woman, I should think—nay, ma'am, I'm sure she would come a week earlier; at least Carter says so?"

"But I cannot conceive," said Jane, "why you are in such a hurry to leave."

"Why, Miss Jane—but why I need I make a secret of it, and so good as you always are? —but I'm going to be married;" and poor Betty looked infinitely ashamed of the confession.

"Married!—indeed!"

"Why, ma'am, Thomas Thackaray has been left Mr. Livingstone's service ever since November; or rather, I didn't like he should go over-seas,—you know it's such a risk—there's such a casualty, ma'am."

"You are going to be married, Betty?" said Miss Ashenhurst, with as much calmness as she could command. "Why, did you say Thackaray had left his place?"

"Why, ma'am, I could not let him go abroad, though it was with Mr. Livingstone! The rectory is given up to a curate, ma'am, and Mr. Livingstone has been gone ever since the end of November; it was a thousand pities, such a sweet place as it is!"

This information was so unlooked for, that Jane could not conceal her surprise: she busied herself, however, with her jewel-box, believing that Betty would continue the subject; and, as she expected, the waiting-woman resumed:—

"Thomas has got a new service, to which he is to go just a month after—after we are married, Miss Jane, if so be you could set me at liberty."

"And you wish to spend the honeymoon together," said Jane, determined to exert herself: "but you will not like to part with your husband so soon."

"Oh, Miss Jane, no; we are to go to Harbury, to his friends and mine for the first month, and then we go into the same service—a place Mr. Livingstone got for us; I shall have washing to do, and get up the linen. We are to have a small house in the grounds, with a pretty garden, Miss Jane, and a honeysuckle porch. It will be a very good situation—at Sir Robert Combe's."

"I will oppose nothing to your plans and wishes," said Jane, sympathising in her exultation: "Thackaray has been a faithful lover, and I am sure you will make him a good wife."

Betty blushed, and declared Miss Ashenhurst was too good to say so. "But, deary me!" said she, emboldened by her lady's kindness, "if you could but have liked Mr. Livingstone!"

Jane looked at her in silence; and Betty, stammering and ashamed, feared she had offended.

"I cannot imagine," observed her mistress, "what cause you have for connecting my name with Mr. Livingstone's the way you do."

"Dear me!" replied Betty; Mr. Livingstone surely loved you as ever a gentleman loved a lady; everybody at Harbury knew it.

"They were a set of impertinent people there," was the lady's answer.

"Yes, ma'am, maybe they were; and I've no business to talk in this way. But only to think of Mr. Livingstone going into foreign parts, and to leave that fine place at Collington-Magna! And Thomas says he was sure something was on his mind—he seemed so cut-up. But, to be sure, if you did not fancy him—Only Thomas says—"

"I desire that neither Thackaray nor you will make me, as connected with Mr. Livingstone, the subject of your conversation," said Jane, coldly.

"Oh dear, Miss Jane! to think of my offending you! Only," continued the pertinacious Betty, piqued at the little value her lady set on the remarks of her husband elect,— "only, I should never like to see another Mrs. Livingstone, as is like enough, seeing the store Sir Robert's daughters set on him, and them all so handsome!"

"This is nothing less than impertinence," said Miss Ashenhurst, with unwonted dignity; "I cannot allow you to continue the subject, and I desire it never may be resumed."

Betty had far overshot her mark: she meant to serve Mr. Livingstone, but she had offended her lady, and, humbled to the very dust, she sat down in her own chamber crying bitterly and wishing her tongue had been cut out before she had said any single word to vex dear Miss Ashenhurst. "Oh dear; oh dear!" sobbed she, "I shall never forgive myself as long as ever I live!"

X

Poor Betty did, however, live to forgive herself: she did liv to wear a wedding-cap trimmed by the fair hands of her dear lady,—to eat a wedding-dinner, for which her lady paid the cost, and to receive from her ten golden guineas in a purse, over and above her wages, to help in the furnishing of that cottage with the honeysuckle porch, and the pretty garden which seemed the paradise of the poor bride's imagination. A proud and a happy woman was Mrs. Thackaray the younger, and she spread the fame and glory of her late mistress throughout and round about the town of Harbury; yet, in spite of her gratitude and of her lady's prohibition, she did wish many a time that "Miss Jane could but have fancied poor Mr. Livingstone."

And now came the time of the banquet. Great and anxious had been the general expectation for many weeks throughout the whole country as to *who* would be invited: it was given out that everybody with claim to rank, family, fortune, or gentility, was to be invited; therefore many were the conjectures, many the secret wishes and fears, that agitated many an individual bosom and many a little circle. "Would Mrs. so-and-so and her daughters be invited?"— "would Mr. such-a-one-and his wife be invited?" Many a restless, anxious night, full of dreams of perplexed disappointment was spent by those who dwelt, as it were, on the border-land between the privileged and non-privileged classes. Everybody felt that it would be really a less honour to be invited, than an eternal dishonour to be excluded. "I shall never bear to go again into company," was the internal murmur of many a spinster and widow-lady of small income but great pretension, "if I am not invited to Denborough Park for the 12th of March."

The time for the banquet was now at hand. The whole house underwent a change: one entire suite of apartments was fitted up for a banqueting-room; the saloon was re-arranged, and a ball-room and orchestra were fitted up in the most expensive and gorgeous style, as if the place had originally been designed for purposes of public entertainment. An immense temporary building was erected, extending from the conservatories into which the saloon opened several hundred yards into the gardens, and into these were introduced whole groves and gardens of oriental and tropical trees and flowers; rich carpets covered the floors, and hangings of inconceivable splendour clothed the walls; couches and sofas the most luxurious that could be devised were placed everywhere; and all was lighted with shaded or richly-coloured lamps, which in burning emitted a fragrant perfume.

An awning of silk extended from the portico to the entrance of the shrubbery, illuminated with innumerable coloured lamps, shining out like stars from among the shrubs and trees which the awning inclosed, giving to them a magical effect, as if they were wrought in topaz, ruby, and chrysolite; while here and there shone out, in Nature's own adorning, the tall and quivering branches of the almond-trees, clothed over with their pale pink blossoms, that looked even paler in that illuminated atmosphere. A carpet of rich green, soft as moss, and intended to represent it, covered the whole way, bordered on each hand with the real flowers of the season, snowdrops, crocuses, primroses, thickly set in a beautiful mosaic; it was the very entrance of an enchanted palace. Beyond this covered walk, at the commencement of which the company alighted, lamps were suspended in the trees through the whole windings of the carriage to the park-gates, producing a fine effect seen from any point, as if a chain of light undulated onward to the grand centre of attraction. The night was fine, but extremely dark, as if made on purpose to assist the general effect.

Of the immense number of delicacies furnished forth to the company it is useless to attempt speaking. Suffice it to say, that it was the most magnificent banquet that art or money could furnish; and that all the country round, who had any pretension to rank, wealth, family, or fashion, were invited, and were there, saving and except Sir Harbottle Grimstone.

But before we dismiss the banquet, we must say, that nothing could surpass the delightful suavity of the nabob, nor the ease, perfect grace, and graciousness of Mrs. Ashenhurst, whose regal dress of purple velvet and ermine, with a tiara of silver tissue spangled with diamonds and plumed with ostrich-feathers, excited universal admiration; and that there was no young lady present so distinguished as Jane Ashenhurst for beauty and every other desirable female quality. Her dress was of the palest pink, of the nabob's own choosing, and she wore the renowned Furnapore diamonds. These important subjects dismissed, let us hasten now to what may be called the event of the night—the event, at least, in which our story has most concern.

In the course of the assembling of the guests, Jane was startled by seeing at a distance a figure so strongly resembling Mt. Livingstone, that for the moment she turned aside to conceal the emotion of which she was conscious. The figure was the same; the same style of person—tall, rather slight, but remarkably well-knit, with a general air rather of high breeding than fashion: the turn of the head, the mode of standing, all resembled Brian Livingstone.

In a while the whole crowd had shifted; he was gone. At dinner she discovered him at a lower table; for the nabob's family and his more noble and dignified guests occupied the dais of the banqueting-room, while he went from table to table paying attention to all alike.

"Who is the gentleman in black, whose back is to us, and to whom my uncle is now speaking?" asked Jane of Lady Cornbury, who sat near her.

"I cannot tell," said her ladyship; "it is so far to look."

Jane repeated her inquiry, but without success; no one knew him.

"Bless me!" said Mrs. Ashenhurst; "he is very like a person I know."

"Can it indeed be Brian Livingstone?" thought she, without venturing to look at her mother; "and if so; why is he here?"

No sooner did the assembly break up, than Mrs. Ashenhurst, who felt no less agitation and anxiety than her daughter mingled among the guests to discover who the stranger was. Jane watched her movements with intense interest, and, to her amazement, saw her after a while formally introduced to him, and, what was more, actually advancing with him towards the place where she stood. The resemblance to Brian Livingstone was of manner and figure; for, strict speaking, the countenance was much handsomer, and the expression more grave and thoughtful. He was introduced, "Mr. Vigors—a relative and guest of our friend Sir Willoughby Doyne," added the lady with a most gracious smile, which intimated to her daughter that she was at liberty to cultivate his acquaintance.

The evening passed away delightfully. As Jane looked on her new friend, her heart warmed towards him;—he, too, was equally charmed with his companion. As the amusements of the evening commenced, they were of necessity parted; but they met and met again as if drawn together by mutual attraction. His conversation was wonderfully captivating, full of earnest and deep thought, which, at times, leaving the place and people among whom they were, revelled on the subjects of art, literature, foreign lands and manners, and the wonders and beauties of our own country; while his mind seemed a perfect creation of original thought and observation, or of that which perhaps strikes the listener equally, the power of presenting accepted opinions and observations in new forms and with new combinations: yet over all lay a shade of tender melancholy—a tone of voice, an expression of the eye, which irresistibly touched her heart, and assured her that he had experienced some deep sorrow which had tinged to sadness one of the most lofty and cheerful of spirits.

While she sang he stood near her, listening with that silent, profound attention, which is infinitely more grateful and flattering to a mind of taste and sensibility than the most extravagant and ecstatic praise. Jane meantime was sensible that she played but for one listener, and never since the days when she played Brian Livingstone's favourite airs at Harbury, had she so completely devoted herself to please—so completely enjoyed the fascinations of sweet sounds as now.

Mr. Vigors did not dance, and so he told her, or he should have requested the honour of her hand. Jane wondered; "It was so charming an exercise, so beautiful in its figures said she, blushing at her own enthusiasm, "I have looked on a set of beautiful dancers, with their inimitable grace and harmony of motion, till it has thrilled me like a fine passage of poetry. I wonder *you* do not dance!"

Mr. Vigors made no reply; but he looked on her, while she spoke, with that admiring, affectionate interest, which the most delicate soul might receive without offence.

"What a singularly interesting man! what a strangely fascinating influence he seems to have over me!" thought she, as, thrilled and yet warmed into a sentiment of affection, she turned from him, to mingle with the fluttering triflers who surrounded her, to be courted, flattered, and annoyed by the fulsome tribute of the men, or to hear the flippant folly of the ladies, which at last drove her to take refuge under the shadow of the monotonous Lady Cornbury's wing, where she had leisure and silence to think how much the one she had shunned gained in comparison with all she had since seen.

The company began to disperse, and Mr. Vigors was again at her side. He assured her it was a long since he had experienced pleasure such as that evening had afforded him, and hoped he might be permitted to renew the acquaintance thus happily formed for himself at an early opportunity. Jane blushed, and said she believed the General and Mrs. Ashenhurst would have much pleasure in his acquaintance.

Mr. Vigors heard the compliment without a smile, adding, in the most impressive tones of his singularly sweet but touching voice, that he hoped Miss Ashenhurst would permit him to introduce to *her*, at an early time, the being most dear to him.

It was now Jane's turn to hear without replying; she knew neither what he meant or what she ought to say. Mr. Vigors seemed not to expect an answer, but, glancing on her one of those peculiar looks of almost holy and affectionate interest, he took his departure.

"That's a fine young man!" said Lady Cornbury; and Jane, startled by such an unusal display of energy from her ladyship, was made aware of Mr. Vigors having left the rooms.

"What could he mean! Was he married?" The thought struck almost painfully upon her heart. She must be a happy woman who could inspire such a being with love; but to be the life-long—the life-loved companion of such a being, must truly be the perfection of human felicity! So thought Jane Ashenhurst—and let her not be misjudged for so thinking—while her jewelled dress was removed, and her long fair hair was smoothed down for the night's repose.

She awoke with the idea of Mr. Vigors's wife in her mind; she must be beautiful—she must be all that could make a woman the fit companion for the most intellectual, the most warm-hearted and high-minded of God's creatures!

XI

A few days afterwards, to escape the throng of callers, many of whom were admitted to pay their respects to Mrs. Ashenhurst and the

General, Jane walked out into a favourite pleached walk, screened from the wind, and which, even at this early season, exhibited signs of coming spring—budding trees, and a thickly-gemmed border of primroses and violets. Here she had walked but for a short time, when Mr. Vigors appeared, excusing himself for interrupting her privacy, by saying, that as that morning his visit was to her, he was most fortunate in finding her alone, and hoped she would not refuse him her company. Jane blushed deeply. Mr. Vigors led by the hand a little boy, whom the next moment he presented.

"This is the being of whom I spoke the other night—my little son. Will Miss Ashenhurst receive him kindly?"

The boy was the most beautiful Jane had ever seen. He was dressed in a complete suit of dark purple velvet, with a black velvet cap and feather; a bright-eyed, fair, but thoughtful child; his features finely chiselled, and more formed than those of children commonly are. He strikingly resembled his father; except that for the deep, dark eye of the father, the child's were of a full violet blue—eyes beaming with the most inexpressible tenderness and love. His hair which was of pale gold colour, much like Jane's own, fell full and curling over a collar of point-lace, which was fastened round his beautiful throat with a diamond button. For the first moment Jane experienced that sensation so happily described by Wordsworth—

'His beauty made her glad.'

The next, as the boy looked into her face with innocent wonder, and his trusting eyes kindled up in affectionate expression so like his father's, the truth flashed on her soul, and tears filled her own eyes as she stooped down and kissed his fair forehead—the child's mother was dead; Mr. Vigors was a widower!

"Thank you, Miss Ashenhurst," said Mr. Vigors, "for receiving my child with so much kindness. I was not deceived—I knew you were all goodness!"

"He is a dear child!" was Jane's involuntary reply.

"God bless you!" said he; and then after a moment's pause he went on, his voice becoming more irresistibly sweet and thrilling as he spoke:—"I never thought till last night of giving a second mother to my boy. I will be frank, Miss Ashenhurst, it is necessary to me, and, I believe, must be most agreeable to you. You have many lovers who seek you for your riches—some you must also have who seek you for your virtues and attractions. Fortune is no object with me—I have more already than I need, therefore I belong not to the first class, but I am proud to acknowledge myself of the latter. It is, however, for the sake of this child that I am most anxious to connect myself with you. Can you, dearest Miss Ashenhurst, accept such devotion as this? so warm, so sincere, pretending so little, yet implying so much?"

Jane took the child's hand in hers, but she made no reply.

The father received it, however, as a sign of acceptance, and, seizing the other, pressed it warmly to his lips.

"Nay, sir," said Jane, suddenly disengaging her hand, "I must speak. Oh! there is so much to tell you, and I know not how to say it!"

"Speak on, dearest Miss Ashenhurst," he said, as she paused in the deepest agitation.

"I have been so surprised into this acquaintance that I know not how to act, nor what to say. I am, I will not deny, warmly interested by you and for this child; but I am not, at liberty to act for myself," said she, with an emotion she could not conceal.

"Certainly not," was Mr. Vigors's reply. "Let me but know you interested for me and my boy, and what can oppose our happiness? If fortune is an object with your uncle, I have enough to satisfy even him;—if family and connexions with Mrs Ashenhurst, there too can be no exception."

"My uncle has prejudices," said Jane.

"How?—what can they be? General Dubois can have no prejudice against me—till within the last week he has never seen me; nor are my family or connexions impeachable in the slightest degree. I cannot, I will not think it possible: Dearest Miss Ashenhurst, you shall not tell me of prejudices, I will hear none from your lips,—for this one morning let me be happy. If sorrow and disappointment are to come, let them not be from you; but I cannot suspect that they can come!" So saying, he linked Jane's arm into his, holding her hand in his, and giving the other to the child.

The contagion of his hopeful spirit seized Jane, and she felt as if difficulties must vanish before the influence of such a being a this. "And I too," thought she, "will be happy for this one morning, come what will on the morrow!"

"No, no, Mr. Vigors," said Jane, at length, interrupting the eloquent outpouring of his new happiness; "you shall not talk thus to me! Talk to me of your child, of yourself, on any general subject. Heaven knows, but, in spite of myself, I tremble to hear you talk thus!"

"Run on, my boy, and look at those sweet flowers," said he to Herbert, disengaging the hand which Jane held.

"Gather me a handful of violets," said Jane as the little hand was drawn from hers.

The obedient and happy boy left them, each following him with admiring eyes as, with the grace of a young antelope, he bounded on before them.

The strangeness of this new friendship irresistibly struck her, and she remarked that that time yesterday they had not exchanged a word.

"It does not require a long time to make two consonant spirits acquainted," was his reply. "I loved you the moment I saw you; I, who for the last four years have had but one sentiment in my soul,—sorrow for the dead."

"It is a sacred subject," said Jane.

"I have never spoken her name since the day she died—I have never spoken of her to any but my boy,—it *is* a sacred subject! yet I feel no desecration in telling you of my Beatrice—how fair, how angelic she was, how like a dream of heaven were the short twelve months of our wedded life! Beatrice was in her twentieth year when she died,—I was three years older. Our love was the growth of our lives. How different from *ours*, dearest Jane! and yet in spirit the same,—the same confiding union of heart, less the growth of passion than of affection;—yet, I was unlike my present self,—full of confidence and joy, without a tinge of sorrow,—believing in, not hoping from, the future. She was a joyous, social being, filling all places with gladness; like me, she had never known sorrow. How happy was her father, how happy was the whole household in her presence! the very sound of her voice, very tread of her foot, brought joy with them. She passed in and out of the house like sunshine! Pardon me, dearest Jane," said he, as he passed his hand over his brow, "pardon this unlover-like subject; but, Heaven knows, I can give you no greater proof of my love, my devotion, than by unlocking my heart on this sacred subject! Beatrice would have loved you. The boy strongly resembles her;—the same eyes, the same oval of countenance, the same hair; but above all, the same trusting, innocent, and happy spirit, though he has grown too thoughtful under my tuition." Mr. Vigors ceased, and the lovers walked for some time in silence, the hearts of both filed with the tenderest emotion.

" My heart blesses you for this confidence," said Jane, at length, in an agitated voice; "but the subject is too painful for you."

"No," he replied, firmly; "I can speak to you of her,—I can tell you, how dear, how deservedly dear she was: the subject which has been locked up in my soul for four years, and which her father and I never dared to speak upon. I can unburden to you even after one day's acquaintance; and yet I have not lived in solitude. I have been through Europe,—in Paris, Vienna, Rome, and London,—seeking, not shunning society; yet, in the multitudes of women whom I have seen, the beautiful, the intellectual, the accomplished, I have never breathed one sentiment on this subject to one of them. They only made me feel how different they were to her: on the contrary, the same cheerful-spiritedness, the same high-toned feeling, the same integrity and simplicity of heart, which bound her to me, and will keep her memory precious to my dying day made you irresistibly attractive! I know the felicity which affectionate intercourse, daily and hourly communion of kindred and confiding spirits, can create! I know that the purity, the peace of such a life, can only be surpassed by existence in a happier state of being! Oh! but to see you as happy entirely and perfectly happy, as was my Beatrice; to be assured that my boy would never know how deep a loss he has otherwise sustained;—would leave me nothing to desire!

"But I am selfish—let me hear you speak, dearest Miss Ashenhurst; sorrows you can have had none—let me hear of your happy life. Nothing is more beautiful, more interesting to my contemplation that the uneventful happiness of a young innocent being!"

"Nay, Mr. Vigors," said Jane, "if I am to try to tell my story, whether, eventful or uneventful, I cannot do it. If we meet again in happiness, there will be sufficient time for that."

"Why, dearest girl, will you forebode evil? We shall meet again, and, please God, a life of happiness lies before us!"

"Look at that sweet child kissing the flowers," said Jane and disengaging herself from her lover, she ran to his side.

"Oh, why do you kiss the flowers" she asked.

"They are so sweet," said the boy: "will you have them?"

"If you will exchange them for a kiss," said Jane, taking the offered flowers, and kissing him on his red lips, and then on his fair forehead.

"But papa must have some—you must give papa some flowers, if you please," said he, rising on tiptoe to reach the violets, which Jane held playfully higher and higher.

"You are a brave boy," said she; "but you have given the flowers to me, and I shall give some to papa."

"Oh!" said the little fellow, perfectly satisfied.

"There are papa's flowers," said she, giving half of them into his father's hand.

Mr. Vigors returned his own affectionate look, and pressed the flowers to his lips.

"Oh, papa kisses the violets!" shouted the boy, with a burst of childish merriment.

At that moment the bell rang announcing the hour of dressing.

"I shall see General Dubois and your mother to-morrow," said Mr. Vigors.

"No, no, not to-morrow!" was Jane's earnest reply, "not to-morrow! Why are you so impatient of our friendship?"

"Why not to-morrow, my dear Miss Ashenhurst?"

"It is Friday," said she, smiling, "if I must invent a reason; and you cannot think of risking so much on a Friday."

"Risking!—no, no," said he; "we will be perfectly happy to-morrow!" and pressing her hand to his lips, and begging her to kiss his child, he parted from her.

Jane walked to the house with slow steps, amazed at the strange engagement into which she had, as it were involuntarily, entered—entered without sufficient reflection, in the very despair of its accomplishment.

"What new sorrow and trouble hang over my head!" thought she, as she took her seat at table. But the conversation was so unusually cheerful—her mother and uncle seemed so perfectly themselves—that she felt confident they had no idea of the interview she had had with Mr. Vigors.

"And who knows," thought she, in the course of the evening, as she recalled that fascinating voice, that noble person, and those engaging manners, and remembered moreover that he was wealthy and well connected, though she knew not how or to whom,—"who knows but my uncle may forego this prejudice, which is in itself so unreasonable, so unfeeling?" The perfections of her lover wrought powerfully on her own imagination, and Jane persuaded herself that all would be well.

"I wish I could see him this morning," was Jane's waking thought, as she opened her eyes from a strange perplexity of dream, in which Brian Livingstone and Mr. Vigors—now one and the same, and now two separate persons, with a fearfully distinct individuality—had haunted her through the night;—I wish I could see him, to prevent his speaking to my uncle to-day!—for surely I might come to love him, even as well as I once loved Brian. How strange that I should have dreamed thus! how strange too that at first he should have appeared so strongly to resemble Brian Livingstone! yet in reality how different they are! Mr. Vigors would never have demurred and doubted, and then at last have given me up, as Brian has done! And yet," continued she, mentally musing, while her maid was assisting in the operation of dressing, "what happier should I have been had Brian come forward? it would only have caused fresh misery!—Nay, nay," mused she, correcting herself, "it would have proved Brian the true-hearted, noble being I believed him: better any pang than to find those we love best unworthy!"—How bitter were these thoughts! Jane dismissed her maid, and finished her toilette alone, that she might indulge her own feelings. "Brian Livingstone unworthy!" how noble then seemed the frank-hearted but unhappy Mr. Vigors! "And yet," thought she, "what a fresh and cruel disappointment even now awaits both him and me!"

"Oh; I am unfortunate!" cried the poor girl, giving way to her emotion, "subjected as I am to unreasonable prejudice and senseless pride, and doomed as I am to wound that noble being! Far better had I been a free, though a poor maiden at Harbury! I might then, had circumstances so willed it, have been the happy wife of Mr. Vigors."

XII

In the course of the morning, Mrs. Ashenhurst entered her daughter's apartment, and sat down with a countenance full of important business.

"Why, my dear," said she, "this is a most unfortunate affair—to think of Mr. Vigors having been married before!"

Jane absolutely felt faint, but her mother went on.

"I cannot think what is to be done! it would be so good a match!"

"Is Mr. Vigors here?" asked Jane, with an effort that a choked her.

"Yes, love, unless he is just gone. He is a charming young man and with such good connexions!—own cousin to Lord Napier; and his wife was the daughter and heiress of Sir William Eland. But there's the misfortune! I cannot think why he should have married before!"

"Nay," said Jane, "why should any one make that objection?"

"Well, my love, you know it is your uncle's way. I have no doubt but he has some reason, and a good reason too, for objecting. It is unfortunate, I allow; but I suppose we must submit—I am sure it is our duty to do so."

"It is an abuse of the word to apply it thus. It is a duty my uncle owes to us, since he has made us dependent on him to overcome prejudices as unreasonable as this! Far better had he left us in our humble independence at Harbury,—we should then have been happy!"

"My love," said her mother, "you forgot that we sought out the General, and are infinitely obliged to him for receiving us in the manner he has; and I am amazed at your talking of him in this way. And as to Mr. Vigors, I have no doubt you will have quite as good offers! Bless me! Mr. Vigors is not the only man in the world! A young lady who is known to be the heiress of General Dubois will be sought after by the best men in the land!"

"Dearest mother," replied Jane, "it is not the mere circumstance of being splendidly married that would satisfy me: I cannot believe there are many such men as Mr. Vigors."

"I can remember," said Mrs. Ashenhurst, laughing, "when you said the same of Mr. Livingstone; and since you have seen two models of perfection, you may see twenty! I have no doubt, love, in twelve months you will find a suitor, as much to your taste as either of these, without his belonging to any of the interdicted classes."

"These are most unjustifiable, not to say wicked prejudices," observed Jane, earnestly; "and I am amazed, dear mother, that you do not attempt to overcome them in the mind of the General."

"Nay, love, make the attempt yourself. I do not pretend to have any right to influence him: I think it our duty to acquiesce. I certainly should have been glad, for poor Mr. Vigors' sake, that he had not been married before; but I have no right to influence your uncle's judgment: at least, that is my view of the case; if you think differently you can try. Only I beseech you, do nothing rash or violent—I know the General better than you do!"

Presently afterwards a servant requested them to walk to the saloon, where General Dubois wished to see them. They found him apparently in high good-humour, reclining as usual on his couch.

"Well, Miss Ashenhurst," said he, as Jane, pale and agitated, entered the room which her lover had just left, "you have run through the interdicted classes—a fox-hunter, a parson, and, a widower, and I hope next time you will start from clear ground! Be so obliging as not to give me the trouble of saying 'no,' the next time; for, upon my soul! this was a pretty young fellow, and I was half sorry for him myself."

Jane could not have replied for the world. Had Brian Livingstone then absolutely been rejected? This was a new subject of doubt and wonder, and for a few seconds she forgot the immediate cause of disappointment and anxiety.

"Come, come," said the General, "do not let us have such melancholy looks. You should imitate your mother, Miss Ashenhurst;—why, upon my life, you look more cast down than Mr. Vigors himself! By-the-bye, that young man has a fine spirit after all; I should very well like to see him at the head of a troop—a noble figure for a uniform! a fine spirit he has, on my soul!" and the General laughed in uncontrollable merriment.

"How long has Mr. Vigors been gone?" asked Mrs. Ashenhurst

"Not two minutes before you entered."

"Uncle," said Jane at length, and with great agitation, "may I know your decision with regard to Mr. Vigors"

"To be sure, my fair niece, you are welcome to know it—that you must look out for another husband."

"May I ask why?"

"Why?—indeed!" said the General, in a tone between anger and mirth. "Why? forsooth!—a pretty question, Miss Jane; do you know why your last lover was refused? Come, there's a Roland for an Oliver!"

"Mr. Vigors is a man of family and fortune," said Mrs. Ashenhurst in a deprecating tone.

"My niece is not going to be any man's second wife," was his reply.

"Dearest uncle, said Jane, "I would not willingly displease you, but—"

"*But!*" interrupted the General, starting up from his couch with a burst of rage that terrified Mrs. Ashenhust and silenced Jane; "who dares oppose a *but* to my will! By Heaven, it shall not be! Why must there be more opposition on your part now than on a former occasion?—how is this man better than the parson? I thought *he* was an old and valued friend—an old lover before you came here. *This* man you never saw till Wednesday, and yet you now come to me with your *buts!*"

"I never knew," said Jane, with desperate courage, "that the other *had* been rejected!"

"God bless my soul, Miss Ashenhurst," said he, stamping with passion, "what does your knowing or not signify to me!"

"Oh, sir, it signifies much to me!" replied the agitated girl. "It is enough for you that I say yes or no!" continued he in the impetuosity of rage; "I expect submission from you; or if it please you better, you can leave Denborough Park!"

Mrs. Ashenhurst burst into tears, protesting that any opposition to his will was the farthest from her thoughts, and that she was confident all he said was right. Jane sat with her hands clasped together, unable to speak or weep.

"Miss Athenhurst," said the General at length, in a milder tone, after he had taken several turns across the room, "let me have no more nonsense of this kind! Your duty is plain before you—to submit."

"To be sure, my dear General, it is her bounden duty; and I will answer for her, that it will be her pleasure also."

Without vouchsafing any reply, the General left the apartment.

"My dear love, how can you be so headstrong! Only to think of your displeasing your uncle in this way, so good as he has always been to you! You make me miserable" said she, bursting again into tears.

"Mother," said Jane, calmly, "has Mr. Livingstone actually been refused?"

"Oh dear yes, love, and I am sure it was done as nicely as could be; there was no rage about it, nor any trouble. I wish to goodness this Mr. Vigors had never come!"

"Why did I not know of Mr. Livingstone's proposals?" asked Jane.

"My dear, how can you talk so! You were at Wilton at the time—when you were there in the autumn. I am sure you ought to be very much obliged to me for sparing you all the vexation and disagreeable of it; you know you could no more have had him than poor Mr. Vigors. I am sure I have always been so anxious to spare you any distress."

"Dearest mother," said Jane, "it might be well meant but it was mistaken kindness; I should not have suffered more from resigning him to your will than I have done in the belief that he had deserted me."

"Really, Jane, you are so strange!" said her mother; "but I wish you would let the subject drop—there can be no good in talking of it now."

"No, dear mother," replied Jane, with a countenance pale, but a manner perfectly calm, "I cannot let it drop thus—I must know more! How did *he* bear it?"

"Oh, exceedingly well! I am sure, love, I never thought so highly of Mr. Livingstone before. He saw perfectly well how the case stood, and that it was no use making any fuss about it; nothing could have been more reasonable than he was, and I wish, love, you would only take example by him."

"Mother," said Jane, with a solemnity that, startled her; "dearest mother, do not mislead me! Do him not the injustice to say so. Brian Livingstone, since he has come forward, could not have resigned me with indifference."

"Well, love, since you appear to know so much better than me, why do you ask me? But," added she, softening the tone of displeasure with which she had spoken, "I tell you he is a man of sense; and knows the insuperable barrier which your altered fortune throws between you. His addresses, I believe, were merely a point of honour; he had no idea, he could have none, that they would, be received!"

"Do not trifle with me," cried Jane, clasping her hands in an agony. "You know not how important it is to my peace, to my mode of action with regard to Mr. Vigors, that I should not be deceived! Heaven forgive me for thinking you would deceive me!—but these never could be Brian Livingstone's feelings. Tell me dearest mother,—I conjure you, whatever took place, nothing will wound me like uncertainty,—I dread my own surmises!"

"Dear love, you really frighten me! What can you mean?—how can it matter to you now? And besides, I have nothing to tell you; I am sure Mr. Livingstone gave me credit for speaking the truth, and it is hard that you cannot do so too!"

"Forgive me, dearest mother; but you do not know my feelings. I owe justice to Mr. Livingstone, I have wronged him so long! You know that he has left England?"

"Well, love, and what then! Many a man goes abroad; and what more likely than that he should take his pleasure, now he can afford it?"

"Pleasure!" repeated Jane, in a tone of unwonted bitterness; "pleasure!—oh, no!—I know him too well to believe he is gone for pleasure."

"Well, love," again said her mother, petulantly, "if you know so well, why do you ask me?"

The poor girl covered her face with both her hands, and, without shedding a tear, bowed her head to her knees in mental agony. Mrs. Ashenhurst, thinking the while how beautiful she looked in that attitude, felt as much tenderness towards her as was in her nature.

"Come, dear love," said she, "do not give way to such distress; I am sure you have no cause but for happiness; and think what good fortune lies all round you, and everybody loving you as they do."

Jane lifted up her marble-like countenance, and repeated her mother's word "happiness." "Happiness!" continued she, in a tone of heart-felt anguish; "to have driven Brian Livingstone from his native country in the belief that I refused him even my friendship! Happiness! to inflict misery on another noble being, who has already only known too much sorrow. No, no, this is not happiness!"

Poor Mrs. Ashenhurst was at her wit's end. "The more I say," thought she, "the worse I make matters,—I will e'en say nothing; there is no fear but this grief will work its own cure. I cannot think who Jane takes after; neither poor dear Captain Ashenhurst nor myself ever made such troubles of nothing. Well, the worst I wish poor Mr. Vigors is, that he had never come near the place." So mused and murmured she, as she wandered about from room to room, declaring to herself that it was the most miserable day she had ever spent at Denborough Park.

XIII

In the course of the morning Jane received a note from Mr. Vigors requesting an interview. Mrs. Ashenhutst warmly remonstrated against such a thing, but Jane was firm in granting it.

"Well, love, if you are determined to turn us out of this place, I cannot help it—remember it is your own doing."

"My dear mother, we had better leave this place than be thus subjected; we degrade ourselves by submitting thus."

"What! and go back to Harbury? What would everybody say?— what would the Parkinsons say? You terrify me, Jane! How can you fly thus in the face of your duty?"

"If I thought my duty forbade it, I would not do it. But, dear mother, this one interview I owe to Mr. Vigors even more truly than obedience to my uncle."

"I cannot think how it is, Jane," replied her mother, "that you see things so differently to everybody else. However, if you are determined to offend your uncle, you must understand I will have nothing to do with it. I will go to Wilton, or somewhere; and remember, Jane, I insist upon it that you give this Mr. Vigors no encouragement."

"How can I," said Jane, mournfully, "feeling as I do what I owe to Mr. Livingstone?"

Mrs. Ashenhurst did not understand her daughter; but she thought it was no use asking for her meaning—it was enough that this interview was to be final with Mr. Vigors. "Now be sure you do not keep him long, and do not let your uncle see him," were, therefore, her parting injunctions.

Accordingly, in half-an-hour's time the carriage bore away the trouble-laden Mrs. Ashenhurst, and Jane was left alone to the performance of the most painful duty.

The calm that succeeded the departure of her mother was of the greatest possible benefit to her. She nerved herself for what she had to do, the sacrificing this new love, less in obedience to the exactions of those about her, than in justice to her outraged affection for her early and ill-used lover. "It is," she inwardly exclaimed, "a difficult, a most painful duty, to inflict sorrow, to withdraw hope, and this to one of the most generous, the most noble beings the earth holds. Alas! it may be to subject myself to misconstruction. But no, I wrong him; his pure, generous nature will understand, will accept my motives! I will unshrinkingly do what I believe right; and may Heaven strengthen me!" ejaculated she, as she awaited her lover's approach in her own apartments, where she was in no danger of interruption.

Mr. Vigors came; he looked extremely pale, yet his manner was perfectly calm, and even as he began his voice was cheerful.

"You were right, dear Jane," said he; "Friday was an unlucky day— I had to encounter unlooked-for prejudices; but all this enhances your goodness—I owe you eternal thanks for this interview."

"My uncle's determination," said Jane, "as you may suppose, has not astonished me, and yet it has given me infinite pain."

"The General has yet to learn—a hard lesson, truly," replied Mr. Vigors—"sympathy with human sorrow; but your sentiments cannot be affected by it."

"I will not deny that my heart is warmly interested for you; but circumstances are too strong for me. Indeed, Mr. Vigors, I have had to endure much."

"Dearest Jane," returned he, tenderly, "why need you submit to these prejudices? Heaven knows, I would not counsel disobedience to your natural guardian, but—"

"Oh! do not talk thus, Mr. Vigors; it cannot, cannot be!"

"If fortune, if connexions—incidental things which weigh as nothing with me," continued he, "influence Mrs. Ashenhurst, as I believe they do, I can offer these. I can offer you a home, less splendid it is true than this, but still a noble home. Would to Heaven I could see you there, dearest girl! What a world of happiness we should make even this!" said he, with the most winning voice, and pressing her hand to his lips.

"No, no!" said Jane, disengaging her hand; "it is a sin in me to listen thus."

"Dearest Miss Ashenhurst, you owe no obedience to your uncle's prejudices. Assert your natural independence; if your uncle be a reasonable man, he cannot esteem you for such weak submission. Pardon the term,—but if he be unreasonable, why must you suffer? Confide yourself to me, dearest of women. I am not one to kneel, and vow, and utter protestations;—in the sincerity of the warmest affection, I can but offer you a heart that has bled, but which is yet capable of the most ardent, the most enduring love. Shake yourself free of these prejudices, in which you are too noble to partake, and be mine. Oh! to see you as happy, to make you as happy, as one who was young and beautiful, and good, like yourself! Pardon me, dearest Jane; but I cannot be with you, and not be of the past. I forget that you cannot know the compliment it implies."

"I can, I can!" said Jane, suppressing an emotion which seemed almost like death,—"I can; but I have a terrible duty before me!" and clasping her hands in an attitude of unspeakable sorrow; "My soul bleeds," she said, "to assure you that I cannot return your affection."

Mr. Vigors started; and Jane, compelling herself to be calm, went on, "Let me consider you as a brother,—let me open my soul to you"

"Say on," said he, in utter amazement, and distressed by her pale, agitated countenance,—"Say on, you may command me to listen even to my own death-warrant."

"It is an extraordinary confession I am about to make," she resumed, "and especially considering the short time of our acquaintance; but I believe you can understand my motives and feelings, and I believe also that I may confide to you circumstances which must be told to explain my conduct." Jane paused scarcely knowing how to proceed, and her lover sat in breathless suspense.

"But to be brief," she continued, "I never knew till this morning that an old and beloved friend had been rejected by my uncle, only lately, on the sole plea of one of those prejudices of which I am doomed to be the victim."

"A clergyman," said Mr. Vigors; "it was mentioned."

"A man," said Jane, "who would have honoured your virtues and won your esteem. I believed, till this morning, that he had resigned me quietly to my new connections. I cannot tell you how such a belief wounded me; but I was unjust to him. It would be additional injustice were I to enter into new engagements, especially in opposition to my friends, in opposition to those very prejudices for which he was rejected. I know him too well not to believe he has endured much, particularly believing me accessory, as I think he may. It is true he has gone abroad; it may be true also that he is now reconciled, and in all probability we shall never meet again. But I despair of making my full meaning intelligible;—I despair of giving the full weight to arguments which are conclusive to my own feelings and sense of honour;" said she, the consciousness of the confession she had made changing the marble-like earnestness of her countenance to a deep blush.

A silence of some minutes succeeded. Mr. Vigors, during the latter part of this confession, had leaned his brow on his hand, and he still remained so, as in a state of the deepest abstraction. Jane watched him with the most intense anxiety, dreading lest she had committed herself unwisely, or out-stepped female delicacy. She saw his fine countepance agitated and full of the most eloquent sorrow; and, as she looked on him, she was filled with admiration and deep sympathy. It was a dangerous moment;—Brian Livingstone and Mr. Vigors alternated with the exactest balance—a word could turn the scale, and that word was spoken.

"You are a noble creature—you have done perfectly right—you have acted honourably; I must confess it, though I lose you by the confession;" said he, looking at her with the utmost tenderness.

The reaction was irresistible—the next moment her face was buried in her hands, her head bowed to the silken cushions of the sofa, she was relieving her overwrought feelings by tears. Mr. Vigors the while bent over her with such tender and affectionate admiration and pity as her guardian angel might have felt.

"Pardon me," at length she said, raising her brow from the cushions on which it had lain; "I ought not to give way to this weakness; but your goodness—your nobility overcame me: can you forgive me?"

"I shall bless you to my dying day!" was Mr. Vigors's emphatic reply, and taking her hand and pressing it tenderly to his lips, he seemed about to depart. Jane took a cornelian heart, suspended by a small gold chain from her neck. "Give this," she said, "to your little Herbert, and do not let him forget me: I will treasure his violets," added she, with a tremulous voice, "among my most precious things!"

Without speaking a word, he pressed the trinket to his lips, and giving her a momentary glance, in which she read the fulness of soul-rending agony, he left the room. The time of weakness now came. The sacrifice had been made, but the strength which had nerved her for the sacrifice was gone. In the moment of natural reaction, she seemed wantonly to have thrown away this noble being for a point of honour. "Could Brian, indeed," thought she, "have been cold and indifferent—willing to give me up without a pang? and do I for this lingering attachment—for a romantic sense of justice perhaps, strip myself thus, and cast that generous and noble creature back upon the solitude of his own sorrow!"

These doubtings and almost self-accusations were the consequent result of her excited feelings; she again wept those passionate tears which women alone weep, and which are given in mercy as an outlet for their emotion.

XIV

When Mrs. Ashenhurst returned from her friends, she found Jane laid upon her couch, her head throbbing violently, her eyes oppressed by the light, and a burning fever consuming her whole frame. Bitterly did Mrs. Ashenhurst blame herself for leaving her daughter, and many and loud were her lamentations over her. The physician was sent for, and pronounced her seriously ill; and then the poor mother's distress was beyond bounds. The next morning she was declared to be worse; nurses were sent for, and Mrs. Ashenhurst, unable to rest in any one place, stole from room to room in her noiseless Indian slippers, wringing her hands and weeping, and wearying the physician with ceaseless inquiries after his patient.

General Dubois at first appeared haughty and indifferent; but as the day advanced, and the physician still sat, hour after hour, in the apartment adjoining her chamber, and the shrill agonised voice of the poor girl, new highly delirious, was heard occasionally to ring through the silence of the house, even he was detected inquiring three times in the course of the evening how she was going on.

Another Physician was called in on the third day, and the rumour of her illness spread through all the neighbourhood. Nothing could exceed the interest that was excited; she, so young and beautiful, who had borne her honours so meekly, had charmed every heart into love and every eye into admiration,—who had, too, but so lately been the admired of hundred of eyes,—now lay insensible in the very grasp of death; and so numerous and incessant were the inquiries after her, that the porter was ordered to answer them, receiving every hour the physician's report of her state. Mrs.

Ashenhurst felt and loved the flattery of all these attentions even in the midst of her distress.

At length the physicians pronounced that all would be decided by the turn of a few hours. No one of the whole household went to bed that night; the General himself sat in his chamber, wrapped in his Indian dressing-gown, his untasted hookah beside him, to watch over the critical period, and even as the hour approached was seen to steal to the anteroom of her apartment without venturing an inquiry. Mrs. Ashenhurst sat in her chair at the bedside subdued by anxiety into perfect quiescence, studying the countenance of those about her, but feeling as if even certainty of death could not make her more perfectly wretched than she was. Throughout that long, anxious night, too, walked another watcher, wrapped in his cloak, to and fro, within sight of her windows. This, it is needless to say, was Mr. Vigors,—the truest-hearted, the most intensely anxious of all her friends. The trinket she had given for his boy rested on his heart, and many a time in the course of the night was pressed to his lips. No astronomer ever watched the transit of a planet with more anxiety than he watched the feeble line of light that marked the almost-closed shutters of her chamber-windows, and the stronger continuous light that burned in the adjoining room where the physician remained to watch over the crisis.

He saw the steady light burning; but as the hour approached, shadows passed the curtained windows in the direction of the chamber: the physicians were on the watch. Oh, the awful passing on of those moments The memory of another sick chamber—the chamber of death, came over him; he saw, as if brought together before him, the being who then died, and the one who might now be dying. His heart bowed before the mighty grief which seemed beyond human strength to bear, and among the trees of the garden he offered up the most earnest of prayers.

The hour was passed—another succeeded, and the physicians pronounced the patient to be in that state when, though danger remained, they could yet give hope. The joyful tidings communicated throughout the house. The General smoked his hookah, and ordered his valet to prepare his bed; Mrs. Ashenhurst gave to each of the physicians a purse of gold for their tidings, and said she would now go to rest. Lights passed from room to room, and Mr. Vigors, believing the omen happy, presented himself at the door of the servants' hall, frightening several of them into the belief that they had seen a ghost, before he could get the blessed intelligence that Miss Ashenhurst was certainly better.

The next day Jane woke to a dreamy consciousness of some fearful catastrophe, feeble in body and feeble in mind, Oh, the dreadfulness of such waking! Where was she?—what had happened? were the strange questionings of her mind, without the power to give the questions words. Throughout the day she alternately slept that profound sleep which, though in its effects so sanative, is so painful to wake from; and though in that state of gathering consciousness, often more full of suffering than bodily pain, the struggling as it were of disjointed knowledge and mental feebleness.

Day after day went on and the youth and natural strength of the patient overcame disease. Jane sat up in her bed, or reclined on her couch, and received her uncle, or her more intimate acquaintance, Lady Cornbury, and a few others, to a daily levee. The memory of all the past was now fully restored; Brian Livingstone's addresses, and the strange events of that parting with Mr. Vigors. A chastened sorrow lay on her spirit when she thought of him, but the approving consciousness of having done right cheered and consoled her nevertheless. She longed to know, yet dared not ask where he was, what had happened to him, or whether any one had seen him. Many a tune was the question on her lips but she was spared the pain of asking it by a conversation which passed in her room.

"Only to think of Mr. Vigors making so short a visit!" remarked one lady.

"What! is he gone?" exclaimed another. "What a fine melancholy creature he was!"

"The most beautiful eyes—the most interesting man; I protest I could have cried when he was gone," said a young lady.

"And, oh?" asked another, "did you see his little boy?—such a love!"

"I cannot think why he went so soon,—thought he was come here for the winter," wondered the second lady.

"Lady Doyne told me," replied a third who had not yet spoken, "that she was sure his spirits were worse than than when he came down; she thought he was some way reminded of poor Mrs. Vigors; and she said, though they were all so sorry to part with him—for he really is the most delightful companion, and makes himself so amiable in a house—and that sweet child too, they were all so fond of him!—yet she was glad for him to go where he could see more general society—to Bath or London. It is a pity he lets his wife's death distress him so much; and she, you know, has been dead four years."

"But she certainly was a most beautiful creature!" said the first lady; "I saw her somewhere soon after they were married,—I think it was at Clifton. We were there with poor Mr. Wilbank, and they came with her father, Sir William Eland; they all lived together—and what a beautiful pair they were!—and he, such a benign, cheerful old man, so proud of his daughter and son-in-law. I am sure everybody admired them, and nobody was thought anything of but Mrs. Vigors; and yet she was the simplest-dressed woman there—and they used to run up and down the cliffs, she and her husband, just like two school-children."

"Oh, you are certainly tired, dear Miss Ashenhurst," said one of the ladies, turning from the talking group to Jane's chair; "you look quite overdone"

"Bless me! and we have been talking at this rate; and never thinking of you, Miss Ashenhurst!"

"Let me ring for your maid," "Let me divide you a orange," "Do smell at this vinaigrette?" overwhelmed her on all sides; and to be rid of her persecutors, and to indulge her own feelings, Jane allowed that she was tired and wished for repose.

All this time we have said nothing of Sir Harbottle Grimstone. The fact is, there was nothing to say. He returned to his home, after the last time he figured in these pages, in one of those brutal passions which vented itself in oaths and outrage upon every being round him, and finally worked itself off in a drunken carouse. The consequence of his rejected suit was, as may be imagined, only greater hatred for the nabob whenever he went among his jovial fox-hunting companions, the nabob was the subject of his unmitigated abuse and of his vulgar ridicule; yet since that time they had never met, at least never come in contact. Sir Harbottle, though a swaggering boaster, a most insolent asserter of his own superiority among his own set, had had already too much experience of the nabob's sarcasm, and dreaded too sincerely the world's opinion, which he knew always went against him in his enemy's presence, not to studiously avoid meeting him. Another cause of the greater infrequency of their meeting was, that since the ladies had become inmates of his house, the General's circle of intimates was much narrowed. Neither Mrs. Ashenhurst nor her daughter went into mixed society—they belonged to the *élite* of the county, and almost unconsciously to himself he adopted their customs: yet was not his dislike nor his ridicule of Sir Harbottle one whit abated. It was a standing joke with the visiters at Denborough Park that Sir Harbottle Grimstone always came on with the dessert, and, to the infinite annoyance of the ladies, the story of the nabob's triumph was invariably told.

Thus much said, let us return to the more interesting persons of our story.

XV

No sooner was the anxiety of Mrs Ashenhnrst set at rest with respect to her daughter's life than she was seized by a new cause of solicitude—fears for her beauty. That Jane should be restored to her less beautiful, less generally attractive than formerly, was an idea that filled her with the most exquisite concern; and every day she studied the poor girl's countenance to discover whether, in place of her former bloom, she acquired any new graces of a more delicate character.

The General too had similar feelings, though with him they never amounted to anxieties; he merely felt that she could not be equally interesting to him were she less beautiful. But they might have spared their anxieties and conjectures; Jane's chiefest beauty was of feature and expression, not dependent on the bloom of unabated health; and as the weeks progressed and her former strength was restored, if she had lost somewhat of the hilarity that characterised the Hebe-like countenance that beamed and brightened first on the General, she had gained what was infinitely more touching— an expression of deeper thought and sentiment. In truth, Jane Ashenhurst had never been so entirely beautiful as now, because *mind* had never been equally developed before.

Both mother and uncle were beginning to be satisfied on this subject when it was confirmed by a gratuitous remark of Lady Cornbury's, "that Miss Asbenhurst was really lovelier than ever!" Nothing more was needed. If the impassive soul of her ladyship was aware of the fact, and could even be excited into an exclamation of surprise by it, there need be no fear of its now making its full impression on eyes ever open to detect female beauty. This important subject therefore being so satisfactorily settled, the General informed his kinswomen that their attendance would be required by him in his customary visit to London, whence he should return during the summer.

To Mrs. Ashenhurst this was the glorification of life; especially as her friends the Cornburys were there at present;—a most unusual event, and only brought about by certain overtures to reconciliation with the contumacious nephew, who, as we have intimated before, notwithstanding the ten 'years' breach, had occupied the place of a spoiled and undutiful child in the hearts of his noble relations.

Mrs. Ashenherst rejoiced as much in this reunion as Lady Cornbury herself. She had certain ambitious projects respecting this unknown personage; and a more favourable opportunity to act upon them, she thought, could not occur than the present; for

though she was by no means unaware of her daughter's decision and
firmness of character, she so sincerely believed that even *she* could
not resist the united influences of rank and fashion, especially when
she was assailed, at the same time, by the idolatry which would be
paid in the capital to the beautiful heiress of General Dubois, that
she made sure of old attachments, which might have withstood
assaults in the country, giving way before these flattering influences,
and, in the sanguine spirit which always governed her, she already
looked upon her daughter as not only the future possessor of
Denborough Park, with all its manors and its untold wealth, but also
of Wilton, with its old title.

To Jane herself the thoughts of the journey brought pleasure. It
was an infinite relief to her to leave, for the present, scenes which
had become connected with such painful passages in her life.
Attractive as Denborough Park in itself was, her soul turned from
it; for in vain she attempted to recall any pleasure which it had
yielded or obtained equal to the quiet, unpretending home which
had been left for it. Painful doubts and uncertainties had met her, as
it were, at the very threshold; she had been made the tool of selfish
cunning, the victim of senseless prejudices, the innocent means of
the most exquisite and unmerited pain to two noble natures. What
associations of tenderness or of comfort bound her to this place?
None! On the contrary, mortification, suffering, and humiliation,
were alone impressed on her memory; and any change, she felt,
must be for the better.

We will leave all the preparation for the journey and set out
with our travellers; the General and his kinswomen in the most
commodious and elegant coach which those days could furnish,
drawn by four horses; and another following, containing their
servants, and such necessaries for the journey as the luxurious habits
of the nabob required, and which he knew even the extraordinary
accommodations of the best inns could not furnish. It was the
first week in May; a full month later than the General commonly
went to London, his present journey having been delayed in
consequence of Jane's illness; and now also, contrary, to his usual

custom, the journey was made much slower, time being allowed to
see everything interesting or beautiful by the way. Relays of horses
were provided all along the road, but they stood harnessed in their
stalls often many hours after the appointed time.

"What contrasts presented themselves to the mind of Jane as
they approached Harbury! which, to the unspeakable delight of her
mother, lay in their direct route, and was by no means to be avoided.
She knew every turn of the road, every coppice, every brook, every
tree;—nay, every breach in an old fence, every picturesque bit of
old lichen-covered paling, was familiar to her. There winded the
dingle, so renowned for its orchises, and which even now, she knew,
was gemmed over, among its mossy hazel roots, with thousands of
primroses: there was the croft already yellow over with cowslips, and
a little way onward the one which was even more beautiful with its
wild daffodils. There peeped the very hill, crowned with its young
plantations, bright in the tender green foliage of spring, where, at
that time, the ground was blue with myriads of nodding blue-bells.
She seemed to hear the thrush sing, the stock-dove coo, and the
multitude of small singing-birds fill with "their sweet jargoning," as
she had heard so many a time in many a former spring. But, above
all, there it was that the last evening walk was taken with Brian
Livingstone; and, who knew but the place had become sacred to him
from that very cause? Nay how knew she but he had there pondered
in bitternes of heart on her supposed fickleness, her worldliness, her
neglect? Her spirit died within her at the very thought. Everything
about her looked the same as formerly; it might have been twelve
months back, for any eternal change in nature; but what a change
was there in her own feelings and in her own experience! Twelve
months back, perhaps this very day, she might be wandering with her
beloved friend by some brook-side, watching the first peeping of the
water plants, or the manœuvring of some shy, timid denizen of the
stream, with no deeper care than it—unapprehensive of sorrow or
disappointment, and alive to every passing influence of pleasure even
when presenting itself in no more uncommon guise than a burst of
sunshine or a sweet sentiment of poetry.

While these thoughts, little calculated to exalt her present condition, were passing through her mind, feelings of a very different character were passing through that of her mother. Her sentiment was something like this: "Here am I, people of Harbury, my former neighbours and acquaintance, and you, the Parkinsons, especially; now drawing near your town in the full blaze of my glory! Come out and amaze your eyes by the spectacle! No delusion of greatness—here I sit in the midst of my real splendour!"

Cæsar entering the Capitol with the subject world at his feet felt less personal pride than did Mrs. Ashenhurst as the postillions whirled round the corner of the street, and drew up at the Queen's Head in the admiring eyes of all the town of Harbury; Mrs. Ashenhurst being all the time conscious that the full sense of her greatness was more conveyed by the carriage that followed than even by themselves. What could her good looks, smiling countenance and rich dress, the elegant simplicity and refined beauty of her daughter, the sumptuous nonchalance of the General, tell them, the good easy people of Harbury, of all the wealth and glory with which she had become endowed and glorified, in comparison with what the travelling equipage of their very servants implied? Her senses were all alive; she heard the drawing up of the satellite-carriage, and felt to herself, "Now you see!"

It had been noised abroad in Harbury that Mrs. and Miss Ashenhurst would pass through in the course of the day, therefore everybody was on the watch; and many more were the townspeople who collected in the street and in the houses about the Queen's Head to get a sight of them; and no sooner had the carriage made a halt than the bells pealed forth a joyous welcome. The smiling faces of the jolly landlord and landlady greeted them with a happy return, and the hope that they would alight.

"No, they were proceeding immediately." Mrs. Ashenhurst felt that this was much more *comme il faut* for her grandeur. Here she sat as on her throne to be worshipped. The parish clerk came with his bow hoping they would "please to remember the ringers:" Mrs. Ashenhurst gave him money far beyond his hopes. The whole place seemed astir. The grocer, his apprentices and customers, were all at his door; the draper at his; the shoemaker and his sons in their leather aprons joined themselves to a miscellaneous knot of people; the cooper and his fat wife, and many a neighbour stood in another admiring group—all with the familiar faces and figures of old townsfolk. Many were those who, at a respectful distance, examined the first carriage, more were they who crowded about the second, wondering, admiring, and declaring they must be grand, they must be happy indeed, who could afford to have such fine servants and provide thus for their accommodation. A crowd of heads was at Miss Farnel's window; and the next moment, the tall meagre lady herself, in the well-known, best visiting carmelite-brown Paduasoy gown, and carefully-kept India scarf, was at the coach-door.

"My dear Mrs. Ashenhurst, I am so delighted to see you!" she began, in her thin, wiry voice. "How well you look! And Miss Jane, I protest I never saw her so blooming in thy life.—Thank you, ma'am, I am better than I have been. I thought of leaving my house, but I shall not now. Oh! what an altered place this is! Everybody one cares for gone; only think of poor Mrs. Burgoyne and all! Well, you'll make a happy day in Harbury!—The Willoughbys—Oh yes,—thank you, they are tolerably; they would have liked to have seen you, but thought they were not intimate enough; and, do you know, the Parkinsons are over the way!—'Don't tell her for the world!' said Mrs. Parkinson; 'but one likes to get a peep as well as one's neighbours;' and, I assure you, there has not been a party worth going to since you left," &c. &c. So talked the overjoyed and much privileged Miss Farnel, glancing between every sentence at the General, and looking alternately from mother to daughter. The officious landlord, with a bow, informed them that "all was now ready."

"Well, God bless you, Miss Farnel!" said the gracious Mrs Ashenhurst, giving her hand.

"And will you, dear Miss Farnel," said Jane, "divide this small sum among my old friends in the almshouses?"

"With the greatest pleasure in the world," returned Miss Farnel, taking the two guineas Jane presented: "and I am so happy to have seen you! That's a mighty becoming hat of yours, Miss Jane. Good-bye,—and a good journey to you! Your Servant, General Dubois." And Miss Farnel, with a deep curtsy, withdrew a few paces backward.

The carriage-door was closed, the postillions in motion, and the housed or window-blind-hidden people came forth or looked out; and amid the ringing of the bells, and the applause of the handsomely-paid and bonused people of the Queen's Head, the first carriage rattled off and the second followed it.

Jane looked down the street where Mrs. Burgoyne had lived, and saw the board nailed to one of its large trees which announced that the house was to be let. Presently afterwards they passed their old home; a thrill passed through her heart, and tears involuntarily came to her eyes. How small it looked—how familiar, and yet, at the same time, how unlike anything that now belonged to them. A servant-maid was drawing along the gravel walk a spotted wooden horse to amuse two fat children; and a stout middle-aged person, with but slight pretensions to gentlemanship, delayed the shutting of the gate to watch the carriages. Two minutes afterwards, they suddenly stopped; and, hurried and out of breath, Mrs. Thackaray the elder presented herself with a nosegay of spring flowers in her hand,

"I beg your pardon, ladies," she said, " but my master seed you come in, and I just ran down to Mrs. Burgoyne's garden—we've the care of the place till it's let—to get you two or three flowers; they are better nor our own; and Miss Jane used to be so partial to a posy."

"Thank you, thank you," said Jane, taking the nosegay.

"Give her this piece of money," said Mrs. Ashenhurst, as the carriage drove on.

"No," said Jane; "the flowers were given from good will, not for reward" and she nodded an adieu to the poor woman.

"Well, Heaven bless her, and send her a good husband," thought Mrs. Thackaray, just as the second carriage drove past and left them thinking; "and there's one sits there as has a good place, of it, if she had only half as much reason to thank her as my son's wife had."

Nothing farther worth narrating occurred on the journey. Jane, invigorated in body, and with spirits sensibly refreshed and lightened by a journey so pleasantly taken, and at so congenial a season, entered the lordly mansion in Grosvenor-square with as much of her former buoyancy of heart as could exist with her late experience.

XVI

The very next day the Cornburys' coroneted coach stood at the door. Mrs. Ashenhurst received her noble friend with open arms; and her ladyship, coming to tell news, had it literally extracted from her—so great was her incapacity for talking, and so much easier was it to answer the comprehensive questions which Mrs. Ashenhurst from experience knew how to put, than to give a substantial relation of what she had to communicate. The sum and substance of all this was the arrival of the Honourable Jacquetta Freemantle, the dominant spirit of this collateral branch of the Cornbury family, together with her so-many-years-junior brother, the Honourable Conyers Freemantle, whom it now was her pleasure to reconcile to his noble relations, after a ten years' dissention, and for whom she was desirous also of forming a matrimonial connexion—the corollary of all this being that Mrs. Ashenhurst and her daughter should be introduced to them the very next day, at Lord Cornbury's house in Berkeley Square, the two families alone being present, in order to bring the young people acquainted before they mixed in general society. The two ladies' understood each other's plans perfectly. Lady Cornbury, too indolent to plot or even devise a plot, was yet desirous of securing to the nephew she had always loved so beautiful a bride, and for the house of Conyers, whose well-being was clear to her as her life's blood—herself being of it—own cousin to the heiress whom the Honourable Mr. Freemantle, her husband's brother, had married—so noble an accession of wealth as the heiress of General Dubois must bring to it. Mrs. Ashenhurst, on her part, with but little delicacy of feeling, and unbounded ambition, bent only to agrandizement, determined to plot, and counterplot, so that she could but bring about a match so entirely to her heart's content as this.

In order to sound the General's thoughts on the subject, she mentioned the call from Lady Cornbury, and the proposed next day's visit, adding, "I can give a shrewd guess as to what is in her ladyship's mind all the time: she wishes to secure your niece for her nephew, knowing as well as any of us, though she says so little, that the first chance is worth having."

The General answered her with one of those sinister looks which she so extremely disliked—they made her uneasy; but his verbal reply was satisfactory. "He would not desire his niece to engage the attentions of a better man than the Honourable Conyers Freemantle—she would have his entire acquiescence in so doing."

All this plotting and assenting, however, was most sedulously kept from the knowledge of the party most interested in it. Mrs. Ashenhurst would not, for the world, that her daughter should have the remotest notion of it; nor was Jane aware of the arrival of the Freemantles, and the consequent reconcilement, till within an hour of making the visit—then nothing more was needed to give interest to a visit otherwise of a most commonplace character. Jane knew the only event perhaps capable of arousing the lethargic spirit of Lady Cornbury was this reconciliation; the only being for whom she had at any time evinced any affection—of whom she appeared to have retained any memory, was this young man—"poor dear Conyers," as she invariably called him; although his lordship many a time so far excited himself as to remind her "that Mr. Freemantle had given them serious cause of displeasure."

Whatever his misconduct had been did not cencern Jane; she thought much less of him than of the pleasure his return must have afforded to his aunt; and accordingly, at her mother's instance, she put on the blue and silver brocade and the suit of Furnapore diamonds, in honour of the reconciliation, not of the guest, as was the design of Mrs. Ashenhurst.

The General congratulated Jane on her appearance; and her mother saw her seated opposite them, as they drove to Berkeley Square, in the firm persuasion that she was the one-day-to-be Lady Cornbury of Wilton and Court Conyers.

Whatever Lady Cornbury's pleasure might be in the reconciliation, to Jane's astonishment it made but very little visible alteration in her countenance and manners. His lordship, on the contrary, was astonishingly animated and alert; he really seemed as if his heart beat the quicker for it. On him devolved the honour of introducing the parties to each other. Jane had not been prepared for the full ceremonial—the meeting with the honourable Miss Jacquetta Freemantle. Jacquetta! she knew the histories connected with that name at Wilton; she knew the fair, meek face of the one Jacquetta who stabbed her lord, as the story told, with "a bodkin;" and the other, the haughty woman of imperial beauty, with eyes full of dreamy, fearful passion, whose crimes people spoke of in whispers, in dread lest the uneasy spirit which had troubled the scene of her guilt so long should again be given up from its awful place; and now certainly here was a third Jacquetta, not unworthy of these ancestors—a tall, haughty woman, of commanding figure and presence, approaching middle age, but evidently using no means to counteract the effects of time; as one regardless of man's opinion, or of women's either; as one would say, "What are these things, what is all the world, to the Honourable Jacquetta Freemantle? and am not I she?" Jane remembered the old housekeeper's story, that the Lady Jacquetta was not dead; that for certain she had been seen in flesh and blood many a long year after people thought she had mouldered in her grave; and that for her part she believed the coffin would be a strong one, and the grave a deep one, that must hold her down. All this which she had listened to, and shuddered at the while, now came back to her mind with a reality and a repelling influence as she saw the proud turn from her mother's greeting with ill-disguised contempt, and then stand with her haughty head thrown back, one arm dropped, and the other held close to her waist as if to still the knocking of her proud heart—the very attitude of the awful Jacquetta.

As Jane was presented, she rapidly eyed from head to foot, and then gave her hand with the air of condescending greatness which the powerful assume to inveigle as much as to honour. Jane felt a repugnance amounting almost to horror, when the lady retained her hand, and, begging his lordship's permission, conducted her half-way down the room. "I must introduce you to each other," said she mysteriously, and the moment afterwards presented her to her brother, desiring him to approve the acquaintance. The gentleman was, in most respects, outwardly unlike his sister. He was singularly fair for a man, with flaxen hair, and those colourless eyebrows and eyelashes which give so unmanly a character to the countenance, and the general expression of his face, though cold, was by no means unpleasing. In person he was above the middle size and of a good figure, but his manners were at times almost awkward and shy, while at others he assumed an air of indifference and haughtiness. A short time, but certainly not this one interview alone, convinced Jane of what was in truth the history of this young man's education. Many years the junior of his strong-minded but imperious sister, to whom the management of the inheritor as well as the inheritance had been intrusted, he was compelled to assume character in some respects opposed to his own. The better parts of his nature were cheerfulness, a certain degree of amiability, and extremely affable manners. He had been trained to be reserved and haughty; but there was a *gaucherie* about him which betrayed the mask, and hence his manners appeared variable and unformed. The only part of his natural character which had been zealously fostered, was what he inherited in common with the whole line, inordinate family pride. His feeling was less that he belonged to the universal human family than to the noblest branch of it—that he was a Freemantle engrafted on the old, true Conyers stock. Besides this, there was another ramification of the same passion—extreme personal selfishness;—that mean selfishness which makes the boy snatch the apple from the lips of his younger brother when he has eaten his own, and makes the man regardless of the feelings and convenience of others, when his own pleasure, caprice, or indulgence comes in the way. He was a charcater and person in the first instance to be seen with indifference; in the second, to interest to a certian degree, because it was discovered that he had some native good properties; but in the end to be despised, inasmuch as petty meannesses outweigh commonplace virtues. So far came to the knowledge of Jane—a little more must be added for the sake of our readers.

As a boy, and as a youth even, Conyers Freemantle had been submissive and obedient to his sister, in virtue of that natural authority which strong minds acquire over weaker ones; but as he advanced to manhood, his spirit began to crave after greater freedom of will; there were certain buddings of rebellion in his mind, and though as yet it had rarely evinced itself in acts, it invariably strove against every command of his sister. Hence at this very time, when he knew his sister's designs to be matrimonial, he vowed with himself not to further them even by the lifting of a finger.

The result of this visit appeared sufficiently satisfactory to bring the parties again in a short time. Little did Jane suspect of private meetings of which she was the subject, when the imperious Jacquetta treated for her hand on behalf of her brother, much in the same style as an ambassador of a sovereign prince might demand in marriage the daughter of an inferior line, with whom policy as much as inclination made it advantageous to unite himself. The matter was satisfactorily adjusted. The Honourable Conyers Freemantle was to take to wife Jane Ashenhurst, the fair heiress of the great nabob of Furnapore. So stated the fashionable newspapers, under the head "Marriage in High Life"—only giving dashes and asterisks for proper names. But Jane read no newspapers, nor busied herself with the passing tattle of the day; and she was, perhaps, the only person in their whole circle who know nothing of what was agitating.

Mrs. Ashenhurst supposed, as was natural, that the lover had gained the good-will of his mistress—felicitating herself the while on the extraordinary success of the scheme; and was perfectly charmed with the acquiescence of her daughter, though, from unpleasant recollections, she abstained from speaking on the subject to her at present.

All this time Mr. Freemantle considered Jane a party in the design upon him; and though at first, as we have said, averse to the scheme from opposition to his sister, his self-love had already accepted the flattery of Jane's supposed willingness, and he was becoming less and less averse. The attentions, however, which he paid her—a large award from him who had hitherto thought no woman worthy of his slightest regard—were still so little beyond common courtesies, that they did not even excite her suspicion, leaving her entirely at liberty to think her own thoughts and pursue her own fancies at will; his self-love, the while, giving all she said and did a reference to himself. This state of cross-purposes must, however, have worked itself straight, had they remained much longer together; but at the end of the third day Mr. Freemantle returned to his country residence, without even a formal leave-taking of Jane, from a temporary pique against his sister.

A week of stately amities succeeded, and then a party was proposed to Court-Conyers—a visit of the bride-elect and her friends to her future home. Little could Jane imagine why the ungracious Jacquetta condescended to spend a whole morning in formally speaking of the family history—of its illustrious descent and alliances—of the Conyers, who were more illustrious than the Freemantles—of the family quarterings—of the family plate and jewels;—"reserving the subject of the rent-roll for her brother; though she understood it as well—nay, certainly better than himself; and it would be found that all future branches of the family were infinitely indebted to her for the zealous management she had so long given to its most minute concerns. But," added she, with dignity, "had I laid down my life, it would not have been too much for so illustrious a name—though certainly you cannot be supposed to understand the responsibility of such an inheritance!"

Haughtily as all this information was given, contemptuous as had been its winding up, and little concern as Jane felt herself to have in it, she had too much general kindness—was too much disposed to give and receive pleasure—to appear indifferent to any gratuitous instance of good-will, even from a person so repugnant to her as the Honourable Jacquetta Freemantle.

XVII

The important day came. The distance to Court-Conyers was twenty miles; the party was to take luncheon there, see the house, and return to London in the evening—which would easily be accomplished, as they were to travel post.

Lord and Lady Cornbury and Miss Ashenhurst occupied one carriage; the General, Mrs. Ashenhurst, and Miss Freemantle the other. There could be no interest to Jane in the meagre conversation of her companions—she therefore occupied herself with her own thoughts, and some little curiosity she felt respecting the mansion they were about to visit, which to her imagination seemed to have something ogre-like about it. How the other triad occupied themselves is not known, further than that they appeared singularly gracious to each other, and to everybody else, on their arrival at Court-Conyers.

Jane's imagination had not pictured a more sombre and forbidding exterior than the place presented. It seemed of large extent, square, heavy, and prison-like, built of stone which was black with age, with low round towers, small windows, and heavy-browed doors. It stood low, in an unpicturesque and unpleasing park; woods of pine thickly interspersed with ilex and yew flanking it on either hand, and stretching behind upward to the brow of the only eminence for miles round.

"This place never looks cheerful," said Lord Cornbury, "come when you will."

"It never does," was his lady's reply.

"But we should not say so to you, my dear Miss Ashenhurst!"

"To me! Oh, sir, you are perfectly welcome to say what you please of this old castle for me!" said Jane, wondering in perfect simplicity what they meant: "for my part, I think it a hideous place!"

The laconic people made no remark, and the carriage waited its turn to draw up to the gloomy door.

If the Honourable Conyers Freemantle had been indifferent and silent in Berkeley Square, he seemed bent to make up for all deficiencies in his own house. Nothing could exceed the elaborate ceremonial of their reception. One thing seen struck Jane's attention most unpleasantly—that she was made, instead, as she supposed herself, the least important person of the party, the one for whom everything seemed arranged—for whom, in fact, everybody seemed to have come there.

When the party had refreshed themselves, the host requested the honour of her hand, and led the way in the domiciliary inspection, desiring her free opinion of all she saw, and begging she would suggest alterations according to her own taste; at the same time insinuating that everything had been arranged by a Conyers or a Freemantle, and therefore of necessity had remained *in statu quo*. Every moment Jane's annoyance and suspicion grew; she longed to join herself to the others, but they seemed to keep aloof, and she feared at the same time to make herself conspicuous or ridiculous. By degrees the whole tribulation of the intrigue came upon her, and she walked on from room to room silent and irresolute, which the lover mistook for passive obedience or timid admiration.

At length Jane found that, either intentionally or accidentally, they had missed their party; and she now stood with him alone in a small room, apparently in one of the towers, and to which they had ascended by a narrow stone stair. They entered the room: its aspect was forbidding, small and gloomy, containing only tarnished folio volumes, arranged on shelves dusty and worm-eaten, two high leather-covered chairs, a desk, and a table. Jane started, for it seemed like the den of the ogre himself. She attempted to retreat, but the door was shut, and her companion already had seized her hand.

"Charming Miss Ashenharst," said he, "why will you persist in this cruel silence? I confess to you that I was once indifferent to this match, but I am not so now. Jacquetta has lorded it so long, she thinks me still a child, and to be awed by the lifting of her finger; but she will find I have the spirit of a Freemantle in me!"

"Let me go!" said Jane, withdrawing her hand, and really terrified.

"We will not trouble our heads about this old place," pleaded Mr. Freemantle, looking at her the while with unfeigned admiration. "You will have time enough to study it hereafter, and I must make up for lost time."

Whether he would have protested his passion on his knees, or by any other approved mode of lover-craft, cannot be known; for Jane, though feeling, as it were, betrayed, and in a place which her imagination made fearful, and with her heart as cold as death, put him back with a dignity he could not withstand.

"Some strange delusion has been practised on you, sir, she said; "for, till within this hour, I had no idea what this visit meant."

"Come, Miss Ashenhurst, I know this is the way with you ladies; but the faster you fly, the faster I shall pursue: and I think I have you pretty safely now," said he, in atone between good humour and triumph.

"I am sincere, Mr. Freernantle," said Jane, coldly and calmly—"I am most truly sincere, when I assure you of my entire ignorance of this scheme till within the last half-hour."

He looked at her for a moment as if he disbelieved his senses, and then burst into a loud laugh. "Come, come, Miss Ashenhurst, this is truly ridiculous; you think it your turn to be cold now. I beg your pardon for my past indifference—punish it any way but by your coldness: but, to speak truth, I was provoked with Jacquetta."

"I wish you were provoked with her now," said Jane, half amused, spite of herself, "if it would insure me your *present* indifference."

"Miss Ashenhurst," he returned, looking impatient, "there has been too much of this—I am tired of this child's play."

"Sir'," said Jane, "your words are enigmas; but I do not care about their meaning. I must now return to my friends."

"No!" anwered he, almost fiercely, "I shall not part with you thus; you were in a different humour in Berkeley Square."

"Because, sir," said Jane, offended and angry, "I never thought about *you* in Berkeley Square."

"Upon my honour!" exclaimed he, in a tone and with a gesture which made Jane involuntarily look at the thickness of the walls. "And this scheme was concocted at Wilton among yourselves! Do you know, madam, to whom you are speaking?"

"To Mr. Conyers Freemantle," she replied, with an indifference that she did not feel.

"Madam!—Miss Ashenhurst" he began, in a tone that sill more terrified her; and, in very despair, she laid her hand upon the iron pin of the door. To her inexpressible relief, it gave way, and the exploring party was in the act of ascending the stairs.

"I beg your pardon, Miss Jane," said Lord Cornbury, who was foremost, and too unapprehensive to observe the disordered countenance of either herself or Mr. Freemantle. "We have certainly arrived inopportunely."

"No, no", said the master of the mansion; and you must see this chamber: it is of some renown in the house, being the one in which our ancestor, the astrologer, punished his contumacious wife."

"Ay, he poisoned her, didn't he?" said Lord Cornbury, as the whole party entered.

Jane, sick at heart, and filled with perfect loathing of the place and the people, walked hastily down the stairs to an open casement-window, that she might look out upon the sunshine; but the wood of dark pine and yew lay all below, stretching to the very horizon. It was a dreary prospect; it seemed as if cheerful sunlight never came there; and an impatience to be gone seized upon Jane's spirit like anger.

"It is an evil place," thought she; "it fills me with feelings of revenge and cruelty!"

The party descended, Mr. Freemantle and his sister bringing up the rear.

"We have now seen all," said Lord Cornbury.

"All except the chapel," said Miss Jacquetta.

"We will not go there," yawned Lady Cornbury, seating herself on a sofa in the chamber through which they were passing.

"We will wait for you here," assented Lord Cornbury, seating himself by his lady.

"Come, Miss Ashenhurst," said Miss Jacquetta, griping her with her hard hand.

Jane, as if under the spell of a destiny, obeyed; and the next moment was conducted through a low arched door, to which they descended by a flight of chilly stone steps into the chancel of a church. She looked behind her for her friends but the door was shut, and she stood alone with this fearful woman, who for two moments gazed into her face with a steady, severe countenance, as if she would penetrate her very soul. Jane's imagination, excited as it was, was filled with terrible and undefined apprehensions; but she stood the scrutiny with an unblenching calmness.

The place was cold and silent as death, striking its sunless chill to the bone, while its influence fell solemnly on the spirit. Lofty and effigied tombs stood round; mural tablets of all ages were on the walls, and the floor was paved with graven stones and dark brazen plates of memorial. Two old, decaying banners, black and heavy with age, which had been borne by the Conyers in the wars of the Roses and the Plantagenets, depended from the roof over the pews of black carved oak, lined with ancient crimson velvet, where the proud Conyers had sat to worship for ages. A sombre light fell through the richly-painted panes of the large window that faced them, leaving the altar in perfect gloom, as if sunshine could not enter there.

At another time, or with less agitated feelings, Jane would have enjoyed this old place with a thorough zest; its antiquity, its solemnity, its gloom, would have produced a frame of mind in perfect accordance with it: but there was a disquiet in her spirit now that unfitted her for any enjoyment; the muttered words, too, of her companion, filled her with a mysterious awe. "By the souls of our ancestors!" she spoke, as if thinking aloud, "if it were——"and then she clenched a key in her strong, bony hand, as if she would make the senseless iron feel.

Jane started, believing this had reference to what had passed between herself and Mr. Freemantle.

"But come," said Miss Jacquetta, "I brought you to see the burial-place of the noble Conyers, and the one Freemantle, its last lord!"

And so saying, with the key she held in her hand she opened a low door in the wall, and descending a few steps into perfect darkness, bade Jane follow her.

Jane hesitated to obey.

"You foolish child!" said Miss Jacquetta, speaking with a stern voice, that seemed sepulchral, "why need you fear to enter this place, where so many of your betters are laid. Come down, and see where the direct line of the noble Conyers, and those as noble, with whom they mated, lie piled, coffin on coffin, for twelve generations."

Jane considered how improbable it was that any evil was intended towards her, and descended the steps.

"Not one foot nearer," cried Miss Jacquetta, speaking from among the cofffins, as Jane had reached the middle of the vault—"Not one step nearer! farther *you* never can enter—here lie only tlhe nobly born! and fathers and sons for twelve generations, with their wives, none below a baron's daughter. You may go back!"

Jane felt displeased at this senseless parade of greatness. "And where," said she, as the lady emerged from the tombs; "where lies the wife whom we heard above was murdered?"

"Nonsense!" retorted the descendant of the Conyers; "do you believe whatever tradition hands down?"

"I heard it from a Conyers!" was Jane's answer.

Miss Jacquetta eyed her for a moment, and then said, bitterly: "That wife was the daughter of a commoner, and here she lies:" pointing to a raised tomb, one of seven which stood side by side, with its well-wrought marble effigy—"she lies here! These others also are wives of Conyers; and one of them a daughter, who married unwisely and came here to die."

"And here I must lie," thought Jane, "if I marry a Conyers—which Heaven forbid! Nay, I will die first," mused she, as she walked down the aisle and saw the arms of the proud Conyers emblazoned above the Decalogue and the Lord's Prayer.

"You see the nobility of this house," said Miss Jacquetta, reconducting Jane into the chancel; "you see who those were that mated with them. It is not for *you* young woman to undervalue a Conyers. Remember what you have seen!"

Jane felt utterly incapable of replying, and Miss Jacquetta, neither seeming to expect or desire an answer, motioned her to follow through the door by which they had entered, haughtily keeping the advance; and presently afterwards they rejoined the party, who waited for them in the chamber.

Refreshments were again offered, of which all partook except Jane, who, though faint and weary, firmly refused; "I will not again break bread nor drink water in this house," was her internal vow; and presently afterwards the carriages being announced, the party left Court-Conyers in the order they had arrived, the master not offering more than the most distant civilities to Jane, and remaining behind.

Jane began only to breathe freely when they left the demesne of the Conyers and entered on the king's high-road. She turned to her companions to relieve herself by talking even on the most trivial passing subjects; but they were both fast asleep, nor did either of them wake till the carriage drew up at their own door at eleven o'clock at night.

When Jane took the place lately occupied by Miss Freemantle, in their drive to Grosvenor-square, she was immediately aware that some unpleasant rencontre had taken place. She could see by the indistinct light of the carriage-lamps,★ the haughty, angry countenance of her uncle, and the perturbed anxiety of her mother's: no word was exchanged, but the very silence seemed full of terrible omen.

Jane ran hastily to her own chamber, and thence sent to request an interview with her mother; but she was informed that Mrs. Ashenhurst also was gone to her chamber and desired not to be disturbed that evening.

What had occurred during the homeward drive Jane could in part conjecture; but her mother's refusal to see her filled her with an exquisite distress, even more painful than the other events of the day. The day itself was frightful in review; and Jane sat down in the state of one who, waking from a terrible dream, finds the realities that encompass him even more distressing.

XVIII

What had occurred during the journey must now be briefly related.

Miss Jacquetta, quick-sighted as she always was, observed the apparent want of understanding between the lovers, and had extracted sufficient information from her brother to decide her line of conduct. Scarcely, therefore, were they seated in the carriage, when, with all the offended pride of a Conyers, she haughtily informed the General and Mrs. Ashenhurst of what she had discovered; adding, that "if Miss Ashenhurst was unaware of the great honour done her by these proposals, it believed her relations to keep her from again offending. That, for her part, she did not now desire the connexion; still, as it was the wish of Mr. Conyers Freemantle that the affair should proceed, she was willing to sacrifice her own feelings only she begged them to understand that a Conyers could not again be thus trifled with!"

Mrs. Ashenhurst internally resented this insolent harangue, but she waited to know the General's sentiments before she spoke. Great was her amazement then to find that, instead of retorting upon the arrogant lady and defending his niece, as she had hoped he would do, he joined entirely with her; reprobated Jane's conduct as childish and unpardonable, as what Mr. Conyers Freemantle could not in honour subject himself to a second time, and gave his word that no farther impediment on the part of his niece should prevent a marriage so entirely accordant with his wishes for her.

In spite of these concessions, good-humour was by no means restored. The General folded his arms as if in repressed anger against his niece; and the haughty Jacquetta sat like an angry porcupine, bristled at all points in her unmitigated wrath for the affront done to a Conyers by a daughter of a commoner.

Poor Mrs. Ashenhurst was like a troubled sea on which the storm comes from all points; she struggled with offended pride, with some maternal sympathy for her daughter, and with the consciousness that by neither General Dubois nor Miss Fremantle was she considered a party in the disposal of that daughter. Again self-interest and ambition bade her bear all patiently and submit; told her that come what would the General must not be offended—that policy as well as duty demanded acquiescence; and that, after all, the match was excellent—in spite of the arrogant Miss Jacquetta, most excellent! What would the Cornburys say if it were given up, especially when things had gone so far?—and perhaps Jane had given Mr. Freemantle sufficient cause of offence. "She is so headstrong!" cogitated the poor lady; and then she remembered Brian Livingstone, and how pertinacious her daughter had been, The more she thought the more she fretted, and as she fretted she grew angry; and long before they reached London she had come to the conclusion so often come to before, that Jane was flying in the face of her duty, and ruining her good fortune!

Now for the first time in her life Mrs. Ashenhurst felt estranged from her daughter, and when she awoke in the morning from a night of uneasy repose, she determined not to see her till she had encountered her friends in Berkeley Square. When Jane, therefore, inquired for her after a night far less refreshing than even her mother's, she was informed that Mrs. Ashenhurst was about leaving the house. Jane felt instantly the displeasure this implied, and without regarding the etiquette her mother had lately established, rushed into her dressing-room. Mrs. Ashenhurst had that moment dismissed her woman, and Jane, seeing her alone, threw her arms about her neck and sobbed on her bosom.

"Oh, mother!" said she at length, "why will you break my heart with this coldness? What have I done to make you, like everybody else, my enemy?"

"Dear love," said her mother, touched by her daughter's sincere grief, "how can you talk so? How can you think of calling me, or any one, your enemy?"

"Does not every one scheme to drive me mad?" cried Jane, with bitter agony. "Oh, mother, mother! and could you countenance this hateful connexion! And did *you* know why I was taken to that horrible place?"

"My love: my dear love!" said Mrs. Ashenhurst, wishing the while she did not feel so deeply sorry for her daughter; "everybody knew why we went. Surely you cannot pretend ignorance."

"Then you were a party in this miserable intrigue!" cried Jane, reproachfully. "You surely cannot wish me to marry that proud half-witted man; you surely cannot wish to put me in the power of that haughty, cruel woman!"

"Jane, Jane," remonstrated her mother, "your imagination runs away with your reason! You really distract me—do be calm, child!"

"I cannot; I feel frantic when I think of it!"

"Oh, then I must leave you till you are calm," said Mrs. Ashenhurst, moving towards the door.

"No, mother, do not leave me thus," said Jane, rising and repressing her emotion. "Oh, you do not know how miserable I am!"

"Well, love, what can I do for you?—you really are so violent!"

"I am calm—I will be calm; but tell me your mind about this wretched affair!" said the poor girl in a heart-broken tone.

"Why, my dear, what can I tell you that you do not know?" replied her mother, wishing sincerely she had never promoted the scheme.

"I know nothing!" said Jane.

"Do you not know that this match has been brought about by our friends the Cornburys?"

"No!"

"Why, my love, Mr. Freemantle himself must have declared his passion before he left Berkeley Square."

"Dearest mother, he never did!" was Jane's earnest reply.

"Really, love, you astonish me. But let me go, love; this is a queer business, and I must know the bottom of it."

"But, mother dear," said Jane, "before you go, let me beseech of you to be my friend. Oh, do, do!" cried she, kissing her mother's hand tenderly, while the tears streamed down her cheeks, "be my friend, dearest mother, and oppose this miserable connexion—you have a right to do it, when you know how wretched it makes me!"

"Let me go, let me go, love," said Mrs. Ashenhurst, truly pitying her daughter, and yet knowing how deeply committed she herself was in this affair.

"Listen to me, dearest, dearest mother, and be my friend— whom can I appeal to but you? Tell my uncle that I cannot marry. It is not Mr. Freemantle that I reject—but I cannot marry; you know, dear mother, I cannot!"

Jane had overstepped the range of her mother's sympathies, and had touched on an offensive topic; her reply was accordingly—"I know no such thing, Jane; but this I know, that it is your duty to obey your uncle!"

"I could lie down and die," said Jane, in a voice of the deepest anguish, "to hear you talk thus, dear mother!—it is so unlike what you used to be."

"It is no use talking," replied Mrs. Ashenhurst; "you know your uncle as well as I do. What can I do! It is ridiculous of you to talk so. What can you do either?"

"I will never marry Mr. Freemantle, ' said Jane, firmly; "that is what I can do; I will go back to Harbury and earn my own bread first!"

"Really, Jane, how you surprise me! Well, you must take your own course—only I am sorry you are in such a temper." And Mrs.

Ashenhurst, wonderfully relieved by the turn the conversation had taken, hastily left her dressing-room, stepped into her carriage, and was driven to Berkeley Square.

The proverb of the "frying-pan and the fire" might not inaptly be applied to the case of poor Mrs. Ashenhurst, were it not so inelegant. But it is too late to seek for another comparison now, as she is at this moment entering the breakfast-room in Berkeley Square.

There sat the still bristled Jacquetta, and there sat the sleek Lady Cornbury, looking ruffled and ill at ease, her Conyers blood mounting to her quiet forehead from the enormous affront put upon the house the day before; and Lord Cornbury himself was walking up and down the room with a letter in his hand, which had come express from Mr. Conyers Freemantle that very morning; in which letter it was stated, "that notwithstanding the young lady's mistake in thinking a Conyers could be played with like a child's shuttlecock, he was more bent on the match now than ever, and should accordingly be in Berkeley Square that evening, in order to prosecute his suit, and accomplish the marriage at as early a date as possible."

The point at issue when Mrs. Ashenhurst entered was, whether, considering the extent of the young lady's delinquency, it became his dignity to do so; nay, whether he would not compromise his honour by doing so.

Miss Freemantle had found an unlooked-for ally in Lady Cornbury, and their opinion was, "that the indiscretion of Miss Ashenhurst forfeited the honour of so illustrious a connexion; that the thing did not admit of debate—a Conyers could not ally himself with such contumacy."

Lord Cornbury, on the contrary, was approving warmly of Mr. Freemantle's spirit, and declaring that Miss Ashenhurst was too charming in herself, and too important a match in point of fortune, to be thrown away for an idle pique of honour—for, after all, perhaps nothing but an idle lovers' quarrel.

The entrance of Mrs. Ashenhurst suspended the subject.—The ladies received her most coldly; she not only wished herself back in Grosvenor Square, but the whole calamity of losing her noble friends' countenance came upon her, and she felt how impossible it would have been to retract, had she come there for that purpose. Without vouchsafing any notice whatever of her greeting, Miss Freemantle haughtily left the room, intending it as a signal punishment and token of displeasure; but her retreat brought assurance to the enemy.—Mrs. Ashenhurst changed her tactics instantly; and now, instead of conciliation, as she had meditated, resolved on attack, confident in her accustomed influence over the indolent minds of her friends.

"It was so strange a thing," she said, "that Mr. Conyers Freemantle, who had such abundant opportunities of declaring his wishes, had not done so! She considered her daughter extremely ill-used, and certainly thought some explanation or apology was requisite from him."

Lady Cornbury opened her eyes, and absolutely stared at Mrs. Ashenhurst.

"To be sure! a most extraordinary lover," replied his lordship, "if the case really be so!"

"It is so," said Mrs. Ashenhurst, warmly; "and now, forsooth, you are all offended because Jane is surprised at the familiarity of a person who has never declared himself! I am sure I would never have gone to Court-Conyers, nor should my daughter, if I had known how matters stood!" added she, with a warmth and dignity that had its full effect on her hearers.

"My dear madam," said his lordship, in his most conciliatory voice, "you have just cause of complaint. But," continued he, assuming a jocose air, "I see how it is,—Mr. Conyers Freemantle was not to be driven into love by Miss Jacquetta; he is now in love of his own head,—things will go on smoothly now never fear. Read this letter, my dear madam,—I think it will satisfy you: or, rather, I will read it, without troubling you," said he, remembering some expressions which might perhaps give umbrage to the lady; and accordingly he read the letter in his own way. "This must satisfy you, I think!" said he, when he had done.

"Certainly, my lord; he could not speak more handsomely," replied she.

"And you are satisfied too, my dear?" said Lord Cornbury, turning to his lady, who was calming down into her ordinary quiet.

"So that Conyers is not to be refused and played with like a common person, I am satisfied," was her answer; and as this was a morning of extraordinary exertion, she added the moment afterwards, "Miss Ashenhurst was always a favourite of mine, or I should not have wished Conyers to marry her."

Mrs. Ashenhurst, with unfeigned pleasure, expressed herself highly complimented.

"Then," said her ladyship, "we are friends again,—I hate the trouble of being angry."

"Oh," returned Lord Cornbory, in perfect good-humour, "we know you are a Conyers, and are privileged to resent a family affront—even when a Conyers is wrong," said he, bowing to Mrs. Ashenhurst.

"I am sure I do not know what Miss Freemantle will say," remarked her ladyship.

"Miss Freemantle is never so happy as when she is angry, therefore she will have reason to thank us," said his lordship, laughing.

The visit ended to the entire satisfaction of all parties; there never had been more amity between them even at Wilton, and Mrs. Ashenhnrst left the house assured that, some way or other, things would work themselves straight. "But," thought she, as she was driven along, "I will be perfectly passive: Mr. Freemantle shall plead his own suit, and to the General shall devolve the office of compelling Jane to obedience,—I never do any good when I interfere!"

A succession of visitors and engagements occupied her through the rest of the morning, much to her satisfaction, for she determined not to encounter a second interview with her daughter.

The General returned to dinner in extraordinary spirits.—He too had been in Berkeley Square, where everything had likewise fallen out to his satisfaction. As a piece of pleasant news, he informed his sister and niece, that he had encountered no less a person than Sir Harbottle Grimstone in Pall Mall, and the nabob was extremely merry at the thought of the diversion he should have with this renowned knight among his London friends. Besides this, he brought with him a letter from Lord Montjoy, wherein his lordship spoke in the most flatttering terms of having made the acquaintance of his excellent cousin Mrs. Ashenhurst, at her own pretty house at Harbury, and that he had not forgotten the extraordinary beauty of her little daughter. Moreover, his lordship promised himself the pleasure of a week's shooting at Denborough Park in the autumn.

Nothing could have been more gratifying to Mrs. Ashenhurst than this letter. She laughed with her brother at the unfortunate baronet, applauded his proposed practical jokes, and once in every half-hour, at least, told what a perfect gentleman was their noble cousin Montjoy.

The evening was spent at the opera, Jane wearing the blue and silver brocade and the Furnapore diamonds, to please her uncle; and Mrs. Ashenhurst having the pleasure of seeing that her daughter attracted universal admiration—nobody thinking the while that a heavy and anxious heart beat under those splendid habiliments.

The next day Mr. Conyers Freemantle presented himself in Grosvenor Square; but the ladies were not at home. He had, however, a prolonged interview with General Dubois, the result of which was entirely satisfactory to both parties. The lover spoke of his unbounded passion, and earnest desire for an immediate marriage,—blamed Jacquetta for everything that had hitherto gone wrong, and hinted of marriage settlements. Whatever the nabob's promises or insinuations were, even the Conyers was satisfied, and internally called himself "a lucky fellow." After several hours thus spent in business, the gentlemen agreed to pass the remainder of the day together, and to close the evening at Vauxhall.

XIX

The next morning, while Mrs. Ashenhurst and her daughter were yet in their beds, the whole house was thrown into the greatest possible state of confusion by the stopping of a hackney-coach out of which was supported, by Mr. Conyers Freemantle and a surgeon, the General himself, faint and bleeding. He was conveyed to his chamber, and the news carried to his kinswoman. Mrs. Ashenhurst was walked from a dream of wedding favours and coronets to hear the shocking tidings, which threw her into violent hysterics. Jane, full of the most incoherent apprehensions, hastily dressed herself and ran to the breakfast-room, where she despatched a servant to request admission for her if she could be of any service to her uncle, or to bring her back particulars of this strange event.

Mr. Conyers Freemantle attended the servant back. Every subject but this one seemed to shrink into minor importance, yet still she felt a momentary repugnance to encounter this man. Fortunately, however, just then her mother entered, folded in wrapping-gown and shawl, leaning on the arm of her woman, and looking well nigh as feeble as the General himself. Mrs. Ashenhurst was seated with great care and state in a large easy-chair; and then, with some little embarrassment both of manner and countenance, Mr. Conyers Freemantle informed them that he and the General had spent the last evening at Vnuxhall; that there they had met a gentleman between whom and the General an old quarrel seemed to exist.

"Good heavens!" exclaimed Jane, clasping her hands, and comprehending at once the whole affair.

"Sir Harbottle Grimstone?" asked Mrs Ashenhurst.

"The same," replied Mr. Conyers Freemantle. "A renewal of the quarrel took place, and a challenge from Sir Harbottle was the result. I had the honour to attend General Dubois as his second this morning; and I must acknowledge that his antagonist took no unfair advantage, though the consequence has been so unlucky."

"Is he dangerously wounded?" asked Jane.

Mr. Conyers Freemantle bowed to Jane with the greatest deference, and informed her, that a skilful surgeon was with him, but as yet had not given his opinion.

Mrs. Ashenhurst again fell into hysterics, and was conveyed to her chamber by her maid and daughter.

Many hours of the most dreadful suspense succeeded; the General resisting every solicitation, not only of the surgeon, but of his friends Mr. Conyers Freemantle and Lord Cornbury, who were now with him, to let his wound be examined. At the same time that he deplored this accident, he imprecated curses and vengeance on the head of Sir Harbottle, and insisted with fierce earnestness that he would not die. The surgeon at length declared that the General would be guilty of a species of suicide if he longer delayed the examination, and that, in fact, he himself would leave the house unless he was allowed to use his own means for his restoration. The General submitted; Mr. Conyers Freemantle and Lord Cornbury withdrew; the valet remained in the anteroom, and the surgeon was left alone with the patient. With what intense anxiety did Jane await the issue: "There is a mystery then about him," thought Mrs. Ashenhurst, in the midst of her agitation; "I wonder what it can be!"

At the end of the examination, they were informed that the surgeon dared not give hopes, but that he earnestly requested to call in additional surgical aid, which the General violently opposed; that now Mr. Mortlake, his lawyer, was sent for instantly at his own request, with whom he was to remain undisturbed for two hours.

At length the surgeon joined them in the drawing-room.

"Dear madam," said he, with a distressed and anxious countenance, to Mrs. Ashenhurst, the moment he entered, "for God's sake, madam, if you have any influence, induce him to let me have assistance! The extraction of the ball might save his life, but I dare not perform it alone!"

"Why does he object?" asked she, her curiosity overpowering her anxiety.

"That, madam, is not the question!" said the agitated man; and then he turned to Jane.

"I will introduce *you* to the chamber if you will plead for me!" said he, in a voice of such distress as might have pleaded for his own life. "Cannot you influence him?"

"Oh, sir, I doubt it, I doubt it!" exclaimed Jane, clasping her hands; "but I will try!—or cannot I do something for you?—I think I could hand you your instruments?"

"No, no," said he; "I want the experienced mannual aid of a brother-surgeon'. He cannot live four-and-twenty hours without surgical aid!" groaned the poor man.

The next moment he was summoned to the General's chamber. A violent ringing of the bell sncceeded; and the voice of the surgeon was heard directly after, reiterating his commands to the servant.

"Fly, as if for your life!" said he; "bring Mr. Haslop back with you as speedily."

The additional surgeon arrived. Again hours of suspense succeeded; again the lawyer was introduced; and the surgeons declining to give an opinion, withdrew to an adjoining chamber, where dinner was served to them.

Mr. Mortlake, like the surgeon, seemed to find the work for which he had, been summoned beyond his skill; and Mrs. Ashenhurst, who was now sufficiently collected to take note of whatever occurred, had a new subject of speculation afforded her by hearing that a second lawyer was also summoned with as much despatch as possible.

In the course of the evening Lord Cornbury called—called again with his solemn condolence, and offers on the part of his nephew, who feared he had displeased Miss Ashenhurst from the coldness with which she treated him, that he might be permitted to remain in the house through the night, in order to render any possible assistance either to General Dubois or to the ladies. Mrs. Ashenhurst most willingly assented, declaring that any gloom which appeared on her daughter's countenance arose from anxiety for her uncle, "she was so extremely attached to her uncle!"

As the night set in, Mr. Conyers Freemantle took his place by the drawing-room fire; Mrs. Ashenhurst, in a rich cloak and shawl, reclining in a large easy-chair, now feebly talking over "these melancholy events," and now dozing into pleasant forgetfulness. The lady's silken repose was contagious, and Mr. Conyers Freemantle also dozed in his chair. In a while, however, the lady's sleep went from her; and as she lay with her eyes open looking to the richly ornamented ceiling, she began to look forward into the future. How bright it all appeared! There was in it neither pride, power, nor pain; neither the haughty Jacquetta to frown her into insignificance, the General to control her, not her daughter's tearful eyes to fill her with an uneasy sympathy. "We shall have everything our own way then," thought she; "and then it will be my turn to frown on the haughty Jacquetta. And Jane, poor girl! shall certainly not marry this man. There's my Lord Montjoy coming down in the autumn; we'll choose a better match for her than this Conyers Freemantle, whom, after all, I never did like!" The ornaments of the ceiling might have been diamonds and rubies, so bright did they seem to the upturned vision of the pillowed lady. But we will leave her to her pleasant fancies, and look after the sterner realities of the night.

Jane all this time remained in her chamber in the deepest anxiety and distress of mind, believing herself the cause, though innocent, of this terrible event; and many and fervent were the prayers she put up that her uncle's life might not at this time be required from him.

In the General's chamber too was all agitation and anxiety. The lawyers sat together, pale and perplexed: the wounded man at one moment dictated to them what they should write, and the next broke forth into terrible imprecations on his enemy, then gave way to frantic passions, threatening to tear off his bandages—or lay back on his pillow, struggling with apparent agony of mind even more terrible than his bodily pain; the cold perspiration standing on his brow like drops of water, his features compressed, and his hands clenched and wrung together as if by a vice. The lawyers alternately gave place to the surgeons, and the surgeons to the lawyers declaring to the other that it was the most fearful death-bed they had ever witnessed. The work of the lawyers was at last completed; and the surgeons with pale lips and low voices declared that the most fatal symptoms had appeared, and suggested to him, that if he wished to see his relatives, or to see any other friend, it would be well to do it soon.

"I know how it is!" said the General in his customary bland voice—so different to what he had lately spoken with, that the surgeons started to hear it;—"I know how it is, I shall die!—I shall die!" screamed he forth in the high key of his fury, as if addressing some far off being—"I shall die!"

"Fetch me here a minister of the Church of England," said he, in a tone of absolute command: "and are you furnished as I ordered, Mr. Mortlake!"

The gentleman in question assured him that his commands had been attended to. The surgeon besought him to be calm, as he endangered his life by these efforts.

"Fools!" exclaimed he, in a tone of increasing irritation; "you know I cannot live!"

He then ordered additional lights to be brought, and the surgeons, thinking he was about to receive the sacrament, assisted the valet to arrange the room.

The minister entered, and the General bade him take his place at the right hand of the bed.

"Bid Mrs. Asheuhurst, her daughter, and Mr. Conyers Freemantle to hasten thither," he said in a hurried voice.

Again the surgeons prayed him to be composed; and the clergyman in his most persuasive tones began to speak of the holy calm of his spirit.

"Fools!" again exclaimed he, waving them back with a voice and gesture of infinite contempt.

The three who had been summoned entered: Mrs. Ashenhurst weeping violently, both from real agitation of feeling, and the effect the whole scene had on her nerves. Jane heard nothing, saw nothing, but her uncle; all past annoyances—all past provocation was forgotten; she saw only the generous, munificent relative who had raised them from obscurity to unbounded affluence, and who now lay at the point of a horrible death, as she believed through her own indirect agency.

"My beloved uncle," said she, falling on her knees at his bedside, and kissing his hand tenderly, "pardon me if I have ever displeased you—if I have been the means of your suffering thus!"

"Rise, Miss Ashenhurst," said the General, interrupting her; "the time is short—rise!"

Jane obeyed trembling. The General took her hand, and looked fixedly in her face. "I have loved you, Jane," he said; "you will find that I have loved you—you must now obey me!"

The calm, low, sweet, tone of voice in which this was said, overcame her, and she wept bitterly. He then took the hand of Mr. Conyers Freemantle and joined it to hers. Both started—a sudden revulsion seemed to turn Jane's heart to stone; she would have withdrawn her hand, but it was too firmly held.

"What hinders it," said the General, "that these two be not even now united in matrimony?"

The second lawyer produced a special license and ring, and the clergyman stepped forward.

"No, no!" screamed Jane, snatching back her hand; "it shall not be—it cannot be!"

Mr. Conyers Freemantle besought her to consent. "Jane!" said the General, in a tone that touched her soul; "I am dying, and I beseech of you to marry this man!"

"I will not!" said Jane, passionately, "I cannot—indeed I cannot!"

"Tell me not of inclination! tell me not of love!" said he, in a deep solemn voice, as if she had spoken of them; "tell me not of passion! It is a dying man who warns you not to trust in these things—it is a dying sinner who warns you that these things have brought damnation to his own soul!"

Jane felt as if her existence was withered up before these blasting words. A silence like death was in the room—the General sank back upon his pillow, and the surgeons rushed to the bed.

For five minutes he lay in one of those convulsions of mental agony which seemed to rack him like an instrument of torture; and Mrs. Ashenhurst venturing one glance on his distressed and distorted countenance, shut her eyes and buried her face in her handkerchief.

General Dubois seemed angry when he woke to the presence of so many spectators.

"Come, come," said he, starting up in his bed, "what folly is this? Reverend sir, do your office. Mr. Conyers Freemantle, you must receive your bride from my hands."

"Brother," said Mrs. Ashenhurst, "delay it, I beseech you, till your recovery!"

"I am dying!" he exclaimed, "and thou knowest it, woman!"

Mrs. Ashenhurst felt like a crushed worm.

The clergyman stepped up to Jane, and prayed her to comply with "the not unreasonable wishes of her dying relative." Mr. Freemantle attempted to take her hand, Jane put him back, and knelt at her uncle's bed.

"Ask my submission—my obedience, in any way but this!—for with this I cannot comply!"

The General made no answer, and Jane prayed fervently in spirit that this great trial might pass from her.

"It will never be done if it be not done now!" said the General, in a low, awful voice, indistinct beyond the bed, and which no one heard but herself. A deep thankfulness filled her soul, and she rose from her knees.

"No! no!" cried the General aloud, but in a broken voice; "it is only thus that I require obedience! It must be now—I am dying—it must be now!" said he, again sinking back on his pillow. Again the alarmed surgeons flew to his bedside.

"Jane!" shouted the General, again raising himself suddenly,

"For God's sake, sir, compose yourself!" said the surgeons. "Mr. Freemantle!" shouted the General, "on your soul, promise me to marry my niece!"

"I promise!" replied he.

"My friend," said the calm voice of the clergyman, "leave these things for the higher concerns of your immortal soul!"

The surgeons consulted quickly together. Mrs. Ashenhurst, her daughter, and Mr. Conyers Freemantle were requested to leave the room. Lockjaw and paralysis had come on, and immediate death was apprehended.

In the course of the early morning, General Dubois expired. Mr. Freemantle, after proffers of the most willing service, retired to Berkeley Square, and Mrs. Ashenhurst retired to rest. Jane's heart meantime was agitated by the most conflicting sensations and emotions;—sincere thankfulness to Heaven that she had been delivered from this hateful marriage, while she deplored with tears the awful cause of its interruption. Self-reproaches filled her spirit for many a bygone rebellious feeling towards her uncle, and then came rushing over her mind the memory of many a gift nobly given, and the poor girl wept with an entire abandonment to sorrow. Sincere, and earnest, too, were the prayers she put up to the Throne of Grace on his behalf. The proud sinner who cared not for his own soul died not unpleaded for; and mercy, perchance, abated somewhat of his penalty for her sake!

The curiosity of Mrs. Ashenhurst respecting the General's penitential garments, or whatever the mystery might be, was only the more stimulated by finding that the surgeon who had first attended him was bound to remain with the body during the performance of these rites which the dead require, and were performed by the confidential valet and an old woman, a perfect stranger to the household, introduced by the surgeon for the purpose.

All Mrs. Ashenhurst could learn was, that the cartilage of the nose had been pierced, and appeared at some time to have suspended a ring, and that one toe of each foot had been amputated. The surgeon never left the body until it was enclosed within its shell.

XX

Of course the sensation which the death of General Dubois, and the occasion of it, produced was immense. Sir Harbottle Grimstone had left London, and fled no one knew whither: it was conjectured that he had gone abroad. But neither with the public nor with Sir Harbottle have we any immediate concern.

The beatific vision which Mrs. Ashenhurst had indulged in her chair was no little deranged by this closing scene in the General's life. It was evident that, from some unknown cause he not only favoured the suit of Mr. Conyers Freemantle, but was extremely anxious for its accomplishment; she did not doubt, therefore, but that its accomplishment was rigorously provided for in the will—perhaps the very heritage itself might depend on that condition. This new view of the case, therefore, of necessity altered again the tortuous line of her conduct: for the present, at least, Mr. Conyers Freemantle must be treated as the son-in-law elect—all future conduct towards him would depend upon the will. "Besides," argued her entire selfishness, "better far that Jane should reject him herself, if rejection is possible. I stand committed with my friends the Cornburys, and their countenance will matter nothing to her with the new connexions she will form; but there is no reason why I should needlessly affront my old friends."

It was late the next morning when Jane woke from the heavy sleep into which she had fallen long after daybreak. It was a melancholy waking to the business of the day. Her first thoughts were of him who but a few hours before had been so full of life and strength and passion, but who now lay a disfigured corpse in a near chamber;—of him who had so fearfully passed from time to eternity amid the agonizing conflicts of a troubled spirit, violent and unaccomplished wishes, and severe bodily suffering—like an angry sun setting among tempestuous clouds. No wonder that her spirit felt sad and desolate: yet, as her mind became accustomed to the awful strangeness of these events, she could not but take a hasty prospective view of her suddenly altered fortunes; but, unlike her mother, there was no general plan of conduct to be altered. She had no doubt but that she was the heiress of her uncle's immense wealth; she had no doubt, either, of his strong desire that she should unite herself to Mr. Conyers Freemantle: but she felt that a high and holy duty—higher and holier than mere obedience to wishes unexplained and apparently capricious—forbade such a union,—nay, though the very inheritance itself depended upon it; for, in common with her mother, she thought the will might restrict her as to marriage; and yet, when she remembered the muttered words of her uncle, "that the marriage never would take place if it remained then unaccomplished," she felt a strong persuasion that it would leave her free as regarded *him*, and for this she was thankful beyond the power of words. She determined, therefore, that since nothing could be positively decided till the will was known, though she would avoid Mr. Conyers Freemantle as much as possible, and give him no reason to expect other than her decided rejection, yet she would make him the cause of debate and misunderstanding with her mother.

Mr. Conyers Freemantle, too, had his thoughts. Jane's coldness—her avoidance of his presence—the horror with which she shrank from his touch, had all roused his self-love to the direst pitch of resentment. Love, admiration were gone: what he craved after now was revenge!—and revenge he vowed to himself he would have in performing the promise made to the dying man, assuring himself that Jane was bound by the will to marry no one but himself.

Never had Mr. Conyers Freemantle felt so strong to act, so filled with determinate character before. He went to his bed in the full intention of his purpose, he rose with it equally energetic. He moved, he looked, he spoke unlike himself—unlike the man of uncertain purpose, who had hesitated hithterto, and puzzled himself in the mazes of his own feeblemindedness. He was great in this one purpose of accomplishing revenge upon the despiser of a Conyers!

Lord and Lady Cornbury could not but observe his altered demeanour; but they, good, easy people, thought it was all in the nature of things—he had so much to think about, he had such serious business on his hands; but they were glad to see him so cheerful!

Miss Jacquetta Freemantle knew better than they; she knew that no ordinary cause could have wrought him to this pitch of decision, of earnestness, almost fierceness of eye. He had determined with himself to stand alone and take counsel with no one in the unwonted strength of his new energy—especially he meant that his sister should have no hand in it; but the wily Jacquetta compassed him about with her snares, and, before he was aware, she was possessed of his secret. It was little that the haughty Jacquetta spoke; but that little confirmed her brother in his purpose, and established an entire working together through the future of this affair. Jacquetta was satisfied—her brother, too, was in her power; and she then sat down to luxuriate on the meditated body-and-soul subjection of their intended victim.

The morning of the General's death, Mr. Mortlake, attended by the confidential valet, set off for Denborongh Park, to carry thither the melancholy tidings, and to take possession of the place.

Lord and Lady Cornbury, apparently more interested in Mrs. Ashenhurst and her daughter than ever were full of attention and kindness; and the Honourable Miss Jacquetta Freemantle, in her haughtiness, condoled on the melancholy event.

General Dubois was to be buried in the tomb which he had built for himself at Denborough Park, and Mr. Conyers Freemantle undertook to accompany the body on its stately homeward journey; while the Cornburys, with Miss Freemantle, proposed returning to Wilton at the same time that Mrs. Ashenhurst and her daughter returned to Denborough Park. The whole journey was to be accomplished as speedily and as secretly as possible.

Mrs. Ashenhurst merely remained in London to give orders respecting the mourning dresses which were to be sent after them; and, in two days' time, Jane found herself travelling on the road by which she had so lately arrived in London. How different was that time and the present! "Surely never," thought Jane, "did contrasts so sad and singular meet in any life before! So lately as he was with us travelling upon this very road, who now will follow us—a corpse. Again, not twelve months past, we two who now sit side by side, so sat when we were driven from Harbury, on our journey to Denborough Park!" A deep melancholy fell on her spirit as she mused on these things—on this mingled retrospect, and all it brought with it, more splendid than consoling, much fuller of sorrowful experience than of even passing gladness.

Mrs. Ashenlhurst, too, was deeply occupied by her own meditations; but they were entirely prospective, and very little varying from her former meditations. It is true that occasionally they were diversified by the recollection of Brian Livingstone, and Jane's pertinacious and determined attachment to him; but then she consoled herself with the thought that the prohibition which sundered them in the General's lifetime, no doubt would be in full operation even after his death, through his will. But, cogitate as she would, puzzle herself with difficulties as she might for a time, the result was always satisfactory; her daughter was the heiress of General Dubois!

That Mrs. Ashenhurst felt either regret or sorrow for the death of her brother, now the agitation and first shock were over, may by no means be asserted. Still, a feeble sort of conventional mourning pervaded her manners and mingled with her conversation. She looked the melancholy gentlewoman most gracefully, and with inimitable propriety alluded to the "dear deceased," her "poor, dear relative," and her "late loss." Nothing could have been more unexceptionably supported than the character of mourner through the journey: while she internally congratulated herself on always being said to look well in mourning, especially as she had not to assume the weeds of a widow, and that the handsome mourning dresses which had been ordered for Jane would become her beautifully, especially since her countenance had so much more thoughtful an expression. But perhaps the most interesting subject of thought and speculation with Mrs. Ashenhurst we have yet omitted—the access she should now assuredly get into the mysterious chamber, together with a knowledge of what the chest contained.

Let us, therefore, pass over the remainder of the journey, and even their drive through Harbury—so different from the last, and yet withal a species of triumph to Mrs. Ashenhurst, inasmuch as they were the objects of intense interest, and appeared to be now going to the fall possession of their glory, even though under a temporary cloud.

All this we shall leave, and accompany Mrs. Ashenhurst, the morning after her arrival, into the General's apartment.

It was with a palpitating heart and a timid step that she entered it, as if fearful of making palpable the invisible presence which even then might lie within its walls. The room itself was no way extraordinary, furnished, like the rest of the house, with the utmost attention to luxurious ease; yet this very absence of anything peculiar to fix the mind upon seemed to give a suspicious character to the most common of its furniture. In what apparent respects did the easy-chair in which he had reclined seem different to the one in her own chamber? Yet she shuddered at the thought of sitting in it, in the same way that one who suspects poison shrinks from a cup of sparkling wine. But, of a veritable truth, the mysterious chest, of which so much had been said, stood at the bed's head, barred and cross-barred with iron, as if it secured the wealth of a kingdom, or held within it an evil genius! Mrs. Ashenhurst did not dare to lay even a finger upon it. The guilt, the mystery, whatever it were, was connected, she doubted not, with the contents of that chest!

As she more calmly considered it, when the first excitement of the discovery was over, she was surprised to see, that though to every other chest, and cabinet, and lock in the room, the seal of Mr. Mortlake was affixed, this was without. Here was a strange subject of speculation. Had Mr. Mortlake in very terror forborne to acknowledge it as a part of the General's property, or had the imprisoned mystery defied the bondage of a human seal? As she was thus pondering in a state of highly-excited curiosity, the door immediately before her, not the one by which she had entered, slowly began to open. She saw the noiseless turning of the lock-handle and the opening advance of the door with the freezing horror of one who believes himself in the coming presence of a spectre. The door opened scarcely one foot's space, and the figure of the valet presented itself. Seeing her before him, he appeared not less astounded than herself, and was about to make a hasty retreat. Mrs. Ashenhurst, who instantly suspected the man's design to be the searching of this mysterious chest, which he had purposely kept from the knowledge of Mr. Mortlake, bade him come forward.

"Robert," said she, with great severity, "you are detected! come forward!"

The man obeyed, pale and trembling: he had the nabob's keys in his hand.

"What are the contents of this chest?"

"I—I know not, my lady;—indeed, my lady, I never saw!"

"Your design was to see—and the keys are now in your hand!"

The man looked like a thief caught in the act.

"Have you courage to open that chest?" asked she. There was something in the question, or in the tone in which it was put, that reassured him.

"If you wish it, I can try, ma'am," was his answer.

"Have you ever seen it opened?"

"No, ma'am; General Dubois only opened it of nights, ma'am—and there was something queer about it; I never could shift it then, though he *could* easy enough; and now one may move it and welcome," said the valet, as if willing to bribe his lady with information which he had tact enough to see she was eager to obtain.

"Do you, then, say it is light?"

"No, ma'am, not light, but so as a man may move," said he, shoving it half an inch along the floor.

"Open it!" said Mrs. Ashenhurst.

The valet selected a key, and applied himself to the task, as if this was not the first time he had practised the mystery.

The sensation at the heart of Mrs. Ashenhurst cannot be told, as she saw the terrible lid about to move—about to reveal whatever mystery lay below it;—nor can any one easily appreciate the coolness and self-command with which she turned to the valet, as she compelled herself to look in—throwing the whole onus of the search upon him.

"You see, sirrah!—a human skeleton—are you satisfied? Close it instantly! and fetch hither Mr. Mortlake to affix his seal!"

The artifice was successful; the valet, confounded and ashamed, closed the chest in humble submission, gave the keys into her hand, and went to do her bidding. The keys dropped from her hand with perfect loathing, and she struggled with a horror that crept to her very heart; here then was the mystery of iniquity—the miserable remains of a human body!

"This chest, sir, awaits your seal!" said she, with a desperate calmness, as Mr. Mortlake entered the room.

"I have looked in vain for that chest!" he replied; "having received from General Dubois especial orders concerning it."

The tongue of Mrs. Ashenhurst clove to the roof of her mouth; and Mr. Mortlake, taking a paper from his pocket book, read in the General's handwriting—"I, Francis Dubois, solemnly enjoin upon those who commit my dust to the grave to lay also with it a certain iron chest, standing at my bed's head—and that, unopened, as it remains; as they trust to their own souls' repose!"

"See that it remains inviolate," said Mrs. Ashenhurst as she left the room, disappointed and yet filled with a new and horrible subject for mysterious wonder—wonder, too, which she was bound to keep in her own breast, and which she believed the valet, for his own credits would also conceal. The valet, however, disappeared from Denborough Park that day, decamping, it was imagined, with treasure to an untold value, the jewels of carbuncle reputation never being found. The immediate pursuit of him was unsuccessful; and subsequent events diverted the attention of all parties to even more momentous subjects of interest.

XXI

We will now pass over a space of ten days, and then look into the saloon the morning after the sumptuous funeral had been performed; assuring our readers that the nabob's magnificence in life was not disgraced by his consignment to the tomb, and that, together with his crimson-velvet-covered coffin, went into holy earth the other mysterious remains in their iron bondage—no small sum being paid to the church for admission, and that only on the secret assurance of Mrs. Ashenhurst to the bishop that it contained merely human dust, according to her solemn belief.

In the saloon, then, which was hung with black velvet, sat in her graceful mourning Mrs. Ashenhurst, full of the dignity of place; Jane Ashenhurst, beautiful, most touchingly beautiful, and solemnly interested as she was in all that went forward; Lord and Lady Cornbury, slient, and with countenances as placidly unmeaning as ever; the Honournble Miss Jacquetta Freemantle, and her honourable brother, who already looked round in proud anticipatory possession of this stately mansion, its great wealth, and its fair mistress;—all likewise in mourning.

Below them, and at a table, sat Mr. Mortlake and his brother lawyer, who had come down for the occasion; "An unnecessary expense," said Mrs. Ashenhurst; "but he had insisted upon it, and he came." There they sat, like solemn judges at a tribunal, the tied-up and sealed document before them, which they seemed reluctant to open.

"It is is a painful duty which devolves upon me—an extremely painful duty," said Mr. Mortlake, as he slowly broke the seals, and then held the open parchment in his hands.

The assembled company started; but Mrs. Ashenhurst thought it was merely a form of words with which this gentleman prefaced such an office.

The whole room was a hush like death, and the deep voice of Mr. Mortlake read, as if the parchment spoke from the tomb—

"In the name of God, amen.

"I, Francis Dubois, sound in mind, but wounded to death by my enemy Sir Harbottle Grimstone, Bart.—whom may the fiends confound!—seeing I am summoned from the deeds of the body to the judgment of the soul;—

"I, Francis Dabois, on this the twenty-seventh of May, in the year of our Lord seventeen hundred and—, in my hired house in Grosvenor-Square, make this my last will and testament, to the cancelling of any former will or deed whatsoever.

"My house, park, lands, manors, situate in the parish of Denborough, in the county of —; together with whatever furniture the house contains, and whatever treasure in jewels, bullion, or coined money may be found in any chest, cabinet, or under any lock whatever—excepting the iron chest which stands at my bed's head; together with my Indian spoil and articles of wearing apparel, my plate in daily use, and whatever the plate-chest, standing in the butler's room, also contains; several pieces of gold and silver brocade, silk-stuffs, and velvets; rings, buckles, and other personal jewels; clocks, cabinets, statues, and pictures, all and sundry which the house contains, excepting the iron chest aforesaid;—my carriages, horses, harness, and whatever is contained within my stables, carriage-houses, stable-yards, and stack-yards; together with all implements of husbandry whatsoever;—in fine, all my real and personal property whatsoever and wheresoever found, saving and excepting what is hereinafter named, I give and bequeath—" Mr. Mortlake wiped the perspiration from his brow—"I give and bequeath, with my eternal curse, to Sir Harbottle Grimstone, Bart. aforesaid—"

Jane started to her mothers side, who, with a scream of horror, fell back in a swoon.

"My good sir!" exclaimed Lord Cornbury.

Mr. Conyers Freemantle started to his feet, and protested that it was beyond his comprehension.

Miss Jacquetta looked on Mrs. Ashenhurst and her daughter in cruel triumph.

Lady Cornbury opened her eyes and wondered what it meant.

"Be calm, dearest, dearest mother!" said Jane, as Mrs. Ashenhurst started up in frenzy.

"This is a colleaguing with Sir Harbottle Grimstone!" said she. "The will, Mr. Mortlake, is a forgery!"

"Madam," said Mr. Mortlake, calmly, "the disposition of the property was not less astounding to myself than to you; and therefore I required the assistance of my friend Mr. Villars, and his presence at this trying moment."

"The will shall not stand, sir!" said Mrs. Ashenhnrst, in haughty indignation. "Read on, sir, and let us hear what further iniquities it contains!"

Mr. Mortlake bowed, and read on.

—"Not from love or favour make I this bequest, but from the eternal hatred I bear him the said Sir Harbottle Grimstone, Bart, and for the sake of the hatred I conceived for him when we first met; and because I know of a surety that these things which are bequeathed to him by myself, Francis Dubois, can never do him good: on the contrary, that certain ruin, misery, and perdition will cling to him who inherits them, to him and to his heirs;— wherefore, lies among the great secrets which the judgment-day will reveal—for this reason shall the inheritor be mine enemy Sir Harbottlc Grimstone, Bart, aforesaid; and hereby I am revenged."

"My good sir," said Lord Cornbury, "my unfortunate friend could not have been in sound mind."

"Certainly not" said Mrs. Ashenhurst, "here are evident signs of insanity!"

Mr. Mortlake shook his head. "Mr. Villars," said he, "you can bear testimony to this subject!"

Mr. Villars declared it to be his solemn opinion that General Dubois was of perfectly sound mind; there was no evidence whatever to the contrary—nothing, in fact, could have been cooler or clearer, or more collected, than his conduct during the whole time they were together.

"But," said Mr. Mortlake, "I foresaw this suggestion, and obtained therefore the evidence of the medical men on this subject." He produced a paper signed to the same purpose by both surgeons.

Mr. Conyers Freemantle stood leaning with his two palms on the table, Mrs. Ashenhurst likewise remained standing, Lord Cornbury drew his chair to the table, and Mr. Mortlake taking up the parchment again read.

"To my sister, Katherine Ashenhurst, widow of Captain James Ashenhurst, of the Life-Guards, deceased, I leave—nothing——"

Jane again started to her mother's side; but her mother put her back with indignation. The face of Mrs. Ashenhnrst was first crimson, and then deadly pale, but she stood firm.

"Read on, sir!" she said.

A laugh-like sound was heard from the chair where the haughty Jacqnetta sat. Lord Cornbury was the only person who turned round to notice it.

"Read on, sir!" repeated Mrs. Ashenhurst, as Mr. Mortlake still paused.

"—I leave nothing, because her weak mind can submit to all circumstances, and she has already assured me of cheerful submission."

Mrs. Ashenhurst still stood calm, though the crimson again mounted into her face, and she would gladly have sunk into the earth, and though again the triumphing laugh of Miss Jacqnetta Freemantle sounded through the room.

"To my niece, Jane Ashenhurst, daughter and sole child of the aforesaid Katherine Ashenhurst, I bequeath the sum of ten thousand pounds funded property, being the fruit of honourable military service in the colony of Madras."

"This," said Mr. Mortlake, "is the substance of the will; and then follows a more circumstantial reiteration of the whole, mainly intended for the secure bequeathing of his landed and other property to Sir Harbottle Grimstone, which it would perhaps be unpleasant for you to hear."

"Does not my name occur in the will?" asked Mr. Conyers Freemantle.

Mr. Mortlake either did not hear or did not choose to answer the question. "Sir Willoughby Doyne and Mr. Fawcett," continued he, "are there named as executors, and, at my instance they wait without for admission; but it appeared to me better," said he, "that you should know the nature of the will first—their presence might have been unpleasant to you."

"We are extremely obliged, sir," said Mrs. Ashenhurst, in scorn and indignation; "but this precious document shall never stand!"

"Madam," said Mr. Mortlake, "you deceive yourself!"

"The will is certainly unjust, sir, and a most extraordinary will, sir!" interrupted Lord Cornbury; "Miss Ashenhurst is unquestionably the true heir!"

"My dear lord!" said Mrs. Ashenhurst, the floodgates of her excited feelings opened by his apparent sympathy, "is it not a cruel will?—is it not a most unfeeling, a most absurd will? If it could be set aside," said she, in a confidential tone, addressed as much to Mr. Mortlake as to Lord Cornbury, "my daughter would be heir-at-law. Cannot it be done?"

Mr. Mortlake shook his head.

"Oh, sir," continued she, compelled to speak plainer, "the law can do anything—such things are done every day: what need to say anything of this will—this absurd, this ridiculous will at all? What claim has Sir Harbottle on our property? Nothing need be said of this will—we are all friends here together. Gentlemen, it shall be worth your while!"

"Dearest mother, no!" said Jane.

"Madam, madam, you are mistaken," said Mr. Mortlake, hastily; "this is such a thing as *the law* cannot do. My good lady, I beseech you to think of what you are suggesting!"

"Is there no mention of me in this will?" again asked Mr. Conyers Freemantle.

"Of you, sir!" exclaimed Mrs. Ashenhurst, turning the wrath upon him which she dared not pour out on the lawyers; "and what right have you to suppose you are mentioned in the will?"

Mr. Conyers Freomantle both looked and felt chagrined, but he kept his eye on Mr. Mortlake.

"Your name, sir, does not occur in the will at all!" replied the lawyer.

"Humph!" said the disconcerted gentleman, and began to wish himself away.

"The will shall not stand," again said Mrs. Ashenhurst, forgetting the temporary diversion of her thoughts; "the will shall not stand if there is a power on earth to set it aside! It is an iniquitous will!" repeated she, in a voice approaching to frenzy.

"Mother," said Jane, "let us withdraw."

"Gentlemen," continued Mrs. Ashenhurst, disregarding her daughter, "if there is power on earth to do it, this will shall be set aside!"

"Madam, I wish you joy of your legacy," said Miss Jacquetta Freemantle, rising, with the most withering scorn, herself more mortified and chagrined than she had ever been before,—I wish you joy of your legacy, madam!" and with a laugh she swept out of the apartment.

Lady Cornbury looked round like one aghast when she was gone, and taking the arm of Mr. Conyers Freemantle, she went quietly out after her; he glad of what seemed like an excuse for his withdrawing.

"Let us leave the room, dearest mother," again said Jane; "Sir Willoughby Doyne will do what is right—his lordship will do what is right!"

"Go, if you will!" replied she, in violent anger; "but I will stay!"

Jane withdrew to her own apartment—her own no longer—and sat down to contemplate this strange termination of their vision of splendour. Surprise and disappointment she certainly felt, and an unpleasant consciousness of the world's coming wonder and idle pity; but her greatest concern was on her mother's account, to whom this was worse even than a death-blow. The agony of her feelings was a deep, living sympathy with her mother: for herself,

Jane knew there could and must yet be happiness and blessings in store; but for her, thus insulted—thus degraded—thus stripped of what made all the glory and desirableness of life—there seemed nothing but darkness and death.

What took place in the saloon after Jane left it, we know not: in an hour's time Mrs. Ashenhurst was supported to the room where her daughter sat, in violent hysterics. Rage the most ungovernable succeeded her restoration; she was frantic with disappointment and anger; and Jane, bewildered and terrified, knew not what to do. The Cornburys were gone, and as hour after hour passed on, and no message came from them, either of condolence or sympathy, Jane began to suspect that yet another cutting pang, the neglect and desertion of friends, would be added to her other sorrows.

In the course of the evening, Mrs. Ashenhurst, exhausted with the vehemence of her excitement, sank into a profound and death-like sleep, which might have been mistaken for death, but for the spasm-like starts which shook her whole frame at intervals. Jane sat by her mother's bed alone, and no wonder that, as the deepening twilight filled the chamber with yet heavier gloom, the full bitterness of this disappointment—the peculiar difficulty of their situation—fell sadly on her spirit. She felt that they were objects of strange and vulgar wonder to the very domestics; that they had been cruelly, wantonly betrayed by their relative;—they had been mocked by the presence of their enemies, as she deeply felt the Freemantles to be;—they were deserted by their friends the Cornburys;—and now, with no one to counsel, no one to sympathise with her, she sat by the bed of her mother, who already seemed fallen a victim to this cruel shock. At this very moment her maid informed her that a gentleman waited in the saloon to see her: he had refused to give his name, but said he came from Harbury, and wished particularly to see Miss Ashenhurst.

"Good heavens!" thought Jane, "can it be Brian Livingstone? What a comfort—what a mercy—if it be!" She consigned her mother to the watchfulness of her maid, and, with a beating heart, hoping and fearing, hastened to the saloon.

The saloon was lighted up as usual; but its black hangings gave a general sombre effect, and for the first moment she did not see who awaited her. A sound of low whistling, however, the next moment directed her to an Indian screen, within which stood the unshapely figure of Mr. Parkinson, resting on his two stout legs, set apart to command solidity of base, and his arms a-kimbo, in the act of surveying the room. What an unpleasant apparition!—What a revulsion of feeling! Mr. Parkinson, instead of Brian Livingstone! Jane felt sick at heart, and would have stolen back as silently as she had entered, but at that moment he faced about.

"Oh! Miss Jane! why, I didn't hear you come in! How do you do? Bad job this of your uncle dying! I was just travelling this way, and thought I must look in on you. Zounds! it's a bad job!—Well! and how's my old friend Mrs. Ashenhurst?"

Jane replied coldly that her mother was not well.

"Egad, Miss Jane, you have managed badly somehow, to let the old fellow leave his money from you in this way!"

"Mr. Parkinson," said Jane, "my attendance is required elsewhere,— I must wish you a good evening."

"Oh, no offence sure, Miss Ashenhurst,—no offence, I hope; but you see this is a thing everybody talks of. Why, they've got the story at Wood Leighton there, as pat as can be; and I'll tell you what now,—there's a pretty little house of mine at Harbury as will just suit you—moderate rent."

"I must wish you a good evening," said Jane, with apparent indifference, and left the room, feeling now indeed the humiliation of this event. Her heart was full to overflowing; nor did she return to her mother's bedside till she had wept away some of the excess of her feelings in her own room.

"Hollo!" said Mr. Parkinson, seeing her gone; "why, bless my soul, she's touchy! Ha, ha! this is a pretty coming down, after all my lady's airs!"

"Sir!" said a footman, entering.

"What! I shan't see Miss Ashenhurst again, shall I?"

"No, sir?"

"Oh, very well!" said Mr. Parkinson, doggedly, as he walked slowly down the room, looking first on one hand and then on the other. "Why, you'll have a new master here soon," said he, at length.

"I know nothing about it, sir," was the footman's reply.

"Oh, very well!" repeated Mr. Parkinson, and began to hum a tune. "I should think young man, you'll hardly suit Sir Harbottle," said he, at length, in vexation, as the footman stood with the door in his hand.

"Sir, I'll thank you to take your leave!" said the man.

"Oh, very well, sir!" returned the visiter, in great wrath; "but you'll please to remember, sir, that I am a gentleman."

Scarcely was Mr. Parkinson gone, when Jane was informed that Lady Doyne prayed for an interview with her. There had been a general good understanding with Sir Willoughby Doyne and his lady, but no intimacy, and Jane questioned for a moment whether this might not be an additional insult which her strange fortune subjected her to; but then she remembered that this lady was the friend of Mr. Vigors—and, so remembering, granted the interview.

Lady Doyne was a clear-headed, straightforward, kind-hearted woman, and without apology or ceremony, or referring in the remotest manner to what had occurred, introduced her errand: Sir Willoughby and herself prayed Mrs. Ashenhurst and her daughter to remove for the present to their house.

Jane thanked her, but hinted of the Cornburys.

"The Cornburys," said Lady Doyne, without explaining herself; "are cold-hearted, selfish people; and I have reason to believe, my dear, that you will not find a home at Wilton."

Jane started; but she remembered the Freemantles.

"I speak advisedly, my dear Miss Ashenhurst," said Lady Doyne, in her business-like manner, and Jane forbore to ask any explanation.

We will not go through the arguments used to induce Jane to accede to her proposal. She did succeed, and then remained through the night in the chamber of Mrs. Ashenhurst; Jane the while forgetting her own personal distress in anxiety for her mother, and filled with admiration for the thoughtful, unpretending, frank-hearted kindness of this Samaritan neighbour.

The next day Mrs. Ashenhurst, in the same lethargic state, was removed to the house of their new-found friend—no message, no token of kindness or care, having reached them from Wilton; but Jane, hearing from Mr. Mortlake that his lordship was gone to a great cattle-show, and her ladyship about to visit a long-neglected seat at two counties' distance, to which the Freemantles were to accompany her—an unheard-of journey for Lady Cornbury.

Let us now hasten over a space of many weeks, leaving untold, for the present, what occurred next at Denborough Park; leaving the world's wonder at these strange events to go by unspoken of; nor will we toll of the devoted attachment of several domestics who prayed to follow the altered fortunes of Jane—many a poor hired servant bears a truer and a nobler heart than the friends of our prosperity;—and saying nothing of the deep and desolating sickness of mind and body which lay heavy as death on poor Mrs. Ashenhurst; nor will we tell the fearful suspense of Jane's watching, nor will we tell the unabated kindness of Lady Doyne.

We must now look in upon a small, quiet residence, many, many miles from the scenes of these latter events, and there find our former Mrs. Ashenhurst, emaciated, shorn as it were of her former honours, the pride and strength of her life gone, a melancholy ruin of her former self, weak in body, and with a total oblivion of memory as to the later years of her life. She is seated, as is her daily wont, in an easy-chair, with the Book of Common Prayer on a small table before her, from which she reads the lessons for the day many a time in the course of the day, and, saying but little, seems yet to take an almost cheerful interest in what passes, however trifling the event. There too sits Jane, the good, dutiful daughter, who, self-forgetting, tended her through her melancholy sickness with holy watchfulness, and now devises a hundred little schemes to amuse and diversify her monotonous life.

Mrs. Ashenhurst and her daughter, even after this cruel destruction of their hopes, were not poor; the gifts alone which they had received from their relative, of themselves, constituted no ordinary wealth; and now, in the elder lady's debility, they were passing rich. At the earnest desire of Jane, Sir Willoughby Doyne had obtained for her this home among strangers, where, unannoyed by passing events, undisturbed even by familiar faces, recalling memories which it was only tranquillity to forget, she might devote herself to her mother, and gather about herself, in humble thankfulness, the blessings and amenities of life which yet abundantly remained for her, in unabated strength, clear and even strong intellect, bright imagination, highly-cultivated taste, and above all, in the holy and cheerful resignedness of her spirit, and its entire trust in Heaven. And here within this new home she had gathered about her her favourite authors, her music, her flowers, her birds. She was not less beautiful than formerly; though, with a beauty somewhat less brilliant and joyous, her countenance, like her spirit, was calm. She feared little, now that her beloved mother was restored to her, and little also dared she hope; though her mind many a time reverted to pleasures which she believed never could return, lingering on them, and retracing them, and feeding her soul with visionary things which often left her sadder then they found her.

So sat Jane one afternoon in November, watching the last gleams of red sunlight on the yet unfallen leaves of a young beech-tree, but occupied less by those outward objects than by thoughts which they produced through some mysterious association, when Brian Livingstone again stood at her side. Jane started as if she had seen a spectre, but the eloquent blood spoke a welcome on her cheek and forehead.

"Thank God!" exclaimed Jane involuntarily; "but who told you we were here!"

"I heard it all from a friend of yours," said he, taking her hand tenderly: " owe this happy meeting to that noble follow Vigors."

Jane again blushed deeply.

"Thank God, we can yet be happy!" said he, clasping her in a long embrace, and impressing the first kiss he had ever given her upon her glowing forehead: it was such an embrace as a husband might have given a much-endeared wife. Oh, the perfect happiness of that time! Holy and chastened as their love was from long disappointment, they met, not as lovers for the first time meeting and embracing, but as most dear, long-tried, and long-parted friends. The misery of the past seemed at once annihilated by the present fulness of joy; and, in the midst of their heart-happiness, Livingstone told how Mr. Vigors had sought him out in his foreign wanderings, and joined him at a cottage by the Lake of Geneva; that the most entire friendship had grown up between them, and thence he had come to know the sacrifice which Jane had made for his sake; and at length, through information Mr. Vigors had received from his friends in England, himself had returned now to claim the happiness which in so great a measure he owed to his noble friend. It was not without emotion that this was either told or listened to; and so the lovers lingered and talked, and lingered yet, till deep twilight had made the colours of the beech-tree one mass of shade.

"Is that Mr. Brian Livingstone's voice!" said poor Mrs. Ashenhurst from the inner apartment, rousing herself up from a nap into which she had fallen. "Do bring him in, Jane; it is so long since I saw him!"

"We have a pretty place here, Mr. Livingstone," said she, when he was seated beside her; "a far prettier place than that at Harbury; a much better house, and more servants too. We only wanted you and dear Mrs. Burgoyne to make it perfect. I am very glad to see you!" and she again offered him her hand.

The tears started to his eyes as he heard her speak thus; but he felt it was in mercy she was thus afflicted. What pain and humiliation were spared her by this oblivion of mind!

And now for weeks and weeks the two rolled on a succession of happiness. Let us again look into this boudoir-like apartment, with its unostentatious comforts and elegancies, on the happy group that sat there one bright morning in April.

"I had such a dream last night of white favours and gloves, of bride-cake and a wedding-ring!" said poor Mrs. Ashenhurst. "I really am glad your wedding is going to be so soon, Jane!"

"We are all glad, dear Mrs. Ashenhurst," said Augusta Livingstone, with an arch smile and bright laughing eyes, a very Euphrosyne in youthful beauty and gladsomeness.

"And so I am to go to Bath with Mrs. Burgoyne—did you say so, Jane, love?"

"Yes, my dear mother; so she wishes, if you do not object."

"Oh dear, no, love—I should like the journey of all things. And you say she has a good house? It must be twenty years since I was at Bath. I shall like it of all things!" And so saying, she turned again to the Prayer Book.

"And pray when is this Mr. Vigors to come?" asked Augusta of her brother,

"He will be here this evening," was his reply.

"And he really is so very handsome?"

"Wonderfully so; and yet unlike any handsome man I ever saw."

"I shall never like him!" said the merry girl. "If you would bespeak my aversion for any man, tell me he is handsome. I hate your handsome men: they have no heart—no sense; they love nothing—they think of nothing but themselves! I never saw a handsome man that I could endure, except yourself, Brian."

"Mr. Vigors is very like Brian," said Jane Ashenhurst.

"Nonsense!" exclaimed Augusta, laughing. "The most charming man I ever saw—the most gentlemanly, the most sensible, polite, and at the same time the most ordinary—was my old favourite, Sir Garton Jellicos. He was a perfect gentleman! I had serious thoughts of proposing for Sir Garton myself, only there was Lady Jellicos in the way—dear, good old lady!"

"Mr. Vigors!" said the servant, opening the door and ushering in that gentleman.

What a happy meeting was that of these friends! and had a spectator stood by, he would have instantly seen the impression which that noble countenance made on the hitherto sceptical Augusta Livingstone; she was a convert in half an hour, though she maintained her old opinion in merry wilfulness all the next day. Mr. Vigors did not meet her as a stranger; he knew her frank true-heartedness, and many a high quality of mind, from letters addressed to her brother; and a few weeks made, as my readers may perhaps already have anticipated, two happy couples instead of one. A few months more, and poor Mrs. Ashenhurst dreamt of another wedding on the eve of accomplishment. And so let us leave them— noble, loving hearts, rich in their own exceeding happiness!

PART II

THE WORKING OF THE CURSE

I

IT WAS A FULL FOUR WEEKS after the death of General Dubois, while Mrs. Ashenhurst lay, to all appearance sick unto death, in the house of Sir Willoughby Doyne, and the Freemantles, sister and brother, unable to avenge the affront put on a Conyers, were giving way to that mutual ill-will which thenceforward became a life-long quarrel; while Mr. Mortlake was sending forth his missives and his emissaries, not only through England, but even on the Continent, in pursuit of the lost legatee; that Sir Harbottle himself, in the ordinary dress of a small farmer—blue coat, flowered waistcoat, corduroy breeches, and boots—took up his abode at the Half-Moon, a small public-house in one of the most retired and out-of-the-world dales in Yorkshire.

It was not an unpleasant life that the baronet led here, giving himself out to be one Mr. Joseph Pickup, a country gentleman's steward, who had fled from the wrath to come in consequence of an amour with the gentleman's only daughter, mystifying his simple-minded landlord, honest Master Cumber, with stories of the wonderful beauty and cruel fate of his fair Mary Ann. Sir Harbottle talked and drank with whatever chance guests came to the house; joined the will-peg and nine-pin players, and beat them on their own ground; angled in the brook below for trout; and when nothing better was to be done, sat down with Boniface within the wooden kitchen-screen, over a brown jug and tankard, to talk over those ideal love troubles in which the landlord—honest man!—took a wonderful interest. So sat they on the sixth day of Sir Harbottle's sojourn, when Daniel Neale, with his wallet on his back and his staff in his hand, walked into the open kitchen of the Half-Moon.

"A long life to ye, and a happy one, and may ye never know want!" began Daniel, as he crossed the threshold. The next moment he recognised Sir Harbottle. "Now may the saints save us both!" exclaimed he, throwing off at once the whine of the mendicant; "may the saints save us, and give us a happy home in Paradise! And is it too that am the happy man to bring ye the news?"

"What! is he dead? or has he given his consent?" asked Master Cumber, his head full of Sir Harbottle's love story.

"You've heard then?" said Daniel.

"No, the deuce, not I!" said Sir Harbottle: "what is it, old fellow?"

"May the saints be about ye, and take away the curse that sticks to the gold! but you're heir of General Dubois! He's gone to his reckoning, and, as I hope to sit down with the blessed Saint Patrick himself, nobody's remembered in his will but yourself!"

"And Miss Mary Ann—is nothing said of her?" asked the compassionate Boniface.

"That's clear beyond my knowledge," said Daniel.

"Daniel," said Sir Harbottle, "this news of thine is somewhat of the strangest: thinkest thou that thy head is of the soberest?"

"Now the Blessed Mary herself help me," returned the beggar, "as what I have told your honour is true; and, more by token, see here what this bit of newspaper says;" and he handed to Sir Harbottle a crumpled and dirty fragment which he had gathered up in his wanderings.

"Now, by jingo!' shouted Sir Harbottle, striking his fist on the table till it danced again, after he had read the paper, "this is the primest bit of good luck that ever came to a fellow of my inches! Thou art a made man, Daniel: give us that old hoof of thine!" and Sir Harbottle shook the beggar's arm till it seemed hardly a part of his body.

"Give this old fellow to eat and drink the best that the house holds," said Sir Harbottle; "and harkee, Boniface, I must have thy shandry as far as Skipton this blessed day! By Jove, we'll have rare doings before I'm a week older!"

"Well, Mr. Joseph, I hope you'll do what is right by the poor young lady; if so be that her father has left you the money, it could only be that you should marry her!"

Sir Harbottle laughed, and swore, and drank, and roared forth songs of riotous jollity in the excess of his triumphant merriment, till honest Master Cumber thought "of a certainty he was gone clean mad!"

In less than an hour the shandry, a most primitive vehicle of some two hundred years old, but the only available carriage within ten miles, stood at the door under the conduct of the one-eyed boots of the Half-Moon, who was to bring it back; and into this vehicle, which creaked and swayed under his vigorous person, mounted Sir Harbottle, after he had kissed the rosy girl who served at the Half-Moon, and promised her a blue ribbon for a keepsake; and kissed even the fat Dame Cumber herself, in the midst of her tubs and steam, as she stood brewing for harvest; leaving the perturbed landlord unenlightened as to his intentions respecting the disinherited and much-suffering Miss Mary Ann.

"I thought there had been some good in the chap," murmured the discomfited Boniface, as he trailed a chair after him to the open door, where the beggar was regaling himself at an entertainment for which Sir Harbottle had amply paid; "but I fear me he'll not do the right thing after all."

"As to that," said Daniel, after he had taken a long draught of "the jolly good ale and old," "it's more than I can say; neither sir Harbottle, nor his fathers before him, have been much famed either for right thinking or right doing."

"What a thick-head thou art!" said Master Cumber, disdainfully; "I'm talking of no Sir Tarbottle, but of yonder young fellow that thou hast sent off as if the devil drove him!"

"Ha! ha! ha!" laughed Daniel, on whom the potations were already taking effect.

"Dost not remember that this was Mr. Joseph Pickup?" asked Boniface, impatient of his guest's merriment.

Daniel laughed louder than ever. "Thou hast picked up a pretty story," said he; "ha! ha! ha! my fine cock-o'-the-hills. Mr. Joseph Pickup! ha! ha! ha! Sir Harbottle Grimstone, that's his Christian name, and surname to boot!"

"Sir Tarbottle Brimstone!" said Master Cumber, laughing in his turn; "Lord love us!—Sir Tarbottle Brimstone!—nay, nay, thou'll pass none of thy jokes on me! But, come, come, friend; you've good eating and drinking there, and I'll maybe find you a night's lodging, only tell me what you think he will do? Will he marry her?"

"What! Miss Ashenhurst?" asked Daniel, "the rose and lily of all England! No; by my consent, that he never shall!"

"Well, there never was such a tangled skein in this world before!" exclaimed honest Master Cumber, half bewildered and half angry: "dost thou say he ought not to do what is right by that poor young woman, and he got all her father's fortune? Goodness guide us! this is a beggar's honesty!"

"Look ye, master,' said Daniel, facing about on his seat, "I know more about these things than you do. I was with the General—Lord have mercy on his soul!—Christ have mercy on his soul!"—muttered he rapidly, and crossed himself: "I was with him, I say, in India, where this money was got; and I saw more than I should like to tell, or you would like to hear. That money, Master Landlord, for which a man sells his soul to the lowest pit of perdition, can do good to neither man nor woman; and Miss Jane Ashenhurst—may the saints love her and give her a good husband!—has had a lucky miss to be left with short-comings. If Sir Harbottle has got the purse, he takes along with it the curse; and there's a rhyme for you, and that's lucky."

"Well, it's clean past my understanding," said the puzzled Boniface.

"I dare say it is," returned Daniel.

"And who is it, dost say, as has left him all this money?" asked Master Cumber.

"General Dubois, of Denborough Park, in the county of S——; and a power of money it is."

"And Miss Mary Ann?" asked the landlord, doubtingly; "that is not her real name, is it?"

"Why, no," said Daniel; "I know of no Miss Mary Ann in our parts."

"*What* dost call this chap?" asked Bonifnce, after a long pause, in which Daniel renewed his attacks on the brown jug and the eatables, and poor Master Cumber had vainly tried to disentangle his bewildered brain.

"Sir Harbottle Grimstone," returned Daniel.

"Brimstone!" said Master Cumber: "it has a queerish sound with it."

"Ha! ha! ha!" laughed Daniel; "thou art a rare scholar! Brimstone! it'll do, it'll do!"

"Well, I must tell my missis," said the honest man, rising; and, before long, Daniel heard a great uproar among the brewing tubs, occasioned by no less an event than the anger of Dame Cumber, who vehemently resented the transformation of Mr. Joseph Pickup into so dubious a personage as Sir Tarbottle Brimstone.

"Begone with you for a nincompoop!" shouted the provoked Dame Cumber, flinging the wooden bowl which she had just been using after her retreating spouse; "begone with you for an old dunderhead, and dont come here slandering honest men with beggars' lies.

"What! and so he's a great gentleman!" said the rosy maiden of the Half-Moon, as she again filled Daniel's jug, and had received from him this strange intelligence. "Well, for certain," added she, blushing yet rosier as she remembered various gallantries that she had received at his hands.

"What do you stand canting here for?" exclaimed the angered landlord, willing to pour upon her the wrath he did not dare to retort upon his wife: "off with you to your scrubbing and scouring—a lazy baggage!"

"A great gentleman and a baronet!" murmured the retreating maiden to herself. "Well, it's maybe no better for me—but, for sure, he'll remember the ribbon—I would not be without a keepsake!"

Master Cumber again sat down. But let us leave him and Daniel Neale to clear up this entangled story as best they are able, and hasten now to the county where the return of Sir Harbottle was so eagerly desired, and where, as we may imagine, nothing can exceed the interest and anxiety which his absence excited. Many, too, were the ineffectual means used by his friends—and everybody seemed his friend now—to discover his retreat. Daniel Neale, however, as we have seen, was the first to carry him the tidings, as if he had some mysterious connexion with the nabob's gold.

Sir Harbottle's domestics were all alive. Morning, noon, and night, their business was to look out for their mister; and, among them all, none were more deeply interested, none more warmly eager for his return, than his poor follower Dummie; and before we introduce Sir Harbottle to his home, to which, at this very moment we must imagine him advancing with the utmost possible speed, a word or two must be said on this his humble dependant.

In the very earliest years of Sir Harbottle's manhood, his mother had a fair maiden named Judith, whose rustic beauty drew the admiring gaze of the young profligate. Like many another trusting heart, she was deceived; and the righteous Lady Grimstone, Sir Harbottle's mother, amazed at the damsel's folly, to which she gave a harsher name, cast her forth upon the world, holding up her pious hands at the awful depravity of the sex "now-a-days."

The poor young woman went forth, no one knew whither; and bitter must the hardships have been which she endured, for when, in three years, she returned to the native village of her betrayer, no one recognised her: she was apparently a care-worn, sorrow-stricken woman; resolute, and stern, and sad; and with her came a deaf and dumb child, her little Edmund, for whom with determined courage she laboured night and day, taking him with her to the harvest-field, or to the gleaning, in almost sullen self-dependence, unbeholden to charity and thankless for compassion. The poor mother made no friends, and she wanted none; all the tenderness and kindness of her heart were centred in her child. Little Edmund, unlike his mother, was a creature of universal sympathies; and, loving all, all loved him in return: in frame he was robust; and, notwithstanding his natural defects, possessed of much personal beauty, with a most extraordinary quickness of intellect. His eye was intelligent and full of observation, and, with a sort of intuitive knowledge, he seemed to understand whatever was transacted before him, while his imitative powers and his manual dexterity were so great that he succeeded in all the little arts or devices he attempted. But his ruling passion was for dogs and horses; and as the hounds and horses of the Grimstones, always renowned Nimrods, were ever before his eyes—for the poor mother, from some unknown cause, established herself near the park-gates, though herself never entered the demesne—Dummie, as he was familiarly called, leaped from his mother's arms at the neigh of the horses or the bark of the hounds, or toddled out in his young independence to clap his hands for joy as his favourite quadrupeds passed in and out, or to seduce by his caresses some strong or sleek sagacious hound to play with him, or to lie unfrequently with him in the sun, in which way they were not unfrequently found together asleep.

This passion for the four-footed race attracted the attentions of grooms and stable-boys, and poor Dummie was indulged with many a ride and many in introduction to stables and kennels of which neither Lady Grimstone nor his mother knew anything. The lady at length died, and then the boy, eluding his mother's eye, and disobedient only in this respect, lived half his time among the grooms at the hall.

When Sir Harbottle came to the estate at the death of his father, he found Dummie a fine, well-grown lad of ten years old, active, bold, and enterprising, the favourite of huntsman and jockeys, a privileged person both in stable and kennel. The favourite racers and hunters neighed to see him, and the hounds wagged their tails and laid down their sleek ears at his approach. Sir Harbottle himself caressed the boy, and he, in his turn, felt for Sir Harbottle the strongest attachment. Could poor Dummie have opened his heart to his mother, he would have talked of the baronet as a faithful, affectionate dog would speak of its master, had it the power to do so. His attachment was like that of the animals, a blind, indiscriminating love. His eye brightened at his presence; he watched his motions, and anticipated his wishes; he was aware of his coming by some unknown instinct, and ran forth to meet him, to hold his horse's bridle, to hold his stirrup, or perform any office whatever, apparently sufficiently rewarded by the consciousness of serving him, and overpaid by a smile, or any passing token of approbation or good-will. It is true, that, like a dog's, his treatment was often not the gentlest; he was the meek recipient of much of Sir Harbottle's wrath, drunken or sober; he was sworn at, menaced, and even beaten by his master, but he resented it not. Though evincing to every one besides a spirit which would brook neither insult nor wrong, to Sir Harbottle he was attached, faithful, and submissive. In return, Sir Harbottle gave him as much love as was in his nature to bestow; he loved him like his dogs and his horses. Though poor Judith kept herself as much aloof as heretofore, she no longer forbade her son's going to the hall. "It is his father's house," said she to herself; "and, though I will never ask for a drink of water there, he has a right to as good as it holds!"

When Sir Harbottle left his home for London, poor Dummie drooped and moped about like a dog that had lost his master; he no longer seemed to take pleasure in the society of his old friends the grooms and jockeys; his only companion was Sir Harbottle's favourite horse, and his only pleasure fondling with the noble creature in his stall, and lying down to sleep under his manger. But when the whole country was astir with inquiries after Sir Harbottle, Dummie went out east and west, north and south, in search of him, aware, in spite of his natural impediments, that some great and desirable event awaited his coming.

The morning after the day with which this chapter opened, Dummie rose up at earliest dawn, and, scarcely allowing himself time to take a hasty breakfast, set out from his home, as if filled with a new vivacity. His mother questioned him by signs, to him perfectly intelligible, as to the cause of his excitement; Dummie made her understand that Sir Harbottle was approaching, and, brooking no longer delay, ascended to a hill, and stood there looking northward.

"What a poor fool it is!" murmured Judith, as hour after hour she looked forth from her door, and still saw the speck-like figure of the boy standing on the hill.

Towards noon, poor Dummie, like the hound that again scents his master's coming, and bounds forward to meet him with joyful impatience, ran eagerly down the hill to the high road, just as the post-chaise came in sight which was conveying Sir Harbottle homeward. With the peculiar cry of joy which the poor fellow made in his moments of ecstasy, he hailed his master. Sir Harbottle welcomed him as the first confirmation of the good tidings; and, calling to the driver to stop, threw open the door, and, snatching him in, seated him beside him. Dummie looked into his face with his animated, intelligent eyes, kissed his hands and his feet, and when his impatient master reproved him for his troublesome joy, meekly and gently smoothed down his shoulder with almost imperceptible caresses, or rubbed against the laps of his coat as an affectionate animal might do in the ecstasy of its attachment.

Sir Harbottle Grimstone came home to find the amazing news true to the minutest particular; came home to find all the world his friends; came home to sit down at Denborough Park, its sole lord and master.

A jovial man was Sir Harbottle; and three days after his return he made a feast in his house which was to be like the feast of a king. "Whatever is this day eaten or drunk," said the joyful heir, "shall be produced from the new heritage—oxen and sheep, fish, flesh, and fowl." Wine and strong drink, whatever furnished forth the potations of the day, Sir Harbottle vowed should be furnished from the nabob's spoil.

Poor Dummie, like all the rest of the household, was full of activity and bustle; and, on the third night after Sir Harbottle's return, accompanied the gamekeepers to take fish from the ponds in Denborough Park. The night, at first still and heavy, with an electric atmosphere, became towards morning wild and terrible, with a tremendous storm of thunder. The whole sky was a vault of blackness, momentarily torn asunder with fierce, red, jagged lightning; and the never-ceasing thunder rumbled, and pealed, and echoed from one horizon to the other. The men sheltered themselves through the fiercest of the storm; but Dummie, whose want of hearing closed his soul to what makes the principal terror of a thunder-storm—the appalling sound—exulted in the wildness of the night, and the sublime and terrible beauty of the lightning. As the morning advanced the storm abated, and the gamekeepers and their attendant fishermen, together with Dummie, sallied forth to take up their night-lines from waters which lay in one of the deepest glens of the park, hidden among old oaks and birches. But no sooner had they reached this place than the storm again collected, concentrating its fury over the hollows in which they stood, as if the very elements resented Sir Harbottle's takmg possession of the nabob's wealth.

The storm had abated, and the morning sun shone out from a cloudless sky over the refreshed and dripping earth, when poor Dummie s mother, who, as we have said, had never entered within the park-gates since the day she was driven from the hall in her deep shame, was seen, to the amaze of her neighbours, with her cloak over her head, and in the greatest possible agitation, hastening up the park. Without ceremony or leave-asking, she rushed into the house, and onward to the breakfast-room, where at that early hour she encountered Sir Harbottle alone, taking his morning meal.

"Where is my boy? exclaimed she.

Sir Harbottle recognised the voice, though the person had long been forgotten. "Bless my life, Judith," said he, "where have you sprung from?"

"Where is my boy?" again asked the frantic woman.

"What, in Heaven's name, do you mean?"

"Where is that poor dumb lad, your own son, Sir Harbottle?" said she, looking wildly round her. "Oh, he is dead! he is dead! I know it!" cried the poor woman. "I saw him this night dead in my dream."

"Judith," said Sir Harbottle, "is that boy——"

"Your son, Sir Harbottle; as I live, before God, your son and mine," said the poor woman; "nor should mortal soul have known it, but my agony has wrenched it from me. Where is my poor dumb child!"

Sir Harbottle leaned his head on his hand, and was thoughtful. "Come, come, Judith," at length he said, as she reiterated her question; "you are as foolish as ever: I remember your dreams formerly."

"Man," said the poor woman, with a voice and gesture of indignant severity, "am I come here to be taunted with those days? Accursed was the hour I saw you first! You were my ruin, and now you are the death of my boy. I dreamed it, Sir Harbottle. O Christ! and so dearly as the poor fool loved you!"

"Sit down, Judith, sit down; this is an idle dream," said Sir Harbottle, much disconcerted, and offering her money.

"I will never touch your gold, Sir Harbottle," exclaimed Judith; "I that have sorrowed and suffered unthought of, that have toiled and struggled uncared for, will have none of your gold. I ask nothing of your hands but my poor dumb boy. Tell me where he is, for I know of a surety he will die in your service."

"Upon my soul," said Sir Harbottle, "I know nothing of him further than that he went to the glen-pools with the men last night."

"I knew it," screamed the poor mother; "I knew that he was dead; I saw him drenched with water last night in my dream!"

"Sir Harbottle rang the bell.

"O the poor fool, the poor dumb fool!" muttered the mother, in heart-broken accents; "and he would run through fire and water for him; he would have worn his poor feet off for him; and burnt his fingers to the bone for him. o the poor dumb fool! and I knew all along that a curse would come."

"Where is Dummie?" asked Sir Harbottle of the servant who, after a considerable time, answered his summons.

"Oh, sir!" exclaimed the man in reply.

"I know it!" screamed the mother; "he is dead! O, my God, he is dead!" and so saying, she rushed past him, as if instinctively, through the well-remembered house to the courtyard, where, blackened by lightning and drenched by water, lay in truth the body of poor Dummie, which the men had just then brought in, and about which a throng of servants had gathered.

Sir Harbottle fell into deep cogitation; and as he sat, oppressed with sadder reflections than he had ever experienced before, the lamentations of the poor bereaved mother came sorrowfully to his ears.

The awful and sudden death of poor Dummie at this particular time struck all the domestics as an omen of evil, and especially as in her frantic grief the mother spoke mysteriously of the connexion between Sir Harbottle and her son. Sir Harbottle himself was disconcerted by the incident, and drank deeply that day to drown the remembrance of it. One while he poured out volleys of wrath upon all who came near him; again, he vowed with himself, in a fit of half-drunken pity and remorse, to repair the wrongs and bereavement of poor Judith with money, which, according to his ideas, was the universal panacea for heart-griefs as well as worldly wants; yet, in spite of his vows of reparation, his sallies of anger, and the potations he swallowed, like all his people, he thought it a bad omen; he remembered the nabob's curse; and this—the death of a poor faithful creature in his service, the child of the injured Judith—seemed like a seal to it. But Sir Harbottle was not a man to detain uneasy feelings, if it was in human means to dismiss them. A few days went on; the acuteness of this excitement wore off; the world thronged about him with congratulations and felicitations; the feast was holden; and poor Dummie was forgotten.

Sir Harbottle Grimstone sat a jovial man among his boon companions, feasting on the good things which the nabob had provided.

"And Heaven send me," exclaimed he in his elation, with a triumphant laugh, as he read to them from his copy of the will the motive of the bequest—"Heaven send me many such enemies, and many such curses!"

Deep and long was the carouse, and Sir Harbottle's oration to his friends was much in this style:

"Egad, I smell the old fox; I fathom the old boy's charitable intentions. He thought me an extravagant dog, and was resolved that I should not want means to take my swing and my destruction. But I will balk him. Yes, my lads, I will turn old man; I will set you an example of moderation and economy, such as few of your fathers can show. Oh, this blessed Godsend of Indian gold! what miracles shall it not perform on good English ground!

"Doubtless, the worthy nabob had many a pleasant vision of hounds and harlots, and the spending of substance upon riotous living, with a proper sequel of Jews and lawyers, and most melancholy means to patch up and support a broken constitution, a battered estate, and a conscience that, finding sly twinges and a continual crying to no purpose, took to downright slashes and stabs of a most deadly character. But not so! O majestic nabob! hadst thou ten tenements, I will make them a hundred. Hadst thou hundreds of acres, I will make them thousands. Thy copper shall become silver, thy silver gold, and thy gold as the very mountain of Ophir itself; and as for iron chests, in those days they shall be without end."

He laughed, and his comrades laughed; but this resolve, so merrily avowed, was in reality formed seriously. He had, reckless as he was, sufficient superstition to dread the curse denounced upon him in the possession of the nabob's wealth; and the death of poor Dummie, the sacrifice of a singularly attached being, and in truth his own son, at the very moment, as it were, of his entering on an inheritance so bequeathed, gave yet greater force to his feelings.

While Sir Harbottle and his friends thus caroused, the bereaved mother and a few neighbours followed poor Dummie to the grave; and the vulgar public, with quick sense of right and wrong, and ever ready to censure their superiors in rank, spoke in no measured

terms of the man who held a revel in his house the very day his
son was buried.

Sir Harbottle, sincere in his desire to repair, as far as money would
do it, the loss and sorrows of Judith, sent down his man to desire
an interview with her. The poor woman was busied putting by her
son's clothes into the little chest whence they could never more be
taken for his use.

"Tell your master," said she, with tearless eyes, still smoothing the
old coat her boy had worn, "that I shall not come at his bidding nor
shall I receive gold at his hands. I asked neither help nor pity in my
sorest need, and I ask them not now, and especially not from him.
Tell him to keep his gold to be a curse to himself, and his pity, if
pity he have, against the day when he may need it for himself. Tell
him I have not another son of whom I can be bereaved; I am utterly
desolate; and though he drank his wine with the drunken while the
poor dumb fool was buried, he may live to see the time when he
may wish the heads of his own sons as low as is the head of mine.
Tell him all this, young man, word for word, or bid him come down
to me and hear it for himself."

The lacquey turned on his heel, believing, as many had done, even
before the boy's death, that the woman was mad. The purport of her
message was delivered to the baronet; and though he laughed loudly,
and swore with a desperate oath that she was ready for Bedlam, it
only gave yet deeper energy to his resolve of counteracting the
nabob's curse by beginning altogether a new life.

II

To begin a new life, or, to use his own phrase, "to turn over a new
leaf," in the most effectual way, would be, Sir Harbottle Grimstone
knew, by taking to himself a wife. He accordingly looked round
among the ladies of his own neighbourhood, but no one of them
took his fancy. If he again thought of, or had still a lingering
passion for, Jane Ashenhurst, certain it is he did not again solicit
her hand. How or where Sir Harbottle met with the wife he

chose, is not for us to say; nor was it known to any of his friends; for great was the surprise of them all when it was given out that the baronet was about to bring home his lady, and to take her to Denborough Park, which would henceforward be his residence. Lady Grimstone made her appearance, without bridemaids, without any bridal attendant or ceremonial whatever; a calm, placid lady; young, but with the staid, sober demeanour of much more experienced years, and withal a Roman Catholic. Sir Harbottle's jovial friends were all thrown aback by the lady who thenceforth was to preside over the mansion; they foretold at a glance that all the jolly doings of the old hall at Knighton were at an end—and they were right. The next thing that was heard of was the dismissal of hunters and hounds: "A most prudent beginning," said every one. The old hall was then let, its furniture sold, the park farmed to advantage; farms were admeasured and relet on higher terms; supernumerary servants dismissed; borrowed money was paid off, and everything put into a train of the greatest possible order and sober regularity.

Courteous reader, by your leave, we must now suppose seven-and-thirty years to pass before we again resume this true history; and so supposing, after this lapse of time we will again look in upon the once-princely demesne of Denborough Park. The very turf of the park itself seemed to have undergone a change: the more distant parts were enclosed, and had already borne the harvests of many seasons; the luxurious herds of deer were gone, and in their stead cattle were grazing at so much a-head; the waters were some of them drained dry, and others overgrown with reeds and choked up with water-plants; all the oaks in the prime of their vigour were cut down, and the unbroken sunlight fell upon many a hollow which for centuries before had lain in the shadowy umbrageousness of its woods. Here and there, on the boundaries where the wall had fallen down, or palings were broken, the breach was defended with the most economical substitutes for the original material. The heavy tree-branches hung low over the richly-wrought cast-iron gates which made of old the principal park-entrance; the massy and deeply-cut stone pillars on either hand were green and weather-stained; while the stone lions-rampant with which they were surmounted were, the one hidden with the over growth of trees, and the other broken by some rude accident. Spiders, season after season, had spun their webs in the iron tracery of the lofty gates, and weeds and gravel encroached on their lower fretwork: all things showed that it was many a year since these gates had been opened. Advancing onward, by the very road by which Mrs. Ashenhurst and her daughter gained the house, the once marble-smooth gravel walks, winding among lawns and shrubberies, were now green and over run with a plentiful growth of weeds, which went to seed and sprang up thicker each successive season. The lawns themselves, rank and untrimmed as the common field, encroached with their seeded grass both upon shrubbery and walks; the once cheerful fountains were now dry, and the marble basins into which they had played unsightly with rubbish or matted with weeds; the shrubberies were wild, overgrown thickets, that told of many years of neglect. Immediately round the house might still be seen some feeble attempts at cultivation: the grass was mown once or twice in the year; the flower borders and shrubberies were roughly dug, and the branches of trees lopped, which would otherwise have impeded the freedom of walking. But the house itself told even a sadder tale of neglect than the surrounding grounds; the exterior had assumed that aspect of disorder and neglect which even the dry brick and mortar or stonework of a house so soon puts on: the woodwork was unpainted; the windows, many of them closed, and others, by their dingy, uncleaned appearance, spoke of discomfort and neglect within. Some, too, there were of the lower and more commonly used apartments, with cracked panes puttied at the extremities; or, if quite broken out, mended with paper, or more effectually with a wooden substitute.

Let us enter and observe the inmates. But our entrance must not be by the splendid, temple-like portico at which Mrs. Ashenhurst and her daughter alighted—it was many a year since it was in use; tall dandelions lifted up their globes of winged seed from the joints of the marble steps, and the carved door was bleached and weathered by the tempests of many seasons; the small, line-like crevice where the well-made doors folded together was filled with dust, and in the keyhole a spider had built its web. It was through a side-door leading to the less dignified apartments that entrance was now to be had. In all the rooms were yet to be seen abundant traces of the once regal plenishing; but everywhere the dominant spirit of sordid parsimony or of brutal misrule made itself felt: it was a degraded den of the most revolting features of the human character, ignorance and avarice, the superb appliances for luxurious enjoyment remained many of them in their tattered and tarnished grandeur, and others were put to uses far different from their original destination.

The history of the gradual steps by which the master of the mansion, the once jovial and lavish Sir Harbottle Grimstone, had advanced from retrenchment to parsimony—from parsimony into avarice—avarice absorbing and insatiable—it is needless to trace; seven-and-thirty years had seen the nabob's curse operate deeply and fatally by the very means Sir Harbottle had used to counteract it. Nor will we tell of the domestic strife and bickering, nor of the conjugal and maternal wretchedness, which had harassed and almost worn down the spirit of the much-enduring Lady Grimstone.

Their descendants were five: the three elder sons, Christopher, George, and Robert, all grown to man's estate, with the rude ignorance of boys, and the determined undisciplined vices of men. Sir Harbottle had soon become too penurious to pay for his sons' education at school or college, and when they again returned to their home they had far outgrown the influence of their mother. Lady Grimstone, from her own slender' funds, provided them for a while with pocket-money; but when, as Sir Harbottle's parsimony grew, and she was obliged to provide for herself and her younger children whatever was beyond absolute necessaries, and as the passions and propensities of the elder strengthened, and their expenditure proportionably increased, she was unable longer to supply them; they filched and eked out their own finances by means which would not have borne too close an inquisition, and which made a perpetual warfare between their father and themselves. They were lawless at home, debauched abroad, and rapacious harpies everywhere, regarding their father as a stingy tyrant, and he the while looking on them as so many vampires ready to suck his blood, and impatient for his death.

The daughter, Julia, had been entirely educated by her mother and the priest, Father Cradock, a poor but pious man, who circulated among the few Catholic families within three counties, and held at Denborough Park the threefold character of priest, preceptor, and counsellor,—at least with Lady Grimstone and her two younger children. Julia, in spite of the atmosphere of debased passion, of sordid and miserable contention, of fearful example and evil communication, in which she had breathed from her infancy, had grown up like a lily among thorns. At the time we revisit Denborough Park she was in her twentieth year; a fair and blooming girl, with a roundness and fulness of figure, a bright and buoyant style of beauty, that contrasted sorrowfully with the worn, anxious, and shadow-like appearance of Lady Grimstone.

The youngest son, Bernard, was at this time eighteen; extremely unlike his sister or brothers; pale, and with an attenuation of frame and face that told somewhat of delicate health, but more of a quick, restless spirit, which excited and agitated within. No one could have looked on Bernard without thinking of the sword and its scabbard: his eye was dark and piercing, flashing with a troubled light, as much the evidence of strong passion as of keen intellect; his mind was grave and meditative; his nature affectionate and deeply sensitive, alive to the least sentiment of kindness, but quick also to resent slight or insult. Like his sister, he had profited to the utmost by what little instruction their peculiar circumstances afforded them. He was the indefatigable pupil of Father Cradock while he remained at Denborough Park; but in his absence wandered in unparticipated solitude about the brook sides, or by the wild overgrown ponds in the park, with his angling-rod and his book, and often, instead of attending to either, sat absorbed for hours in visionary day dreams, fostering still more an idealism of mind which must eventually unfit him to struggle with the commonplace realities of the world, and leave him an easy prey to the designing, or the victim of certain disappointment. Both Lady Grimstone and Father Cradock designed him for holy orders—nor had Bernard himself opposed his destination: for the present, however, he was essentially a poet—a poet, though he had essayed but little verse. He saw everything with a poet's eye, he felt it with a poet's heart, and within his soul lay those unfathomed wells of sentiment and deep moral feeling which are a vitality to true poetry; at the same time that his temperament was that of electric passion. Much of all this at present slept, but the elements were there, ready to be kindled into being at a word.

Bernard Grimstone was a solitary enthusiast; neither his mother, his sister, nor Father Cradock himself knew as yet the susceptibility and depth of his feelings; yet to all of them he was extremely dear, and the source of much deep and almost painful interest. Of his son Bernard's existence Sir Harbottle Grimstone appeared to have no consciousness; the young man went in and out before him without attracting the least attention. His favourite son—in fact, his favourite child, in spite of his continual offences—was Christopher, his first-born; his affection apparently decreased in seniority; the spirit of avarice, as it had grown, lessened and deadened his natural affections, till his younger children might be said to claim no paternal regard whatever. If the world censured Sir Harbottle, such censure either did not reach him, or if it did, he was too callous to be affected by it: besides, the interests of his property, and the strict guard he was compelled to keep over all to preserve it from the harpy clutches of his sons—like the dragon-watch of his own golden apples—occupied him so entirely that he had no time to mix in general society. True it is, he was in the commission of the peace, and might be seen upon the bench and at quarter sessions; but except there, Sir Harbottle could only be found walking with sturdy steps, dogged countenance, and watchful eye, that peered with quick glances from under his shaggy grey eyebrow, as if looking out for a depredator under every bush or behind every tree on some of his broad manors; or when at home, busied over his strong escritoir with his multiplied bonds and mortgages, leases and immense rent-roll; with the strong ring which held his keys over his left thumb, while his palm held fast the keys, from suspicion and experience of lawless hands which were ever ready to seize upon these keepers of his treasure.

Lady Grimstone, naturally a retiring and domestic woman, with strong affections and quiet good sense, had, as we have seen, not sought society even at her first coming to Denborough Park; now, how much more would she have avoided it had it been pressed upon her! For years she had been struggling to counteract the growing avarice of her husband, and the profligate propensities of her elder children, and in acting as peace-maker between them and their father. Besides this was another deep and anxious work of love, the education of her younger children, whose dispositions, naturally different, filled her with intense solicitude, from the consciousness of their fearfully dependent state, when her declining health entirely failed her—a consummation she had looked forward to for years. Her sole counsellor in all her cares was the good Father Cradock—one friend, too, she had of her own sex, though subordinate to the priest. This lady, whose name was Constable, was the last and decayed remnant of a once proud old Catholic line, and lived with her son at the small and ancient house of Westow, whose lands adjoined, or rather were entirely surrounded by, those of Denborough—the last fragment of their once noble possessions, and one of the most insignificant jointure houses in the flourishing days of the family, and whence Mrs. Constable visioned to herself that the family was again to take root and spring forth into fresh glory through the talents and influence of her only son.

Far differently educated was the poor Walter Constable to the rich sons of his mother's friend. Mrs. Constable had husbanded her son's income, and hoarded from her own private purse, denying herself both indulgences and comforts, to obtain for her son the education of a gentleman. Father Cradock had been his early preceptor, and at fourteen, when he had acquired all that the humble priest could teach him, and far more than the roistering Grimstones had ever learned, he was sent to St. Omer's to complete his studies, and perfect himself in the arts of rising in the world—arts which his mother intended he should practise to the utmost. At three-and-twenty he returned to the old house at Westow, a profound scholar, an accomplished gentleman, the delight of his mother's heart and the glory of her eyes—active, enterprising, ambitious, with splendid connexions abroad, and offers of patronage from the first Catholic families in England.

Many a time, in the fulness of her maternal pride, was the heart of Mrs. Constable filled with a generous compassion and sympathy for her friend, doomed as she was to humiliation and sorrowful anxiety about her children.

"Poor woman!" said the self-satisfied mother, "how thankful I am that my Walter never caused me a moment's uneasiness!" and then, while she saw in fancy the certain degradation and misery of the young Grimstones, and their heartbroken mother, she luxuriated in sunny visions of prosperity which her son would assuredly gather about her declining years.

But week after week, month after month, went on of the summer after Walter's return, and, to his mother's astonishment, he seemed becoming indifferent about his future career; the at-first eagerly discussed plans of ambition occupied him no longer, and the letters of his most influential friends remained unanswered. She remonstrated, but his reply was an idle excuse. She then watched him narrowly; and the proud, intellectual Walter Constable might be seen angling in a beautiful brook that divided the lands of Denborough from those of Westow: she saw him carry out books of poetry which did not return with him; she saw him seated on the grass with Bernard Grimstone; and Bernard, the shy youth who had avoided her presence when she visited his mother, was now not an unfrequent guest at Westow. All this Mrs. Constable saw, but she suspected it was not all; and her suspicion was right: it was for

the sake of Julia Grimstone that the ambitious man trifled away a
summer among sunshine and green leaves; for her sake that even
more than a brother's interest warmed him towards her sensitive and
ardent-spirited brother.

III

A new existence opened upon Julia Grimstone from her intercourse
with Walter Constable. Her mind, full of natural refinement and
purity, had shrunk from the grossness and vulgarity of her elder
brothers, and from the sordid, selfish spirit of her father, turning
itself inward with an earnest, unsatisfied craving after companionship
with gentler and nobler natures; for though a close bond of union
existed between her mother and herself, Lady Grimstone, subdued
by long suffering, yielded to, rather than resisted, the difficulties and
annoyances of her lot, while Julia lived in a restless daily warfare
with them. In Walter Constable all that she had visioned and desired,
whether as friend, counsellor, or companion, was realized: his graceful
person and the easy polish of his manners, the frank simplicity of
his address, the lofty tone and purity of his sentiments, contrasting
as they did with those of her hourly annoyance, were, in the first
instance, irresistibly attractive; but when beyond this, on further
acquaintance, she felt the force of a strong mind, opening before her
new and extended views of all subjects of thought; when she heard
him speak on topics, of which she had only dim conceptions, as
familiar matters of every-day experience; she looked upon him as a
being of a superior order, come down, as it were, to irradiate the dark
sphere of her mortal existence. To him this profound reverence of his
intellect, which Julia in the simplicity and integrity of her heart took
no pains to conceal, was flattering. The admiration of a beautiful
woman finds its way to the heart of the deepest philosopher; and
Walter, be it remembered, was young, fresh from the seclusion of a
college, and with a heart peculiarly alive to the influence of beauty.
No wonder was it, therefore, that the docile pupil who sat by his
side, reading with him the same book, opening to him timidly the

speculations and fancies of her own mind, and drinking in his deeper knowledge with an undisguised and reverential admiration, became more to him than the mere pupil of his school-learning.

But the exact manner in which the passion had directly revealed itself is not for us to say. At the very time we introduce the youthful pair to our readers, they were lovers, and in the daily habit of meeting; sometimes wandering together through the hollows or by the overgrown ponds of the park; or to some dingle, open moorland, or secluded ruin in the neighbourhood: and often the deep twilight shadows gloomed over the landscape, or the summer moon shone out, before they turned their faces homeward. But the more favourite place of meeting, and which many and many an hour was spent beside, was an old ruinous summer-house, which in the bygone days of the Denborough Park glory had shown forth from the midst of its parterre and shrubbery on a wooded hill side, with its painted windows, its gilt vane, and an internal decoration of marble and ornamental painting, but which now stood a picturesque, half-ruinous object; its garden overgrown with weeds, and with but desolate remains of its shrubbery, in the midst of a growing plantation of younger trees,—the old generation of full-grown timber having been felled by Sir Harbottle when he came to the estate. Doubtless the place was sacred to the lovers for something beyond its picturesque character, its sylvan site overtopped by the vigorous growth of its trees, or for the extensive view over many a county which the hill-top commanded at twenty yards' distance. Thither their steps, as if by instinct, were mostly directed, standing, as it did, most conveniently at the very point where the two neighbour lands met, and whence it commanded a view of the two homes—Denborough Park, yet magnificent in its desolation, showing at that distance perhaps even a more imposing aspect than in its grander days, like an old picture darkened and mellowed, though somewhat damaged, by time and neglect; and the ancient though small house of Westow, built of dark brick, with its balconied and turreted porch rising like a low tower over the roof; its old arched gateway and its double avenue of venerable elms—the only timber of which its fallen fortunes could now boast, and upon which its possessors looked with pride and respect almost equal to their family quarterings, or the achievements of their renowned ancestor John Constable, by whom these trees were planted.

Week after week, week after week, went on of summer weather, and the blades of corn which the lovers had seen shoot from the ground were in ear, and the leaves which they had seen bud were now darkened into the monotonous green of the full-blown summer. Walter to all appearance and forgotten the schemes of busy life in which but shortly before he had been so impatient to engage, and Julia's home-griefs and vexations had lost half their power of disturbing.

Blissful were those days of first, unclouded, unreflecting love, when all happiness—all existence even—seemed concentrated in its consciousness.

The intercourse with this accomplished neighbour was not less delightful and beneficial to Bernard Grimstone than to his sister. Walter was of that order of spirits which, full of mind itself, enkindles and calls forth the mind of those about it. Never did Bernard feel himself so overflowing with bright imaginings, so conscious of his own intellectual power, or so much disposed to revere and yearn after intellectual beauty, as when, out in the open air reclining on the turf, or walking with him and Julia, linked arm in arm, he listened to, or conversed with, Walter Constable. At first, it is true, he had been cast back, overpowered and dazzled, as it were, by the exhaustless and varied stores of his mind—for in learning poor Bernard felt as a little child before him; but when his friend, who understood his character at once, and the peculiar tendencies and gifts of his mind, brought out and showed him wherein his own strength lay, commending and encouraging his genius, a new and brighter future seemed to open before him, easy of access and certain in its reward; at the same time an eternal weight of gratitude seemed laid upon him, and in the overflowings of his heart he made Walter the confidant of many a hope, many a day-dream, many an

ardent aspiring which he had believed but a few short hours before
were as the sacred treasures of a holy place, not to be revealed to
eye of man.

All this opening of the heart, this new sunshine of life, occasioned
a closer and more intimate union between Bernard and his sister,
and warmly and deeply did she sympathise in all those feelings
which had hitherto been locked up in his own breast with such
jealous care. Julia, the beloved, the chosen of Walter Constable,
ranked next, for judgment and knowledge, in the eyes of the young
poet, to Walter himself and sometimes even above him; for Julia
would be enraptured by the sentiment of a stanza, while the wiser
and sterner critic would demur about the rhythm of a line or the
propriety of a new phrase.

Such was the state of affairs when Mrs. Constable, who had looked
on with jealous eyes for some time, and forborne to reproach or
reason with her son, only from the hope that it was but a passing
friendship which would die all the sooner if unopposed, began to
think her silence wrong; and especially as, in confirmation of her
own suspicion, a rumour had reached her of the love between
her son and Julia Grimstone, at which her informant had arched
her brows and looked willing to wonder and talk if the lady had
given encouragement, which, however, she did not, being perfectly
satisfied with the hint. But when Bernard came next to Westow she
determined to sit in company with them, and even endure those
poetical rhapsodies and reveries with which she had no sympathies,
and then take the opportunity afterwards of representing to her son
the folly and imprudence of such acquaintance, and still more of any
closer connexion with the family. Accordingly, no sooner was the
resolve made than an opportunity occurred of acting upon it. Bernard
came to visit her son that very evening; and though she saw the
restraint which her presence imposed on him, and the distress visible
on his countenance as Walter commenced the customary topics,
still she sat by in silent irritation, pursuing with redoubled speed
her knitting—work in which she was everlastingly engaged, having
already knit, during the nine years of her son's absence, hangings to a

bed, chair and sofa covers, and, above all, a rug some four yards square
of worsted, curiously and elaborately emblazoning forth the arms of
the Constables, with all their quarterings, in colours proper—gules,
or, azure, and argent—in which lions pawed the air, and armed arms
displayed their daggers; and though the four-footed creatures and the
weaponed gauntlets did not materially differ from each other in form,
whatever they might in colour, and required verbal setting forth, still
it was a grand piece of work, and, fringed as it was with scarlet and
purple, made no inconsiderable show in the centre of the old black
and polished oak floor of their sitting-room, where it was laid down
in especial honour of her son, to be consigned again to lock and key
the very day on which he left Westow—the dark wainscotted walls
of the same apartment displaying divers renowned ancestors of the
family, grim and faded in their dull, gilded frames; among whom was
the gallant John Constable, with his well-used sword; and Blanche, the
lady of his second son, conspicuous for her angelic beauty through
the dimmed colours of the canvass.—But to return to Mrs. Constable,
who sat busied and troubled in this apartment. Her present work was
now a counterpane, in which she exhibited endless imaginings of
pattern, in every diversity of diced, diamonded, starred, waved, and
scrolled pattern—a very paradise of dainty devices, and which site
intented as a wedding present to her son's wife, when, after having
achieved greatness, or won the heart of some noble lady, the family
tree, like the banyan, again shot root, to become even greater than the
parent stock. For such a time this exquisite piece of work was now
preparing, and it is possible that the good lady felt somewhat jealous
that all this labour and pains, designed for some highly-dowered
and nobly-allied bride, might, after all, be bestowed on a Grimstone;
although Lady Grimstone was her friend, and the daughter, by her
own confession, an excellent young woman; but then, there was the
family! So thought Mrs. Constable, as she knit stitch after stitch, and
the point of the great diamond grew wider and wider, enclosing
within itself a succession of yet smaller diamonds, and then again
decreased to the opposite point. So thought she, always ending
with an exclamation against the awful disgrace of marrying into

the Grimstone family! How many diamonds were mined while she
fretted and listened to what seemed to her the solemn folly and high-
flown nonsense of the two young men, it is impossible to say—she
knit and drew out the needles, and began again, and yet the thing
went wrong; while Walter, in rich and finely modulated voice, read
the verses which Bernard timidly laid before him.

> "Away, vain power of song! why make the gift
> Of thy enchantments torture? Are there not
> Thousands who down time's smoothest waters drift,
> And curse the o'erflowing fulness of their lot;
> Flying from scheme to scheme, from spot to spot,
> In emptiness of soul? There launch the fire
> Of thy quick lightnings, let the dreary blot
> And blankness of their bosoms feel desire,—
> Why should my care-bound heart be tempted to aspire?
>
> "Oh, what a mighty and resplendent world
> Lies there around! Yet what avails it me?
> Like a sea-reptile in its shell upcurl'd,
> Whelm'd in the waves, half-conciously, I see.
> Abroad, abroad all natures wander free:
> The waters leap in gladness; wild winds ring
> On their far journeys; through the forest-tree
> The fleet birds glance with joy-uplifted wing,—
> Freedom, and light and bliss, visit earth's smallest thing!
>
> "The shepherd ranges the lone mountain proud;
> Blithely his furrow the poor ploughman sows;
> In wood and dell the labourer carols loud,
> As on his cheek the free wind freshly blows;
> Wildering delight the lowliest wanderer knows,
> For round him peace and beauty are dispersed:
> But me alone thy necromantic shows
> Beset in crowds—with sudden light they burst.

And mock my heart with dreams, and madden It with thirst.
"O for a glimpse of Ocean! the wild roar—
The fluttering breeze, like breath of distant lands;
The waves' glad riot on the rocky shore;
The calm blue stretch of far reposing strands!
Oh! the fair scene where livingly expands
The waste of waters that, with heave and bound,
Rejoice in their sublimity—the sands
Where the wild sea-flocks piping blithe are found,
Or send their lonely cries, blent with the billows' sound!

Stand not the lonely hills as they have stood
Through solitary ages? There the cloud,
From far lands sailing, loves to pause and brood:
There haunts the wind, and there the torrent loud
Shouts in its joy; the eagle circles proud;
There crouches the red stag; there roams the flock:
Why, why am I, as they, not thus allow'd
To climb their lonely ridges, and unlock

Thought's solitary flow, like waters front the rock!
"I pine for those wild slopes and glooms—I yearn
To feel the free winds of the heath; to slake
My thirst at waters that through moss and fern
Run sparkling to the forest-skirted lake;
Through morning dews and odorous dells to take
My joyous way, to where the northern seas,
Mid screaming wild-fowl, ever sounding break
Round isles which know no shade of summer-trees,

But mid the misty crags green lie the silent leas.
"My soul is haunted with the sights and sounds
Of the vast world; I hear, I hear the roar
Of the great ocean, whose delight surrounds
The glorious earth, and rushes evermore

With an immortal strength on every shore!
Rapt o'er its waters, on the spirit's wing,
What palmy hands my fancy doth explore,—
What sea-like floods, and forests tall that fling

Their spicy branches wide o'er no familiar thing!
"So dost thou, soul of Poetry, at will
Catch up and whirl me to all climes remote;
Through storm and darkness—through the arctic chill,
Like an unbodied essence do I float;
War's wasting myriads, drum and trumpet note,
And merchant-caravan, and city-show;
Here fleets, and there the famine-haunted boat,
Driven far, the terrors of the sea to know:
Man's pride and misery all before me come and go!

"I wake, and what am I? With closed eyes,
As the chain'd captive in time galley's hold
Dreams of free-footed winds and cloudless skies,
Till the chain pinches, and his fate is roll'd
Back on his bosom—so to thirst and cold
And darkness do I wake! These visions fair
Pass, and life's most unspiritual things unfold,—
Things which I would not—hopes I scorn to share—
And souls—can *they* be souls!—those drudges of low care?

"This, my friend, is in the true spirit of your art," said Walter,
as he gave back the paper; "and the versification is as good as the
sentiment: your images are not incongruous either. It is a noble
poem, Bernard!"

The tears started to the poet's eye, and his pale cheek was yet
paler, as he received the verses back, and heard the few words of
commendation. Much talk of poetry ensued, and poor Mrs. Constable
knit yet faster than ever, and wondered her son had no more sense.
No sooner was the young guest gone than she began:—

"I think, Walter Constable, you might find somethmg better to do than to fill that young man's head with such high- flown and sentimental nonsense! What good can all this verse-making and rhodomontading do for either of you?—can it alter the Grimstone reputation, or stand Mr. Bernard in the stead of a decent education?—or can it, I pray you, in your own case, answer those letters which have needed your attention these so many weeks?"

"He is a fine fellow!" was Walter's irrelevant reply. "What a fine intellectual head!—what a keen yet tenderly expressive eye! I have never seen the poet so beautifully marked in countenance and in mind as in this young man."

"And what good, I should like to know, can all this do for him, cursed as he is with his Grimstone connexions?" asked Mrs. Constable.

"Do for him?" repeated Walter. "It will raise him high enough above his connexions! The highest men in the land will be proud to connect themselves with him, if his future years fulfil the promise of his youth!"

"And I suppose, son Walter, you desire to connect yourself with his family, in anticipation of all this wonderful greatness!" said she, sarcastically.

The colour mounted to Walter's brow, self-collected and full of self-command as he commonly was.

"It is a cruel disappointment to me," continued she, "that you should thus waste your time and neglect your interests for the sake of the first fair face that comes in your way."

Walter looked displeased, but he still made no reply, and his mother again went on.

"Your education—an education worthy of an earl's son—has cost me many privations and much painful economy; but I regret it not—I would make even greater sacrifices for you! But now that you should neglect your natural advantages, and offend and neglect friends willing and able to seve you, and all for the daughter of a miserable wretch like Sir Harbottle Grimstone, the sister too of those profligates with whom any connexion would be like having the plague itself, is ingratitude to me—and for yourself, nothing short of absolute folly"

"Miss Grimstone," returned Walter quickly. "is guiltless of the crimes of her family; and the man who united himself to her would insure his domestic happiness."

"And pray, sir," replied Mrs. Constable, "what have you to do with domestic happiness for the present, further than you may occasionally find at this fireside at Westow? A public life, with its rich reward of wealth and honour, is what you must follow; for this your education has fitted you—and your talents, Walter, also, in an eminent manner, unless you abuse them over rhapsodical nonsense!"

"Which life would produce the greater sum of happiness," replied Walter, "I think hardly admits of a doubt."

"What!" exclaimed his mother, losing her patience, "will you indeed throw away those already splendid offers which solicit your notice, as if you conferred the honour by accepting, not your friends by bestowing?—will you throw away the patronage of the Marquis of A—?—and all, forsooth, because Christopher Grimstone's sister has bright eyes and raven hair! Son Walter, I might have neglected you, as these your friends have been neglected—I might have lived in bodily comfort, and as my station required—and yet you have been quite good enough to have matched with a Grimstone. Little did I think, while I condescended to economy which almost verged on parsimony— though, I thank God, it was not to lay up under lock and key like your friend Sir Harbottle—I little thought, son Walter, for what a poor reward it was done."

Walter sat with his arm folded and his eyes fixed on his mother's face, but without replying; and Mrs. Constable, drawing out her needles in her energy, continued—

"It is the extreme of folly thus to have entangled yourself. What business had you to engage the affections of Julia Grimstone!"

"I am master of my own actions!" retorted he, stung by his mother's words; "I have arrived at the years of discretion."

"Years of consummate folly, say rather!" replied the disturbed lady.

"You that have no means of supporting yourself must yet encumber yourself with a wife and family!"

"You are over hasty," said her son; "marriage for the present is out of the question. I hope before then to achieve some of the greatness of which you have had such bright visions!"

"An impossibillty—a pure impossibility!" exclaimed his mother. "No sooner will Lady Grimstone be dead—and her life is already as a lamp without oil—than Miss Julia must look out for a new home. Good God! what a dependant state she will be in! and who must provide for her? Why, yourself! This young man, too, whom you puff up with such empty and extravagant hopes, how, I pray you, can he contend with the gross natures to whom he will be subject?—you must provide for him also! You ought to have had a fortune rather in possession than one to make, with these dependants whom you have taken to yourself!"

Mrs. Constable had given a most impressive view to the subject, and Walter fell into deep thought.

"You are right," at length he said; "I have too long neglected my friends; the letters you speak of shall be attended to this day. I have deeply involved myself in responsible duties."

Walter sat down to address his honourable and his right honourable friends, and to declare his readiness to embrace whatever offers of employment, at home or abroad, they might propose to him. Mrs. Constable, in the mean time, re-arranged her knitting.

The letters finished, Walter laid them before his mother, for whose judgment he had the profoundest respect.

"Thank you, my son," said she, when she had gone through them; "you have now done your duty to yourself, and to me also; for, Heaven knows, you owe no duty to the one in which the other is not intimately connected."

"Let us not misunderstand each other," said Walter, taking a seat beside her. "These letters, or even my going abroad, do not abrogate my engagement with Miss Grimstone; whenever I am in a condition, as regards worldly prosperity, to marry, I am bound to her."

"I can but think it a precipitous step," said his mother, "and a most unadvised one; you had done far better to have kept free of any such engagements for the present, but most of all with this family."

"On the contrary," said Walter, "I esteem myself most fortunate to have secured such a wife, and such a daughter for you!" said he, taking her hand, and smiling in her face affectionately. "The long winter evenings, of which you made such pathetic complaints in my absence, would be short with a companion like Julia;—Julia, whom you have styled a sweet, lively, affectionate girl—of whom, too, you sent me such pretty pictures of filial duty and meekness and forbearance while I was abroad. You may thank yourself, dear lady," said Walter, laughing, "for my entanglement, as you call it; you had already bespoken my love for her!"

Mrs. Constable smiled. "No, no, I have nothing to say against her; she has, to be sure, been an excellent daughter; nor can I object one word against this young poetical friend of yours, nor their poor mother; but still it will require some time to reconcile me to the thought of your marrying a Grimstone!"

"You are an excellent, reasonable woman," returned Walter, "and I do not doubt your being perfectly contented with it."

So concluded this conversation, which, on Mrs. Constable's part, was begun with the design of ending the connexion with the Grimstones.

IV

In the foregoing conversation, Mrs. Constable had said two things which were very true—that it would take a long time to reconcile her to her son's marriage with a Grimstone; and that the life of Lady Grimstone was but as a lamp in which the oil is exhausted.

The first truth impressed itself again on her mind within the first hour after the apparent acquiescence she had been, in a manner, decoyed into by the concession of her son; and, thenceforth daily, nay hourly, were her struggles with herself to see this connexion other than foolish and impolitic, though she forbore to renew the subject.

The second truth, together with the consequences she had foreseen, at Walter's very next visit to Denborough Park, revealed itself as if to verify his mother's words.

Lady Grimstone sat in her large easy chair at the open window, to enjoy the sunshine, and the warm, fresh, and yet odorous air of the garden, into which she was now no longer able to walk. Julia was absent from the room; and while Walter stood by her chair, apparently observing the long, lithe sprays of a jasmine, starred over with flowers, which the breeze was lightly waving to and fro, he saw of a certainty that the head which had so long been bowed with suffering and sorrow would shortly neither know the one nor the other. In the pale and hollow countenance, Death had already done half his work; and Walter wondered how, hitherto, he had been so unobservant of this decay of life. A sentiment of the most profound sympathy and affection filled his heart; and wishing to amuse her by passing conversation, he pointed out the whitening of the corn upon the opposite slope of what had once been park, but was now converted into tillage fields, and which might be seen through an opening in the shrubbery.

"I see it," returned the sick lady; "it will soon be ready for the reaper; and, my friend, by the time that corn stands in shock, I shall be carried to the grave!"

"My dear lady!" began Walter, distressed at the application she had made of his words.

"Yes, my friend," she continued, "it will be so! I, like that very field, am ripening for the harvest, and shall be carried to last home before it is carried to the garner; my time therefore is short; then let me speak now what is so deeply on my mind!"

She raised herself in her chair, and Walter, impressed by solemnity of her manner, seated himself beside her in silence.

"May the Almighty Father and Preserver bless you for your kindness to my daughter and my son Bernard!" said she, laying her thin, pallid hand upon his arm. "I know, Mr Constable, the disgrace, the infamy—I speak plainly what I yet shudder to acknowledge— the infamy of a connexion with this house! And you, with your virtues—with your talents and your prospects in life—might look forward to an alliance of honour. May the Almighty therefore bless you that you have condescended to us!"

Walter endeavoured to interrupt her; but she motioned him to silence with her feeble, attenuated hand, and continued:—

"I know the extent of our obligation to you—I know the nobility of your heart, Mr. Constable, and it wounds me to the soul to think of the sacrifice you must make for our sakes; but, my friend, my whole life has been one of humiliation and self-denial; I have loved deeply, but have either received coldness and neglect in return, or have found myself, as now, unable to pour out on those I loved the essential and available blessing which they deserved and I coveted for them! I leave my Bernard and Julia to your care! God bless you with them! God Almighty, in whose keeping are the hearts of all men, open the heart which is now shut, and incline it towards them—touch the hearts which are now hardened, and turn them from sin, that they may no longer be a disgrace to the guiltless, and as a stumbling-block in their way!"

"Amen!" said the low voice of Father Cradock, who had stolen in unperceived and now joined them.

"Have I done well, Father Cradock?" asked Lady Grimstone.

"Yes, my daughter," answered he; and then turning to Walter, "Will you do these things?" inquired he.

"To the best of my poor ability, and so help me every good saint!" exclaimed Walter, fervently, taking from his breast at the same time a small crucifix, which he pressed to his lips.

"May the Father of Mercies, and the Mother of our dear Lord bless you, for the kindness which you have already shown to us, and for the kindness which is in your heart to show!" ejaculated Lady Grimstone in a trembling but earnest voice.

"Amen!" repeated Father Cradock.

Lady Grimstone sank back in her chair, apparently exhausted.

"Leave me, my dear friend," said she, at length, turning to Walter; "I am much spent, and the good father will remain with me."

Without seeking for an interview either with Julia or her brother,

Walter left Denborough Park with a deep sense of the serious duties laid upon him, and with an earnest prayer in his heart to be enabled to the utmost to perform whatever those duties required.

The days went on, and Mrs Constable's knitting many a time went wrong as she thought of this unwelcome connexion with even more than her unwonted disapprobation, hearing now, as she did, almost daily, of the declining health of the lady of Denborough Park, and watching with the closest scrutiny the grave and anxious countenance of her son, who seemed never to have regained his former buoyant-heartedness since the day of that conversation which we have recorded.

The lovers met not less frequently than formerly; but their meetings were short, and darkened by natural sorrow—no longer in the freedom of the ruined summer-house, or for half a day's ramble many a mile from home—but for the few minutes which Julia stole from attendance in her mother's chamber, spent in the wilderness of garden or shrubbery, or perhaps for a longer time in the stillness and shaded light of the sick room—mournful meetings, but meetings full of even more than ordinary heart-union.

Within two weeks after Walter had written to his noble friends, he received an answer from the Marquis of A——. The letter was the most gracious that patron ever penned. It expressed the entire pleasure which Walter's application had given him—and still greater, as at that very moment he could offer him employment which, he believed, would meet with his entire approbation. What it was, however, was not stated; but the patron went on to hint of the highest trust being reposed in him, of great emolmnent and honour, and proceeded to say that he should be at his country-seat in a few weeks, where he hoped Mr. Constable would join him, ready to enter upon his post immediately, supposing that the proposed employment accorded with his own views and wishes when it was made known to him. Beyond all this, the writer inquired in a postscript whether, among the clever and trustworthy young men of his acquaintance, Mr. Constable could recommend one who could act as private secretary to a noble man, and perhaps accompany his son abroad, less as a tutor than as a travelling companion.

Nothing could have been more entirely to Walter's satisfaction than this letter, promising not only himself honourable and lucrative employment, but enabling him at the same time to provide for his young friend.

Mrs. Constable herself was warmed into self-forgetting and generous enthusiasm on the occasion.

"Poor Lady Grimstone!" said she; "this will make her death-bed happy; and, to be sure, Mr. Bernard is a well-conducted young man; and if the whole family had been like him, there had been pleasure in knowing them!"

Walter took the letter with him, and hastened to Denborough Park, passing in his way through the very corn-field to which Lady Grimstone had given so ominous a character.—The ears were heavy and ripe, and, in spite of the good tidings he bore with him, his mind dwelt with sad meditation on the words of the dying lady. "What," thought he, as he entered the house and advanced along the well-known passages without encountering a single domestic, if she be even now dead!"

He passed Sir Harbottle's room, and opened the door softly to gather even there some knowledge of what he almost dreaded to know. Sir Harbottle, as usual, was sitting before his escritoir busied among his papers.

"Body o' me!" exclaimed he, huddling his papers together, closing the escritoir suddenly, and grasping the keys in his hand as they hung in the lock. "Body o' me!—Christie, lad! George! Bob! away with you!—Oh! Mr. Constable, is it you?" added he in a softer tone as he faced round to the intruder.

"How is Lady Grimstone?" asked Walter somewhat assured by the baronet's manner.

"I can't say, sir,—I don't exactly know, sir!" replied Sir Harbottle in the hurried voice of a thief guarding his booty, dropping at the same time a heavy bunch of keys, which he had disengaged, into his capacious pocket; "I really cannot say, sir; but you'll find somebody in her room."

Walter retreated from the miser's den, which he had never before entered, scarcely knowing whether he might understand evil or good from his words: and no sooner had he left the door, than he heard the lock turned and the bolts drawn, as if to intimate to him how unwelcome his intrusion had been, or to secure himself against similar incursions.

Walter paused at the door of Lady Grimstone's apartment. The sweet, cheerful voice of Julia reached him outside as she sang, Bernard the while accompanying her with the low tones of his flute. There was the most delicious assurance in these sounds; and Walter, unwilling to interrupt them, listened to the words which Julia sang.

> "Father, we praise thee,
> Father, we bless thee
> Yet how can we raise thee
> Such hymns as thou needest
> Poor are we and lowly,
> Thou, mighty and holy
> All Heaven thy throne is;—
> Yet each heart to thee known is,
> And its sorrow thou heedest
> Its sorrow most secret
> Thou knowest and heedest!
> Father, we bless thee,
> We praise, we revere thee!
> For the groans of our feebleness
> Ever come near thee!"

When the hymn was concluded he entered. Lady Grimstone, looking unusually cheerful, sat in her chair by the window, through which the setting sun streamed with a golden radiance, warming into a ruby glow the crimson damask curtains, which were only partly put back. At her feet sat Julia, on a low seat, more animated and beautiful than common, looking upward to her mother's face, the rich light seeming to irradiate her whole figure. Bernard stood a little apart from them, with an open book in his hand, from which he was selecting another hymn.

Nothing could have been more beautiful than this group which, as Walter opened the door, presented itself before him,—a gronp which expressed so exquisitely maternal and filial affection. What a striking contrast to the sordid-spirited Sir Harbottle, terrified over his money-bags, and suspectimig a thief in broad daylight, and that too in the person of one of his sons! What a delightful contradiction too of all his fears!—The next moment Walter was among them. He congratulated Lady Grimstone on her improved looks; he impressed an ardent kiss on Julia's rosy and smiling mouth, and shook Bernard so resolutely by the hand as to make him drop the book, scattering abroad from between its opening pages many a scrawled and blotted manuscript.

"I will lay you the worth of that book, though it were a Wynkin de Worde itself; that I can match any of those lucubrations in value—nay, exceed them—by a manuscript I have at this moment in my hand, though the caligraphy is none of the rarest!"

"Let us see," said Bernard, "for among these are some of your own exquisite scholarship."

Walter explained the contents of the letter, and dwelt particularly on that part which he intended should refer to Bernard.

"Give me your hand!" said Lady Grimstone, when he had finished; "you are the friend I believed you! I shall die in peace,—my prayers have been answered, my children will be provided for!"

All that was said, all that was planned at that happy time, need not be told; everything, like the light of the chamber, seemed rose-coloured. With the most entire union of heart, and full of confidence in the flattering future they talked on, till the sudden gathering gloom of the chamber attracted their notice.

"Alas!" said Lady Grimstone, with a voice that sounded sad, as a prophecy of woe, "these are clouds which have darkened the sunset! Heaven grant that this be not a warning for us! To-day we are full of confidence and joy,—what may not happen on the morrow!"

The young people all thought she spoke of her own probable death, and elated as they had been, their spirits were saddened by her ominous words.

V

Walter replied to the marquis's letter, accepting with confidence whatever employment his noble patron had in prospect for him; recommending, at the same time, his young friend with the most unhesitating zeal.

The next and most important step to be taken was the obtaining from Sir Harbottle Grimstone a sufficient sum of money to enable Bernard to begin his career with the outward appearance of a gentleman and. that he might not be penniless till he received the reward of his own labours. Three hundred pounds was the sum which was thought necessary,—very little to begin the world with, and yet as much as it was dared to demand from the bags of Sir Harbottle.

Bernard had hitherto been scarcely chargeable to his father; and while, at one moment, the domestic conclave, to which Walter Constable was admitted, flattered themselves this might be a plea on which to advance their claim, at another they feared, and not without reason, that Sir Harbottle would never yield to so unaccustomed a demand. The affair, however, did not admit of delay, and Walter was commissioned to urge the subject with the baronet, after his lady had found her most urgent prayers unavailing.

Accordingly, a few mornings afterwards, Walter again presented himself at the door of Sir Harbottle's room. It was that very apartment which in former years had been the private room of the nabob, opening into his chamber, and which also, as by a strange fatality, was Sir Harbottle's own. This room, light and splendid as it had been in the days of its first possessor, was now dingy and sombre. One window only was ever opened, the shutters of the others being closed with their heavy iron bars; what remained of the damask hangings was heavy with dust; cobwebs hung in long waving lines

on the ceiling, or festooned the rich cornice, which was deeply
shadowed by its long-accumulated dust; the thick rich carpet, in
many parts entirely unworn, was trodden even into holes in the
particular parts where the heavy feet of Sir Harbottle Grimstone
had been for so long, almost mechanically, set down as it were to
an inch. Some of the furniture must have been removed, for there
was an air of vacancy in the room: one chair only beside the one
he himself used by the fire—the identical chair in which the nabob
had reclined—stood by the wall, as if to intimate that the miser did
not receive guests; one other also there was, which he used as his
escritoir—a leather-covered armed-chair, with a remarkably low
back, suggesting the idea that it was used, not for comfort truly, but
to enable him to see behind without impediment in case intruders
entered: it was an incongruous piece of furniture, and one which
the refined taste of the nabob could never have selected,—it had
been brought probably from Sir Harbottle's old house at Knighton.
A richly-wrought table of curious Indian wood stood in the centre
of the room, as it had stood in the days of General Dubois; and upon
it, in place of the superb Persian cloth with which it had formerly
been covered, was thrown a piece of faded yellow damask which
had been torn from the hangings. In the untrimmed and unpolished
stove remained the untidy ashes of the last season's fires,—Sir
Harbottle never admitting a domestic within his door excepting on
the most indispensable occasions; hence it was that the room had
never been swept or otherwise cleaned for many years. The escritoir,
a grand piece of cabinet work, and on many accounts the most
remarkable piece of furniture in the room, had been placed where
it stood by the former possessor; and, rumour said, contained among
the accumulated parchments and papers, and swelling money-bags
of Sir Harbottle Grimstone, many a manuscript of the nabob's own
writing, which it had been worth anything to the romance-writer
or the chronicler of the human heart to have read; but their author
could not have guarded them with more inviolate care than did his
successor,—none but Sir Harbottle ever knew if such things there
were.

Such was the room into which Walter entered, not for the first time, it is true, but which now for the first time, he leisurely examined. He found Sir Harbottle sitting in the large armed-chair opposite the door. He was a large-made, heavy, though not corpulent man, in a well-worn snuff-coloured suit, without wig or powder, extremely bald and grey, with a shaggy eyebrow almost entirely concealing the smell, deeply-set, grey eye, cold, and apparently passionless. The whole expression of his face was in unison,—a dogged, hard character of countenance, totally without sentiment, and appearing incapable of emotion. He was sitting upright in his chair—his legs set firmly on the ground—feet together, but knees apart—the bunch of keys in the closed palm of his left hand, the iron ring as usual over his thumb, and in his right he held a small parchment deed, upon which he was poring through his old steel spectacles. He glanced off the parchment at Walter's entrance, but, without returning his salutation, again employed himself as before. The purport of his visit he knew, and thought within himself he would make him wait.

Walter drew the one chair from the wall, and sat down, intending to arrest his attention when he had gone through the parchment, which, on account of its small size, could not occupy him long; but Sir Harbottle might have been spelling it through letter by letter, so slow was his progress; and Walter in a while began to suspect that his intention was to tire him out, especially as he saw a latent smile about his cold mouth, which he had occasionally remarked on former occasions, and knew intimated malice rather than good-will.

"I hope, Sir Harbottle," he therefore began, without, "you have decided on advancing this money for your son Bernard?"

Sir Harbottle appeared to read without seeming to hear.

"Nothing could be more advantageous to your son than this post, which may so readily be obtained for him, but which yet requires an outfit."

It seemed like striking a rock with a feather to talk to Sir Harbottle.

"Your son Bernard," continued Walter, "is an excellent young man, with talents most unquestionably of a fine order. "You must not stand in the way of his fortune, Sir Harbottle."

The baronet might have been deaf and dumb, for any visible impression which the words made upon him; and Walter, almost out of patience, determined to assail what was more penetrable to his senses—his love of money.

"If, Sir Harbottle," said Walter, "you will not advance this sum, it must be taken up in your name."

Sir Harbottle laid down the deed and took off his spectacles at once.

"There are two things," said he, "Mr. Walter Constable, which I should like to be informed upon,—why you intermeddle with my affairs, and why I am to do all this for Bernard?"

"Simply, sir, because Mr. Bernard is a noble-minded and most excellent young man. The last few months have made me intimately acquainted with him; and an opportunity now presents of his acquiring both fortune and reputation."

"Let him acquire them then, sir!" was Sir Harbottle's reply.

"Sir Harbottle," continued Walter, "you have known something of life; you know that a young man cannot enter it, and especially move in an elevated sphere, without money: a few hundreds therefore it will be necessary that you advance for him."

"It will save time and breath, Mr. Walter," said Sir' Harbottle, "for you to know at once that I am not intending to advance him any money."

"I cannot allow you to decide so hastily, Sir Harbottle."

"As you please," said the baronet, with the most rigid apathy.

"It is not possible that you would ruin his prospects in life thus wantonly, Sir Harbottle!" exclaimed Walter with rather an unphilosophical warmth of temper, "and that for the sake of a few paltry hundreds!"

"Oh, sir, if you think money so paltry," returned the baronet, "why I presume you have plenty. I can have no objection to your advancing him the money—a man is perfectly at liberty to do what he likes with his own," said he, again taking up the parchment.

"My good sir," replied Constable, "I cannot do it—I wish I could!—but money is not so plentiful at Westow as at Denborough Park."

"You take tolerable liberties for a man of your years, Mr. Constable," returned the baronet. "If I had wanted your advice, sir, I doubt not but I could have sent for you."

"Sir Harbottle," said Walter, "I am not come to affront you, but to beseech you, on behalf of one of the most deserving and highly-gifted young men—on behalf of one whom you may be proud to esteem your son—"

"Wheuh wheuh!" whistled Sir Harbottle contemptuously.

"—To beseech from you, Sir Harbottle, a small sum which is as nothing from your abundance—which you will never miss, but which will ensure your son's fortune and happiness."

"I have already told you," returned he, "that I am not going to advance him any money."

"Consider, Sir Harbottle, what you are doing! Every child has a natural claim upon its parents for the very best assistance they can give! You are bound by the most sacred bond before both God and man to provide for your children."

"Why, I might be one of the most godless wretches under the sun, and you one of the most profound of teachers!" said Sir Harbottle in wrath. "Pray, sir, in what respect have I neglected my duty to this son of mine, or to any of my sons? Did I not send those three scapegraces to school and college, and a pretty sum it cost me! and what were they the better for it? Am I not cheated by them, and robbed by them, and, for aught I know, shall have my throat cut by them? They are the very plagues of my life! And yet you come here upbraiding me because I will not throw my money away to them by handfuls!"

"It is not for these your sons, Sir Harbottle, that I am soliciting your assistance, but for your son Bernard."

"Bernard!" retorted Sir Harbottle with contempt, as if the idea were perfectly new to him; "a mere stripling! what can he want with money?—a child that has never been away from his mother's apron-strings, and knows nothing of the world, what can he do with money? Why, you might as well give it to sharpers at once! Bernard, i' faith, that knows nothing either of men or manners! If you had asked it for Christie, there might have been some sense in it; for he would have his pennyworth, though it were of folly—never fear him! But Bernard! 'tis absurd!"

"Allow me to tell you, Sir Harbottle, that you have very little knowledge of your son Bernard."

"Very well, sir, I must have more, then, before I shall trust him with even three pounds, much less as many hundreds! And so, sir, I beg you will drop the subject."

"No, Sir Harbottle," continued Walter; "I cannot let you thus lay up repentance for yourself! How can you answer it to God that you have neglected to provide in the best possible manner for your children—for this son at least? What have you done for Bernard?— in what way have you advanced his fortunes? Give him, sir, a sum equal to what you expended on his brothers for their education! Bernard has hitherto cost you but little!"

"Spare your breath for a better purpose, Mr. Constable," said Sir Harbottle; "I have already told you my determination."

"Will you send him penniless into the world?"

"He has a home here," replied Sir Harbottle—"a good roof over his head, and plenty to eat; his mother provides him clothes—she can very well afford it! What in reason can he desire more!"

"Bernard," replied Walter, "was never designed for an inglorious, inactive life; he may be an honour to his country, Sir Harbottle, and, before heaven and earth, I again enjoin it upon your conscience— you are bound by the most righteous of ties to provide in every possible way both for the spiritual and temporal well-being of your children!"

"Pray, sir, are you in orders?" asked Sir Harbottle in cool contempt.

"No; but I am not stepping out of my vocation as a man—as a friend to your family, and to yourself, Sir Harbottle—in urging this upon you. Besides, in a politic point of view, the money will be well employed; it will enable your son to maintain himself honourably— he will be less chargeable to you in the long-run."

"Sir," replied the baronet, "you talk about what you do not understand; his living makes no difference in the family expenditure—one more or one less is never felt; and as to the rest, Lady Grimstone provides for him."

"My dear sir, are you unaware of the precarious state of that excellent lady's life? Your son will become more chargeable to you on his mother's death!"

"Look ye, Mr. Constable, you talk like a greenhorn," answered Sir Harbottle. "Shall I not then come into the possession of the allowance she receives from me—a hundred a year, as you may see by this paper—a copy of the marriage-settlement?" and he pointed to the small deed which he had been reading. "Though, to be sure, this says two hundred—and two hundred she received for fifteen years at least, and then everything dropped in price; the lands at Knighton were lowered half an acre, and I could not afford it. A hundred she has had ever since, and Lady Grimstone will not say but she has had it regularly. Two hundred a year for fifteen years makes three thousand; and one hundred for twenty-two years is two thousand two hundred. Five thousand two hundred pounds for pin-money! I wonder how the deuce it is that women spend so much!"

Walter was shocked and indignant at the unnatural unsusceptibility of his soul, hardened as it was against every generous and kindly sentiment or affection; but he made no remark upon it, and renewed the former topic, determined to bring the interview to a close.

"If, Sir Harbottle," said he, "you are not disposed to advance this small sum as a portion of your son's just claims on you as a father, you cannot object to advancing it as a loan—as money for which you shall receive legal interest!"

"Bernard is not of age," returned Sir Harbottle quickly—"who will be security for him?"

"I will," replied Walter.

"Why, that somewhat alters the case. But look ye, Mr. Constable, I have not as much loose cash by me; I am compelled to put out

all I get, as much to secure it from the rapacious hands of those
lads—who never scruple breaking a lock, I promise ye, to get at
money, the dogs!—as to make it yield some return;—all right and
fair, Mr. Constable—a man must do the best he can for himself; and,
therefore, it would be inconvenient to me just now to advance it;
and besides, who will pay the cost of drawing up a bond?"

"Deduct it from the money you advance for your son, Sir
Harbottle—we will not make difficulties," said Waiter.

"Ay, ay, the money is to be lent to you, Mr. Constable. You
will allow me to ask, sir, whether your property is already much
encumbered?" Walter's brow reddened, and his eye flashed indignant
fire. "For you see, sir," continued Sir Harbottle, "I am accustomed to
have unexceptionable security for my money."

"Sir, your money will be secure!—my bond ought to satisfy
you; and considering that the benefit of your own son is my only
inducement for resorting to this loan, and of which I shall not touch
one single sixpence, your scruples are extremely unhandsome—
extremely ungentlemanly!"

"So, so, Mr. Constable," said Sir Harbottle soothingly, who was only
too well pleased to have acquired thus unexpectedly a power, however
small, over the lands of Westow, on which he had long looked with a
jealous eye, lying as they did in the very midst of his own possessions—
"So, so, there is no need for you to be angry! all in the way of business,
sir! Well, three hundred pounds is the sum you want?"

"Yes, sir."

"Pretty soon, I presume, too."

"The sooner the better."

"Very well, sir, I will see to it;—to be advanced to you at the usual
rate of interest; the interest to be paid half-yearly, and the principal
to be paid back on demand?"

"No, sir," interrupted Walter, "not on demand: that might ruin
your son. Consider, Sir Harbottle, it is to your own flesh and blood
that you are making this Jew-like loan! Heaven and earth! have you
no more conscience than to lay a trap like this for your son?"

"So, so, Mr. Constable, you are hot this morning! The loan, sir, is advanced to you—with my son I will have nothing to do. If you choose to relend you can; and you can make your own terms. I make mine: I am no novice, sir, in affairs of this kind—fifteen thousand I put out only the last month."

"More shame to you, Sir Harbottle, and yet make all this demur and difficulty about giving your son less than the means of beginning the world with!"

"But my security was good, sir—unexceptionable security."

Nothing but his earnest desire to save Bernard would have induced Walter to continue the negotiation; but for his sake he subdued his feelings.

"I will sign no bond, Sir Harbottle," he continued, "in which the money is payable on demand. Six months' notice, if please, sir; but not otherwise."

"Very well, sir; I will endeavour to accommodate you," replied Sir Harbottle, not at all disposed to lose this slight hold on the proprietor of Westow.

And so the interview closed.

VI

Nothing could exceed the gratitude of Lady Grimstone and her son and daughter, when on signing the bond, Walter Constable put the required sum into their hands.

The answer he again received from his noble patron was favourable to all their hopes. Walter and his young friend were requested to join the marquis at his country seat in a few weeks, where Bernard would be introduced to his new connexions. Lady Grimstone, worn and feeble as she was, revived like the reviving flame of the renewed lamp in the promise of honourable and secure provision for her son; and even Mrs. Constable herself, under the influence of anticipated prosperity, visited again the sick-chamber of her friend, to the inexpressible delight of her son and the Grimstones.

A portion of the money was immediately appropriated to the supply of Bernard's wardrobe, and the remainder was carefully reserved to furnish

a fund for any further expenditure. Hope and prosperity seemed again
to dawn upon them; and could security have been given for the life of
Lady Grimstone, all would have been perfect happiness. Again the lovers
met in the ruined summer-house, and enjoyed their former confidence,
even more than renewed. Bernard was the life of every place; his sanguine
and buoyant heart filled itself with glorious anticipations—anticipations
of poetical achievement, and consequent reputation, nobler and loftier
than poet ever acquired; while visions of beauty and peace which were
to come surrounded him on all hands, and made even the present an
elysium. He even persuaded himself that his mother would live—live to
partake with him the realities with which to his fancy the rose-coloured
future teemed, and which his unselfish nature could not have enjoyed,
had not those most dear to him enjoyed them with him. He rambled
through his former haunts, by brook and through weedy hollow, and
reclined for hours on the sunny and dry slope of a meadow, or among
the ferny knolls of some unreclaimed woodland. Happy poet! The hard
realities which in truth pressed him on every hand were unregarded—all
was bright, all was tanigible; and over all lay the heart-refining sense of a
noble and devoted friendship. Life seemed life indeed; and many were the
lays which Bernard poured forth in his full-souled enjoyment.

The intimacy between Bernard and Mr. Constable had not all
this time escaped the notice of the elder brothers, and many had
been the advances which the three had made individually and
collectively to draw him to their faction; well knowing, if little were
to be obtained from him in the way of money, yet, lightly esteemed
as they were by the world, and continual as were the perplexing
circumstances into which their follies and misdeeds were throwing
them, that the countenance of a man like Walter Constable
would ensure them acceptance, and entitle them to attentions
which, for their own merit's sake, they could not command. Most
persevering, therefore, had been their attacks upon him, which
he had strenuously withstood, although Julia had many a time
besought him not to withhold the influence of his countenance and
encouragement, believing that through him a salutary effect might
be produced upon them.

Whether it was in consequence of what Walter Constable had obtained for their brother Bernard, we knew not; but certainly about this time the three, and especially Christopher, sought more than ever to gain his intimacy. Christopher had been now at home for about a week; had gone to bed sober every night, and had been guilty of no domestic outrage for that length of time; and so far had gained extraordinary credit, and on the strength of it importuned Walter to accompany him in a day's excursion to the bull-running at Tutbury, which was then shortly to take place. Walter ridiculed the idea of *his* going to such a scene—the spectacle itself could afford him no pleasure, and yet he had so invariably resisted all the impertinities of the brothers hitherto, that he conceded in this one instance, hoping withal to restrain their excesses by his presence.

Of the outward demeanour of the three elder Grimstones a word may be said. Christopher was a tall and nobly-formed young man, singularly handsome in feature, but with all that reckless expression which marks the confirmed libertine: his dress was always good, and thereat the world wondered—yet it was worn with the characteristic freedom of the debauchee; his hat set knowingly on one side of his head, displaying his richly-coloured black hair, handsome temple, and laughing eye, which seemed always roguishly winking: he wore his cravat loose, and amply displayed, from his half-unbuttoned waistcoat, his shirt-frill, pinned with an immense brooch. His younger brothers, though in style similar to Christopher, were far inferior to him in person, with infinitely less address, and less natural talent also: accordingly, they were even less scrupulous than he in their associates or their actions—two beings admirably calculated to be both the dupes and tools of their elder brother; more especially as, with all their faults, they were recklessly good-natured and unselfish, while Christopher was cold-hearted, crafty, and selfish.

Walter was returning to Westow two days previous to the one on which this sport at Tutbury was to take place, when he saw Christopher at the top of a field waiting for his approach. Christopher beat the hedge, and marked little circles with the heel of his shoe, and larger ones with the whole length of his foot, in the dry marly soil of the headland on which he stood, till Walter reached him, and then with an unusually polite bow he accosted him.

"I am sure, Mr. Constable, I am very glad you will give us your company on Tuesday—prime sport it will be!"

"So Mr. George Grimstone tells me," returned Walter, walking on, Christopher accompanying him.

"What! has he told you of all old Haughton's schemes to make the day full of diversions?—of the grinning matches, and the jumping in sacks, and all that?"

"Yes," said Walter, "and of a fair lady who is to be there beside."

"The devil he has!" exclaimed Christopher.

"It is a lucky thing for you, Grimstone," said Walter, laughing, "that a lover is not, like a servant, obliged to produce a character."

"Why, look ye, Mr. Constable," returned he, "I am perfectly steady now—and I mean to reform in good earnest. Hang it! I've sown all my wild oats; and they turn out such a bad crop—so confoundedly smutty, I e'en try what good sound oats will produce. You'll certainly see, Mr. Constable, what a creditable fellow I shall grow;" and Christopher laughed loudly.

"I am glad that you even *think* of reforming," said Walter.

"You see, Mr. Constable," said Christopher, "the world thinks so much of who a man is with—Heaven bless the world for the most faultless of judges!—but that has been my misfortune."

"You have not had the credit of the best companion certainly," was Constable's reply.

And yet many of them were good fellows enough," returned Grimstone; "but that won't do now-a-days. You, on the contrary, have a famous good name; I want you therefore to help me with it. I tell you, seriously, I mean to reform; d— it, I do!"

"You will always find me ready to assist you in so good a work as your own reformation; but you must explain yourself farther," said Walter, who had no confidence in Grimstone's professions; "for, to be candid with you, I cannot give you credit for this proposed reformation, without imagining you have some covert motive— some end to be obtained of personal advantage or convenience."

"You are a deep hand," replied Grimstone; "but I too will be honest with you. I *have* a motive, and an end of personal advantage: I want to many Miss Hammond!"

"Excellent!" exclaimed Walter.

"A glorious creature she is!" continued the other; "a prodigious heiress, and cousin to some dozen of earls."

"Upon my word, you are aspiring! But are you not outrunning chances?"

"Yes, yes," replied Grimstone; "you think that a lady highly connected, divinely handsome, and immensely rich, as Miss Hammond is, will have nothing to say to a fellow like me. My reply is, that all women are not alike. I have been a lucky dog in my day; and if the girl fancies me, why, that's everything."

"To be sure!" said Constable, laughing.

"Now, if a good fellow like you would stand by me, I am a made man," said Christopher. "You must speak a good word for me!"

"How?—this lady is a perfect stranger to me."

"This lady's friends know you, and think mighty well of you," replied Grimstone: "she told me so herself."

"Hammond?—Hammond?" repeated Walter, endeavouring to recall any former knowledge of the name.

"Oh, hang it!" interrupted Christopher, "their names may not be Hammond."

"And does your fair one present herself at a scene like this at Tutbury?"

" Oh, Lord bless you! she will come with the Haughtons, and half the gentry of the country—everybody will be there: and, besides, she is not one of your she-saints, Constable. Gad ! if you were not an honourable fellow, I would not introduce you to her.—But you'll speak a good word for me, will you?"

"I must know to whom it is to be spoken first," said Walter.

"Oh, that you'll know when you are there. I do not know myself who they are,—but somebody that thinks confoundedly well of you. You'll promise me!"

"No, certainly not," replied Walter.

"Well, this is enhancing a favour with a vengeance!" returned Grimstone. "I'd have been hanged before I would have asked a favour from you if I had thought you would have hummed and ha'd in this way."

"I cannot, in my conscience," replied Walter, "promote a connexion which, I fear, might end in disappointment and misery. I have not sufficient confidence in you, Grimstone."

Christopher suddenly stopped, and looking at Walter with an expression of unwonted earnestness and sincerity, addressed him—

"Mr. Constable, I never knew the worth of a good name till I knew you. You love Julia—she is an excellent creature; you are the friend of Bernard, and he deserves your friendship; for me, who am beginning to lead a new life, and, of you, you demur as if I wanted to pick your pocket."

"Give me cause to suppose your reformation real," replied Walter, moving onward, "and no one will be more ready than I to assist you in everything reasonable."

"Well, if you won't promise me out and out, you'll think about it—mention it to Julia?"

"Yes, yes, I will think of it," said Walter, hesitating to open the gate leading to Westow, and at which they had now arrived, unwilling to present to his mother so unwelcome a visiter as Christopher Grimstone.

"Oh—ay, think of it!" repeated Christopher, in a tone of vexation, as he turned from Walter, and perhaps comprehending why rather inhospitably he delayed to open the gate of his own demesne—"yes, think of it! and go to the devil with you, for an ill-natured, cold-blooded, sanctimonious curmudgeon!"

The next evening, when Walter entered the apartment of Lady Grimstone, he found her more deathlike and feeble than hitherto, relapsed into her former worn and debilitated state. She was still, however, sitting before the window in her large cushioned chair, and Julia was leaning over her, weeping bitterly.

"You are come as usual at the right time," said Lady Grimstone, turning her sunken countenance upon Walter with a smile of sorrowful but cordial welcome. "My eyes are dim," continued she, directing her sight through the window; "but to me it seems that the reapers are busy with the corn. Tell me, Walter; your eyes are strong, for this poor girl cannot see for weeping."

"Your sight has not deceived you, dearest lady," replied Walter cheerfully, and thinking it best to make light of the subject.

"My time grows short, then," returned Lady Grimstone; "a week perhaps—at farthest ten days—and I shall be at rest."

"These are superstitious notions," said Walter; "life is uncertain to us all."

"I know it, Mr. Constable, I know it; but for me, my days are numbered. Sit down beside me, my friend; I have earnestly desired to see you."

Walter sat down; and Julia, assured as she always was by the presence of her lover, dried her tears and leaned on the back of her mother's chair.

"My son Christopher has been with me even now," said the dying lady. "Oh, Mr. Constable, what a hope has arisen on my waning life! Heaven has surely sent you for the salvation of this degraded house; you will not withhold your countenance—you will stand by him in this affair?"

"Dearest lady," replied Walter, "Miss Hammond is totally unknown to me: besides, I cannot feel justified in promoting such a connexion." The words seemed harsh to Walter as he spoke them, and he qualified them by a look and tone of sympathy and kindness.

The tears streamed from the sunken eyes of Lady Grimstone. "Ah," said she, "if you cannot stand by us, who then will?"

"God knows," returned Walter, deeply moved; "I would stand by you even to the death."

"Pardon me, pardon me,—I am unreasonable; but oh, Mr. Constable," replied Lady Grimstone, with an energy that seemed incompatible with her feeble frame, "this is my first-born; and none but a mother knows how dear is her first-born. Christopher may be reclaimed, think of that! and so much, so very much, depends upon him!—he has unknown influence with his brothers, with his father too—everything depends upon him! Do not abandon him! he voluntarily seeks to you for help—for example! Oh, my friend, you who are rich in a good name, do not withhold it from a poor brother. What a heavenly light will stream in upon my dying hour when I think of all my children in bliss!—their father too! Oh, Mother of Mercies, I bless thee, and thy dear Son who bore his agony on the cross, and suffered shame and want for the sake of sinners!" exclaimed she, kissing with devotion the crucifix which lay on her breast. Julia, again unable to restrain her emotion, buried her face in the cushions of her mother's chair. Walter replied not, for his heart was torn with conflicting sentiments.

"Let me put my poor sinful children, as well as my guiltless ones, under your care," continued she, after the passion of her emotion had a little subsided; "and remember, that he who turneth many to righteousness shall shine forth as the stars in the firmament of heaven! Remember this, and may the Almighty Father and Ruler of events abundantly bless and reward you!"

Walter still hesitated to answer; but he felt, in spite of his better judgment, his resolution giving way before the words of Lady Grimstone and the beseeching eyes of his beloved Julia.

"I demand no promise from you," said the dying mother, feeling the reluctance which Walter's silence implied; "you have already made us deeply your debtors; I bind you by no promise, but I confide in your goodness."

"For the reverence I have for you, dearest lady,—for my love for Julia, my friendship for Bernard,—I will do my utmost for the reclaiming of these young men," was Walter's reply.

Lady Grimstone took his hand and poured a solemn benediction upon him; and the tearful eyes of Julia spoke gratitude and affection beyond words.

VII

On the morning of the fifteenth of August, Walter Constable mounted his horse and rode down the avenue, at the gate of

which he found Christopher unaccompanied by his brothers,
already waiting. Walter could not help noticing the unusually
handsome appearance of his companion, apparelled as he was in
a most fashionable and even costly suit, and mounted on a horse
far superior to any which the miserable stud of Sir Harbottle
Grimstone could have furnished. Christopher was in exuberant
spirits, and would have edified his companion by all imaginable
sallies of merriment, but that Walter that morning was in no mood
for jest or conversation. His mind was at war with itself; he felt that
he would fain oblige Lady Grimstone and Julia by attempting to
reform or assist her brothers; but his understanding represented the
attempt as hopeless to them, and very possibly injurious to himself.
He felt therefore ill at ease, and after several unsuccessful essays on
the part of Christopher, he gave them up in despair, cursing him
as the greatest flat under the sun, and thenceforward confining his
animation to his own breast, or giving it only occasional vent in the
humours of a half-sung song or half-whistled air.

The morning was as splendid as an autumnal morning could be.
The atmosphere was in that state of resplendent transparency peculiar
to the season; the most distant horizon shone out clearly defined, and
the whole landscape lay as it painted in colours of light. On every
hand stretched out meadows green with the abundant after-crop of
grass, in which herds of cattle were luxuriantly pasturing; and on
every slope the corn stood in sheaves, fell before the busy sickle of
the reapers, or was borne away in the loaded wagon. Gleaners and
harvesters were abroad; and not a field but presented some group or
figure of rural beauty or interest. By the dry and dusty wayside the
light harebell nodded, and the minutely-flowered spikes of the yellow
bed-straw were seen among the white and wiry bents; the crimson
foxglove and the golden snapdragon contrasted their beautiful colours
on the hedgebanks, and the long sprays of the blackberry bowed with
their yet crude but heavy clusters of fruit.

Minute as these individual features of the splendid and abundant
autumn were, they formed a whole of extraordinary beauty, and of
that silent yet strong influence which operates on the mind of the

beholder. Walter felt its full effect; his mind was tranquillized by the harmonious beauty of earth and sky, and without thinking of enjoyment he rode on, finding in everything that presented itself to him a source of deep and earnest delight.

The whole landscape, too, was one of extraordinary and Arcadian beauty. The valley of the Dove, the Needwood, the richly-timbered park and farms of Sudbury and then, the finely-varied champaign of meadow, corn-land, and wood, in the midst of which rose the hill of Tutbury crowned with the far-seen ruined towers of its castle; its castle famous in history, the once almost regal abode of the Dukes of Lancaster, and of the most potent of them, John of Gaunt himself, to whose minstrels he ordered to be given, on this holy day of the Assumption of the Blessed Virgin, a bull, not to be contended for in song, but by strength and dexterity of limb.

This custom, the well-known Tutbury bull-running, though the race of Lancaster was extinct, their castle a pile of ruins and the order of minstrels, like other feudal institutions, gone to dust, yet remained—a rude sport, honoured but little by the noble and the fair, but yet religiously observed by the peasants of the counties of Stafford and Derby, on whose confines Tutbury stood.

At the time of which we write, and but a very few years before the custom was abolished altogether, it had been attempted by one Colonel Haughton, a man of large property, but of eccentric habits and tastes, and a great patron of all rural sports and festivities whatever, to revive the custom of the bull running with somewhat of its ancient honours. Neither pains nor expense were spared by him to give the occasion a general interest and *éclat*; he even proposed instituting for the purpose a band of minstrels, who, harp in hand, and habited in robe and girdle, were to edify the assembled multitude with their strains, and afterwards contend for the bull by the more legitimate means. But this laudable endeavour was abandoned from the difficulty of finding a sufficient number of qualified persons: hundreds could run over meadow, and even swim the river itself, in pursuit of the four-footed guerdon; but not five men could be found who were capable of chanting a stanza to the tinkling of a harp. Instead thereof, every rural game was to be exhibited, no matter how absurd or ridiculous: grinning through horse-collars, running-matches of old women, or jumping in sacks—these were to occupy the morning; the bull-running, the grand event of the day, according to ancient usage, commenced in the afternoon.

As Walter and his companion advanced on the road, they saw, from all the villages through which they passed, groups on foot, or in every variety of vehicle, setting out on their way to the scene of attraction. Sturdy and athletic countrymen, too, with sunburnt faces and hands, who had left the harvest-field, the forge, and every variety of handicraft trades, and wearing their broad ribbon scarfs of blue or red, according to which county they belonged, might be seen on the road singly, or in companies of threes and fours, increasing in frequency as they approached the town. From the topmost tower of the castle also had been seen to wave, from the time the ruins first came in view—in fact, had waved there from the earliest morning—two banners of the rival colours; and as they neared the town, the sounds of music reached them, coming with a full swell, or dying away to the low breathing of remote melody, according as the wind or the turns in the road brought it nearer or made it more distant.

But before we enter the town, an incident must be related, at the moment considerably amused Walter, and was characteristic of the person in whose company he was riding. In passing the little village, before they reached Tutbury, two grooms in livery rode out from the yard of the small public house, and touching their hats to Christopher, took their place in attendance.

"You have not been negligent in the style of your retinue, Mr. Grimstone," said Walter.

"Why, plague take it!" replied he, "one must do as others do."

Walter might have said, what he thought, that the means by which these things were done were mysterious, seeing that Sir Harbottle would not advance one hundredth part of what they must cost; but he forbore, knowing that suspicion went sorely against the brothers on this subject. They had not ridden far, however, before Christopher stopped his horse to speak to his attendants, evidently desirous at the same time of speaking to them unobserved by Mr. Constable. Walter was struck instantly with a resemblance which, notwithstanding their disguise, the two bore to the younger Grimstones; and the thick under-tones of George's voice, which could not be disguised, as he replied, confirmed his suspicion. The young men were evidently acting as servants to their brother, to whom on this day, perhaps, some extraordinary outward show or ceremonial was considered necessary; doubtless they were to be rewarded out of the fair lady's coffers.

"Your brothers act as grooms to-day, Mr. Grimstone," said Walter, determined to show that he was not unobservant.

"No, d—me, not they!" was his quick reply.

"Come, come," said Walter, "I might pardon the practical lie, but not a deliberate falsehood like that."

"Why, look ye now, Mr. Constable," replied he, evidently chagrined, and yet desirous of soothing him, "I did not mean to offend you; but, hang it, one's forced to all sorts of schemes to make a decent show."

Walter fell into a thoughtful silence, and with this concession he and his compaions entered Tutbury.

The little town was full of bustle and animation: townspeople were passing nimbly to and fro; the bells were ringing; booths covered with white awnings stood in the wider parts of the streets, where various kinds of confections and cheap refreshments were offered for sale; country vehicles, driven in by countrymen in their clean carters' frocks, or Sunday coats and hats, and filled with gaily-attired women and ever and anon; and before the only inn in the place, two or three gentlemen's carriages and post-chaise horses had been taken, told that some more had already taken place; and through the open upper windows might be now and then seen the lovely fair maiden who had thence alighted, an object of bright attraction to the yonng men who crowded the street below, upward many a furtive glance.

Christopher, who objected to enter this inn on account of the crowd who would be at it, and the indifferent accommodation there would be for their horses, proposed their riding to a small, but to him, well-known, hostelry, where they would have no reason to complain of their treatment. All this was a matter of indifference to Walter Constable, and he cheerfully agreed. They, therefore, rode through the town, and stopped at a small house kept by one Milly Freckleton, who, as the painted board over her door intimated, offered good accommodation for man and horse.

Christopher, giving his own and Walter's horses to his *pro tempore* grooms, entered the house, and without ceremony opened the door of a neat, small parlour, looking into a garden shady with trees and bright with autumn flowers, into which he ushered Walter Constable. No sooner had Christopher entered, than the old landlady, who saw him from her kitchen, advanced, receiving him with almost maternal kindness.

"Ay, Mr. Christopher, and so you are come at last! Well, I says, says I to Peggy, if aught will fetch him, this day will!" She stopped suddenly on seeing a stranger, and, dropping a curtsy, begged Walter's pardon, saying she was "always main glad to see Mr. Grimstone."

"Let us have a good luncheon, mother!" said Christopher; "quick! the best you have; and these fellows of mine must not too often see the bottom of your brown jug! D'ye hear!"

"Your landlady welcomes you cordially," said Walter.

"She is a good old soul, and nursed me night and day for three weeks this very spring: I might have been a dead man now but for her care," was Grimstone's reply.

Christopher presently afterwards went out, and the old woman bustled in again with a clean napkin and tray.

"I mun e'en serve you myself, for my grand-daughter is out o'call. Young folks is so thoughtless," said she, as she arranged the new white loaf, the rich cheese, and the delicate butter on the table.

"And you are a friend o' Mr. Christopher's?" said she, looking at him attentively, when, after fidgeting about, dusting the tables and chairs with her apron, she could find nothing else to do; "and yet you was not here with him in the spring!"

"No," replied Walter.

"What, th'ould man's living yet, I reckon?"

"Sir Grimstone?" asked he.

"Ay."

"He is living and likely to live," replied her guest.

"What's naught lasts th' longest," muttered she. "Well, I wonder where this wench is! But I'll get you summut to drink—Mr. Grimstone reckons our tap none of the worst;" and so saying, she again went out.

A quarter of an hour elapsed, and Christopher did not make his appearance; and Walter, invited into the garden by its sunshine, its shade, and its old-fashioned tidiness, leaped through the large open casement into it. For some time he amused himself with studying the effusions of country wit inscribed on the benches and the little tables before them, and marvelled at the extraordinary patience which it must have required to cut sundry well-defined true-love knots and intricate stars into the hard wood with a penknife, which had probably been the only tool, when his attention was diverted by the low weeping voice of a female in an adjoining arbour; and looking round through the woven branches, he saw to his amazement a very lovely young woman leaning on the shoulder of Grimstone, and evidently pleading with him in the bitterest distress. Christopher had his arm round her waist, and was speaking in a tone of kindness, though the words seemed to give the poor girl no consolation. The next moment the old landlady hobbled into the garden, calling, at the top of her voice,—

"Peggy! Peggy Woodhouse!"

The young woman hastily disengaged herself; and answered that she was coming. She wiped her eyes with her apron, put a small packet in her bosom, and ran out; while Christopher apparently embarrassed, pulled to pieces a branch of early-blowing phlox which he held in his hand.

Walter walked onward and stood before the arbour, and Christopher instantly assumed a perfectly unconcerned air. For the first time in his life almost, Walter Constable knew not how to act; he had been a spy on the lovers, and though he was convinced of heartlessness and villany on the part of Grimstone, he forbore to upbraid him, because by so doing he must in some measure compromise himself. He resolved, therefore, to watch for some opportunity of so doing, which he doubted not would occur in the course of the day, and returned with him to the parlour, where they sat down to their refreshment.

The fair Peggy, however, did not make her appearance, the old grandmother herself waiting on her guests with the most devoted attention, though, as if by a signal from Christopher, refraining from all familiarity.

When the two had refreshed themselves, they walked out into the town, which was now thronged with its assembled people and visitors, to witness the various sports which were going forward.. As Christopher had said, many of the gentry were there, though as yet but few ladies; and as if to parade his companion, on whose arm he ostentatiously leaned, he went from sport to sport, thrusting into the thickest crowds, and attracting attention by his loud jests and observations; and Walter found that, if not with one of the most honourable, he was with one of the most known, of the Tutbury visiters,—and with one, at the same time, who entered into every sport with the most earnest zest, and whose opinion was not unfrequently appealed to as decisive.

An hour before noon, however, the arrival of the grandees—an earl, the guest of Colonel Haughton—the earl's ward, the beautiful Miss Hammond, and a numerous and splendid train who attended them, diverted public attention from all minor persons, and even for a few minutes interrupted the grinning-match itself. To Christopher's disappointment the ladies did not honour these inferior games by their presence; but, before long, the gracious nobleman and an accession of gentlemen joined the assembled spectator's, the public attention being for the first five minutes about equally divided between the rival combatants and the new-comers, while the visages protruded through the horse-collars grinned even into redoubled grotesque hideousness in honour of the noble eyes that looked on. Walter immediately recognised the nobleman to be the Earl of N—, whom he had met while abroad, a remarkably proud and aristocratic person; and he marvelled what could be the strange chance which had brought him to a scene like this. Walter supposed himself barely known, if at all remembered, by him, and therefore thought not of introducing himself to his notice; but this was one of the relations of whom Grimstone had spoken, and accordingly he urged him to present himself for the purpose of introducing him.

"The Earl is looking this way, Constable; his eyes are on you at this moment;—let us go to him! He wants to catch your eye."

"Perhaps so," replied Walter, with assumed indifference, now feeling the sense of the situation in which he had placed himself by consenting to accompany Christopher hither, more disagreeable and mortifying than he had anticipated. While he supposed that there would be merely a concourse of country people there, or of those neighbouring gentry who were not too refined or elevated to see much that was strange in such a conjunction of casual association as that of Walter and Christopher, it mattered little; but now that he found a different class was likely to be present, he shrunk into himself with feelings of shame and vexation.

"Come, you'll introduce me," urged Christopher. "Why, you'll not shy off now—you'll never be so shabby, will you? You promised to introduce me."

"I shall not even introduce myself," replied Walter, "much less another person."

At that very moment, the Earl, who, as Christopher had said, had been observing Walter for some time, left his own party to accost him, and, offering his hand, expressed his sincere pleasure in thus unexpectedly meeting him.

While Walter was making his acknowledgment, his lord's attention was demanded by Colonel Haughton, to decide between two rival grins; and he again joined his own party

"Well," said Christopher, with an oath, "you're the most shame-faced, chicken-hearted fellow in the universe!" and flinging from him, he joined himself to a knot of his own associates. After a while, when this match was over, and the spectators began to disperse, Christopher again returned, begging pardon for his rudeness and violent temper, and endeavouring by all means to regain Walter's favour, which he thought he might have lost; but Christopher's ebullition of anger had made no difference to him, and without either noticing that, or the pains he took to flatter him to forgiveness, accompanied him out of the crowd. Grimstone conducted him into a set of dissolute fellows, low gamblers, who were betting on a donkey-race. They all had deep designs on Walter Constable, and Grimstone thought he would here revenge the affront he had just received at his hands. But Walter was not a man to be the dupe of such as these; at the same time he was a curious inquirer into human nature, and an interested spectator of every development of human character and passion, and stood among these choice spirits of the day and scene, penetrating all their designs, and baffling their arts. They were a set of brutal, swaggering, and reckless men, many of them wearing the garb of gentlemen, but with manners and avowing sentiments which were only worthy of the most hardened and unprincipled profligates. It was soon seen that Constable, instead of being a dupe, could only be a spy upon them—a hindrance and a restraint; and many, therefore, were the efforts which Christopher used to free himself from him. But here, at least, Walter would not be shaken off, hoping that the restraint of his presence, or the desire still to preserve his favourable opinion, would withhold him from any gross act of indiscretion. But Walter was mistaken. Christopher found it better, from some cause or other, to disconnect himself from him; and, before long, he was alone. The three were gone, he knew not whither; and hardly knowing whether to be vexed or pleased at losing control over them, he dismissed them from his thoughts, resolving to enjoy the humours of the day since he was there, and leave them to take care of themselves.

At the exact hour of noon, the various games being finished, the bull, a noble creature, bred in the rich meadows of the Dove, brindled like a pard, with sharp short horns, curved like the crescent moon, a thickly curled front, and eyes of intense lustre, though of mild expression, was led through the streets by a strong chain passed over his horns, drawing away man, woman, and child from all minor spectacles—the first immediately to fall into the procession, and the second to flee away to covert, till, re-assured by the meek demeanour of the creature, they joined the rear of the crowd. A more beautiful animal of his kind never fed in the meadows of ancient Thessaly; and Walter, as he saw him garlanded with flowers, and bound with shining ribbons, led onward, strong yet passive, faultless in form, and attended by a thronging multitude, bethought himself of the old days of Grecian rites, when processions like this, and of which even this might perhaps be a remnant passed along through grove and valley, and from every little town, and were immortalized in bas-relief on many a marble frieze, or in poetry, living and breathing, like the reality itself.

VIII

The crowd went by, and Walter turned to the castle-hill, noticing with admiration on his way the fine old church, with its low, broad, and circular entrance of exquisite Saxon architecture, adorned with its grand moulding of alternate grotesque figures and zigzag work, a part of the old Priory Church. All the world as well as Walter Constable were bound to the castle-hill, not only for the view of the sport below, but because it had been given out that Miss Hammond and the *élite* who attended her would be there on horseback, themselves no undesirable show.

It was with no common interest that Walter ascended the ruin-crowned hill.

It was a beautiful scene on which Walter Constable looked. The whole area of the ruins was filled with a gay and gathering assesmbly; the clear blue sky was stretching above them; the silent, majestic ruins encircled them on three sides, while on the north-west it lay open to that glorious landscape of meadow, river, and forest, with an open Arcadian country, including towns, villages, and noblemen's seats, to an extent of thirty miles.

The area of the castle-hill itself was a fine turf, green and smooth as a lawn, on which was met that gay and motley assembly; some standing in groups, some strolling leisurely about, and others perched upon tower or crumbling wall. Two tents were pitched upon the very verge of the hill, whence the more dignified company might witness the sport in the meadows below. Gay ribbon-streamers were fluttering from the poles of each tent; and a small company of musicians, who had stationed themselves among the ruins, filled the warm, bright air with the melody of wind instruments,. Walter's pulse quickened with enthusiasm as he gazed round, and felt at once the picturesque and beautiful effect of the whole scene and its accompaniments.

Presently the crowd dispersed to right and left from before the old gateway, and, with trumpets blown before them, by half-a-dozen men in quaint liveries and with badges on their arms, a long and stately cavalcade rode leisurely in, three a-breast—a lady escorted by a gentleman on either hand.

The cavalcade passed into the court, the rear being brought up by serving-men, mounted, and in rich but ancient dresses. After a circuit round the western side of the court, which brought them to the tents, the trumpets ceased to blow, and about half the company dismounted and entered them, their horses being led away by grooms, and the remainder of the cavalcade arranged themselves promiscuously. Walter observed that Christopher Grimstone was there on horseback, and attended by his grooms; but he was so much engrossed by watching Miss Hammond as to appear unconscious of him.

Walter saw that Grimstone's report had not exaggerated the beauty of this fair lady. She was such as Cleopatra might have been—of a haughty and regal style of beauty; and he wondered yet more and more at the presumption of Grimstone. Her dress was singularly simple—a green riding-habit, with a velvet hat; her hair, of an intense blackness, was tightly braided on her forehead; and the small and delicately-chiselled ear—between which and the smooth, round cheek, as if for contrast, went the narrow black ribbon that fastened her hat—was bare; the throat, too, was bare, in its pure whiteness set off even by the small but richly-wrought cambric collar that surrounded it; while the close-fitting riding-dress revealed a bust of the most perfect symmetry. Walter contemplated her with unfeigned admiration; she was, indeed, the finest woman he had ever seen; and though Grimstone's passion seemed to his mind more hopeless, more like fatuity than ever, he pardoned him for indulging it.

On her right was an older lady, the one who had ridden first in the procession, escorted by Colonel Haughton and the Earl, habited like Miss Hammond, excepting that the colour was many shades darker, and the whole style less youthful: she, too, was a haughty and beautiful woman, and from the younger lady's resemblance to her, Walter concluded this to be her mother. On the left hand of Miss Hammond was a young man of slight and effeminate person, remarkable for his singularly fashionable dress and entirely self-satisfied air. Other gentlemen paid their court to the beauty, and came and went, receiving a haughty smile or a passing word; but this cavalier maintained his place at her side as he had entered the court—patted her horse, was privileged to jest with her, and received from her fair hand an admonition with her riding-whip, which even showed more like favour than all the words and looks which, as if intending to do him honour, or as if he alone were worthy of her regard, she from time to time lavished upon him. He was evidently a favoured lover, and Walter looked to Grimstone to see how he bore the discovery. His countenance was flushed, and his eye riveted upon him in angry jealousy; he pricked his horse with his spurs, and then suddenly checked him, till the creature, fretted and impatient, pawed and reared, and would have thrown his rider had he not been perfectly master of his saddle. All eyes were turned upon him, even those of his mistress and her young lover. Walter thought he perceived a smile of derision on the lips of the lady; he was sure that the youth was permitted a jest at his expense.

"Who is the gentleman that occupies so much of Miss Hammond's attention?" asked he of one who stood by him.

"The Honourablt Henry Finch," was the reply: "his uncle, the Earl of N—, is in the tent with Colonel Hanghton."

Walter again turned to look at Grimstone; but he had assumed an apparent self-command and was at that moment speaking to his brothers. What, however, was Walter's indignation to see him, the very next moment, ride straight into the middle of the crowd, and forcing his horse between that of Miss Hammond and Mr. Finch, address her with insolent confidence! He felt as if his breath were suspended, and yet with intense anxiety waited for whatever would next take place.

The reception of Grimstone was that of annihilating disdain; and without appearing to return his salutation, she urged her horse forward. Mr. Finch was again in attendance; and wheeling round with an evolution worthy of a horse soldier, she took her place on the other side of her mother, with her more favoured cavalier still beside her. The action was instantaneous, and Christopher, as instantaneously, again thrust between them, swearing he would knock any man from his saddle who attempted to displace him; and, at the same time, he struck his rival's horse so violently on the flanks, that, it sprang suddenly aside, and its rider was thrown. The whole company was in instant confusion. The ladies, escorted by part of the gentlemen, retired to a distance. The company within the tents, alarmed by the confusion, rushed out, increasing the confusion still more by not knowing exactly what had occurred. One crowd gathered about Mr. Finch, who, however, was not hurt, and soon remounted; and another about Grimstone. Loud and angry were the vociferations which assailed him, and most vehement the indignation. He was compelled to dismount; and in spite of the violent efforts he used to free himself, and the volleys of angry oaths which he poured forth, he was consigned into more strong but less gentlemanly hands, and conducted out of the castle yard, his brothers, or grooms, to whom his horse was given, following after.

Walter, equally indignant with the rest at this audacious outrage, had rushed in upon them; but his reproof and remonstrance were lost in the vehemence of the general displeasure, and supposing him to be drunk, and seeing him borne away as he hoped to some place of confinement for the rest of the day, though he could not help feeling infinitely annoyed at the occurrence, dismissed further care about him—and especially as Miss Hammond, her young lover, and their gay attendants, were again drawn up apparently in reassured equanimity, and the trumpet was blown which announced the sport about to begin, and the attention of every one was diverted to other subjects. Walter, chagrined as he was, hoped that this offence of Grimstone might not be otherwise considered than as a drunken sally; whereas Mr. Finch and the lady's friends looked upon it as a personal insult, and for reasons which are afterwards to be disclosed, the Earl took especial umbrage at it. Christopher was taken into custody for an assault on the noble person of Henry Finch, and at this very time was being conveyed to the house of Justice Halliday, the nearest magisrate, for committal.

In order to have a yet more perfect view than the crowded area of the castle court afforded, Walter descended the hill about one-third, as many besides himself had done, till the whole hill-side was alive with people. What an animated scene lay below him! It mattered not to him. What the occasion was which had assembled those eager crowds, they in themselves were beautiful.

The parts of the meadow near the town were inclosed with strong palisades, within which were booths erected, each displaying some sign or blazonry painted in gaudy colours, and whence issued music and sounds of revelry. Everything was full of exhilaration and happiness. Beyond the palisades, and stretching onward for several hundred yards, were drawn out the two bands of runners—Derbyshire and Staffordshire men, stripped to their shirts and pantaloons, with bare heads, and scarfed with their respective colours of red and blue, waiting for the bull which was about to be led out. The trumpet was again blown from the castle-hill: the music below instantly ceased, as well as every other sound; the faces of the hundreds below were all turned upwards, and the long, clear clangour of the trumpet seemed to fill the whole extent of the landscape. The trumpet ceased, and even while the ear was filled with the sound, it was sensible of a universal silence. The next moment a movement was observed below; a shout burst forth, and the bull, still wearing his garlands, was led forth between the two bands of runners. The bull had been rubbed over with soap in order to render him slippery to the touch, and therefore less easy to be caught: the barbarous custom of mutilation had been long abolished. The chain was disengaged from his horns, he was pricked on with a goad, and then, with a bellow like low thunder, he burst through the men of Staffordshire, who sprang right and left from before him, into the freedom of the meadows. The garlands with which he was bound burst from him, as he put forth the mighty sinews of his frame, as if he had flung them off in very derision.

Away he went, tossing his head in the joyous belief of regained liberty. The crowd rushed after him with impatient shouts, pursuing him in two eager but separate parties. The bull faced about upon his pursuers, but with no appearance of hostility, allowing them to approach almost within arm's length. A murmur of disapprobation passed through the spectators, in the belief that the animal, powerful and thorough-bred as he was, would show no sport, but suffer himself to be tamely captured. The moment, however, the hands of a party were almost upon him, he wheeled round with, perfect coolness, and as if in contempt of them, levelling the inner circle to the ground with one sweep of his head, and then with a cry, more like a scream than a bellow, dashed through the surrounding crowd, overturning many a one, and again scoured off over the meadows, bearing his tail aloft and shaking his head as he went. The discomfited parties again turned in pursuit, leaving their fallen comrades to shift for themselves; and these also, of whom none were hurt, were soon on their feet again and in active pursuit.

The bull prepared hiunself to practise the same manoeuvre, but the men were not equally confident, and approached with much more caution. Each party advanced in a firm semi-circular phalanx from opposite sides, each desiring to get the start of the other, and yet neither coming within many yards of him, and gradually completing their circle so as to inclose him on all sides. The creature seemed to find sport in all this, and looked slowly round him from side to side:—it was like the child's play of "the bull in the park," and he seemed as if looking round for the weak place through which to make his escape. Instead, however, of bursting through them, he cleared them with a bound, as he would have cleared the low fence of a field. Not a single man had fallen; and so instantaneous was his movement, that the circle remained entire when he was on the other side; and then, as if in perfect contempt of them, he began quietly to graze.

The spectators saw wonderful amusement in all this, and shouts and acclamations echoed from the hill. The pursuers, however, either thought themselves fooled by the bull, or they were impatient of his good temper, and used therefore every possible means to irritate him; they pelted him with stones, railed at him, bellowed, and shook their handkerchiefs in his face, while others, with long sticks sharply pointed with iron, pricked him in various parts of the body. The blood followed the wounds, and the creature was excited to rage. The sport then began anew, he being no longer the pursued, but the pursuer. He roared, he tore the ground with his horns, his eyes flashed fire, and his dilated nostrils seemed to emit steam; he leaped here and there; he dashed through the crowd wherever it collected, with shrill, short bellowings, and occasionally singled out an individual whom he pursued with determined enmity, goring and tearing him till he was covered with blood, and was only diverted from killing him outright by some new and ingenious mode of torment which the others employed to turn his fury to new objects. The courage of the men was amazing, and yet now and then a cry of human terror or agony was made frightfully audible through the general silence with which the contest was witnessed. No attempt was now made to take the bull; all were employyed in preserving themelves, and for the present it was their object to excite him to the most violent exertions in order that he might tire himself ou. His colour no longer was dark—the soap with which he was smeared had worked into a snow-white foam which covered him all over, and, as it trickled from his forehead into his eyes made his fury yet more terrific. Many men in the course; this transport of pain and rage were disabled by him, and either crept away to the booths, or were carried thither by their companions.

The bull, in the mean time, burning with thirst and mad with pain, plunged into the river, dashing the water to an amazing height, and changing it into white foum with the lather that was washed from his sides. Here he found some relief from his torments, and plunging yet deeper into the stream, stood and bellowed at his pursuers, who ranged themselves on the banks, impatient to plunge in after him.

Walter had seen all this with intense interest, forgetting in the animation of the sport whatever his sober reason might have objected against it; but his attention was now entirely diverted from the whole scene by seeing a boy, one of the very few servants employed at Denborough Park, who, hurried and hot, hastily descended the hill to where he sat. The boy presented him with a letter, which he begged him to read instantly, and then sat down at some distance wiping his hot brow, and gazing with eager delight on the scene below.

The letter was from Julia, and was as follows:—

"DEAREST FRIEND.—The saddest of events is befalling me; my beloved mother is indeed at the point of death! Ah, how can I write it?—but I must control my feelings, for I am alone—Bernard is gone for Father Cradock.

Alas, my friend, what a heavy sorrow hangs over me! Come hither with what speed you can; you only can comfort me—you only can teach me to resign her. But what is far more important, my poor mother prays earnestly to see you, and to see my brothers also: bring them with you—who knows the blessed influence of such a meeting? and, oh, my friend, of such a parting!

"I confide all to your goodness. Come quickly!

"I write with a breaking heart, and eyes swimming with tears.—Adieu!

"Yours ever, in sorrow as in joy.—Joy! what a word is that to write at this moment!

"J.G."

To ride instantly to Denborough Park was the first impulse of his heart; and without bestowing another glance on the scene which but a few moments before had occupied him so deeply, he ascended the hill and was presently in the town.

No sooner had Walter entered the small hostelry, than the fair Peggy, inviting him into the little parlour, accosted him with streaming tears.

"Oh, sir, you are his friend, and can save him: let him not be committed to prison!"

"Is it Mr. Grimstone of whom you speak?" asked Walter touched with the poor girl's distress.

"Oh yes, sir, yes!" replied she, blushing deeply in the midst of her tears; "and his lordship, they say, and Colonel Haughton, insist on his committal."

"Is his folly treated thus severely?" said Walter. "But of a truth he deserved punishment."

"Then you will not befriend him!" exclaimed she in despair. "O that I were a man!" added she, forgetting or regardless of Walter's presence; "then I would go to prison for him: but what can a poor girl do!"

Just then the old woman also entered, and looking on her grand-daughter with displeasure, bade her get about her own business, and not stand talking to every handsome gentleman who came to the house, like an idle hussy as she was. Thus reproved, Peggy withdrew, and the grandmother presented a slovenly-folded paper to Walter, telling him that it was come for him from Justice Haliday's; adding—

"This is a sore job of Mr. Christopher's! but you mun be off, sir; we munna let him go to gaol. I'll order your horses to be saddled—it'll save you the time." And so saying, she left Walter to read his second billet, which ran thus:—

"Take horse and ride instantly; I want your help! Stay not to reason about it—for God's sake, come! I am the most unfortunate of men; let not my past misconduct, or rather madness, provoke you. On my soul, I will give you no further cause for offence or regret!

"Your most unfortunate servant,

"C. GRIMSTONE."

The case was clear, and was much more serious than Walter had imagined; and however he might have felt disposed to act towards Grimstone for his own sake, the desire which Lady Grimstone had expressed to see her sons was so natural and reasonable, that Walter, forcibly drowning the voice of reason in what he deemed a sacred though severe duty, inquiring the way to the justice's, put spurs to his horse, and very soon gained the house, his intention being to get Grimstone liberated if possible.

Walter found the justice a solemn, portly little man, who in his cocked-hat, light blue coat, and with his gold-headed cane, was walking leisurely among his flower-borders in the front of his house, in the warm light of the setting sun. His worship, who reverenced wealth and rank with most laudable goal, inasmuch as he held poverty and crime synonymous, perceived instantly that Walter was a person to be treated with respect;

"Your servant, sir," said he, therefore, in acknowledgment of Constable's much less submissive salutation. "Your servant, sir," and lifted his cocked hat so as to reveal the smooth, bald crown, white over with powder.

Walter's business was soon told, but not as soon transacted. The justice would not believe Grimstone to have been drunk; the earl, he said—Colonel Haughton—none of the gentlemen—considered him to be drunk; and, according to his humble opinion, he appeared perfectly sober: the action was a cool assault, and his worship had no other means of liberating him but by sufficient bail for his good behaviour. Walter persisted in arguing that it was but a drunken frolic, of which the shame and consequent apologies of Christopher, when sober, would convince the earl, and lead to his liberation. But there was too much responsibility on the justice to allow *him* to be so persuaded; and Walter saw that if he must keep faith with Lady Grimstone, or indulge the earnest desires of Julia, there was no alternative but to be bound for him. He felt that it was like running a course, ruinous to himself and useless to Christopher, with open eyes; but honour and affection seemed now to demand it of him. He felt compelled to make a wilful plunge into a desperate gulf; and at once inwardly blaming his own folly, and yet vindicating himself as under a stern necessity, he made the sacrifice with a groan, and was bound, in order that that very hour Christopher and his brothers might return with him to Denborough Park.

This being agreed to, the justice set forth in pompous terms the offence of which Grimstone had been guilty—an assault on the person of the Honourable Henry Finch. "It would have been a melancholy duty," he averred, "to have committed the son of a brother magistrate—the son of a man of unquestionable honour—a most worthy man—as Sir Harbottle Grimstone was." All men of wealth were, in the good justice's eyes, men of unquestionable honour and worth. "To have committed such a one to his majesty's county gaol for a misdemeanour of so serious a nature—a misdemeanour of which any poacher or common cut-throat might have been guilty—would certainly have been a most trying duty; but that, on his entering into a recognisance of three hundred pounds to appear in court at the ensuing sessions, and in the mean time to keep the peace, Mr. Walter Constable himself being surety therefor, he should be at liberty to attend him." Time pressed and Walter had not even a moment to deliberate: if his good angel warned him, he regarded him not. The recogniance was prepared, and Walter was introduced to the room where Grimstone remained a prisoner. Without having pictured to himself how the disgrace had been borne by him, Walter certainly felt rather surprised and extremely provoked, especially after the urgent summons he had received from Grimstone himself, to find him asleep on a sofa—where, too, he had evidently taken great pains to insure his bodily convenience—and to see him then

rise up with an air of perfect indifference and on hearing what had
been done for him, snap his fingers and swear it was a good joke!

Christopher had ridden to the justice's attended by his grooms,
and they now came forth rosy from the kitchen, and with many
an outward sign beside of the good cheer they had been enjoying
there. Walter related to them the melancholy news which he had
received from Denborough Park—told of their mother's earnest
prayer to see them—and urged them to speed; in that they might
find her alive.

They had unfortunately yet to return through Tutbury, the justice
living beyond, upon another road. As they entered the town, the
bull, which had been captured by the Staffordshire-men—but not
without a violent contention with the other party, and even a long
and bloody battle, the uproar and tumult of which were even heard
that night even at Wood Leighton—had subsequently been killed,
and was just at that time borne through the streets on a platform
raised shoulder-high, decorated with ribbons, flowers, and large
branches of laurel, preceded by torches and music, and followed by
an immense and unruly concourse, shouting, reeling, singing, and
dancing—a procession worthy of the wildest rites among the groves
and mountains of Crete.

In crossing the street, they became entangled with the crowd;
and when it was gone by, Walter looked round in vain for his
companions. Provoked beyond measure at this, which he thought
might be intentional, in order that they might remain to partake
the license of the evening, he turned his horse, and pursued the
tumultuous company, looking on all sides for the Grimstones—but
they were not to be seen. He rode down to the small hostelry, but
they were not there and, without stopping to answer the inquiries
of the fair Peggy, or of her not less anxious grandmother, and
mortified to have lost thus much time, spurred his horse to a gallop,
and took for the high road to Wood Leighton, thinking it possible
that they might have ridden on before him; but neither were they
on the road, nor could he hear of their having been seen upon it.
It was long past ten o'clock when he reached Denborough Park;

and as Walter advanced along the silent and dimly lighted passages, his heart warned him truly of the tidings that awaited him. Lady Grimstone was dead. And after a melancholy meeting with Julia, Bernard, and Father Cradock, Walter hastened to Westow.

It would be in vain to attempt to describe or unravel his feelings as he rode homeward. A sense of the folly into which he had been, as he now thought, weakly betrayed by his synmpathy with Lady Grimstone and his love for Julia, hung on him with a dark and most depressing weight. "Fool!" he continually exclaimed to himself, "how could I be so weak? how could I hope for a moment to produce the slightest good effect on such abandoned wretches as those brothers? how could I be deluded into so Quixotic an enterprise as to accompany them to such a scene?" And yet he continually again questioned of himself, in the fond desire to do away the impression that he *had* been weak and foolish, "Yet, how *could* I help it? could I be so barbarous as to let that worthy and afflicted woman go down to the grave with the blunt assurance that I would not move a finger for the promotion of her dearest wishes?—so barbarous as to tell her to her face that her sons were hopeless reprobates, and the very attempt to reclaim them certain destruction to the firmest character?" Yet, in spite of all his fond self-persuasions, the sense of a weak imprudence, and sense of vague apprehensions, and fearful and destructive consequences—he could not tell what—from this rash undertaking, haunted him, and caused him to pass a sleepless night of the saddest, most depressing, and torturing state of mind that he had ever endured.

IX

The next morning, before Walter had left his bed, his mother presented herself in his chamber, with a countenance of such unusual agitation as immediately confirmed his worst apprehensions and made him instantly demand what awful tidings she brought.

"Father Cradock waits to see you," said she; "rise, my son—here is strange news!"

"Is Julia dead!" asked he, with terror.

"No, no!" replied Mrs. Constable, vexed that his thought was of a Grimstone; and bidding him again hasten she left him in no enviable state of suspense.

Walter dressed with almost incredible speed and entered the room in which Father Cradock and Mrs. Constable sat together in deep consultation. The old man's countenance of a certainty indicated anything but good news, and Walter impatiently demanded what tidings he brought.

Father Cradock stroked his white hair; and said sorrowfully that they were not such as he would like to hear.

"Tell me then instantly!" exclaimed Walter; "you torture me by this suspense."

"Of a surety," said the priest, "if such things were permitted now-a-days, I should believe the Evil One to have bodily possession of Christopher Grimstone!"

"That he has, there is no doubt of it!" exclaimed Mrs. Constable.

"What of Christopher Grimetone?" asked Walter, in a tone of angry impatience. "Speak it out at once!"

"Peace, my son, peace!" said the old man, again stroking down his high, bald forehead. He then inquired at what place Walter had left the Grimstones, and how much of the day before had been spent in their company.

Walter, though still burning to know the exact tidings which Father Cradock had to relate, told circumstantially the events of the day.

The old man crossed himself when he had ended, and muttered a few words of thanksgiving; "I believed you innocent!" said he, with emphasis.

"I told you he could not be otherwise," said Mrs. Constable.

"Of what am I suspected? Speak out, Father Cradock!" said Walter, "if you would have me keep my senses."

The old priest then related, that an express had just arrived from Justice Haliday, with warrants for the apprehension of the three Grimstones, on these grounds of suspicion; that it had been proved that Christopher and his brothers had ridden from Tutbury to Hanbury, on the edge of Needwood Forest, where they had regaled themselves, and which place they had left about half-past nine o'clock, taking the road onward to the forest; that the Earl's coach, containing himself and two ladies, with his nephew on the box and two out-riders, had also passed through about a quarter of an hour afterwards, on their way to Lichfield, which place, late as it then was, and unfrequented and lonesome as were the road and the district through which they had to pass, they intended to reach that night. That somewhere near the by-road that led to the Hoar-cross, in the depths of the forest, the coach was stopped, as was supposed at first, by highwaymen, for the purpose of plunder. Accordingly their money and watches were offered them without hesitation. This, however, was not their object; nothing was taken from them, but a forcible attempt was made to carry off the younger lady; but in consequence of resistance offered by the younger gentlemen and the two out-riders, the villains, who also were three in number, were defeated; but, woful to relate, one of them had paid dearly for his temerity—his life was the sacrifice. The fact of the man being dead was clearly ascertained; the two decamped, and the body was thrown by the way-side; the coach then, with its inmates more dead than alive from terror, drove at its utmost speed to Yoxall, which lay but a few miles onward, where, instead of going forward, they remained through the night.

Many were the exclantatious both of indignation and surprise with which Walter interrupted this relation. He again bitterly cursed his own facility of temper, which had made him responsible for so desperate a ruffian. "And which of these villains," asked he, "has been killed in this outrage!"

"That," said Father Cradock, "I have yet to relate. From Yoxall persons were instantly despatched for the body, accompanied by one of the out-riders to point out the exact spot; but the body was not to be found: the survivors, it is supposed, returned and conveyed it away, to prevent their persons being identified. No traces were discoverable beyond the blood where the body had fallen and afterwards been laid: it had been removed carefully and expeditiously. The whole country, however, is roused in pursuit both of the living and the dead, which last, it is imagined, has been thrown into some pond or thicket of the forest.'"

Walter sat for some time without speaking, his countenance darkened, his brow knit, and his consciousness growing into a burning desire for vengeance.

"Well, my son," asked Mrs. Constable in triumphant resentment, "what think you of your friends now?"

"Do you consider *me* the friend of these ruffians, Mrs. Constable?" demanded Walter, with a tone and glance which made her feel how unjust and unkind had been her taunt.

"By G—d!" exclaimed Walter, "I will rouse heaven and earth but these villains shall be brought to punishment!"

"Vengeance is the Lord's, and he will repay it," said the mild voice of the priest. "Besides, there are those who deeply suffer from this awful visitation: of a truth that sainted woman was removed from the evil to come!"

"But said you not," asked Walter, "that *I* was implicated in this affair?"

Father Cradock then went on again to say, that though the persons who were guilty of this outrage had not been sworn to as the Grimstones; for owing to the darkness of the night, the thickness of the forest, and the general confusion of the scene, their persons had not been distinctly visible, though that they were there was clearly ascertained; and moreover, as the body had not been found, it had not been identified;—still suspicion was strong against the Grimstones. The conduct of Christopher on the castle-hill, and their being at the very time on the road—a road so entirely out of their homeward course—seemed to leave no doubt that they were the perpetrators of the outrage; that perhaps the circumstance of Walter's being seen with him the day before, or because he had procured the liberation of Christopher, might have in some degree turned public attention upon him. True, however, it was, a warrant

at that very time awaited to carry him before the nearest magistrate
to answer to this suspicion. Beyond this, Father Cradock told that
the warrant he understood, had been issued at the express desire of
the Earl of N—, who, it was said, had taken serious umbrage against
Walter, the cause whereof, however, he could not ascertain.

The proud and sensitive spirit of Walter felt the very suspicion
itself as the most cruel wrong. "Yet" said he, "is it no more than the
natural consequence of being seen in such company; and moreover
giving security for such fellows."

"Thank God, however," continued he, "that this suspicion has
taken a tangible form! The very publicity of the impeachment must
be accompanied by an acknowledgement of my hononr at once—it
must and shall."

In obedience therefore to the warrant, Walter presented himself
before the magistsates, who were that day met at Wood Leighton.
The circumstance had got wind; the affair of the Grimstones
was the univesal theme and that Walter Constable could by any
possibility be implicated with them is the strangest thing of all.
The justice-room was crowded and Walter had the satisfaction of
finding that public opinion acquitted him even before the case was
examined. And when he stated in a clear and candid manner that
every one must have felt how repugnant his appearance with such
a man as Christopher Grimstone in such a scene must have been,
and that nothing but the solemn dying request of Lady Grimstone
made in the fond hope of saving him from some foolish act and
consequent deeper disgrace and recklessness could have induced
him to accept the office he had so fruitlessly undertaken, Walter
was cleared in the most honourable manner; not the shadow of
a doubt remained against him. This implication of an honourable
and unimpeachable man, as every one felt Walter Constable to be,
excited public indignation still more against the Grimstones. That
Christopher Grimstone should have rendered himself amenable
to the laws by a second, even more audacious outrage, at the very
time when Constable had made himself responsible for his actions,
not from personal regard to him, but in order that he might hasten

to the death-bed of his mother, was an accumulation of guilt, and indicated a more base, a more selfish nature than even public opinion had hitherto believed him capable of.

Walter's anxiety had been intensely great, as to the means by which the forfeit sum for which he was become responsible should be raised. True, until the body was found and identified as a Grimstone, the case rested on suspicion; but that suspicion was considered by all as a certainty—Christopher was already convicted by public opinion. This anxiety, however, was set at rest by a sealed packet being brought into the justice-room, and delivered to him—from Denborough Park, as was said, and, as was also understood, from Sir Harbottle Grimstone. It contained three hundred pounds, and a slip of paper purporting that it was to cover the demand upon Mr. Walter Constable, in case of the conviction of Mr. Grimstone.

There was nothing extraordinary in the circumstance itself: it was but common justice, common honesty; and Walter, inexpressibly relieved, returned to Westow, having placed the money in the hands of the magistrates, to answer his recognisance in case the Grimstones were legally proved to have been guilty of this outrage, otherwise to be returned to Sir Harbottle Grimstone, neither to hold Sir Harbottle's money, nor to have any public obstacle to his own departure from the country which his anticipated engagements with the marquis might require. We said there was nothing extraordinary in the circumstance; but we were wrong: both Walter and the gentleman to whom he consigned the contents of the packet agreed, that, as the action of Sir Harbottle Grimstone, it certainly *was* extraordinary; but all agreed that, doubtless, the death of his lady had touched his heart with a natural sorrow, and opened it to more generous sentiments than commonly operated upon it. Sir Harbottle gained great credit by this act of gratuitous justice.

What was the cause Walter Constable did no got that evening to Denborough Park, it is impossible to say. He doubted not the distress of his friends, and he did not need telling that his presence there would be consoling to them: still he did not go there, and even when Mrs. Constable remarked, in the course of their conversation, "that her heart truly bled for Miss Julia Grimstone, yet her utter disgust for the family outweighed even her sympathy for her," he heard the remark without reply.

Walter talked that night again of his former schemes of personal advancement, spoke of the weariness of a life of inaction, and declared himself impatient till the time came when he should leave this neighbourhood altogether. He did not forget, it is true, that Bernard Grimstone's views in life were connected with his own, nor did he wish the connexion between them annulled; but, for that night, he made no mention of his name.

It cannot be supposed this while that his friends at Denborough Park were equally as apparently regardless of him. Acute as was their grief for the death of their mother, still more agonising were the events which had succeeded it, made yet more distressing from the implication of Walter, and the way in which he might become a sufferer in the guilt of their brothers.

It was within the chamber of death that these two noble minded young people sat together that morning, mingling their tears, and humiliated in the degradation of their house. Their intense mourning for the dead was over; for how could they sorrow for her who had so evidently departed from the evil to come? The most immediate subject of anxiety was how to free Walter from the bond he had subjected himself to; and, as the most legitimate means, they resolved upon applying to their father.

Had Bernard demanded his father's life, his surprise could not have been greater than it was on hearing for what he asked. It was the first time that Bernard himself had ever asked his father for money, and the strangeness of the circumstance did not escape Sir Harbottle's notice.

"And pray, sir," asked the father, when both Bernard and Julia had gone through all their arguments of equity and honour—"And pray, sir, who desired Mr. Constable to make himself responsible for the actions of that d——d rascal? who invited him to meddle or to make? and what, I ask ye, have we to thank him for in so doing? Is not the whole of this confounded business his own bringing about? Christopher and the rest of the pack should have gone to the devil for me! I shall not raise the money: he that was fool enough to do it may abide by his own folly! When I ask Mr. Walter Constable to advance money, why then I'll pay him, and not till then! I am not going to throw my money to every blockhead who puts himself in the shoes of every one that calls himself Grimstone—d'ye hear that? and, by—, if you come here asking for money, why I'll e'en make it scarcer than it has been!"

Still Bernard remonstrated, and Julia seconded his arguments by tears and the most tender persuasions; but the more they pleaded, the more resolutely determined became the father, until, at length, he overpowered them with oaths and threats, and sent them, silenced and heartbroken, back their own apartment.

"This money, then, shall go," said Bernard, bringing forth the sum which had been advanced for his own outfit in life. Julia had remembered this money, but had not ventured to hint of its being so applied.

"Heaven reward you, dearest Bernard!" exclaimed the weeping Julia, and kissing his outstretched hand; "but it is such a sacrifice!"

"No, no," replied Bernard, firmly; "it is but justice—it is but what our honour demands; it must go!"

The money was still deficient many pounds—far more than they themselves had any means of supplying; and to apply again to their father, even for this smaller sum, was what they did not dare to do. Without saying a word, and blinded by her tears, Julia opened the small cabinet where her mother kept her few valuables, and where she knew was deposited her carefully-husbanded allowance; but the purse contained only a couple of guineas. Julia's eye, however, fell upon another, an ancient one long disused, which appeared tolerably filled, and to it was attached a small paper. The paper contained the handwriting of Lady Grimstone, feeble and scarcely legible, written the day before her death. "The money," it said, "contained within this purse, was of many years' saving, by long and painful economy, aud was left to be divided between her two dear children, Julia and Bernard Grimstone; not to purchase mourning ornaments with—they did not need such to keep their mother in their memory—but for their own proper use, or to be applied to any urgent need, as they might see fit."

Both brother and sister read the paper. Julia did not speak—she did not even dare to think—but, falling on her knees before the crucifix which had always hung over her mother's cabinet, poured out the emotion of her soul in silent devotion. Bernard, touched beyond expression by this proof of his mother's tender, thoughtful affection, and with feelings too powerful almost to be contained within his breast, covered his face with his hands, and wept like a woman.

The sacrifice was made: the sacred bequest—little as it was, yet enough to eke out the required sum—was applied to an urgent need, as their honourable hearts felt this indeed to be, and the money was received into the hands of Walter Constable without its exciting any sentiment of gratitude—any emotion whatever.

X

The next morning Walter awoke with renewed fealty of soul to his one-day-slighted Julia; and writing her a hasty but affectionate note, excusing his absence at a moment when his presence was doubly needful to her, ordered his horse, and set out on his way to the house of Colonel Haughton, principally with the design of clearing himself with the Earl, and ascertaining the cause of that nobleman's displeasure and suspicion.

It was a long ride, and the noon was past when he arrived there. Colonel Haughton was a frank, cordial-hearted man, and received Walter with the greatest good-will, assuring, him, even before he introduced the subject, that he entirely acquitted him; that, in truth, he had not for a single moment suspected him; "although his noble friend," he said, "had some queer notions, at the bottom of which he could not get."

He then excused himself with Walter, as the Earl was at that moment leaving his house. The carriage was at the door, he said; the ladies and Mr. Finch were already gone.

Walter insisted on seeing the Earl. His desire was immediately granted. The nobleman was naturally proud and implacable, and the interview was unsatisfactory.

He stood with his foot on the step of his carriage, and intimated that he was not to be detained. Walter, however, did detain him; but it was merely to hear "that nothing would give his lordship greater pleasure than to be convinced of his disconnexion with Mr. Grimstone; but he believed he had proofs to the contrary, more conclusive even than Mr. Walter Constable's present asseverations."

"What were they?" asked Walter, with forced submission: "would his lordship be good enough to state them?"

The Earl looked at him, as if amazed at his insolence, and declined to say further, desiring that his time might not be intruded upon.

Walter withdrew, incensed and bewildered to the utmost, and the carriage drove off.

It was in vain that Walter turned over and over in his mind the insinuation of the Earl: so entirely had he hitherto been disconnected with the three elder Grimstones, that he could find no circumstance on which to ground the insinuation. At length it occurred to him that it must be owing to something which Christopher had himself said; for did he not speak of a conversation with Miss Hammond, of which himself had been the subject? The idea was plausible; and Walter burned with yet stronger impatience for the detection of the traitor. The more he thought of it, the more indignant he became: he was maddened almost to frenzy; he longed to challenge the Earl—to make him prove or retract his words—to show to the whole world his detestation of the Grimstones—his entire disconnexion with them! "And this," thought Walter, in his indiscriminate passion, "is the bitter fruit of this alliance: my name blasted—myself degraded into the reprobate associate of these outcasts of society!"

To a young man like Walter, with his keen sense of honour, his high moral purity, and fervent desire for distinction, what more cruel blow could have been given? He vowed with himself to discover the traitor, be he where he would; and for this purpose again mounted his horse on his way to Justice Haliday's.

It was a melancholy ride. The afternoon was close and sultry; low electric clouds seemed to weigh heavy upon the very face of the earth. Walter's road, too, lay through the forest, where not a breath of air was stirring; the broad leaves of the trees stood motionless, as if fixed in an atmosphere of quicksilver. Beyond this, it was the very road upon which the outrage had been committed; and in that depressing and stifling atmosphere, Walter felt an impatience and restlessness of spirit painfully at variance with the torpidity of his animal frame. He approached that part of the road where the dark and livid traces of blood yet remained frightfully distinct. It was with unmingled horror that he reached it, and looked down upon the ghastly witness of the deed. Was it the blood of Christopher himself, or one of his brothers? Walter shuddered as he asked himself this question; and as he pondered upon the answer, his reflections grew awfully melancholy. There, at his very feet, lay the life-blood of a being whom, but a few hours ago, he had seen living, and, in the full intoxication of reckless and guilty youth, who had died a sudden and frightful death in the commission of outrage. What had followed, God, of his just but awful judgment, alone knew!

Walter's heart was overcome by these reflections; and spite of the inveterate hatred with which he had ridden up to the spot, he drew forth the small crucifix which lay upon his breast, and kissing it devoutly, offered up a prayer for the soul of the miserable departed.

This done, with much calmer and more Christian sentiment Walter proceeded on his way.

The justice, like Colonel Haughton, received him with the most entire friendliness; regretting extremely the annoyance to which he had been subjected, and deploring yet more and more the distress which his respected brother magistrate, the worthy Sir Harbottle Grimstone, must endure on account of his reprobate sons.

"A far greater mercy, Mr. Constable, it is," said his worship, in a voice of solemn and unfeigned thanksgiving, "to have no sons, than to have to see them thus peril and disgrace themselves, and thus bring sorrow on the grey hair of their parents! I am thankful to say, Mr. Constable, that I have no children!" And of course Walter congratulated the excellent magistrate on the happy circumstance.

The storm, which had been collecting the whole afternoon, came down shortly after Walter had arrived; and as it was then getting late, and there appeared no prospect of its present subsiding, Mr. Haliday, who was greatly pleased with his guest, insisted on his remaining there for the night. Walter consented, not without fears for the anxiety which his mother might feel on his account.

The storm, which abated towards bed-time, returned with force in the course of the night; and Walter, who could not sleep, rose from his bed, and partly dressing himself, looked out upon the deluged landscape, which ever and anon shone out in fierce brightness, as the broad universal flashes of lightning descended at once, as if from every part of the heavens. He saw the near forest lying in profound blackness—lying like a wall of solid darkness against the illuminated sky. His eye became irresistibly attracted towards it, and he seemed to see, within some hidden thicket of its profound depths, as the lightning flashed downward into them, the disfigured and ghastly dead body! Walter thought he must dream, and roused himself into strong consciousness. Again the chilling horror crept over him, and the besetting vision was there; and as the succeeding glare flashed by, he saw again the ghastly upturned eye, and the bloody death-wound. Walter again believed that he had slept, though but for a moment, and that this was the creation of his excited imagination. He turned, therefore, to his bed, intending to compose himself to rest; but, in spite of himself, yet once more returned to the window. At that very moment the dense black clouds seemed rent asunder, and the lightning, as if grasped into a gigantic handful, was hurled into the very centre of the forest. A frightful concussion succeeded—peal upon peal of deafening thunder, which shook the walls of the house, and made every pane in the windows vibrate. A profound stillness succeeded; the lightning flashed again; but each succeeding flash grew paler, and the thunder less loud, till by degrees the storm entirely abated.

Walter returned to his bed; but, excited by what he had seen, and the fearful vision which had so frightfully haunted his imagination, it was long before he again slept. Nor did he wake till the slow, pompous voice of the old magistrate summoned him at his chamber-door, with the information—not the most agreeable for an unrobed guest to hear—that he had been up for half an hour, and should be happy to take his breakfast whenever it was Mr. Constable's pleasure to make his appearance. It was fortunate for Walter that his host's patience was not made of glass. The two sat down to breakfast with mutual good-will.

Walter spoke of the storm of the preceding night; but his host had not been disturbed. "He had," he said, "one deaf ear, and he always lay with that uppermost."

He had related to his host, the evening before, the whole particulars of the day passed at Tutbury, not omitting the apparent interest which Christopher Grimstone had in the good-will of Milly Freckleten and her grand-daughter. The justice had thought these things over; and now suggested to Walter that Grimstone might perhaps be concealed with these people. The same idea had occurred to him.

Attended, therefore, by proper officers with a search-warrant, as soon as breakfast was over, he took his way towards the small hostelry at Tutbury, having promised, at Mr. Haliday's urgent injunction, to return again to an early dinner, in order that he might know the result.

Walter alighted at the door of the small public-house, and, without ceremony, entered the little parlour. All stood in the exact order in which he had last seen it. The old woman entered after him.

"Ay, bless you, sir," she began, wiping her eyes with her apron, "here is a pretty job! War it Mr. Christopher as lighted of his death! Pray, sir, tell me, if you know!"

"I know not," replied Walter, "but am come to you for information."

"Eh, sir, but you are come to a wrong body for that!—And, heyday!" exclaimed she, fixing her eyes on the men who attended Walter, and had followed closely upon him, "and what have we here?"

The warrant was produced, and the old woman informed that her premises must be searched.

"Ay, ay, search and welcome!" said she; "I'll give ye leave to take whatever ye find that'll bring shame on Milly Freckleton!"

"How is your grand-daughter?" asked Walter.

"How is she?—why, not much better for your asking after her! It's like to be the death of her; and of me too, for what I see; and now ye mun come here with your search-warrants, as if I harboured stolen goods!"

"My good woman," returned Walter, "nothing is wanted but the persons of these ruffians: you will do the country good service by delivering them up to the law!"

"I am no but a poor widow woman," she replied, "and live by my credit; and it can do me no service to have my house rauked over by a couple of catch-thieves. At that rate, I should like to know who is secure by his own fireside? Onybody may get a search-warrant, if this is law, and enter his neighbour's house night or day! It's not what I've been used to, and I'm none so fond of it!"

The constables entered, declaring they found no cause for suspecting the persons of the Grimstones to be concealed there.

"Ay, so I tould ye—I tould ye, ye might look and welcome, ye'd get nothing for your pains! A couple of bulking varlets! Get out of my house with ye—for turn you out I will, though I, maybe, was forced to let you in!"

The men went out, and Walter offered her half-a-crown, apologizing for the disturbance they had occasioned. She pocketed the money, but still looked far from pacified.

"I took you for one of his friends," said she; "but I war mista'en, it seems."

Walter again inquired after the grand-daughter, and if she were at home.

"Ay, ay, her's at home!" replied poor Milly, petulantly! you havn't a search-warrant for her, have you?"

Walter smiled and replied that she was a pretty and a modest young woman, therefore he had inquired after her.

"Why, if that's your business, it is soon done." Walter was not satisfied, for he suspected that where Peggy was, there might Christopher be also; but he could get no further information—the old woman was angry and sullen. But in going out, he saw the fair Peggy engaged in household work. She was down upon her knees whitening the hearth-stone of a little side-room; and as she pursued the work unconscious of any observer, he saw the tears fall from her eyes upon the stone she was rubbing.

It was a simple picture of real sorrow, that touched Walter deeply. "Christopher Grimstone is not here," thought he, "or that poor girl would not weep thus at the moment of his escape!" Walter, nevertheless, was wrong. Christopher and his brother were both there, hidden in a small chamber of the roof. They were her own deep and secret heart-griefs which made Peggy Woodhouse water her household-work with her tears.

As Walter was returning to the house of the old magistrate, he saw the small, light figure of Daniel Neale stepping along to no measured pace. There was important meaning in his very gait; and it was not without a firm persuasion that the beggar had something to tell, that Walter overtook him, slackening his pace as he approached.

"Lord love you, Mr. Walter Constable!" exclaimed he, raising up both his hands at once; "you are the very man of all others that I wanted to see! Dismount, sir, and hear what I have to tell you."

Walter dismounted, and Daniel then related, that being on his travels, though he must confess somewhat out of his usual round, he was the last evening overtaken by the storm in the midst of the forest, and had taken shelter under a miserable hut. That in truth, to him, who was used to be out at all times and in all weathers, it was a matter of but little moment, for he could sleep as well in storm as in shine—at least when the storm was in a common way, but the last night's storm had been no common one, but one of God's messengers of judgment, said Daniel, crossing himself both on breast and forehead. He had lain awake, he continued, most of the night, and had seen old Malabar, the deer-stealer, out on his marauding even at such a time as that. But, however, that was neither here nor there with what he had to relate, he saw every distinct flash of lightning as it came; and, at last, down from the very top of heaven, as if it had been a huge fiery ball, he saw the red thunderbolt itself come down right over his head; and thinking at the very moment that his hour was come, he prayed every saint to have mercy on his soul. However, sure enough the prayer was only thought, not said; for, before there was time to speak three words, the bolt fell at about ten yard distance, right upon a large forest-oak, riving it from top bottom, splitting it asunder with a dreadful crash, and dividing it right and left. Dazzled and stunned with this strange and frightful death, which had been at hand, and yet slain not, Daniel described himself to have fallen flat on his face, and to have lain he knew not how long; he supposed, believing himself dead. When he came to himself again, it was daylight and he got up thinking he had been in a dream; but the fallen and splintered tree was an evidence of the reality of what he had seen. He got up, and went to the spot to examine more narrowly, "And may the blessed saints in paradise be about me!" exclaimed Daniel, "what should I see but the body of George Grimstone—I knew it well by the cut over the left eyebrow: that was done when he was a lad. What should I see but his body, bloody and disfigered, lying in a thicket of holly which the thunder-stricken tree had parted in falling! Tell me there's not a Providence in these things!" exclaimed he, striking his staff upon the ground with energy;—"why otherwise was the thunderbolt sent to strike that one tree only in the forest; and why was I sent there, out of my regular course, but for one and the same purpose?" So saying, Daniel crossed himself with deep devotion and repeated a Paternoster. Walter did not deny what the beggar had asserted of the agency of Providence; on the contrary, he thought him right; and, inviting him to follow to Justice Haliday's, again mounted his horse, and carried the news forward at full speed.

The magistrate, being informed of this, set himself about to take all proper steps respecting it; and Walter, directed by the beggar to the exact spot rode forward to see for himself a place and event which had been so singularly visioned to him in the night.

The place itself was a small lawn-like opening in the very heart of the forest, and to which there was not even a foot-track—a spot admirably chosen for the purpose of concealment. Impenetrable thickets of holly surrounded it, with but narrow openings between; and in the very centre of this oasis had grown the tree which the lightning had struck. He found it cleft exactly down the middle, as Daniel had said, the two halves falling opposite ways; a strong branch of one division having completely opened the thick clump of holly in which the body had been concealed. The shed which Daniel had mentioned stood at right angles with the tree, and had been erected by bark-peelers at some distant time. It was now a picturesque object, half fallen to decay, such as a painter would have loved, and no one, save an out-of-doors dweller like Daniel Neale, would have thought of passing a night in.

At another time Walter might have looked on it with pleasure, as an excellent and beautiful accessory of a fine bit of forest scenery; but he was in no mood now for such thoughts or such contemplations. The place was not solitary; several peasants were already there, sent thither by some rumour of discovery which had got abroad. The body had been drawn forth from its concealment, and laid under the shed. It was, without a doubt, the body of George Grimstone, in the identical groom's livery which he had worn on that fatal day. A sickness, as of death, came over Walter as he recognised the body, and he leaned against the broken wall for support. An old woman, wrapped in a long grey cloak, and with a black handkerchief tied over her head, was looking on the body; and the peasants, seeing one with the appearance of a gentleman arrive there, hastily joined him.

"Ay, ay," said the old woman, observing Walter's emotion, "this is a Grimstone come by a violent death—where's the wonder? and the others are hiding in dens and caves of earth! Well, well, it's all right! There was a storm last night!—ha! ha! ha! Poor Dummie was struck with lightning. They told me so; and now, and now, you all see there lies a Grimstone! I knew what would happen—I knew it five-and-thirty years ago. Well, I'm an old woman now, and they call me mad; but I've lived to see my words come true, and I may yet live to see more than this. Sorrow strikes as deeply as sin! But what of that?—they are all Grimstones!" And so saying, she turned herself round and walked away, leaving the peasants looking one upon the other.

"Who is she?" at length asked Walter.

He was told that she was a poor woman, afflicted with periodical insanity, who lived in one of the forest villages, and was suspected at some former time to have lost a dumb child by lightning. Her name was unknown to every one, except that she called herself Judith.

Walter was unaccountably agitated by the words of the poor maniac; and taking from his pocket a slip of paper, upon which he wrote a request that his friend, Justice Haliday would pardon his taking leave without further ceremony, and desiring one of the peasants to hand it to him without fail when he arrived there, as he shortly would do, with the coroner and other official persons, he remounted his horse, took the forest-road through Newborough and Marchington homeward.

XI

The news of the body being found was carried to Denborough Park by the good Father Cradock; and however strong had been the conviction of Julia and Bernard that it had to be their brother, the certainty was not received with less poignant distress.

Sir Harbottle heard the tidings with an unmoved countenance. "The rascal!" exclaimed he: "what! and I shall have two funerals on my hands at once!" He then turned round again to his bonds and mortgages.

The inquest taken on the body found a verdict of "Accidental death caused by a wound given in defending the person of Miss Hammond from himself and his brothers."

The next evening, in the dusk hour, Father Cradock and Bernard saw the body decently interred in the nearest churchyard. Sir Harbottle Grimstone afterwards defrayed the expenses which had been laid down by the priest, but not without his demurring as to the necessity of several small items.

No sooner was it gone abroad that the dead man was of a surety George Grimstone, than tradesman after tradesman, and claimants of both sexes, who in a variety of ways had deemands upon him, beset Sir Harbottle in his house, and when he walked abroad. "How," he exclaimed, "was he likely to pay money for which they had nothing to show?" No sooner was this said, then out came notifications and certifications that such and such sums were justly due, and should be faithfully discharged on the demise of Sir Harbottle Grimstone, all properly signed by the veritable hand of his son George.

"But," replied the baronet, with imprecations on his son which were terrible to hear, "that desirable event has not yet taken place!" And the unsatisfied claimants were dismissed, denouncing vengeance on Sir Harbottle and his family, and leaving him even more than ever filled with distrust and aversion to his children.

Four days had now passed since Walter Constable had been at Denborough Park; and Julia, almost overwhelmed by their misfortunes, was agonized at his apparent indifference. She made excuses for him to herself; and yet, at the same time, she listened for his step, and started at every sound, in the fond hope that he was coming; and then, in the continually-recurring disappointment, felt as if this doubt and suspense were more than she could bear. All this Bernard saw; and though neither spoke of it to the other, the pale and anxious countenance of his sister, of which he too well divined the cause, weighed as heavily on his soul as either their family grief or shame. Like all highly-poetical but ill-regulated minds, he was irritable and suspicious; and once excited the sympathy he felt for Julia became resentment against Walter. He recalled looks and expressions which, though not unobserved at the time, might yet have been entirely forgotten, had not events and suspicions brought them back, and given them even deeper meaning; and he condemned Walter Constable, as less generous, as less unworldly than was the ideal standard of excellence by which he had so long measured him. "I have imagined as I have wished him to be, not as I might have known him to be," said Bernard: "I have partly imposed upon myself, and I have been bitterly punished!" Again he thought of the sympathy and encouragement which he had received from him, and of the bright prospects that had been opened before him; and he felt hurled, as it were, from the sunny heights of confidence, of trusting friendship, and intellectual delight, into the dreary abysses of suspicion, deceived hopes, and the solitude of his own troubled spirit;—and dark indeed were those alternate seasons of depression!

"I shall never believe in virtue or friendship again!" exclaimed Bernard indignantly, when, returning from the interment of his brother, he asked the desperate question, whether Walter Constable had been there, and received from his sister the answer "No," spoken, spite of herself, reluctantly, as if his partook of her brother's suspicions. "I shall put no faith in fair promises again! And I thank Heaven that he will have to make no sacrifices for us! Had I sold myself into slavery for it, Mr. Constable should not have lost one sixpence by us."

"Oh, Bernard, dearest Bernard," said Julia, "you make me miserable—you misjudge him. But supposing he were offended, has he not had enough to offend him ten times over?"

"What has passed between yourselves," replied Bernard, with asperity, "I know not; but as to anything farther, I can only answer you by this question; had he been in your place, and you in his, could you have thus neglected him?"

Julia's heart, not her lips, made the direct reply. "Well, Bernard," she said, "leave the subject—I cannot contend with you; and if it were possible that he had deserted and forgotten me, you, I know, never will." And so saying, she kissed his forehead tenderly, and

hastened to her own chamber to think over the anxious subject
with tears; while Bernard, yet more confirmed in his own opinion,
and filled with yet hotter resentment against Walter, because of the
anguish which Julia strove in vain to conceal, went forth into the
solitudes of this old park, not to think, not to tranquillise his mind,
but to see cause of irritation in everything that surrounded him—in
twilight, in silence, and even in the fair round moon herself.

The next day was Sunday, and its calm bright evening brought to
the soul of Walter Constable those heart-cementing, heart-softening
influences, which are as if the passing of an angel's wing overshadowed
us, leaving behind some of it celestial essence of love. A golden light
streamed in between the trees that formed the western side of the
avenue barring the turf with light and shadow; and, as if the blasting
events of the last few days were forgotten, Walter gave himself up to
the beauty of external things. He saw the rich and mellow light lie in
broad masses alternated with intense shadow on the wooded slopes
and hollows of Denborough Park; and to the right, just overtopping
its dark trees, upon the very highest ground, the gilt vane of the old
summer-house. All at once a renewed sense of Julia's goodness—her
blameless suffering—her beauty—the natural joyousness of her heart,
gloomed and saddened as it must now be—came upon and with
self-condemnation which would have entirely reconciled Bernard
to his friend, could he have known it, he vowed with himself to go
even then to her, and receive all her full-hearted sorrows into his
own breast. He leaped over every stile that came in his way with
the alertness of a schoolboy and the impatience of a lover; "And of
a truth," thought he as he wondered at his own hilarity of heart and
limb, "my soul is taking holiday!"

Denborough Park was in sight, but a reception awaited him for
which he was not prepared.

" So, young man, what is your business?" asked the gruff voice
of Sir Harbottle Grimstone, as Walter entered the park and came
suddenly upon the baronet, who, in his old threadbare dress
and walking-stick, furnished with a small spade at the end—his
invariable out-of-doors companion—was stubbing up the thistles in

all the energy of ill-humour, counting the while the prodigious costs of two funerals at once, with all the necessary mourning, though none would be wanted for Chrisopher and Robert, of which circumstance he by no means lost sight;—"So, sir, and you have yet to learn, at your time of life, a seemly behaviour and carriage on the Lord's Day! What urgent business are you upon, that you must needs come leaping and vaulting like a sky-rocket at this rate?"

"This is a goodly crop of thistles!" returned Welter, sarcastically, meaning the remark to apply to the temper as well as to the field.

"Sir," said the baronet, understanding the allusion, "was it to affront me that you came jumping here like a mountebank!"

"By no means, Sir Harbottle."

"Then, sir, what is your business here at all ?"

"I am not come for a brawl, Sir Harbottle," returned Walter, offended, and yet willing to keep peace; "my intentions were the most friendly in the world both to yourself and your family—my object was to see Miss Grimstone."

"Oho! that was it, was it? Lookye, Mr. Constable, there go two words to every bargain. Has my leave been asked in this business?"

"You amaze me, Sir Harbottle!"

"Perhaps so," replied he, coolly; "but I will put to you one simple question: to whom am I obliged for the death of one son, and for the d—d confounded trouble that the others are got into!"

"To yourself, Sir Harbottle—to yourself, who neglected them in their youth to be disgraced by them in their manhood."

"It was myself who took them to Tutbury, eh?" ejaculated Sir Harbottle, almost breathless with passion; "it was myself, who, when that rascal was in safe keeping, thrust my neck into the noose on purpose that he should be at liberty to get into further mischief, oh!"

"Do you insinuate, Sir Harbottle, that I have been the cause of your sons' misdemeanours?"

"I not only insinuate it, but I speak it out plain!"

Provoked as Walter was by these insults, he remembered the money which he supposed Sir Harbottle had advanced to release him from his responsibility, and he in some degree excuse his anger.

"Come, Sir Harbottle," said he, "your feelings are excited—you are not in a fit state to speak of these things, and I cannot hear you reflect thus upon me in silence; therefore, if we must needs talk, let it be on subjects less personal, less exciting."

Sir Harbottle was pale with passion, and without noticing Walter's observation, he replied with the former charge: "I not only insinuate it, but I speak it out, sir; and I should like to know what the devil you must meddle in this matter for?"

"I wish to Heaven I had not meddled, Sir Harbottle," said Walter, extremely provoked by this renewed accusation; "but I by no means wish to quarrel with you; therefore, I wish you good evening, Sir Harbottle."

"No, sir, I shall not let you off so easily," said the baronet. "You take extraordinary liberties, let me tell you, Mr. Constable: this, that, and the other you do, interfering in affairs, without as much as, 'by your leave;' and now, having got my sons out of the way, you think of marrying my daughter. You have an eye to the money, sir! But let me tell you, you are counting without your host!"

"This is most extraordinary behaviour, Sir Harbottle!" said Walter, subjecting his passion by the most resolute self-command.

"Extraordinary behaviour! Heyday! the world is come to a pretty pass, when a man has not a voice in disposing of his own! My daughter, sir, is as much my own as this land is!"

"Let not Miss Grimstone's name come between us, Sir Harbottle; neither you nor I are cool at this moment; for God's sake, sir, do not make her a subject of strife between us!"

"I am perfectly cool—never was cooler in my life," replied Sir Harbottle; "and I shall say what I please, and be controlled by no man. I told you that you took great liberties, and now forsooth I am not to say anything but what it pleases you to hear! Egad! you are for making yourself master of Denborough Park with a vengeance!"

"Sir Harbottle," remonstrated Walter, "why should we work ourselves to this state of animosity? My addresses to Miss Grimstone cannot have been unknown to you!"

"Lookye now, Mr. Constable," returned he, "my daughter will some day have a pretty fortune, if she marries to please me—a hundred thousand pounds, or something like it. But money must have money, sir. This old place at Westow, seventy acres of land, a tumble-down house, and not a spare hundred pounds to bless yourself with, will not do for me. I do not live here with my eyes shut, Mr. Constable; I know how things are going with you. You had better cut down your trees, and trade with the money—an old avenue and a head full of family pride will not do for me, sir; I shall never give my consent; that you may both of you understand—and let her marry without it if she dare!"

"What in Heaven's name, Sir Harbottle, is your motive for this strange behaviour?" asked Walter.

"Lord bless me! am I to explain myself down to the dregs of actions and motives? I tell you, you shall not marry her!"

"Leave this subject, Sir Harbottle, or both you and I will say what we shall bitterly wish unsaid. By God! sir, I would not have borne from any other living man what I have this night borne from you," said Walter, with a flashing eye, and his excitement of tone which he vainly struggled to command.

"What I have to say, sir, I'll say now," replied Sir Harbottle. "I know what you, with your miserable place at Westow, and your beggarly income, look after my daughter for. You think of being master here, sir—you have got these lads out of the way, and that simpleton, Bernard, completely under your thumb, and now you think of settling yourself here."

"I will hear no more, or I shall forget that you are an old man," said Walter, turning away with a low suppressed voice of the most tumultuous passion.

"Pay me the money you owe me!" exclaimed Sir Harbottle, "and come again to Denborough Park at your peril!"

Who can describe the tempest of passion that agitated the soul of Walter Constable? He had gone there with a heart overflowing with tenderness and affection, disinterested as the daylight itself; he had been insulted, taunted with his poverty, subjected to the most injurious accusations, and finally rejected. The indignant anger which had been suppressed at the time, boiled over when he found himself alone, and for many hours he remained in the fields in a state of mind bordering on frenzy. A burning sense of insult seemed to drive him on to some act of desperation; he despised himself intensely for having tamely borne these insults—even Julia seemed an inadequate reward for the wounds his honour had received. It was a miserable time of passion; and when the paroxysm had gone by, he was terrified at his own excitement.

The next morning he rose from a night of broken slumber, with the firm determination to leave Westow as soon as possible, that he might lose in constant occupation the haunting sense of Sir Harbottle's insults, and the annoyances which must of necessity beset him while he remained in the neighbourhood of Denborough Park. All this excitement of mind did not escape the watchful eyes of Mrs. Constable, but with commendable forbearance she pressed for no explanation; and Walter, highly incensed as he was, resolved to keep Sir Harbottle's injurious behaviour strictly from her knowledge. She would not readily have pardoned his submission, nor would she ever after have extended sympathy or kindness to Julia, who more than ever, Walter was well persuaded, would need them both.

He intrusted a letter to Father Cradock which he enjoined him to deliver to Julia praying her to meet him at their old resort, the ruined summer-house, as soon as she could and begging her to name the day and hour.

Unconcious of the unhappy encounter between her father and her lover, the day was still passing heavily and sorrowfully with Julia; she sat alone in their melancholy apartment, with the full sense of her stripped and desolate state upon her, Bernard, too, was gloomy and ill at ease—there was a bitterness and a fierceness in his few brief expressions, from which she shrank as from the sting of a serpent. She dreaded to inquire why he was thus irritated, because his reply would be bitter invective against Walter. A presentiment, in spite of herself, lay heavy upon her, that the intercourse with Walter was near its close, when Father Cradock delivered to her the letter.

The sight of his handwriting was an inexpressible relief; and Julia read the letter twice before she discovered that it was unsatisfactory. "Why did he write at all—why did he not come as formerly; but why, especially, did he write a cool, constrained letter like this? Oh! it was so cruelly unlike her own feelings!" Julia meant her answer to be equally guarded; but, in spite of the short-comings of his letter, hers, written with many tears, was full of kindness. As soon, she said, as the mournful rites had been performed for the dead, she would meet him at the appointed place. "May the dear Mother of Mercies bless you!" she concluded. "I write this with an aching heart, and a dread of yet coming sorrow which weighs on my spirit like a mountain of lead. There is but one voice which could assure me, and that I can never more hear! I think at times this is more than I can bear; but, oh, Walter, we know not what we can bear! Who could have persuaded me, but a few days since, that I should have sat with tearless eyes by the dead body of my mother, and have been thankful even that she could not return to share the sorrow that overwhelms me? We know not indeed what we can bear, till some greater anguish than the last has tried us; and then we wonder, as well we may, that our hearts are not broken."

Walter read and re-read this letter, and even with tears vowed upon it to be true, eternally true, to the heart that had dictated it.

Lady Grimstone was buried; and that same evening the corn was cleared from the field which she had so prophetically pointed out.

Julia had agreed to meet him at the summer-house on the following afternoon; and but one single hour before the appointed time, he received a letter from the Marquis of A—. He broke the seal with impatience, supposing it an immediate summons for himself and Bernard. What was his consternation, his agony, to read a letter of this import!—

"That the marquis had received from his friend and relative, the Earl of N—, information of a most unpleasant nature, relative to certain disgraceful occurrences which taken place at Tutbury and in its neighbourhood, in which Mr. Walter Constable, was implicated; that, for his part, he could not but imagine Mr. Constable able in some way to palliate his own share of the offence; but still, in consequence of even a suspicion being breathed on his character, he regretted extremely being unable to offer him the employment about which he had formerly written." The letter went on further to say, "that it certainly showed either very little moral honesty, or an uncommon audacity of purpose, to endeavour to introduce into the house of his noble friend, and as a companion to his nephew Mr. Finch, a character so notoriously abandoned as Mr. Grimstone was, and one, at the same time, who had signs upon his noble friend's ward, Miss Hammond. That he might have supposed Mr. Constable ignorant of his character, or imposed upon by him, though that would not have argued much for Mr. Constable's sagacity, but the fact of his accompanying him to Tutbury, and obtaining his liberation after the first offence, unquestionably implicated him in the guilt, and convinced him, however reluctant he might otherwise have been to believe him guilty of so imprudent an imposition, that his noble friend was right in the severe judgment he had passed upon him;" and, in conclusion, "as one who had some experience of the world, he advised him to let his associates for the future be few, and those few choice."

Walter felt as if he had received a stunning blow as he read this terrible letter. The whole mystery was at once clear before him. The Earl of N— was the friendly patron of Bernard Grimstone, and Christopher was supposed to be he. Well might the resentment of all be kindled against him! Walter could not bear to think of the implication.

"What a base hardihood of purpose am I accused of!" exclaimed he; "and yet the thing is plausible!" And in the very recklessness of desperation, he threw the letter before his mother: "There is an end of all my hopes! I am a blasted, ruined man!" he exclaimed; "and all for the sake of these accursed profligates!"

He ground his teeth in rage, folded his arms, and walked with hurried steps through the apartment, feeling the while as if the compass of the room was too narrow for his excitement—as if the walls pressed upon him.

Mrs. Constable, who had laid down her knitting at the first glance of her son's countenance as he read the letter, took it up and read it also.

"Walter," said she, "you must hasten to the marquis and clear yourself: this imputation must not rest against you—the name of Walter Constable must be unstained."

"It shall be done instantly; I will be off this evening." And immediately preparations were made for his journey, and in the agitation and occupation of the time, the appointed hour when Julia was to meet him went by.

Julia had reached the place at the appointed moment. The summer-house met her like an old friend; her very heart warmed towards the old bleached door, with its wide, gaping joints and broken mouldings.

"What a dear place it is!" thought she; "what happy hours have I spent in it!" And then she ran over in memory many a time of especial delight, of heart-union and communion, that stood pre-eminently happy among all the happy memories of the place. But this triumphant state of mind gradually subsided, and then she began to wonder he was not there—to look out for him, to wish he would come, and in the end to think it was but like the other strange parts of his later conduct; what could it mean? And then it seemed, by the impatient reckoning of her heart, as if she had waited there for hours. She looked out again towards Westow: she could see the house through an opening in the plantation at a few yards distance from the summer-house. There it stood, with its character of old family stateliness about it, its arched gateway, its magnificent avenue, its tower-like porch, its large chimneys; the very chamber which she knew to be Walter's, she could see with its open casement; nay, she could see the very dog, a remarkably white hound, which lay sleeping under the parlour window, upon the sunny flower-border. Walter of a certainty was not on his way, or the dog would not be lying there. Her pride was touched by this apparent slight and neglect, and she returned to the summer-house, questioning with herself whether it beseemed her maidenly dignity to wait any longer for a lover who appeared so regardless of her; but before she had answered herself a step approached—it was Bernard. The sight of him recalled her fealty to Walter, at least so far that she would have been extremely unwilling for Bernard to knew how aggrieved she felt at that very moment.

"Have you waited thus long, and he is not come?" asked he, with an acrimonious tone.

"For whom do you mean?" said she, with some confusion; "I am waiting here for my own pleasure."

"Fie, Julia!" said he, "you cannot impose upon me thus; you are waiting for Mr. Constsble. I watched you come here an hour ago."

"You cannot have been studying very deeply," she remarked, looking significantly at the book between the pages of which he still kept one finger—"you cannot have found your volume interesting, Bernard, if you have had an hour to spend in watching me."

"I know," continued Bernard, in his low but earnest voice, and without noticing her interruption, "that Mr. Constable wishes this connexion at an end! I know it well, Julia—I have seen it long—I had reason enough to knew it months ago, but I was so blind I would not see."

"You are unjust," said she: "you are so suspicions—you are as you used to be before we knew Walter; and why will you distress me thus?"

"He is ashamed of us, Julia! It is his honour, not his inclination, which yet binds him to you," replied Bernard, "if he still considers himself bound at all—you see how his engagement is kept."

"It is not kind of you, Bernard," said Julia, with emotion, "why do you thus pry on our intercourse?—why do you thus wish to deprive me of the only consolation I have left? You are unjust to Mr. Constable, and you would make me so too; besides, what business have you to suppose me here with any expectation of seeing him at all?"

"You may deceive yourself, dear sister," said Bernard, with emotion equal to her own, "but you shall not deceive me; and as to your intercourse with him—Heaven knows, I wish to pry into no secrets, nor to deprive you of consolation; but have a strong heart, a proud, womanly heart, dear Julia, and do not let him give up this connexion: it will be easier for you to give him up by your own act than for you to find him faithless. How could you bear that?"

"I shall never have to bear that," said she, persisting against the anxieties of her own heart. "I know him better than you do, Bernard—I know that he is too noble to desert me for the faults of others; and so long as he willingly continues our love, I will never give it up. Why should I, Bernard? I could bear rather to die than to find him unworthy!" And the tears that Julia had restrained so long flowed freely.

Bernard looked on her with pity mingled with reproach.

"It is not kind in you, brother," continued she, no longer repressing her feelings, "to seek to deprive me of the only poor consolation I have in this world! What could you give me instead? at what price would you buy from me the affection of Walter Constable?"

"Heaven knows," replied Bernard, with bitterness, "that we are poor enough in friendship and the world's esteem; but I can promise you peace of mind and self-esteem."

"Do you, Bernard, enjoy them yourself?" asked Julia, fixing her dark and beautiful eyes upon him. "No, dearest Bernard," said she; "leave me as I am. In a little while I shall be yet more forlorn; you will be gone, and Walter; and my only consolation will be the memory of your love, and your mutual friendship for each other. Let us not, dear brother, wantonly throw away from us those friends we have; my happiness can only be insured by Walter's truth, which I will not doubt, and by your restored friendship."

"Julia," said Bernard, solemnly, "listen to my determination. I will receive no favour from the hands of Walter Constable. What he does for us now is done grudgingly; he wishes the alliance broken—it is broken on my part. Had he been the firm friend you take him for, would he have neglected us thus long in our sorest heart-needs?—

would he have kept you at this your first meeting after all that has passed? No, Julia, my resolve is taken—I will have no favour at his hands. Thank God that money is paid; we owe him no debt, and we will receive no favour."

"Oh, Bernard, Bernard! you will break my heart!" exclaimed Julia; "you are so ungenerous, you are so suspicious, so proud. You deceive yourself. This, you think, is manly independence, it is pride, it is pique—it is even more unworthy than what you charge Walter Constable with; he at least has had reason for offence, if offence there be—you have had none."

Bernard looked at her in silent astonishment. "I will wait for you," at length he said, "below the wood: you must learn the truth more bitterly than I had wished. When you are tired of waiting, you can join me." And so saying, he went out; and Julia, depressed beyond expression, leaned her head on the window-sill and wept bitterly.

"Miss Grimstone!" said a voice, a few moments afterwards, which roused her like an electric shock. Julia lifted up her tearful eyes, and notwithstanding the coldness of the address, looked joyfully up into her lover s face. Her mourning dress, her sorrowful countenance, the angelic purity and tenderness of her eyes, touched his heart with the deepest love.

"I have not deserved all this goodness," exclaimed Walter; "I have kept you waiting, and even now my time is but short."

"The time is always short with you," replied she; "all the long summer days that we spent here, how short they seemed."

"You are an angel to forgive me thus; but I must clear myself."

"It is enough, it is enough," said Julia, "to have you here—to know that you are the same kind friend as ever—to know that we shall again meet as hitherto."

"Julia," said Walter, letting go the hand was holding, and recalled by her words to what he had especially appointed that meeting to say, "you know that we meet in disobedience to your father's commands; that in loving me, in being here, you are guilty of disobedience to him; that our meeting, our intercourse, for the future must be clandestine?"

Julia felt as if her heart had suddenly become stone, pale, and almost lifeless, she heard these strange words, spoken in that cold, severe tune which Walter unconsciously assumed in the very recollection of Sir Harbottle's insults.

"Do you know this?" asked Walter again, while his heart bled for her.

"No," returned Julia, summoning an extreme force of mind, "I know it not, nor can I understand what you mean."

"I ask you, Julia, are you prepared to continue our intercourse in opposition to your father's commands?"

"I cannot understand you: what has my father to do with this now?" asked she, in a tone of heart-agony.

Walter then related what had passed between Sir Harbottle and himself—concealing, however, all but what he applied to this attachment, that he might wound her feelings as little as possible.

"It is for you, Julia, to decide the steps I shall take," said he. "If you can love me on these terms—if you can continue our intimacy with these restrictions, and their consequence of Sir Harbottle's inveterate opposition—my heart is still yours and my hand too, whenever fortune shall enable me to make you mine."

This was perhaps as much as Julia could have expected her lover to say; but still it wanted something—it came far short of the energy of her own affection, which would have laid down life for his sake—it seemed cold, and Julia bethought herself of her brother's words.

"Mr. Constable," she replied, "I would rather have died than you should have been thus insulted, and that you must know: besides, my father's character and temper were not strangers to you when our acquaintance commenced. I could only have been chosen by you as disconnected with my family. I am as guiltless of this great wrong which has been done you as of all the other offences, and they are manifold, which you have received at their hands; and, Heaven knows, not one of them but has wounded me deeply! But Bernard said," continued she, still deathly pale and with tearless eyes, "that you were changed—that your absence from Denborough Park was occasioned by disgust for our family—that your connexion with me was continued from a sense of honour, not of inclination. Oh, Walter, these are cruel things to surmise only—to know them of a truth is the saddest, the heaviest, of all my misfortunes!" And, spite of herself, her voice faltered, and the tears filled her eyes, though not one fell.

"Bernard was partly right, dear Miss Grimstone," returned Walter; "but he did me grievous wrong as to my affection for you: never was I more devotedly attached to you than since these unhappy events have occurred. The very circumstance of my offering to continue the connexion, after what has passed between Sir Harbottle and myself, may assure you of my devotion. I am not a man, Julia, lightly to bear an insult; and yet—"

"And yet, Mr. Constable, you would say," interrupted she, "though you have been thus injuriously treated by my father, if I desire it, you consider yourself in honour bound to me. I release you on these terms."

"No, Julia, you have misinterpreted my meaning. I would have said—and yet I cannot resign you without the most painful struggle—your love is dear to me as life itself!" replied Walter, with an earnestness and truthfulness that Julia could not resist.

"Thank God that you have said so! But, oh, Walter! I have sometimes questioned with myself whether I ought not voluntarily to release you from your engagement to me—perhaps I ought—this connexion has already cost you so much," conceded she in the generosity of her overflowing heart.

"No, dearest Julia," he replied; "not from considerations of wordly interests must this connexion be given up—not unless your duty to Sir Harbottle demands it."

"God forgive me if it be sin!" returned she; "but my blessed mother sanctioned it. Have you forgotten her words?"

"No, no, my own Julia; I have not forgotten them; and sacred as is the memory of the dead shall be the promise I then made her. And now, come what will of further trial, sorrow, or disappointment, they shall not sunder us."

A long embrace sealed these words, and for those few happy moments all anxiety—all care—all sorrow—were forgotten.

"And now, my Julia," said Walter, "this our blessed meeting is but, in fact, our parting: I must leave Westow this very night."

"And Bernard, must he go with you?"

"No," replied Walter; "I must go alone."

Julia, in spite of the reassurance of his good faith, started at these words. "And you disconnect yourself from Bernard?" asked she. "Oh, Walter! this is hardly kind—hardly generous. Bernard is as guiltless as myself."

"Do not question me, nor judge me," replied Walter, not willing to disclose to her the nature of the marquis's letter. "Some little difficulty—some little impediment—has occurred which I hope to remove; in the mean time, hope for the best—yet be not surprised even by utter failure and disappointment."

"What does this mean?—has it not reference in some way to my family?" asked Julia.

"Do not pry into it, dearest girl—do not drag new troubles into being before their time," said he; "I shall return yet again to Westow after my interview with the marquis."

Julia saw a gloom settle on Walter's brow, and she again remembered the words of her brother. "Oh, do not let me think you repent our acquaintance—do not speak the words which I tremble to hear from your lips!"

"No, Julia," said he, solemnly; "I shall say nothing at this our parting which you shall wish unsaid; I will carry with me the remembrance that your heart has received no sorrow from me. And yet, dearest Julia, of the particulars of my present journey I cannot now speak; do not seek to pry into them; but be assured of this, that my soul is faithfully and devotedly yours—that the love we plighted in our happier days shall not be shaken by adversity, nor influenced by opposition. Brighter days will come, never fear! and my energies, both of mind and body, shall be employed in enabling me to return and claim you for my own."

"Now the Eternal Father of Love bless and prosper you!" said she, with an energy of affection she could not conceal. "I will inquire into nothing—I desire to know nothing beyond the assurance of your continued faith. And, dearest Walter, pardon me if doubts—dark and cruel doubts and despondings—have crossed my mind, and made even gloomier the path of my life. But it is enough to know that you are faithful. I am satisfied—I am more than satisfied—for myself; and I trust to the goodness of your nature not to forsake poor Bernard—not to think hardly of him."

"Of *him!*" replied Walter; "oh, no; for, if there be a high-minded pure, and noble creature on the earth, it is your brother Bernard."

Julia was reassured. And so talked they; and hours passed on in that close and endearing communion of heart and soul, though it may be mingled with sighs and tears, serves yet for the heart to live upon, and take hope from, through years of sorrow and separation. The hours slid on imperceptibly; many a parting was essayed and many an embrace taken, and then the gathering twilight recalled to Julia's remembrance that her lover had his journey to commence. Walter accompanied her through the wood; and then, Bernard presenting himself at a short distance, one more embrace sealed their parting, and each went a separate way.

XII

Walter's interview with his patron was extremely unsatisfactory. He found the earl just gone, and the marquis filled with prejudice. It was in vain that Walter explained—he was coldly believed; and after all was done, the marquis declared he could not comprehend how there should be two Grimstones of characters so opposite, for both of whom Mr. Constable showed so much zeal. He could not understand, besides, how one of the Grimstones, who, it seems, had designs upon Miss Hammond, supposing it were not the guilty young man himself, should be introduced into the most private connexion with his noble friend's family, where he would have daily opportunities of seeing the lady;—unless it had been with design—"base design"—said the marquis, exciting himself to passion; "for these accidental coincidences do not occur in real life, whatever they may do in books, Mr. Constable."

Walter started up, declaring it was useless to urge anything further to one who had prejudged the case. He asserted again that he was entirely blameless—was falsely accused; and though he deeply deplored that any event should have cost him the favour of the noble marquis, from what he had seen he was convinced not even justice was to be expected at his hands.

This was not the spirit to conciliate the proud noble. The marquis, nevertheless, condescended to say, "if Mr. Walter Constable suceeeded in clearing himself, and could assure him connexion with this family was at an end, perhaps, at time, he might be able to serve him." Walter thanked the conceding patron, but begged he would trouble himself no further on his account, as he was by no means at liberty to bind himself, nor could he wait for contingencies.

The breach was irreparable; and Walter left the house with the feelings of one who has been playing for desperate stakes, and knows not yet what may be the extent of his loss.

Instead of returning to Westow, he pursued his journey to London, and thence to St. Omer's, where his firmest friends were. He remained there several weeks; and as if ill-fortune had set in against him, it was not long before he heard from his London friends that an implication of his character, to his disadvantage, was abroad; and, at the same time, that the breach with the marquis, and his abruptly leaving England gave sanction to it. Walter's pride was deeply touched, and in the irritation of the moment he embraced an offer which was made him in Germany, and engaged to remove shortly to Vienna. This done, he again returned to London with the determination of clearing his character, which he happily suceeded in doing.

All this necessarily oecnpied many weeks—it was the middle of October when he returned to Westow. In the mean time, the two Grimstones had left their hiding-place at Tutbury, and taken refuge at the old house at Knighton, Sir Harbottle's former residence, which had been now unoccupied for many months. They had not enjoyed their retreat long before their father himself discovered them. The exact particulars of their rencontre are not known; but rumour said that Sir Harbottle actually meditated delivering them up to justice, in order to secure to himself the reward offered for their apprehension; but this we cannot vouch for. Their meeting, however, was one of anger on the part of Sir Harbottle, the effects of which were felt by every member of his family at Denborough Park. The two young men were taken at Knighton, at the very at the very moment they were jovially carousing over a tankard of ale and a mutton-chop—which they had obtained and cooked, nobody knew how—and were lodged in the county gaol.

Julia experienced her father's anger in his threat of disinheritance, if she encouraged the addresses of Mr. Constable; and Bernard, in an unceasing attack of reproof and insulting taunt, for his want of spirit—his love of books—his idle, dreaming life, which had not even the pretence of manly sport about it, as it must be allowed Christopher's life always had, whatever else there might be bad about him.

Bernard had of late become even more gloomy and self-occupied than before. He no longer made his sister the confidant of his thoughts and feelings, though his manner was kind and full of consideration towards her; nor had he any intercourse, either of a studious or spiritual nature, with Father Cradock. And these incessant, invidious reproaches were a new cause of suffering and irritation to his morbid spirit, and chafed it beyond endurance. Packing up, therefore, a few favourite books, with a change of linen, and pocketing the amount of his finances (but a few shillings), he took his fishing rod in his hand, and, on the plea of a fishing excursion, left his home, scarcely taking leave even of his sister.

Nothing could be more melancholy than the situation of Julia. Walter did not write; Bernard was gone, she knew not where, nor for how long; Mrs. Constable evidently shunned her. There was no one to sympathise with her—no one to whom she could even hint of her peculiar unhappiness, except Father Cradock; and to her the good old man devoted himself with the zeal of a lover. Most touching were his endeavours to divert her: he would bring her a flower from his walks, or go a day's journey to borrow her a book, or to fetch her a piece of music which he thought would give her pleasure; he even established himself amid the discomforts of Denborough Park, that he might be constantly at hand to enliven or solace her. Julia felt all these delicate attentions, this devotedness of friendship, to the very core of her heart. She kept her tears for her own chamber, her miserable reflections for her own bosom, and expended her smiles and her forced cheerfulness upon the kind old man till he half persuaded himself that she was happy.

Walter Constable returned to Westow; and his mother, after the first joyful emotions of meeting were over, and after the anxious concern was expressed which his care or travel-worn countenance gave rise to, laid before him Sir Harbottle's demand in legal form for the repayment of the money he was indebted to him.

"How is this," asked she, "that you have borrowed money from Sir Harbottle Grimstone?"

Walter explained. It was money which could be instantly repaid, as nearly the entire sum remained in Bernard's hands.

The lovers met again in the ruined summer-house. The cheerfulness of the summer was gone; there had come that change over everything, both of earth and sky, which is beautiful or sad according to the tone of mind of the beholder. The leaves were tinted brown, red, and yellow; many had already fallen, and lay matted and damp underfoot from the effects of several days' rain; others were scattered by the autumnal wind which went sobbing and wailing at intervals through the branches, over the broken roof; and among the loose casement-panes.

"How melancholy it is!" said Julia, after she had listened to it some time in silence. "At first, when I entered and found you here, I thought everything was delightful, and that wind seemed to me like cheerful music: now it is sadder than an Æolian harp—you know not how how utterly it depresses me."

Walter talked cheeringly of everything; his spirits were even gay, and under their influence Julia's spirits rose again.

"But," said he, when they were about parting, he having first recollected the subject at that moment, "Sir Harbottle demands the money which was advanced for Bernard. Poor fellow! How unfortunate we have been! I am more grieved for Bernard than for myself even. Disappointment cuts him up so completely!"

"Oh, Walter!" said Julia, who saw a new trouble before them, "you know we have not the money."

"How so?" asked he; "it was put into the hands of Bernard at the time: he has it, there is no doubt."

Julia then told how it had been applied. Walter was amazed. "Surely," said he, "that money was advanced by Sir Harbottle Grimstone!"

Julia explained still further, and told him, with tears, of the sacred deposit which had gone with it.

"And for this," exclaimed Walter, with generous enthusiasm, "you had no thanks! I might have that such prompt consideration could only come from you!" And, filled with admiration of her and her brother, and the noble sacrifice they had made, he disregarded for the time the demand that it flung back upon himself.

The lovers parted, each carrying away increased affection, and that deep joy of spirit which a pure and ardent attachment alone can give, and against which misfortune itself has no power—nay, like the carbuncle in the midst of darkness, which shines out clearest and brightest when fortune seems set in array against it.

In the sobriety of after-reflection Walter took a survey of this affair. Bernard had sacrificed what, in the prospect which he thus had of honourable employment, might be considered his own money, although Walter was surety for it. That money he had now to refund; in fact, he was but again finding the consequences of making himself responsible for Christopher Grimstone—deeply indeed was he punished for that act! As to remonstrating with Sir Harbottle himself that was not to be thought of; he had put himself in this difficult position, and he must abide by it. The question was, how the money was to be raised;—a difficult question indeed for Walter to answer! Small as the sum was, he knew not where to borrow it; for, being a Catholic, though of an old, respectable family, surrounded only by Protestant gentry, at a time too when these religious differences made wider separation than they do at present; and having himself lived so much abroad, while his mother led the life almost of a recluse, he had no intimate friends among his neighbours, therefore he could not borrow. He was thrown upon his own resources, and Heaven knows, they were small enough! Sir Harbottle had said truly that he was poor. His mother had already made immense sacrifices for him. He could not possibly ask her to do more, and especially not ask her to advance money for this Grimstone connexion; and whatever money he had the power of raising, he himself would need for his present means of support. Walter cursed his own folly in being surety for any man, as many another has done before him, and vowed to make it a lesson for life; and then set himself to consider what he could turn into money. Farming-stock he had none—the land was all let, and thence came part of his mother's income—field-timber there was none, for it had already been cut down to bear in part the charges of his education. There was not even a gravel-pit or a stone quarry at Westow—these good things were in Sir Harbottle's lands: nothing remained but the avenue, and of those sacred, inviolate trees not one had been touched for their own needs. Walter thrust the idea away as if it were sinful—it would be like cutting up the old family tree itself.

The next day he walked in the avenue admiring the goodly array of trees, three hundred and sixty-five sufficient witnesses to the stateliness of his house—the supporters of the family arms were certainly less respectable than these. "And suppose," thought Walter, "it were possible to sacrifice a sufficient number of these trees, which of them must go?" They were all so much alike—not one had outgrown its fellows, not one had decayed—it would be impossible to select. "The trees must stand!" was, therefore, his concluding remark.

The third day the same idea beset him, and he thought of the man who was haunted with the idea of murder till he actually committed it. Wherever he went, the thought of the trees went with him; he looked from his window, but he saw only the avenue: and two gentlemen, two of his foreign friends, calling upon him, began immediately to extol the wonderful beauty of the avenue, the grand cathedral-like vista, the extraordinary fine effect of light within it; and Mrs. Constable, who, good lady, never missed an opportunity to relate its history, gave it at full length, adding, that "the loss of any one of those trees would be to her like the death of a dear friend."

Walter felt strangely disturbed; and no sooner were his guests gone, than, as if by some irresistible impulse, he began to calculate aloud the value of the trees, exclaiming against the necessity of felling any of them.

"Walter," said his mother, "are you dreaming?"

"I am only too much awake!" was his reply; "yet how is this money to be raised but by felling some of this timber?"

Mrs. Constable had yet to be shown the necessity there was for her son's repaying the money; she laid down her knitting before he had finished—a certain sign how deeply she was affected.

"Sir Harbottle Grimstone," said she, "received the greater of his property, the whole of the Denborough Park property, as a curse—a curse upon him, his heirs, and whoever connected themselves with them. You see how it works. Sorely against my will has this connexion been from the first!"

"Curses cannot come by inheritance," replied Walter: "this is an idle superstition!"

"The very means," returned his mother, "which Sir Harbottle has taken to nullify this curse has made it operate only the more deeply. This connexion will be your ruin—you see it has already brought you nothing but confusion! Your character is tarnished—you have lost the favour of your noblest friends—you have banished yourself from England; and now you will tear up by the roots our old family honours, all for the sake of these Grimstones! Walter, this is cruel. Take everything I have, leave me but one change of raiment—take away my very income itself, but leave the avenue touched: at all events, let me be dead before you put axe to the root of any one of those trees!"

"Dearest mother," replied Walter, who felt most acutely every word she had said, "I grant you I have done a marvelously unwise thing to make myself liable to this payment, but having done so, I must submit."

"Submit!" repeated his mother with an emphasis of extraordinary scorn; "and what business has a Grimstone to ask for any sacrifice from us! Good Heavens! we are poor enough, and have difficulties enough to encounter, without sacrificing ourselves and involving ourselves for *them*!"

Notwithstanding the conversations he had with his mother, a specimen of which we have given above, Walter tried to reconcile himself to the idea—to persuade himself to the idea that the family honours were independent of these trees; that with his uncertain prospects, narrow finances, and already encumbered estate, it would be far wiser to cut down the whole avenue, than to add even the small sum of three hundred pounds to present encumbrances which weighed so heavily upon his mother. But it would not do—this rhetoric of reason was weak against sentiment, family pride, and old attachments. What would Westow be with a broken avenue! The family glory was, that the trees had stood from the days of their great ancestor, just as he had planted them—not one had perished. Walter's boyish memories, too, were all connected with them. His only distinct recollection of his father—the tall, stately man, who in middle life had silver hair—was of his walking up and down this avenue of a summer's evening, with himself—his latest-born and only living child—by the hand; and of his relating the family history over and over again; of the the stout-hearted John Constable and the thirty years' war; and of the fair Lady Blanche of such wondrous beauty, whose sad story made both man and child weep. And with those retracings of gone days came back many a thing else forgotten—the violets which grew by thousands among the swelling roots of some particular trees, and which he was sent out to gather for his mother every day throughout the season. He remembered the very birds which, in the undisturbed quietness of Westow, were so wonderfully tame, that they hopped about, they and their broods, picking the seeds of the dry summer-grass within the avenue, and filling his boyish heart with intense delight. Walter was living over again those former years in perfect forgetfulness of the present, one day shortly after the conversation we have given above, when Mrs. Constable, again putting down her knitting, began—

"I would say nothing about it, Walter, if the money had been laid out for any advantage to yourself, or for any imagined advantage; but that you should have been duped out of it for that profligate, and in the end for it to serve worse than no purpose— to enable him to get into yet deeper disgrace, and in fact to ruin you—does, I must confess, provoke me. But, however, that was not what I meant to say: it never was in my nature to put my own personal convenience in comparison with your advantage, and especially, Walter, could I not do it at the expense of your good name!"

"You have been a noble, a most self-forgetting mother," replied Walter, emphatically: "would to God I saw the means of raising this miserable sum without distressing you!"

"Walter," said she, solemnly, "the trees must not be cut down. In the eyes of your former noble friends you are a dishonoured man— to cut them down now would be to chronicle your disgrace!"

"I have been deeply unfortunate," said Walter.

"Yes, my dear son," she continued, "you have been so: but I keep a heart above misfortune, and all may yet be well. What your mother can do to help you shall be done."

"No," replied Walter, "you shall make no further sacrifice for me."

"It is a parent's duty," said she, "to sacrifice every personal consideration to her children, provided those children be worthy." Walter was about to speak. "Listen," she said and do not interrupt me. There is a religious house near Bruges, where I spent some happy months of my maiden life—thither I will go; a small sum will suffice for me there. I leave Westow for two years, and my income for that time will be mortgaged. You will thus not only have the ready cash to cover this demand, but something wherewith to cormmence your career handsomely. I thank Heaven that I have thought of this plan!"

Walter was unable to reply; he knew what this sacrifice must have cost her. To leave Westow at any time, even for a few days, had always been a great trial. She had not even thought of living abroad, to be near him, formerly; and now, to relieve him from difficulties into which the Grimstones had brought him, she volunteered so much!

Nevertheless, he saw the feasibility of the scheme, though he had never thought of it—he could not. None but a noble-hearted, generous mother like his could have thought of it; and his heart overflowed with gratitude. He did not even oppose the scheme, but he made her feel how deeply sensible he was of her goodness.

"Well, thank God," said she, "that this is decided!" I have not slept, Walter, since you talked of felling the trees! I believe it would have killed me. And now, though the thought of leaving this dear place at another time would have been terrible, I am reconciled. I shall return to Westow, and find all its unshorn honours yet about it!"

No sooner was it decided than it was done. The money was advanced by a London money-dealer, who was empowered to receive the income for the next two years. Mrs. Constable dismissed her few domestics, retaining only one ancient woman of undoubted fidelity, to whom the house was confided, with free permission to Father Cradock to be there whenever he pleased. So great an event as this, the voluntary absence of Mrs. Constable, had not happened at Westow since the death of its master; and unbounded was the amazement of every one to whom her habits and character were known, when the rumour got abroad. It was one of the world's wonders of nine days.

Sir Harbottle received his money; and Father Craddock, who was commissioned with the payment, took the opportunity of remonstrating with him on the singular hardness of his nature, on his avarice, his unfatherly conduct to his children; and Sir Harbottle, applying it all to this repayment, dwelt in answer, like Shylock, upon the strength of his bond. But the good priest undeceived him, and set a long array of sins before him. Sir Harbottle heard him without interruption, smiled, and bade him go on. Father Cradock did so, and pleaded for the lovers. The old house at Knighton, he said, was standing vacant at that very time; and that it would be a joy which angels themselves might envy him, to endow them richly, and give them Knighton for their home. The old man was eloquent, and spoke feelingly of domestic life, and of the beauty and the endearments of children. It was a beautiful picture that he drew, giving the grandfather a place in it—he wept as he spoke: but he had reason presently to wish he had held his peace. The answer which Sir Harbottle made was one of concentrated rage; imprecations and threats against his daughter if she ventured to marry thus in opposition to his will, and threats against the old man if he dared to advocate such a step with her.

Father Cradock withdrew, absolutely putting his fingers to his ears, that his soul might not be afflicted with the impieties of the angry man.

XIII

The evening had arrived before the day of departure. The house at Westow already looked deserted; the household dismissed, the shutters of many windows were closed; and Mrs. Constable was in readiness for her journey.

The lovers were met to part in the ruined summer-house; and Julia, conscious that on these passing moments she must live through dreary and melancholy years, stood overwhelmed with grief, her cheek resting on Walter's shoulder, when Bernard, dusty with travel, with a pale and agitated countenance, suddenly entered. Julia, delighted to see him, flew to meet him; he returned her welcome with the utmost affection.

"Mr Constable," said he offering his hand to Walter, "I have done you a great wrong—from my soul I beg your pardon! I believed you less noble than you have proved yourself."

Walter grasped the offered hand with friendly warmth, and Julia wept to see this unlooked-for reunion.

"I have heard what you have done for us," said Bernard.

"I have come past Westow even now. It must not be, Constable,—
my father cannot submit to it! My God! what a dishonour it is to
us that your household must thus be broken up for this paltry sum,
and all the money that lies unappropriated at Denborough Park the
while! It must not be, Constble—it shall not be! I will go to my
father myself." And turned instantly to go out.

"Bernard," said Walter, after he had prevailed upon him somewhat
the vehemence of his feelings, and Julia had informed him of the failure
of Father Cradock's interference,—"Bernard," said he, "follow me to St.
Omer's: I have firm friends there; I will insure you no disappointment
among them—there you will find the most intellectual, the most
noble-hearted men. Your blessed mother herself would have advocated
this step; you must not forget your holy destination."

"Yes, dearest Bernard," exclaimed Julia, reconciled to parting
with her brother in the prospect of their restored friendship,—"Yes,
dearest Bernard, go! I can bear all things if I know you are happy.
There you will have books—there you will have quiet—there you
will have peace of mind."

Bernard struck his open hand upon his forehead, and stood
in agonized silence. "No," replied he, at length; "this cannot be!
Heaven knows, from the depths of my soul, how I bless you for
your great kindness; but this cannot be,—I am not a Catholic! I
see your horror—you regard me now as a renegade from God! Do
not misjudge me: my mind has striven with conviction till it can
withstand it no longer—I am a Protestant! Let not this, however,
make strife between us; our paths through time may be different we
shall meet at the same point in eternity."

"Brother!" exclaimed Julia, her hands clasped and her countenance
pale as death, "this is the grief I least of all looked for." And, unable
to restrain her feelings, she burst into tears.

Walter, too, who, like Julia, was a religious Catholic, heard the
avowal with the most unqualified sorrow and regret.

It was an evening of bitter grief—grief for parting, grief over the
beloved apostate; while his feelings were of such intense suffering as
it would be impossible to describe.

The Constables, mother and son, were gone; and Julia had received her first letter, sent to the care of Father Cradock at Westow, written from Bruges;—a letter consolatory from its spirit of affection, and comfortable from the hope it held out for the future.

Christopher and George Grimstone were convicted of the offence charged against them, and were sentenced to two years' imprisonment in the county gaol, and to find, on liberation, sureties in heavy recognizances for the preservation of the peace. It was well for Julia that the entire seclusion of her life at Denborough Park kept her from the personal sense of the ignominy that hung over her family. She knew, indeed, of its existence; but she was spared in a great measure the humiliation of being made to feel it.

The intercourse between Julia and Bernard in the mean time was of the tenderest kind; though the subject of religious opinion, at first warmly entered upon, was soon entirely abandoned, from the jealous solicitude which she felt lest it should produce any breach or coldness between them. Julia gave him up to what she considered the better skill and experience of Father Cradock, who, she fondly hoped, would bring him back to his old allegiance; but Bernard was too honest to let the good Father expect a proselyte, and too deeply convinced of the faith he had adopted to be readily shaken. Father Cradock cared not to tell Julia the result of their conferences.

In appearance Bernard was wonderfully changed. The quick, restless eye, the flushing cheek, the timid and almost bashful manner, were gone, and had given place to the most grave, earnest, and decided manner and cast of countenance; he seemed to have grown at once from the visionary youth to the man whose life is devoted to momentous purposes. Julia wondered as she looked upon him, wishing earnestly that she could have known the whole secret of his spirit. She could hardly believe, at times, that this could be the gentle, doubting being whose mind might have been fittest emblemed by an April day, and whose hand had shaken like an aspen-leaf as he had presented to her. The song or sonnet he had been too sensitive to read aloud to her, in truth, however, his spirit was the same as ever,—equally sensitive, equally irregular,—now elated, now depressed; but principle and moral feeling had been developed, which gave an aim and character to his mind; and a necessity was now upon him which called forth energies both of mind and body, and, like any other stimulus, raised him for the time above weakness or sense of inability. What this necessity was we will make known to our readers.

"Have you no sonnet, or sweet little song, dear Bernard?" said Julia, one dull morning in November, as they sat together in their room; "it is so long now since you read me anything. Oh, Bernard! those were blessed times when you wrote something new every day: do you not remember them? All was flowery and sunshiny then—my heart has grown old since those times; there is no poetry now—all is dull prose."

"I cannot write now, Julia," said he; "I shall never write poetry as long as that old house at Westow stands desolate. A blight, a desolation has come over my spirit. You know not the agony it is to me to see those smokeless chimneys—those closed windows."

"Alas!" said Julia; "but is it in our power to alter these things?"

"I have a vow with myself," replied Bernard, "to see justice done to those noble beings. Why should they suffer for the guilt—the absolute dishonesty—of our house! I am crushed as with the weight of a mountain when I think of this great wrong that is done them."

"Think of the abominable pelf that is heaped together within these walls, from which the paltry sum that would do but bare justice to them would be no more missed than a child's handfull of sand from the sea-shore; and yet this I cannot obtain!"

"And these are the things," said Julia, "that make you so grave!"

"These are the things," replied Bernard, "that sear my spirit as with a hot iron,—that make my nights sleepless and my days miserable. The silence and desertion of Westow proclaims to the world the dishonour of our house; and upon me the whole weight and sense of that dishonour seem to have fallen."

Julia could not console him; on the contrary, his acutely sensitive spirit communicated its anguish to hers.

Drearily the winter wore on; and few and far between came letters from Walter Constable. Julia could not deceive herself with the persuasion that he was prosperous: his letters were dated each from a different place, without any cause being assigned for this circumstance. At length a long pause occurred. Julia's anxiety was intense; and to exhibit Bernard's state of feeling, we must give an interview between him and his father.

"I am come," said he, as he was admitted through the barred door into his father's room, "yet once more to demand from you a small sum of money to enable me to undertake a journey—in fact, to commence life for myself."

"You have had your answer already," returned Sir Harbottle, with more coolness than might have been expected; for even he, like Father Cradock, could not altogether resist Bernard's force of character, which had revealed itself in the many though ineffectual interviews that there had of late been between them;—"You have had your answer—I shall advance not one sixpence."

"My present life," continued Bernard, "is miserable to me beyond description; you cannot conceive the irksomeness of my daily inactivity."

"If that be all," replied Sir Harbottle, "work! I grant you, you have been idle—work, and welcome! I pay no inconsiderable sum to my labourers; occupy whatever place you like. I shall never object to your working."

"Father," replied Bernard, "I should not come here to ask your permission to perform day-labour. It is extremely hard for a young man to be compelled to solicit thus painfully the miserable sum which I ask: how could ten or twenty pounds impoverish you?"

Sir Harbottle looked fixedly on his son without replying, and then turned doggedly to the newspaper that lay before him.

"I have heard," continued Bernard, knowing that his father would hear while he seemed to read, "that this estate came to you as a curse;—a singular and fearful bequest. God knows why such a curse—denounced perhaps by a sinner—should be permitted to have a terrible fulfilment; but of a truth so it is! It has operated frightfully, and even now has not lost its power. Heaven knows, I say, why it is thus permitted; but, of a certainty, the hand of Almighty God is sorely against us."

"Young man," said Sir Harbottle, deeply struck by these unexpected words, and with a countenance agitated as Bernard had never seen before, "you talk of bygone things—of which you do not understand."

"I speak only from too deep experience," replied he, "of things which are only too present with us. My father, can it be aught less than a sinner's curse which closes your heart against your children,—which makes money, and only money, of worth in your eyes? My comfort, my well-being, are less important to you than twenty pieces of gold!"

"Had I lived the life of a spendthrift—of an imprudent, thriftless profligate, wasting my substance in riot and debauchery—the thing might have been as you say: I might have deserved these reproaches from you. But I did not so: I married a prudent woman—I retrenched my expenditure—I lived carefully, and practised the most rigid economy. I had the benefit of my descendants in view; I meant to do the best I could for my children. It is hard to be thus censured. I gave my sons, as far as I could judge, the education of gentlemen; and what has been the return? Ingratitude!—ingratitude, young man, and insolent profligacy!"

"That is but too true," replied Bernard, "of your elder children: of your younger, at least, sir, you must make an exception."

"I have been robbed, threatened, circumvented," continued Sir Harbuttle, without noticing Bernard's interruption; "you know not what I have borne from them. I have laid up money, as you say—I have amassed wealth which would buy a kingdom; but have I been happy? My God! no! The ingratitude of my sons has cut me to the heart."

Sir Harbottle spoke as if thinking aloud; his lips quivered, his voice trembled, and he covered his face with both his hands when he had done.

"My father," said Bernard, laying his hand upon his arm, and deeply touched by so singular a display of emotion; "it is not the will of Heaven, which is full of blessing and mercy, that a sinner's curse should have power over our resolute determination to do right."

"Lookye," said Sir Harbottle, withdrawing his hands from his brow, and gazing fixedly at his son, "they have been scoundrels; I will cut them off with a shilling! I will make you the eldest son—and my curse light upon you if you relieve them in their sorest need by the value of one farthing!"

"Nay, nay," exclaimed Bernard; "that must not be: if thine enemy hunger, give him bread—if he thirst, give him drink—how much more our own flesh and blood!"

"I will do it," said Sir Harbottle, vehemently; "I will make an elder son of you."

"Not with such restrictions as these," interrupted Bernard; "for this inheritance already has suffered too bitterly from a curse. But since you permit me the privilege of speaking with you on this subject, let me induce you to allow to Julia and myself such an income as your children may demand. On my soul, Sir Harbottle, we are both of us penniless; the beggar is better off than we. We will render you an account of its expenditure; only insure to us an income."

"I have told you what I will do—but I will not be dictated to," replied his father: "I will make you my sole heir! This very day I will do it."

"Let it be without the curse you speak of, then," said he; "for on such terms I would not accept the inheritance."

Sir Harbottle looked at his son with a mingled sentiment of surprise and contempt. "Thou art a chicken-livered fool!" said he: "I ate, and drank, and made merry, when this inheritance came to me; thou settest light by it tenfold—But," continued he, after a pause, "to be candid with you: I have already destroyed my will; another is about being made; and look here—I will show you the worth of this inheritance; I show not this to every one." And he laid before him bonds and mortgages—deeds and securities of money without end. "All this,' said be, "is mine, and may be yours, besides this manor of Denborough, the manor of Knighton, and whatever is contained within these sealed bags." The bags of which he spoke were contained within the escritoir, and in an iron chest in the wall.

"And with all this wealth," said Bernard, almost bewildered by what he had seen, "you refuse to advance me even ten guineas!"

"This shall all be yours," returned Sir Harbottle: "I will cut those scoundrels off with a shilling! Hang them!—would you think it?—they have had their clutches in my bags! But body o' me, they shall not touch another crown of mine!"

Bernard thought of his poverty, then looked at the temptation that was presented to him, and for some time he could not reply.

"How these vampires will stare," muttered Sir Harbottle, "when they hear the will read!" The words decided Bernard.

"I ask not undue heirship," said he,—"nay, I refuse it. I would not entail upon myself the deadly feud between my brothers and myself which must thence ensue, with all its fearful consequences. I should consider myself answerable for whatever crimes they committed,—I could not accept the inheritance on such terms."

Sir Harbottle looked angrily on his son, and yet he replied calmly, "I will give you till to-morrow to consider it."

"No," said Bernard; "I should think to-morrow as I think now; or, if there were a chance of my thinking otherwise,; I would reiterate my answer ten times this day. I cannot take advantage even of my brothers' misconduct—of their absence, though in prison. But, my father, instead of hoarding up in your lifetime to leave deadly hatred and animosity among your children after your death, take to yourself the noble privilege of doing justice—of using wealth for its true end while you yet live. Make it the instrument of good. The time will come when one good action will outweigh mountains of gold!"

Sir Harbottle regarded him in amazement and anger: he had expected the most unbounded gratitude for his offer, and instead of appreciating the high principle of his refusal, despised him as a spiritless contemner of money.

"Give me the means of leaving this place," said Bernard in reply to his father's scorn. "One-hundredth part of the sum you can count any day will suffice for me. I have hitherto been but little chargeable to you; I will be less so in future."

"You are one of Father Cradock's followers," said Sir Harbottle. "Your intention is to take orders, I presume."

"I am not a Catholic," replied Bernard, humbly. "From sincere conviction I have embraced the Protestant faith."

"And pray what mode of life is it your intention to follow? The sum you want is too little for a profession—too little even for a handicraft tradesman to begin his calling upon. You know nothing of the value of money. But let me know your wise schemes."

"It may perhaps appear foolish to you," said Bernard, a crimson blush covering his pale countenance; "but my intention is to support myself by writing."

"What!" replied Sir Harbottle, contemptuously; "engrossing at a halfpenny a line in some pettifogging lawyer's office?"

"No," said Bernard; "by original composition. I have thought deeply, I have read much; I am conscious of no inconsiderable powers of mind; and I doubt not but in London—"

"Simpleton! greenhorn!" exclaimed Sir Harbottle, and then, burst forth into a laugh of utter contempt. "Thank you, sir, continued he; "you have given proof of considerable originality of mind! And what the devil can you write about? or what do you know that would be worth putting on paper, of which has not been said a thousand times better before? This is some of the confounded nonsense which that fine scholar Constable has put in your head."

Bernard, though he knew that the sordid spirit of his father could not possibly be a judge of these things, felt for one moment humiliated and ashamed.

"Yes," continued Sir Harbottle, scornfully, "write down that you have this day refused to be made heir of Denborough Park; that you have refused the inheritance of half a million, and there will be a piece of original composition! Write down also, like Dogberry, that you are an ass, and there will be an incontrovertible truth!"

"Father," said Bernard, roused into energy by these taunts, "all this is the miserable sophistry of sordid avarice against your own reason. You know that this is cruelly unjust—you know that my request is humble—you yourself have acknowledged it; and as to my rejecting the offered inheritance, I did so because I will not take such an advantage of my brothers—not even of their crimes. Despise me as you will, my own soul tells me I have done right, and your own soul tells you so too; but I pray that you will not refuse me this small sum."

"I have told you," replied Sir Harbottle in his usual dogged tone, "that you shall get no money from me. I know the league between you and that fellow Constable, and my money shall not go into that quarter."

"As to Mr. Constable," said Bernard, "his absence from Westow at this time is a perpetual dishonour to our house, if anything can dishonour it. We are the country's talk, its execration, already. The world knows that Mr. Constable is a ruined man because of us,—we are chargeable with his misfortunes."

"Very well," returned his father in his coldest tone.

"These things do not affect you," said Bernard: "they are to my spirit like fire applied to a wound."

A long pause ensued, and then again Bernard besought his father in his most energetic and persuasive manner to enable him to leave hence. But Sir Harbottle remained inexorable.

"There are," at length, said Bernard, "certain pictures in this house of considerable value; they have been to me like dear and faithful friends—I owe them much; they are the same to Julia. Give me but one of these pictures, then, since you refuse me money."

"Ay," said Sir Harbottle, a new light breaking in upon him; "they are of great value, you say?"

"Unquestionably," replied he; "they are divine works, and are attributed to celebrated masters: give me but the smallest picture among them, and I will be content."

"It would lessen the value of the house," said Sir Harbottle.

"The pictures might be destroyed by fire; and the damp of the unaired walls has already injured some," was Bernard reply.

"Ho!" said Sir Harbottle, "a good idea! certainly, certainly, certainly! fire might destroy; damps will endamage;—they shall be sold!"

"Sold!" repeated Bernard.

"Yes, yes," said Sir Harbottle,—"sold. And look you here young man, I have an inventory of every picture in this house, and touch one at your peril!" Sir Harbottle drew forth from his multitudinous papers the one he spoke of, and sat down to study it.

Bernard, thunderstruck at the idea he had suggested to his father, sat in perfect consternation, provoked to the utmost also at having suggested it at all. To argue, he knew, hopeless,—to remonstrate would be vain; the sale of the pictures promised too rich a harvest for the cupidity of Sir Harbottle ever to relinquish it. And, worse than all, how deeply—how cruelly—would not Julia feel the loss of these pictures, endeared as many of them were by the reverence with which Lady Grimstone had regarded them!—and to Julia also, as to her mother, they were blended with religion. That divine Madonna, clasping the infant Saviour to her breast; that terribly sublime Crucifixion, which they together had reverenced, kneeling at their mother's knee; Christ's Agony in the Garden, which Bernard himself had studied so profoundly for its depth of mental and heart anguish, and which Julia could not see without tears; that triumphant picture of the Angels announcing to the Shepherds the birth of the Saviour, where the burst of heavenly radiance seemed to swallow up the clouds and darkness of night, like a sublime Christianity over the ignorance and superstition of the world—a glorious picture, fit to be the altar-piece of the noblest of cathedrals;—how could all these be given up! Bernard felt almost frantic at the idea.

"Would that I had gone penniless from this place," exclaimed he in anguish that he could not control, "rather than have brought this new bereavement upon Julia!"

"Every picture is set down here; and remove one of them at your peril!" said Sir Harbottle, glancing up from his paper as he heard Bernard's voice, though the meaning of his words had escaped his mind.

Bernard made no reply, but, internally cursing gold, and the lust of gold, he went out.

It was early in the month of February, and the evening had already set in, when Bernard, feeling it impossible to meet his sister in his perturbed state of mind without adding to her uneasiness, hastily threw on his cloak and rushed out of the house to give way to the vehemence of his feelings, as was his wont, in the silence and solitude of the old park. It mattered not to him that the evening was one of the most comfortless of a comfortless season: the air damp and chilly, the earth wet and forlorn; and that from every tree under which he passed the heavy moisture dropped as if from the roof of some damp and dripping cave. Bernard neither saw nor felt the desolate landscape which lay around him, yet dimly discernible through the gathering darkness. His whole consciousness was absorbed in pondering on the miserable destiny that seemed to entrammel him as with iron bonds; and he walked on, unheeding whither he went, till he stood within the avenue at Westow. Bernard was like the spectre of this old place; many a night had he thus wandered about it, led there, as it seemed to him, by an irresistible spell. He started to find himself once more at this place, and his senses were at once acutely alive to every sound and object that were about him. He heard, through the deep silence of the scene, the heavy waterdrops fall upon the masses of leaves that lay in heaps blown together under the trees; he heard the rustle and fluttering start of birds and small animals here and there as he passed; and then he saw before him the tall arched gateway, the closed gate—and beyond, the black, cheerless walls of the old mansion, with its tower-like porch rising up dark and silent into the night. All was profoundly still; there was no sign nor token of life. At length, as Bernard approached still nearer, the dog sent up a long and startling howl-like bark, that seemed to echo through the desertion of court and building, and sounded to Bernard's excited feelings like an ominous voice of yet coming misfortune.

"We have made this place desolate!" exclaimed Bernard internally; "we have driven its once cheerful inhabitants into exile; and whatever farther ruin hangs over them will be ours to answer for. But, so help me Heaven! justice shall be done to them. This one dishonour, at least, shall be removed from our house, though I die to accomplish it!"

Again the dog sent forth a long and dismal howl, and a black spectral-like figure seemed gliding under the shadow of the walls. Bernard stood still, his imagination excited to the utmost;— shadowy forms seemed to dance before his eyes, and strange, unearthly sounds to ring in his ears. Again the dog howled dismally, and the black figure stood at his side.

"Ah, Father Cradock," said Bernard, "is it you?"

"I would to Heaven," returned the old man, "that the dog were silent; for after the news I have had, I like not that howling."

"What news!" demanded Bernard.

Father Cradock then related that he had received a letter from Mrs. Constable, dated Berlin, whither she was gone to attend upon her son, who was ill. The letter contained also the suspected truth that Walter's fortunes were unpropitious,—he had been disappointed in a hundred ways. It was in every sense of the word, a melancholy letter. Poor Mrs. Constable poured out in it all her unrestrained feeling to the Father,—to him at least, she said, she could tell all; and it was some satisfaction, even in the midst of a strange land, and a people whose language she could neither speak nor understand,—it was some satisfaction to pour out her heart thus freely to an old friend, and to think that the letter would be read in the dear house at Westow, from which both she and her son were unhappy outcasts, doomed perhaps to lay their bones in a foreign land. Mrs. Constable did not even say, "God's will be done!"

Father Cradock, who forbore to speak his entire mind to Julia on the misfortunes of the Constables, that he might not add to her anxieties, felt less scrupulous on this subject with her brother. Every word, however, that he spoke entered Bernard's heart like a dagger. And when he parted from the old man, he shook him cordially by the hand, internally blessing him, as before a long parting; resolving with himself that he would leave Denborough Park, penniless as he was; convert his very wardrobe into money, and retrieve by his single hand the fortunes of his friends.

A mind like Bernard's, in its hour of enthusiasm, casts a glory about whatever it contemplates; dangers affright not, nor can difficulties impede; it is as a strong angel whose wing can compass heaven and earth. In such a mood, Bernard through the darkness and cheerlessness of the late evening, paced his old and well-known haunts, a happy visionary, achieving prosperity for his friends, and crowning himself with a poet's renown.

It was past the usual hour of retiring to rest when Bernard returned home. Julia was in her chamber; the domestics were dismissed to theirs; and Sir Harbottle, as was his night custom, was about to fasten bar and chain when Bernard entered. He glanced upon his son a look of surprise and displeasure, but no word passed between them. Bernard sat down by the almost extinguished embers of the kitchen hearth, still occupied by thoughts which were too engrossing to be lightly dismissed. But the enthusiasm was gone by—a heavy, crushing weight of duty seemed laid upon him, and his weakness, his friendlessness, his utter penury, came also fearfully before him. He thought of his youth—of his proper station in society—of what life might have been to him, could he but have enjoyed the natural advantages of that station. He was the very being of all others to have enjoyed to the utmost the most noble and elevated pleasures of life. Then, from the beautiful vision he created he turned to what he was—penniless in the midst of accumulating thousands;—a nature keenly sensitive, and endowed with the nicest moral perception in the midst of natures callous and gross as the common clods of the field. The very beggar in the street had advantages which he had not—for the beggar at least was fitted to his fortunes. Bernard looked round through the large, gloomy kitchen in which he was seated; the wind came down the wide, tall chimney with hollow and unearthly sounds; the remote parts of the room seemed filled with a moving darkness, and his lamp flickered and threw up fantastic circles and shapes of light upon the lofty and darkened ceilling. All this, which would have excited a common mind to terror, harmonized with Bernard's feelings: he regarded himself as one acted upon by a strange destiny, and, in a sort of intoxication of mind, laughed as he thought of struggling with it.

The last ember had long been cold, and the hour of midnight
had gone by, when Bernard bethought himself of taking repose. As
he passed the room occupied by Sir Harbottle, and opening, as we
have said, into the chamber he used, Bernard was surprised to see a
light still burning there. "Does my father, then, count his money by
night as well as by day?" thought he. The next moment it occurred
to him that his father had perhaps fallen asleep in his chair, and
Bernard returned to the door and knocked, intending to make him
aware of his situation—perhaps of his danger. No answer, however,
was returned, and Bernard knocked still louder, not supposing but
the door was fastened inside. Again his summons was unanswered,
and Bernard then turned the handle of the lock. To his surprise the
door opened freely. Sir Harbottle, as Bernard had imagined, sat fast
asleep in his chair; his lamp had burned low in the socket, and the
escritoir was open before him; and before him, also, was an open
bag of money, which he perhaps had been counting. The inventory
of the pictures had fallen from his hand; sleep seemed to have
overtaken him in the midst of calculations on this new source of
money. So profoundly was he asleep, that the noise which Bernard
made on entering the room, which was without any attempt at
silence, did not wake him. His breathing was regular and inaudible,
as that of one who slumbers calmly. Bernard looked upon his father
with surprise: that he could sleep calmly was strange to him—for
his own rest was painful and unquiet. His next thought was of the
singular circumstance of a man who guarded the contents of this
room—and especially the escritoir, the immense value of whose
contents Bernard had been himself shown that very day—with such
jealous care through the day, should yet thus leave it unprotected
during the night. "What would hinder," thought Bernard, "but that
any one might carry off much of that treasure!—Even I myself
might do it!"

A strange sensation passed over Bernard's heart—he felt tempted
to do it. "What were that one bag to him?—to me it would be
everything!" thought he. He fixed his eyes intently on the gold, but
he felt as if he dared not touch it. "Shall I make myself a thief—a

night-robber?" said he, internally. "No, no! I would to God he were awake!" So thought he, and yet he did not wake him; for he began to think of the vast hoard that Sir Harbottle possessed—of its utter uselessness with him—nay, even how it was a snare to his soul: and with a sincere loathing he cursed the spirit of avarice. He remembered his own unsuccessful pleading with him, day after day, for fifty, for twenty—nay, only for ten guineas; and now, here lay ten times the sum before him, as if for his behoof! "Oh," thought Bernard, "that I could but possess myself of it without sin—that it were but mine! Yet how do I know but this is an interposition of Providence on my behalf?"

The very idea brought with it its reproof and its reply. "What! to steal?" said the internal voice. "No! had it been Heaven's will, the heart of Sir Harbottle would have been softened! God wills not evil that good may come."

Bernard thought he had resisted the temptation, and he suffered himself to look upon the money before him. "I am as the veriest beggar," mused he to himself. "I have not wherewithal to provide for my smallest needs—yet this very day I have refused the whole inheritance; and why? because I would not injure my brothers."

How weak is human nature at the best! Bernard felt disturbed and angry as he had never felt till then. He had refused the whole inheritance from pure principle but a few hours before, and now he was disturbed and fascinated, as it were, by the sight of the gold. "He could not miss ten pieces—what were ten pieces to his abundance?" argued the weakness of his tempted heart. "No, no," again returned the internal monitor; "thou shalt not steal! Bear all things—suffer all things—but degrade not thyself!"

Bernard smote his hand upon his forehead, and wished he had not been tempted; he put forth his hand to wake his father, but he withdrew it again, for he felt as if he could not bear that his father should see him.

"I should not have been tempted for myself," reasoned Bernard, trying to silence the voice of self-accusation that *would* be heard; "I could not have been tempted to take it for my own pleasure: it is to enable me to do justice—to do what is barely honest—to subject myself to unknown difficulties, trials, and hardships, so that I might but restore to Mr. Constable that sum whereby he is impoverished for our sakes. Accursed were I to desire this gold for my own pleasure—for my own gratification—for my own advantage; but a heavy, an imperious duty is upon me!"

"God forgive me if I commit sin!" said Bernard, as, suppressed breath, a throbbing heart, and a feeling of desperation, he softly put forth his hand, and took up ten gold pieces.

"I am a thief!" muttered he, as he felt the money in his hand; "I have robbed my own father! God Almighty forgive me!" And with a countenance pale as death, a noiseless step, and trembling limbs, Bernard went out.

"I am a thief!" murmured he, as he stole onward to his chamber; and then barring the door and flinging the money from him, he threw himself into a chair, and sat like one stupefied by some overwhelming blow.

"The curse has indeed lighted upon our house!" groaned he at length. "Has it not made me a thief—a night-plunderer? What hinders now but that I should do murder?"

"My God! my God!" again exclaimed he, in an agony of inexpressible anguish; "it is I myself that have brought this curse upon me—by my own pride I have fallen! I have prided myself on intellect, on high principle, on purity of heart! I have called myself better than they; and what am I? I could not resist temptation—I could not wait thy hour—miserable wretch that I am!"

Bernard wrung his hands, smote his breast, and then sat in a stupor of utter misery—deeper, heavier, more soul-agonizing than death.

Before the morning had dawned, Bernard, wrapped in his cloak, and with his hat pulled over his brows, stole out of the house; and with the hurried steps of one who flies from the Avenger, hastened through the park down to Wood Leighton, and then to the nearest town, whence a stage-coach passed on its way to London. He took no change of raiment with him; he left no token whatever behind him, not even to Julia; but, utterly self-degraded, went forth, desiring never to repass the threshold—never to behold the face of his sister—till he had cleansed from his soul the miserable stain which his misfortunes and his hour of weakness had affixed upon him.

XIV

When Sir Harbottle woke, his lamp had burned out, and it was with the utmost terror that he discovered the situation in which he had been; his escritoir opened—his treasures undefended. The room was perfectly dark, and it was only by groping about that he ascertained his valuables to remain much as he had left them. The ten guineas which had been abducted he did not then miss. He closed the desk, and pocketed his keys with the satisfaction of one who has rescued his all from destruction. This important point ascertained, Sir Harbottle set himself about procuring a light; and then going the round of his apartments, and assuring himself, after the fearful discovery his door actually was unbarred, that no robber lurked within them, the clock struck three, and he went to his bed, wondering still with himself how so unparalleled an event could have happened, and blessing himself that Christopher and Robert were within strong walls at a moment which otherwise they could not have failed to avail themselves of.

The morning light made known to Sir Harbottle the loss he had sustained; ten guineas were of a certainty gone, and, his suspicious terror was ready to believe, much more. He rushed from his room with the alarming information that he had been robbed, as he declared, to what amount he knew not. The few domestics were questioned; even Julia herself underwent scrutiny. Bernard was the last suspected; but when the whole day passed and he did not make his appearance, the father, with imprecations and terrible vows of vengeance, declared every one of his sons thieves. Julia maintained and solemnly believed him incapable of so base an action. His absence, she said, might appear suspicious at that particular time, but in itself was not extraordinary. Bernard had often absented himself from home for weeks, and this absence was but as those. It was morally impossible, she declared, for one so noble, so pure, so unsolicitous for money as he was, should have taken so desperate a means of obtaining any; the bare suspicion went to her soul. Sir Harbottle persisted in his opinion, and hinted of the conversations his son had of late had with him—of his pertinacious desire to obtain the money for Mr. Constable; and, taking for granted what he was willing to believe possible, he declared his loss to be upwards of three hundred pounds, which left no doubt upon the fact. Bernard was gone off to Mr. Constable with the money, Sir Harbottle maintained, endeavouring to persuade himself that his loss was to that amount, though the ten guineas were all he could actually miss. "But," reasoned he with himself, "is it likely that so small a sum would content him? were not thousands of pounds as ready to his touch as one single ten? It is not likely that so little would satisfy him; I have been robbed to the amount of Constable's money at least."

Days went on, and weeks, and no tidings came of the fugitive. The weeks grew into months, the spring came, and summer, but nothing could bring pleasure to Julia. She had heard from Walter— no word was said of her brother, and the most dreadful anxiety and apprehension filled her mind. What had become of him? Was it indeed possible that he had been guilty of theft, and had left his home a dishonoured man forever? No; she could not wrong him so far as to entertain the belief. What seemed far more probable to her, yet still terrible to her to believe, was, that he had absented himself as he had done before, to leave behind him the annoyances of Denborough Park; and was perhaps dead, in poverty among strangers, or was enduring even then she knew not what hardship, privation, and suffering. But why then had he not taken leave of her?—why had he not spoken to her of his intention? He must have known the dreadful anxiety she would suffer on his account.

Father Cradock took many a journey to gain, if possible, some information respecting him; but all was fruitless—not even the slightest clue could be obtained by which to discover his movements or the place of his concealment. It was a dark and inextricable subject—one on which it was misery to think but one at the same time which it was impossible to forget. Even Walter Constable was much less the object of Julia's solicitude than formerly, and every night her sleep was haunted by dreams of her brother. She saw him dead, dying, imploring for help, reduced to unimaginable suffering. She went through floods to rescue him, and through fire; she passed through every infliction of fantastic misery to afford him help, and then seemed mocked by fearful spectres, hurled down precipices, or whirled through the air at a mad and bewildering speed; and she woke fevered, terrified, and filled with indefinite horrors. A settled melancholy rested on her spirit; she felt incapable of exertion; and feared many a time that terrible suspense, this friendless, incommunicable grief, would leave her a feeble maniac.

Father Cradock saw with intense anxiety the change that was coming over her, and exerted himself in a hundred ways to divert her thoughts. Excellent old man! she was to him dear as a daughter. He prayed for her, he wept for her, he never ceased to think of her—devising, with unwearied love and sympathy, many a source of amusement and employment of thought, so that her mind might be turned from this most painful and bewildering subject of interest. The necessity for exertion, in order to appease the good man's anxieties, was of incalculable benefit to her. Julia's sense of gratitude, and her religious faith, mastered her intensest anguish; and, as the summer went on, she again began to see and feel the healing spirit of external nature. She and Father Cradock walked forth together in the park, even into those very dingles and woodland hollows so long the resort of Bernard, and which seemed filled with remembrances of him. She saw again the beauty of flowers, of running waters, of trees—nay, of all created things; and her soul overflowed with love and thankfulness, though her heart never ceased to bleed.

All this time Sir Harbottle Grimstone had been occupied by the idea which Bernard had suggested—the sale of the pictures. The first intimation Julia had of such a design was by a London picture-dealer being introduced into the apartments which had always been considered as sacred to herself, her mother, and Bernard, as in the former days they had been devoted to Mrs. Ashenhurst and her daughter, and which, even in spite of the general discomfort and neglect of the house, had such an aspect of elegance and comfort as was necessary to their more refined spirits. In these rooms were those pictures we have particularly enumerated—pictures said to be by Raphael, Carlo Dolci, and Annibal Caracci; and pictures, of a truth, they were, worthy of their reputed authors, and which had become objects of reverential regard to Lady Grimstone and her children. To Julia they had been as friends, counsellors, and companions; and many a time in her hours of darkness, and almost despair, had she gathered strength and comfort in their contemplation. What then was her astonishment, her grief, in discovering that it was the design of her father to despoil her of them! But it was at the very time that her soul was overwhelmed, and utterly subdued by her painful anxieties for her brother; and, as one incapable of resistance, she passively sat by—heard the chaffering between her father and the dealer—saw the bargain struck—and though she felt as if the only light of her life was put out, yet she made no opposition.

As strength returned to her spirit, and she in some measure had overcome the agony of her grief for the loss of her brother, the full extent, however, of this new and unexpected trial came sensibly upon her, and she felt how cruelly she was about to be bereaved.

In a few weeks more, whatever pictures were of any value were gone; and instead of them remained only the unsightly, discoloured, or yet unfaded spaces of wall where they had hung. What a blank on every side! The walls seemed to her as faces from which all intelligence was gone. She felt as one whom a sudden calamity had deprived at once of many friends—on all hands their places were vacant.

Sir Harbottle sat counting over this unlooked-for accession to his treasure, which wanted but ten guineas to make up a large round sum, when a packet was presented him. He opened it. It was from Bernard, and contained ten guineas with a letter. The sight of the money—the exact sum—at the very moment when it was wanted, filled the soul of the miserable man with such delight as a child feels when it finds unexpectedly the toy for which it has been longing. Sir Harbottle chuckled over the money, shook it within his closed palms, and, with a burst of exultation, added it to the heap before him.

When he had satisfied his soul with the contemplation of the perfected beauty and the goodly display of so much coined money, he broke the seal and read as follows:—

"—*July,* 17—"

"I charge you not with having compelled me to the degrading act of which I have been guilty. In the hour of temptation my souls strength failed me—I became a thief!

"This consciousness has haunted me—It has been a spectre by my bed—it has pursued me in crowds—it has been with me in solitude! My father, you have been revenged! It matters not to me that the sum was small—was as nothing in comparison with your abundance: I took it while you slept—I robbed you to possess myself of money. In vain I have argued that my intention was upright—the fulfilment of what my soul held to be a sacred and imperious duty; the act has poisoned my peace! I have abhorred myself because if it. You have indeed been avenged!

"I need not tell you of bodily suffering, of privation, of cold and hunger; of friendlessness, disappointments, soul-weariness; toils and watchings, which I have gone through to purge from my soul this deadening and desolating self-accusation. I have done it as far as in me lay. I return you the money which I deprived you. God Almighty blot out the remembrance of the act!

"I shall now begin to live! I shall dare to look my fellow-men in the face; for if I have sinned, I am no longer degraded by that sin; and, humbled yet not abject, I can crave your forgiveness, doubting not but Heaven has forgiven me. Your son,

"BERNARD"

Sir Harbottle's immediate sentiment, on reading this letter, was one to which he had hitherto been a stranger. He was sorry for his son; the letter made him uneasy, and he wished it had never been written. He thought at the time that he would rather never have seen his ten guineas again than have regained them accompanied by such a letter; and he determined to do something for him—to advance him even a handsome sum. Before long, however, Sir Harbottle had counted over again his ten thousand guineas, and he hardly remembered Bernard's ten—they looked no way different from the nine hundred and ninety others: he could see in their shining surfaces neither toil of body nor suffering of mind; he only remembered that his sum of money was completed.

When he thought of Bernard again, he wondered to what place any money could be sent to him. He turned to the letter; it left him without a clue. It was clearly impossible that he could remit to him; Bernard had given no address. "And," argued the miser, willing to satisfy his own conscience by doing nothing, "perhaps after all he does not desire my assistance; ten to one but he is even now well off, or why did he so readily part with his money?" The argument was conclusive, and Sir Harbottle contrived to think very little more of his son.

The packet also contained a letter for Julia. In it Bernard acknowledged the crime of which he had been guilty, and prayed her forgiveness, her forgiveness also of what must have appeared his cruel desertion of her. "But," said he, "I was driven from your presence by a sense of degradation and sin; nor could I write to you till I was enabled to remove the stigma from me by restoring the money. He told her, however, nothing of his present condition, of his past sufferings, nor of what he intended to do for the future; still he spoke cheerfully—spoke of hope and assurance, and poured out such overflowings of affection, of consolation—of what seemed almost like joyous-heartedness,—for he *was* at that moment, in the approving consciousness of clearing his soul from a haunting memory,—that although Julia bathed the letter with tears, she could not but gather comfort from it. In the end Bernard promised to let her hear again from him; but he furnished no address by which she had any means of communicating with him.

The particulars of Bernard's absence, where he was, what he had suffered, and how he had obtained the ten guineas, it is not for us at present to relate. Our readers, like Julia, must remain a while longer in ignorance. In the mean time, the year wore on; autumn succeeded summer, winter succeeded autumn; and the next year passed on also. These two years saw the bloom vanish from the countenance of Julia Grimstone: how could it be otherwise? Sir Harbottle, on the public disgrace of his sons, had resigned his commision of the peace—because even he, callous as he was, could not but feel the odium of his family—and thenceferward confined himself most entirely to Denborough Park, but rarely indeed going out of his own rooms—except into the kitchen to keep an exact look-out upon the domestic expenditure. This sedentary and inactive life soon produced visible effects upon him. He grew heavy and unwieldy in person; irritable and morose in temper; full of jealousy and suspicion; doling forth every shilling with hard parsimony, as if it were the very wringing out of his heart's blood, drop by drop. Melancholy indeed was his daughter's life, and her home-annoyances increased daily. —The domestics were mostly dismissed, for none would live with the miser who had a chance of better service elsewhere,—and who, indeed, had not? Poor Julia herself sometimes thought the domestics were less to be pitied than she; for they could mend their condition—she was bound to endure it.

Just about the time when Denhorough Park was in a fair way of being left without domestic of any kind, our old acquaintance Milly Freckleton, who left her hostelery at Tutbury shortly after the Grimstones' committal, and whose grand-daughter, the fair Peggy Woodhouse, fatally connected as she was with Christopher Grimstone, was working day and night to support herself and her child, as well as to afford to its father many a little comfort and indulgence in his prison, volunteered her services at Denborough Park as general the domestic manager, on such extraordinarily low terms as insured her acceptance with the master. Milly had now lived there for several months, contriving, for reasons which she would have been extremely sorry to reveal, to make herself a valuable and not unimportant personage in the miser's household.

Most melancholy, as we said before, was Julia's heart and home; and more especially so, because a cloud still hung upon the fortunes of Walter Constable. His letters came but rarely, and Julia felt too deeply that he was no longer the buoyant-hearted man he had been; he was striving against fortune.— Mrs. Constable's return to to Westow was yet longer delayed and Julia could not doubt for a moment as to the cause of that delay. But one lettor also had been received from Bernard and that left her still in anxious uncertainty. The nabob's curse was indeed fulfilled both upon Sir Harbottle and his descendants. But we have not yet done with poor Julia's troubles. Father Cradock, who was far advanced in years, and become of late greatly enfeebled in body, died at the house of a rich Catholic at two counties' distance, whither he had gone to take his leave, being himself conscious of decaying strength, and intending for the future to decline all journeys and take up his residence at Denborough Park or Westow, so that he might supply to Julia the friends she had lost; to be always at hand to be the counseller and comforter that she so deeply needed.

Excellent old man! He was indeed a true disciple of Christ, humble, patient, long-suffering; kind as a tender-hearted woman, simple-minded as a little child! Nor was her sorrow for his loss lessened by the affecting proof of his more than paternal regard which she received with the intelligence of his death—that the poor priest had made her the heir of his painfully accumulated little property, amounting to somewhat less than six hundred pounds.

The death of Father Cradock left Julia indeed bereaved, and, in the desolation of her heart, she questioned what was the next anguish she would have to bear. Were all those she loved to be removed from her? was she to stand alone like a blasted tree in the midst of a wilderness? There are times when the meekest spirit raises a cry of remonstrating agony. "Lord, if it be thy will, let this cup pass from me!" Such was the bitter cry of Julia's spirit as she looked round and saw herself so stripped and so forlorn.

XV

Before the term of the Grimstones' imprisonment had expired, the Earl of N—— died, and Miss Hammond was married to her honourable lover. Sir Harbettle Grimstone, as might be expected, peremptorily refused to become surety for his sons in the recognizance which was demanded from them; and they might have remained seven years instead of seven months longer for want of bail, had they not been liberated without it by the intervention of Mr. Finch himself. Men like these could not be improved by a thirty months' residence in a gaol; their return to Denborough Park even yet more added to the humiliations and griefs of Julia.

It was many weeks before Sir Harbettle would see his sons, and more before he would permit them to sit down at table with him; for he knew full well that the longer he kept up enmity with them, the less prospect was there of a demand being made upon him for money; and Christopher, he knew, was not as easily to be denied as Bernard. Sir Harbottle bought a new patent lock for his iron chest, took more than usual care not to lose sight or hold of his keys, and made up his mind to maintain this coldness towards them as long as possible. In a short time, however, Christopher, who better than any one living knew how to manage his father, regained some of his old influence over him, and even obtained money from him, Sir Harbottle making this a new and convenient plea for the indulgence of his beloved parsimony. "He had to find money for Christopher"— "Christopher, or Christie, he familiarly called him, was the very deuce for money;" or, "he had just left himself penniless by paying bills for Christopher—the devil take him!" So said Sir Harbottle many a time when called upon for money which an excuse would save him from advancing. And the world, who knew both father and son, while they wondered not at the extravagance and recklessness of the latter, held up their hands and marvelled not a little that the former would open his bags to him, especially after the warning he had had already.

Considerable as seemed to be the influence Christopher had over his father, there were many points he could not carry with him, and especially his favourite one of obtaining from him the house at Knighton, now long uninhabited, with a sufficient allowance to maintain him there as eldest son. "When Christopher was married, if he married to please him," Sir Harbottle replied, "he would talk about it: the house wanted a deal of repair, and he was not going to lay out money upon it without something to look forward to. A wife's fortune would alter the case, and till then Christie must run with the rest; there was plenty of room at Denborough Park for all of them."

Christopher knew that the house at Denborough Park was large enough; but he wanted more room for him and his than he dared to let his father know of. He shrugged his shoulders, bit his lips in his father presence, cursed and swore behind his back, and then sat down by the kitchen fire to talk over, with old Milly Freekleton, affairs which nearly concerned them both; for Peggy Woodhouse, who was by this time the mother of three children, had induced Christopher to marry her, and both Christopher and the old woman had to keep their wits at work to maintain this young family.

Christopher and Robert Grimstone, to all appearance, returned to a life similar to the one they had practised before their imprisonment. The elder brother ruled, the younger served. They still dressed well, and to all seeming were not without money. They went and came as they listed, and not unfrequently were absent from Denborough Park several weeks together, no one seeming aware of their movements but Milly Freekleton, who always carefully provided for their return. Julia could not but remark the good understanding between them, and wondered that the jealous eyes of her father should appear unaware of a circumstance in itself not without suspicion; but, in truth, Sir Harbottle was too well satisfied with the old woman, who refused all domestic help, who asked but small wages, and was always assiduous to please him, to see willingly anything faulty or suspicious in her. Milly, he persisted, was the very jewel of housekeepers; he had a fair word and a smile for her whenever they met: and Milly, on her part, was too desirous of maintaining her post for the sake of her grand-daughter and her children, to give the miser offence willingly. Julia soon saw that the old woman had an importance and value in Sir Harbottle's eyes beyond what she herself could boast of. All these things cost her many a sigh, but she looked on and was silent.

In the course of the next winter four new inmates were discovered at Denborough Park. It happened in this way. There was among the outbuildings a small dwelling-house, which in the munificent days of General Dubois had been inhabited by the family of the head groom. The place itself, like all the outbuildings, through many years of neglect and disuse, had fallen into decay; yet here for several months had been secreted Peggy Woodhouse—Grimstone, as she was now—and her three elder children, and here a fourth had been born. When first they entered upon their abode, it contained only such few articles of indispensable use as Milly could abstract from the hall without fear of detection, and was indeed a comfortless place; but, by degrees, as they remained week after week undiscovered, Christopher and the old woman grew bolder, and removed into it many a piece of luxurious grandeur from the locked-up rooms, which, in the days of the nabob, it was little expected would ever be removed to furnish forth the house of the groom; and poor Peggy's little rooms, while they presented a curious display of incongruous plenishing, assumed a comfortable and home-like appearance; and Peggy herself, pale, anxious, and care-worn, as her countenance had been, regained somewhat of her former beauty, as day after day, week after week, went on, and she remained undisturbed in what she began to look upon as her settled home. Add to which (and it was the great whole of Peggy's happiness), Christopher was constantly at Denborough Park, and, what was more, constantly or nearly constantly sober the whole time; for the necessity of preserving the secret of his wife's residence there kept him always watchful over himself as well as over his father. Sir Harbottle, unknown to himself, was well nigh a prisoner in his own rooms, which, it must be confessed, he was never very willing to leave when his sons were at home.

How it was managed that five mouths were daily secretly supplied from the parsimonious larder of Sir Harbottle, is more than we can tell; but supplied they were. It is also mysterious how the children were kept silent, and within the bounds of their concealment; for the eldest was a strong-limbed, active, and most indomitable lad, with all the elements of his father's character about him. Some one of these causes, it might have been imagined, would have led to their detection; but it was not so: their detection was occasioned by the thin column of smoke which Sir Harbottle observed to ascend from among the outbuildings at various times. Christopher knew that this could not be seen from his father's room, nor from the kitchen; where, in the winter season, to save the expense of a fire in the great dining-hall, they commonly took their meals. It could only be seen from the window of the lobby, through which Sir Harbottle passed from the kitchen, but through which window there was no necessity for him to look at all. The sight of this smoke however, now and then did catch his eye, and he jealously inquired the cause of it. Milly or Christopher, either of them, had an answer ready. At one time the smoke came, Christopher said, from the saddle-house, where he had lighted a fire for his own purposes; another time Milly was washing, or Robert was mending a cart, and needed a fire for his work; or, if none of this would serve, Christopher would outface his father, and persist in there being no smoke at all.

At length Sir Harbottle, who had slily glanced through this window for several days, and either morning, noon, or night, seen this suspicious smoke, began to think, as he said to himself, that all was not right, and therefore, without remarking the circumstance either to his son or to the old woman, hastened to discover the fire for himself. Through many a labyrinth of court-yard, ruinous stables, and half-falling outbuildings, he traced out the smoke which issued from the house of the whilom groom. Without making any attempt on the door, Sir Harbottle looked through the window, the lower half of which was fastened up with boards, intended partly to serve as a shutter, and partly to defend the broken panes of glass; and, to his astonishment, he beheld the inmates, his son

Christopher, Peggy, and her four children. The rage of Sir Harbottle cannot be described; he felt choked with passion, and ascending the seven steps of the door at two strides, shook it violently, and, with almost inarticulate anger, demanded admittance. When Sir Harbottle entered, Christopher had vanished, and poor Peggy, pale and trembling, stood before him.

Sir Harbottle, unable to speak from rage, glanced round the room, and recognised the furniture of his own house—tables, chairs, carpet, looking-glass, and all. He had never been in such a paroxysm of anger before; he would gladly have trampled everything to dust that he saw before him: it was several seconds before he could articulate his indignation.

"Oh! sir," I am his wedded wife!" exclaimed Peggy, in reply to Sir Harbottle's coarse accusations—"I am his wife, sir, and these are his innocent children!"

Sir Harbottle's reply was a denial of her words.

"Nay, nay!" exclaimed Peggy; "what I tell you is true—I am his wedded wife: he himself would not deny it!"

"Where is he?" demanded Sir Harbottle; "let him tell me so if he dare!"

"He will not deny it—he cannot deny it!" said poor Peggy; weeping, and endeavouring vainly to pacify the younger children, who, terrified at the loud and angry voice of Sir Harbottle, clung crying to her.

The noise of the crying children irritated him still more; and now shouting to his son and bidding him come forth from his hiding-place, and then pouring forth imprecations upon the distressed and terrified group that stood before him, Harbottle worked himself into a frenzy of passion, which left him no power of coherent language, and made him hideous to look upon.

"You are a wicked, ugly man, and I will thrash you!" screamed out the eldest boy, seizing a stick that lay on the floor, aud, with a face inflamed with passion, attempted to strike at Sir Harbottle even while he shrank from his furious eye.

"You are a wicked, ugly man, and I hate you!" repeated the boy, while his mother, in a perfect agony, endeavoured to silence and keep him back.

Sir Harbottle stalked up to him, and, griping him by the shoulder, flung him on the floor. The heavy sound of the fall, the child's sudden silence, the blood that started from his mouth, and the thrilling scream of the mother that he was dead, recalled Sir Harbottle in some measure to himself. Peggy threw her youngest child into the cradle, pushed the others aside, and snatching him up, took him on her knee, and began to rub his temples.

Sir Harbottle stayed to see that the child was not dead; and then muttering an indistinct murmur of anger, like the distant growling of thunder, went out.

It was a fortunate thing for Peggy and her children that this happened. Sir Harbottle was really moved; some mysterious, electric link of associations was touched—the unhappy, long-forgotten Judith and her poor dumb boy returned to his memory, and for their sakes his hard nature relaxed. Sir Harbottle shut himself in his rooms, and was seen by no one of his household again that day.

Had Christopher known what his father's feelings were, he would not have failed to take advantage of an occurrence so favourable to him; but as it was, he carefully avoided meeting him for at least a week. Peggy, in the mean time, was unremoved, and Milly undertook to introduce the subject to Sir Harbottle.

"But, ay, dear-a-me!" said Milly, as if in surprise, when she had heard his observations on the new inmates, and in reality had been amazed at the moderated severity of his temper— "But, ay, dear you would not let her be starved!"

"You have taken good care not to let that happen; she does not look in a starving condition," rejoined he.

"She is a decent, pretty-behaved young woman," said Milly, anxious to get Sir Harbottle's approval in any shape. "He might ha' married a lady-born, and had one less of a lady in look or manner either; or he might ha' brought home some tasseling wench that would ha' been more plague nor profit."

"What the deuce must he marry for at all!" asked Sir Harbottle, wrathfully, "unless he could marry a woman with money?"

"Young folks," replied she, "isn't like old ones! I'd uphold her for coming of a decent family and having had a good bringing up!—she's so pretty behaved."

"Pretty the devil!" muttered Sir Harbottle in contemptuous anger; "don't talk to me about her."

"Dear heart!" replied Milly, "for sartain you don't mean her to be starved, and she the mother of your son's children, and his wedded wife into the bargain?"

"Let those that brought her here maintain her," said Sir Harbottle, doggedly; "it is no business of mine."

Milly knew from experience that Sir Harbottle's sullen humours were more difficult to manage than his violent ones; and muttering therefore a "Dear heart!" and a "Lord bless us!" she went out, intending to urge with Christopher his taking advantage before long of the forbearance which his father, in spite of his ill humour, was disposed to extend to the intruders. Christopher did so, and bore the scornful vials of his father's indignation and anger. He had his own purposes to serve, nnd therefore he bore them patiently. "He behaved extremely well," as Sir Harbottle internally said; and though it was yielded but slowly, and with the worst grace in the world, yet Christopher obtained permission that Peggy, whom he acknowledgcd as his wife, and her children, might yet continue to inhabit their former dwelling, provided neither she nor they ever entered the Hall. Christopher was satisfied; whatever further was needed, old Milly, at some more favourable time, would obtain. He, however, carefully kept from his father's knowledge Milly's relationship to his wife; and fortunately for all parties Sir Harbottle was too willing to forget the existence of Peggy and her children, to make inquiries about her family.

Julia, who before this discovery had been, like her father, aware of some secret connected with the outbuildings in which both Milly and her brother Christopher were much interested, had forborne to inquire into it from fearing that the discovery might only add yet more to her discomforts; and that since her influence in that ill-regulated household was so small, it was far more to her peace to remain in willing ignorance. Her own apartments, at least, were sacred from intrusion: she had but to take her meals with her family, and then, for the rest of the day, she could close the doors and shut in there her own sorrows, indulge her own thoughts and memories, and fear intrusion; for she was too unimportant a person to be sought after or needed by any one. Add to this, her spirit had insensibly received the impression of early death; and though her eye was sunken, and her cheek, instead of the bright bloom of her youth, was now marble-pale like her brow, and her frame had lost much of its roundness and elastic buoyancy, yet excepting these, which no one had kindly and anxiously regarded, her general health had not failed. The impression was heavy on her spirit, and in the deep religion of her soul she dedicated herself to good works through the remnant of her days, blessing God that, although the death of the good Father Cradock had made her solitary life yet more solitary, still his sacred bequest furnished her with a small fund at her own disposal, and enabled her to set about those benevolent schemes which she had planned many a time without power hitherto to accomplish. She visited the poor in the neighbouring hamlet, hearing all their domestic troubles and grievances, sympathising when she could not succour, and in many cases giving what was better than money— the benefit of her experience and good counsel. The blessings of this intercourse of Christian love were mutual; there was healing for Julia's own heart in the interest it took in the cares and sorrows of others. At home likewise she found it a consolatory employment to make up garments, like Dorcas of old, for their comfort and use. Our hearts are made for human sympathies, for the admission of human kindness; and stripped and heart-broken as Julia had been, she found in these works of love, that even for her there were peace and joy. All this, however, was strictly kept from the knowledge of Sir Harbottle; for though the money was her own, the fact of giving away even *that* would not have failed to make a breach between her father and herself.

The strict embargo which had formerly confined Peggy and her children within the narrow limits of their concealment being removed, it was not long before Julia became acquainted with the persons of all. The eldest boy, John—or, as he was more character-istically called, Jack—she met at every turn, always in mischief, and perpetually in danger; a strong-limbed, bold-visaged, and audacious boy—a very Christopher in youth. As she walked through the wilderness of shrubbery, a tree-branch would crack, and down would drop the urchin to the ground, from a height which would have broken another boy's leg, or perhaps neck, but only left him with a bruise, a scratch, or a torn jacket. She was never safe from the stones he was continually hurling in every direction. There seemed to be a sort of ubiquity about him. If she avoided one part of the grounds because he was there, two minutes afterwards he would be whittling sticks, or blowing through a shrill whistle behind the very tree where she was standing. Nor was he a boy to be impressed with either fear or reverence; he stalked up to the very windows of Sir Harbottle's room, scrawled with a pebble on the glass, which he had been at some pains to reach, or sent forth a screaming shout of a sudden, without aim or meaning—unless it was with the graceless intent of frightening Sir Harbottle. Julia tried in vain to attach him to her, in the hope of taming him and bringing him into subjection; for his bold black eye and his laughing face did not fail to draw her early attention. But he was not a child for a woman to train; he whistled while she talked to him, or started off after a rabbit or a bird at the very moment when she hoped his attention was fixed on her words. Julia sighed as she looked upon him, and thought what such a character would become, with training and example such as he would have. Far different from Amy, his twin-sister—a meek, fair-haired, and delicate child—the very counterpart of her brother: She, likewise, Julia met many times in the grounds, wandering in quiet thoughtfulness, or leading by the hand her younger brother careful and overflowing with love, as if she had been a tender and gentle-hearted mother. Amy, whose nature was alive to kindness, and who had a quick perception of whatever is graceful and amiable, soon distinguished Miss Grimstone as a being to be loved; and while the same kind feelings were growing in Julia's heart towards her, her own soul was yearning towards Julia with an enthusiasm of love. Julia knew not that often little Amy had stood behind a bush to watch her go by, and had sent a kiss after her—nay, that once as she was seated on the grass, deeply engrossed by her own thoughts, the little maiden, whose heart could resist the impulse no longer, had stolen quietly behind her and kissed the hem of her garment, and then as quietly stolen back again unperceived. Such were the elder children of Christopher Grimstone.

For some time Julia carefully avoided meeting the mother in the belief that she must be a degraded, vulgar woman, such as the associate of her brother Christopher might be expected to be; and Peggy, modest, retiring, and deeply conscious of the suspicion that naturally attached to her; and with many a sore heart-grief of her own, so far from obtruding herself upon Miss Grimstone's notice, shrank back at her approach; or if they did chance accidentally to meet, dropped an humble curtsy and went on. Poor Peggy! like little Amy, her heart yearned to the gentle sister of her reprobate husband; and "Oh," sighed she many a time, "were it but possible for her to know all, she would not shun me."

This modest demeanour soon attracted Julia's attention; and though no nature could possibly be fuller of unsuspecting kindness and true charity than hers, yet so little confidence had she in whatever was connected with her elder brothers, that she doubted if this modest seeming might not be a deeplaid trick to gain her notice.

At length the love which we have said little Amy had conceived for Miss Grimstone could contain itself no longer; and one morning in May, as they met in the shrubbery, Julia having looked kindly upon her, the little girl, in spite of her natural timidity, thrust her hand softly into hers, and in a low gentle voice asked "if she would please to talk to her."

There was so much good faith and perfect artlessness in the child's manner, that Julia's heart received her at once. She kissed her forehead and blessed her. A happy child was Amy that day—an exceedingly happy child; and from that time she became Julia's constant out-of-doors companion; Sir Harbottle rigorously interdicted them the house. Through Amy, Julia also became acquainted with the mother, and by degrees deeply interested for her.

That poor young woman's heart was an overflowing fountain of love. By little and little the whole story of the unhappy connexion with Christopher was related. Peggy had been deceived, betrayed by him; had suffered endless privation and hardship for his sake, and had borne from him every neglect, wrong, and unkindness, which man can inflict on trusting women; yet still she loved him—how devotedly, her meekness, her forbearance, her endeavours to win back his faithless heart by every loving and gentle wile, told far more than words. "Oh," said poor Peggy, many and many a time, "I will do ten times more for him; I will bear even more than I have already borne for him—if not for affection only, for gratitude; for has he not made me his wife?"

One thing, however, there was which Peggy did not reveal—that was the relationship between herself and Milly. This was a secret which was rigorously enjoined upon her both by her husbaud and the old woman. Milly had a hundred opportunities of serving all parties, as the careful housekeeper in the confidence of Sir Harbottle, which she would have lost entirely as the grandmother of Christopher's wife; and Peggy loved her children too well to betray a secret in which their wellbeing was involved.

Juila could not but respect and admire the devotedness and the submissive fidelity of this young woman; and Peggy, on her part, looked cheerful, and might even be heard singing, morning, noon, and night. To Sir Harbottle, however, she was always invisible; or if he saw her, it was as though he saw her not; and Peggy retained such an awful remembrance of his first introduction to her that she would as soon have encountered a lion as him.

XVI

No sooner were his wife and children understood to be permitted residents of Denborongh Park, than Christopher Grimstone dismissed all care or concern for them, and in the course of the next summer absented himself for some months, accompanied by his brother, without having given any intimation of his absence to his wife or even to old Milly. Day after day, week after week, they were expected, and yet they came not; and Milly resented extremely the omission of his usual confidence in her. Whither he was gone no one knew; but though Peggy shed tears about him many a time in the day, and watered her pillow with tears at night, yet she was not as one who refused to be comforted. The hours went cheerfully on when Julia came in and talked with her, and Peggy felt as if she could not be miserable; and when Milly wrought up into a pitch of vehement indignation against Christopher for his neglect of her and the children, and in suspicion of the profligate life he was even now leading, Peggy defended him and invented excuses for him—excuses which her own heart could not accept.

All this time Julia's strength was wearing away; and though her spirits found relief in the interest her heart took in the unsophisticated and innocent Peggy and her children, she became every day more assured of her declining health. But she was now no longer without a sympathising, anxious eye to regard her, or a friendly voice to speak kindly to her. Peggy watched over her as one tender sister might watch over another; her admiration for her and her humble love were without bounds. Julia's gentle mauners, her refinement of taste and sentiment—and above all, her piety—were deeply felt by her and had a marked influence upon her. Julia could not but see the gradual change which was wrought in her manners and feelings, and her heart bled for her. She was doomed, she foresaw, to be even a more unhappy victim than the former Lady Grimstone had been, inasmuch as Christopher was many grades more debased than his father. Other trials, too, Julia could foresee for this loving, gentle-hearted woman; the fierce indomitable spirit of the eldest child, self-willed as he was with but weak affections, would strengthen with his strength and grow with his growth into a character, aided by paternal example, which would be a thorn in his mother's side; while little Amy, all love, all gentleness, with knowledge and thought far beyond her years, was too good, too pure to live—or if life were spared her—which her feeble health as much as angelic purity of her spirit hardly premised—what would not be the pains and humiliations which she must endure! Peggy's soul was wrapped up in this child; she loved her with a passionate love that had no words to express itself in; she loved her all the better too for the affection Julia showed towards her mother—and to Julia the child was as a daughter. These new sources of interest and affection, though they brought with them anxieties, did not fail to make Julia's time pass much more happily than it ever had done since the death of her mother. She daily met eyes that beamed upon her with affection; the consciousness of conferring happiness upon some living thing, it matters not how humble, brings with it a rich and abundant reward.

All this time we have said but little of Walter Constable or of Bernard. In these passing years, Julia had received several letters from Bernard—letters that were full of unabated affection, but unsatisfactory, because they filled her with undefined anxieties. They breathed, in spite of their assumed cheerfulness a tone of melancholy resignation, that persuaded her he was enduring, she knew not what, of privation, hardship, or suffering, and they never furnished her with the means of communicating with him. Still, as long as he wrote, she knew he was alive—and that in itself was some consolation. The letters, however, which she of late had received from Mr. Constable were of increasing satisfaction: the tide of fortune was turning with him; and now, in the autumn of the year, at which we are arrived, after mehanchly residences in Vienna, Rome, Constantinople, Smyrna, and a journey to Egypt, he was looking forward to a permanent return to London, with full ability to visit Westow at his will, and also to fulfil his engagements with Julia. It was a joyous letter—a letter that spoke as Walter used to talk; and Julia, as she read it, forgot the intervening melancholy years, and was transported back to the old summer-house. The letter added that Mrs. Constable also, who had refused to leave the Continent while her son's prospects were uncertain, was beginning now to look forward to her return to Westow; and preparations were already making, through the agent who had managed their affairs during their absence, for her return. All this was like a blessed streaming in of daylight to the eyes of the captive. She read the letter again and again, shed abundant tears of joy, and then, falling upon her knees—she had no benign and beautiful Madonna to address now—returned thanks to Heaven.

It was many and many a month now since Julia had been so far as the old summer-house; but in the gladness of the precious memories which this letter restored and in the strength of its joyful tidings, she set forth, taking little Amy by the hand, that she might look down upon Westow—dear, happy Westow! which was so soon to receive back its true inmates.

"Oh, that Bernard could but be with me—could but know these Happy events!"—sighed she, as she went along.

It was a fine breezy morning late in October, and little Amy now skipped on before her, catching the threads of gossamer, that, shining like silver in the sun, floated lightly in the air, or were carried on by a passing gale, and then gathered her little handful of the most fairy-like of flowers, the graceful and slender harebell, appealing to Julia with her sweet, cheerful voice to admire them with her. But Julia was silent and disinclined for talk, and the child then walked on demurely and mutely by her side, occupying herself with her own pleasant little fancies. Julia was thinking deeply; perhaps it was the only time she had ever been with this dear child and wholly disregarded her. Her thoughts, joyful when she set out, became, as she went on, insensibly full of heaviness. Her decreased—nay, almost utterly failing strength was made painfully sensible to her long before she reached the brow of the hill. How different was it when she had bounded thither with an elasticity of step, totally unconscious of fatigue, five years ago! Yes, indeed, it was five years since that evening in October when she went there to meet Walter Constable on the eve of his departure. She remembered how, though it was to part from him, she had ascended these slopes, unconscious of effort, with the free-footedness of a young deer;—now, when it was to look down upon the home which was so shortly to receive him—perhaps to receive her—she crept on with feeble steps, beating heart, and a general debility of frame. Julia felt that death was before her; the long-hoped-for happiness which a union with Walter Constable would bring might never be hers—and oh, the painful knowledge which thus awaited *him*! for she had jealously avoided hinting of her melancholy forebodings, or of her failing health, that she might not add one uneasiness to his anxious life abroad. She had hitherto hoped, or tried to hope, that it was but the solitary unhappiness of her lot that filled her spirit with gloom, and even depressed her physical frame; but she could not now deceive herself. By the time she reached the summer-house, she was completely exhausted, and sank down powerless upon the threshold. All that poor Amy could do for her she did; she supported her head upon her knees, kissed her, and gently rubbed her temples, as she remembered to have seen Julia when her mother had fainted,

"Bless you, my child!" said Julia, opening her eyes, and seeing the distressed face of the little Amy looking down upon her; "I am better—nay, I am well"—continued she, raising herself and kissing Amy tenderly.

"Oh, I thought you were dead!" exclaimed Amy, bursting into tears.

Julia exerted herself to the utmost, smiled, and strove to pacify the child.

"I thought you were dead!" again she said, scarcely able to speak for weeping—"and I dream so often that you are dead! Do not die; for mother says, if you die, I shall not see you again!"

"Yes, my dearest one!" said Julia, mingling her tears with the child's; "you will come to me in Heaven; you are kind, and gentle, and obedient, and such go to Heaven."

"Yes, mother says so," replied Amy; "and she says sometimes that you will die, and it makes her cry sadly; and I mean to die when you do—but I do not want to leave mother and the baby yet." And poor Amy wept again as if her heart would break.

Julia was deeply impressed by her words, and by the intimation thus given of Peggy's fears respecting her, according as they did with her own melancholy forebodings; and though she would fain have made light of it to soothe the child, she felt incapable of trifling with a subject awful in itself, or of belying her own feelings. The two sat silently together side by aide, each pondering on death, bound to the earth by strong affections, and desiring life, if so might be the will of Heaven.

Two beautiful beings were they, and pure as angels, though the world's disesteem lay heavy upon them.

Julia, at length, reproaching herself for allowing the spirit of the child to be gloomed with thoughts so unnatural to her years, assumed a cheerfulness which she did not feel, and began to point out to her the decayed paintings on the walls and ceiling, which had once been frescoes of no inconsiderable merit; and to speak of what she herself had been told in her childhood of the singular history of the former possessors a Denborough Park, with whom this summer-house had been a favourite resort, though it was now but one of a thousand tokens of magnificence that belonged to those days. There was a strange, fascinating interest to Julia's mind in the traditions of those times the fame of Jane Ashenhurst's beauty—her mother's pride and its fearful punishment—and the dark, mysterious nabob, whose memory continued to haunt the hall like a spectre;—these had been stories to which Julia and Bernard had listened with thrilling regard, and they had deeply impressed themselves on both their imaginations. It was many a day now since Julia had talked of them: in their younger days, she and Bernard were now weary of them, and it was the most favourite of all their plays to act the nabob and the ladies. Julia told Amy all this.

"Ah!" said Amy, who had listened with her sweet lips apart and her dark, large eye fixed on her aunt with intense interest, "the all is true that old Milly says."

"And what does Milly say, dearest?"

"She says," replied Amy, drawing closer, "that she would not for the world go into many of the chambers; and that an old man with a long beard walks o' nights; and that there is a lady so beautiful and yet so dark, that comes now and then, with a baby in her arms."

All this Julia had heard in her childhood—it was one of the traditions of the house. "And anything more?" asked she, for she had heard much beside.

"Oh yes," said Amy, shuddering; "all about the proud lady; and how the nabob was chained in his coffin, and how he used to torture himself every day. I heard old Daniel Neale, that comes now and then, talking to Milly, and he said he knew all about it; and Milly says she can hear groans plain enough as soon as the clock strikes twelve at night. And, oh, aunt, how old Daniel must be if he can remember such things!"

Julia was sorry to find that one with so excitable a mind as Amy had heard so much, and blamed herself for having perhaps given force to those impressions by this very conversation.

"You must not believe such tales as these," said she. "The house is large, and the rooms are gloomy, but no beings worse than ourselves inhabit them. I have lived in it longer than Milly, and never saw either the old man or the lady. The wind blows down the wide chimneys at night, and sounds hollow. I have heard this myself; but any spectral groans I never did. You must believe what I tell you, Amy."

"Yes, aunt, yes," replied she; "but you are so good. Milly says they come to frighten wicked people; she says Sir Harbottle hears them as well as she does. And she says," continued Amy, with great animation, "that there is such money in the house, and that she has seen crowns, and rings, and such beautiful jewels!—and *Milly* has a deal of money!"

"Has she!" exclaimed Julia, reverting instantly to her own suspicions of the old woman, "But she does not give this money to your mother?" asked she, hoping not to receive an affirmative answer.

"No; but I have seen her give a deal of money to my father," said Amy, in perfect simplicity.

Julia determined to ask no more. Whatever poor Amy knew was to her innocence—it burdened not her soul with knowledge of sin. Julia wanted to know no more; and rising hastily, she took Amy's hand, and led her out, saying—"There is an old house below this wood; let us look for it." Julia was alarmed to find, as she attempted to move, how feeble and exhausted she was. They reached, however, the height of the ascent whence Westow was formerly visible; the plantation had grown so much since she had been there last, that although some of the trees had already lost their leaves, the house was completely concealed: they must go yet further on before they could obtain the view. Julia hesitated for a moment whether it would not be wiser to return home than to add, even though it might be but a few hundred yards, to the walk; but her heart urged her onward. "To see Westow once again, perhaps for the last time, and she within so short a distance of it! Yes, she must see it—it would be a sight to do her good."

The top of the hill, however, for a considerable distance entirely shut out the view, and they had to go, on and on, a full half-mile farther, before she could obtain a free view below. At length, she stood upon the very promontory of the ridge. The woods shelved down with a sudden descent, and Westow lay immediately below her. She looked down, as it were, upon the very roof of the house with its broad leads and its tall turreted porch; and the first that she saw was the smoke cheerfully ascending from four out of its six chimneys. The shutters, too, were opened; the casements stood wide; and two men were busied in the garden.

"Thank God!" exclaimed Julia, forgetful of fatigue, or, if conscious of it, feeling abundantly recompensed by the sight for even greater fatigue than she had endured; "O that Bernard could but see it with me!" She felt as if she could not satisfy her eyes with looking on these happy tokens of restored prosperity of the Constables; and little Amy, in her thoughtfulness, had to remind her that they were a long way from home before she thought of returning.

A weary and painful return was that; and Julia's spirit as well as her strength, were completely exhausted before she reached the hall. Through the night she could not sleep: an indescribable apprehension of she knew not what of horror and grief lay on her spirit; every sound startled her—she seemed to see phantoms in the darkness, and the very silence itself appalled her. It was a miserable night; and though towards morning she slept, she woke unrefreshed and feeble. The two succeeding nights were the same, and on the third day she found herself unable to rise. She knew she was ill but how was she to obtain medical aid? Father Cradock dead; for Father Cradock, who had been possessed of considerable skill in medicine, had acted as physician of the family excepting in the extraordinary case of Lady Grimstone's illness, when a medical man was called in a few weeks before her death. Sir Harbottle, robust himself,—and, in fact, priding himself on never having taken a drachm of physic in his life,—had no sympathies for invalids. His wife's chamber he but very rarely visited: all illness, he maintained, originated in people not being employed. "Get up betimes, work hard, and eat a hearty dinner," said he to all who complained, "and you will soon be better." Julia could have done none of these, and therefore she was obliged to throw herself on the tender mercies of old Milly, although she had anything but a favourable opinion of her, believing her an artful woman, in some way or other bound to serve her brother Christopher, and sent there by him, as she suspected, to serve his own ends. But Julia had no other resource, since Peggy was forbidden to enter the house, and therefore she submitted.

"Ay, dear-a-me," said Milly, when she saw and heard how seriously indisposed Julia was; "but we mun have a doctor. You munna be lost for want of help. I'll go and hear what th' ould master says?" And Milly, without ceremony, entered Sir Harbottle's room, and demanded medical aid for his daughter.

Milly, however, had come in an evil hour. Poor Sir Harbottle had fretted his soul with the consternation of a discovery he had just made, during which he had dragged off the forty-years-old carpet. Milly was half stifled with dust as she entered, and looked round the room for a second before she discerned through its thick atmosphere Sir Harbottle down on his knees before a suspicious hole in the floor.

"Oh, Lord!" said Milly, "what's your honour after!"

"It is a strange thing," said Sir Harbottle, grubbing down in the hole like a terrier after vermin,—"It is a strange thing. But shut the door, woman."

Milly did so, and then looked on. "Have you lost owt?" asked she, presently, as Sir Harbottle still kept groping downward, first with two fingers, and then with three.

"Lost anything!" repeated he; "I've lost a deal! It is a strange thing that rats should come here, where there's neither candle-ends nor cheese and look here," said he, rising from the floor, and shoving down his coat, which hitched up at the shoulders,—"look you here!" And by laying her face close to the wall, as Sir Harbottle did, she discovered a hole the size of a man's hand at the back of the escritoir, which he had loosened from the wall, and in the wall itself a corresponding hole.

"Ay, they are rats sure enough," said Milly; "the varmint! they dearly love paper."

"And something besides paper," said Sir Harbottle, fiercely.

"Well now, only think," said Milly, without seeming to understand his words; "how do you ever think all this rubbage can be got out, and these things sided, and only one pair of hands, and Miss so badly as her is?"

"I tell you what," said Sir Harbottle, "I have missed money; and if I did not strongly suspect rats myself, I'd have you all searched, that I would—every one of you!"

"Ay, for sartain they are rats," replied she; "I hear 'em scratting at my bed's head like so many moudiwarps; and o' summer mornings I've seen the mice washing their faces on my pillow—the impudent huzzies! It's a great gayshous place, your honour—But come, sir, we mun have a doctor for Miss Julia."

"What's amiss with her?"

"Ay, dear-a-dear, sir, she's clean going in a waste; can't sleep never a wink o' night; falls into faints every now and then; can't eat as much as a sparrow, and is as weak as a cat."

"She sat at table with me yesterday," said the hard voice of Sir Harbottle.

"But she ate nout," replied Milly. "What's the use of sit at table if a body can't eat? We mun have a doctor."

"I'll have no doctors," said he,—"I'll not have my pocket picked with doctors; and so you know my mind—a set of lazy vermin! I've plague enough with the rats, without giving my money to doctors," and poor Sir Harbottle again began to examine his floor. "Look here," said he, weighing with his heavy foot upon the broken board, "I must have a new floor; and deal-boards are raised a halfpenny a foot. Harkye, woman, I've lost somehow about nine hundred pounds—part Bank of England bills, and part gold—no trifle that; and now you come here wanting a doctor."

"Well, sir, she's your own daughter—she's none of mine," said Milly.

"Begone with you!" said Sir Harbottle, growing angry. "After the losses I have had, it is as well not to have too many people in my room."

"And what's to be done for Miss Julia?" asked the old woman, feeling herself compelled to decamp.

"Make her plenty of kitchen physic," returned he, driving her on step by step to the door. "No good comes of giving fees to doctors, it's what I neither can do nor will do. There's more virtue in a slice of beef and a penny loaf than in all the doctors' stuff in ten parishes. Make her kitchen physic, and she'll soon be better."

"And who, pray ye, is to wait on her, I should like to know?" asked Milly. "It's no sham badliness; and her wants looking after night and day, and who's to do it? for it's more than I'll undertake—I've enough work o' my own, believe me."

"The woman in the yard can come in and nurse her," said Sir Harbottle; "there is no sense in her being kept to nothing."

Milly shrugged her shoulders as she heard the miser's bolts drawn after her, and laughed as she repeated "the rats!"

Julia was grateful beyond measure to be allowed the attendance of Peggy, and to have the little Amy seated by her chair or her bed. It was cheering to hear the low, sweet voice of the gentle child singing or talking soothingly; it was cheering to know her present, even when, profoundly silent, she watched beside her—never so happy as when employed in her service. Melancholy though those days and nights of sickness were, they were not altogether sad: Julia was conscious of affection—the most patient, unwearied, devoted affection, both of poor little Amy and her gentle-hearted mother. Her own soul, too, overflowed with love to all. Her affection for Walter Constable, chastened as it had been, grew yet more deep and holy; and for Bernard her love seemed surpassing—as if a union of spirit were taking place between them—as if they were even now drawing nearer and nearer to a joyful and eternal communion. She seemed already sensible of some mysterious spiritual intercourse with him, which was all love, all peace, all joy. An absorbing ecstasy of affection filled her spirit, and her pale countenance was irradiated by it, as if it had been the face of an angel. Sweet Amy looked at her in silent reverence, her own little heart kindled into a yet warmer glow of love; and Peggy stole in and out of the room like a ministering spirit, feeling a sentiment more like veneration than love: in her eyes Julia was almost divine.

XVII

At the very time Julia walked with little Amy to the hill-top to get a sight of Westow, the Constables arrived in London. Walter's engagements were diplomatic; a brilliant future had opened before him, and his mother was again to all appearance a happy woman; but she was not, like her son, capable of forgetting the difficulties and hardships of the last five years. Walter thought that his present greatness and future prospects were cheaply purchased by them: Mrs. Constable, with a sigh, thought that his prosperity had been dearly bought.

"Thank God," she would say, "you are at lengths worthily employed! This is the life I have coveted for you—an honourable life; but you have had a sore up-hill tug."

"I shall be the better for it all my days," he would cheerfully reply; "such a breaking-in as this will do me good—has done me good already; it was the very thing I needed."

"Ah, well, the back is mercifully made for the burden. I am thankful for the dawn of prosperity that has opened on you; but I shall carry the effects of the last five years with me to the grave."

Mrs. Constable would have laid down her life cheerfully for her son: strong to bear and to suffer in the hour of adversity, prosperity threw her back upon a temper somewhat querulous, and a spirit proud, open to prejudices, and tenacious of the world's esteem. No wonder was it, therefore, that with such feelings all her old aversions to the Grimstones remained nothing abated.

Walter had intended to accompany his mother to Westow immediately on their arrival in England; but he soon discovered the design impracticable: two weeks, at least, must elapse before he could leave London. Mrs. Constable, therefore, was impatient to be again established in her old home, though the season was late and the weather severe, undertook to the journey without him, escorted thither by the agent, who through their absence, had proved himself a faithful steward. This journey was to be performed, be it understood, in the days when the facilities of travel were much less than at present; and a long, weary journey it was. They took the London stage to Lichfield, the nearest town to which such a conveyance came, and thence they proceeded in post-chaises. The last day of the journey was one intensely cold—a black, cheerless November day—a day of all others to make places and objects unsightly; yet with what real satisfaction did the good lady look through the closed windows of the chaise on familiar prospect on either hand! Yes; in spite of the regrets that would spring up, because she had been an exile from home so long, Mrs. Constable was a happy woman.

Her travelling companion, with praiseworthy delicacy, left her at Wood Leighton, pretending business there, and promising to follow her in the evening. His absence was a great relief; her heart was full of emotion, and since her son was not with her, she desired no other eyes to observe it. As she drove out of Wood Leighton, within less than an hour's drive Westow, sitting alone in her chaise, she was a happy woman but when, before long, they came to the road bounded by the line of ancient, lichen-covered park-wall, and she could see at some turn, or from some higher part of the road, the home of the Grimstones, grey and dark, showing neglect even at that distance, annoyances sprang thick about her; and she remembered that her dearly-beloved Westow was surrounded by the lands of Denborough Park, and that the inhabitants of Denborough Park were the root of all the evil which had come upon either herself or her son. Poor Mrs. Constable! she was baptizing her spirit with these eternal regrets, when the road swept round, the park-wall took another direction, and the long, noble avenue opened before her—its gates standing wide as if with outspread arms to receive her. At the farther end she saw the tall arched gateway, and, beyond all, the trim garden, with its spired and ample evergreens before it; the dear old house, with its irregular front, its bay windows, its tall tower-like porch, richly escutcheoned with the arms of the Constables, its balustraded roof, high-pointed gables, and chimneys of solid masonry. Mrs. Constable, calm woman as she was, who seldom displayed external emotion, felt a choking sensation come over her, and the unrepressed tears flowed from her eyes, as the chaise, with slow motion and deadened sound, drove into the gloom of that goodly avenue. It was with a proud delight that she looked onward through the vista, and upward to the trees, every one of which had been purchased, she felt, by this painful absence, and by all the anxieties, fears, and bodily pains she had borne through it. None but such as love home with the proud, reverential regard which Mrs. Constable had for Westow, can understand the emotion of this return.

At the door of the house, the ancient and faithful domestic who had remained there in her absence received her. This meeting was that of friend with friend.

"The Lord be praised that I see you well at home again!" said the poor servant, wiping the tears, which flowed plentifully, with the corner of her apron.

"Thank Heaven!" responded her lady, in a low, suppressed voice, feeling overcome by her sensations; and then, seating herself once more in the cushioned arm-chair, which stood, as it did formerly, upon the parlour hearth, she felt the sentiment too deeply in her soul for it to again find utterance in words.

Full of satisfaction as Mrs. Constable's re-establishment at home might be supposed to be, she could not but miss the friend whom death had removed during her absence. Father Cradock had been dead a considerable time; and although she was aware of the event, and had mourned it sincerely during her foreign sojourn, the fireside at Westow did not seem right without him. She had again to mourn his loss; she had now to feel, of a certainty, that Father Cradock, the long-tried, faithful friend, the ghostly comforter, the cheerful companion, was dead. He had been, even more than her son, her associate at Westow; she could imagine the house without Walter, but not without Father Cradock. His own chair stood by the fire vacant; when the door opened, she looked for him to enter; and even in this hour of fulfilment, both heart and soul were made conscious of wants which only he could have supplied. Mrs. Constable's return to Westow was a practical illustration of the incapability of what the world calls "good fortune" entirely satisfying the human heart.

Having now established Mrs. Constable at home, we must return to her son, who, after having seen his mother off in the stage-coach, strolled carelessly towards his hotel, and in his way passed the shop of Mr. Charles Stevens, one of the principal booksellers of the day, and was detained for a moment by the title-page of a political pamphlet which was just then exciting an intense sensation throughout London. Walter stepped in to purchase it, and found the shop crowded with people—men of fashion, men of rank, eager and hot politicians, loiterers of all descriptions, such as met there constantly to discuss the events of the day, and whatever new lampoon, caricature or pamphlet, the agitation of the time had produced.

Now, however, nothing was talked of but this production so clever, so witty, so true; full of such noble sentiments, right views, such cutting and annihilating sarcasm, such pure and wonderful eloquence. All joined in extolling it, and all were inquisitive after the author. One great cause of interest connected with it was, that the author, who called himself: "Marcus," and who for the last three years had produced a vast number of similar works, all on the passing subjects of the day, in this his latest took leave of his readers, and of the public at large, in one of the most pathetic and eloquent adieus that ever had been written. On all hands were regrets over him. His works, it was said, were perused by the cabinet as well as the people at large, and had had no inconsiderable influence upon the sentiments of several influential persons. The author, it was declared, was a made man, would he but reveal his name; and Mr. Stevens, who was likewise the publisher; was importuned to reveal it. This was what Walter Constable gleaned up, as he stood with the pamphlet in his hand, turning over its pages the while, and catching glimpses of its extraordinary style, and of the wonderful force and reach of the author's mind. Mr. Stevens declared himself not at liberty to say who it was; it was a secret he was in honour bound to keep; but report hinted, he said, of a certain noble lord about his majesty's person, and again, of a right reverend bishop, but he could not say which rumour was nearer the truth;—this, however, was certain, that the writer was one of the most extraordinary men of the day. All parties agreed in this; and the sapient man of books elevated his eyebrows, folded his arms and looked very knowing.

Walter listened to what was said with great interest, and then addressed him to the reading of his pamphlet, which soon so completely engrossed his attention, that he took no farther heed of what went forward around him, nor was able to leave it till he had finished with the last words. He then applied to the master of the shop with the same eager queries that the others had done, expressing at the same time his unbound admiration of the talent displayed in this production, and still more, a reverence for the right-minded, unflinching principle with which it abounded; and ended by desiring that the whole of this singularly-gifted author's writings might be sent to his address, which he furnished.

Walter was deeply engaged over their pages upon the evening of the next day, when a small packet was brought in for him. He opened it, and, to his extreme astonishment, found it to be from Bernard Grimstone, enclosing three hundred pounds and the following letter:—

"MY MUCH-VALUED AND DEAR FRIEND,

"What a singular series of providential interpositions has my life been! and how consoling is the belief that such has been the case! I will not in this place explain to you what these instances have been, but will now speak of what more nearly concerns yourself.

"After five years I restore to you the sum of which you were impoverished by our family, principally through regard for my beloved sister and myself. Would to God it could have been returned to you earlier—at a time when money was more needful to you than, I thank Heaven, it is at present! I have heard of your success—that you stand high with not less than two crowned heads. May your good fortune be equal to your virtues! may the trials and difficulties you have had to encounter be the only ones your life may experience!

"And now you will naturally require some account of myself—some cause for my so carefully concealing my mode of life and place of abode, and some explanation of the means by which I am enabled to restore you your own. I will give it to you. I am the 'Marcus' with whose name the town rings. I was in Mr. Stevens's shop at the time you were there; but not even Mr. Stevens himself knows my name or my history, although he knows me for the author whose writings are enriching him.

"I came to London—let me confess it—with the sin of theft upon my soul! I stole from my father ten guineas to enable me to undertake this journey; and venial as the world's morality might have held the offence, it was a crushing load of enormity,

of self-degradation, which trammelled and galled me worse
than a slave's fetters. I did not dare to look an honest man in the
face; I could not speak of probity, morality, or any, of the virtues
of social life, even through my pen; I could not reprobate any of
its vices while my conscience accused me of theft! O miserable,
miserable time! I came into this vast city a self-condemned
wretch. Busy and happy faces surrounded me, but I had neither
companion nor friend, I walked alone all day—I passed the
night, it matters not how; I regarded myself as the one isolated
drop—as the one incongruous particle—in this immense ocean
of life, in this great whole of social existence. The traveller in the
heart of the Great Desert has a less oppressive sense of solitude
upon him than had I in the crush and throng of London—;
he looks forward to the end of his journey, when he shall be
received again into the bosom of society; I could foresee no
such termination of my dreary pilgrimage. The necessity which
is laid upon man to earn his daily bread, is one of the mercies
of God. How fain would I have consorted myself with the
handicraft man at his trade, but that, like the unjust steward
of the Gospel, 'I could not dig!' I therefore applied myself to
what I conceived my own vocation; but a paralysis had come
over my soul—I could not pour forth my thoughts in words
as I had done, and whatever I produced then was feebleness
indeed. Many a time I walked into the fields—into the most
secluded and beautiful scenes, that I might refresh and comfort
my soul with sunshine, green trees, and bubbling waters, fondly
persuading myself that it was the unusual circumstances of
city-life that warped and deadened my energies; but my brain
was dry, the once free-flowing fountains of poetry were sealed.
I saw the kindly aspect, I felt the amenities of external nature,
but they were as waters poured upon a thirsty desert, which
sink into the sand and produce no vegetation!

"My expenditure was reduced to the lowest possible scale; still
my money was diminishing day by day, and at length I had but one
shilling left. I was reduced to despair. I could not write, my faculties

were all prostrated before absolute misery. I despised myself. I believed I had over-estimated my powers, or that I was cursed for my crime, and I looked forward to a death by starvation. Yet, my friend, this appalling prospect distressed me far less, as my own personal suffering was concerned, than that I should die without removing the charge of theft from my name.

"It was on the 17th of April—a night never to be forgotten, when I dared not enter under a roof, because I had not wherewith to pay for its shelter,—after I had been four-and-twenty hours without food, and with a brain that ached with the labour of fruitless thought,—that I walked on London Bridge, resolved—yes, my friend, resolved in that desperate misery to cast myself from its walls into the waters below. What a repose seemed to my spirit to lie under those waters—I wished I was there! My God! I tremble now to the horribly calm state of feeling with which I contemplated suicide! 'When it is dusk,' I said, 'I wlll do it;' and I paced backwards and forwards with more composure of mind than I had ever experienced since I entered London—"My God, it was of thy mercy that I was preserved from such offence against Thee—that I was made thy instrument of mercy to another despairing and abandoned soul!

"The clocks of the city had tolled nine; the evening was dusk, and the bridge unusually free of people; my hands were laid on the wall of the bridge with the intention of assisting my spring over; when a sudden shrill cry, and the fall of a heavy body into the water, arrested my attention. It was a woman who had precipitated herself into the river from one of the quays. I saw it done, and instantly forgot my own desperate intention; I thought of nothing but saving her, and the next moment was upon the stairs. I threw off my coat, cast myself into the water, and amid a throng of watermen, and of persons who had congregated on the spot, succeeded in rescuing her.

"The further particulars of that night I need not dwell upon; enough that it was an epoch in the history of my life and in

the operation of my own mind. The entire self-forgetting—the
arousing of my sympathies, and of my mental and physical
energies, which it had occasioned, created a new existence in
me. The moral atmosphere was cleared by the tempest that had
agitated it, and I looked on life and on the purposes of life
with new views and better knowledge. The fountains too of
my intellectual being were immediately unsealed; the rock had
been smitten, and the waters gushed forth plenteously. From the
inane torpor of my former miserable self, sprang forth sensation,
knowledge, aim. I was as the blind man who had received sight;
as the lame man leaped up in renewed strength; as the dead
who was raised! The healing hand of the Redeemer's love had
been laid upon me, and I was no longer poor and miserable,
blind and feeble!

"The young woman whom I had been the instrument of
saving was restored to her mother, her only parent, and I became
their inmate—I was no longer without friends or without home.
Of these good people, however, I cannot stay to say much; nor
need I relate the cause of the young woman's desperation—hers
was a common history. They were in what the world calls the
lower class of society, but hearts such as theirs ennoble any class.
I boarded myself with them, and inhabited an upper room
which they had been accustomed to let to casual lodgers. My
first object was now again to obtain the ten guineas of which I
had deprived my father; for until that burden was removed from
my conscience, I was not free to lay by one farthing for what
otherwise was the great business of my life.

"Of course my experience as an author was small; but I wrote
for magazines, for newspapers, for every publication of the day. I
penned odes, sonnets, songs, and epistles; I wrote short histories
and imaginary travels; I essayed my skill in tragedy and comedy.
My pen was never idle; and incessant as was my labour, small
my remuneration, and many and various my disappointments,
nothing could daunt me. My personal expenses were small; I
was content to be poor, and to seem so, that I might be able

to lay by even from my pitiful gains. Good Heavens! when I look back to those times, when pence even went to swell the slowly-growing amount, I am amazed at the undismayed ardour that sustained me!

"At length the time came when I saw the sum completed; and with the exultation of a child, I wept for joy My friend, life could not afford me, were it prolonged to the fourscore years and ten, more perfect fufilment of peace than I partook then. I felt like Christian when the burden of his iniquity fell from him; and I went out at noonday, poor as was my appearance, into the very throng of the city,—on to the Exchange; into the parks; down to the palace itself, that I might indulge myself with looking proud, and rich, and honest men in the face! You will smile perhaps at all this, and call it folly; but you know not what it is to rise up from under the agonizing weight of self-accusation, and walk forth in the light and strength of an approving conscience!

"I wrote to my father; I wrote then also to Julia; but I could not give her the full knowledge of my condition, and I kept the place of my residence a secret from her—for I yet had a purpose to accomplish, and I did not venture to receive her regrets, nor even her sympathy, lest my purpose might be shaken, or my mind diverted from it.

"In all the events of my life I can trace the interposing hand of Providence; and, oh! what an ennobling, encouraging, preserving consciousness has this been. How could I doubt when I knew that the power of the Almighty Father would uphold me! I had been on the brink of self-destruction, His hand had mercifully held me back; I had been dismayed with the prospect of utter want, He had provided me food; I was homeless, and He gave me a shelter! I saw these things, and blessed Him! Again, it was surely by the Divine interposition that I was led out of the unprofitable track of light ephemeral literature, to which only I had hitherto devoted myself; and the manner of it was thus: I was walking down Whitehall on the evening of one of those remarkable debates which occupied the house three years back;—at the very commencement of these great national agitations which at present interest not only our own country, but Europe also;—when two persons passed me, and the elder of them seeming to glance upon me as he went by, said 'Go to the House of Commons tonight, and listen to the debate.' I heard the words distinctly, but supposing them addressed to his companion, took no further heed of them. Shortly afterwards the same persons met me again, and the same words were repeated. I was struck by the repetition, and immediately a desire sprang in my mind to go there. Hitherto I had never been—in fact, I did not commonly care to present myself in public, because of the worn and ill-conditioned state of my wardrobe, and I was in the very act of questioning with myself whether I should follow this momentary impulse, when the person who had so singularly arrested my attention before again came up alone. Whether he actually the third time spoke the words or not, I cannot tell; but so strongly was my mind impressed on seeing him, that, as in a dream, the words seemed spoken, and I involuntarily said, 'I would fain go to the House, but I know not how.' The gentleman stopped, and looked at me as if in surprise, and then said, 'To the House of Commons is it you would go?—come then with me!' I followed him, and, to my surprise, was led into the body of the house. The crowd opened obsequiously before my conductor, and the best place under the gallery was instantly conceded to me; I saw him immediately afterwards take his seat,—it was the great Edmund Burke.

A new world was presented to me. The vast importance of these great political questions, their immense influence upon the happiness and social condition of thousands, impressed me at once, and I became a constant attender of every debate; and through the rest of the day, and even through the night, I read and studied them profoundly in books. Able as had been the minds that treated on those subjects, I seemed to see many things in new points of view, and felt, or believed I felt, the truth in many an intricate maze in which cunning or ignorance had involved it; and as I pursued out these subjects, day after day, with increased avidity, I was amazed at the clearness and strength of my own perceptions. I sat down and wrote; page grew upon page, and at length my first political treatise was finished. My views were widely different from those of old politicians, and I almost trembled at my own audacity; but the more I examined them, the more I was satisfied of their soundness; and though I asked myself the humiliating question, 'is it possible that they are all wrong, and I only right?' my internal conviction upheld me, and assuming the name of 'Marcus.' I ventured to send it to Mr. Stevens for his approbation. He demured for some time at the startling nature of the sentiments—they were out of the common way, so unlike what everybody believed; and yet he agreed to publish it, giving me two guineas for the entire copyright, making great merit of this, and talking greatly of the certain risk he was about to incur.

"The work soon attracted the public attention: it was read by all, from the prime minister down to the artizan; the public papers were filled with it, and the name of the author was eagerly demanded. But, before I was by any means aware of its full popularity, Mr. Stevens, with the bearing of a man who is doing an act of benevolence, engaged me in a bond to furnish him with a series of similar essays for the next five years, on the questions of the day, whatever they might be, for each of which he engaged to pay me twenty guineas. For some little time I was extremely well satisfied with the engagement; but the necessity there was for me to read the daily papers soon made me aware of the extent of my popularity, and consequently of the folly of the bargain I had made, or rather of the advantage which had been taken of my inexperience. But it was timed too late; and mortified though I was, the interest of the work in which I was engaged bore me up.—In three months afterwards my second essay was published, ten thousand copies of which were sold on the day of publication: it was an unexampled instance of sale. And so I continued to write during the next two years, sometimes with more, sometimes with less success. Mr. Stevens in the mean time was realizing a fortune; and I, with all my assiduity and expense of strength and thought, had laid by but little more than one hundred pounds, although I practised the most rigid economy—nay, almost parsimony. But do not, my friend, believe that during this time I was unhappy—by no means. Setting pecuniary advantages entirely out of the question, the author has a pure, an elevating, a sufficient happiness in the very exercise of his mental powers; the athlete has less positive pleasure in the buoyant use of his limbs, than the literary man in the expression of his thoughts on paper. This perhaps was the portion of my literary life which was most filled with positive pleasure; no satiety of mind, no exhaustion of body had yet come on. I sat in my solitary room, small, meanly furnished as it was, in the very midst of a toiling population, and sent forth thoughts and words which kindled a spirit wherever they came, and established themselves into the rallying cry of liberty. Tell me, my friend, was not this a noble prerogative? The necessity there was upon me to lay aside the greater amount of my gains, preserved me from the excitements of personal vanity: I coveted not to be known in my own person as the 'Marcus' whose name was on every tongue. The very men who lauded 'Marcus' most vehemently, passed me by in the streets as one unworthy of their notice, or suffered my words to drop unanswered, if, when we did chance to meet, I ventured an humble sentiment. But in the very height of my popularity, my health began to decline. I had been aware for some time of such indications, and had disregarded them; but at length I could resist them no longer. I was visited by long fits of depression; doubts and anxieties took possession of me. The very work which formerly had been as my life's blood to me, became irksome if not distasteful; the high and splendid views which I had accustomed my mind to contemplate, of the moral regeneration of man, and of the omnipotent nature of trruth, seemed commonplace or delusive. My hand trembled, my appetite forsook me, and sleep brought less than no refreshment, for it was filled, with harassing and distressful dreams, that fevered and wore me out worse than waking disquiets of the day. The good woman with whom I lodged compelled me to have a physician; but his prescription was one which I could not adopt,—entire relaxation of mind and body,—nay, if possible, the very absence of thought. Little as I believed myself capable of obedience, I promised it, and dismissed my physician; and, as it was fortunately the summer season, spent the greater part of my days for many weeks in the beautiful country that surrounds the metropolis.

"You may wonder why my employer, Mr. Stevens, did not seek me out. It was not his fault that he did not do so. The truth was, I had a repugnance to have my exact circumstances known to him, and jealously kept from him both my name and residence; he know me only as 'Marcus,' and saw me only at his own place, for such was my part of the agreement between us.—But to return to the summer of which I was writing. My favourite haunt was in the neighbourhood of Windsor. There is a little churchyard, green and quiet as a land of dreams, where I spent my most happy time—forgetting politics—forgetting the contending, toiling multitude from whom I had escaped, and throwing my mind back upon memories that consoled and refreshed it. There, too, came back the full gush of poetry which the world and the world's cares had choked up so long. Walter Constable—I was indeed happy! I was, however, violating the prescription of my physician, as I fatally found. But it is not in the power of art to stop the workings of mind: as well chain up the torrent that leaps with headlong fury, in wild and beautiful strength, from the rock! I knew that I was hastening my own death, but I could not cease to think, nor to pour out those feelings which, whether they had had an outlet or not, must have worn me away.

"The sunset is glorious from the churchyard of Ensfield, and

I never witnessed it without the idea of the deathbed of the Christian being present with me. Yes, it was here that I learned to think of death not only with calmness, but with desire; my eternal hopes had their births in the golden sunset-light of that little churchyard!—My friend, before I proceed, let me unfold my wishes to you. It is where the golden stream of sunset falls between the two poplars that I would wish to be buried. Start not at the word! the time is approaching; and the good providence of God, after enabling me to accomplish the great purpose of my life, has sent you hither to perform the last duties of humanity. Said I not with abundant cause that he had been merciful to me? You are come to close my eyes, and to see me buried in the churchyard of Ensfield!"

Walter Constable, overcome by emotion, laid down the letter when he had read these words, and then started up, impatient to hasten to him; but it was then past midnight, and yet he knew not where Bernard was to be found: therefore, again seating himself and taking up the letter, with a heart that would ache, and eyes dim with tears, he continued to read.

"In spite of the incessant flow of thought that I indulged through this summer, my bodily strength was in a considerable degree recruited, and with it my former activity of mind returned, and I again found pleasure and interest in public affairs. But before I recommenced my career, I went to Mr. Stevens, who professed himself overjoyed to see me; and doubtless his professions were sincere, for I was the mainspring of his trade. My desire was not in any way to take advantage of him; for, however unfortunate our agreement was for me, I considered it binding; but I represented to him the impaired state of my health,—that I was compelled to overwork myself to live, whilst he was making a fortune at my expense. Mr. Stevens by the reckoning of the world was an honourable man, and he declared himself such over and over again. This is the custom of many persons when they have a design of overreaching another: I learned to know him well in the three years of my dealings with him. The result of this interview, was however, to my advantage. He agreed to give me fifty pounds for whatever I might produce, provided it ran into a certain number of pages, instead of twenty as heretofore; and beyond this, offered to purchase the secret of my true name for fifty more. But this, great as was the temptation, I resolutely refused; and henceforth Mr. Stevens pretended to consider me, not as real 'Marcus,' but as his agent, and gave it out, by hints and inuendoe that 'Marcus' was not of lower rank than an earl, and as much higher as people chose to conjecture. With one part of the public the bait took; Marcus was more in fashion than ever. The design of this was to pique me to the disclosure of my secret but it had a contrary effect,—I guarded it more carefully than before; it was my revenge, and I hope not a sinful one, upon Mr. Stevens for the Shylock-like measure that he dealt out to me.

"The town had now been a long time without a 'Marcus,' as those works came to be styled; and Mr. Stevens was proportionably impatient for me to produce one. My next appearance was at Christmas, and was the most successful of any I had written; and my fund being increased one-half at once, I too was satisfied. But these works could not now be written with impunity—my former indisposition returned, and another long pause succeeded I again appeared before the public. During this time I one day called on Mr. Stevens: a gentleman was talking with him, and as they appeared in confidential discourse, turned to leave the shop. 'Mr. Marcus,' said the publisher, stepping aside to me, 'you must not go;' and then he introduced me to the gentleman as one in the confidence of Marcus, without mentioning to me the name of the person to whom I was introduced. The gentleman held out his hand, and saluted me most cordially; and then, withdrawing me into an inner room, and motioning to Mr. Stevens, much to his visible chagrin, to keep back, empowered me in no equivocal terms to state to my friend Marcus, that such noblemen, whom he named, were desirous of serving him. 'How?' said I, astonished—for these were the very advocates of the oppressions and malversations against which I had been warring, 'They would be most happy,' replied the stranger 'to induct him into the church, or to provide him an official appointment abroad—highly lucrative—provided the works which appeared under his name might be discontinued.'—'Marcus is poor,' I returned, with an indignation I could not restrain, 'but he will not be bribed to silence!'—'Sir,' resumed the gentleman, not apparently displeased by my warmth, 'Marcus may take time to consider this offer; but he must not go on at this rate! Good God! he will overturn all the old institutions,' said he, kindling up; 'he will teach the rabble to think! Marcus may rise to what height he chooses in the church: let him make his own terms, so that he keeps silence, or, what is better, employs his pen on the other side.'—'No, sir,' I returned; 'Marcus, though poor—though wearing a coat threadbare as this—cannot sell his principles!'— 'Then Marcus is a fool!' was his reply. 'And yet,' continued he, softening the tone with which he had spoken, 'my employers would not pardon me for losing you thus lightly. Consider, sir, Mr,—, and—, and—, all our most distinguished writers, have been purchased, or are secured by pensions. Marcus must not rate himself as more immaculate than these men!'—'Go back,' I said, roused by these taunts of the tempter, 'and tell your employers that there is one honest man in London who will not sell the great cause of God and of his fellow-creatures for a mess of pottage!' And without staying to hear his further remarks, I went hastily.

"A few days afterwards I met Mr. Stevens in the street. He looked extremely angry, and with an oath demanded why I had insulted Sir James — in his shop; for that several noble persons, whom he named, and with whom Sir James was connected, were patrons of his own, and that they would now never come near his place;—that I had done him irreparable mischief, and it would have been better for him that he had never known me than that I had done thus. I then briefly related to him, with some little retaliation on my side, the object of Sir James ———'s mission; and that, had I acceded to his proposals, 'Marcus' would have been no more, and consequently *his* own profits at an end: that I had evidently, in adhering to my principles, lost an advantage for myself; but that his interests were secured by it. Mr. Stevens was amazed at what he heard, begged my forgiveness for his haste, and, in the excess of his civility, voluntarily offered me one hundred pounds for the next work I would produce, provided it were immediate.

"It was at the very moment of an important crisis, and the work was written in a few days. I was abundantly thankful, for my hoarded gains were growing apace—and this seemed again like the hand of Providence rewarding me for my adherence to the right. I had now two hundred and fifty pounds laid by; for in the intervals between my larger efforts I produced many small things which amply supplied my expenditure.

"Unfortunately, the sale of this work was much less than usual—perhaps it was designed to keep me humble—but the work went off heavily, and Mr. Stevens treated me with so great coolness that I very rarely went near him. It was at the commencement of the present year; and, what with discouragement from him, the daily wearing away of my strength, and the consequent depression of spirit that accompanied it, the summer wore on gloomily: I was unable as formerly to reach even the nearest fields. The summer went on, and I saw neither trees nor running waters. O the insatiable yearning that filled my spirit for the sights and sounds of Nature! The good woman with whom I lodged,—a Samaritan in soul, though poor, and winning her daily bread with hard labour,—often brought me flowers—fresh field-flowers, which she purchased based out of her own small earnings; and not a Sunday came but her daughter went out purposely into the country many miles to bring me home as many as she could gather. The love of flowers was to me as an appetite; I felt as if I must die if it could not be indulged; and though I many a time bathed them with my tears, those very tears were an infinite relief. Ah! my friend, let me pass over that season of impatient weakness, when the earth from which I was departing seemed to be so desirable—when I wished with passionate longings for the wings of the dove, so that I might flee away and cast myself down under the shadow of trees, or upon the breezy tops of mountains, and pour into the bosom of the great genial mother the unparticipated woes and anguish of my spirit!—when not only the beauty of the physical world, but of our moral and intellectual nature, was so clearly revealed, and an unappeasable cry was in my soul for companionship—for the interchange of affection! But it is past! I go where the fulness of love shall satisfy the heart—where the very springs of intellectual being have their birth!

"The physician whom I had formerly consulted, I again called in towards autumn; but he gave me now no hope. This was, however, no surprise to me; and as I accustomed myself to the daily—nay, hourly—contemplation of death, and as the duller, darker days of the year advanced, when I was no longer excited by sunshine, clear skies, and the voice of birds, which I could not go forth to enjoy, a calmer state of feeling succeeded, and my only prayer was to be enabled to make up the three hundred pounds, of which I still wanted fifty.

"The comparative failure of my last production had so far discouraggd me, that I felt aversion to the thought of further authorship; and as I had not had courage through the whole of the summer to read a single newspaper, I was so far behind the present time, that this was still another impediment in my way. At length, one day, when I was in better spirits, I took a hackney-coach, for I was no longer able to walk, and presented myself before Mr. Stevens. He appeared much shocked at my altered appearance, and received me with extraordinary kindness, volunteering me the help of money, physicians, his country-house, his carriage,—in short, whatever he possessed. I was much amazed; glancing my eye upon my last production, which still lay about, all the mystery was solved by my reading the words 'fourth edition' upon the title-page. 'Ha,' said he, seeing my eye had caught the fact 'the thing went off after all. And,' said he, reproachfully, 'you have lost you know not what by your obstinately keeping me ignorant of your abode. Mr. Burke called to inquire after "Marcus," with very significant glances: it is a thousand pities you did not confide your name to me!' I could not feel sure, notwithstanding Mr. Stevens's show of candour and regret, whether he would willingly have given up my address had he known it; I suspected not, and therefore I did not coverwhelm him with gratitude. Still, indifferent as I appeared to him, I will not deny that what he told me was extremely gratifying; and I even for some time contemplated making myself known to Mr. Burke, who had been in truth so singularly the instrument of turning my mind to public affairs. But as the fever of self-gratulation subsided, my desire for personal distinction subsided also, and I set about the work which I too well knew would be my last; I disregarded my bodily weakness, and applied myself with unremitting diligence to regain the time I had let slip. My work was finished—it was by far the shortest I had ever written, and attained but the size of a pamphlet. Whilst it was printing, I wrote that farewell to the public, which it appears has given it even more signal success. I received fifty pounds for it. And, which was another proof of the signal mercy that cared for me in so remarkable a manner, on the the same day I received another fifty from some unknown hand: it came to me in an envelope, containing these words,—'For the use of Marcus.' Thus, after restoring you your own, I have more than sufficient left for my own remaining wants.

"Many have been the providences which have marked my pilgrimage—the last not the least. I was sitting yesterday morning, considering with myself how the money would best be conveyed to you—for I still supposed you abroad—when an impression came strongly upon me that I must go to Mr Stevens. Why I should go there, I could not tell; I was not in the habit of seeing him except on matters of business, and such a suggestion had no connexion whatever with my thoughts. I endeavoured to dismiss it; but it had taken possession of my mind so strongly, that it was not to be put aside, and, in obedience to the strange mission, I ordered a hackney-coach, and was driven there. Mr. Stevens was surprised to see me, and with the greatest considersation placed me beside his own desk, where he said, unseen by the crowd who were thronging the place, I might have the pleasure of hearing what was said of 'Marcus.' This, I doubt not, he supposed to be the object of my coming. I had not been long there when your voice attracted me, but I was too much agitated to acknowledge you. I saw again the merciful hand of the Almighty extended for me; and I was about to rise and request an interview with you in the inner room, when you voluntarily furnished your own address. I regarded it as the Divine will that our meeting should not then take place, and returned to my own lodgings to address you thus.

"This has been painfully and wearily written, but I owed this information both to you and to my beloved sister. My work is now done; the blessing of the Heavenly Father has been with me—He has crowned me with success; and now, though young in years, I fold my arms in peace and await my hour, assured that the accomplishment of hopes and desires which I once indulged will be granted me in the land whither I am hastening.

"Farewell! May the God of peace, the God of love, the Universal Father, watch over you and bless you—This will be the latest prayer of yours,

> "My dear friend, most faithfully,
> "BERNARD GRIMSTONE.

"No. 7, — Court., — Street, Nov. 4th."

It may be imagined, but it cannot be told, what were the sensations with which Walter Constable closed this letter.

XVIII

"Is your name Constable?" asked a meek-browed young woman, opening the door of No. 7, — Court, at which Walter presented himself by eight o'clock the next morning. "It is," he replied, concluding instantly that she was the unfortunate young woman of whom Bernard had spoken.

"He expected you," she said, bringing him in and offering him a chair: "sit down, sir, for a minute, and I will let him know that you are here."

Walter glanced round the room. It was meanly but scrupulously clean: the people were evidently sacking-bag makers, for work of this description lay on the floor, and, early as it then was, the young woman had been busied at it that very morning. The upper room of this poor habitation was the abode of that 'Marcus' whose name the rich and great were curious to learn, and whose writings were known and honoured, not only through London, but through the whole extent of the island. Walter thought of Sir Harbottle, and of the useless abundance which surrounded him, and wished he could have been brought hither to feel the lesson which this scene might have taught him. His thoughts, however, were interrupted by the sounds which proceeded from above,—the hoarse, hollow voice of a consumptive patient, and then the deep distressing cough. He could not control the emotion which these but too intelligible tokens gave rise to, and he reproached himself as being the innocent means of this noble being's sufferings. Again all was silent above; and then an elderly woman descended the stairs, and with quivering lip and eyes full of tears, without speaking one word to him, but with a most melancholy shake of the head, motioned him to ascend to the chamber. Walter repressed his feelings that he might meet his friend cheerfully, and obeyed her: the young woman left the chamber as he entered.

Prepared as Walter was for the change in Bernard's appearance; it was even greater than he expected. He was wrapped in a cloak, and reclined in a large chair, pale and shadow-like, evidently in the last stage of consumption,—bald, and already grey. The expression of cheerful greeting with which Walter had entered the chamber vanished at the first sight of Bernard; his soul melted into an unutterable anguish of sympathy; and, without attempting to speak, he grasped his hand, turned his face aside, and wept. Bernard was not less affected, and several minutes elapsed before the silence was broken. "Sit down beside me, my kind friend," at length said Bernard; and then, after a considerable pause, he asked, "Have you read my letter?"

"I have," replied Walter, compelling himself into calmness; "and my admiration—my almost reverence—of you is unbounded. I cannot reproach *you* for this self-sacrifice, but myself I do. I have been the means of shortening your noble career. O that I could purchase your life at the price of my own success!"

"Peace, peace, my friend," said Bernard, speaking with difficulty; "it is not to talk of these things that you are come. Do not regret me: life is but desirable, it is but valuable, inasmuch as every duty it involves is accomplished. Were mine to be prolonged to the most extended date, I might not be as fully prepared to resign it as now! No, no; my hour is come! One by one, the links which held me fast are dissolved. Even to my sister, heavenly-minded as she is, my heart no longer clings with the agony of love which once oppressed it. Had you any belief in spiritual influences," said he, half raising himself in his chair, and speaking with animation, "I could tell you of mysterious but blessed communion, that has been as the ministering of angels; but you were always a sceptic!" and a smile of playful reproof, such as common to him in former days, passed over his features. He sank back into his chair, and then again spoke with deliberation and difficulty. "You will supply to Julia what I might have been—my place will not be vacant. You weep, my friend;—ah! well, our human nature is weak." A long pause succeeded these words, and then Bernard, as if pursuing the train of his own thoughts, said in a low and impressive voice, as unconscious of the presence of any one, "O my Father, except for thy everlasting love, I had bowed down in the bitterness of despair;

but thou didst uphold me—thou didst pour into my bruised heart the oil and wine of thy consolations. I bless thee, my God, I bless thee!" Bernard throughout had spoken with difficulty, and now the cough interrupted further utterance. It was a long and distressing fit, and then he sank exhausted upon the bosom of his friend. Walter heard again the ineffectual voice attempting to speak; he felt his hand grasped—a deep sigh was heaved—the breath fluttered and then the head sank down heavily. His eye was fixed the whole time upon the countenance; a smile was upon the lips, a heavenly expression upon the brow; but the pure and noble spirit had departed for ever!

What need to say more? Walter Constable closed his eyes and saw him buried, as he had desired, in the beautiful churchyard of Ensfield. The vast mass of his papers he found arranged and confided to his care, together with instructions respecting what little property remained after his decease which, with upwards of twenty pounds in money, he had bequeathed to the good people with whom he lodged.

XIX

Mrs. Constable had returned, as we have said, with her aversion to the Grimstones nothing abated; and though it had been her intention to drive up to Denborough Park "some day soon," yet day after day had gone on, and the visit was unpaid. The weather was so winterly, she argued with herself; and after her long journey, it was such a luxury to be quiet—to sit down for the day, and feel that there was no necessity to cross the threshold. Besides all this, there were many domestic arrangements that must be attended to before her son's return: there were hangings to put up, and carpets to lay down; and the works she had found leisure to do, even in the unquiet times of her foreign sojourn, to be fitted to furniture and particular places for which they had been designed; and this was found too large, and required making less; and that too small, and had to be made larger. Nobody knew what a vast deal Mrs.

Constable found to do;—the exertion of her journey was nothing to the exertion she used on these first days of her return. And then, besides all this, the much-thought-of and elaborate counterpane, which she had finished among the good Ursuline nuns at Bruges, was to be examined; and the examination excited a desire to do divers other things to match it; and they had to be devised and begun; so that if Mrs. Constable left her bed with the sincerest intention in the world to drive to Denborough Park on that one day, it was sure to be too late before she had got through the multifarious concerns that presented themselves. Seven days thus went on, and the severity of Julia's indisposition was past, when Mrs. Constable received from her son a letter, briefly relating what has occupied the last two chapters.

Strong as were Mrs. Constable's prejudices, her heart was placable, and the surest key to it was attention or regard exhibited in any way towards her son; consequently, this self-sacrifice of poor Bernard's melted her down into the most relenting of moods. The sins of the Grimstones were no longer remembered. On the contrary, she recalled to mind her early friendship with Lady Grimstone, when all the sorrows of that unhappy woman were poured into her own breast. She remembered Julia, the beautiful and joyous girl, the most dutiful of daughters; and Bernard, the young visionary. His friendship for her son, his quiet visits to Westow, and all the hard judgments which, even against her own better feeling, she had pronounced upon him, came before her. Then she thought of his early death, a martyr to high principles and her heart was filled with uneasy self-reproach and though she was in the most interesting crisis of a new pattern of knitting, without stopping to see what it would turn out, she ordered her ancient and long-disused barouche to be got ready, and, apparelling herself in an ample furred travelling cloak and hood, she stood prepared to go forth, upon a morning of driving snow, a full half-hour before the vehicle itself came up to the door. The old housekeeper, full of amazement, wondered "what, for sure, madam could mean by going out on a day like this!"

Mrs. Constable knew nothing of the misunderstanding between

Sir Harbottle and her son. She supposed him to be the lover of Julia, acknowledged and accepted by all the family; and though Walter, on this her return, had not expressed a wish that she should visit Julia, she took it for granted that it was from knowing her disapprobation of the family; but she flattered herself that her doing so would not only be gratifying to him, but was the highest compliment she could pay him.

Ill-conditioned as Mrs. Constable knew Denborough Park to be, she found it even worse than she had imagined; for when she had been there last, some show of external care was visible, and there was then kept such a number of domestics as to give some appearance of life to the place. Now, the only living object that she saw was the audacious figure of Jack, who was treading down the snow to make himself a slide, and who, on seeing so singular a phenomenon as a carriage approaching, set up a shout, clapped the gate to, which he had set open for his own diversion, and then gathered up a snow-ball, with which he saluted the postillion. The barouche drove on without deigning to the urchin even a reproof, though the postillion was obliged to dismount to open the gate. They drove past the principal front, round two sides of the house, but still no sign whatever of life was visible; and even when they drew up at the customary entrance, the door seemed as firmly shut against them as if it had been fastened with bars of iron. The postillion struck upon it heavily, first with the large but broken knocker, and then with the butt-end of his whip; but though the sounds echoed from within, no answer was given to their summons: old Milly was smoking a pipe at her grand-daughter's. After they had waited so long that even the patience of the calm Mrs. Constable was exhausted, she desired the boy to try if access were indeed possible that way. The door opened readily, giving to view the one, desolate, and not over-clean arched passage, which led to the kitchen. As the house was perfectly familiar to Mrs. Constable, she dismounted, making sure of finding somebody within. The neglected and forlorn internal arrangement caught her eye wherever she came. A very small fire was burning in the immense kitchen-grate, giving, almost more than anything else could have done, the character of miserable parsimony. It was absolutely chilling to see that handful of fire, on that dreary winter's day, laid within the compressed creepers, leaving almost a yard of cold iron-bars on either side; and to see that thin, feeble line of smoke passing up a chimney as large as an ordinary room. Still nobody was to be seen. Mrs. Constable, therefore, determined to proceed onward to the apartments that had been used by her friend, lying at the other end of the house, not doubting but she should find Julia there. Onward accordingly she went, without encountering Sir Harrbottle—he was in his den, busied about his own affairs— room after room, the doors of which were all shut, and up flights of broad, magnificent stairs, bare and long-neglected; and along once richly-decorated galleries, making her own observations as she went, and pausing for a moment to look how the rain had come in by the window and broken ceiling; until, at length, she reached the apartments whither she was bound. Here again she knocked, but without success. It was like the very house of death and desertion. She entered the room, and the first thing that caught her eye was the denuded walls;—was it possible, she inwardly exclaimed, that those holy pictures could be gone! Still, here were the signs of habitation, and abundant proofs of an elegant and refined taste: many a beautiful decoration—books, and music, and vases which had held flowers; and the furniture, which had been of the most costly kind, was all well preserved—and, beyond this, all was neat and perfectly clean. But Julia was not there; nor, from the appearance of the grate, could have been there that day. She then advanced to the inner apartments, and, as was most natural, made her first attempt at the door of Lady Grimstone's chamber; but it was fast. Julia's came next, and there Mrs. Constable entered. The light of the chamber was dimmed, and Julia was reclining in her easy-chair, asleep by the fire; for she could not sleep through the night, a heavy slumber came upon her in the course of the morning.

The shock which her son had felt on seeing the wasted form of Bernard was even surpassed by Mrs. Constable's sensations on seeing the figure now before her, so unlike the bright, healthful Julia of five years back. It was a figure as of pure marble; the lips still red, though the eyes wore sunk; and every feature so richly chiselled, that, though attenuated, the contour of the face was the most exquisite that can be conceived: the expression, too, one of angelic sweetness, as of a sleeping seraph. The rich, black, and abundant hair was simply put up in one large knot; contrasting, as did the finely-lined dark eyebrow, and long, dark lashes, with the pure whiteness of the almost transparent skin. She lay back, her head turned slightly aside, in the most perfect repose, wrapped in a loose white dress, the shoulders enveloped in the folds of a dark India shawl, her small white hands lightly laid together upon her bosom. Her chair was of crimson damask, richly carved and luxuriously cushioned. The cushion, however, upon which her head rested, belonged to some other piece of former magnificence; it was of ancient white damask tasselled with gold. We have been thus particular in this description, because Mrs. Constable, who had a remarkably acute eye for such things, was not only struck with the wonderful and touching beauty of Julia herself—with that chastened melancholy of countenance and that evidently drooping, suffering frame—but also with the striking harmony of the auxiliaries. She thought that she had never seen so lovely yet so affecting a picture; her eyes filled with tears, and a sentiment as of maternal love warmed her heart and melted it into deep sympathy.

Fearful to disturb her, Mrs. Constable drew her chair softly to the opposite side of the hearth, and sat down intending to await her waking. She had not sat long, when, without raising her head, Julia opened her eyes in that quick consciousness which in sleep makes us aware of an approach. Her last thoughts had been of Westow, and of its dear returning inmates: what wonder then, if, on seeing the figure before her, she doubted her senses and believed it a deception of the brain? A sudden flush of crimson, however, mantled her cheeks, and a faint scream of joyful recognition escaped her, as Mrs. Constable proved her own identity by rising with a "God Almighty bless you, my poor child!" taking her hand and folding her to her bosom. So singular a mark of favour from the mother of Walter Constable had never been extended before, and the poor girl, overcome as much by this welcome but unexpected show of affection as by her unexpected appearance, wept out her full-hearted emotions as if there could be no end to her tears.

Mrs. Constable had formed a determination while she had watched Julia sleeping, and the exchange of but a few more sentences with her still more confirmed it. "How long had she been ill?" "Oh, she was not ill—could not be ill now!" persisted Julia; but Mrs. Constable was not to be so persuaded. "Whom had she to nurse her?—what domestics were there in the house?" Julia confessed the truth—"There was but Milly in the house; but Peggy was her nurse;" and then she digressed to tell who Peggy was. Mrs. Constable shook her head. "But Peggy," she said, "was kind as a sister; and, little Amy, she was like an angel! Oh, if Mrs. Constable could but see that sweet child!" Mrs. Constable again shook her head, as if she would convey that the child's parentage was enough for her, "She did very well," Julia said, "through the day; Peggy and Amy came in constantly: but, oh! the nights, they were long, and she felt so far from help if she were worse; and, besides, at night she could not sleep."—"And where are the pictures and the crucifix?" A deep blush overspread Julia's face, and for a moment she hesitated to reply; she felt jealous of Mrs. Constable's knowing all the secrets of the house; and it was only after a pause, in which she satisfied her own mind that it was better to be candid at once, that she told how they had been disposed of. "Poor-child! poor child!" exclaimed Mrs. Constable, extremely shocked; "to take from you even your religious helps! But you shall go home with me: Westow from this time shall be your home; I will nurse you myself, and Walter—But, bless me! what is the matter!" Julia had fallen back in her chair like one dead, at once overcome by the uncontrollable ecstasy of feeling. Mrs. Constable was alarmed, and instantly produced pungent salts and reviving essences from her pocket. "Shall I go to Westow?" murmured Julia, returning to consciousness—"to dear,

dear Westow!" and then she clasped her hands and looked upward in unutterable thankfulness. "Is it possible?" she exclaimed the next moment: "is it not a dream? Dear Mrs. Constable, you will think me beside myself; but you know not what you promise me—you know not what it will be to exchange Denborough Park for Westow—how should you?"

Winterly as was the day, and perilous as Mrs. Constable in her own mind feared the immediate removal of Julia might be, she could not satisfy herself to defer it even for milder weather: the whole winter was before them, and the weather, instead of improving, might entirely cut off all communication between the two houses. Julia must be wrapped up securely; the cushions must be carried to the barouche; and under its spacious head, with its curtains drawn in front, Mrs. Constable persuaded herself the business could be managed without risk. And Peggy entering shortly afterwards, Mrs. Constable, with considerable kindness of manner—for, in spite of her prepossessions against her, she was struck by her mild, intelligent countenance—turned to consult her on the subject, telling her at the same time that she felt obliged to her for the attention she had shown Miss Grimstone. This condescension made poor Peggy the most grateful of creatures; and finally to her was entrusted the packing up Julia's clothes and what ever else belonged to her, for which Mrs. Constable promised to send.

The loss of Julia was like an earthquake shock to the kind-hearted and affectionate young woman; and little Amy, who had followed her mother, and without being observed, had heard what was going forward, stood, in her meek unobtrusiveness, like one paralysed, her hands laid together, and the large tears chasing each other down her cheeks, without venturing a word or introducing herself into notice by praying for a farewell.

Julia thought of her father, and spoke of the propriety of asking his permission, or at least taking leave of him; but Mrs. Constable, who, after what she had seen since she entered the house, had conceived even a stronger dislike to Sir Harbottle than she had before, had no desire to see him, and therefore silenced, and in a great measure satisfied Julia, by saying, "Make yourself easy, Miss Grimstone—I will take all responsibility upon myself; and you know, my dear young lady, Sir Harbottle's temper is not of the evenest—we had better get off quietly if we can; and besides, it is high time I was at home."

Julia, perhaps even more impatient than Mrs. Constable herself to be at Westow, made no farther resistance; and then folding dear Amy to her bosom, and kissing, and blessing, and consoling her with an assurance that she should see her at Westow was conducted by Peggy to the barouche, taking also of her a grateful and affectionate leave.

In less than one hour afterwards, Julia, with such feelings as it is impossible to describe, found herself within the home of Walter Constable's mother, less as a visiter than an inmate. It was such a blessed change, so instantaneously brought about, that, like one overpowered by a sudden translation to heaven from the penalties and pains of earth, she sat in silent happiness, enjoying the all-sufficient consciousness of being so supremely blest. By degrees the more tangible, not to say commonplace, causes of her bodily comfort made themselves felt: there were on all hands warmth, plenty of domestic order, and still more, the unstinted and affectionate forethought and watchfulness of Mrs. Constable herself, with the full ability not only to wish, but to accomplish; and then, beyond all, came the crowning felicity of being at Westow—in the very rooms where Walter had read, and spoke, and thought, and where she knew not how soon he might again be. Thus Julia sat, on the first evening of her removal, by the glowing fire in Mrs. Constable's most snug and most old-fashioned of dressing-rooms, her own chamber also opening into it. Could she be other than supremely happy? The interest Julia, for her own sake, had already inspired in the heart of Mrs. Constable, even more than the reaction which the death of poor Bernard had occasioned there, made her seem altogether like another person; and as she sat in her high-backed needle-worked chair, busied at her knitting, smiling and talking cheerfully, Julia could hardly believe that beamingly-kind face, that actively-affectioned spirit which spoke in almost every sentence, could belong to the cold, measured Mrs. Constable, whose manners had formerly repelled her. "It is thus," thought Julia, "that she appears to Walter!"—and even more than for her kindness to herself, Julia loved her from this consideration.

And now my readers must please to imagine, if they can, how Julia felt, when, after a parting kiss and benediction, and reiterated instructions from Mrs. Constable as to how she was to be summoned if Julia wanted her in the night, she laid her head upon her pillow, and saw, through her half-closed curtains, the cheerful fire blazing in her room, and lighting fitfully many a dim and ancient portrait, or formal group of flowers, or more ambitious basket of fruit in faded needlework, the much-admired labour of some fair lady whose portrait adorned either this or some other more dignified apartment. It would be no longer wearisome to lie awake at nights, Julia thought—nay she felt as if to go to sleep, and to lose the assurance of all this great happiness, was what she did not desire. But sleep did come, sweetly and balmily as it had seldom done at Denborough Park; and then came the waking again—the certainty, even through the dimmed light of the room, that it was all reality—that she was in the very home in which Walter Constable was born, and whither he would return—for what?—to make her his wife. Happy Julia! she forgot her weakness—the cruel malady that had destroyed her bloom and bowed her down towards an early grave. But in this sense too, "perfect love casteth out fear;" and Julia could not fear— could have no presentiment of evil in this great happiness, this "perfect love."

XX

It was a full hour after Julia's departure from Denborough Park before either Milly or Sir Harbottle knew what had taken place. Sir Harbottle, as may be supposed, was not a little indignant. It was a great liberty—a most unheard-of liberty. What! did the woman suppose that there was neither bread nor water at Denborough

Park, but she must carry off his daughter to such a miserable hole as Westow? Why, there were not more than seventy acres in the whole estate at Westow. He would disinherit his daughter—that he would, he knew what she was gone for—it was to marry that Walter Constable. And so Sir Harbottle went on, excepting that a plentiful intermixture of oaths came in, like seasoning to a dish, to add force to his words. Milly, however, who in her heart was glad to be rid of Miss Grimstone on many accounts, soothed him down surprisingly; and, without noticing what he had alluded to of her attachment to Walter Constable, took up a view of the subject which she did not doubt would influence him. "It was better," she said, "that Miss Julia should be with somebody as could nurse her; poor thing, she was dying by inches as it was—and then only think of the coal that must have been burnt to keep up a fire night and day in her chamber, and of the money it would cost, say nothing of trouble, to find her in nice little dainties, such as she could fancy; for as to eating boiled beef and batter-pudding—say nothing of the bread that was often mouldy, his honour ate it so stale—why her very heart went against 'em. That for her part she thought it a very neighbourly good action of the old lady to take her off. And then," continued she, in a low tone of particular emphasis, "supposing her gets worse—as, be' leddy, I think her will, for I buried a daughter myself as was just in her way; why, you see, them as have her mun pay the doctor—for as to doing without a doctor, that's clear nonsense. His honour," she persisted, "was in luck's way to have such friends: a poor body's child might have been dead and buried afore any one would ha' thought it worth their while as much as to ask after it." And so the old woman talked; and Sir Harbottle, though sorely against his will, listened, and listening, though he grumbled out his oaths and threats still, saw some reason in what she said. "Since Mrs. Constable," he muttered, more angry with her than with his daughter, "had chosen to remove her from under his roof, why she must provide for her." "Ay, to be sure—to be sure," echoed Milly, "and a pretty saving it will be to your pocket!"

Still, although Sir Harbottie was somewhat mollified by this important consideration, he kept his resentment hot both against Julia and her friends. "Anywhere," muttered he over and over, to himself, "but to Westow! It is a d——d liberty, and I never will forgive it."

Exactly one week after Julia had been under Mrs. Constable's roof, as she lay in bed about midnight, she fancied she heard a carriage drive to the door and a bustle in the house. What could it be, but that Walter had arrived? Her heart beat violently, and she felt ready to faint. She listened eagerly if she could catch his voice, but all again was profoundly still; nothing was to be heard but the beating of her own heart; Julia was too full of excitement to sleep, and getting up, and throwing on her large furred cloak, she looked into Mrs. Constable's dressing-room: all was dark and still there, and the fire had burnt out as it was suffered to do when Mrs. Constable retired for the night. It must be fancy, she thought; or perhaps she had slept, and it was a dream; and with such an unsatisfactory belief she again lay down to rest.

In the morning, she anxiously studied the countenance of Mrs. Constable. But it was calm; and, which seemed farther to improve her fancy, breakfast was served as usual in the dressing-room, where, for the accommodation of Julia, Mrs. Constable had taken it, always saying that when her son came she would have it with him below. It was an unusually silent breakfast, and it was not till Mrs. Constable was taking her second cup of chocolate that she began to talk. "I hope you will be able to dine down-stairs to-day. I shall have that nice pheasant which Dr. Shackleton sent" (and, by-the-bye, we must interrupt this little speech, to say that this Dr. Shackleton was a physician whom Mrs. Constable had called in the day after she brought Julia to Westow); "that nice pheasant," she said, "which Dr. Shackleton sent, I shall have cooked—a little slice would be quite a relish for you." "Yes, I certainly am much better, dear Mrs. Constable; I think I can go down." "I shall have company to dinner, my love." Julia gasped for breath. "Is he come then?" she said in an almost inarticulate voice.

"Do not excite yourself," said Mrs. Constable; "I will tell you. A friend of my son's is come; we may consider him as a forerunner of Walter. An excellent friend this has been to him. I hope he may supply to us the place of our poor dear Father Cradock."

"He is a priest then?" said Julia.

"He is: I could not be satisfied that you should be so long without such comforts as our religion can give us."

Julia grasped the hand of Mrs. Constable, and her heart was deeply touched by this new proof of regard—this new promise of consolation.

"My dear child," returned Mrs. Constable, in a tone of great kindness, "we must make use of all means in our power to keep you with us; and, independently of your own spiritual advantage, I have great faith in the intercession of a holy man. We are told to ask and we shall receive. You remember these promises?"

Julia kissed the hand which she held without being able to speak, and a long thoughtful silence ensued. "I had a fancy," at length said she, unable to lose the idea that had possessed her, "that Walter came last night."

"Well, my dear young lady, and suppose he did?"

"Then he *did*!" exclaimed she, growing at once deathly pale, and then a burning glow lighting up her countenance. "Dearest Walter! Oh, Mrs. Constable, I will be so calm—you shall see how calm, only let me see him."

The very next moment Walter himself clasped her in his arms, and she was weeping such a passion of tears upon his bosom as entirely discredited all the assurances of calmness she had given to Mrs. Constable but a minute before.

Although Walter had been prepared by his mother for the sorrowful change he would find in Julia, he was not prepared for it in its full extent. The chastened, angel-like expression—that peculiar, holy look which seems to belong less to this world than the next—which had been impressed upon her countenance from the commencement of this illness, touched him more deeply, and filled him with a more intense and affectionate solicitude, than even the drooping and attenuated frame; and he held her to his

heart with such an overpowering agony of love as made him think
fortune, rank, youth—whatever is held most desirable—as light,
nay, as absolutely nothing, in comparison with but one assurance
that her beloved life might be spared. And then, after the first
excitement was over, what hours of cordial, endearing intercourse
followed! How much was to be told! how much to be heard! what
gentle reproof to be given for sorrows and anxieties concealed!
what pauses that were filled up with long embraces, and with
looks, fuller even than words, of tenderness! And so let us leave
them to be happy for two days, and in the mean time tell our
readers that, melancholy as had been the effect of these five years
upon Julia, Walter in appearance was improved, although he looked
more than five years older. He was a fine, noble, and distinguished-
looking man. He was one who impressed the beholder at once
with respect and admiration—admiration for the nobility of his
person—respect for the stamp of intellect and high principle which
was upon him.

And now, on the third evening after his return, we will look
in upon the evening party round the parlour fire. There, on the
warmest side, reclined Julia, cushioned and wrapped in rich shawls
and furs, upon the large couch-like sofa, with its curious cover of
needlework; and by her side, upon a low scat, sat poor little Amy,
who the day before had walked up in the frost and snow to Westow
to see her, and had been detained, happy child! to wait upon her.
There she sat meek and quiet, her heart full of grateful love, and
her large blue eyes every now and then turned upward to Julia
with a very peculiar expression. Walter leaned over the back of the
sofa; and while he held one hand which he often pressed to his lips,
he was pleading some cause with Julia which called up a crimson
blush over her marble-like countenance. What this cause was Mrs.
Constable shall explain. "Nay, my dear," she said laying down her
knitting, and turning to Julia, "why should you hesitate? there is
nothing either unusual or improper in it. Father Jerome is here,
and Dr. Shackleton too; they are playing at chess in the little room.
And as to bridesmaids, why there you are unlucky, I grant you. I am

somewhat too old, and this little friend of yours too young; but I do not fear our managing. What say you to it, Amy?—shall Miss Julia be married?" said she, playfully turning to the child. Amy blushed deeply, but made no reply.

Julia spoke something in a low voice, and the tears fell as I she spoke. "No, no, my beloved," replied Walter, in his tenderest tone; "our dear Bernard's memory would be honoured by it. God knows it is a holy rite, and the blessed spirit of our friend will sanctify it by his presence."

After a moment's pause, Julia raised her beautiful head, and with her dark, eloquent eyes, without speaking one word, looked at Walter. He understood the expression and impressing a long kiss upon her lips, and fervently blessing her, came forward. Mrs. Constable saw that consent was given, and rolling up her knitting, kissed Julia also, brought her a small glass of wine, which she insisted on her drinking, and then taking little Amy by the hand, went out.

"I did not think once that this happy event would happen thus," said Julia, with a deep sigh, looking at her dress. "Oh, dearest Walter, may God forgive me if I cling too much to the world now!—if I am less willing to meet the things that he has appointed than I was!"

"My beloved," returned Walter, his own heart deeply affected, "God himself has ordained our happiness!"

"O that I had health and strength—that I were such as I once was!" said Julia, in a voice of anguish. "Your wife, dearest Walter, should not be such as I am now!" And then, in an agony of overwrought feeling, she covered her face and wept.

"Julia, my dearest one," said Walter, "you are to me ten thousand times dearer than ever. Look up, my love—think what miracles true affection can do, and from this hour we shall not part again. You do not consider the long life of happiness that lies before us. Look up, my own Julia! you shall recover if there be power in medicine—if there be power in love; and there is—there is, my dear one! I know it."

Walter spoke his passionate wishes, not his belief; and Julia, willing to believe, was willing also to be comforted.

Presently after came in the servants, with six tall candles; and next Mrs. Constable and Amy reappeared, the child wearing a broad sash of white silk, and Mrs. Constable in her best cap and best cambric apron. Immediately after entered Father Jerome in his priest's vestments, bearing an open book in his hand, and Dr. Shackleton, the most of kind of physicians, followed. It seemed an awful thing this while to poor Julia, who, agitated and trembling, sat pale as marble, conscious of, yet hardly comprehending one-half of, the tender and assuring words which Walter spoke in his low, rich voice.

And now the ceremony was over, and the servants brought in wine and chocolate with great state. That old parlour, with its dark oak wainscot, and its grand portraits—John Constable, the fair Lady Blanche, and all the rest—looked exceedingly well: so did the group that was in it—little Amy standing against the carved wood-work of the chimney-piece, full of wonder and awe; Mrs. Constable, an excellent figure for an old lady, and in good keeping with her house, talking confidentially with Dr. Shackleton; and Walter again leaning over the sofa where Julia was reclining—the very emblems were they of honour and virtue; and lastly, Father Jerome emptying a glass of wine to the happiness of the newly-married pair.

The next day, as Sir Harbottle Grimstone sat in his room, he was startled by a knock at his door, so unlike that of the old woman, that he rose instantly to open it, not even thinking it might be his son's.

"Well, sir!" said he, with kindling anger, when, after a moment's pause, he recognised his visiter to be Walter Constable.

"You must pemit me a few minutes' conversation with you, Sir Harbottle." The baronet, out of humour as he was, made way for him to enter, and then closed the door, muttering to himself that it was "a great liberty!"

Walter, without waiting for an invitation, sat dawn; and Sir Harbottle, looking at him in utter astonishment at what he considered his assurance, sat down also, saying at the same time, "I am very much, amazed, Mr. Walter Constable, after what passed between us, to see you here: you are taking a great liberty, let me tell you."

"I remember our last interview, Sir Harbottle, but I am willing to forget it: your money has been paid you—cannot there now be good-will between us."

"Good-will!" exclaimed he; "good-will with a vengeance! when your mother comes here and carries off my daughter without any leave of mine, and especially after what had passed between us."

"Sir Harbottle, you know the state of your daughter's health!"

"I tell you what, sir," said, he; "if my daughter marries you, I will cut her off with a shilling—you know my mind."

"When you forbade me to address your daughter, you considered me as a poor man. I remember your taunts, Sir Harbottle."

"If you are come on such a fool's errand as to ask my consent now, why, I tell you you'll never get it."

"I am not come for that purpose, sir!—nothing was farther from my mind."

"Well, then, send my daughter home again: it is not a reputable thing for her to be under your roof."

"Your daughter is my wife."

"Wife!" roared Sir Harbottle, in rage; "tell me that again!"

"When you are calm, Sir Harbottle."

"I will not give her a shilling!" continued he, fiercely; "I will see her die at my own door before money of mine shall go to patch up Westow."

"Thank God," said Walter Constable, "your money is not needed, nor will my wife want: I am not as dependent on fortune as I was five years ago, but could make a handsome settlement on your daughter."

"Stuff!" said Sir Harbottle, in contempt. "You think yourself a mighty clever man—I should like to know what your cleverness has ever done for my family: there was that fool, Bernard—"

"Sir Harbottle," said Walter, with a solemnity that made the angry man pause instantly, "Bernard is dead. And if ever a blessed spirit passed from death unto life, it was he."

"Do you know that he robbed me?" said Sir Harbottle, trying to stifle the troublings of his conscience.

"Did he not return you the money?—Sir Harbottle, you have

been a hard, a cruel, a most unjust parent! Heaven blessed you with a son and daughter such as but few men possess, and what have you done for them? Did you not neglect them in their youth, and in their more mature years subject them to degradation—Bernard at least—suffer them to endure privation and hardship of every kind, that you might accumulate about you that miserable pelf which will be squandered to the winds and made the instrument of every degrading vice by your elder sons?

"Bernard," continued Walter, "might have died of starvation in the streets of London—he might have committed suicide in his desperation. What did it matter to you? But, Sir Harbottle, there was a Father who did not abandon him; who saved him through these extremes of misery—even the great God to whom you must account for your neglect! The very money which that poor fellow restored to you was drained, as it were, from his very life's blood. Good Heavens! when I consider what Bernard has done, less to ennoble himself than our common nature, and look at you sitting here, like an earth-worm in the darkness of its own miserable prison-house. I am filled with the most sovereign contempt of money." Walter paused, expecting some remark; but Sir Harbottle only turned in his chair, and Walter continued,—

"I am wearing mourning for your son at this time. Two weeks are scarcely past since I closed his eyes, and saw him buried in the place which he had chosen for his interment. Thank God, you are not without feeling!" said Walter, seeing a tear actually hang on Sir Harbottle's eyelid: "give me your hand—I honour you for this emotion."

Sir Harbottle, offended that this emotion had been observed, and especially by Walter Constable, kept back his hand and muttered that "the lad was a fool—there was no need for him to have left home—that here he might have had food and clothing, and have led a nice idle life; but that since he would go, of course he would have to abide the consequences."

Walter then produced Bernard's letter, which he offered to leave with him; but Sir Harbottle declared he could not read so much written-hand—it seemed to him to be a very bad hand too; and since the poor lad was dead, he did not see what would be the use of it. "But," said he, "if you laid any money down for-funeral expenses or such, why I have no objection to refund you."

"Poor fellow!" said Walter, "he had sufficient for all he needed. Upwards of twenty pounds remained after all expenses were paid."

"Ay!" said Sir Harbottle, quickly; "and what became of that?"

"It was bequeathed by himself to persons who had shown him much kindness: to a poor woman and her daughter with whom he lodged."

"Well, then, you see he did not want," observed Sir Harbottle, with considerable self-satisfaction. "There has been a pretty stir about nothing—but, however, I am as well pleased that the poor fellow did not want."

Farther impression than this Walter could not make; he and Sir Harbottle, however, parted better friends than they had ever been before.

But little more need now be said. The perfect happiness of Julia, and the affectionate care that was extended to her, in some degree restored her health for a time; but the seed of death had too surely been sown amid the discomforts and anxieties of her former home; and though she was taken by her husband into Italy, and attended by the most skilful of physicians, and nursed with the most extraordinary care, she returned to Westow, as was her wish, within four years of her marriage, to die.

A few words must now be said of little Amy. She remained with Julia as long as she continued at Westow, and then, feeling as if she could not attach herself to Mrs. Constable, by her own desire returned to her mother. The history of that poor child's heart would be a beautiful illustration of what our nature is capable of. She was uncomplaining, and meek as an angel, and willing to endure all things for those she loved. She was her mother's nurse, her confidant, her comfort. She was the only blessing her poor mother ever had.

Of Denborough Park as little shall be said as needful; it is an unpleasant task to turn again to crime and degradation, but it must be done to make our history complete.

Within five years of the time when Julia left her home, the insolent and shameless depravity of Christopher Grimstoiie grew into such frightful excesses that his father forbade him the house. Next, a daring burglary was committed, and the escritoir of the miser completely rifled. The boy Jack (then grown into a daring reprobate), his father, and his father's tool, Robert Grimstone, were strongly suspected; and Sir Harbottle then called in the arm of the law to protect him against his sons. The condition of Peggy was miserable in the extreme. She and her family were driven from their home in the stable-yard, and afterwards inhabited a small house in the village of Denborough, where they were still provided for, unknown to Sir Harbottle, by the old woman. Milly was now the sole living being about the premises; and though she hated Sir Harbottle, and hated still more his son Christopher, she remained at Denborough Park that she might secure to her grand-daughter and her children the means of life. Sir Harbottle, grown ten-fold suspicious, became morose and irritable to such a degree as made his very life a burden to himself; and though he dared not dismiss old Milly, because he feared to see a new face, he looked upon her as a harpy ready to snatch the keys from his bosom, and plunder his treasures before his face. Such, it was reported, was indeed the case on the night of his death, when, old Daniel Neale, then in his ninety-seventh year, summoned our reverend friend from Wood Leighton to attend him, as was related at the commencement of this history.

"It was a wonder to himself," the beggar said, "why he went there. It was in no expectation of an alms, for an alms never was given at Sir Harbottle's door; but it was because he felt persuaded that he must go. He reached the outer door—it was open; he knocked, but no one came; he entered; feeling his way with his long staff in the pitchy darkness; he stumbled over an old table, he hammered upon it with his stick and shouted, but no one appeared. At length, still advancing onward—amazed, yet filled with desperate curiosity—he went on: presently he heard a faint groan, another and then another. He followed the sound after a moment pause, in which he felt as if a sudden spasm of fear had compressed him into half his natural size, for he thought of the nabob, and of all those mysterious secrets to which he alone was privy. Presently a faint glimmer caught his eye; it was the expiring fire in Sir Harbottle's chamber, and on he went into that large ghastly room, where he perceived, directed by his ear, and by the dubious twinkling of a small lamp, a fearful object of dying misery.

"God help you, Sir Harbottle!" exclaimed Daniel, holding up both his hands.

"Off with you! away!—thief! plunderer!" screamed the dying man.

"I am no thief," said 'Daniel; "I would not finger your gold. But Christ and all his saints help you, Sir Harbottle!"

"There's nothing left!—nothing! nothing!" still cried the miser.

"Oh, your poor lost soul! Shall I run for Father Cradock," said Daniel, forgetting that the poor priest was dead.

"Run," said the dying man, faintly comprehending the words addressed to him, "run for Lawyer Wolfe. I am robbed—I am ruined! That hag has robbed me, and those cursed lads will be coming to carry all away!"

Daniel departed with a swifter step than he entered, and sped at an almost incredible rate to the house of Mr. Somers, and then to the lawyer's; but before either lawyer or minister had arrived, the spirit of the miser had departed.

Sir Harbottle died without a will, or at least no will was ever found; all, therefore, came to the hands of his elder son. Sir Christopher Grimstone will long be remembered as the abhorrence of the whole country; Robert sank into a weak-spirited dependant, to whom his brother allowed a weekly stipend, and for many years he filled the post of gamekeeper.

Strange to say, Sir Christopher established himself at Knighton, and within ten years of his father's death the house at Denborough Park was taken down and the materials sold, We visited the spot where it had stood; but nothing remained excepting the inequality of the ground and one solitary plane-tree, to mark either its site or that of its once extensive grounds: inhabitants—house—everything—had vanished before the mysterious working of the nabob's curse.

INTRODUCTION

ONE OF OUR FIRST RAMBLES was to the picturesque village of Henningly, about three miles from Wood Leighton, lying on the other side of the river, and, indeed, on its banks. The village consisted but of about half a dozen farmhouses, with their dependent cottages, principally of one story, thatched and whitewashed, built round a large green, in the middle of which grew an immense sycamore. Round the tree trunk was placed a wooden seat, on which, when the day's work was done, on a summer night, or on Sunday evenings, the cottagers sat, their children or grandchildren playing on the green turf before them.

No more perfect pictures of rural happiness can ever be presented than may be found every day upon this green, or under this tree. Three things I could not fail remarking in this village: the neatness and general aspect of comfort of these cottages; the affection that seemed to subsist between the labouring men and their families; and the universal taste for gardening which reigns throughout it.

The church is an extremely pretty one, with a low but well-built tower and the chancel end entirely covered with ivy, the trails of which run up the stone tracery of the large eastern window, and give it a very novel effect. The river runs round one side of the churchyard with a fine sweep, and a cheerful rushing sound that is perfectly delicious in hot weather. The, churchyard, however, is considerably higher than the river and is separated from it by a narrow slip of green meadow which slopes down to the water's edge. On this same side also grows a row of tall, full-grown elms, among which, in a little plantation of flowering trees end evergreens, stands a pleasant summer-house, entered from the churchyard, but looking out over the river,—a singular object, but of good effect, and marvellously pleasant to spend a summer's day in. Hither came Elizabeth and I, one hot day in June. The churchyavd was, as usual, the principal object of attention: there were all the epitaphs to look over, the long flat stone, curiously carved in deeply-cut crosses, to be speculated upon, and the particular window to be found which gave a view of the interior of the church. When all this was done, we walked to the other side; and there my attention was arrested by a large solitary grave on that gloomy, shady side, while there was abundant unoccupied room in the sunshine; and on a low stone at the head was merely engraved the seventh verse of the twenty-fifth Psalm:—

"Remember not the sins of my youth, nor my transgressions; according to thy mercy remember thou me for thy goodness' sake, O Lord!"

"There must be a story attached to this grave, Elizabeth," said I.

"Yes, indeed," she replied, with an unusual solemnity of manner: "she was a most unhappy woman who was buried here; and fortunately for you, my father has her life, written by herself, and left to the then rector of this place at her death. My father knew her well; she was indeed an unhappy lady! and when the rector died it came into his hands. You shall see it."

Elizabeth kept her word the next day. The manuscript copy was as follows, and with my readers' permission we will call it:

The Sinner's Grave

I

I KNOW NOT WHY I SHOULD write of myself:—that I might be forgotten, totally blotted out from the memory of man, has been my most fervent prayer; why, then, should I perpetuate the memory of myself? why, but as a momentous warning to others? The past is to me inconceivably terrible; yet I will go back to it, and trace out my wanderings, my errors, my sorrows; and may God bless the reading of it to inconsiderate beings like myself, who, seeing my fall, shall learn not to do likewise!

I was the daughter of General Sir John Cleave. My father died in my infancy. My mother was a beautiful and fashionable woman;—fashion, and that which the world calls honour were the gods she worshipped. I, too, was reckoned beautiful and at sixteen my education was said to be complete. *Education*! I had no moral principles, I had no religion, I had no higher motive for action than pleasure—no dread of consequences beyond the world's ridicule and yet I heard it said of all hands that I was well-taught—that my education was complete!

My mother, retaining her beauty almost undiminished at six-and-thirty, joined with her whole soul in all the dissipations and follies of fashionable life. These things, and the making me attractive to men of fortune and fashion, were the business of her life. We hurried from place to place, wherever splendour and pleasure could allure us; and wherever we went, found ourselves courted and flattered as among the most shining attractions of the gayest circles. O scenes of folly and heartlessness! would that I could blot you from the years of my life—that I could wither those seeds of vanity and sin which sprang up afterwards to such accursed growth, and made my life, and the life of the thoughtless mother who bore me, as a howling and frightful wilderness!

In my seventeenth year I was sought in marriage by Mr. Edward Staunton. He was the most fashionable man of the season— distinguished at Bath and Tunbridge Wells, and in the most select circles of the metropolis. My mother was flattered by his attentions, less because she was willing to secure him for her son-in-law, than that his notice was of itself distinction, and by it she hoped to attract the addresses of some more wealthy suitor. He was a younger son, and, having but a younger son's portion, was not considered an eligible match. For myself, I desired but to marry him; I preferred him to any man I had ever seen, I was too ignorant of right and wrong to know that a man frivolous, heartless, and immoral as Edward Staunton was, could not make either a good husband or father; but my foolish heart loved him: he was the handsomest man of my acquaintance—the most fashionable, the most popular among women. I believed him witty, because his repartee was always ready; and his sayings were quoted as the finest specimens of wit: I believed him clever, because he had always something to say when wiser men were silent. Of qualities and qualifications beyond the exterior I had no idea. My mother allowed that he was unexceptionable as an acquaintance—nay, an acquaintance to have been desired, but she resolutely forbade anything further. My husband, she said, must produce rent-rolls, and be able to make a splendid deed of settlement; and could only purchase my hand by making me mistress of broad manors, and wealth, it mattered not how much superior to my own.

I parted from my lover as, I believed, inconsolable. I went to flutter again in the glare and whirl of fashion; and I was taken a tour to the North, to divert my mind, and to restore a complexion which my mother fancied was less blooming than befitted a being created only to captivate the richest man of our acquaintance, let him be whoever he might.

Within three months after this I was married. I still preferred Edward Staunton to every other man—yet I was the wife of Charles Worthing! My husband was a dozen years my senior,—calm, sedate, domestic: I was the very antipodes of his nature—restless, giddy, and dissipated. Why did he marry one so unlike himself! My mother was abundantly satisfied with this union: my home was noble—unlike, it is true, the home I had been used to—all was old, stately, and solemn. Our domestics were such as had lived half a century in the family: they, too, were solemn and grave—full of old histories of the lords and ladies of the house, and as jealous of its honour as if they had been of its blood, or personally interested in and allied to its fortunes.

At first I was proud of being the mistress of so noble a home, and was amused with the novelty of my new life. I received and returned the visits of ceremony of my neighbours, among whom were some of the oldest and noblest families of the county; and I entertained myself with laughing at and contrasting their heavy, punctilious state, or their simple courtesies, with the fastidious etiquette and glittering show of London society, which seemed to me to make up the glory and perfection of human existence. But of these things I soon tired: I grew peevish and discontented; the country appeared to me insipid and dull. I longed for excitement. My husband devised a hundred schemes to amuse me, but I would not be amused. O thankless, impenetrable heart! mailed in by the selfishness of fashion, how could it resist the patient striving of that affectionate spirit?—why did it close itself against the purest, the best happiness? O why was I permitted to make my own misery so complete? It was for natures cold and hard as mine that the blessed Saviour bled upon the cross—nothing but the dear blood of the Redeemer could save me—but, blessed be God! there is hope even for a sinner like me.

I was the mother of two children. Beautiful spirits! their mother should have been a creature of human kindness—their glad, affectionate natures should have been fostered by a being all affection, and joy, and purity—for me, senseless and unnatural as I was, not even they could wean me from the follies and the vanities of my past life. My children, it is true, were my pride; I was proud to look upon beings so beautiful, so richly endowed, and to say, "These are mine;" but then I coveted to exhibit them to the flattering and the gay; and, in an evil hour, my long-resisted pleadings were granted—I was permitted again to enter the gay world.

My husband knew the weakness of my character, and, with affectionate and patient forbearance, had striven against it.—He appeared to me cold and unimpassioned: I knew not then the depth and strength of his love. I could not prevail on him to leave his retirement;—alas! I did not endeavour to do so. I regarded him as a check upon my pleasures, and therefore rejoiced to launch forth unrestrained and unupbraided even by his silence. Taking, therefore, my younger child, who was beautiful as an angel, with me, I went to London, determining to make up by the splendour and diversity of my life for the months and years of seclusion which I had borne so wearily. My circle included Sir Edward Staunton—not now a younger son, but the titled inheritor of his father's and brother's possessions. He was still the sun of fashion; not only the same showy, bold, admired being as formerly, but still more sought after, more admired, because wealthier.

I was a wife and a mother, but these sacred names were disregarded by Sir Edward Staunton.

I forgot everything—husband, children, God! O let me be spared this wretched career of sin! I have sunk so deep in its consequent misery, that I will spare myself its details.

My mother's doors were closed against me; her resentment was bitter and implacable, and yet I was but the victim of follies to which I had been trained. Alas, alas! and this my mother went down to the grave dishonoured and mourning over my fall, ignorant and unaware that she had fostered the very causes of my ruin.

Like Eve, when I had eaten of the forbidden tree, my eyes were opened, and I then knew good from evil. I was as one who, unconscious of the precipice that yawns below him, finds himself hurled to the bottom, astonished and confounded. With agonizing yearnings I now looked back to my husband and children, from whom, in the madness of my folly I had separated myself for ever. The contrast between Sir Edward, and my husband seemed as that of light and darkness: I could understand and appreciate the quiet virtues of the one; I detested the heartlessness and the vanity of the other.

My husband neither challenged his rival nor sought a divorce: he was therefore branded as spiritless and mean. Wretched was the life of guilt which I led. We hurried from one city of dissipation to another: we went into Italy, and Greece, and France. I persuaded myself that somewhere I should find the peace I had lost; but the sense of my sin, my utter separation from innocence and the nobility of virtue, like a haunting, blasting spectre, went everywhere with me.

At length, in Paris, at the opera, as I sat covered with jewels, hiding under the gorgeousness of my exterior and the extravagance of my gaiety the canker which was within, I beheld my husband near me. My first sensation was a shuddering amazement. Why was he there? why had he left the seclusion of his home? why was he in a scene so little accordant with his nature? I could only imagine one motive—seeking after me; like the father in the parable of the prodigal son, while he was yet a long way off going forth to meet him. Oh, miserable sinner that I was!—there was I sitting in my shining guilt, present to his eyes only as the unabashed, unrepentant adulteress; yet I longed to throw myself at his feet and exclaim, "I have sinned before Heaven and in thy sight; make me as one of thy hired servants!" But this he knew not—could not know; he could see in me only levity and hardened sin. For some time I believed myself unobserved—I appeared not to have met his eye. To a common observer, he would have seemed engrossed by the performance; but I recognised his peculiar look of abstraction: I saw, too—and the sight drove into my soul like the sword of judgment—furrows upon his brow; that his hair was almost white; and that, if I had known him before as a man of thought, he was now before me a man of sorrow. An agony of self-accusation, strong and tertible as death, passed over me; and yet, to outward seeming, I was calm, my eyes riveted on that countenance; and "Oh!" I only exclaimed, "that I could have understood thy worth and returned thy affection!—would to God that even now I could lay down my life for thee!"

Without appearing at all to have noticed me, after he had sat through about half the performance, he rose and went out. Regardless of time and place, thinking only of him, and fearing to lose him, I rose too, and went out unperceived by my party.

I met my husband in an outer passage.

"Charles!" said I, throwing myself at his feet, "forgive me!—Oh, forgive me!"

"Adulteress!" he muttered sternly, and would have moved on.

"I know it!" I exclaimed; "you cannot reproach me more bitterly than I have reproached myself!—How are my children?"

"Your children!" he said, in a deep, hollow voice, "your poor, deserted children!"

"How is my daughter?" I exclaimed in an agony—"how is thy boy?"

"He is dead!" said my husband, with a voice that seemed to enter my spirit like lightning.

I heard the words and understood their dreadful meaning, but I know not what happened next. When I returned to consciousness, a crowd was about me, my husband was gone, and Sir Edward, in great indignation, was ordering his carriage.

That very evening our separation took place—I never saw Sir Edward Staunton again.

I left Paris and returned to England, not knowing where to go nor whom to seek. I longed to meet my husband again to bear even his reproaches, his scorn, his hatred, so that I might but see him.

These terrible words "He is dead!" rang in my ears day and night. That beautiful being, all joy, and strength, and love, was no more! I seemed to hear his voice calling for me—I imagined his imploring looks, his first sad lesson of a mother's desertion, and my soul passed through an agony, in comparison with which mere mortal pangs would have been sweet.

II

My mother had died while I was abroad, bequeathing to me only reproaches, unkind as curses. Her property she had left to a distant relative, with whom we had formerly kept up no intimacy, but who had sought my mother after my flight, and by exciting her anger towards me, and flattering all her weaknesses, had sundered her heart from me for ever; or, if at last she relented and forgave, had kept such consolation from my knowledge. Thus desolate and alone, after three years' absence I was again in London; the world's wonder at my flight had ceased—I was forgotten—and the obscurity in which I found myself was an inconceivable relief.

By parting with jewels, which I resolved never more to wear, I obtained ample resources for my need. I took retired lodgings, and for a while felt as a ship which has found safe harbour after the perils and terrors of a tempest. But ere long unappeasable yearnings after my husband and child again awoke in my heart, and they seemed to become as necessary to my being as the air I breathed. Conscience again cried aloud, like the angel of eternal damnation; self-accusation was for ever in my soul. All day I sat as in torpor, not perceiving outward things, consumed with remorse; and at night my dreams were even more terrible: yet in the morning I said, "Would God it were night!" and at night, "Would God it were morning!" At times I woke up from this stupor, and then I observed external objects with an acuteness and reality of vision which contrasted horribly with my former insensibility. In these alternations of mental light and darkness I believed I had been mad, or in the end should become so. Terrified at this new apprehension, I resolved to place myself near the objects of my soul's desire, and, by making my torture even more acute, cast off this frightful morbid wretchedness.

I took coach to—, a long journey in the winter season; but seasons mattered little to me,—indeed at that time I scarcely knew whether it was winter or summer,—the external world was a blank to my outward senses—my life was concentrated in the desolate misery of my own heart. The journey was to me as a dream, from which I seemed only to wake at—by the landlady's question of what I would please to want.

I now made a desperate effort at self-possession: I was within three miles of my husband and child, and my impatient, yearning affection seemed to give life and new energy to my existence. I was like the camel in the desert, that has dragged on, feeble and ready to die for lack of water, but that gathers up its wasted powers into one great effort when the well is within reach. Hardly allowing myself time for refreshment, I set out to that precious home from which I was however but an outcast. How blessed and beautiful it then seemed! Afar off I beheld the vast woods, now leafless and dark, that surrounded it, and concealed it from my sight. "Oh," I exclaimed, "that those dear ones would receive back their wanderer to their arms—that even now the meanest place in that beloved home could be appointed for me!" I had never prayed before—my cries had been only the ejaculations of despair; but now my soul poured forth its repentant misery before God, and I begged for reconcilement, if not reunion with those who were precious to me as Heaven itself. Strengthened by this new unburdeniug of my grief, I went on.

Every step brought me in sight of some familiar object, disregarded and undervalued formerly, but now inexpressibly dear and beautiful: my senses, which a few hours before were dull and unapprehensive, now seemed full of a strange vitality; I saw and felt as I had never done before. Presently. I entered the demesne: I stood upon the very turf on which it might be my child had played—over which, perhaps, her buoyant feet had even that day passed. For hours and hours of a dull yet mild winter day I wandered within sight of the house, not venturing to approach it, lest I should be driven thence, like our unhappy first parents from paradise, never to enter it more.

The smoke went cheerfully up from the chimneys and, tracing it downwards in imagination, "That," I said, "comes from my child's nursery—that from my husband's room. Oh! sacred and most blessed hearths, ye are not made utterly desolate. There, even after the unworthy one had deserted you, the inmates have gathered comfort to themselves, and even now are filling those rooms with the cheerfulness and blessedness of home." My soul was comforted at the picture; I had not made them irrecoverably forlorn. I had dimmed their light, it is true, but I had not put it out for ever. And with this self-consoling belief I ventured yet nearer as the shades of evening came down. I did not wish to hold intercourse with any one; I only desired a nearer vision of their happiness. "I will dwell," I said, "somewhere within the influence of their presence, in some humble cottage, where I may see them daily, and perhaps be seen of them: I will not make myself known as yet; enough for me that I can see them happy."

I was now within a bow-shot of the house. Lights were in many of the rooms, some stationary, and others passing about: there was an air of activity and bustle even in these little things which astonished me: blinds were hastily drawn down, and lights carried quickly, not as was the wont of those ancient and stately domestics. The change struck upon my heart. "Ah!" I said, "my husband could not bear the silence and solitude of his desertion; he has gathered friends about him—I am forgotten!" and the thought came like a fresh pang. In this belief I felt desperate, and entered the court-yard. How little could the poor travel-worn, spirit-crushed wanderer, stealing in here in the darkness of evening, and dreading detection like a thief, be known for the once idolized and cherished wife—for the once proud and courted mistress of this mansion. The desolation of guilt had passed over me, and I stood an alien on my own threshold. In a moment I encountered a servant. He stared at me with the insolent effrontery of his office, and inquired my business. "This is Mr. Worthing's?" I said, scarce knowing what to answer. "Yours is a fool's errand," said he, imposed upon by my humble appearance; "no Mr. Worthing lives here—this is my Lady Mordaunt's, as any one could have told you. You had better be gone, for my lady never encourages vagrants."

Disgusted less with his insolence than oppressed by his intelligence, I turned quickly away; and regaining the high road as speedily as possible, I went on like one stunned by a thunderbolt. At nightfall I entered my inn, scarcely aware of the curiosity which my bewildered manner excited. The landlady, however, followed me to my room, and, with a kindness of look and voice which while it recalled me to myself almost overwhelmed me, inquired what she could do for me, adding that she feared I was ill. Gladly availing myself of her suggestion, I replied that I was; and taking the refreshment she offered, begged to be left alone. On the morrow I found myself seriously indisposed: I was restless, irritable, consumed with fever, and I tossed to and fro in my bed as if stung with scorpions; an impression of some impending and yet unexpericnced woe hung upon me, and, in the bitterness of my soul, I wished again and again that I might die.

In answer to my summons for attendance, my landlady again made her appearance. Oh! how can I do justice to the Christian kindness of that good woman. I was an outcast sinner, a friendless stranger; yet for three weeks, during fever and delirium, she moved about my bed with silent alacrity, regardless of trouble and weariness, like an angel of mercy. When I regained my consciousness, I dreaded that I might, in some paroxysm of delirium, have made myself known: if I did, I never was tortured by any reference or allusion to it on her part. I received from her only the most respectful attention; and when, in reply to her inquiry whether she should inform my friends of my situation, I replied, 'No, no—I have no friends!' she made no further remark than by redoubling her attentions, as if her good faith in my friendlessness called for more devotion on her part. And yet I half suspected that she knew me; and I still more felt the delicacy of her nature, for one day, during my recovery, she began, as if to amuse me, to speak of the families in the neighbourhood, and, merely hinting at distress which had occurred in Mr. Worthing's family, told that he and his daughter had gone to London, and that the house had since then been occupied by Lady Mordaunt; that she had understood the younger child had died, and that the girl was now educated at a convent in Paris. My soul blessed her for the information, so opportunely given if unintentional,—so nobly, so delicately, if she suspected the interest I had in it. May God Almighty return tenfold the kindness I received at her hands! My prayers have gone up to Heaven on her behalf; and, still more availing, her Samaritan deeds to a stripped and broken-hearted stranger were seen and accepted by the Eternal Father himself!

I remained but a short time in London, and, hateful as was the memory of Paris I hastened there with all possible speed, intending to take up my abode in the convent which contained my daughter, and flattering myself that I should find in her love and the seclusion of the place, balm and healing for my wounded spirit, and an abundant recompense for all I had suffered. I had no clue to the particular convent: but that was of small importance; for now that I seemed so near upon the attainment of my object, a momentary pause between my desire and its accomplishment was almost a relief. I accordingly went from convent to convent, wherever children were instructed, eagerly inquiring if Miss Worthing were among them. At length at an Ursuline convent my inquiry was thus answered, "She had been there, but was now removed. Would I see the abbess?"—"Yes," I replied, my soul again sinking within me. I was ushered into the abbess's parlour, and veiling my face so as to conceal my emotion, repeated my inquiry. "The dear child," replied the meek and fair woman, "had been removed from them by her father, some months ago,—very suddenly," she added after a moment's pause, "and she believed her to be again in London." I inquired the cause of removal. The abbess knew not exactly; "The father appeared unhappy; some sudden cause, unknown to them, had removed him from Paris." "Did they see much of Mr. Worthing?" I inquired. "Very little," the abbess replied: "he appeared prejudiced against the sex in general, and had placed his daughter with them that she might be removed from the influence of women of the world; and even from us," the abbess said with a smile, "he appeared to dread contamination." My heart died within me at her words, and yet I encouraged her to say more: here only had I gained intelligence of those dear ones, and I wanted to know more. "Was his daughter happy?" I asked, dreading her answer. "She was happy in a peculiar way," replied the abbess. "She was a quiet, timid girl; cheerful, but not gay. She was too thoughtful, too anxious for a child; devotedly attached to her father, and yet afraid of him. He was very unfit," the abbess said, "to be much with a child like her: he appeared fitful, and of uncertain spirits. She was much generally cheerful after she had been in the convent some time, and appeared very unwilling to leave it." "Had she a mother?" I inquired. The abbess believed not; "Mr. Worthing was very reserved, and never spoke of his wife; the child believed her mother to be dead." This was the whole information I could obtain, but to me was most precious, though containing much to agonize my heart.

My daughter, my beloved daughter! how glad would I have laid down my life to have purchased for her the undimmed—the buoyant spirit of a child. I saw my husband bowed down with grief, petulant and unhappy: I saw my daughter timid and desponding; her beautiful youth gloomed and full of unnatural cares: and all this was my work! And again, with a heart consumed by the severest remorse, I returned to London.

In London I again settled myself hoping by some chance circumstance to gain information of my husband and child. I walked for hours in the streets and parks hoping to meet them. I persuaded myself I should know my daughter, though she was then ten years of age; and with fond and yearning heart did I gaze upon the faces of fair young creatures of that age. If I saw one with a pale and anxious countenance, I believed it must be my child, and fain would have clasped her to my bosom. How often have I looked with a fond solicitude upon such a one, till she has been half startled; and we have turned again and again to look after each other. Many a time have I followed her to her home, with beating heart and trembling steps, till I there ascertained that she was not the one whom I sought. Often, too, I have gone out hoping to meet my husband,—his image so vividly stamped upon my brian, that I have believed I saw him in almost every person I met: sometimes all men at a distance seemed to wear his form, and then gradually disenchanted themselves as they approached me. What was this but a hallucination of mind which would end in madness? Again I feared this would be my fate. I could no longer depend upon my senses. Imagination was becoming stronger than reason.—Blessed be the Father of mercies! I was enabled to rouse myself and put aside the evil that threatened me:—the efforts I made were painful, but successful.

I determined to leave London, to go into the quietness of the country, and submit, if possible, to circumstances which myself only had made so melancholy. All this was not soon done; for one while I resolved and believed myself capable of acting, again I relapsed into my old habits, or sunk into despair, and said, "Let me die—let me sit down, fold my arms, and wait for death—why should I care to preserve a life which is dear to no one?—let me die." It was of the mercy of God that the idea of suicide did not then present itself: I longed to die, but thought not of taking my own life. The Almighty Preserver even then was with me, and kept me from my own despair, reserving me for after miseries, and for the loving kindness which cast a light almost of happiness over my after days.

The terrible sense of approaching poverty at length roused me to exertion. I collected together my few possessions, discharged the few debts I owed, and retired to a quiet, secluded village in North Wales, where I hoped my diminished and yet small finances might yet last a considerable time.

III

A new life was now before me; and here for the first time I began to feel repose and security, and, in some degree; submission and patience. A new colouring gradually stole over my mind, and I looked upon external nature with a sentiment; if not of pleasure, at least of sympathy. The quietness and peace of all that surrounded me entered into my spirit, while the sublimity of the scenery elevated my mind to devotion. God seemed present with me—not the God of terrors and judgment, who had passed through my soul like the thunders and earthquake heaved these mountains and hollowed out these valleys—but the God of mercy and love, who had clothed them with verdure, and made the clouds, suffused with sunshine, to rest upon the mountains, and cast over all a benignity like the protecting spirit of fatherly love.

When I returned from Paris the first time, I adopted my mother's maiden name of Winton, that I might sink, if possible, all exterior connexion with myself; and be a stranger among strangers; and here, therefore, for the same reason, I was only known as Mrs. Winton, a widow. The district where I had fixed myself was peopled principally by the lower class; the clergyman and his wife were the only educated persons—the only persons who spoke English within several miles; but kind offices are soon understood, and sorrow wears that universal expression that appeals to all hearts. The people, I was told, in their language; called me "the unhappy lady;" and I daily received from them kindness either of word or deed. A rough farmer would ride half round his field to open me a gate; children, sent by their mothers, would run to meet me with an offering of flowers; and the mothers themselves would bring me offerings of milk, oat-bread, or even a pitcher of water, obtained with difficulty from some remarkably fine spring of the mountains.

With the clergyman and his wife, who were aged people, I spent much of my time. It was enough for them that I was unhappy and a stranger; they pried not into the causes of my grief; nor desired to know more of my history than it was expedient for me to tell them. At their house, I met a rich widow lady of the name of Vickars, who lived seven miles off near a little sea-bathing town much frequented in the summer. She was a woman of great benevolence and activity, full of schemes to improve the condition of every one about her. For the young women of the district she obtained domestic situations, and farms for the men; she was her own steward, an enthusiastic agriculturist, and, like those of Solomon's days, "her talk was often of bullocks;" yet she was an excellent, most kind hearted woman. While the little town was full of strangers, she was occupied in making their acquaintance; bringing them acquainted with each other, and in filling up her subscription-lists for the poor bathers; but when the season was over, she returned with renewed zeal to her neighbours and friends, and would willingly have made them inmates of her house, for the sake of their society if they would have become such.

I was soon distinguished by her particular notice. At first, I had an utter repugnance to her; I believed that through her my present peace would be broken up. I was confident that a person like her must have heard of my history, and I already felt, as it were, withered under the terrible discoveries which she must make sooner or later. But I did her injustice; she was often troublesome, but never malicious; she was indeed the innocent cause of my peace here being broken up, but then, I owed to her the most pure, the most exquisite enjoyment that my heart was capable of—too short—but as if of Heaven. Yet let me not anticipate events which were even then approaching.

One day I was sitting with my friends, the clergyman and his wife, consulting with them on some means of providing for my own maintenance; for my funds, which, if they had at first been wisely invested, might have provided a sufficient annuity for my now humble way of life, had by this time become reduced so low, that I began to fear absolute penury being added to my other causes of uneasiness, and I was now anxious to devise some mode of supporting myself which would enable me to remain in the quiet and seclusion of this beautiful country. While I was in consultation with my friends, Mrs. Vickars entered; and they, knowing her good-will to me, but not my repugnance to her interfering in my affairs, laid the subject before her, and requested her counsel. Never was Mrs. Vickars so happy as when called to a council of this kind. "Oh yes, she could benefit me in twenty ways;" and already had her active mind arranged plan upon plan for my comfort; but the one most to her heart was the establishing me with herself as friend and companion. To this I could not consent; and cutting the conversation short, abruptly left them, but not before I had heard Mrs. Vickars say, "Well, well, the season will soon commence; and among the gay people of my acquaintance it will be strange if I cannot provide for her." This was the very fear that had haunted me ever since I had known her—I should be the talk of the idle, the vain, the impertinent. My blessed seclusion was at an end—I should be dragged before the world again, more miserable than ever, inasmuch as I was now poor.

The tone of my spirit again relaxed, and I sank back into my former depression. Terrible forebodings again possessed me; I became restless and irritable, and even meditated making my escape, that I might again bury myself among strangers. "Let me earn my daily bread," I exclaimed, "by the most menial service, rather than become an object of wonder and derision The curse of my folly shall not thus come upon the head of my living child—I will hide myself in obscurity, and humble myself to the penury I have drawn upon me."

While these determinations had possession of my mind, and I was even meditating whither I should direct my steps, the season anticipated by Mrs. Vickars advanced, and I was accordingly one day distressed by seeing her enter my room.

"Come, my dear," said she, gaily, "since there is no getting you to me, I must e'en come to you. And so you keep your determination—you will not live with me?"

"It cannot be," I replied—"it cannot be, Mrs. Vickars."

"Well, well, my dear," said she, "you know your own concerns best, and, upon the whole, I think you are right."

"I thank you," I said, relieved; "you acquit me of insensibility to your kindness?"

"Certainly I do; but I have now a scheme, which if you object to, I shall quarrel with you, you may depend upon it."

"Let me hear it," I said, trembling for what might follow. "It is but early in the season," she went on, "very early, and, yet many families are already arrived, and among them are a relation of my own, very unexpectedly—a Mr. Cathcart—Mr. Worthing Cathcart.

He has taken the latter name with an estate, of no great value it is true, nor was it legally necessary for him to do so; it was the condition on which the next heir was to have taken the estate in case of Mr. Worthing's death. But he was glad to change his own name; poor man, he had no very agreeable associations with his own. You perhaps might have heard, so nine or ten years ago, of his wife—a mighty pretty woman—who who went off with a Sir— Somebody, I forget his name—"Mrs. Vickars was so intent upon her story that she did not, for a few minutes, perceive my distress; and then, interrupting herself, exclaimed, "Bless me! my dear, but you are ill!"—"I am," I answered; "I have been indisposed several days."

"Poor dear soul!" said Mrs. Vickars, "you are ill! And you have no doctor here, nor within many miles. Well, well I am more bent on this scheme than ever. I must have you to the town, and we shall soon make a new creature of you." And so ran on good Mrs. Vickars, giving me time by the greatest possible efforts to compose myself, and prepare for what would come next. When she saw me tolerably recovered, she again went on. "Well, you see, my cousin has one daughter—a poor, delicate thing she is; wants air and exercise, and some kind motherly person about her. Her father is the most improper man in the world to bring up a young creature like that; he is a good sort of person, but of the old school; has no conciliation in the world, and thinks mighty ill of women, I assure you. True it is, he has no great reason to think otherwise; but then, for his poor child's sake, I wish he would let some respectable gentlewoman be about her, and not be dragging her from place to place for the benefit of her health as he thinks, but, as I told him, the very way to kill her. Well, my dear, and what do you say to my scheme."

"Dear Mrs. Vickars," I replied with difficulty, "go on; I am interested in what you say. Let me know your scheme."

"Bless me!" exclaimed she, "have I not told you? Why, you see my cousin Cathcart must be in London to attend his parliamentary duties; for, strange enough—there is no understanding these men—he is now in parliament, and an active member too—he that for years never went out of his own parish. I will lay my life, if that young wife of his had found him a more cheerful companion, she never would have left him. But then," she added, after a moment's pause, "I never can excuse her leaving those poor little children. But, however, to return to my subject—I am heartily glad to get my cousin out of the way; and then, I think, you and I, between us, can manage to bring that dear child about. He is a strange being. He will not consent to her living under my roof; I have too many visitors, he says; I dare not raise any objections, or I shall ruin my plan altogether. The girl, he says, shall live in close retirement, under the care of a sober, conscientious woman—if such can be met with. You, my dear, are the very person for this charge. Mr. Cathcart, dare say, will require to see you, and question you about Heaven knows what. But that matters nothing—you can answer discreetly enough; only mind one thing—not to promise that the girl shall not be out in the open air half her time, and that she shall not be brought to see me, nor ride on the pony. I have no notion of men pretending to understand how a delicate young creature like that should be brought up. Will you undertake it?"

"I will," I replied, trembling from head to foot; "only let me not see Mr. Cathcart," I added, for I felt that it would kill me.

"Why, no, no," said she; "there is no need of it; I surely know whether you are qualified for such a charge or not. But then, you know, he is obstinate; and if he will see you, he must not be thwarted."

"No," I replied, feeling that I would encounter any trial rather than lose this chance of becoming again a mother to my precious child.

"I am rejoiced," said Mrs. Vickars, "that you are willing to be guided by me. Go now, and lie down—I will send you my physician."

By entreaty rather than argument, I prevailed on her not to do so; since, as I assured her, my illness arose only from anxiety about the future, which she had now removed, and that I needed only rest, which I would take, to enable me to commence my new office whenever she pleased.

IV

The remainder of the day was passed in the most overwhelming emotion. For one while, an extravagance of joy, which seemed to elevate me above every possible chance of evil, took possession of my soul I felt as it I could defy my fortune to assume its deepest colour, could I once hold, that dear child in my arms, and make her the companion of my solitude. In the insanity of my rejoicing, I determined, once possessed of her, never more to be separated from her, but to assert a mother's claim to her offspring;—nay, I even felt angry and aggrieved that she had so long been withheld from my bosom. "She shall be mine!" I exclaimed; "henceforth and for ever she shall be mine!" But this transport was only as a passing tempest; a voice within me cried, "Woman, hast thou deserved thy child?" And, like one hurled from a precipice, I sank humbled and spirit-crushed into a state of the most fearful despondency. An oppression of terror and foreboding lay upon me, such as the guilty must feel when summoned to the bar of eternal judgment. "I have sinned! I have sinned even now!" I exclaimed, in a passion of remorse; "when shall I cease to sin?" And throwing myself on my bed, I buried my face, and poured out my soul before God in an agony of torturing self-condemnation. My misery was accepted; I arose comforted, and subdued into the acquiescent spirit of a little child. "Take me into thy arms, O my Saviour!" I cried; "deliver me from evil—I say not from sorrow—but oh, deliver me from evil! and let me be accepted, even as thou didst accept the sinful women of the Gospel!" As the calm succeeds the storm, a holy tranquillity followed this agony of spirit, and I sat down calmly to await whatever trial might next present itself.

For two days I saw no one; my eyes were for ever fixed on the road, of which I could catch distant glimpses from my cottage windows, but no one approached my gate. On the third morning I was startled by the approach and stopping of a carriage; a sudden

faintness came over me, and a momentary blindness; but the
necessity for firmness nerved me, though dared not lift up my
eyes. Presently a shadow passed my window, and steps were at my
door; I felt my lips dry and bloodless, and my tongue cleave to the
roof of my mouth; nevertheless, I mechanically arose, and with
the firmness of a martyr conducting himself to the stake, I opened
the door;—there, to my inexpressible relief, stood Mrs. Vickars
alone.

"Bless me, my dear," she exclaimed, "how ill you look! and you
refused a physician! I had twenty minds to have sent you Dr. Sandys,
for all that—and I wish I had."

"Oh no, I am not ill," I said. "Are you alone?"

"No," she replied; "Miss Cathcart is with me, but I have left
her in the carriage; I want to have a moment's talk with you. My
cousin is summoned to London quite suddenly, and by the greatest
persuasion in the world I have got him to entrust the young lady
to our care till the session closes; but I am to impress this upon you,
that her mother is never to be mentioned to her—as if one were
likely to do it!—so I told him; but then he is the most perverse man
that ever was created, and must have his way. But, in fact, to tell
you the truth, if I had not been sorry for the poor child, and been
determined to find a nice, genteel employment for you, since you
will not live with me, I would not have had anything to do in the
business. There were so many conditions—so many instructions—as
if I did not know how a young lady should be brought up! But
go in, go in, my dear; you look dreadfully ill—you shall have Dr.
Sandys. Go and sit down—I will bring Miss Cathcart to you in a
moment."

Inconceivably relieved by the information which Mrs. Vickars
had poured like a torrent upon me, I awaited with composure,
astonishing even to myself, the precious moment which should give
my inexpressibly dear child to my arms.

Thus was the desire of my soul accomplished—after nine years'
separation I was again restored to my daughter. Oh! when I look
back to those times of heavenly enjoyment, and then to the agony

that followed, wonderful is it that a human spirit could have passed through such extremes, and yet live! Dear moments of pure and exquisite bliss, let me dwell npon you for ever!—too short were you in passing; and yet you brought such a fulfilment of all the wants of the soul, that your yery memory might have sufficed me even in the after desolation of my spirit!

With a tenderness that surpassed even a mother's love, I received my daughter to my bosom, and holding her dear hands in mine, looked into her face with an insatiable gaze, with which I sought to fill the whole capacity of my being. Love—deep, inextinguishable, inexpressible love—flowed towards her, and I secretly vowed to dedicate my life to her service.

"Thou shalt not know what I am to thee, thou beloved being!" I only exclaimed; "but I will be more to thee than a mother. Thou shalt be a holy bond between my injured husband and myself; I will be a servant to you both, that I may become your friend—your friend never to be parted from you."

And thus secretly I made my rejoicing over her, blessing the Almighty, that he had restored her to my arms.

My poor child was pale and delicate as a flower which the frosts and winds of an ungenial season have visited too roughly; her frame was languid, and her spirit depressed, as if unused to the encouragements of tenderness and love. She spoke of her father with great affection, and yet I soon found that she did not desire his return. Her nature was enthusiastic—she threw her whole soul into whatever she did; but every excitement was an emotion which left her only more languid and depressed. She was the meekest and kindest of God's creatures; her whole being was one sentiment of love.

I soon won her entire confidence, her entire affection. Never can I forget our many delicious rambles, when I endeavoured to infuse into her spirit a cheerfulness and a hopefulness gathered up from the outward objects of nature; never can I forget our many communings together, nor the unfoldings and outpourings of her youthful but melancholy experience. Many a time have we sat together in solitary places of the mountains, her hand locked in mine, or her dear head resting upon my bosom: one time especially I remember.

"I am forbidden," said my Emily, "to speak of my mother; sometimes I think she is dead, and that grief for her loss makes my father shun the subject; but, I know not how it is, he has terrified me so much by his anger when I have wished I had a mother, that now I never speak of it. I used to wish, when I saw happy children with their mothers, that I was but like them. I have wept for hours, dear Mrs. Winton, when I have thought how happy a mother would make me; and then they called me fretful and unamiable. Oh! no one knew how I wished to love everybody, and to be happy and make every body happy!

"Sometimes I tried to love a dog or bird, but then I never could be sure that they loved me very much in return: I have often wished to have a little child to love; and once—I will tell you, Mrs. Winton, about something that I thought would break my heart. We were spending one winter at Brighton: we had a house at some little distance from the town, and at the next door to us was another family. My father never visits, and had told me I must not do more than just acknowledge the little kind attentions which the lady of the next house was continually showing me. I was very sorry for this, because I could not help loving her.

"There was a balcony in front of the houses filled with orange-trees and myrtles; it was quite a little wood; and here I used to sit concealed among the evergreens, that I might peep into the lady's drawing-room, and see her little boy, and how she loved him. It was very silly, I am sure, but I used to feel every kiss she gave him, and I could fancy her arms were about me; and I felt exactly how it must be to live with a person who would love one so much. And then the lady used to play on her piano, and little Augustus used to dance about in his pretty red shoes. Oh! I never saw anything so lovely in my life; it made me happy only to look at him and his kind and cheerful mamma!

"One day the lady saw me, and opened one of the windows and said, 'Will you come in, my dear?' I knew it would be wrong, for that if my father knew he would be angry, and therefore I refused; but then little Augustus ran to me, and took hold of me with his pretty, soft hands, and said I must, for that he wanted me to dance with him; and so I went in. I was very much frightened, because I knew I had done wrong; but the lady kissed me, and so did Augustus; and though I could not help crying, I never was so happy before in my life. 'You shall come and see me every day,' she said; 'you shall be Augustus's sister—will you?' and she put his little hand into mine. Augustus burst out into a loud laugh, and said I should be his sister, and then jumped about for very joy. He was so pretty, with rosy cheeks, large bright blue eyes, and thick curling hair, that shone like sunshine. Oh! how I loved him! and I never should have promised to go there again if it had not seemed to make him so happy.

"When I got home, I was afraid of seeing my father; but he said nothing, he did not know that I had been there; and so I went again the next day, and the next day, and every day for a week. How happy we were! Augustus sat on my knee, with his soft, warm arms round my neck, and would even go to sleep with his head resting on my bosom; the lady sang and talked to us, and kissed me every day, and that made me very, very happy.

"At last my father found it out. He was not so angry with me as I expected; but when the lady came herself to beg I might go there every day as usual, he grew quite displeased, and made me tremble exceedingly. He declared he would leave Brighton directly; and two days afterwards we went. I heard Augustus, in the balcony, calling to me, as I got into the carriage, but I dared not look up; poor little fellow! and I could fancy all the time I saw him with his dear face peeping through the iron railing of the balcony, and pushing out one little red shoe. I thought I should never be happy again;" and, overcome by the recollection, she wept bitterly.

"Since then," the dear girl went on, "I never loved any one so well as Augustus, till I knew you,—and you I love even better. Will you let me call you mamma? Why do you cry, dear Mrs. Winton?" she said, throwing her arms round my neck, for I could no longer keep my emotion; "do you think it would be wicked for me to call you mamma?"—"My best beloved," I replied, "think of me as your mother; pray for me as such, love me as such, but do not call me so! God knows, but I think it might be the sundering of us if you did; and so dear as you are become to me, it would be my death to part with you!"

Day after day went on, week after week, and we were more to each other than parent and child. Emily moved about my cottage like a spirit of gladness. What music was so delightful to me as her light step in the chamber above, or her voice heard among the shrubs of my little garden! The angels that walked in paradise with our first parents brought not such joy with them as did this beloved being to my desolate abode. Most consoling too was the change already produced in her appearance: her frame was braced with the fresh mountain air and regular exercise; her step was buoyant, and her countenance had lost its anxious expression: she was no longer subject to that alternation of spirits which had distressed me so much at first; she was now uniformly cheerful, and having an extraordinary talent for drawing, found a never-ceasing fund of amusement in sketching. The country people and their children, their picturesque abodes, many a solitary nook, and many a bold outline of mountains, furnished her with amusement for many hours of every day, and enriched me with treasures which money could not purchase.

I have passed through a sea of anguish; years, twice her blessed life told, have passed over my head since then; yet I can recall the fair, smiling face which would look in, among the jessamine leaves, through my open casement, only to speak, in the overflowing of her affectionate heart, some sweet word of love, or to show me some sketch which she had been making among the trees of our garden. The peculiar softness of her low yet rich voice has never left my ears; and even now, in the silence of the night, I often hear, as it were, the voice, though I know not what is spoken. In the extreme of my after misery, it was a dear consolation to believe those ever-present tones the spiritual intercourse of the blessed one who, though I could no longer see her on earth, was still permitted to be near me!

V

Week after week went on, month after month, and the summer waned to its close.

Emily and I sat together, as usual, one morning, full of mutual confidence, and without an apprehension of coming sorrow, when suddenly my husband stood before us.

Emily sprang to his arms with the most eager affection; but a sickness as of death passed over me, and I felt that I stood as a criminal before his judge. Without returning his daughter's embrace, he sternly put her aside and fixed his eyes on me. I knew how momentous was my calmness—how important it was, if possible, to remain unknown; but I saw in a moment, by the severity of my husband's glance, that the attempt would be vain.

I rose, making a sign of welcome, though I dared not speak.

"I certainly am not mistaken," said my husband, in a tone of such awfully calm severity, that I felt already detected and condemned— "I certainly am not mistaken in your person; you are—the woman I saw in Paris!"

"Leave us, Emily," I said, turning to my terrified daughter —"leave us, my beloved one!"

"You are right," I said; "I am indeed your wife!—But, oh, Charles!" I exclaimed, falling on my knees before him, "by the God of mercy, I pray you to pardon me!"

"Adulteress!" muttered he, indignantly, "God may pardon, but it is not in the nature of man to pardon wrongs like mine! Kneel to Him not to me!"

The hour of retribution seemed now only to have come, and in an agony of unutterable despair I stood silent before him.

"Woman!" said he, "you have steeled the heart that loved you— you have turned my human nature to gall!"

"I have sinned," I said, humbly—"I have sinned grievously but my sin has been visited on my own head!"

"Your sin," he replied, "has been visited on mine—on the innocent head of that little one who died calling in his fever pangs for you!"

A burning and desolating agony withered me up, and I remained silent while he went on.

"While the child died, you were parading your guilt in the eyes of Europe. With a fond credulity in your not yet utterly lost nature, I followed you—fool that I was!—hoping to lure you back to virtue, if not to happiness, till your hardened guilt burst upon me in Paris! Needed I more? Was the sin visited on your head then, when you sat bedizened with your paramour at the most public places! That sight extinguished pity, and shut out pardon!"

"God pity and pardon me!" I cried, wringing my hands. "Why should I speak in my own behalf? it is unavailing. But, oh, my husband! even then my heart yearned towards you, and my prayer was in the words of the repentant prodigal!"

"It is too late now!" said my husband, with a composure that overcame me more than his wrath,—"It is too late now! I might have forgiven before that night—I cannot now! I am not what I was! I am a hard, stern man; prayers and tears do not move me as they used."

"I am the mother of your daughter," I said: "let that plead with you!"

"You are the mother of my daughter—and as unworthy to be a mother as a wife! Nevertheless, you shall not want; had I known your retreat, I should have provided for you ere now: but my daughter must leave you."

"Never! never!" I exclaimed, with a passion which was the animal instinct of the tigress about to be robbed of her young,—"Never will I part with my child! She is my only comfort;—if you cast me off for ever, leave me my child!"

"Did you not yourself abandon your children?" asked the stern man, "and think you now to reclaim a mother's part whenever you list? One you left to die—the other belongs to me."

"Oh, my husband!" I exclaimed, "I am bereaved if I am severed from my child."

"Is an adulteress," asked he in reply, "the fit companion and teacher of a young girl?"

"I have sinned—I know that I have sinned—nor has that sin left me scatheless; but, oh, my husband, you yourself do not abhor my guilt more utterly that I do myself. I have suffered too deeply—too bitterly—not to teach my precious daughter other lessons than those which my youth received! Leave her with me: you have many friends—you have a part to act in society—you have comforts and companionship; you will not miss her as I shall, who am poor, and friendless, and spirit-crushed, and solitary. Leave her with me!—if you would have her pure, leave her with me. The angels of God would not guard her from taint of evil more jealously than shall I!"

"The past," he replied, with an unmoved countenance, "has decided the future. My daughter cannot—shall not—remain with you."

What followed I cannot relate. It was a day of desolation. My precious Emily, overwhelmed with grief, pale and terrified, followed her father to his carriage; and I, who had subdued in some measure my unutterable woe, that I might reassure my child, found myself before evening robbed of a treasure dear beyond life itself.

My spirit was wrought up to frenzy; I scarce knew what I did; and hardly were they out of sight when I felt compelled to follow them.

Like one bewildered and confounded, I went forth, without any object save the instinctive one which makes the timid ewe desperate in defence of her lamb. A mighty void was in my heart which my child only could fill. I feared not a second meeting with my husband—that had far less terror than the loss of my daughter. The madness which I had formerly apprehended had at last taken hold on me; and though I still retained some volition of mind, it was but a feeble struggling against the approach of that awful malady which hung upon my soul like iron chains for five dark and terrible years.

At Shrewsbury, I recollect—and that is my last distinct recollection, till it pleased God to remove his fearful visitation, and restore me to my perfect reason, for which let my soul praise him unceasingly—as I sat wearied and forlorn in a small upper room of the inn at Shrewsbury, I heard one of two voices in an adjoining room, say—"She is dead! What a grief, that one so young, so beautiful, should die."

And the other voice replied, "If ever heart was broken, it was hers."

And half an hour afterwards I saw a hearse pass from the inn yard followed by a single mourning-coach. I heard the words; I saw the procession, and I believed that my daughter was dead! But in so absorbed and uncertain a state was my mind, that they seemed to me only a part of the phantasmagoria of misery which for ever passed before my excited fancy; and not till five years afterwards did I know, for a certainty, that though my adored child died in the interim, still it was not she who was carried thence a dead body.

VI

A fearful gulf of time succeeds—a confusion of painful unconsciousness, mingled with a sense of suffering and wrong.

The events that had happened at Shrewsbury had been passively received into my mind; and, without any accession of grief, I believed that my daughter was dead; and, as marked before, her spirit-voice seemed to bring sweet consolation to my darkened and forlorn soul.

The beauty and the hope of my being had passed away with my idolized child; but it pleased the Almighty not to forget me in the pit, any more than he forgot his prophet in the den of lions.

As the rock gave forth water at the wand of Moses, so does the implacable and hard nature of man melt at the touch of sorrow. The death of our sainted child melted the heart of the father. In the years of my darkness I was conscious of a friendly voice that frequently spoke kindness to me; and of a pitying face, though it seemed as the face of a stranger, which often looked in among the fearful and fantastic visages that presented themselves before me. This face and that voice were those of my husband.

In five years' time it pleased the Almighty to let the darkness pass away from my soul; and I awoke, as from a long and distressing sleep, to a chastened sorrow and an humble abiding of his judgments. There was now no new agony for my soul to go through; but many consolations—many smoothings down of the thorns of life— which instilled patience, confidence, and a better hope into my being.

My kind friend, Mrs. Vickars, who had often, I found afterwards, visited me in the season of my affliction, was sent for by my husband to remain with me on my recovery, and afterwards I was conducted by her to the home which was henceforth appointed for me—this quiet home in the village of Hennningly, which you, my reverend and dear friend, to whom this memoir of my unhappy life is consigned, have helped so much to make an ark of rest and peace. Manifold are the mercies that have surrounded my latter years, for which let my soul magnify thy great and adorable name, O my God!

Many and earnest were my petitions to see my husband; but though he had watched over my misery, and had now so abundantly provided for my comfort, the indulgence was denied—nor was I permitted to address him by letter.

At length—O sad and heart-rending recollection!—eight years after my restoration, I was suddenly summoned to his presence by the following letter, dated from ——, his former residence, and whither he had retired on the death of our beloved daughter.

"My dear Wife,

"It does not befit a human being on the brink of eternity to withhold forgiveness from his fellow-sinner. I hasten where I myself must plead for mercy and pardon, and may God so regard my soul's need as I extend them to you!

"My sickness has been heavy and painful; and I have seen

that I have been unjust and severe,—not remembering that you
were in the hands of God, who would punish as he saw meet,
and that man is not more just than his Maker. These thoughts
have been the companions of my sick-bed; and my prayer now
is, that you will hasten to close the eyes of him who in death
is yours,

"Charles Worthing Cathcart."

I lost not a moment in complying with a prayer so precious; but
the punishment of my guilt followed me even here! The journey
was long, and I arrived one quarter of an hour after my husband
had expired;—only one short quarter of an hour!—but it had
deprived me of what a life could not restore—of what I would
thankfully have given my own life but to have obtained—pardon
and reconciliation from the hand of my injured husband. It was too
late! a few tickings of the clock had made me utterly, hopelessly
desolate!

Regardless of the attendants, I threw myself on the bed where
my dead husband lay, trying to disbelieve the assurance of my senses,
and franticly praying to hear from his cold lips words of love and
pardon.

"Speak!" I cried, "thou who wast living even now! Speak to
me,—let me recall thy spirit but for one word—one look!"

Ah, miserable woman that I was!—my only hope was gone
for ever; and, exhausted and insensible, I was removed from the
chamber of death.

In the early dawn of the next morning I woke from a long and
heavy sleep. The curtains were drawn round the bed, the room
was profoundly still, and for some time I was bewildered beyond
the power of remembering where I was. Gradually, however, I
disentangled my confused recollection, and the events of the
preceding night rushed over my soul like an overwhelming flood.
I had arrived too late—my husband was dead! And here was I, too,
in the very house to which I had been brought a bride—in which
my children had been born! What anguish came over me with the

remembrance of these things! I groaned aloud in the agony of my spirit, and watered my pillow with my tears!

I put aside the curtains—I was in the very chamber, in the very bed which had been mine in those former years! The old female attendant, who had, unknown to me, watched me through the night, now reclined asleep in a large chair before the half-decaying fire. I was known to the household as the unfaithful wife, and yet I had been received with the greatest respect: could this be by the orders of my husband, who, making sure of my arrival, had provided for my comfort even in death!—And so I found it afterwards to have been.

What a heart-sickness came over me as I lay in that accustomed chamber, the furniture of which remained exactly as I had left it! How dark, how fearful seemed the history of my life, as event after event passed through my brain in connected and yet such dissevered succession!

Four-and-twenty years since, I had come here as a bride. Could that young, thoughtless, inexperienced, and frivolous being, be the same as now tenanted that chamber—a guilt-stricken, heart-broken, sorrowing, and repentant woman? Once, too, I had crept about the place with stealthy steps; a stranger in the home of my children; fearing to be seen, and shunning the daylight which might reveal the guilty intruder!

Again I was here—could it be the same?—an authorized mourner, called hither by the voice of an injured but pardoning husband! That husband too I had undervalued and deserted, and then prayed to be reconciled to with tears of blood, through years of suffering and sorrow: I had hardened and alienated his once gentle and affectionate nature; yet he had cared for me, and comforted me in the gloom and agony of madness, and at last summoned me to perform a wife's duty in the hour of death! O miserable, heart-rending reflections! how did they set my guilt in array before me! I was unworthy, I then saw, to take a wife's place, even in closing the eyes of the dead: it was by the justice of God's judgment that I was not permitted that melancholy privilege! I was humbled, and I dared not murmur!

The home of my children has passed into the hands of strangers; and here now, in this quiet retirement, I await patiently the time till death cometh, humbly hoping to be permitted a reunion with those of whom I was not worthy in this life.

Let the thoughtless and imprudent take warning by my example. The indulgence of one guilty desire involves misery, and ruin, and shame!

The Lord have mercy on my soul!

So ended the manuscript of this unhappy woman. What further was appended was in the handwriting of the Reverend Thomas Fellows, the late rector of Henningly, and was as follows:—

"In the year 17— I received a visit from Mr. Worthing Cathcart, respecting a small house at the end of the Leasowes, which was at that time advertised to be let. The house was a small, genteel residence, retired among ample shrubberies, and almost hidden from the eye of the passenger; a sweet, pretty place, though it had been for the last several years much tried by its ever-changing tenants. He wished to take it, as he signified, on a lease for the life of the lady who was to occupy it, or for twenty-one years. The terms he offered were liberal; and as it was glebe property, I considered that I was doing my successor a benefit by closing in with his proposals. I should have been glad to secure a permanent tenant even on less advantageous terms; and I hoped, besides, that my parish might be benefited by the new occupier, as well as that we might find in her an agreeable addition to our little circle of friends.

Mr. Cathcart made, at his own expense, several alterations in the house, all tending to its comfort and convenience. He had the garden entirely relaid out and replenished; he repaired and heightened the walls with six new courses of bricks, and completely new-gravelled the walks. He took down the old ruinous dovecot, and opened a small conservatory from the drawing-room, which he intimated would be the apartment principally used by the new inmate; and this he had well supplied with choice plants sent down from London, and arranged by his own gardener, there being neither nurseryman nor working-gardener in Wood Leighton whom he thought qualified for the management of his work.

The house was excellently well furnished, though in a simple manner; and my wife could not help, at the time observing that no provision seemed made for the lady receiving and entertaining guests. Women are generally quick-sighted to these things; I confess that I should not have observed It, but so it was: the cause thereof and the generally retired manner of our poor friend's life were of course known, till the above melancholy history came into my hands after her death. Two aged servants, a man and woman, were sent down from Mr. Cathcart's own establishment to take charge of the house; and to these were added the daughter of a respectable parishioner of mine, by my wife's recomendation, being the sister of our own cook, Becky Cleavers. These composed the whole small establishment.

During the time the alterations were going on, I saw but little of Mr. Cathcart, although he was here for several weeks at a time, having a couple of rooms fitted up for himself in the house; but he was of a gloomy, reserved character, and I did not think it my place to press an intimacy which he appeared to avoid.

When the house was so far completed as to be ready to receive its furniture, our afterwards well-known and excellent friend Mrs. Vickars came down to see the finishing stroke put to the work; and no sooner was Mr. Cathcart gone, than she called on my wife, and invited her assistance in several little matters respecting the arrangement of furniture and so forth. From Mrs. Vickars we learnt that our new neighbour, that was to be, was a near relative of Mr. Cathcart; that she had known many misfortunes, and was but even now recovered from a five years insanity: and thus in some measure our sympathies were enlisted toward her. This place, she told us, had been chosen as the afflicted lady's residence, because of its retirement and its

quiet natural beauty,—and certainly, in these respects, no better
place could have been selected. Of the real cause and nature
of her misfortunes, and of course her true relationship to Mr.
Cathcart, I knew nothing till after her decease.

By Mrs. Vickars was arranged on the walls of the sitting-
room I have before mentioned those wonderfully beautiful
and expressive heads, and those sweet sketchings of landscape,
peasant people, and flowers, which my poor friend alludes to in
her memoir as being the drawing of her daughter, and which
afterwards, according to her request (though it seemed a pity to
suffer them so to perish, and I should have liked some of them
myself to hang in my study, especially those which represented
Madonnas and other Scripture characters), were taken from
their frames and buried with her in her coffin—all except those
three, which, with a handsome mourning ring, were sent, as she
had desired, to Mrs. Petersham, the married daughter of the late
Mrs. Vickars, she having died upwards of three years previous
to her friend.

Of this excellent lady's manner of life while among us, it is
but right to say a few words, which may testify to the sincerity
of her repentant and altered life.

In her the poor of my parish have lost an invaluable friend.
In times of sickness or family distress, who was ready like her to
stand by the bed and administer help both to the suffering body
and afflicted mind? No abode was too mean; no condition,
whether of penury or guilt, too revolting for her Christian
spirit to contemplate and pity. In winter as in summer she
actively visited the distressed; her benevolence was not like a
garment, put on and off at pleasure (like that of so many), but an
earnest active principle of the soul: she had the largest share of
true Christian charity, the bearing and forbearing spirit of love,
that l ever saw in any human being. This I say, not to extenuate
her former evil life; but I speak of that which I saw during the
last twelve years of her existence.

Of the ordinances of the church she was a regular observer,

with the exception of the blessed sacrament, of which, till within three days of her death, she steadily refused to partake, as being unworthy of that blessed rite; many was the time that I reasoned with her on this subject, showing to her that the arch-traitor, Judas Iscariot, was made a partaker of it even at its Institution, and adducing her praiseworthy life as a reason (by her own showing) why she might join us at this most holy of the church ordinances. I feared much that her neglect in this particular might have been a scandal among my people, or a cause of this sacred institution being undervalued, for all looked up to her as an example; but though she obstinately refused to participate herself, she was zealous in all those about her preparing themselves for its benefits, by purity and sobriety of life and conversation.

By her own request she was interred on the north side of the church, with no other inscription on the head-stone than the text from the twenty-fifth Psalm which she had selected for that purpose. She died in her forty-seventh year, and her funeral was as private and simple as might be, according to her own desire.

Her history I have kept from public knowledge, because, though I believed it to contain a deep and awful moral, I was unwilling to lessen, in any way, the force of those virtues which had shone forth so conspicuously among us. I endeavoured, however, to improve the occasion of her death by a sermon on the exceeding sinfulness of sin, which amazed and angered my people rather than did them good. Nor, though I was three days in composing the discourse, in order that it might be written with the greatest care and enforced with my choicest rhetoric, do I believe a single person in my congregation was affected or benefited by it, it being considered a sermon both inappropriate and ill-timed;—a remark which my wife heard, not only in the pew of Thomas Guest, Esq., whose family was assembled to hear the funeral sermon, but also from Goody Grundy and the mother of our own Becky Cleavers.

Little reputation as I got by my sermon, I did not (as some might have done) clear myself at the expense of my unhappy friend's memory. The virtues and the charity of the poor Magdalene had done more to aid true religion than ten sermons on sin could ever do, and therefore I was willing to be censured for her sake.

She is gone to the reward of her good deeds, and to know her sins washed white in the blood of the Lamb. She is gone to sit down with the sinful woman of the Gospel, to whom likewise much was forgiven!

"T. FELLOWS."

MAY SCENES
AND STROLLS

THE SEASON HAD NOW ADVANCED into the richness of May. To a real lover of the country not a week can pass without bringing change, without presenting some object that gives him pleasure. In spring and summer this is especially the case. From the moment that frosts and snows take their flight, almost every day comes accompanied by some cause of delight. Even in January you perceive what you can only describe as a feeling of heart-gladness, of renewed hope, of something akin to the delicious sensations of youth. There is a greater light and cheerfulness in the face of day,—the landscape has an indefinable but certain brightening of hue, though not a leaf is out and scarce a bud is visible. The gale that blows upon your cheek is cool, but fresh—gratefully fresh. A note of the thrush will be heard here and there—a carol or the lark already overhead in a brief glimpse of sunshine; and besides all this, there is a dancing and expanding of the heart that is partly influenced by these circumstances, but yet more perhaps by the influence of the sea on the frame than by their direct effect on the mind. Be it, however, explainable as it may, there it is; we feel it in body and soul. And from day to day all this goes on: days become longer, fairer, more gladsome; the country greener, fuller of buds, leaves, flowers; the sun rejoices above, the running water flashes in his beams, and seems rejoicing below, in rivers and brooks, and little runlets through fields and over heaths, and in cascades amongst the woods. Birds, one tribe after another, open anew their concerts; young lambs are seen, white and curly, and with looks of the most innocent beauty, and fill the meadows with their tender bleatings; and the foal gambols and gallops in its new life round its mother. But it is in vain to trace all the delightful and accumulating amenities of spring; we go on from day to day, meeting them, till the country is all one wide paradise.

But when we meet them in a new place, we have a double pleasure. As we see them come out in succession, they appear like old friends in new situations; we welcome them with a double gladness; and they give to the scene where we now meet them features of beauty and estimation they had not before. They commend them to our hearts. With what delight did we see the first pure snowdrop appear in our garden at Wood Leighton! First, a single flower or two hastening before their fellows to show themselves beneath our windows, and then whole tufts of them embellishing our borders and the edges of the shrubberies. And hepaticas and cerulean hounds-tongue, the yellow aconite, and the brave, familiar orange of the crocus, like little clusters of flame bursting from the fresh, brown soil, intermingled with tufts of their purple brethren. And then violets as purple, and ten times fuller of the sweetness of bountiful spring. These had been succeeded by a thousand blossoms and clustering leaves on plant and tree, till our garden was become a new place to our eyes, its beauty enhanced beyond conception; a place all sunshine and sweetness—a circumscribed and umbrageous fairy-land. And abroad the same process in all our walks.

Daily we sallied forth on our walks with our children, from whose memories all the country sweetness of these discoveries will never be effaced. But I must speak more particularly of our different walks, as each had its own character, and possessed its own peculiar objects of attention.

At one time we bent our way to Bramshall Wood. This lay about a mile and a quarter from the town. A little side street led you at once to the outskirts of the place. Here you passed the ropemaker's yard—a pleasant little paddock, surrounded with high hedges and trees—where you could see through the gate, the man going backward and forward on his level walk, while his boy sat under his shed at the end turning his wheel. On the other hand was the sieve-maker's shop with his door thrown open, and a confused heap of shavings and ashen-hoops, and sieves of all sorts and sizes, seen within. Anon you came to gardens, with their little, sunny, old-fashioned cottages in them; then to the crofts, where the towns-people kept each his horse or cow. Then you passed the lawyer's pleasant villa amongst its trees, with its goodly gate, and well-rolled gravel-walk leading up to it; and then the retired tradesman's more capacious mansion, close to the roadside, as if its inmates were not desirous in their retirement to shut out all knowledge of the passers-by, and yet showing over its garden-walls the tops of trees and shrubs that spoke of a pleasant place within their limits. Then you were out amongst the fields, with nothing but the toll-bar and turnstile between you and the wood; and then you were in it.

A quiet, shady place it was, though of no great extent, but large enough for you not to see one end from the other, and therefore leaving you to imagine as much space as you pleased. A beautiful clear stream came running all through it, with its bright gravelly bottom; and the starwort, and the blue-bells, and the bright yellow gem-like flowers and emerald-green leaves of the golden saxifrage dipping into it. In much earlier days of the season, there were the pale flowers of the wood-anemone all scattered about; and then the bushes of the wild rose became all covered with their beautiful leaves; and there were primroses by thousands, and blue-bells, till the wood was azure with them. The blackbird and thrush shouted to each other from the tops of its fresh-budding oaks; and the whitethroat, and the chiff-chaff, and the willow-wrens, made a mingled harmony, delightful to the quiet listener. On one side of the wood ran the high road, but so much below it, and so banked out with a huge turf mound, that it was unseen; and you might ramble about and plunge into the most delicious hollows and thickets, or lie down amongst the fern or the long dry grass of a former year, under the trees, and see the hare go hopping about, the rabbits peeping out of their holes, and the little creeper running up and down the stems of the trees about you. It was a delightful place to take a book to on a fine, dreamy summer day, and throwing yourself down amongst the grass and flowers, or amongst the green bilberry-bushes, hear the water bubbling and gurgling between its grassy banks, and the woodpecker sending its gay laugh through the foliage above.

Beyond this charming little wood ran the footpath, through fields that seemed seldom visited by men, for you rarely saw any one there. And yet you found cattle grazing, and sheep and lambs occupying the still fields; and here and there a farmhouse; and beyond, a region of woods and hills most inviting to the eye, but which we never thoroughly explored.

Again, those fair wide meadows I described as lying below the town tempted our feet in many directions—for in many directions lay footpaths across them. One took us down through its broad expanse of grassy greenness past Crakemarsh Hall, with its pleasant conservatory and gardens lying in full view from the footroad, and its bank-full stream winding through its lawn, and its noble trees scattered here and there, with Eaton Banks in full view on the other side of the valley, dark and shaggy with wood.

Another path led us to these very Eaton Banks, across another part of the meadows where that flower, of such a mysterious and sombre beauty, the spotted fritillary (the *Fritillaria meleagris*), grew in the grass, to the old bridge over the river Dove, and then up into the woods. A charming stroll was this in a summer's evening, when the sun was travelling westward; and from the woods and cliffs above the river, which comes sweeping to their very feet, we could look out and see the town, with its old church, and its intermingled houses and gardens, all lying in brightness; and along the winding river banks the anglers standing with their rods, or seated in profound attention to their object. And these Eaton Banks were not like the little fairy wood of Brashall—they stretched away far along the steep eastern side of the valley, dark and silent. Ever and anon as you wandered through them, you came to deep glens and impassable thickets: a strong odour made you aware that the fox there had his abode; and you might stand and hear the wood-pigeon send its deep, solemn voice through the solitude, and find on the tops of the old oak the nests of the hawk and carrion crow. And all along below ran steep, green declivities to the meadows, scattered here and there with large old crab-trees, which, if it were April, were each a rose-tinted mass of blossom; and in the watery hollows the great coltsfoot (*Tussilago petasites*) showed its pink tufts of flowers in the early spring, and in a later day spread out its large broad leaves. Here and there, in some quiet hollow of those green, wood-screened slopes, you came upon a farmhouse, the very picture of retired peace and plenty.

I seem at this moment to be seated in a cloof of those old woods while the evening sun shines serenely over all the scene; and the smoke from the farm-house rises blue and perpendicularly into the calm air against the mass of woods beyond; and everything is hushed into a beautiful repose that one is loth should pass away. But the sun is this moment hiding himself behind the old church spire; a grey, damp gloom steals over the landscape; a mist, like the floating veil of a water-nymph, hangs along the river; the wood-pigeon seems to send a deeper note of farewell to the day from the dark glen above; and as we return through the mossy wood, our eyes, dimmed with gazing on the evening splendour, discern only the delicate blossom of the white wood-orchis.

A sweet walk, too, we had from the town at the very opposite side of the meadows, with wooded banks on our right hand from amongst whose thickets and ivied boles of trees we saw in summer; the Canterbury-bell showing its tall stems and large cerulean flowers, while, on our left, winded the river in many a fine sweep. This led us to an old mansion-like farmhouse called Wood-ford, and for containing a view of which a pocket-book found favour in my eyes the last Christmas; perhaps from the sketch of some wandering artist, who, like ourselves, had been struck by the solitude and the sylvan beauty of the place. Passing through this farmyard, we returned over upland fields full of grass and corn; to our amazement, the crops seeming to top the very hedges—a land of fertility and a thousand singing larks.

But of all our walks in the immediate neighbourhood of the town, I think the one right up the hilly crofts opposite our own garden was the favourite. Here we could strike into footpaths in almost every direction that we pleased, through the most quiet fields, surrounded by high, ancient hedges, and adorned by some old picturesque barn or hovel, and their groups of cattle; while, as we ascended, the scene behind us became every moment more beautiful. The town then appeared in a hollow at the feet of this range of hill, half buried in trees, or only partially seen through the hedge-row trees about us, but its tall taper spire standing up high above every impediment in graceful majesty, while beyond lay the meadows and the river and the woods I have described.

But perhaps even more alluring than these footpaths was that dear old Timber-lane, which ran winding up from the very town itself to the top of the hill. Yes, it was, and is, a thorough old English lane: the very haunt made for a poet, or poetical naturalist; for a Gilbert White, or Bewick, or Evelyn, or a Goldsmith—for Miss Mitford, Bloomfield, or Clare to stroll in—or for old Christopher North to hobble down with his crutch, and rhapsodize into an article of fifty pages on the delights of the country. The moment you enter it, you behold the blue periwinkle luxuriating on a green bank above a little runlet, stretching its long runners and green glossy leaves into it, and clambering up into the neighbouring hedge with its cheerful azure flowers. Presently you pass the very prettiest of white cottages, small and picturesque as heart can wish, standing on a little green slope, overtopped by its tall fruit trees; and in the garden, which runs along the lane-side, many a time you may see the old dame—the true picture of a cheerful cottage-woman—or her more portly, though lame husband—talking to one of their stout, yeoman-like sons, who has come from his own home to give their garden a day's labour. It is a picture of rustic comfort and good feeling to warm and gladden one's heart. As you advance, you find yourself between tall hedges of fragrant hawthorn that seem never to have suffered from pruning-hook or shears; and the farther you go, the higher they rise—the higher the mossy banks on which they grow rear themselves—till, above your head, the green boughs of hawthorn, and oak, and shining alder, form a whispering and twinkling canopy, lighted up with yellow sunshine, struggling to get through, and snatches of sky as blue as ever bent over happy regions; while a stream of water, as clear as light itself comes gushing and murmuring from under dark banks, and spreads itself across the gravelly path, as if it resolved to keep you in its gladsome company. And then the violets and primroses again—there they grow by thousands, as they had grown, you felt, from generation to generation. And so you wind up the hill, hidden still, hemmed in by banks all mossy and ferny, and hedges waving with wreaths of hawthorn flowers, and odorous with dangling bushes of honeysuckle; and amid the flitting wings of birds that fly to their nests, or away into the sunny fields, till you come out on the open ridge of the hill, breezy and lavish of magnificent prospects. On the one side all I have been telling of—on the other the high busy banks of Needwood forest, running in woody promontories or receding coves for many a mile. Here it was delightful to sit on a stile, or on the warm, dry turf, to enjoy the whole ample scene, or to convert it into a picture by looking at it with downward heads—a mode that is worthwhile for any lover of landscape to try, giving to the living scene all the character of a glorious picture in a most magical manner. The cause of this curious effect I leave to the philosophical to explain, contenting myself with pointing out the effect itself.

Here, too, as we saw the various farm or gentlemen's houses in the great landscape, our fair friend Elizabeth Somers, or our mercurial attendant Charles Harwood would edify us with many a curious history of their inmates.

MAY FAIR

WHOEVER WOULD SEE THE BUXOM maidens and the sturdy and cordial-spirited swains of this rural district in the perfection of their jovial-heartedness and in their trimmest array, should visit Wood Leighton on the afternoon of May-fair day. The morning is devoted to the business of the fair, to the buying and selling of those herds of cattle brought thither from the whole country round; the meadows the night before being filled with them, some lying luxuriously to rest after the day's fatigue, others pasturing on the rich herbage, and others ill at ease, though in the midst of plenty, filling the air with their lowing;—and the weary-footed, dense flocks of sheep and bleating lambs that entered the town in the early morning, or of the long-tailed shaggy colts, and the huge, elephantine farm horses that all through the morning are careered along the streets at an awkward trot, or still more awkward canter, to exhibit their action to the purchasers, to the no small peril of any daring pedestrian who may venture out on business less important than the buying one of these heavy quadrupeds—fine specimens as they are, every one of them, of what the meadows and uplands of this sweet pastoral land can produce. A wonderful thing did it seem to me, who watched all the chaffering, the pro-ing and the con-ing, and the consequent length of time which the sale of one only of these creatures required, how all the selling and buying could be got through in so few hours—for the business was over by noon. At noon the streets were swept and the causeways washed; but long before these needful ablutions were finished, the groups who came hither for pleasure only might be seen entering the town at all its inlets. Every cottage, farm, and hamlet, for ten miles round, had sent forth its inmates in every variety of holiday guise; antiquated and picturesque habiliments many of them, but all most characteristically English, harmonizing beautifully with the occasion and the whole scene, and proving, moreover, whatever may be the case now, that fifty years ago our peasantry might be said to have a costume—the men, blue coats, all of precisely the same cut, horizontally striped waistcoats of yellow and brown, with blue worsted stockings;—the women, black bonnets, short red cloaks, or scarf-like ones of black mode; with a very small cape on the shoulders, and trimmed with narrow black lace, a flowered gown, and a black or green quilted petticoat. Many such dresses as these, all of the same invariable cut, might be seen, their wearers hale old people with venerable white hair and cheerful conntenances, attended by their children and grandchildren, a goodly company, all with eager faces set townward, as if they were impatient of the intervening streets and houses that hid the market-place from their eyes. But these pleasure-seeking people did not invariably approach the town on foot; many a vehicle as rustic and antique as the dresses we have been describing might be seen on the way; and many a cart, too, bearing evident traces of less dignified employment, conveyed thither its holiday companies, seated on chairs, close-packed as could be—often three generations together. The town once entered, and the vehicles disposed of, all bent their way to the market-place, which was crowded with caravans and shows of every description—wild beasts, learned pigs and ponies, gigantic ladies and renowned dwarfs, fat children and living skeletons; the mountebank, the rope-dancer, and the great king of the conjurors, together with the theatre of mechanism, wherein was to be exhibited the interesting murder of Mr. Weare, with all its various details, as real as life, for the low price of one penny each; while, duly ranged among and beside these, were the booths of ribbons and trinkets, toys and sweet-meats, where the true fairings could only be bought. Oh, the innumerable attractions of this one open space! While, at the same time, placards—in red, and green, and blue—announced to the public, at every corner, that the celebrated fire-eater, who had astonished all Europe, performed his wonderful feats in one large club-room; that some French Monsieur, with an unpronounceable name, exhibited his tame harnessed fleas, or his wonderful talking birds, in another; or that the well-known and much-admired panorama of the battle of Waterloo, or the taking of Quebec, might be seen at a third. No wonder was it that old and young, grave and gay, came trooping hither, where so much was to be seen and so much to be enjoyed. But, mercy on us! what aching eyes and muddled brains those must have been which, amid the racket and the din—the contending discords of the rival caravans—the crushing, the squeezing, the heat, and the turmoil—went through all the wonders of the fair. If they could go unconfounded through that ordeal of sound and sight, there was nothing that could ever distract them afterwards.

A great delight was it to me to stand a looker-on, and to see the happy children, each with its fairing in hand; a little wooden horse, spotted black and white, with rabbit-skin tail and mane; a rosy-faced doll peeping out of the paper that wrapped it, and upon which the eyes of its possessor were ever and anon turned with exquisite delight; a penny trumpet, blown every now and then; or a little box-organ, adorned with green and red flowers, that tinkled forth its chiming music to the admiration of every neighbouring group of little ones. Here was happiness indeed, and many a kind heart beside! But even beyond this—beyond the heart-and-soul enjoyment which all seemed to find in what surrounded them, was it a delight to me to observe the cordial greetings that passed between these country people; the long, hearty shakes of the hand—the loud-spoken welcome—the joy at some unexpected rencontre—the inquiries after this branch and that branch of the family; and, by the shade of sadness and the lowering of the voice that followed now and then a question, one could see that sorrow indeed was universal: there was some dear dead daughter to be deplored, or some prodigal son whose memory brought heart-ache and bitter tears.

I was carried away in fancy from this gay scene of bustle and country merriment to the homes where these sorrows and desolations had come—sweet seclusions of quietness and rural beauty—the small farm-house, the little picturesque mill in the valley, or the cottage under the wood, surrounded each with its garden, its orchard, and its crofts, where poets might have fancied health, and peace, and innocence to be dwellers, but where, as those looks told me too surely, heart-ache and trouble had been, and left sad memories, not lightly to be foregone.

Summer Rambles

SUMMER WAS COME! OUR PLEASANT walks in the spring were over. We had anticipated all its beauties and its pleasures, and then watched the progress of the one and deeply enjoyed the other. We had seen the snowdrop, the crocus, the bluebell, the primrose, the cowslip, successively come out and disappear. We had wandered with our friends, the Somerses, all round about Wood Leighton, and seen the green grass spread over the fields, the green plants spring freshly and vigorously on the banks, the green leaves bud and unfold themselves on the fine old tall hedges that surround its fields and lanes. We had seen tribe after tribe of sweet flowers come out and beautify all places—the sloe, the wild cherry, and the hawthorn enliven the air with their snowy blossoms, and fill it with their odours. By the old Dove bridge we had plunged about amid the deep wilderness of giant leaves of the greater coltsfoot, to gather its thyrses of pink flowers; in Eaton Wood we had pulled down the boughs of the witch-elm, laden with its pale yellow-green blossoms, and ransacked the wilding on

the slopes below for its blooming branches. We had gathered the
oxalis, with its delicate purple-rimmed petals, and the fern, with its
curled head, as it first springs from the earth, in Bramshall Wood.
The children had scampered over the April fields after the lovely
orchises, over the May meadows to gather the spotted fritillary;
and in Marchington holts and forest banks, had clapped their hands
in delight at the broom that, in all its gorgeous gold of blossom,
threw itself in splendid masses over the top of hedges, and from
among the boughs of copses, in such magnificence as few citizens
have ever beheld it, growing not less than ten or twelve feet high.
But now these, and the prime glory of the furze, that covered the
commons and heathy lanes everywhere with heaps of living gold,
were gone by—summer was come, and with it its own favours and
enjoyments.

I have before me now one charming afternoon. We were sitting
in the Somers's croft, and they were haymaking. It was one of those
pleasant crofts that ran down to the stream that flowed also at the
bottom of our meadow. It had rising slopes beyond it, and was
cut off by houses and gardens on this side, and, by there being no
foot-road on the other, from the intrusion of strollers. All was quiet,
and sweet, and fresh, and the whole family had turned out, Mr. and
Mrs. Somers, Charles and Elizabeth, too, to enjoy the pleasure of
haymaking; and we were invited to partake of this piece of rurality.
The reverend pastor himself had been working away from the very
morning with his gardener, a labourer of the name of Thomas
Bishop, on whom he used to cut some of his good-humoured jokes,
calling him now "Thomas-à-Becket," and now "my right reverend
diocesan;" saying that he was certainly *his bishop*, and therefore he
must take care how he behaved himself before him. With these two
men, and two stout old women who regularly turned out to work
in the fields, either picking stones, or weeding corn, or helping in
harvest, and had faces weather-beaten, and limbs as strong and free
as those of many men, he had been working most of the day, taking
out of it, to be sure, a pretty good siesta during the heat of it—tossing
the hay about and raking, and as full of chatter and enjoyment as

any of them, and working harder by half, because it was a novelty. He and his work-people formed a very pretty group—his coat thrown off, and his head and handsome good-humoured features shaded with a broad straw hat. Now was tossing the greener grass from beneath the hedges—now following one of the women with his fork, turning over a swath at such a rate that the poor dame had to scamper on at a most unmerciful speed to keep before him, her bustle and her anxiety not to break off her gossip, notwithstanding her haste, affording him no little amusement; and now he was standing, with his rake leaning against his shoulder, examining his hands, which, as one might see, began to exhibit symptoms of blistering with all this unusual work. The old women, with their blue checked or striped bed-gowns, pinned up behind, one side over the other, showing their stout brown quilted petticoats, their broad black gipsy bonnets, their red and yellow handkerchiefs thrown over their shoulders, looked exceedingly well, and the men too in their rustic habits. And then, there was a cordial conversation going on between the parties, with so much respect on the one side and familiar kindness on the other, that it was delightful to witness it, and no less interesting to hear. For, at these times, it seems as if the sunshine, the pleasantness of all nature—the very harvest work itself; which has always a boon character about it, opened the hearts of these good, simple people; and such endless recollections are poured out of the annals, accidents, adventures, and peculiar characters of all the country-side, as they call it, as seldom are heard at any other time, except it be by the Christmas fire. Mr. Somers took a strong interest in all these things, as every uncorrupted heart must do who hears them told in the manner they usually are—with such simple earnestness, natural pathos, or bursts of native wit or merriment, as are not to be transferred to books, but must live and die and revive again under summer hedges, amongst haycocks and shocks of corn, where groups of peasants assembled to their meal, with their ruddy, sunburnt faces and many-coloured garments—or as they roll the fragrant hay to and fro in happy files, with the blue sky above them, their native fields about them, and the memory of things and past times thronging upon them with a feeling that none but they, in their simple and unexhausted spirits, can know:—their adventures, ludicrous or serious, at wakes and fairs; the stories of murders in solitary lanes, and robberies in by-paths; of unlucky and lucky families; of the enlistment and good or evil fortune of young men; the sorrowful love-tale of the village damsel—betrayed, forsaken, or leaving her own land with her husband and little children for the woods and wilds of America; and all the news of troubles, disappointments, deaths, or success, that at long intervals have come thence. The story of the man transported to New South Wales or Van Diemen's Land; his poverty and idleness here—there the wondrous growth of his fortune; all the strange catalogue of his houses, farms, sheep, and cattle, and the invitation sent, and money sent, for his family to go and join him in his greatness.

In the afternoon, when the heat was over, we joined them—that is, Mrs. Somers, Charles and Elizabeth, ourselves, and two children. It would be hard to tell whether our little boy and girl, each supplied with a light fork, or ourselves, enjoyed it most. A delightful air was blowing about us; the people were all in high spirits, talking and joking; and the hay, which was now quite dry, was to be thrown up into long rows, called wind-rows, I suppose for the wind to blow through them, and then into cocks till the next day, when it was to be carried away and stacked. Charles, with his usual vivacity, talked and worked, and made no little merriment; while Elizabeth and one of the women got into a conversation that began very drolly, and then turned upon some concerns of the poor woman's that touched her nearly; for many a poor person's heart has an aching in it that it is obliged to shut up, because nobody cares to be troubled about it, and is obliged to wear an outward show of hardness and complacence; but touch it with a kind tone, and it flies open, and claims mightily the sympathies of our common nature. I saw that Elizabeth was planning good for the poor old creature another day—but she only said, "Well, well, Molly, we will talk of it another time" and Molly wiped her eyes with the corner of her apron, and went on raking.

Mr. and Mrs. Somers and ourselves were deep in the local traditions of the coming of the Scotch rebels into the neighbourhood in 1745, and the coming of the Duke of Cumberland there, and all about the house he lodged in, and the charter he procured the good old town, when there was a call to tea, and turning round, we beheld our tea-table set under the hedge beneath the broad shade of an oak. It was a delightful evening: the sun was shining with his calm setting splendour over the green fields and hills around. There is a peculiar beauty in the aspect of the smooth new-mown field, contrasting with the free and unshorn boughs of the hedges and trees waving around, and our spirits and feelings were full of the enjoyment of the season.

The children having done their tea, had gone rambling all along the sides of the field; and soon shouted to us to come to the brook, where, it seems, they had found many wonders. The younger of us obeyed the summons, leaving the worthy pastor and his lady to sit and look about them at their leisure. The children were eager with delight at the various beauties of the brook, and wanted our assistance to gain different flowers that grew in it. And truly it was a pleasant watercourse, as almost all watercourses are in summer. Its banks were thick with a luxuriance of vegetation that stood up in higher and bolder relief from the close mowing of the field. There were whole expanses of the water poa, standing up with its broad green leaves like giant corn, and flags and arrow-heads without end. The yellow flag showed its flowers above its green, sword-like blades; and in the stiller places of the stream, lay, amongst their large oval leaves, the yellow and white water lilies: the yellow, like flowers carved in thick gold; the white, like glorious ones chiselled in the purest marble—large, and snowy, and regal—the very queens of all English water-flowers. It was no easy matter to satisfy the children with gathering them by means of a rake; they must have some to place in water in the drawing-room; they must have roots to set, up in our own part of the stream. And then there were those beautiful blue geraniums, that grow in sweet lovely tufts all about the banks of summer rivulets, with petals as vividly cerulean as the summer sky itself, and falling as quickly as the most fragile of summer's pleasures; and the butomus, or flowering rush, as it is called, though it is as little like a rush as a lily is, lifting up here and there, from amongst the abundance of green things, its tall stems and crowning umbels of rosy flowers. And then, in the swiftest place of the brook, might be seen a swarm, or rather conglomeration, of little eels, not longer than one's hand, nor thicker than a quill, all with their heads turned up the stream, swimming and undulating in a little crowd, all seeming desirous to get up the water, and yet not moving an inch from their place. And in every direction flew and darted, and settled, dragon-flies of various sizes and hues, giving their short-lived beauty to the summer brook.

"How delightful everything is!" cried Elizabeth, as she at length ceased her good-natured exertions for the children, reaching to get this and that—"How delightful everything is now!" How sweet Croxden would be to-day! How pleasant Chartley! how charming Wootton and Dovedale! And she was determined to visit each of those places, and to begin with Croxden the very next day.

And the very next day to Croxden we went. It is about four miles from Wood Leighton, the road to it leading through some of the most delightful woody scenery imaginable. We set out after breakfast, and strolled through fields, some mown, some with the fragrant hay lying about, and troops of merry people amongst it; others standing yet unmown, with all their flowery grass; and everywhere were trees—sweet, umbrageous trees. Around every field they grew, stretching their branches far over the sward, and dealing out bountiful shadows; and all before us was a sea of wood, terminated by the blue Weaver hills. Sometimes we came into deep, hidden lanes, where the damp coolness was delicious; and from the high banks hung ferns and polypodiums, and such like plants, and flowers that love the summer shade. Then we came to some beautiful stream, too large and too plentiful to be termed a brook, and yet not large enough to be dignified with the title of a river—its just appellation being, I take it, that of rivulet It ran across our way; and a single plank ran across it; on which we stood and regarded its beauty. What, indeed, is there so beautiful, so refreshing to heart and mind, as such a stream in such a secluded, solitary, summer place? Over bright sand and pebbles it goes, rushing, and hurrying, and talking, a thousand little sweet voices together, from as many little ripples, like a crowd of eager children, borne on by some intense topic, through a populous city, which they see not through their own busy thoughts. Away it goes streaming in crystal clearness; and the leafy thickets and the humid flowers stoop in very love to its face, and the long grass floats on its surface from the banks. What a place for trout! And there they go, ever and anon, darting past like arrows from a bow or rather like swift shadows through a clear sky. What a place for a poet to haunt, with his favourite book, and his own fair dreams and fancies!—to see the water flowing and flowing on; to see the sunshine playing on bank, and stream, and tree; to feel the breeze come in its pure delight; and yet to see and feel them not, but as in a golden dream; to have the consciousness upon him that he was far from the working-day race and intrusions of the world; and to convert the amenities about him into parts of that fairy-land of love and beauty, and nobility of heart—of all that is dreamed of by poets, and lies far off in antiquity, in some Atalantis of a summer sea, or in a glorious future, the very milienium of the imagination. How delectable! But having drunk of the fair stream, and sat on the end of the plank, and on the grass, and talked to our heart's content of a thousand things as unapproachable as our supposed poet could dream of; we went on—on through meadows all overshadowed with wood, till in the valley rose, over the tops of the trees, the tall ruinous walls of Croxden Abbey.

The historians of the county say that it was built in the reign of Henry II and tradition adds that it was one of the first of the abbeys destroyed; but whether it be exactly so or not concerns me little. It is enough for me that it is a place of quiet delight. It is enough for me that a picturesque beauty hangs about it, and a profound tranquillity; that around it solitude lies on the fields like a dream, and far-stretching shadowy woodlands extend, so hushed, so unallied to the daily aspect of the life we lead, that one should

not much wonder to see satyrs skipping or reposing in them, or
to meet some person who had here lived on for ages, forgotten
by death. A noble arch, extremely tall lancet windows, and lofty
walls finely hung with ivy, stand amid uneven ground whose turf
evidently covers extensive ruins, and yet shows through it the stone
coffins of the long-departed monks. Near it stands a church, and in
the meadow below runs a lovely little trout-stream. A farm-house is
built amongst the ruins, with its sheds and stables; pigs luxuriate in
sties formed by beautiful cloister cells; and amongst the weeds of the
garden we beheld a richly-sculptured stone crucifix, with figures
of the Virgin and Child at the back, once, no doubt, adorning
the abbey chapel. Over all brooded a monastic stillness. The farm
maidens, stripped to their stays and petticoats, looked at us with a
wild sort of stare, as if they rarely saw strangers, as they scoured their
great brass pans in which they form the curd for cheese, their milk-
pans and churns, and ranged them at the back-door, under the great
trees; while another of them, going into the neighbouring croft,
blew, on a huge ox's horn, a long, deep blast, as a signal to the cows
to come home to be milked; and presently we beheld them coming
out from the far-off shady extremities of the field, and moving
homeward in an orderly troop. We climbed up a ladder over the roof
of a shed, and found to our delight a place fit for the thinking-place
of a philosopher; a broad space on the top of a wall, overlooking a
ruined apartment of the abbey, with another wall at its back from
which sprang bushes of lilac and other trees that made a delightful
canopy. Here you were hidden from all below, and yet looked out
from amongst the foliage of trees into a pleasant landscape. The
farmer had evidently discovered this snug retreat, and had placed
a bench in it, so that, drawing up the ladder, he might smoke his
pipe, and take his quiet pot of ale, and bid defiance to all intrusion.
Here we ate our luncheon with much mirth and contentment,
and then, descending, strolled over the pleasant fields by another
route home to dinner. It was a day without an adventure, and tells
but little upon paper; but the calm pleasure of such a day, and its
sunshiny peace in the memory, are worth a score of adventures. So

much did we enjoy those rambles, that the very same week we set off to Chartley Moss.

This place was not less, I suppose, than seven miles distant; yet we took our way over the fields on foot, made the walk at our leisure, and highly enjoyed it too. I have a vivid recollection of the pleasantness of the day and the scenery. Now we went up over pleasant hills, which in spring were covered with the wild daffodil, and then down into retired dales where ran a swift stream as beautiful as the one we had crossed to Croxden, all overshadowed by alders with their dark shining leaves; passed a delightful rustic parsonage, through old pastures, and then along the highway for some distance, the lively breeze tossing the long branches of the wild rose, and the large white umbels of the elder, as we passed; and then turning into the fields to the left, we were at the Moss. Many inhabitants of towns, and of the country indeed, have no idea what a moss is, not having lived in the days when mosses and moors covered three-fourths of merry England; when many a knight could say with Sir Bertram, in the Hermit of Warkworth—

"All day o'er moss and moor I've rode
To see my lady fair;"

nor having had the luck to travel into Scotland, in the days of the moss-troopers. With our heaths, forests, and commons, our mosses too have generally vanished; and when we say that they were merely a species of bog, my readers will be apt to say, "A good riddance of them;" and, indeed, as a general proposition I agree with them; but a moss is, after all, a pleasant thing to me. In the first place, it is become a curiosity; in the next, it is an ancient thing, and one of those ancient things where a delicious solitude lingers in the midst of this new, populous, spinning, weaving, thumping, rolling, tearing, flaring, steam-engine, railroad, coach and car, and cart-driving, and rattling country; and I love to look over it, and think it is just as it was a thousand years ago—that if an old Briton or an old Englishman were to come back, he would at least recognise this spot, when he could recognise nothing besides in the whole farmed and ploughed, and hedged and ditched country; and I love to seat myself on a heathy bank, with all its crimson bells rustling and breathing a wild fragrance round me, with the boughs of goodly trees over my head, and say, "There—good-bye to king, lords, and commons—to whig, tory, and radical—to church and state, and all corruptions in them, and reforms wanted in them; good-bye to ye all—I have gone into the land of fairy." And to the lover of the country and the naturalist, a moss is a perfect treasure-house of things that are rooted out of every other place by ploughs and harrows, corn bills, and taxes. It is full of natural beauty, and of plants and insects nowhere else to be found. This moss was a level of perhaps a hundred acres, lying amid cultivated fields and woods in its native brownness; covered over with heath and moss, whence it derives its name. In winter and early spring, it would, I suppose, be impassable for wet; but now it was dry enough to cross it in any direction, taking care to avoid certain spots, and to leap across, here and there, a natural watercourse: yet it shook and vibrated under our feet, as if we were trampling over a mighty jelly-bag, and were about to be let in every moment. It was regular bog-trotting. I seem to see it at this instant as we saw it when we reached its margin. The sun was shining brightly, and it lay brown and gloomy before us, surrounded by shadowy woods, and scattered over with green bushes and trees of birch. We could occasionally hear the short crow of the pheasant; and when we penetrated into the interior, up rose some of those beautiful birds, with their startling whir of wings, and flew into the woods; and, at their alarm, up flew here, there, all about, wild ducks, with their loud quacking, and the whispering voices of the mallards; and up went the solitary snipe that here stays through the summer to build in its sedgy recesses, and, in its eccentric flight, darted off with a shrill "tweek! tweek!"

We went joyously on amid these wild cries, and the clamours of the harmless *feræ naturæ*; the children delighted with them, and looking about sharply for their nests; and our feet sinking at every step into a deep cushion of elastic moss. But we soon encountered

what was not quite so attractive—a great viper coiled up on the
stump of a tree, basking in the sunshine, which immediately raised
itself up on its tail, and with waving head, and rapidly brandished
tongue, bid us defiance. As we had nothing in our hands to defend
ourselves, Mr. Howitt and Charles ran to a heap of rods that lay at
some distance, cut for hedge-bindings, at the sight of which the
venomous reptile immediately glided away into a hole under the
stump. The sight of this creature, and Charles's assurance that they
abounded here, did not prodigiously delight us. At every step we
expected to tread on one of them, as they lay concealed in the moss,
and to be bitten; and every large brown lizard that we saw—and
there were plenty of them—called by the country people esks,
and askers, startled us; but on went Elizabeth Somers, and on went
Charles Harwood, and we felt it a point of honour to go on too
with a bold face. And we went on with safety; for though we saw
several others, we allowed them time to escape—and they always
seemed glad enough to do it, and they generally are: the one that
defied us being, I suppose, suddenly startled from his sleep, and
seeing himself nearly surrounded, hardly knew which way to
retreat. Deeper and deeper we proceeded into this wild fragment
of Nature's antiquity, and it was delightful. The cranberries, though
not ripe, were lying thickly on their slender crimson runners about
our feet; and various flowers, the yellow asphodel, the curious sun-
dew, all glittering with the crystal drops whence it takes its name;
and tall flags, the typha or club-rush, the yellow flag, and thickets
of the rough, branched, dark-green cyprus grass, grew here and
there. We reached a place of open, soft turf, nearly in the middle;
and here, amid the green birchen bushes, we sat and enjoyed the
contents of our provision basket. The sounds of the wilderness were
novelly pleasant. The grasshopper with its dry chittering note; flies
and bees keeping up the perpetual hum of summer noon abounded;
the reed-sparrow sent its monotonous, metallic, laboured note from
a distant part of the moss; in the green bushes sang the thrush and
various smaller birds; and the cuckoo came and shouted in the tree
over our heads repeatedly, and then flew into a neighbouring oak in

pursuit of caterpillars. We all enjoyed the newness of the situation; and the children were full of interest in listening to Charles as he told them that all the ground under them was full of phosphoric fire, produced by the decaying vegetation; and that, as he had ridden across the moss one summer night, following Mr. Somers's horse, he was quite startled to see the horse's hoofs at every step throw up fire, and leave flaming prints and fiery sparkles behind him.

Having refreshed, and somewhat satisfied ourselves with the peculiar features of the place, we crossed a farm to the castle and park. On a gentle hill we found the remains of the castle where the Queen of Scots was confined under the care of Sir Amias Paulett at the time that Anthony Babington of Dethic and his accomplices attempted to rescue her; maintaining a correspondence with her by means of a hole in the wall, which they closed with a loose stone; the attempt, however, only ending in their own destruction, and the Queen's removal to Tutbury and to the care of the Earl of Shrewsbury. Like every other place of her confinement, it is a ruin. Crumbling walls, trees growing where rooms once were, and inscribed with the names or initials of hundreds of visiters—tall weeds, and melancholy yews spreading around their shade—mark the spot as one fraught with many subjects of thought on the past and the present, on the changes of time and national character.

Below this decaying place stands an old house of the Ferrers; and one close by it, built by one of its more recent possessors, but never inhabited or even finished, stands an evidence of the eccentricities that have marked more than one descendant of the earl whose death forms such an anomaly in the history of noble executions. But we had an object to show to the children far more interesting to them—the herd of original, wild, white British cattle; the only herd remaining, I believe, except at Alnwick. They are entirely white except the nose, ears, and tips of the horns, which are black. They are said to be fierce and dangerous, and will surround a careless intruder in a circle and gore him to death. There is a tradition in the family, that when they are suffered to exceed a certain number, or a calf is produced differing from the general breed, it portends misfortune to the house; and many curious proofs of it are related, from the hanging of the notorious earl to the death of the last Lady Ferrers.

Having satisfied our curiosity with these wild cattle, we returned home, and concluded a charming day.

Many a summer day we spent in this simple but happy manner, and extended our visits to more distant places. One day we drove to Alton Towers, the seat of the Earl of Shrewsbury; walked in those splendid gardens, and enjoyed not less the picturesque scenery of the neighbourhood. Another day we ascended to the solitary Wootton Lodge, where, through the means of Hume the historian, Rousseau came once to sojourn; and we did not wonder that he so soon became weary of it. Truly did Byron say, that

"Quiet to quick bosoms is a hell;"

and to such a bosom as that of Rousseau these profound solitudes and sombre woods must have been awfully trying. Thence we ascended to

"Wootton-under-Weaver,
Where the sun comes never,"

if the local rhyme be true; and climbed the Weaver hill which, in the blue distance, had often attracted our gaze. We ranged along airy ridges whence wide and magnificent prospects were given, and looked down into deep Arcadian valleys where the haymakers were busy in their steep fields, and their laughing voices came from distant slopes with a strange distinctness in the deep silence of this wild, high region. We came into villages where the inhabitants seemed to live under the shade of thick trees in their rustic abodes, as if they had no connexion with, and felt no influences from, the rest of the moving world, so quiet, quaint, and old-fashioned were they.

Another time we extended our drive to Dovedale, and spent a long day in the green meadows and grey caves, amongst the spiry cliffs and by the rapid waters that good old Izaak Walton loved. And thus sweetly glided away the summer months.

We made a wide acquaintance with a delightful though little known part of the country, and found many causes of growing attachment to it.

An Autumn Day
in the Forest

TIME HAD ROLLED AWAY,—SPRING, Summer, were gone; but it had rolled away to our perception rapidly, and in that word rapidly, we say that it had not gone without being enjoyed. Highly, indeed, had the passing seasons been enjoyed. With our pleasant friends we had made acquaintance with a pleasant neighbourhood, and every day grew more and more attached to it. Many a delightful day we had spent in beautiful and retired places, amongst green fields, flowing waters shadowy woods, and picturesque abodes and people;

"The world forgetting, by the world forgot:"

and many a pleasant project we had conceived which we were never able to carry into effect. One of these was to spend a grand summer-day with a gay party in Needwood Forest, to dine and take tea under the great Swilcar-lawn oak. Everything indeed was arranged; all the committees, cogitations, and contrivances preparatory to such an important event, had been passed through. In the first place, the number, and the persons to constitute that number, had been decided upon. There were to be twenty people! Twenty people to be selected for a pic-nic out of that little place! At first it was proposed to be select, but it was suggested that it would be better to be more merry; and to be very merry, it was absolutely necessary to have hearty people, and odd people, and funny people, and people that could tell a good story, crack a good joke, and sing a good song. And then it was as absolutely necessary to have useful people in a rustic party; people that could turn a hand to anything; that were capital at pitching on snug and eligible places for encampment—constructing seats of moss, or heather, or logs of wood, or even of good substantial stones; placing tender people out of the wind, and propping weak-backs with good old trunks of trees; that could help to pitch the poles and hang the kettle, to blow the fire, and even run and collect sticks occasionally. Do my readers think that such persons are not to be found? They are much mistaken. We know snch persons, and they are rich people, too, that would delight to take upon themselves these Gibeonite functions in a social pic-nic, and so far from thinking it any sacrifice of dignity, would pride themselves on their adroitness in them. And it is well known on such occasions, that the fewer the servants, the fewer the annoyances; and even where there are ever so many of them, one good and ingenious person of this kind, bustling and ardent, puts life and spirit into all about him.

Well, then, it was necessary to consider who in all Wood Leighton bore these various and estimable characters; and next, it was as necessary to balance likings and antipathies, and eschew family feuds and jealousies of rank and wealth: for, alas! Wood Leighton was no more exempt from these earthly cankers than any other sweet place on this rolling globe. It was soon clear enough that this person would not go if that person went; and if that person went, this would not; and yet, if this or that were left out, oh! the dudgeon and the heart-burnings there would be! And, what was more, one thought this person quite a bore—a that person too grave—another, that too giddy and giggling; and as for Mrs. or Miss Such-a-one, oh! they always spoiled every party they went into; they got out of temper, or they could see no fun in what was going on. There were the over-wise, the yawners, the cold-water-throwers, in poor, dear Wood Leighton. And on the other side there were the racketty—people who could not discern any bounds of propriety, who took riot for wit, cracking bottles for cracking jokes; and some who were apt to get muddled and foolish when they did not intend it, and were betrayed into a troublesome condition of maudlin fondness and importunity by sheer gaiety of heart and desire to be agreeable. There were, too, a certain class who would set off in the highest delight, and before they had well got to the place of rendezvous began to wonder what they came for; were afraid of taking cold, or suddenly remembered some engagement that a fortnight's notice had never once made apparent, and were driving off back again just as the rest sat down on the grass to enjoy themselves.

Was not this enough to damp a whole regiment of pleasure-takers? Is it not enough any day? And yet everywhere such things exist, and everywhere such parties are formed; and so it was here. All these difficulties were got over amazingly; characters and dispositions selected, assorted, and amalgamated with great ingenuity, and the invitations sent; when, lo! there was a new species of difficulty developed. Some of the most desirable individuals could not go! This was inextricably engaged; that going a journey; a third expecting company; a fourth had given up all intention of indulging in such pleasures for the future: a fifth would love it above all things, but dare not venture, having caught a dreadful lumbago last summer by sitting only five minutes on a green bank. Here were awful gaps in the circle. But on the other hand there were heaps of volunteers ready to fill them up;—half-a dozen begging they might bring this or the other friend; Mr.—, such a very entertaining person, or Miss —, so very poetical; and these even begging to extend the favour to third parties. I shall not say how all these contingencies, that sprang up thick and unexpectedly as mushrooms, were disposed of; but they were disposed of. The carriages were determined upon,

gigs, phaetons, pony-carriages, car and shandrydans, and who were
to fill each; and moreover all the baking of cakes and sweetmeats,
packing of wine, and of all the various requisites for a substantial
dinner and tea, were finished and brought to an end;—everything
was ready but the day, and that too came—as fine a day as ever
shone out in the finest of summers! At twelve o'clock, the time
fixed on to set out, first one carriage and then another rolled up to
the door, and our drawing-room was soon half-filled with a lively
and anticipating group, who said that they had merely called to see
that all was right, and that no untoward circumstance had occurred
to prevent the going of the whole party, and they would now be
driving on towards the forest. Just at this moment in came Charles
Harwood, who said Mr. Somers was afraid a storm was coming on:
a cloud was forming in the east, which had all the appearance of
being the nucleus of a thunder-cloud and was growing and coming
up in the very face of the wind. "Surely not!" exclaimed every one
at once; and out all rushed into the garden, to see if this portentous
cloud were visible there, and there sure enough it was, black as
night, growing and creeping on with a lowering and tumultuous
aspect, with a dark train extending to the horizon, and yet all in
front the whole sky clear as crystal, and the sun shining in his noon
splendour.

While we were looking at this gloomy apparition, which seemed
to have arisen to chase away our long-concerted scheme of pleasure,
others of the intended party came hurrying in one after another
with eager looks and inquiries. "Well; what do you think? Will it
pass over or not?" And some thought it would, and others thought
it would not; some thought it would be a mere flying cloud, and
others that it would be a most awful tempest. Now one thought
it was passing off to the south, and others that it grew thinner
and paler and would presently disperse; while in fact it was every
moment becoming broader, nearer, vaster, and more intensely lurid.
And now there appeared a tumultuous and whirling motion in the
centre of the nimbus, with an ashen appearance of the clouds. There
depended, as it were, a huge funnel, with the mouth applied to the

cloud and the narrow end downwards, which hung as in a dense column towards the earth, near which its lower extremity swept in hair-like lines, like the tail of a gigantic horse. All exclaimed at the singularity of the spectacle; but of its cause or nature there were opinions as various as on everything else. Some thought the cloud had burst, and was raining in that one singular dependent train; others, that it was a waterspout that was actually sucking up the water front the river; and in fact it actually seemed to hover over the river and to follow its course. On this it was suggested that if it burst we should all be drowned; and at the fearful idea the ladies fled away into the house in a moment. The gentlemen stood to watch the further progress of this strange object; and now the thunder began to crash and growl overhead, peal after peal, most magnificently, but without any visible lightning; and in another instant lumps of ice as large as pigeons' eggs began to fall and rattle about us, at first distant from each other by several yards, but with wonderful rapidity increasing their proximity to each other, till they came in a deluge of the most astonishing hail we ever witnessed; no stones less than marbles, many much larger, and all dancing and leaping around, from trees, walls, and roofs, and in the grass lying one whole white expanse as of snow.

It is needless to say that the gentlemen vanished into the house with a hop, stride, and jump; and all stood gazing from the windows in silent admiration of the magnificent rage and plenitude of the storm. The thunder rolled and roared, and crashed all over the heavens; the lightning flashed in the most vivid gleams past us; the hail fell as abundantly as ever, and amid deluges of rain that seemed as if they would drown the very world. For an hour at least this continued, till all around us was a sonorous hum of falling and rushing waters, from the heavens, from the houses, and along the streets, in one wide, discoloured flood. Here was an end of our pic-nic; and instead of regret, for a time at least we seemed to feel glad and thankful that we were not on our way, and exposed to "the peltings of this pitiless storm." But when it began to abate, regrets began to show themselves. The memory of the plannings and contrivings, of the getting together of carriages and provisions, came upon the mind of all, and especially of some of the ladies. Some thought that we might still go tomorrow; but a dozen voices all at once cried, "No! *they* couldn't go. They had pushed off engagements from this day to that—*they* couldn't go!"—"What a pity! But, after all, could not we really go to-day?"—"What!" said the prudent, "go through a river, and into a sea, as the forest must be?"—"Oh!" said the sanguine, "it will all be gone by in half an hour, and the sun will shine and the ground be as dry as ever,—nay, who knew that it had fallen in the forest at all?" And truly some would have been hardy enough to set off; but the rain, though its fury was gone by, still kept up a slight drizzling; the sky was filled with one dense grey cloud, and so remained till night. It was soon obvious to all that the plan must for this time be abandoned; and so with many a sigh it was given up. And presently came news and motives of curiosity and wonder that diverted all further thoughts from this ill-fated expedition. The gardens were found to be battered and perforated as with bullets; trees and plants of all descriptions were cut through, leaf and blossom, and hot-houses and conservatories were one enormous smash of glass; while the houses had suffered in their windows nearly as much, and looked for all the world as though they had been attacked by a mob. The whole town was one scene of ludicrous disasters, if that can be ludicrous which is full of real trouble and domestic loss. Suddenly, people sitting on their hearths listening to the storm found the water flowing in upon them from the flooded streets. Cellars were speedily filled; barrels were all afloat; many that were not securely bunged got muddy water mingled with their stout old ale; and others, swimming about, dashed the goodly contents out of congregated wine bottles. In low kitchens and cottages, tables and chairs began to swim about; and the inhabitants fled upstairs with cradles, crying infants, and what dry linen and provisions they could collect. One little shoemaker, who worked in a sort of cellar under his house, that had a descent of steps and a door from the street, having given his wife some provocation, and being threatened with a retributive visit by his Amazonian dame, had bolted his door inside, and was thumping away on his lap stone in great inward satisfaction, and chuckling at the idea of his own security and the disappointment of his spouse, when down rushed torrents of water from the streets through door and window, in such a deluge that the alarmed man was speedily up to the middle, and in his consternation and the darkness that accompanied the inrush of the water could not find the bolt he had fastened on the door inside. He therefore set up a most stentorian shout, and beat on the door with his fists,—his hammers were all now at the bottom of the flooded cellar—but neither could he make himself heard nor beat in the door with his whole might, and there was a full prospect of drowning, when luckily his wife suddenly called him to mind, and looking out saw the door of his working-cell shut, and the water rushing in a perfect river. Her anger instantly converted itself into terrified affection. She cried out, "Oh! my poor Johnny! he'll he drowned! he'll be drowned!" and rushing to the door, battered it in with a coal-hammer, and had the satisfaction to see her worthy husband standing up to the chin in water, and soon come creeping up the steps like a half-drowned rat.

This incident furnished a fund of merriment that set all Wood Leighton in a roar of laughter, and will no doubt serve for a standing joke against the poor Crispin while he lives. And indeed we heard that his wife already, on all occasions when she feels herself unhandsomely used by her husband, casts a very scornful and significant look at him, and says, "Eh, you poor rogue! where would you have been now had it not been for me in the great thunder-flood?"—the name by which this awful tempest generally now goes. And an awful storm it was. The very next day we heard that it had fallen on the forest with unexampled fury; had actually shattered to fragments several vast oaks, and killed several horses that were sheltering beneath them.

This was our grand day in the forest put aside as by the hand of Providence, and was given up entirely. But now, in the fine days of October, Elizabeth Somers and ourselves resolved to go, our own snug party of the two families, and spend the rest of the day amid the fading splendours of its solemn woodlands. We drove first to the neighbourhood of Bagot's Park, through a region of retired farms where no change seems to have come from age to age—tall old hedges, old pastures with quiet cattle, old picturesque cottages and farmhouses thinly scattered, and silent fields and dark woodlands. I cannot express how strongly the profound calm of these primitive scenes affects my feelings and imagination. I could not help thinking, as we went along through embowered lanes, and then through little snatches of common and heath, now shut in by high banks and thick foliage, and now catching wide prospects over the country, how the tumult of towns, and the careful anxiety of trade, and the ten thousand wheels of manufactories were going; what countless human creatures were devoured by the perplexities of ill-requiting business or the greater curse of an avaricious mania—what strugglings and contentions of commercial interest and political party were going on, while here lay an everlasting peace as the delicious heritage of an unambitious race.

The glories of October were around us. We had set off directly after breakfast and the dews lay thick on the grass by the wayside; the waters ran here and there, sparkling and bubbling across the road; the gossamer stretched its fine lines from bush to bush and tree to tree, and its agglomerated webs came floating on the golden air in flakes as of the lightest cotton. On the green furze-bushes the geometrical spiders exhibited their webs, concentric wheels of exact workmanship, made more visible by innumerable dewy globules; the hedges were grown beautiful with the rich colour of their dying leaves and their various berries—the black privet and the buckthorn, the hips and haws of bright scarlet and deep crimson. The air had that feeling of cool freshness and that marvellous transparency never seen in our climate but in autumn; and the woods, in all their solemn magnificence of colours, scarlet, crimson, tawny, pale yellow, and richest russet—the woods, and the smoke of peacefullest cottages, rising up in blue and busy columns in front of their deep masses of foliage—Oh! they were beautiful! This was the feeling with which we rode along; and the only words we found to express our sensations were those of beauty,—peaceful, shining, and heart-satisfying beauty. In all my experience of human life I know of no portion of it in wich the goodness of Heaven and the blessings of a virtuous and refined friendship make themselves so sensibly and blissfully felt as in such moments as these, when the buoyancy of health felt through the whole frame is itself a perfect enjoyment, and the deep reposing loveliness of nature inspires us with feelings of gratitude to Heaven and affection for each other.

We put up our horses at a farm-house, the master of which was well known to Mr. Somers, and walked through some pleasant fields into Bagot's Park.

Passing the end of a keeper's house, we seemed to step at once out of modern England into the feudal ages. We seemed to have gone back with a thought through a thousand years. All round us lay the green and cultivated lands of the present times; yet we were in a grey and ancient region—a fragment of the past—a space apparently secured by a spell from the influence of time and change, except that silent and irresistible change into the aspect of the old and venerable. A belt of oaks stretched along a vast circumference enclosing this ancient park. They were of a great growth; and of a remarkable height for oaks; trees of sixty and seventy feet in the boll, yet so old that scarcely one of them was without a scathed and broken top: and issuing from beneath these you looked into a silent region, amongst other oaks of equal age, some scattered far apart, others condensed into dark masses of wood,—some widely spreading, others shattered and sinking into naked decay. There were birch-trees too of great antiquity, with stems rugged and gashed near the ground; thence rising in silvery whiteness and hanging their lithe and graceful branches almost to the earth. We walked in a quiet delight over the dry and mossy turf amongst the tall red fern, startling the deer from their repose amongst it or seeing them lightly trooping up some distant slope, and belling, some in hoarse and others in musical notes—a truly forest sound! The ruddy squirrels were busy on the ground beneath the beech-trees that grew in some places, feasting on their fallen nuts or scampering up the trees at our approach; and the varied and peculiar cries of the woodpecker, the jay, and the solitary raven were all imbued with a woodland charm.

We soon came to a noble oak that seemed in the very prime of its existence, and spread such a mighty circle of shade beneath as created a perpetual gloom, well meriting what Pope calls the "brown horror of the wood." When we had walked up to its foot we were struck with strong admiration; its massy trunk spreading out in gnarled heaps at the ground, and above us extending its horizontal arms, each an enormous tree, to the width of forty feet. Great care was evidently and very justly taken by the noble proprietor to prevent decay or injury. Some of these vast arms were supported by stout pillars of timber, and plates of lead were nailed over every spot where a bough had fallen. From this giant of the woods—called the Beggar's Oak, I know not wherefore,—we wandered along, visiting others of nearly equal dimensions; Mr. Semers evidently impressed strongly himself and trying to impress us with the advantages of an aristocracy and the law of primogeniture by which these noble parks and specimens of forest grandeur were preserved. And truly, if primogeniture has any one popular advantage it is this. One would not like to see these venerable solitudes and giant trees swept away by rapid changes and divisions of property. They are rest and breathing-places to the imagination. Square fields and rectangular fences are good things, so far as our animal wants go; but as we feel wants beyond those of the mere animal—wants of the heart and the spirit we would willingly have old parks and forests preserved, where we may occasionally retire from the noise of towns, from their artificial influences; from the rush of steam-coaches—the very sounds and indications of progression in the arts and facilities of social life—from the strife of politics, and the claims of conflicting modes of religion; and there drink in the quiet spirit of nature, and feel that religion which haunts these shades and falls on the heart with all the holy power of Heaven, without one questioning doubt from a too fastidious understanding. One would have had them left to refresh the imagination; to call back our thoughts to the simple days and habits of our ancestors, and to imbue us with that loftier mind, that poetry which Milton, Spenser, and Shakspere have gathered up and again diffused over such places with a tenfold glory. Yes, we would not have the traces of antiquity, the vestiges of a past state of existence, the manners of men and things connected with the stirring history of this great country, razed out amid the new and imposing forms of life: they should remain for their own venerable beauty and peace, or fall only as a sacrifice to the furtherance of all that is desirable for the great family of man. I say, we would not willingly allow them to disappear, though we could resign them as a sacred duty; and while we hold the law of primogeniture to be fraught with great injustice and many evils, we will accord it the one good quality of having preserved many of these venerable domains, though it must be allowed that it has not kept open a great number for the enjoyment of the public.

Talking of these things each with his or her peculiar views of them, we returned to the farm-house, and we drove into the forest. We first visited the great Swilcar oak, a glorious old tree, sixty-five feet high, forty-five in the width of the boughs, and thirty feet in the trunk near the earth. Here it was that we were to have held our summer pic-nic, and a superb tent it would have been for such a party—

Such tents the patriarchs loved:

but we now enjoyed a quiet delight in gazing on its regal immensity, and thence progressed far onward through the forest; sometimes admiring the rich farms and broad, good roads made where formerly stood one mass of woods; sweet villas and ancient royal lodges; sometimes coming upon a gipsy encampment or a little hamlet half hidden in trees. In one of these Mr. Somers drove up to a little rustic inn, saying here we could dine. As the carriage stopped under the great sycamore before the door, out came the landlord, out came the landlady, and out came the maid—a short, stout-built country lass, looking as if she had health enough in her to set up a score of delicate people. Our host was a tall man, looking more of the farmer than the publican—as he was in fact—and his wife as motherly-looking a woman as you could wish to see. There were bows, and curtsies, and smiles, which showed that our friends were both known and respected here. "Well, Mr. Brewin," said Mr. Somers, "still on the old spot, I see. I am glad to see both yourself and Mrs. Brewin looking so well. I hope you can find us something to eat, Mrs. Brewin; for I assure you we are *forest* hungry, and there is a good carriage-full of us, you see."

"Well, sir, I think I can find you something," said our good-natured-looking dame, with another low curtsy. "I was going to take up the dinner for the ploughmen; it is just one o'clock, and that is the hour they come home. They go out as soon as it is light in the morning, and they had need live well—that is, what we call living well in our countrified way; and though it is but ploughman's fare, yet I fancy you and Miss Somers, and Mr. Charles, and these other gentry, will be able to make a dinner of it for once in a while."

"Oh! no doubt on't, no doubt on't," said Mr. Somers. So we all bustled into the house, leaving our host to take out the horses. We were soon comfortably seated in a nice, clean, old-fashioned little parlour, looking into a garden as neat as the house, full of Michaelmas daisies, French marigolds, China asters, and those splendid flowers the dahlias, now got into every cottage garden, and other autumn flowers, and terminated by a vast and noble walnut-tree. Speedily our little sturdy maid spread a cloth white as the driven snow, and arranged the dinner apparatus with many bashful smiles and rosy blushes, as Mr. Somers kept chatting to her in a voice of friendly jocularity. Presently she set on the table a capital piece of boiled beef—enough, one would have thought, for a regiment of ploughmen—with an accompaniment of nicely-dressed turnips, carrots, and potatoes. Then came a dish of barm dumplings, light as foam-balls on a river. There were sweet home-made bread, butter and cheese fit for a king, a glass of primest Burton ale, and water so cool, so crystalline, that Elizabeth exclaimed, "Why, Millicent"—so our maid was called—"you might have just fetched this from the Elf Spring in the dingle, only that you certainly have not had the time."—"Master has fetched it, ma'am. He knows you are fond of that spring, and so he thought you would like your dinner better with some of it."—"Well, I am really obliged to Mr. Brewin," said Elizabeth, "though the dinner does not need such a luxury to make it acceptable: a forest stroll makes such a meal ten times more delicious than a palace banquet," We all joined heartily in the opinion; and Millicent, who had adroitly drawn the cloth while we were speaking, now reappeared from the kitchen with a plate of fresh Whiking pippins and another of damascenes; and Mr. Brewin followed with one of grapes from the house-side and one of Catherine pears from the tree that adorned the outside of the kitchen-chimney; and we had scarcely expressed our admiration of this country dessert when in came Millicent again with a little basket of filberts, and walnuts from the great tree. To complete so abundant a feast Mr. Somers ordered wine—for our host was licensed to sell wine and spirituous liquors—and Mrs. Brewin brought in a bottle of her elder-flower wine, which she did not sell, but gave to her particular friends. "It was what the ladies," she said, "always fancied:" and truly it was as living and sparkling and grape-like in its flavour as any Frontignac that ever crossed the sea. Our rural entertainment, so far beyond our expectation, and the hospitable heartiness of our entertainers, put us all into high good-humour. Our host and hostess were invited to join us, having themselves dined at twelve o'clock; and they came. Millicent, being deputed to supply the appetites of the ploughmen, and who were making a famous rattle with pewter plates and knives and forks in the kitchen, now came in as hungry as we had been half an hour ago. Charles and Mr. Somers sat and talked past affairs over with our host and hostess, and we sat and listened to the most extraordinary stories of deer-stealers that used to haunt the purlieus before the enclosure of all but the Crown lands, and especially of the exploits of old Malabar, the most celebrated of them. I know not when my imagination has been more excited; and Charles and Mr. Somers seemed as highly interested as the old people themselves. Every now and then Mr. Somers kept saying, "Well! we must be going, for we must take our friends to see Mr.—They must see him and his collection of forest curiosities." This was a gentleman who was a perfect enthusiast about the forest, as most dwellers near a forest generally are; for as in mountains, so in them, there is a wild charm that seizes forcibly on the imagination, and in people of any taste and sensiblity becomes a perfect passion. It was the delight of this gentleman to roam about the forest at all hours, day or night, and at all seasons. All its native inhabitants, and their haunts, their habits, their mysteries, their occasional increase or decrease or extinction, were all known to him; and his house, situated in a retired glen, was a complete museum of forest relics and antiquities, and of stuffed owls, hawks, ravens, curlews, weasels, stoats, squirrels, otters, and I know not what. We were anxious to reach his house, but it was not then to be. Mr. Somers' repeatedly said, "Well, we *must* go! " but still the talk went on till pulling out his watch he started up, and showed by his countenance and exclamation of amazement at the discovery that it was six o'clock! The shadows of evening were already falling, and it was at an end with reaching Mr. —'s. Our carriage was hastily ordered out, our bill discharged, our worthy host and hostess and our good rosy-armed Millicent were bid a hearty good-bye to, and away we drove home.

In a little time we found ourselves in the village of Hanbury. The immense and splendid prospect there we had seen before, or we should now have been disappointed. But as it was a clear and rather breezy evening, there was yet light enough to make us sensible of its vast extent; and the valley of the Dove lay before us in the wildness of twilight and of autumn, solemn and gloomily beautiful. We could still discern the hill and turrets of Tutbury down the valley; the hall of Sudbury opposite amongst its woods; and below us the smoke ascending from the antique chimneys of Fauld Hall. The only sounds that reached us were the wind soughing among the woods, the low of cattle in the Dove meadows, and the music of some village bells ringing cheerfully. The sound of those bells seemed to touch more deeply feelings already excited. As the carriage paused a moment and we cast our eyes down over the sombre masses of forest-trees below us, several voices claimed at once, "How beautiful!" Mr. Somers, over whom the woodland enjoyment of this day seemed to have brought more enthusiasm than I had ever seen in him before—an enthusiasm as of ardent and happy youth—took up the exclamation, "How beautiful! Yes, it *is* beautiful! The longer I live the more do I become attached to this fine country. I know not whether many would not deem it unbecoming of the character of a Christian, and especially of a Christian teacher, to own a growing attachment to the things of this earth; but to my own heart I justify it by the reflection that they are the works of God; and that the loveliness which calls forth so strongly my affectionate admiration is that with which he has adorned the abode of his acknowledged children. I feel that I do not love earth with a sordid love: I do not covet it and grasp at it with any selfish end, but with a love and a delight in which every child of humanity is embraced, and everything however humble that is formed by the same hand, and lives, and feels, and enjoys, may and does in some degree partake. I love these quiet regions for the refreshment and the sober blessing that they breathe upon my spirit. And shall I not feel a strong attachment to the scenes in which my days of the deepest happiness have passed? Shall I not love these? There are other spots in my native and distant county—the spots in which my youth went over—that are dear to me with a peculiar and imperishable feeling; yet I do not hesitate to say that these scenes are still dearer to me, because I have experienced here a second youth—the renewal and crown of my existence—the youth of affection and the life of the heart.

"We hear a great deal of the unsatisfiedness of the human heart, and as a general proposition no doubt it is true; but, God is my witness, there is no wish of my heart that has not been amply gratified in placing me here and enriching me with the gifts and affections that he has done. Is there any lot that I would choose in preference to my own? Not one! Could the widest walk—could the most brilliant reputation—could cities, or courts, or Fortune in any of her many Protean splendours—tempt me to a single sigh? No! let me pass calmly the remainder of my days in the beloved scenes and with the beloved people I have so long shared

it with, and they may write upon my tomb the epitaph of at least
one satisfied man.

"I know not how it is; I cannot comprehend the feeling with
which many quit this noble country for ever for strange lands. And
yet it may be said that hundreds do it every day; and for thousands
it may indeed be well. For those who have had no prospect but
the daily struggle for existence—for those whose minds have not
been opened and quickened to a sense of the higher and more
spiritual enjoyments which this country affords—for the labouring
many—the valleys of Australia or the vast forests and prairies of
America may be alluring. But to me, and therefore it seems equally
to other men with like tastes and attachments, to quit England—
noble, fearless, magnanimous, and Christian England—would be to
cut asunder life, and hope, and happiness at once. No! till I voyage
to 'the better land' I could never quit England. What! after all the
ages that have been spent in making it habitable and home-like;
after all the blood shed in its defence and for the maintaining of
its civil polity; after all the consumption of patriotic thought and
enterprise—the labours of philosophers, divines, and statesmen—to
civilise and Christianise it; after the time, the capital, the energies
employed from age to age to cultivate its fields, dry up marshes,
build bridges and lay down roads, raise cities, and fill every house
with the products of the arts and the wealth of literature; can there
be a spot of earth that can pretend to a tithe of its advantages, or
a spot that creates in the heart that higher tone necessary for their
full enjoyment? Why, every spot of this island is sanctified, not only
with the efforts of countless patriots, but as the birthplace and abode
of men of genius. Go where you will, places present themselves to
your eyes which are stamped with the memory of some one or
other of those "burning and shining lights" that have illuminated
the atmosphere of England with their collective splendour, and
made it visible to the men of farthest climates. Even in this secluded
district—which, beautiful as it is, is comparatively little known or
spoken of amongst the generality of English people—how many
literary recollections surround you! To say nothing of the actors

in great historical scenes—the Talbots, Shrewsburys, Dudleys, and Bagots of former ages, or the Ansons, Vernons, St. Vincents, and Pagets of the later and present ones—in this county were born those excellent bishops Hurd and Newton, and the venerable antiquary and herald Elias Ashmole. To say nothing of the quantity of taste and knowledge that resides in the best classes of society hereabout, we have to-day passed the houses of Thomas Gisborne and Edward Cooper, clergy men who have done honour to their profession by their talents and the liberality of their sentiments. In that antiquated Fauld Hall once dwelt old Squire Burton, the brother of the author of the 'Anatomy of Melancholy;' and there is little doubt that some part of that remarkable work was written there. By that Dove, Izaak Walton, that pious old man, that lover of the fields, and historian of the worthies of the church, used to stroll and meditate, or converse with his friend Charles Cotton, a Staffordshireman too. In the woods of Wootton, which are very visible hence by daylight, once wandered a very different but very distinguished person—the wayward Rousseau. In Uttoxeter that great but ill-used and ill-understood astronomer, Flamstead, received the greater part of his education; and from Lichfield, the spires of whose cathedral we have seen to-day, went out Johnson and Garrick, each to achieve supremacy in his own track of distinction. And there too lived Anna Seward, who with all her egotism and faults of taste was superior to the women of her age, and had the sagacity to perceive amongst the very first the dawning fame of Southey and Sir Walter Scott.

"If this comparatively obscure district can thus boast of having given birth or abode to so many influential intellects, what shall not England—entire and glory-crowned England? And who shall not feel proud to own himself of its race and kindred, and if he can but secure for himself a moderate portion of its common goods, be happy to live and die in it?"

The spirit of patriotism seemed to have completely taken possession of the good old man. I never heard a discourse which carried me on with so kindling and absorbing a feeling, for my present recollection of it is a very faint and feeble one.

As the carriage stopped, and Mr. Somers's tongue stopped with it, Elizabeth pressed my hand and said in a whisper of evident emotion, "*Can* I help being proud of such a dear, good, true-hearted father?"

We were at the vicarage, and the day in the forest was over; but I would not exchange the recollection of it, simple and uneventful as it was, for that of the most brilliant display of city life in theatre or saloon, nor for the most exciting one of its assembled wit and intellect.

CONCLUSION

THE STORIES AND SKETCHES WITH which I have filled these volumes are some of the many I was enabled to glean up in our year residence at Wood Leighton. Many still remain; but in these days it is not as it was when Richardson put forth his seven and nine volumes: we of the modern school are restricted to three,—and three volumes will not hold everytlnng.

Wood Leighton is a rare treasury of old histories—blessings on the ancient town, and the beautiful country that lies around it! There is not a cottage there without its pleasant or its sad little bit of human history, nor a grange nor hall but has traditions and memories lying thick about it as leaves in the woods of Vall'ombrosa. And the best of it is, there runs no canal thereabout; there is no projected "main" or "branch" line of railroad which will cut up its sweet woodlands and pastoral meadows, and bring thither a bustle and a stir, and change the quiet simplicity, old-fashioned faith, and cordial hospitality of its people into the misbelieving, suspicious, worldly-wise, money-getting spirit of present manners.

Blessings on the old town I say again, with its antiquated houses, venerable cross and church! Blessings on its people, quaint and kind and simple-hearted as they are! And our friends the Somerses, ten thousand blessings on them! we came to them strangers, but we part from them as if we were all of one family.

And yet what changes will probably happen in that united and happy family in a very little time! Elizabeth will be married to a distant place; a sweet parsonage in a distant county will ere long receive her. Charles Harwood's passion for the sea grows and assumes a determination that will not be controlled. Mr. and Mrs. Somers will in all likelihood be soon left in their pleasant habitation, but shorn of many of the charms of their existence. Yet why anticipate? All yet is there happiness, vivacity, enjoyment of life, and hope in the future. So let it be; and on so sweet a portion of human life let these volumes close.

ALSO AVAILABLE IN THE NONSUCH CLASSICS SERIES

For forthcoming titles and sales information see
www.nonsuch-publishing.com